SLAY-RIDE

A British jockey, riding in Norway, has disappeared—and a day's takings from a racecourse turnstiles have gone with him, it seems. Neither the Norwegian nor the British police can find any trace of him, and the case appears likely to be filed as just another unsolved theft. In response to an appeal from the racecourse management, the Jockey Club investigator, David Cleveland, is sent to Norway. He goes without much expectation of success, and he soon finds that he is in waters as deep and dark as those of the fjords. . . .

THE SILVER MISTRESS

Sir Gerald Tarrant, of British Intelligence, is kidnapped to undergo ruthless and protracted interrogation. His captors —led by Colonel Jim, a master criminal—have staged his apparent 'death' in a well-faked road accident. Modesty Blaise and Willie Garvin, however, are not entirely convinced, and they follow some slender clues and their own intuition on a trail which leads them to the remote chateau in the Pyrenees where Tarrant is imprisoned. Here they encounter Colonel Jim's villainous gang: the girl, Angel, with the wire garrotte; Mrs McTurk, the genteel assassin; and Mr Sexton, who rightly claims to be the greatest combat-man in the world. . . . Even Modesty and Willie cannot possibly hope to outwit this formidable trio.

A REPORT FROM GROUP 17

Some little distance up the Potomac River from Washington, stands the Villa Petrograd—a kind of miniature Kremlin surrounded by high walls—built early this century by a Russian ambassador to the United States, and still used by the Russians. There are several things about the place that are disturbing to US Intelligence: the secrecy, the private zoo, the microbiological equipment and the presence of Dr Helmuth Schutz, a former Nazi scientist, who has a laboratory in the grounds. Fergus O'Neil is called in to investigate the whole set-up, and the suspense builds up as he gradually realizes the horrifying nature of Schutz's research. . . .

The volumes in this series do not constitute a lending library and all books issued become the personal property of members. Membership is open to all, and involves no enrolment fee or any payment beyond the low price for each exclusive three-in-one omnibus volume. Details of membership will gladly be sent on request.

Please write to:

Odhams Books, Rushden, Northants.

MADE AND PRINTED IN GREAT BRITAIN
BY ODHAMS (WATFORD) LTD
600779297
11.74

SLAY-RIDE

Dick Francis

★

THE
SILVER MISTRESS

Peter O'Donnell

★

A REPORT
FROM GROUP 17

Robert C. O'Brien

ODHAMS BOOKS
LONDON

CONTENTS

SLAY-RIDE

Dick Francis

'Slay-Ride' is published by
Michael Joseph Ltd

The Author

Dick Francis, a former champion National Hunt jockey, had to abandon his riding career as a result of injury. Since then he has become even more successful as a thriller writer, although he says he found race-riding much easier than writing. In 1970 he won the American Edgar Allan Poe Mystery Award, and he is considered to be one of the leading best-seller authors of today.

CHAPTER ONE

COLD GREY WATER lapped the flimsy looking sides of the fibre-glass dinghy, and I shivered and thought of the five hundred feet straight down to the sea-bed underneath.

An hour out of Oslo with the outboard motor stilled and my friend Arne Kristiansen taking all afternoon to answer some simple questions.

A grey day, damp, not far from rain. The air sang in my ears with stinging chill. My feet were congealing. The October temperature down the fjord was giving the land a twenty degree lead towards zero, and of the two of us only Arne was dressed for it.

Where I had a showerproof jacket over an ordinary suit and no hat, he had come equipped with the full bit: a red padded cap with ear flaps fastened with a strap under his chin, blue padded trousers tucked into short wide-legged gumboots, and a red padded jacket fastened up the front with silver coloured press studs. A glimpse of black and yellow at the neck spoke of other warm layers underneath.

He had arranged on the telephone to meet me at the statue in the Radhusplassen by the harbour, brushing aside my suggestion that he should come to the Grand Hotel, where I was staying. Even in those wide open spaces he had gone muttering on about being overheard by long range bugging machines (his words) and had finally insisted on taking to the dinghy. Knowing from past experience the quickest way in the end to deal with his perennial mild persecution complex was to go along with it, I had shrugged and followed him along the quay to where the small pale green craft bobbed beside a flight of steps.

I had forgotten that it is always very much colder out on open water. I flexed the stiffening fingers inside my pockets and repeated my last question.

'How would you smuggle sixteen thousand stolen kroner out of the country?'

For the second time, I got no answer. Arne produced answers as prodigally as tax collectors offer rebates.

He blinked slowly, the dropping of the eyelids marking some intermediary stage in the chess-like permutations going on in his head. He was no doubt, as always, considering every foreseeable consequence: if answer A might produce any one of five responses,

7

and answer B lead on to six subsidiary questions, wouldn't it be wiser to answer C, in which case, though. . . .

It made conversation with him a trifle slow.

I tried a little prompting. 'You said it was all in coins and used notes of small denominations. How bulky? Enough to fit in a small sized suitcase?'

He blinked.

'Do you think he just walked out with it through the customs?'

He blinked.

'Or do you think he is still somewhere in Norway?'

Arne opened his mouth and said grudgingly, 'No one knows.'

I tried some more. 'When a foreigner stays in one of your hotels, he has to fill in a form and show his passport. These forms are for the police. Have your police checked those forms?'

Pause. 'Yes,' he said.

'And?'

'Robert Sherman did not fill in any form.'

'None at all? What about when he arrived from England?'

'He did not stay in an hotel.'

Patience, I thought. Give me patience. 'Where, then?'

'With friends.'

'What friends?'

He considered. I knew he knew the answer. He knew he was eventually going to tell me. I suppose he couldn't help the way his mind worked, but this, God help us, was supposed to be an investigator.

What was more, I had taught him myself. 'Think before you answer any question,' I'd said. So now he did.

In the three months he had spent in England learning how the Jockey Club ran its investigation department we had grown to know each other well. Some of the time he had stayed in my flat, most of the time we had travelled together to the races, all of the time he had asked and listened and blinked as he thought. That had been three years ago. Two minutes had been enough to re-suscitate the old warm feelings of tolerant regard. I liked him, I thought, more because of the mild eccentric kinks than despite.

'He stayed with Gunnar Holth,' he said.

I waited.

After ten seconds he added, 'He is a racehorse trainer.'

'Did Bob Sherman ride for him?'

This dead simple question threw him into a longer than ever session of mental chess, but finally he said, 'Bob Sherman rode the ones of his horses which ran in hurdle races while Bob Sherman was in Norway. *Ja*. He did not ride the horses of Gunnar Holth which ran in Flat races while he was in Norway.'

God give me strength.

Arne hadn't actually finished. 'Robert Sherman rode horses for the racecourse.'

I was puzzled. 'How do you mean?'

He consulted his inner man again, who evidently said it was O.K. to explain.

'The racecourse pays appearance money to some foreign jockeys, to get them to come to Norway. It makes the racing more interesting for the racegoers. So the racecourse paid Robert Sherman to ride.'

'How much did they pay him?'

A rising breeze was stirring the fjord's surface into proper little wavelets. The fjord just below Oslo is not one of those narrow canyon jobs on the Come-To-Scenic-Norway posters, but a wide expanse of sea dotted with rocky islands and fringed by the sprawling suburbs of the city. A coastal steamer surged past half a mile away and tossed us lightly in its wake. The nearest land looked a lot further off.

'Let's go back,' I said abruptly.

'No, no . . .' He had no patience for such weak suggestions. 'They paid him fifteen hundred kroner.'

'I'm cold,' I said.

He looked surprised. 'It is not winter yet.'

I made a noise which was half laugh and half teeth beginning to chatter. 'It isn't summer either.'

He looked vaguely all around. 'Robert Sherman had made six visits to race in Norway,' he said. 'This was his seventh.'

'Look, Arne, tell me about it back at the hotel, huh?'

He attended to me seriously. 'What is the matter?'

'I don't like heights,' I said.

He looked blank. I took one frozen mitt out of its pocket, hung it over the side of the boat, and pointed straight down. Arne's face melted into comprehension and a huge grin took the place of the usual tight careful configuration of his mouth.

'David, I am sorry. The water to me, it is home. Like snow. I am sorry.' He turned to start the outboard, and then paused to say, 'He could simply have driven over the border to Sweden. The customs, they would not search for kroner.'

'In what car?' I asked.

He thought it over. 'Ah yes.' He blinked a bit. 'Perhaps a friend drove him. . . .'

'Start the engine,' I said encouragingly.

He shrugged and gave several small nods of the head, but turned to the outboard and pressed the necessary knobs. I had half expected it to prove as lifeless as my fingers, but the spark hit the gas in an orderly fashion and Arne pointed the sharp end back towards hot coffee and radiators.

The dinghy slapped busily through the little waves and the crosswind flicked spray on to my left cheek. I pulled my jacket collar up and made like a tortoise.

Arne's mouth moved as he said something, but against the combined noises of the engine and the sea and the rustle of gaberdine against my ears, I couldn't hear any words.

'What?' I shouted.

He started to repeat whatever it was, but louder. I caught only snatches like 'ungrateful pig' and 'dirty thief', which I took to be his own private views of Robert Sherman, British steeplechase jockey. Arne had had a bad time since the said Bob Sherman disappeared with the day's take from the turnstiles of Øvrevoll, because Arne Kristiansen, besides being the Norwegian Jockey Club's official investigator, was also in charge of racecourse security.

The theft, he had told me on the outward chug, was an insult, first to himself, and secondly to Norway. Guests in a foreign country should not steal. Norwegians were not criminals, he said, and quoted jail statistics per million of population to prove it. When the British were in Norway, they should keep their hands to themselves.

Commiserating, I refrained from drawing his country's raids on Britain to his attention: they were, after all, a thousand or so years in the past, and the modern Vikings were less likely to burn, rape, pillage and plunder than to take peaceable photographs of Buckingham Palace. I felt moreover a twinge of national shame about Bob Sherman: I had found myself apologizing, of all things, for his behaviour.

Arne was still going on about it: on that subject unfortunately he needed no prompting. Phrases like 'put me in an intolerable position' slid off his tongue as if he had been practising them for weeks—which, on reflection, of course he had. It was three weeks and four days since the theft: and forty-eight hours since the Chairman of the racecourse had telephoned and asked me to send over a British Jockey Club investigator to see what he could do. I had sent (you will have guessed) myself.

I hadn't met the Chairman yet, nor seen the racecourse, nor ever before been to Norway. I was down the fjord with Arne because Arne was the devil I knew.

Three years earlier the hair now closely hidden under the red padded hood had been a bright blond fading at the temples to grey. The eyes were as fierce a blue as ever, the wrinkles around them as deep, and the bags below a good deal heavier. The spray blew on to skin that was weather-beaten but not sunburned; thick-looking impervious yellowish-white skin lumped and pitted by forty-something winters.

He was still breaking out in bursts of aggrieved half-heard monologue, trudging along well-worn paths of resentment. I gave up trying to listen. It was too cold.

He stopped in mid-sentence and looked with raised eyebrows at some distant point over my left shoulder. I turned. A large speedboat, not very far away, was slicing down the fjord in our general direction with its bow waves leaping out like heavy silver wings.

I turned back to Arne. He shrugged and looked uninterested, and the outboard chose that moment to splutter and cough and choke to silence.

'*Fanden*' said Arne loudly, which was nothing at all to what I was saying in my head.

'Those people will help us,' he announced, pointing at the approaching speedboat, and without hesitation he stood up, braced his legs, and waved his scarlet clad arms in wide sweeps above his head.

Twisting on my bench seat, I watched the speedboat draw near.

'They will take us on board,' Arne said.

The speedboat did not seem to be slowing down. I could see its shining black hull and its sharp cutting bow, and the silver wings of wave looked as high and full as ever.

If not higher and fuller.

I turned to Arne with the beginnings of apprehension.

'They haven't seen us,' I said.

'They must have.' Arne waved his arms with urgent acceleration, rocking the dinghy precariously.

'Hey' Arne shouted to the speedboat. And after that he screamed at it, in Norwegian.

The wind blew his words away. The helmsman of the speedboat didn't hear, didn't see. The sharp hard shining black prow raced straight towards us at forty knots.

'Jump' yelled Arne; and he jumped. A flash of scarlet streaking into the sea.

I was slow. Thought perhaps that the unimaginable wouldn't happen, that the bow wave would toss the dinghy clear like it would a swan, that the frail craft would bob away as lightly as a bird.

I tumbled over the side into the water about one second before the bow split the fibre-glass open like an eggshell. Something hit me a colossal bang on the shoulder while I was still gasping from the shock of immersion and I went down under the surface into a roaring buffeting darkness.

People who fall off boats die as often from the propellers as from drowning, but I didn't remember that until the twin screws had churned past and left me unsliced. I came stuttering and gulping to the daylight in the jumbled frothing wake and saw the back of the speedboat tearing away unconcernedly down the fjord.

'Arne,' I shouted, which was about as useless as dredging for diamonds in the Thames. A wave slapped me in the open mouth and I swallowed a double salt water, neat.

The sea seemed much rougher at face level than it had done from above. I floundered in high choppy waves with ruffles of white frothing across their tops and blowing into my eyes, and I shouted again for Arne. Shouted with intensifying concern for him and with fear for myself: but the wind tore the words away and battered them to bits.

There was no sign of the dinghy. My last impression was that it had been cut clean into two pieces, which were now, no doubt, turning over and over in a slow sink down to the far away sea-bed.

I shuddered as much from imagination as from cold.

There was no sight anywhere of Arne. No red-padded head, no red waving arms above the waves, no cheerful smile coming to tell me that the sea was home to him and that safety and hot muffins were *this* way, just over here.

Land lay visible all around me in greyish misty heights. None of it was especially near. About two miles away, I guessed, whichever way I looked.

Treading water, I began to pull my clothes off, still looking desperately for Arne, still expecting to see him.

There was nothing but the rough slapping water. I thought about the speedboat's propellers and I thought about Arne's wide legged gumboots which would fill with water in the first few seconds. I thought finally that if I didn't accept that Arne was gone and get started shorewards, I was very likely going to drown on that spot.

I kicked off my shoes and struggled with the zip of my raincoat.

Ripped open the buttons of my suit jacket underneath and shrugged out of both coats together. I let go of them, then remembered my wallet, and although it seemed crazy I took it out of my jacket pocket and shoved it inside my shirt.

The two coats, waterlogged, floated briefly away and started to go down out of sight. I slid out of my trousers, and let them follow. Pity, I thought. Nice suit, that had been.

The water was very cold indeed.

I began to swim. Up the fjord. Towards Oslo. Where else?

I was thirty-three and hardy and I knew more statistics than I cared to. I knew, for instance, that the average human can live less than an hour in water of one degree centigrade.

I tried to swim unhurriedly in long undemanding strokes, postponing the moment of exhaustion. The water in Oslo fjord was not one degree above freezing, but at least five. Probably not much colder than the stuff buffeting the English beach at Brighton at that very moment. In water five degrees above freezing, one could last . . . well, I didn't actually know *that* statistic. Had to take it on trust. Long enough anyway to swim something over two miles.

Bits of distant geography lessons made no sense. 'The Gulf Stream warms the coast of Norway . . .' Good old Gulf Stream. Where had it gone?

Cold had never seemed a positive force to me before. I supposed I had never really been *cold,* just chilled. This cold dug deep into every muscle and ached in my gut. Feeling had gone from my hands and feet, and my arms and legs felt heavy. The best long-distance swimmers had a nice thick insulating layer of subcutaneous fat: I hadn't. They also covered themselves with water-repelling grease and swam alongside comfort boats which fed them hot cocoa through tubes on demand. The best long-distance swimmers were, of course, usually going twenty miles or so further than I was.

I swam. The waves seemed frighteningly big: and I couldn't see where I was aiming unless I lifted my head right up and trod water, and that wasted time and energy.

The nearest-looking land seemed to my salt-stinging eyes to be as far away as ever. And surely Oslo fjord should be a Piccadilly Circus of boats? But I couldn't see a single one.

Dammit, I thought. I'm bloody well not going to drown. I'm bloody well *not.*

I swam.

*   *   *

Daylight was slowly fading. Sea, sky, and distant mountains were all a darker grey. It began to rain.

I travelled, it seemed, very slowly. The land I was aiming for never appeared to be nearer. I began to wonder if some current was cancelling out every yard I swam forward: but when I looked back, the land behind was definitely receding.

I swam mechanically, growing tired.

A long way off, straight ahead, pinpricks of light sprang out against the fading afternoon. Every time I looked, there were more. The city was switching on in the dusk.

Too far, I thought. They are too far for me. Land and life all around me, and I couldn't reach them.

An awful depth beneath. And I never did like heights.

A cold lonely death, drowning.

I swam. Nothing else to do.

When another light shone out higher up and to the left, it took at least a minute for the news to reach my sluggish brain. I trod water and wiped the rain and sea out of my eyes as best I could and tried to make out where it came from: and there, a great deal nearer than when I'd last looked, was the solid grey shape of land.

Houses, lights, and people. All there, somewhere, on that rocky hump.

Gratefully I veered fifteen degrees left and pressed on faster, pouring out the carefully hoarded reserves of stamina like a penitent miser. And that was stupid, because no shelving beach lay ahead. The precious land, when I reached it, proved to be a smooth sheer cliff dropping perpendicularly into the water. Not a ledge, not a cranny, to offer even respite from the effort of staying afloat.

The last quarter mile was the worst. I could *touch* the land if I wanted to, and it offered nothing to cling to. There had to be a break somewhere, if I went far enough, but I had practically nothing left. I struggled feebly forward through the slapping waves, wishing in a hazy way that I could surge through warm calm water like Mark Spitz and make a positive touchdown against a nice firm rail, with my feet on the bottom. What I actually did was a sort of belly-flop on to a small boat slipway bordered with large rock slabs.

I lay half in and half out of the water, trying to get back breath I didn't know I'd lost. My chest heaved. I coughed.

It wasn't dark; just the slow northern twilight. I wouldn't have minded if it had been three in the morning: the cold wet concrete beneath my cheek felt as warm and welcoming as goose feathers.

Footsteps crunched rhythmically along the quay at the head of the slipway and then suddenly stopped. I did a bit towards lifting my head and flapping a numb hand.

'*Hvem er der?*' he said; or something like it.

I gave a sort of croak and he walked carefully, crabwise, down the slipway towards me, a half-seen, well-wrapped figure in the rainy gloom.

He repeated his question, which I still didn't understand.

'I'm English,' I said. 'Can you help me?'

Nothing happened for a few seconds. Then he went away.

So what, I thought tiredly. At least from the waist up I was safe in Norway. Didn't seem to have the energy to drag myself uphill till my feet were out, not just for a minute or two. But I would, I thought, given time.

The man came back, and brought a friend. Ungrateful of me to have misjudged him.

The companion peered through the rain and said, 'You are English? Did you say you are English?' His tone seemed to suggest that being English automatically explained such follies as swimming in October in shirt and underpants and lying about on slipways.

'Yes,' I said.

'You fell off a ship?'

'Sort of.'

I felt his hand slide under my armpit.

'Come. Out of the water.'

I scraped myself on to the slipway and with their help more or less crawled to the top. The quay was edged with railings and posts. I sat on the ground with my back against one of the posts and wished for enough strength to stand up.

They consulted in Norwegian. Then the English speaking one said, 'We will take you to my house, to dry and get warm.'

'Thank you,' I said, and by God I meant it.

One of them went away again and came back with a battered old van. They gave me the front passenger seat though I offered to drip in the back, and whisked me about a quarter of a mile to a small wooden house, standing near two or three others. There was no village, no shops, no telephone.

'This is an island,' my rescuer explained. 'One kilometre long, three hundred metres across.' He told me its name, which seemed to me like 'gorse'.

His living room was small and bright, and warmed by the huge stove which took up at least a sixth of the floorspace. Seen clearly in the light he himself was a short friendly man of middle age with hands that were used for work. He shook his head over me and produced first a blanket and then, after some rummaging, a thick woollen shirt and a pair of trousers.

'You are not a sailor,' he said matter-of-factly, watching me fumble off my shirt and pants.

'No,' I agreed.

My wallet fell on the floor. I was surprised it was still there; had forgotten it. The Norwegian-only rescuer politely picked it up and handed it to me, smiling broadly. He looked very like his friend.

Between hopeless bouts of shivering I told them what had happened and asked them how I could get back to the city. They talked to each other about it while I dressed, first with a lot of shaking heads but finally with a few nods.

'When you are warmer we will take you by boat,' said the English-speaker. He looked at the wallet which lay now on a polished pine table. 'We ask only that you will pay for the fuel. If you can.'

Together we took out my sodden money and spread it on the table. I asked them to take whatever they liked, and after debate they chose a fifty kroner note. I urged them to double it. It wouldn't cost so much, they protested, but in the end they put two notes aside and dried the rest for me quickly on the stove so that the edges curled. After more consultation they dug in a cupboard and brought out a bottle of pale gold liquid. One small glass followed, and a moderate tot was poured into it. They handed it to me.

'*Skol*,' they said.

'*Skol*,' I repeated.

They watched interestedly while I drank. Smooth fire down the throat, heat in the stomach, and soon a warm glow along all the frozen veins.

They smiled. 'Aquavit,' said my host, and stored the precious bottle away ready for the next needy stranger who swam to their doorstep.

They suggested I should sit for a while on the one comfortable-looking chair. Since various muscles were still trembling with weakness this seemed a good idea, so I rested while they busied themselves putting out businesslike sets of oilskins, and by the time they were kitted up my skin had returned from a nasty bluish purplish white to its more usual shade of sallow.

'D'you feel better?' my host observed, smiling.

'I do.'

They nodded, pleased, and held out a spare set of oilskins for me to put on. They took me in a big smelly fishing boat back up the twinkle-edged fjord to the city, and it rained all the way. I spent the journey calculating that I had been in the water for about two hours, which didn't prove anything in particular about the current in the fjord or the inefficiency of my swimming or the distance I had travelled, but did prove pretty conclusively that the temperature was more than one degree above freezing.

CHAPTER TWO

THEY WAITED while I changed at the Grand, so that they could take back the lent clothes. We parted with warm handshakes and great camaraderie, and it was only after they had gone that I realized that I didn't know their names.

I would have liked nothing better than to go to bed and sleep for half a century, but the thought of Arne's wife waiting for him to come home put a damper on that. So I spent the next couple of hours with various Norwegian authorities, reporting what had happened.

When the police finished taking notes and said they would send someone to tell Mrs Kristiansen, I suggested that I should go too. They agreed. We went in an official car and rang the bell of Flat C on the first floor of a large timber house in a prosperous road not far from the city centre.

The girl who opened the door looked inquiringly out at us from clear grey eyes in a firm, friendly, thirtyish face. Behind her the flat looked warm and colourful, and the air was thick with Beethoven. 'Is Mrs Kristiansen in?' I asked.

'Yes,' she said. 'I am Mrs Kristiansen.'

Not in the least what I would have expected. Oddballs like Arne shouldn't turn out to have slender young wives with thick pale blonde hair falling in loose curls on their shoulders. She looked away from my own less striking face to the policeman behind me, and the eyes widened.

'I'm David Cleveland,' I said. 'I was with Arne this afternoon. . . .'

'Oh were you?' she exclaimed. 'Oh, do come in . . . I'm *so* glad. . . .'

She held the door wider and turned to call over her shoulder. 'Arne,' she said. 'Arne, see who's here.'

He stepped into the hall. Very much alive.

We stared at each other in consternation. My own face must have mirrored the surprise and shock I saw on his, and then he was striding forward with his hand outheld and his face creasing into the most gigantic smile of all time.

'David! I don't believe it. I have reported you drowned.' He clasped both my hands in both of his and shook them warmly. 'Come in, come in, my dear fellow, and tell me how you were saved. I have been so grieved . . . I was telling Kari. . . .'

His wife nodded, as delighted as he was.

The policeman behind me said, 'It would seem Mr Kristiansen wasn't drowned after all, then,' which seemed in our high state of relief to be extremely funny. We all laughed. Even the policeman smiled.

'I was picked up by some fisherman near Nesodden,' Arne told him. 'I reported the accident to the police there. They said they would send a boat to look for Mr Cleveland, but they weren't very hopeful of finding him. I'd better call them. . . .'

'Thank you,' said the policeman. 'That would be helpful,' and he smiled once more at us all and went away.

Kari Kristiansen shut the front door and said 'Do come in, we must celebrate,' and led me through into the living room. Beethoven was thundering away in there, and Kari switched him off. 'Arne always plays loud music when he's upset,' she said.

Out in the hall Arne busied himself with the telephone, and among his explanatory flow of Norwegian I caught my own name spoken with astonishment and relief.

'It is wonderful,' he said, coming into the room and rubbing his hands together. 'Wonderful.' He gestured to me to sit on a deep comfortable sofa near a cheerful wood-burning fire. 'The Nesodden police say they sent a boat out to search for you, but it was too dark and raining and they could see nothing.'

'I'm sorry they had the trouble,' I said.

'My dear fellow. . . .' He spread his fingers, 'It was nothing. And now, a drink, eh? To celebrate.' He filled glasses of red wine from a bottle standing already open on a side-table.

'Arne has been so depressed all evening,' Kari said. 'It is truly a miracle that you were both saved.'

We exchanged stories. Arne had torn off the red clothes and kicked his boots off instantly (I suppose I should have known that a man at home on the sea would wear *loose* gumboots), but although he had called my name and searched around for some minutes he had caught no sign of me.

'When I last saw you,' he said apologetically, 'You were still in the dinghy, and I thought the speedboat must have hit you directly, so when I could not see you I thought that you must be already dead.'

He had started swimming, he said; and knowing a lot more than I did about tides and winds, had taken almost the opposite direction. He had been picked up near the coast by a small home-going fishing boat which was too low on fuel to go out into the fjord to look for me. It had however landed him in the small town where he reported my loss, and from there he had returned by hired boat to the city.

My story was so much the same that it could be told in two sentences: I swam to an island. Two men brought me back in a boat.

Arne searched among an untidy pile of papers and triumphantly produced a map. Spreading it out, he pointed to the widest part of the fjord and showed both Kari and me where we had been sunk.

'The worst possible place,' Kari exclaimed. 'Why did you go so far?'

'You know me,' said Arne, folding the map up again. 'I like to be moving.'

She looked at him indulgently. 'You don't like to be followed, you mean.'

Arne looked a little startled, but that complex of his stood out like Gulliver in Lilliput.

I said, 'The police asked me if I saw the name of that speedboat.'

'Did you?' asked Arne.

I shook my head. 'No. Did you?'

He blinked through one of those maddening pauses into which the simplest question seemed to throw him, but in the end all he said was 'No, I didn't.'

'I don't think there was any name to see,' I said.

They both turned their faces to me in surprise.

'There must have been,' Kari said.

'Well . . . I've no impression of one . . . no name, no registration number, no port of origin. Perhaps you don't have things like that in Norway.'

'Yes we do,' Kari said, puzzled. 'Of course we do.'

Arne considered lengthily, then said, 'It was going too fast . . . and straight towards us. It must have had a name. We simply didn't see it.' He spoke with finality, as if the subject could hold no more interest. I nodded briefly and let it go, but I was certain that on that thundering black hull there had been nothing to see but black paint. How were they off for smugglers, I wondered, in this neck of the North Sea?

'It's a pity,' I said. 'Because you might have got compensation for your dinghy.'

'It was insured,' he said. 'Do not worry.'

Kari said, 'It's disgraceful he did not stop. He must have felt the bump . . . even a big heavy speedboat, like Arne says it was, could not crush a dinghy without feeling it.'

Hit and run, I thought flippantly. Happens on the roads, why not on the water?

'Arne was afraid you could not swim.'

'Up and down a pool or two,' I said. 'Never tried such long-distance stuff before.'

'You were lucky,' she said seriously.

'Arne too.' I looked at him thoughtfully, for I was younger by a good ten years and I had been near to exhaustion.

'Oh no. Arne's a great swimmer. A great sportsman, all round. Very fit and tough.' She smiled ironically, but the wifely pride was there. 'He used to win across-country ski races.'

There had been several sets of skis stacked casually in an alcove in the hall, along with squash rackets, fishing rods, mountain walking boots and half a dozen anoraks like the lost red one. For a man who liked to keep moving, he had all the gear.

'Have you eaten?' Kari asked suddenly. 'Since your swim, I mean? Did you think of eating?'

I shook my head. 'I suppose I was worried about Arne.'

She stood up, smiling. 'Arne had no appetite for his supper.' She looked at the clock. Ten minutes before ten. 'I will bring something for you both,' she said.

Arne fondly watched her back view disappearing towards the kitchen. 'What do you think of her, eh? Isn't she beautiful?'

Normally I disliked men who invited admiration for their wives as if they were properties like cars, but I would have forgiven Arne a great deal that evening.

'Yes,' I said, more truthfully than on many similar occasions; and Arne positively smirked.

'More wine,' he said, getting up restlessly and filling both our glasses.

'Your house, too, is beautiful,' I said.

He looked over his shoulder in surprise. 'That is Kari as well. She . . . it is her job. Making rooms for people. Offices, hotels. Things like that.'

Their own sitting-room was a place of natural wood and white paint, with big parchment-shaded table lamps shedding a golden glow on string-coloured upholstery and bright scattered cushions. A mixture of the careful and haphazard, overlaid with the comfortable debris of a full life. Ultra-tidy rooms always oppressed me: the Kristiansens' was just right.

Arne brought back my filled glass and settled himself opposite, near the fire. His hair, no longer hidden, was now more grey than blond; longer than before, and definitely more distinguished.

'Tomorrow,' I said, 'I'd like to see the racecourse Chairman, if I could.'

He looked startled, as if he had forgotten the real purpose of my visit.

'Yes.' He blinked a bit. 'It is Saturday tomorrow. It is the Grand National meeting on Sunday. He will be at the racecourse on Sunday.'

Don't let a thieving jockey spoil the man's day off, Arne was meaning, so I shrugged and said Sunday would do. 'I'll maybe call on Gunnar Holth tomorrow, then.'

For some reason that didn't fill Arne with joy either, but I discovered, after a long pause on his part, that this was because he, Arne, wished to go fishing all day and was afraid I would want him with me, instead.

'Does Gunnar Holth speak English?' I asked.

'Oh yes.'

'I'll go on my own, then.'

He gave me the big smile and jumped up to help Kari, who was returning with a laden tray. She had brought coffee and open sandwiches of prawns and cheese and pineapple which we ate to the last crumb.

'You must come another evening,' Kari said. 'I will make you a proper dinner.'

Arne agreed with her warmly and opened some more wine. 'A great little cook,' he said proprietorially.

The great little cook shook back her heavy blonde hair and stretched her elegant neck. She had a jaw-line in the same class and three small brown moles like dusty freckles high on one cheekbone. 'Come any time,' she said.

I got back to the Grand by taxi at one in the morning, slept badly, and woke at seven feeling like Henry Cooper's punchbag.

Consultation with the bathroom looking-glass revealed a plate-sized bruise of speckled crimson over my left shoulder-blade,

souvenir of colliding boats. In addition every muscle I possessed
was groaning with the morning-after misery of too much strain.
David Cleveland, it seemed, was no Matthew Webb.

Bath, clothes and breakfast didn't materially improve things,
nor on the whole did a telephone call to Gunnar Holth.

'Come if you like,' he said. 'But I can tell you nothing. You will
waste your time.'

As all investigators waste a lot of time listening to people with
nothing to tell, I naturally went. He had a stable yard adjoining
the racecourse and a belligerent manner.

'Questions, questions,' he said. 'There is nothing to tell.'

I paid off my taxi driver.

'You shouldn't have sent him away,' Gunnar Holth said. 'You
will be going soon.'

I smiled. 'I can go back on a tram.'

He gave me a grudging stare. 'You don't look like a Jockey
Club official.'

'I would appreciate it very much,' I said, 'if you would show
me your horses. Arne Kristiansen says you have a good lot . . . that
they've been winning big prizes this year.'

He loosened, of course. He gestured towards a large barn on
the other side of an expanse of mud. We made our way there, him
in his boots showing me I shouldn't have come in polished shoes.
He was short, wiry, middle-aged and a typical stableman, more at
home with his horses, I guessed, than with their owners; and he
spoke English with an Irish accent.

The barn contained two rows of boxes facing into a wide central passage. Horses' heads showed over most of the half doors and
three or four lads were carrying buckets of water and haynets.

'They've just come in from exercise,' Holth said. 'We train on
the sand track on the racecourse.' He turned left and opened the
door of the first box. 'This fellow runs tomorrow in the Grand
National. Would you look at his shoulders now, isn't that a grand
sort of horse?'

'Bob Sherman won a race on him the day he disappeared,' I
said.

He gave me a sharp wordless glance and went in to pat a
strong-looking character with more bone than breeding. He felt
the legs, looked satisfied, and came back to join me.

'How do you know?' he said.

No harm in telling him. 'Arne Kristiansen gave me a list of Bob
Sherman's last rides in Norway. He said that this horse of yours
was likely to win the National, and if Sherman had had any sense

he would have come back for that race and then stolen the National day takings, which would have been a better haul all round.'

Holth allowed himself a glint of amusement. 'That's true.'

We continued round the barn, admiring every inmate. There were about twenty altogether, three-quarters of them running on the Flat, and although they seemed reasonable animals, none of them looked likely to take Epsom by storm. From their coats, though, and general air of well-being, Holth knew his trade.

One end of the barn was sectioned off to form living quarters for the lads, and Holth took me through to see them. Dormitory, washroom, and kitchen.

'Bob stayed here, most times,' he said.

I glanced slowly round the big main room with its half dozen two-tiered bunk beds, its bare board floor, its wooden table, wooden chairs. A big brown-tiled stove and double-glazed windows with curtains like blankets promised comfort against future snow, and a couple of mild girlie calendars brightened the walls, but it was a far cry from the Grand.

'Always?' I asked.

Holth shrugged. 'He said it was good enough here, and he saved the expense of a hotel. Nothing wrong there now, is there?'

'Nothing at all,' I agreed.

He paused. 'Sometimes he stayed with an owner.'

'Which owner?'

'Oh . . . the man who owns Whitefire. Per Bjørn Sandvik.'

'How many times?'

Holth said with irritation, 'What does it matter? Twice, I suppose. Yes, twice. Not the last time. The two times before that.'

'How often did he come over altogether?'

'Six perhaps. Or seven . . . or eight.'

'All this summer?'

'He didn't come last year, if that's what you mean.'

'But he liked it?'

'Of course he liked it. All British jockeys who are invited, they like it. Good pay, you see.'

'How good?'

'Well,' he said, 'They get their fare over here, and a bit towards expenses. And the fees for riding. And the appearance money.'

'The racecourse pays the appearance money?'

'Not exactly. Well . . . the racecourse pays the money to the jockey but collects it from the owners who the jockey rode for.'

'So an owner, in the end, pays everything, the riding fees, the winning percentage, a share of the fares, and a share of the appearance money?'

'That is right.'

'What happens if after all that the jockey rides a stinking race?'

Holth answered with deadly seriousness. 'The owner does not ask the jockey to come again.'

We stepped out of the barn back into the mud. It hadn't actually rained that day, but the threat hung in the cold misty air.

'Come into my house,' suggested Holth, 'Have some coffee before you catch the tram.'

'Great,' I said.

His house was a small wooden bungalow with lace curtains and geraniums in pots on every window sill. The stove in the living-room was already lit, with an orange metal coffee pot heating on top. Gunnar dug into a cupboard for two earthenware mugs and some sugar in a packet.

'Would the owners have asked Bob Sherman to come again?' I said.

He poured the coffee, stirring with a white plastic spoon.

'Per Bjørn Sandvik would. And Sven Wangen; that's the owner of that dappled mare on the far side.' He pondered. 'Rolf Torp, now. Bob lost a race the day he went. Rolf Torp thought he should have walked it.'

'And should he?'

Holth shrugged. 'Horses aren't machines,' he said. 'Mind you, I don't train Rolf Torp's horses, so I don't really know, do I?'

'Who trains them?'

'Paul Sundby.'

'Will Rolf Torp be at the races tomorrow?'

'Naturally,' Holth said. 'He has the favourite in the National.'

'And you,' I said. 'Would you have asked him to ride for you again?'

'Certainly,' he said without hesitation. 'Bob is a good jockey. He listens to what you say about a horse. He rides with his head. He would not have been asked so many times if he had not been good.'

The door from the yard opened without warning and one of the lads poked his head in: he was about twenty-five, cheerful, and wore a woollen cap with a pompom.

'Gunny,' he said, 'Will ye be takin' a look at that bleedin' mare now? She's a right cow, that one.'

The trainer said he would look in a minute, and the head withdrew.

'He's Irish,' I said, surprised.

'Sure. I've three Irish lads and one from Yorkshire. And three from here. There's a lot of British lads in Norwegian racing.'

'Why is that?'

'They get a chance of riding in races here, see? More than they do at home.'

We drank the coffee which was well boiled and all the stronger for it. I said, 'What did Bob do for transport? Did he ever hire a car?'

'No. I don't think so. When he stayed here he used to go with me over to the course.'

'Did he ever borrow your car? Or anyone's?'

'He didn't borrow mine. I don't think he ever drove, when he came.'

'Did you take him anywhere except to the races, the day he disappeared?'

'No.'

I knew from a file of statements which had been awaiting my arrival at the hotel that Bob Sherman had been expected to leave the racecourse by taxi to catch the late flight to Heathrow. He had not caught it. The taxi driver who had been engaged for the trip had simply shrugged when his passenger didn't show, and had taken some ordinary racegoers back to the city instead.

That left public transport, all the taxi drivers who didn't know Bob by sight, and other people's cars. Plus, I supposed, his own two feet. It would have been all too easy to leave the racecourse without being seen by anyone who knew him, particularly if, as the collected notes implied, the last race had been run after dark.

I put down my empty coffee mug and Gunnar Holth abruptly said, 'Could you be doing something about Bob's wife, now?'

'His wife? I might see her when I go back, if I find out anything useful.'

'No,' he shook his head. 'She is here.'

'Here?'

He nodded. 'In Oslo. And she won't go home.'

'Arne didn't mention it.'

Holth laughed. 'She follows him round like a dog. She asks questions, like you. Who saw Bob go, who did he go with, why does no one find him? She comes to every race meeting and asks and asks. Everyone is very tired of it.'

'Do you know where she's staying?'

He nodded vigorously and picked up a piece of paper lying near on a shelf.

'The Norsland Hotel. Second class, away from the centre. This is her telephone number. She gave it to me in case I could think of anything to help.' He shrugged. 'Everyone is sorry for her. But I wish she would go away.'

'Will you telephone her?' I said. 'Say I would like to ask her some questions about Bob. Suggest this afternoon.'

'I've forgotten your name,' he said without apology.

I smiled and gave him one of the firms' official cards. He looked at it and me in disbelief, but got the Norsland Hotel on the line. Mrs Emma Sherman was fetched.

Holth said into the receiver, 'A Mr David Cleveland . . . come from England to try to find your husband.' He read from the card, 'Chief investigator, Investigation Office, Jockey Club, Portman Square, London. He wants to see you this afternoon.'

He listened to the reaction, then looked at me. 'Where?'

'At her hotel. Three o'clock.'

He relayed the news.

'She'll be waiting for you,' he said, putting the receiver down.

'Good.'

'Tell her to go home,' he said.

CHAPTER THREE

SHE WAS WAITING in the small lobby of the Norsland, sitting on the edge of a chair and anxiously scanning the face of every passing male. I watched her for a while through the glass doors to the street, before going in. She looked small and pale and very very jumpy. Twice she half stood up, and twice, as the man she had focused on walked past without a sign, subsided more slowly back to her seat.

I pushed through the doors into air barely warmer than the street, which in a totally centrally heated city spoke poorly of the management. Emma Sherman looked at me briefly and switched her gaze back to the door. I was not what she expected: the next man through, sixtyish and military-looking, had her again half way to her feet.

He passed her without a glance on his way to collect his room key at the desk. She sat slowly down, looking increasingly nervous.

I walked over to her. 'Mrs Sherman?'

'Oh.' She stood up slowly. 'Is there a message from Mr Cleveland?'

'I am,' I said, 'David Cleveland.'

'But,' she said, and stopped. The surprise lingered on her face among the strain and tiredness, but she seemed past feeling anything very clearly. At close quarters the nervousness resolved itself into a state not far from total breakdown.

Her skin looked almost transparent from fatigue, dark shadows round her eyes emphasizing the pebbly dullness of the eyes themselves. She was about twenty-two and should have been pretty: she had the bones and the hair for it, but they hadn't a chance. She was also, it seemed to me, pregnant.

'Where can we talk?' I asked.

She looked vaguely round the lobby which contained three chairs, no privacy, and a rubber plant.

'Your room?' I suggested.

'Oh no,' she said at once, and then more slowly, in explanation, 'It is small . . . not comfortable . . . nowhere to sit.'

'Come along, then,' I said. 'We'll find a coffee shop.'

She came with me out into the street and we walked in the general direction of the Grand.

'Will you find him?' she said. 'Please find him.'

'I'll do my best.'

'He never stole that money,' she said. 'He didn't.'

I glanced at her. She was trembling perceptibly and looking paler than ever. I stopped walking and put my hand under her elbow. She looked at me with glazing eyes, tried to say something else, and fell forward against me in a thorough-going swoon.

Even seven stone nothing of fainting girl is hard to support without letting her lie on a cold city pavement. Two passing strangers proved to have friendly faces but no English, and the third, who had the tongue, muttered something about the disgrace of being drunk at four in the afternoon and scurried away. I held her up against me with my arms under hers and asked the next woman along to call a taxi.

She too looked disapproving and backed away, but a boy of about sixteen gave her a withering glance and came to the rescue.

'Is she ill?' he asked. His English was punctilious stuff, learned in school.

'She is. Can you get a taxi?'

'*Ja.* I will return. You will . . .' he thought, then found the word . . . 'Wait?'

'I will wait,' I agreed.

He nodded seriously and darted away round the nearest corner, a slim figure in the ubiquitous uniform of the young, blue jeans and a padded jacket. He came back, as good as his word, with a taxi, and helped me get the girl into it.

'Thank you very much,' I said.

He beamed. 'I learn English,' he said.

'You speak it very well.'

He waved as the taxi drew away: a highly satisfactory encounter to both parties.

She began to wake up during the short journey, which seemed to reassure the taxi driver. He spoke no English except one word which he repeated at least ten times with emphasis, and which was 'doctor'.

'*Ja*' I agreed. '*Ja*. At the Grand Hotel.'

He shrugged, but drove us there. He also helped me support her through the front doors and accepted his fare after she was safely sitting down.

'Doctor,' he said as he left, and I said, '*Ja*.'

'No,' said Bob Sherman's wife, in little more than a whisper. 'What . . . happened?'

'You fainted,' I said briefly. 'And doctor or no doctor, you need to lie down. So up you come . . .' I more or less lifted her to her feet, walked her to the lift, and took her up the one floor to my room. She flopped full length on the bed without question and lay there with her eyes closed.

'Do you mind if I feel your pulse?' I asked.

She gave no answer either way, so I put my fingers on her wrist and found the slow heartbeat. Her arm was slippery with sweat though noticeably cold, and all in all she looked disturbingly frail.

'Are you hungry?' I said.

She rolled her head on the pillow in a slow negative, but I guessed that what was really wrong with her, besides strain, was simple starvation. She had been too worried to take care of herself, and besides, eating came expensive in Norway.

A consultation on the telephone with the hotel restaurant produced a promise of hot meat soup and some bread and cheese.

'And brandy,' I said.

'No brandy, sir, on Saturday. Or on Sunday. It is the rule.'

I had been warned, but had forgotten. Extraordinary to find a country with madder licensing laws than Britain's. There was a small refrigerator in my room, however, which stocked, among the orangeade and mineral waters, a quarter bottle of champagne. It had always seemed to me that bottling in quarters simply spoiled good fizz, but there's an occasion for everything. Emma said she couldn't, she shouldn't; but she did, and within five minutes was looking like a long-picked flower caught just in time.

'I'm sorry,' she said, leaning on one elbow on my bed and sipping the golden bubbles from my tooth mug.

'You're welcome.'

'You must think me a fool.'

'No.'

'It's just. . . . No one seems to care any more. Where he's gone. They just say they can't find him. They aren't even looking.'

'They've looked,' I began, but she wasn't ready to listen.

'Then Gunnar Holth said . . . the Jockey Club had sent their chief investigator . . . so I've been hoping so hard all day that at last someone would find him, and then . . . and then . . . you. . . .'

'I'm not the father-figure you were hoping for,' I said.

She shook her head. 'I didn't think you'd be so young.'

'Which do you want most,' I asked. 'A father-figure, or someone to find Bob?' But it was too soon to expect her to see that the two things didn't necessarily go together. She needed the comfort as much as the search.

'He didn't steal that money,' she said.

'How do you know?'

'He just wouldn't.' She spoke with conviction, but I wondered if the person she most wanted to convince was herself.

A waiter knocked on the door, bringing a tray, and Emma felt well enough to sit at the table and eat. She started slowly, still in a weak state, but by the end it was clear she was fiercely hungry. As she finished the last of the bread I said, 'In about three hours we'll have dinner.'

'Oh no.'

'Oh yes. Why not? Then you'll have plenty of time to tell me about Bob. Hours and hours. No need to hurry.'

She looked at me with the first signs of connected thought and almost immediately glanced round the room. The awareness that she was in my bedroom flashed out like neon in the North Pole. I smiled. 'Would you prefer the local nick? One each side of a table in an interview room?'

'Oh! I . . . suppose not.' She shuddered slightly. 'I've had quite a lot of that, you see. In a way. Everyone's been quite kind, really, but they think Bob stole that money and they treat me as if my husband was a crook. It's . . . it's pretty dreadful.'

'I understand that,' I said.

'Do you?'

The meal had done nothing for her pallor. The eyes still looked as hollowed and black-smudged, and the strain still vibrated in her manner. It was going to take more than champagne and soup to undo the knots.

'Why don't you sleep for a while?' I suggested. 'You look very tired. You'll be quite all right here, and I've some reports which I ought to write. I'd be glad to get them out of the way.'

'I can't sleep,' she said automatically, but when I determinedly took papers out of my briefcase, spread them on the table, and switched on a bright lamp to see them by, she stood up and hovered a bit and finally lay down again on the bed. After five minutes I walked over to look, and she was soundly asleep with sunken cheeks and pale blue veins in her eyelids.

She wore a camel coloured coat, which she had relaxed as far as unbuttoning, and a brown and white checked dress underneath. With the coat falling open, the bulge in her stomach showed unmistakably. Five months, I thought, give or take a week or two.

I pushed the papers together again and returned them to the briefcase. They were the various statements and accounts relating to her husband's disappearance, and I had no report to write on them. I sat instead in one of the Grand's comfortable armchairs and thought about why men vanished.

In the main they either ran *to* something or *from* something: occasionally a combination of both. To a woman; from a woman. To the sunshine; from the police. To political preference; from political oppression. To anonymity; from blackmail.

Sometimes they took someone elses' money with them to finance the future. Bob Sherman's sixteen thousand kroner didn't seem, at first sight, to be worth what he'd exchanged for it. He earned five times as much every year.

So what had he gone *to*? Or what had he gone *from*?

And how was I to find him by Monday afternoon?

She slept soundly for more than two hours with periods of peaceful dreaming, but after that went into a session which was distressing her. She moved restlessly and sweat appeared on her forehead, so I touched her hand and called her out of it.

'Emma. Wake up. Wake up, now, Emma.'

She opened her eyes fast and wide with the nightmare pictures still in them. Her body began to tremble.

'Oh,' she said. 'Oh God . . .'

'It's all right. You were dreaming. It was only a dream.'

Her mind finished the transition to consciousness, but she was neither reassured nor comforted.

'I dreamed he was in jail . . . there were bars . . . and he was trying to get out . . . frantically . . . and I asked him why he wanted to get out, and he said they were going to execute him in the morning . . . and then I was talking to someone in charge and I said what had he done, why were they going to execute him, and this man said . . . he'd stolen the racecourse . . . and the law said that if people stole racecourses they had to be executed . . .'

She rubbed a hand over her face.

'It's so silly,' she said. 'But it seemed so real.'

'Horrid,' I said.

She said with desolation, 'But where is he? Why doesn't he write to me? How can he be so cruel?'

'Perhaps there's a letter waiting at home.'

'No. I telephone . . . every day.'

I said, 'Are you . . . well . . . are you happy together?'

'Yes,' she said firmly, but after five silent seconds the truer version came limping out. 'Sometimes we have rows. We had one the day he came here. All morning. And it was over such a little thing . . . just that he'd spent a night away when he didn't have to . . . I'd not been feeling well and I told him he was selfish and thoughtless . . . and he lost his temper and said I was too damn demanding . . . and I said I wouldn't go with him to Kempton then, and he went silent and sulky because he was going to ride the favourite in the big race and he always likes to have me there after something like that, it helps him unwind.' She stared into a past moment she would have given the world to change. 'So he went on his own. And from there to Heathrow for the six-thirty to Oslo, same as usual. Only usually I went with him, to see him off and take the car home.'

'And meet him again Sunday night?'

'Yes. On Sunday night when he didn't come back at the right time I was worried sick that he'd had a fall in Norway and hurt himself, and I telephoned to Gunnar Holth . . . but he said Bob hadn't fallen, he'd ridden a winner and got round in the other two races, and as far as he knew he'd caught the plane as planned. So I rang the airport again . . . I'd rung them before, and they said the plane had landed on time . . . and I begged them to check and they said there was no Sherman on the passenger list . . .' She stopped and I waited, and she went on in a fresh onslaught of misery, 'Surely he knew I didn't really mean it? I love him . . . Surely he wouldn't just leave me, without saying a word?'

It appeared, however, that he had.

'How long have you been married?'

'Nearly two years.'

'Children?'

She glanced down at the brown and white checked mound and gestured towards it with a flutter of slender fingers. 'This is our first.'

'Finances?'

'Oh . . . all right, really.'

'How really?'

'He had a good season last year. We saved a bit then. Of course he does like good suits and a nice car . . . All jockeys do, don't they?'

I nodded. I knew also more about her husband's earnings than she seemed to, as I had access to the office which collected and distributed jockeys' fees; but it wasn't so much the reasonable income that was significant as the extent to which they lived within it.

'He does get keen on schemes for making money quickly, but we've never lost much. I usually talk him out of it. I'm not a gambler at all, you see.'

I let a pause go by. Then, 'Politics?'

'How do you mean?'

'Is he interested in communism?'

She stared. 'Good heavens, no. '

'Militant in any way?'

She almost laughed. 'Bob doesn't give a damn for politics or politicians. He says they're all the same, hot air and hypocrisy. Why do you ask such an extraordinary question?'

I shrugged. 'Norway has a common frontier with Russia.'

Her surprise was genuine on two counts: she didn't know her geography and she did know her husband. He was not the type to exchange good suits and a nice car and an exciting job for a dim existence in a totalitarian state.

'Did he mention any friends he had made here?'

'I've seen nearly everyone I can remember him talking about. I've asked them over and over . . . Gunnar Holth and his lads, and Mr Kristiansen, and the owners. The only one I haven't met is one of the owner's sons, a boy called Mikkel. Bob mentioned him once or twice . . . he's away at school now, or something.'

'Was Bob in any trouble before this?'

She looked bewildered. 'What sort?'

'Bookmakers?'

She turned her head away and I gave her time to decide on her answer. Jockeys were not allowed to bet, and I worked for the Jockey Club.

'No,' she said indistinctly.

'You might as well tell me,' I said. 'I can find out. But you would be quicker.'

She looked back at me, perturbed. 'He only bets on himself, usually,' she said defensively. 'It's legal in a lot of countries.'

'I'm only interested in his betting if it's got anything to do with his disappearance. Was anyone threatening him for payment?'

'Oh.' She sounded forlorn, as if the one thing she did not want to be given was a good reason for Bob to steal a comparatively small sum and ruin his life for it.

'He never said . . . I'm sure he would have told . . .' She gulped. 'The police asked me if he was being blackmailed. I said no, of course not . . . but if it was to keep me from knowing something . . . how can I be sure? Oh, I do wish, I do wish he'd write to me. . . .'

Tears came in a rush and spilled over. She didn't apologize, didn't brush them away, and in a few seconds they had stopped. She had wept a good deal, I guessed, during the past three weeks.

'You've done all you can here,' I said. 'Better come back with me on Monday afternoon.'

She was surprised and disappointed. 'You're going back so soon? But you won't have found him.'

'Probably not. But I've a meeting in London on Tuesday that I can't miss. If it looks like being useful I'll come back here afterwards, but for you, it's time now to go home.'

She didn't answer at once, but finally, in a tired, quiet, defeated voice, said 'All right.'

CHAPTER FOUR

ARNE WAS HAVING DIFFICULTY with his complex, constantly looking over his shoulder to the extent of making forward loco-motion hazardous. Why he should find any threat in the cheerful frost-bitten looking crowd which turned up at Øvrevoll for the Norsk Grand National was something between him and his psychiatrist, but as usual his friends were suffering from his affliction.

He had refused, for instance, to drink a glass of wine in a comfortable available room with a king-sized log fire. Instead we were marching back and forth outside, him, me, and Per Bjørn Sandvik, wearing out shoe leather and turning blue at the ears, for fear of bugging machines. I couldn't see how overhearing our present conversation could possibly benefit anyone, but then I wasn't Arne. And at least this time, I thought philosophically, we would not be mown down by a speedboat.

As before, he was ready for the outdoor life: a blue padded hood joined all in one to his anorak. Per Bjørn Sandvik had a trilby. I had my head. Maybe one day I would learn.

Sandvik, one of the Stewards, was telling me again at first hand what I'd already read in the statements: how Bob Sherman had had access to the money.

'It's collected into the officials' room, you see, where it is checked and recorded. And the officials' room is in the same building as the jockeys' changing room. Right? And that Sunday, Bob Sherman went to the officials' room to ask some question or other, and the money was stacked there, just inside the door. Arne saw him there himself. He must have planned at once to take it.'

'What was the money contained in?' I asked.

'Canvas bags. Heavy double canvas.'

'What colour?'

He raised his eyebrows. 'Brown.'

'Just dumped on the floor?'

He grinned. 'There is less crime in Norway.'

'So I've heard,' I said. 'How many bags?'

'Five.'

'Heavy?'

He shrugged. 'Like money.'

'How were they fastened?'

'With leather straps and padlocks.'

Arne cannoned into a blonde who definitely had the right of way. She said something which I judged from his expression to be unladylike, but it still didn't persuade him to look where he was going. Some enemy lay behind, listening: he was sure of it.

Sandvik gave him an indulgent smile. He was a tall pleasant unhurried man of about fifty, upon whom authority sat as lightly as fluff. Arne had told me he was 'someone at the top in oil', but he had none of the usual aura of big business: almost the reverse, as if he derived pleasure from leaving an impression of no power, no aggression. If so, he'd be a board-room opponent as wicked as a mantrap among the daisies. I looked at him speculatively.

He met my eyes. Nothing in his that shouldn't be.

'What was it intended to do with the bags, if Sherman hadn't nicked them?' I asked.

'Lock them in the safe in the officials' room until Monday morning, when they would go to the bank.'

'Guarded,' Arne said, eyes front for once, 'by a night watchman.' But by the time the night watchman had clocked in, the booty had vanished.

'How did the officials all happen to desert the room at once, leaving the money so handy?' I asked.

Sandvik spread his thickly gloved hands. 'We have discussed this endlessly. It was accidental. The room can only have been empty for five minutes or less. There was no special reason for them all being out at one time. It just happened.'

He had a high-register voice with beautifully distinct enunciation, but his almost perfect English sounded quite different from the home-grown variety. I worked it out after a while: it was his 'l's. The British pronounced 'l' with their tongue lolling back in the throat, the Norwegians said theirs with the tongue tight up behind the teeth. Retaining the Norwegian 'l' gave Sandvik's accent a light, dry, clear-vowelled quality which made everything he said sound logical and lucid.

'No one realized, that evening, that the money had been stolen. Each of the officials took it for granted that another had put the bags in the safe as they were no longer to be seen. It was the next day, when the safe was opened for the money to be banked, that it was found to be missing. And then, of course, we heard from Gunnar Holth that Sherman had disappeared as well.'

I thought. 'Didn't Gunnar Holth tell me that Bob Sherman stayed with you once or twice?'

'Yes, that's right.' Sandvik briefly pursed his well-shaped mouth. 'Twice. But not the time he stole the money, I'm glad to say.'

'You liked him, though?'

'Oh yes, well enough, I suppose. I asked him out of politeness. He had ridden several winners for me, and I know what Gunnar's bunk room is like . . .' He grinned slightly. 'Anyway, he came. But we had little of common interest except horses, and I think he really preferred Gunnar's after all.'

'Would you have expected him to steal?'

'It never crossed my mind. I mean, it doesn't does it? But I didn't know him well.'

Arne could not bear the close quarters of the crowd on the stands, so we watched the first race, a hurdle, from rising ground just past the winning post. The racecourse, forming the floor of a small valley, was overlooked on all sides by hillsides of spruce and birch, young trees growing skywards like the Perpendicular period come to life. The slim dark evergreens stood in endless broken vertical stripes with the yellow-drying leaves and silver trunks of the birch, and the whole backdrop, that afternoon, was hung along the skyline with fuzzy drifts of misty low cloud.

The light was cold grey, the air cold damp. The spirits of the crowd, sunny Mediterranean. An English jockey won the race on the favourite and the crowd shouted approval.

It was time, Sandvik said, to go and see the Chairman, who had not been able to manage us sooner on account of lunching a visiting ambassador. We went into the Secretariat building adjoining the grandstand, up some sporting print-lined stairs, and into a large room containing not only the Chairman but five or six supporting Stewards. Per Bjørn Sandvik walked in first, then me, then Arne pushing his hood back, and the Chairman went on looking enquiringly at the door, still waiting for me, so to speak, to appear. I sometimes wondered if it would help if I were fat, bald and bespectacled: if premature ageing might produce more confidence and belief than the thin-six-feet-with-brown-hair job did. I'd done a fair amount of living, one way or another, but it perversely refused to show.

'This is David Cleveland,' Sandvik said, and several pairs of eyes mirrored the same disappointment.

'How do you do,' I murmured gently to the Chairman, and held out my hand.

'Er . . . ' He cleared his throat and recovered manfully. 'So glad you have come.'

I made a few encouraging remarks about how pleasant I found it in Norway and wondered if any of them knew that Napoleon was promoted General at twenty-four.

The Chairman, Lars Baltzersen, was much like his letters to my office, brief, polite and effective. It took him approximately ten seconds to decide I wouldn't have been given my job if I couldn't do it, and I saw no need to tell him that my boss had died suddenly eighteen months earlier and left the manager-elect in charge a lot sooner than anyone intended.

'You sound older on the telephone,' he said simply, and I said I'd been told so before, and that was that.

'Go anywhere you like on the racecourse,' he said. 'Ask anything . . . Arne can interpret for those who do not speak English.'

'Thank you.'

'Do you need anything else?'

Second sight, I thought; but I said, 'Perhaps, if possible, to see you again before I go at the end of the afternoon.'

'Of course. Of course. We all want to hear of your progress. We'll all gather here after the last race.'

Heads nodded dubiously, and I fully expected to justify their lowly expectations. Either briefed or bored or merely busy, they drifted away through the door, leaving only Arne and the Chairman behind.

'Some beer?' suggested Baltzersen.

Arne said yes and I said no. Despite the glow from a huge stove it was a cold day for hops.

'How far is it to the Swedish border?' I asked.

'By road, about eighty kilometres,' Baltzersen said.

'Any formalities there?'

He shook his head. 'Not for Scandinavians in their own cars. There are few inspections or customs. But none of the frontier posts remember an Englishman crossing on that evening.'

'I know. Not even as a passenger in a Norwegian car. Would he have been spotted if he'd gone across crouching under a rug on the floor behind the driver's seat?'

They pondered. 'Very probably not,' Baltzersen said, and Arne agreed.

'Can you think of anyone who might have taken him? Anyone he was close to here, either in business or friendship?'

'I do not know him well enough,' the Chairman said regretfully, and Arne blinked a little and said Gunnar Holth, or maybe some of the lads who worked for him.

'Holth says he drove him only round to the races,' I said: but he would have had plenty of time to drive into Sweden and back before Emma Sherman had rung him up.

'Gunnar tells lies whenever it suits him,' Arne said.

Lars Baltzersen sighed. 'I'm afraid that is true.'

He had grey hair neatly brushed, with a tidy face and unimaginative clothes. I was beginning to get the feel of Norwegian behaviour patterns, and he came into the very large category of sober, slightly serious people who were kind, efficient, and under little stress. Get-up-and-go was conspicuously absent, yet the job would clearly be done. The rat race taken at a walk. Very civilized.

There were other types, of course.

'The people I hate here,' Emma Sherman had said, 'are the drunks.'

I'd taken her to dinner in the hotel the evening before, and had

listened for several hours, in the end, to details of her life with
Bob, her anxieties, and her experiences in Norway.

'When I first came,' she said, 'I used to have dinner in the
dining-room, and all these men used to come and ask if they
could share my table. They were quite polite, but very very persistent. They wouldn't go away. The head waiter used to get rid
of them for me. He told me they were drunk. They didn't really
look it. They weren't rolling or anything.'

I laughed. 'Considering the price of alcohol here, you wouldn't
think they could.'

'No,' she said. 'Anyway I stopped having dinner. I needed to
make my money go as far as possible and I hated eating on my
own.'

Arne said, 'Where do you want to go first?'

Arne came into a third group: the kinks. You find them everywhere.

'Weighing room, I should think.'

They both nodded in agreement. Arne pulled his hood back
over his head and we went down into the raw outdoors. The
crowd had swelled to what Arne described as 'very big', but there
was still plenty of room. One of the greatest advantages of life in
Norway, I guessed, was the small population. I had not so far in
its leisurely capital seen a queue or a crush or anyone fighting to
get anywhere first: as there always seemed to be room for all, why
bother?

The officials checking tickets at the gates between different
enclosures were all keen young men of about twenty, most of
them blond also, all with blue armbands on their anoraks. They
knew Arne, of course, but they checked my pass even though I was
with him, the serious faces hardly lightening as they nodded me
through. Lars Baltzersen had given me a five-by-three-inch card
stamped all over with *adgang paddock, adgang stallomradet,
adgang indre bane* and one or two other *adgangs*, and it looked
as if I wouldn't get far if I lost it.

The weighing room, black wood walls, white paint, red tiled
roof, lay on the far side of the parade ring, where the jockeys were
already out for the second race. Everything looked neat, organised
and pleasing, and despite an eye trained to spot trouble at five
hundred paces in a thick fog, I couldn't see any. Even in racing,
good nature prevailed. Several of the lads leading the horses
round wore sweaters in the owner's colours, matching the jockeys;
a good and useful bit of display I'd seen nowhere else. I commented on it to Arne.

'*Ja,*' he said. 'Many of the private stables do that now. It helps the crowd to know their colours.'

Between the paddock and the U-shaped weighing room buildings, and up into the U itself, there was a grassy area planted thickly with ornamental bushes. Everyone walking between weighing room and paddock had to detour either to one side or the other along comparatively narrow paths: it made a change from the rolling acres of concrete at home but took up a lot of apology time.

Once inside the weighing room Arne forgot about bugging machines and introduced me rapidly to a stream of people like the secretary, clerk of the course, clerk of the scales, without once looking over his shoulder. I shook hands and chatted a bit, but although they all knew I was looking for Bob Sherman, I couldn't see anyone feeling twitchy about my presence.

'Come this way, David,' Arne said, and took me down a side passage with an open door at the end leading out to the racecourse. A step or two before this door, Arne turned smartly right, and we found ourselves in the officials' room from which the money had been stolen. It was just an ordinary businesslike room, wooden walls, wooden floor, wooden tables acting as desks, wooden chairs. (With all those forests, what else?) There were pleasant red-checked curtains, first-class central heating, and in one corner, a no-nonsense safe.

Apart from us, there was no one there.

'That's all there is,' Arne said. 'The money bags were left there on the floor . . .' he pointed, 'and the lists of totals from each collecting point were put on that desk, same as usual. We still have the lists.'

It had struck me several times that Arne felt no responsibility for the loss of the money, nor did anyone seem in the remotest way to blame him, but by even the most elementary requirements of a security officer, he'd earned rock bottom marks.

'Do you still have the same system,' I asked, 'with the bags?'

Arne gave me a look somewhere between amusement and hurt. 'No. Since that day, the bags are put immediately into the safe.'

'Who has the keys?'

'I have some, and the secretary, and the clerk of the course.'

'And each of you three thought one of the other two had stowed the money away safely?'

'That is right.'

We left the room and stepped out into the open air. Several jockeys, changed into colours for later races but with warm coats on at the moment, came along the passage and out through the same door, and they, Arne, and I climbed an outside staircase on to a small open stand attached to the side of the weighing room buildings. From there, a furlong or more from the winning post, we watched the second race.

Arne had begun looking apprehensively around again, though there were barely twenty on the stand. I found I had begun doing it myself: it was catching. It netted, however, the sight of an English jockey who knew me, and as everyone after the finish poured towards the stairs I arranged to fetch up beside him. Arne went on down the steps, but the jockey stopped when I touched his arm, and was easy to keep back.

'Hallo,' he said in surprise. 'Fancy seeing you here.'

'Came about Bob Sherman,' I explained.

I'd found that if I said straight out what I wanted to know, I got better results. No one wasted time wondering what I suspected them of, and if they weren't on the defensive they talked more.

'Oh. I see. Found the poor bugger, then?'

'Not yet,' I said.

'Let him go, why don't you?'

Rinty Ranger knew Bob Sherman as well as anyone who'd been thrown together in the same small professional group for five years, but they were not especially close friends. I took this remark to be a general statement of sympathy for the fox and asked if he didn't think stealing the money had been a bloody silly thing to do.

'Too right,' he said. 'I'll bet he wished he hadn't done it, five minutes after. But that's Bob all over, smack into things without thinking.'

'Makes him a good jockey,' I said, remembering how he flung his heart over fences regardless.

Rinty grinned, his thin sharp face looking cold above his sheep-skin coat. 'Yeah. Done him no good this time, though.'

'What else has he done that was impulsive?'

'I don't know . . . Always full of get-rich-quick schemes like buying land in the Bahamas or backing crazy inventors, and I even heard him on about pyramid selling once, only we told him not to be such a bloody fool. I mean, it's hard enough to earn the stuff, you don't actually want to throw it down the drain.'

'Were you surprised when he stole the money?' I asked.

'Well of course I was, for Chrissakes. And even more by him doing a bunk. I mean, why didn't he just stash away the loot and carry on with business as usual?'

'Takes nerve,' I said, but of course that was just what Bob Sherman had. 'Also the money was in heavy canvas bags which would take a lot of getting into. He wouldn't have had time to do that and catch his flight home.'

Rinty thought a bit but came up with nothing useful.

'Stupid bugger,' he said. 'Nice wife, kid coming, good job. You'd think he'd have more sense.' And I'd got as far as that myself.

'Anyway, he's done me a favour,' Rinty said. 'I've got his ride in this here Grand National.' He opened his sheepskin a fraction to show me the colours underneath. 'The owner, fellow called Torp, isn't best pleased with Bob on any account. Says he should've won at a canter that last day he was here. Says he threw it away, left it too late, came through too soon, should've taken the outside, didn't put him right at the water, you name it, Bob did it wrong.'

'He got another English jockey, though.'

'Oh sure. D'you know how many home-bred jump jocks there are here? About fifteen, that's all, and some of those are English or Irish. Lads they are mostly. You don't get many self-employed chaps, like us. There isn't enough racing here for that. You get them going to Sweden on Saturdays, they race there on Saturdays. Here Thursdays and Sundays. That's the lot. Mind you, they don't keep the jumpers to look at. They all run once a week at least, and as there are only four or five jump races a week—all the rest are Flat—it makes life interesting.'

'Were you and Bob often over here together?'

'This year, three or four trips, I suppose. But I came last year too, which he didn't.'

'How long is a trip?'

He looked surprised. 'Only a day usually. We race in England Saturday afternoon, catch the six-thirty, race here Sunday, catch the late plane back if we can, otherwise the eight-fifteen Monday morning. Sometimes we fly here Sunday morning, but it's cutting it a bit fine. No margin for hold-ups.'

'Do you get to know people here well, in that time?'

'I suppose it sort of accumulates. Why?'

'Has Bob Sherman made any friendships here, would you say?'

'Good God. Well, no, not that I know of, but then likely as not I wouldn't know if he did. He knows a lot of trainers and owners, of course. Do you mean girls?'

'Not particularly. Were there any?'

'Shouldn't think so. He likes his missus.'

'Do you mind thinking fairly hard about it?'

He looked surprised. 'If you like.'

I nodded. He lengthened the focus of his gaze in a most satisfactory manner and really concentrated. I waited without pressure, watching the crowd. Young, it was, by British standards: at least half under thirty, half blonde, all the youth dressed in anoraks of blue, red, orange and yellow in the sort of colourful haphazard uniformity that stage designers plan for the chorus.

Rinty Ranger stirred and brought his vision back to the present.

'I don't know . . . He stayed with Mr Sandvik a couple of times, and said he got on better with his son than the old man . . . I met him once, the son, that is, with Bob when they were chatting at the races . . . but I wouldn't say they were great friends or anything. . . .'

'How old is he, roughly?'

'The son? Sixteen, seventeen. Eighteen maybe.'

'Anyone else?'

'Well. . . . One of the lads at Gunnar Holth's. An Irish lad, Paddy O'Flaherty. Bob knows him well, because Paddy used to work for old Tasker Mason, where Bob was apprenticed. They were lads together, one time, you might say. Bob likes staying at Gunnar Holth's on account of Paddy, I think.'

'Do you know if Paddy has a car?'

'Haven't a clue. Why don't you ask him? He's bound to be here.'

'Were you here,' I asked. 'The day Bob disappeared?'

' 'Fraid not.'

'Well. . . . Mm . . . anything you can think of which is not what you'd've expected?'

'What bloody questions! Let's see . . . can't think of anything . . . except that he left his saddle here.'

'Bob?'

'Yes. It's in the changing room. And his helmet. He must have known, the silly sod, that he'd never be able to race anywhere in the world again, otherwise he'd never have left them.'

I moved towards the stairs. Rinty hadn't told me a great deal, but if there had been much to tell the police of one country or the other would have found Bob long ago. He followed me down, and I wished him good luck in the National.

'Thanks,' he said. 'Can't say I wish you the same, though. Let the poor bastard alone.'

At the bottom of the steps, Arne was talking to Per Bjørn Sandvik. They turned to include me with smiles, and I asked the offensive question with as much tact as possible.

'Your son Mikkel, Mr Sandvik. Do you think he could've driven Bob Sherman away from the races? Without knowing, of course, that he had the money with him?'

Per Bjørn reacted less violently than many a father would to the implication that his son, having entertained a thief even if unawares, had nonetheless kept quiet about it. Scarcely a ripple went through him.

He said smoothly, 'Mikkel cannot drive yet. He is still at school . . . his seventeenth birthday was six weeks ago.'

'That's good,' I said in apology; and I thought, that's that.

Per Bjørn said 'Excuse me,' without noticeable resentment, and walked away. Arne, blinking furiously, asked where I wanted to go next. To see Paddy O'Flaherty, I said, so we went in search and found him in the stables getting Gunnar Holth's runner ready for the Grand National. He turned out to be the lad in the woolly cap with uncomplimentary opinions of a mare, and described himself as Gunny's head lad, so I am.

'What did I do after the races?' he repeated. 'Same as I always do. Took the runners home, squared 'em up and saw to their scoff.'

'And after that?'

'After that, same as always, down to the local hop. There's a good little bird there, d'you see?'

'Do you have a car?' I asked.

'Well, sure I have now, but the tyres are as thin as a stockpot on Thursday and I wouldn't be after driving on them any more at all. And there's the winter coming on, so there's my car up on bricks, d'you see?'

'When did you put it on bricks?'

'The police stopped me about those tyres, now . . . well, there's the canvas peeping through one or two, if you look close. Sure it's all of six weeks ago now.'

After that we drifted around while I took in a general view of what went on, and then walked across the track to watch a race from the tower. This looked slightly like a small airfield control tower, two storeys high with a glass-walled room at the top. In this eyrie during races sat two keen-eyed men with fierce race-glasses clamped to their eyes: they were non-automatic patrol cameras, and never missed a trick.

Arne introduced me. Feel free, they said, smiling, to come up into the tower at any time. I thanked them and stayed to watch the next race from there, looking straight down the narrow elongated oval of the track. Sixteen hundred metres for staying two-year-olds: they started almost level with the tower, scurried a long way away, rounded the fairly sharp bottom bend, and streamed up the long straight to finish at the winning post just below where we stood. There was a photo-finish. The all-seeing eyes unstuck themselves from their raceglasses, nodded happily, and said they would be back for the next race.

Before following them down the stairs I asked Arne which way the Grand National went, as there seemed to be fences pointing in every direction.

'Round in a figure of eight,' he said, sweeping a vague arm. 'Three times round. You will see when they go.' He seemed to want to be elsewhere fairly promptly, but when we had hurried back over to the paddock it appeared merely that he was hungry and had calculated enough eating time before the Norsk St Leger. He magicked some huge open sandwiches on about a foot of french loaf, starting at one end with prawns and proceeding through herring, cheese, pâté and egg to beef at the far end, adorned throughout by pickled cucumber, mayonnaise and scattered unidentified crispy bits. Arne stayed the course, but I blew up in the straight.

We drank wine: a bottle. We would come back later, Arne said, and finish it. We were in the big warm room he had shunned earlier, but the listeners weren't troubling him at that moment.

'If you're going home tomorrow, David,' he said, 'come to supper with us tonight.'

I hesitated. 'There's Emma Sherman,' I said.

'That girl,' he exclaimed. He peered around, though there were barely six others in the room. 'Where is she? She's usually on my heels.'

'I talked to her yesterday. Persuaded her not to come today and to go back to England tomorrow.'

'Great. Great, my friend.' He rubbed his hands. 'She'll be all right, then. You come to supper with us. I will telephone to Kari.'

I thought of Kari's hair and Kari's shape. Everything stacked as I liked it best. I imagined her in bed. Very likely I should have allowed no such thoughts but you might as well forbid fish to swim. A pity she was Arne's I thought. To stay away would make it easier on oneself.

'Come,' Arne said.

Weak, that's what I am. I said, 'I'd love to.'

He bustled off instantly to do the telephoning and soon returned beaming. 'She is very pleased. She says we will give you cloud-berries, she bought some yesterday.'

We went out to the raw afternoon and watched the big flat race together, but then Arne was whisked off on official business and for a while I wandered around alone. Though its organisation and upkeep were clearly first class, it was not on British terms a big racecourse. Plenty of room, but few buildings. Everyone could see: no one was pushed, rushed or crushed. Space was the ultimate luxury, I thought, as I strolled past a small oblong ornamental pond with a uniformed military band playing full blast beside it. Several children sat in bright little heaps around the players' feet and one or two were peering interestedly into the quivering business ends of trombones.

Øvrevoll, someone had told me, was a fairly new racecourse, the only one in Norway to hold ordinary Flat and jump races. Most racing, as in Germany, was trotting, with sulkies.

For the Grand National itself I went back up the tower, which I found stood in the smaller top part of the figure of eight, with the larger part lying in the main part of the course, inside the flat track. Twenty runners set off at a spanking pace to go three and a half times round, which set the binocular men in the tower rotating like gyros. Soon after the start the horses circled the tower, cut closer across beside it and sped towards the water jump and the farther part of the course, took the bottom bend, and returned towards the start. In the top part of the course, near the tower, lay a large pond with a couple of swans swimming in stately unison across from two small devoted black and white ducks. Neither pair took the slightest notice of the throng of horses thundering past a few feet from home.

Rinty Ranger won the race, taking the lead at the beginning of the last circuit and holding off all challengers, and I saw the flash of his triumphant teeth as he went past the post.

The misty daylight had already faded to the limit for jumping fences safely, but the two races still to come, in a card of ten altogether, were both on the Flat. The first was run in peering dusk and the second in total darkness, with floodlights from the tower illuminating just the winning line, bright enough to activate the photo finish. Eleven horses sped up the dark track, clearly seen only for the seconds it took them to flash through the bright patch, but cheered nonetheless by a seemingly undiminished crowd.

So they literally did race in the dark. I walked thoughtfully back towards the officials' room to meet up with Arne. It really had been night-black when Bob Sherman left the racecourse.

There was bustle in the officials' room and a lot of grins and assurances that the takings this day were safe in the safe. Arne reminded several of them that the Chairman had said they could come to the progress-report meeting if they liked: he said it in English in deference to me, and in English they answered. They would come, except for one or two who would wait for the night watchman. A right case of bolting stable doors.

The Chairman's room had too many people in it, as far as I was concerned. Fifteen besides myself. Every chair filled up, coffee and drinks circulated, and the eyes waited. Lars Baltzersen raised his eyebrows in my direction to tell me I was on, and shushed the low-key chatter with a single smooth wave of his hand.

'I think you've all met Mr Cleveland at some time today . . .' He turned directly to me and smiled forgivingly. 'I know we have asked the impossible. Sherman left no traces, no clues. But is there any course of action you think we might take which we have not so far done?'

He made it so easy.

'Look for his body,' I said.

CHAPTER FIVE

IT SEEMED that that was not what they expected.

Per Bjørn Sandvik said explosively in his high distilled English, 'We know he is a thief. Why should he be dead?' and someone else murmured, 'I still think he is in the south of France, living in the sun.'

Rolf Torp, owner of the Grand National winner, lit a cigar and said, 'I do not follow your reasoning.' Arne sat shaking his head and blinking as if he would never stop.

Lars Baltzersen gave me a slow stare and then invited me to explain.

'Well,' I said. 'Take first the mechanics of that theft. Everyone agrees that the officials' room was empty for a very few minutes, and that no one could have predicted when it would be empty, or that it would be empty at all. Everyone agrees that Bob Sherman simply saw the money lying handy, was overcome with sudden temptation, and swiped it. Sorry . . .' I said as I saw their puzzlement, '. . . stole it.'

Heads nodded all round. This was well-worn ground.

'After that,' I said, 'we come to a few difficulties. That money was enclosed in five hefty . . . er, bulky . . . canvas bags fastened

with straps and padlocks. Now a hundred and thirty-three pound
jockey couldn't stow five such bags out of sight under his coat.
Anyone, however big, would have found it awkward to pick all
of them up at once. To my mind, if Sherman's first impulse was
to steal, his second would instantly be to leave well alone. He had
no way of knowing how much the bags contained. No way of
judging whether the theft would be worthwhile. But in fact there
is no evidence at all to suggest that he even felt any impulse to
steal, even if he saw the bags on the floor when he went earlier to
ask some question or other. There is no evidence whatsoever to
prove that Bob Sherman stole the money.'

'Of course there is,' Rolf Torp said. 'He disappeared.'

'How?' I asked.

There were several puzzled frowns, one or two blank faces,
and no suggestions.

'This must have been a spur of the moment theft,' I said, 'so
he could have made no preparations. Well, say for argument he
had taken the bags, there he is staggering around with the swag
. . . the stolen goods . . . in full view. What does he do? Even with
a sharp knife it would have taken some time to slit open those
bags and remove the money. But we can discount that he did this
on the racecourse, because the bags in fact have never been found.'

Some heads nodded. Some were shaken.

'Bob Sherman had a small overnight grip with him, which I
understand from his wife was not big enough to contain five
canvas bags, let alone his clothes as well. No one has found his
clothes lying around, so he could not have packed the money in
his grip.'

Lars Baltzersen looked thoughtful.

'Take transport,' I said. 'He ordered a taxi to take him to
Fornebu airport, but he didn't turn up. The police could find no
taxi driver who took one single Englishman anywhere. Gunnar
Holth says he drove him round to the racecourse at midday, but
not away. Because the theft has to be unpremeditated, Sherman
could not have hired himself a getaway car, and the police anyway
could trace no such hiring. He did not steal a car to transport the
money: no cars were stolen from here that day. Which leaves
friends . . .' I paused. 'Friends who could be asked to take him say
to Sweden, and keep quiet afterwards.'

'They would be also guilty,' said Rolf Torp disbelievingly.

'Yes. Well . . . he had been to Norway seven times but only for
a day or two each time. The only friends I can find who might
conceivably have known or liked him well enough to get them-

selves into trouble on his account are Gunnar Holth's head lad Paddy O'Flaherty, and perhaps . . . if you'll forgive me, sir . . . Mikkel Sandvik.'

He was much more annoyed this time, but protested no further than a grim stare.

'But Paddy O'Flaherty's car has been up on bricks for six weeks,' I said. 'And Mikkel Sandvik cannot drive yet. Neither of them had wheels . . . er, transport . . . ready and waiting for Sherman's unexpected need.'

'What you are saying,' Baltzersen said, 'is that once he'd stolen the money, he couldn't have got it away. But suppose he hid it, and came back for it later?'

'He would still have much the same transport problem and also the night watchmen to contend with. No . . . I think if he had stolen and hidden the money, he would not have gone back for it, but just abandoned it. Sense would have prevailed. Because there are other things about that cash. . . . To you, it is familiar. It is *money*. To Bob Sherman, it was foreign currency. All British jockeys riding abroad have enough trouble changing currency as it is: they would not leap at stealing bagfuls of something they could not readily spend. And don't forget, a large proportion of it was in coins, which are both heavy and even more difficult to exchange in quantity than notes, once they are out of Norway.'

Per Bjørn Sandvik was studying the floor and looking mild again. Arne had blinked his eyes to a standstill and was now holding them shut. Rolf Torp puffed his cigar with agitation and Lars Baltzersen looked unhappy.

'But that still does not explain why you think Sherman is dead,' he said.

'There has been no trace of him from that day to this. . . . No one even thinks they might have seen him. There have been no reports from anywhere. His pregnant wife has had no word of reassurance. All this is highly unusual in the case of a thief on the run, but entirely consistent with the man being dead.'

Baltzersen took his bottom lip between his teeth.

I said, 'It is usually fairly easy to account for a man's abrupt disappearance . . . during an investigation his motive emerges pretty strongly. But there seems to have been no factor in Bob Sherman's life likely to prompt him into impulsive and irreversible flight. No one would exchange a successful career for an unknown but not huge amount of foreign currency unless some secondary force made it imperative. Neither your police, nor the British police, nor his wife, nor Arne Kristiansen, nor I, have found any suggestion, however faint or unlikely, that there was such force at work.'

Arne opened his eyes and shook his head.

'Suppose,' I said, 'that someone else stole the money, and Bob Sherman saw him.'

The Stewards and officials looked startled and intensely gloomy. No one needed to have it spelled out that anyone caught red-handed might have had too much to lose, and from there it was a short step to imagine the thief desperate enough to kill Bob Sherman to keep him quiet.

'Murder?' Baltzersen spoke the word slowly as if it were strange on his tongue. 'Is that what you mean?'

'It's possible,' I said.

'But not certain.'

'If there were any clear pointers to murder,' I said, 'your police would have already found them. There is no clarity anywhere. But if there are no answers at all to the questions where he went, why he went, and how he went, I think one should then ask *whether* he went.'

Baltzersen's strained voice mirrored their faces: they did not want me to be right. 'You surely don't think he is still *here*? On the racecourse?'

Rolf Torp shook his head impatiently. He was a man most unlike the Chairman, as quick tempered as Baltzersen was steady. 'Of course he doesn't. There are people here every day training their horses, and we have held eight race meetings since Sherman disappeared. If his body had been here, it would have been found at once.'

Heads nodded in unanimous agreement, and Baltzersen said regretfully, 'I suppose he could have been driven away from here unconscious or dead, and hidden . . . buried . . . somewhere else.'

'There's a lot of deep water in Norway,' I said.

My thoughts went back to our little junket in the fjord, and I missed some lightning reaction in someone in that room. I knew that a shift had been made, but because of that gap in concentration I couldn't tell who had made it. Fool, I thought, you got a tug on the line and you didn't see which fish, and even the certainty that a fish was there was no comfort.

The silence lengthened until finally Per Bjørn Sandvik looked up from the floor with a thoughtful frown. 'It would seem, then, that no one can ever get to the truth of it. I think David's theory is very plausible. It fits all the facts . . . or rather, the lack of facts . . . better than any explanation we have discussed before.'

The heads nodded.

'We will tell our police here what you have suggested,' Baltzersen said in a winding-up-the-meeting voice, 'but I agree with Per. . . . After so long a time, and after so much fruitless investigation we will never really know what happened either to Sherman or to the money. We are all most grateful that you took the trouble to come over, and I know that for most of us, on reflection, your answer to the puzzle will seem the one most likely to be right.'

They gave me a lot of worried half-smiles and some more nods. Rolf Torp stubbed out his cigar vigorously and everyone shifted on their chairs and waited for Baltzersen to stand up.

I thought about the two graceful swans and the two little black and white ducks swimming around quietly out there on the dark side of the tower.

'You could try the pond,' I said.

The meeting broke up half an hour later, after it had been agreed with a certain amount of horror that the peaceful little water should be dragged the following morning.

Arne had some security jobs to see to, which he did with painstaking slowness. I wandered aimlessly around, listening to the Norwegian voices of the last of the crowd going home. A good hour after the last race, and still a few lights, still a few people. Not the most private place for committing murder.

I went back towards the weighing room and stood beside the clump of ornamental bushes on the grass outside. Well . . . they were thick enough and dark enough to have hidden a body temporarily, until everyone had gone. A jockey and his overnight grip, and five bags of stolen money. Plenty of room, in these bushes, for the lot. There were lights outside the weighing room, but the bushes threw heavy shadows and one could not see to their roots.

Arne found me there and exclaimed with passionate certainty, 'He can't be in those, you know. Someone would have seen him long ago.'

'And smelled him,' I said.

Arne made a choking noise and 'Christ.'

I turned away. 'Have you finished now?'

He nodded, one side of his face brightly lit, the other in shadow. 'The night watchman is here and everything is as it should be. He will make sure all the gates are locked for the night. We can go home.'

He drove me in his sturdy Swedish Volvo back towards the city and round to his leafy urban street. Kari greeted us with roaring logs on the fire and tall glasses of frosty thirst-quenching white wine. Arne moved restlessly round the apartment like a bull and switched Beethoven on again fortissimo.

'What's the matter?' Kari asked him, raising her voice. 'For God's sake turn it down.'

Arne obliged, but the sacrifice of his emotional safety valve clearly oppressed him.

'Let him rip,' I told him. 'We can stand it for five minutes.'

Kari gave me a gruesome look and vanished into the kitchen as Arne with great seriousness took me at my word. I sat resignedly on the sofa while the stereophonics shook the foundations, and admired the forbearance of his neighbours. The man who lived below my own flat in London had ears like stethoscopes and was up knocking on my door at every dropped pin.

The five minutes stretched to nearly twenty before Arne stopped pacing around and turned down the volume.

'Great stuff, great stuff,' he said.

'Sure,' I agreed, because it was, in its place, which was somewhere the size of the Albert Hall.

Kari returned from exile with little wifely indulgent shakes of the head. She looked particularly disturbing in a copper-coloured silky trouser suit which did fantastic things for the hair, the colouring and the eyes and nothing bad for the rest of her. She refilled our glasses and sat on some floor cushions near the fire.

'How did you enjoy the races?' she asked.

'Very much,' I said.

Arne blinked a bit, said he had some telephone calls to make, and removed himself to the hall. Kari said she had watched the Grand National on television but rarely went to the races herself.

'I'm an indoors person,' she said. 'Arne says the outdoor life is healthier, but I don't enjoy being cold or wet or cut up by the wind, so I let him go off doing all those rugged things like skiing and sailing and swimming, and me, I just make a warm room for him to come back to.'

She grinned, but I caught the faintest of impressions that wifely though she might thoroughly appear to be, she had feelings for Arne which were not wholeheartedly love. Somewhere deep lay an attitude towards the so-called manly pursuits which was far from admiration; and a basic antipathy to an activity nearly always extended, in my experience, to anyone who went in for it.

Arne's voice floated in from the hall, speaking Norwegian.

'He is talking about dragging a pond,' Kari said, looking puzzled. 'What pond?'

I told her what pond.

'Oh dear . . . his poor little wife . . . I hope he isn't in there . . . how would she bear it?'

Better, I thought, on the whole, than believing he was a thief who had deserted her. I said 'It's only a possibility. But it's as well to make sure.'

She smiled. 'Arne has a very high opinion of you. I expect you are right. Arne said when he came back from England that he would never want to be investigated by you, you seemed to know what people were thinking. When the Chairman asked for someone to find Bob Sherman and Arne heard that you were coming yourself, he was very pleased. I heard him telling someone on the telephone that you had the eyes of a hawk and a mind like a razor.' She grinned ironically, the soft light gleaming on her teeth. 'Are you flattered?'

'Yes,' I said. 'I wish it were true.'

'It must be true if you are in charge when you are so young.'

'I'm thirty-three,' I said. 'Alexander the Great had conquered the world from Greece to India by that time.'

'You look twenty-five,' she said.

'It's a great drawback.'

'A . . . what?'

'A disadvantage.'

'No woman would think so.'

Arne came back from the hall looking preoccupied.

'Everything all right?'

'Oh . . . er . . . ja.' He blinked several times. 'It is all arranged. Nine o'clock tomorrow morning, they drag the pond.' He paused. 'Will you be there, David?'

I nodded. 'And you?'

'Ja.' The prospect did not seem to please him; but then I was not wildly excited about it myself. If Bob Sherman were indeed there, he would be the sort of unforgettable object you wished you had never seen, and my private gallery of those was already too extensive.

Arne piled logs on the fire as if to ward off demons, and Kari said it was time to eat. She gave us reindeer steaks in a rich dark sauce and after that the promised cloudberries, which turned out to be yellowy-brown and tasted of caramel.

'They are very special,' Arne said, evidently pleased to be able to offer them. 'They grow in the mountains, and are only in season for about three weeks. There is a law about picking them. One can be prosecuted for picking them before the right date.'

'You can get them in tins,' Kari said. 'But they don't taste the same as these.'

We ate in reverent silence.

'No more until next year,' Arne said regretfully, putting down his spoon. 'Let's have some coffee.'

Kari brought the coffee and with amusement declined half-hearted offers from me to help with the dishes.

'You do not want to. Be honest.'

'I do not want to,' I said truthfully.

She laughed. A highly feminine lady with apparently no banners to wave about equality in the kitchen. Between her and Arne the proposition that everything indoors was her domain, and every-thing outside, his, seemed to lead only to harmony. In my own sister it had led to resentment, rows, and a broken marriage. Kari, it seemed to me, expected less, settled for less, and achieved more.

I didn't stay late. I liked looking at Kari just a shade too much, and Arne, for all his oddnesses, was an investigator. I had taught him myself how to notice where people were looking, because where their eyes were, their thoughts were, as often as not. Some men felt profound gratification when others lusted after their wives, but some felt a revengeful anger. I didn't know what Arne's reaction would be, and I didn't aim to find out.

CHAPTER SIX

MONDAY MORNING. Drizzle. Daylight slowly intensifying over Øvrevoll racecourse, changing anthracite clouds to flannel grey. The dark green spruce and yellow birch stood around in their dripping thousands and the paper debris from the day before lay soggily scattered across the wet tarmac.

Round the lower end of the track, Gunnar Holth and one or two other trainers were exercising their strings of racehorses, but the top part had been temporarily railed off.

Shivering from depression more than cold, I was sitting up in the observation tower with Lars Baltzersen, watching the dragging of the pond down below. Hands in pockets, shoulders hunched, rain dripping off hat brims, Arne and two policemen stood at the water's edge, peering morosely at the small boat going slowly, methodically, backwards and forwards from bank to bank.

The pond was more or less round, approximately thirty yards in diameter, and apparently about six feet deep. The boat contained two policemen with grappling hooks and a third, dressed in a black rubber scuba suit, who was doing the rowing. He wore flippers, gloves, hood and goggles, and had twice been over the side with an underwater torch to investigate when the grapples caught. Both times he had returned to the surface and shaken his head.

The swans and the black and white ducks swam around in agitated circles. The water grew muddier and muddier. The boat moved slowly on its tenth traverse, and Lars Baltzersen said gloomily, 'The police think this is a waste of time.'

'Still,' I said, 'they did come.'

'They would, of course.'

'Of course,' I said.

We watched in silence.

A grapple caught. The swimmer went over the side, submerged for a full minute, came up, shook his head, and was helped back into the boat. He took up the oars: rowed on. One each side of the boat, the two men swung the three-pronged grapples into the water again, dragging them slowly across the bottom.

'They considered emptying the pond,' Baltzersen said. 'But the technical difficulties are great. Water drains into it from all the top part of the racecourse. They decided on dragging.'

'They are being thorough enough,' I said.

He looked at me soberly. 'If they do not find Sherman, then, will you be satisfied that he is not there?'

'Yes,' I said.

He nodded. 'That is reasonable.'

We watched for another hour. The swimmer made two more trips into the water, and came up with nothing. The boat finished its journey, having missed not an inch. There was no body. Bob Sherman was not in the pond.

Beside me, Baltzersen stood up stiffly and stretched, his chair scraping loudly on the wooden boards.

'That is all, then,' he said.

'Yes.'

I stood and followed him down the outside staircase, to be met at the bottom by Arne and the policeman in charge.

'No one is there,' he said to me in English, implying by his tone that he wasn't surprised.

'No. But thank you for finding out.'

He, Baltzersen and Arne spoke together for some time in

Norwegian, and Baltzersen walked across to thank the boatmen personally.

They nodded, smiled, shrugged, and began to load their boat on to a trailer.

'Never mind, David,' said Arne with sympathy. 'It was a good idea.'

'One more theory down the drain,' I agreed philosophically. 'Not the first, by a long way.'

'Will you go on looking?'

I shook my head. The fjords were too deep. Someone in the Chairman's room had reacted strongly to my mention of water, and if Bob Sherman wasn't in the pond he was somewhere just as wet.

Baltzersen, Arne, the senior policeman and I trudged back across the track and into the paddock enclosure, on our way to the cars parked beside the main entrance. Baltzersen frowned at the rubbish lying around in the shape of dropped race-cards and old tote tickets and said something to Arne. Arne replied in Norwegian and then repeated it in English.

'The manager thought it better that the refuse collectors should not be here to see the police drag the pond. Just in case, you see. Anyway, they are coming tomorrow instead.'

Baltzersen nodded. He had taken the morning off from his timber business and looked as though he regretted it.

'I'm sorry,' I said. 'To have wasted your time.'

He made a little movement of his head to acknowledge that I was more or less forgiven. The persistent drizzle put a damper on anything warmer.

In silence we passed the stands, the ornamental pond (too shallow) and secretariat, and it was probably because the only noise was the crunch of our feet that we heard the child.

He was standing in a corner of the Tote building, sobbing. About six, soaked to the skin, with hair plastered to his forehead in forlorn-looking spikes. The policeman looked across to him and beckoned, and in a kind enough voice said what must have been 'Come here.'

The boy didn't move, but he said something which halted my three companions in mid-step. They stood literally immobile, as if their reflexes had all stopped working. Their faces looked totally blank.

'What did he say?' I asked.

The boy repeated what he had said before, and if anything the shock of my companions deepened.

Baltzersen loosened his jaw with a visible effort, and translated. 'He said, "I have found a hand".'

The child was frightened when we approached, his big eyes looking frantically around for somewhere to run to, but whatever the policeman said reassured him, and when we reached him he was just standing there, wet, terrified, and shivering.

The policeman squatted beside him, and they went into a longish quiet conversation. Eventually the policeman put out his hand, and the child gripped it, and after that the policeman stood up and told us in English what he'd said.

'The boy came to look for money. The racing crowd often drop coins and notes, especially after dark. This boy says he always squeezes through a hole in the fence, before the rubbish collectors come, to see if he can find money. He says he always finds some. This morning he found twenty kroner before the men came. He means before the police came. But he is not supposed to be here, so he hid. He hid behind the stands, up there.' The policeman nodded across the tarmac. 'He says that behind the stands he found a hand lying on the ground.'

He looked down at the child clutching his own hand like a lifeline, and asked Arne to go across to his men, who had packed up all their gear and were on the point of leaving, to ask them to come over at the double. Arne gave the child a sick look and did as he was asked, and Baltzersen himself slowly returned to businesslike efficiency.

The policeman had difficulty transferring the boy's trust to one of his men, but finally disengaged himself, and he, two of his men, Baltzersen, Arne and I walked up to and around the stands to see the hand which was lying on the ground.

The child was not mistaken. Waxy white and horrific, it lay back downwards on the tarmac, fingers laxly curled up to the rain.

What the child had not said, however, was that the hand was not alone. In the angle between the wall and the ground lay a long mound covered by a black tarpaulin. Half way along its length, visible to the wrist, the hand protruded.

Wordlessly the senior policeman took hold of a corner of the tarpaulin and pulled it back.

Arne took one look, bolted for the nearest bushes, and heaved up whatever Kari had given him for breakfast. Baltzersen turned grey and put a shaking hand over his mouth. The policemen themselves looked sick, and I added another to the unwanted memories.

He was unrecognizable really: it was going to be a teeth job for the inquest. But the height and clothes were right, and his overnight grip was lying there beside him, still with the initials R. T. S. stamped on in black.

A piece of nylon rope was securely knotted round the chest, and another half way down the legs, and from each knot, one over the breastbone, one over the knees, led a loose piece of rope which finished in a frayed end.

One of the policemen said something to his chief, and Baltzersen obligingly translated for me.

'That is the policeman who was diving,' he said, and 'he says that in the pond the grapples caught on a cement block. He did not think anything of it at the time, but he says there were frayed ends of rope coming from the cement. He says it looked like the same rope as this.'

The policeman in charge pulled the tarpaulin back over the tragic bundle and started giving his men instructions. Arne stood several yards away, mopping his face and mouth with a large white handkerchief and looking anywhere but at the black tarpaulin. I walked over and asked if he was all right. He was trembling, and shook his head miserably.

'You need a drink,' I said. 'You'd better go home.'

'No.' He shuddered. 'I'll be all right. So stupid of me. Sorry, David.'

He came with me round to the front of the stands and we walked over to where Baltzersen and the top policeman had rejoined the little boy. Baltzersen adroitly drew me aside a pace or two, and said quietly, 'I don't want to upset Arne again . . . The child says the hand was not showing at first. He lifted the tarpaulin a little to see what was underneath . . . you know what children are like . . . and he saw something pale and tried to pull it out. It was the hand. When he saw what it was . . . he ran away.'

'Poor little boy,' I said.

'He shouldn't have been here,' he said, meaning by his tone, serve him right.

'If he hadn't been, we wouldn't have found Bob Sherman.'

Lars Baltzersen looked at me thoughtfully. 'I suppose whoever took him out of the pond meant to return with transport and get rid of him somewhere else.'

'No, I shouldn't think so,' I said.

'He must have done. If he didn't mind him being found, he would have left him lying in the pond.'

'Oh, sure. I just meant . . . why take him anywhere else? Why not straight back into the pond . . . as soon as it was dark? That's the one place no one would ever look for Bob Sherman again.'

He gave me a long considering stare, and then unexpectedly, for the first time that morning, he smiled.

'Well . . . you've done what we asked,' he said.

I smiled faintly back and wondered if he yet understood the significance of that morning's work. But catching murderers was a matter for the police, not for me. I was only catching the two-five to Heathrow, with little margin for what I still had to do first.

I said, 'Any time I can help . . .' in the idle way that one does, and shook hands with him, and with Arne, and left them there with their problem, in the drizzle.

I picked up Emma Sherman at her hotel as I had arranged, and took her up to my room in the Grand. I had been going to give her lunch before we set off to the airport, but instead I asked the restaurant to bring hot soup upstairs. Still no brandy. Not until three o'clock, they said. Next time, I thought, I'd pack a gallon.

Champagne was emotionally all wrong for the news I had to give her, so I stirred it around with some orange juice and made her drink it first. Then I told her, as gently as I could, that Bob had died at the time of his disappearance. I told her he was not a thief and had not deserted her. I told her he had been murdered.

The desperately frail look came back to her face, but she didn't faint. 'You did . . . find him, then.'

'Yes.'

'Where . . . is he?'

'At the racecourse.'

She stood up, swaying a bit. 'I must go and see him.'

'No,' I said firmly, holding her elbow. 'No, Emma, you must not. You must remember him alive. He doesn't look the same now, and he would hate you to see him. He would beg you not to see him.'

'I must see him . . . of course I must.'

I shook my head.

'Do you mean. . . .' It began to dawn on her. . . . 'That he looks *horrible*?'

'I'm afraid so. He's been dead a month.'

'Oh God.'

She sat down with weak knees and began to cry. I told her about the pond, the ropes, the cement. She had to know sometime, and it couldn't be much worse than the agony of spirit she had suffered through four long weeks.

'Oh my poor Bob,' she said. 'Oh darling . . . oh darling . . .'

The floodgates of all that misery were opened, and she wept with a fearful outpouring intensity, but at least and at last it was a normal grief, without the self doubt and humiliating shame.

After a while, still shaking with sobs, she said, 'I'll have to get my room back, at the hotel.'

'No,' I said. 'You're coming home to England today, with me, as we planned.'

'But I can't . . . .'

'Indeed you can, and indeed you will. The last place for you now is here. You need to go home, to rest, recover, and look after that baby. The police here will do everything necessary, and I'll see that the Jockey Club, and the Injured Jockeys' Fund perhaps, organizes things from the English end. In a little while we can have Bob brought home to England, if that's what you would like. . . . But for today, it's you that matters. If you stay here, you will be ill.'

She listened, took in barely half, but in fact raised no more objections. Maybe the police would not be overjoyed at her leaving, I thought, but they'd had her around for a month, and there couldn't be much she hadn't already told them. We caught the flight on schedule, and she stared out of the window all the way home with tears running intermittently down her cheeks.

Her grandfather, alerted from Oslo, met her at Heathrow. Tall, thin, stooping and kind, he greeted her with a small kiss and many affectionate pats: her parents, she had told me, had died during her school days, leaving her and a brother to be shuttled between relays of other relations. She liked her mother's widowed father best, and wanted him most in her troubles.

He shook my hand. 'I'll see she's looked after,' he said.

He was a nice scholarly man. I gave him my private address and telephone number, in case she needed an inside edge on official help.

CHAPTER SEVEN

TUESDAY MORNING from nine to ten I spent in the office finding out that everyone had been doing just great in my absence and would undoubtedly continue to do so if I disappeared altogether. On my desk lay neat reports of finished inquiries: the man we had suspected of running a retired high-class 'chaser under a hunter's name in a point-to-point had in fact done so and was now in line for a fraud prosecution, and an applicant for a trainer's licence in the Midlands had been found to have totally unsuitable training facilities.

Nothing to make the hair curl. Nothing like weighted bodies in Norwegian ponds.

The whole of the rest of the day was spent with two opposite numbers from the New York Racing Commission who had come to discuss the viability of a world-wide racing investigatory link-up, something along the lines of Interpol. It was one of a series of talks I'd had with officials of many countries, and the idea seemed very slowly to be staggering towards achievement. As usual the chief stumbling block to any rapid progress seemed to be my own apparent youth: I supposed that by the time I was sixty, when I'd run out of steam, they would begin to nod while they listened.

I talked my throat dry, gave away sheaves of persuasive literature, took them to dinner at Inigo Jones, and hoped the seed hadn't fallen on stony ground. At farewell time the older of them asked a question I was by then well used to.

'If you succeed in setting this thing up, do you have it in mind to be head of it yourself?'

I smiled. I knew very well that if the baby was born it would very smartly be found to be not mine after all.

'Once it's set up,' I said, 'I'll move on.'

He looked at me curiously. 'Where to?'

'Don't know yet.'

They shook their heads and tut-tutted slightly, but gripped hands with cordiality as we separated into a couple of homeward taxis. It was after midnight when I reached the house where I lived behind the Brompton Road, but as usual the lights were still on in the rooms below my own small flat. The street door banged if you let it go, reverberating through the walls, and perhaps that, I thought, as I shut it gently, explained the ground floor tenant's hypersensitivity. He was a self-contained man, greyish, fiftyish, very neat and precise. Our acquaintanceship after six months of living stacked one over the other extended simply to his trips to my door urging an instant lessening of decibels on the television. Once I had asked him in for a drink, but he politely declined, preferring solitude downstairs. Hardly the *entente cordiale* of the century.

I went up, opened my own door, and shut that quietly also. The telephone bell, starting suddenly in all that noble silence, made me jump.

'Mr Cleveland?' The voice was hurried, practically incoherent. 'Thank goodness you're back at last . . . This is William Romney . . . Emma's grandfather . . . She didn't want me to ring you so late, but I must . . . Two men were searching her house when she went in and they hit her . . . Mr Cleveland . . . she needs your help. . . .'

'Stop a minute,' I said. 'First thing you need is the police.'

He calmed down a fraction. 'They've been here. Just left. I called them.'

'And a doctor for Emma?'

'Yes, yes. He's gone, too.'

'What time did all this happen?'

'About seven this evening . . . we drove over from my house just to fetch some things for her . . . and there was a light on . . . and she went in first and they jumped on her . . . they hit us both . . . I do wish . . . well . . . tell you the truth . . . I think we're both still frightened.'

I stifled a sigh. 'Where exactly are you?'

'At Emma's house, still.'

'Yes, but. . . .'

'Oh, I see. Near Newbury. You go down the M4. . . .' He gave me details of the journey, certain in his own mind that I would hurry to their aid. He made it impossible for me to say take a tranquilliser and I'll come in the morning, and anyway by the sound of his voice nothing short of a full anaesthetic was going to give him any rest.

At least at night it was a fast straightforward journey, so I took the M.G.B. down there in fifty minutes flat. The Shermans' house proved to be a modernized pair of farm cottages down an uninhabited lane, a nerve-testing isolation at the best of times.

Lights were on in every window, and at the sound of my car William Romney's anxious figure appeared in the doorway.

'Thank goodness, thank goodness,' he said agitatedly, coming down the short path to meet me. 'I don't know what we would have done . . . if you hadn't been coming. . . .'

I refrained from saying that I thought they should have gone back to his house or otherwise stayed in a hotel, and once through the door I was glad I hadn't, because it wouldn't have helped. Shock prevents people from leaving the scene of personal disaster of their own accord, and of the scope and depth of their shock there could be no doubt.

The house was a shambles. Pictures had been torn from the walls, curtains from the windows, carpets from the floor. Furniture was not merely turned inside out, but smashed. Lamps, vases, ornaments lay in pieces. Papers and books scattered the wreckage like autumn leaves.

'It's all like this,' Romney said. 'The whole house. All except the spare bedroom. That's where they were when we interrupted them. The police say so. . . .'

Emma herself was in the spare bedroom, lying awake with eyes like soot smudges. Both of her cheeks were swollen and puffy, with red marks showing where blows had landed. Her lower lip had been split, and one eyebrow ended in a raw skinned patch.

'Hullo,' I said inadequately, and pulled up a chair so that I could sit beside her. Her grandfather hovered around making fussing noises, obviously freshly worried by the darkening bruises but tiring Emma beyond bearing. He looked more upset than ever when I asked him if I could speak to her alone, but in the end he reluctantly returned to the devastation below.

I held her hand.

'David. . . .'

'Wait a bit,' I said. 'Then tell me.'

She nodded slightly. She was lying on the blankets of the unmade bed, still wearing the brown and white checked dress, her head supported by two coverless pillows and with a flowered quilt over her from the waist down.

The room was hot with a pulsating gas fire, but Emma's hand was cold.

'I told the police,' she said, 'I think they were Norwegians.'

'The two men?'

She nodded. 'They were big. . . . They had thick sweaters and rubber gloves. . . . They talked with accents. . . .'

'Start at the beginning,' I said.

She loosened her mouth, obviously troubled by the split and swelling lip.

'We came over to get me some different clothes. I was beginning to feel better. . . . There was a light on upstairs but I thought Mrs Street who has been looking after the house had left it on . . . but when I unlocked the front door and went into the hall they jumped on me . . . they switched all the lights on . . . I saw the mess. . . . One of them hit me in the face and I screamed for Grandad. . . . When he came in they knocked him over . . . so easily, it was awful . . . and they kicked him. . . . One of them asked me where Bob would hide papers . . . and when I didn't answer at once he just went on . . . punching me in the face . . .

with his fists . . . I didn't answer because I didn't know. . . . Bob
doesn't hide things . . . didn't . . . oh God. . . .'

Her fingers curled tight round mine.

'All right, all right, Emma,' I said, meaning nothing except
that I understood. 'Wait a bit.'

We waited until some of the tension left her body; then she
swallowed and tried again.

'The telephone rang then, and it seemed to worry them. They
talked to each other, and then suddenly they just threw me into
a chair . . . and they went away . . . through the front door. . . .
Grandad got up off the floor but the telephone stopped before he
reached it . . . but anyway he called the police. . . .'

The tired voice stopped. I said, 'Did the men wear masks of
any sort?'

'No.'

'Would you know them again?'

'The police asked . . . they want me to look at photographs . . .
but I don't know . . . I was trying to avoid being hurt . . . I tried
to put my hands in front of my face . . . and I shut my eyes. . . .'

'How about your grandfather?'

'He says he might know them . . . but it was over so quickly.'

'I suppose they didn't tell you what papers they were looking
for?'

She shook her head miserably. 'The police asked me that, over
and over.'

'Never mind,' I said. 'How does your face feel now?'

'Awfully stiff. Dr West gave me some pills, though. He
says he'll look in again tomorrow.'

'Here?'

'Yes . . . I didn't want to go back to Grandad's. This . . . this
is . . . home.'

'Do you want the bed made properly?'

'No thank you. I'm comfortable like this . . . too tired to move.'

'I'll go down, then, and give your grandfather a hand.'

'All right. . . .' Anxiety flooded her suddenly. 'But you won't go,
will you?'

I promised her, and in fact I slept in trousers and shirt on the
sofa in the sitting-room on a cleared oasis amid the rubble.
William Romney, taxed almost too far, snored gently with a
strong sedative on the double bed in the Shermans' own room,
and from three o'clock to five the cottage was dark and quiet.

I awoke suddenly with a soft wail in my ears like the sound of
a lamb in a snowstorm.

'David. . . .'

It was Emma's voice from upstairs, urgent and quavery.

I tossed off the rug, stood up, and beat it up there fast. I'd left her door open and the fire on, and as I went in I could see the ultimate disaster looking out of her great dark eyes.

'David. . . .' Her voice filled with unconsolable desolation. 'David . . . I'm bleeding.'

She lost the baby and very nearly her life. I went to see her three days after she'd been whisked away in a bell-ringing ambulance (three days because no one was allowed in sooner) and was surprised to discover that she could and did look even paler than she had in Oslo. The swellings had gone down in her face, though the bruises showed dark in patches. Her eyes were dulled, which seemed a mercy.

The five minutes visit passed on the surface.

'Nice of you to come,' she said.

'Brought you some grapes.'

'Very kind.'

'Sorry about the baby.'

She nodded vaguely, but some sort of drug was dealing with that pain also.

'Hope you'll soon be better.'

'Oh yes. Yes, I will.'

William Romney shook with fury, stamping up and down my office with outrage.

'Do you realize that it is a week tomorrow since we were attacked and no one has done *anything*? People can't just vanish into thin air . . . those men must be somewhere . . . why can't the police find them? It isn't right that thugs should just walk into a defence-less girl's house and tear things to pieces and hurt her so much that she nearly dies of it . . . It's *disgraceful* that the police haven't found those despicable *bastards*. . . .'

The word was a strong one for him: he looked almost surprised that he'd used it, and nothing could have more clearly stated the fierceness of his feelings.

'I believe neither you nor Emma could identify the men from police photographs,' I said, having checked via a friendly police contact that this was so.

'They weren't there. There weren't any pictures of them. Can't say that's surprising . . . why don't the police get photographs of *Norwegian* crooks for us to look at?'

'It would probably mean your going to Norway,' I said. 'And Emma's in no state, physical or emotional, to do that.'

'I'll go then,' he said belligerently. 'I'll go, at my own expense. Anything . . . *anything* to see those men punished for what they've done to Emma.'

His thin face was flushed with the strength of his resentment. I wondered if part of his fury sprang from unnecessary guilt that he hadn't been young and strong enough to defend or rescue her from two aggressive toughs. Amends in the shape of effort and expense were what he was offering, and I saw no reason to dissuade him from a journey which would bring him mental ease even if no concretely helpful results.

'I'll fix it for you, if you like,' I said.

'What . . . ?'

'To go to Norway and look at the mug-shots.'

His resolution took shape and hardened. He straightened his stooping shoulders, calmed his voice, and stopped wearing out so much of the Jockey Club's carpet.

'Yes. Please do that. I'll go as soon as I can.'

I nodded. 'Sit down,' I said. 'Do you smoke? And how's Emma?'

He sat down, declined a desk-box of cigarettes, and said that last evening, when he'd seen her, Emma was very much stronger.

'She says she'll be out of hospital in two or three days.'

'Good.'

He didn't look as if it were good. He said in recurring worried anger, 'What on earth is that poor girl to do? Her husband murdered . . . her home wrecked . . . I suppose she can live with me, but. . . .'

'I'm sure she'll live in her own house,' I said. 'For a while, at least. Best if she does. Get her grieving done properly.'

'What an extraordinary thing to say.'

'When can you go?' I said, reaching for the telephone.

'At once.'

'Right.'

Øvrevoll racecourse answered in the shape of the manager, who gave me the home and office telephone numbers of Lars Baltzersen. He answered from his office, and I explained the situation. Of course, he said in dismay, of course he could arrange it with the police. For tomorrow? Certainly. Poor Mrs Sherman, he said, please give her my condolences. I said I would, and asked if there had been any recent progress.

'None at all, I'm afraid,' he said. He hesitated for several seconds, and then went on, 'I have been thinking . . . I suppose

. . . if the police don't solve this crime . . . that you wouldn't come back yourself, and see what you can do?'

I said, 'I'm not experienced in murder investigation.'

'It must in essence be the same as any other sort.'

'Mm. . . . My masters here might not be willing for me to take the time.'

'If I asked them myself, as an international favour? After all, Bob Sherman was a British jockey.'

'Wouldn't Norway prefer to ship him home and forget the whole nasty incident?'

'No, Mr Cleveland,' he said severely. 'A murder has been done, and justice should follow.'

'I agree.'

'Then . . . you'll come?'

I thought. 'Wait another week. Then if neither your police nor ours have formed any new leads, and if you still want me to, well, maybe I can. But . . . don't expect too much, will you?'

'No more than before,' he said dryly, and disconnected.

William Romney had adjusted by then to the prospect of travelling the next day, and began to fuss mildly about tickets, currency and hotels. I shooed him out because he could do all that for himself, and I had a good deal of work on hand to start with, and more still if I had to clear time for another trip to Oslo. The police, I hoped, would quickly dig down to the roots themselves and save me from proving to the world that I couldn't.

William Romney went to Norway, spent two full days there and returned depressed. The Norwegian police did not have photographs of the intruders, or if they did, Romney did not recognize them.

Emma left hospital and went home to put her house straight. An offer from me to help her do that was declined; one to come down and take her out to lunch was accepted.

'Sunday?' I suggested.

'Fine.'

Sunday found the carpets flat on the floors, the pictures back on the walls, the broken mess cleared away, and the curtains bundled up for the cleaners. The house looked stark and unlived in, but its mistress had come a long way back to life. For the first time since I had known her, she was wearing lipstick. Her hair was newly washed, her clothes neat, her manner composed. The pretty girl lurked not far away now, just below the still over-pale skin, just behind the still unhappy eyes.

'It's his funeral on Thursday,' she said.

'Here?'

She nodded. 'In the church in the village. Thank you for doing everything about bringing him home.'

I had delegated the whole job. 'I only got it done,' I said.

'Anyway . . . thanks.'

The October day was calm and sunny and crisp around the edges. I took her to a Thames-side pub where pointed yellow willow leaves floated slowly past on grey water and anglers flicked maggots on hooks to wily fish. We walked along the bank; slowly, because she was still weak from haemorrhage. 'Have you any plans?' I asked.

'I don't know . . . I've thought a lot, of course, while I've been in hospital. I'll go on living in the cottage for a while, I think. It feels right, somehow. In the end I suppose I'll sell it, but not yet.'

'How are the finances?'

She produced a flicker of smile. 'Everyone is being fantastic. Really marvellous. Did you know, the owners Bob rode for in Norway clubbed together and sent me a cheque? How kind people are.'

Conscience money, I thought sourly, but I didn't say so.

'Those two men who burst into your house, do you mind if we talk about them?'

She sighed. 'I don't mind.'

'Describe them.'

'But. . . .'

'Yes, I've read what you told the police. You didn't look at them, you shut your eyes, you only saw their sweaters and their rubber gloves.'

'That's right.'

'No. What you told the police was all you could bear to remember, and you would have shut out even that if they hadn't pressed you for answers.'

'That's nonsense.'

'Try it another way. Which one hit you?'

She said instantly, 'The bigger one with the . . .' Her voice stopped uncertainly.

'With the what?'

'I was going to say, with the reddish hair. How odd. I didn't remember until now that one of them had reddish hair.'

'What about the other?'

'Brown. Brown hair. He was kicking Grandad.'

'The one who was hitting you . . . what was he saying?'

'Where does your husband keep secret papers? Where does he hide things? Tell us where he hides things.'

'Good English?'

'Ye-es. Pretty good. He had an accent.'

'What were his eyes like, while he was hitting you?'

'Fierce . . . frightful . . . like an eagle . . . sort of black and yellow . . . very angry.'

There was a small silence, then she said, 'Yes, I do remember, like you said. I shut it out.'

After a few seconds, 'He was quite young, about the same as you. His mouth was very tight . . . his lips were stiff . . . his face looked hard . . . very angry.'

'How tall?'

'Same as you, about. Broader, though. Much heavier. Big thick shoulders.'

'Big shoulders in a thick sweater. What sort of thick sweater? Did it have a pattern?'

'Well, yes, that was why . . .' She stopped again.

'Why what?'

'Why I thought at once that he was Norwegian . . . before he even spoke. Because of the patterns in his sweater. They were sort of white patterns . . . two colours, though, I think . . . all over a brown sweater. I'd seen dozens like it in the shops in Oslo.' She looked puzzled. 'Why didn't I think of that before?'

'Memories often work like that. Sort of delayed action.'

She smiled. 'I must say it's easier remembering things quietly here by the river than in all that mess with my face hurting and policemen asking me questions from all sides and bustling about. . . .'

We went indoors for a drink and a good lunch, and over coffee I asked her other things.

'You said Bob never hid papers. Are you sure?'

'Oh yes. He wasn't secretive. Never. He was more careless, really, than anything else, when it came to papers and documents and things like that.'

'It seems quite extraordinary that two men should come all the way from Norway to search your house for papers.'

She frowned. 'Yes, it does.'

'And to search it so violently, so destructively, so thoroughly.'

'And they were so angry, too.'

'Angry, I expect, because they'd worked so hard and hadn't found what they'd come for.'

'But what *did* they come for?'

'Well . . .' I said slowly. 'Something to do with Norway. What papers did Bob ever have that had anything to do with Norway?'

She shook her head. 'Nothing much. A few receipts, for the accounts. Race-cards, sometimes. A cutting from a Norwegian paper with a picture of him winning a race. Nothing, honestly, that anyone could want.'

I drank my coffee, considering. I said, 'Look at it the other way round . . . Did he ever take any papers *to* Norway?'

'No. Why should he?'

'I don't know. I just wondered. Because those men might have been looking for something he hadn't taken to Norway, not for something he had brought away.'

'You do think some weird things.'

'Mm. . . .'

I paid the bill and drove her home. She was silent most of the way, but thoughtful, and the fruit of that was a plum.

'I suppose . . . well, it's stupid, really . . . but it couldn't have anything to do with blue pictures?'

'What sort of blue pictures?' I asked.

'I don't know. I didn't see them. Only Bob said that's what they were.'

I pulled up outside her gate, but made no move to leave the car. 'Did he get them in Norway?'

She was surprised. 'Oh no. It was like you said. He was taking them over there with him. In a brown envelope. It came by hand the night before he went. He said they were blue pictures which a chap in Oslo wanted him to bring over.'

'Did he say what chap?'

She shook her head. 'No. I hardly listened. I'd forgotten all about it until you said. . . .'

'Did you see the brown envelope? How big was it?'

'I must have seen it. I mean, I know it was brown.' She frowned, concentrating. 'Fairly big. Not an ordinary letter. About the size of a magazine.'

'Was it marked "photographs", or anything like that?'

'I don't think so. I can't remember. It's more than six weeks ago.' Her eyes filled suddenly with tears. 'He put it in his overnight grip, so as not to forget to take it.' She sniffed twice, and found a handkerchief. 'So he did take it to Norway. It wasn't in the house for those men to find. If that's what they were looking for . . . they did all that for nothing.' She put the handkerchief to her mouth and stifled a sob.

'Was Bob interested in blue pictures?' I asked.

'Like any other man, I suppose,' she said through the handkerchief. 'He'd look at them.'

'But he wouldn't collect them himself?'

She shook her head.

I got out of the car, opened the door her side, and went with her into the cottage. She looked at the racing pictures of Bob which hung in the hall.

'They tore all those photographs out of the frames,' she said. 'Some of them were ruined.'

Many of the prints were about ten inches by eight. A magazine-sized brown envelope would have held them easily.

I stayed another hour simply to keep her company, but for the evening ahead she insisted that she would be all right alone. She looked round the barenesses of the sitting-room and smiled to herself. She obviously found the place friendly, and maybe Bob was there too.

When I went she gave me a warm kiss on the cheek and said, 'I can't thank you enough . . .' and then broke off and opened her eyes wide. 'Golly,' she said. 'That was the second lot.'

'What of?'

'Blue pictures. He took some before. Oh . . . months ago. Back in the summer.' She shook her head in fresh frustration. 'I can't remember. I just remember him saying . . . blue pictures.'

I kissed her in return. 'Take care of yourself,' I said.

'You, too.'

CHAPTER EIGHT

A LITTLE MATTER of doping-to-win took me to Plumpton races in Sussex the following day but I saw no harm in some extra spadework on the side. Rinty Ranger, busy in second and fifth races, was comparatively easy to pin down between the third and the fourth.

'What did you say?' he repeated in exaggerated amazement. 'Take pornography to Scandinavia? Christ, that's like wasting pity on bookmakers. They don't need it, mate. They don't bloody need it.'

'Bob Sherman told his wife he was taking blue pictures to Norway.'

'And she believed it?'

'The point is, did he?'

'He never said a word about it to me.'

'Do me a favour,' I said. 'Find out in the changing room here today if anyone ever asked any jockey to act as a messenger . . . a carrier . . . of any papers of any sort from Britain to Norway.'

'Are you serious?'

'Bob Sherman's dead.'

'Yes.' He thought. 'O.K.'

He gave me a noncommittal wave as he walked out to the fifth, in which he rode a bright, tight, tactical race to be beaten half a length by a better horse, but came straight out of the weighing room after he had changed and put an end to my easy theory.

'None of them who have ridden in Norway has ever been asked to take over any papers or pictures or anything like that.'

'Would they say, if they had?'

He grinned. 'Depends how much they'd been paid to forget.'

'What do you think yourself?'

'Hard to tell. But they all seemed surprised. There weren't any knowing looks, sort of, if you see what I mean.'

'Carry on asking, would you? Tomorrow and so on. Say they can tell me hush hush, if they like. No kick backs if they've been fiddling currency.'

He grinned again. 'Some copper you are. Bend the rules like curling tongs.'

That evening I telephoned Baltzersen at his home. There was no news, he said. He had consulted his friends in the police, and they would raise no objections if I joined the hunt. On the contrary, they would, as before, let me see what they'd got, to save me reploughing their furrows.

'So, Mr Cleveland, will you come?'

'I guess so,' I said.

With flattering relief he said, 'Good, good,' explosively, and added, 'Come tomorrow.'

' 'Fraid I can't. I have to give evidence in court tomorrow, and the case may last two days. Soonest would be Thursday morning.'

'Come straight to the racecourse then. We have a meeting on Thursday and another on Sunday, but I fear they may be the last this year. It's a little colder now, and we have had frost.'

I wrote 'warm clothes' in large letters on my memo pad and said I'd see him at the races.

'By the way,' I said. 'You know I told you the people who broke into the Shermans' house were looking for papers? Mrs Sherman now remembers that Bob took with him to Norway a packet which had been entrusted to him, which he believed contained blue pictures. Did anyone mention to you, or to the police, or to Arne in all those preliminary investigations into his disappearance, anything at all about his bringing such a packet with him, or delivering it?'

There was an unexpectedly long silence on the other end of the line, but in the end he only said uncertainly, 'Blue pictures . . . what are those?'

'Pornography.'

'I see.' Another pause. 'Please explain a little.'

I said, 'If the package reached its destination, then it cannot be that particular package that the men were searching for. So I could stop chasing after innocent blue pictures and start looking elsewhere.'

'*Ja.* I see.' He cleared his throat. 'I haven't heard of any such package, but perhaps Arne or the police have done. I will ask them. Of course you know it is unlikely that anyone would need to bring pornography secretly into this country?'

'It would have to be special,' I said, and left it at that.

All Tuesday and Wednesday morning I spent in court giving evidence for the prosecution in an insurance swindle involving grievous cruelty to horses, and Wednesday afternoon I sat in the office juggling six jobs at once like some multi-armed Siva. Looked for Bob Sherman's murderer had meant advancing myself a week's leave when I was too busy to take one, and by seven o'clock when I locked up and left, I was wishing he'd got himself bumped off at any other time.

I went home on tube and feet, thinking comforting thoughts about a large scotch indoors followed by a stroll round to a local grill for a steak. I shut the street door without letting it bang, put one foot in front of the other up the carpeted stairs, unlocked the door to my own flat and switched on the lights; and it was at that point that the day stopped operating according to schedule.

I heard, felt, maybe assimilated by instinct, a change in the air behind me. Nothing as definite as a noise. More a current. Undoubtedly a threat.

All those useful dormant jungle reactions came to my rescue before a thought process based on reason had time to get off the ground. So I was already whipping round to face the stairs and pushing further through my own doorway when the man with the knife did his best to send me early to the cemetery.

He did not have reddish hair, angry yellow eagle eyes, or a

Norwegian sweater. He did have rubber gloves, a stocky muscular body, a lot of determination and a very sharp blade.

The stab which had been supposed to stop my heart from the back ripped instead through some decent Irish tweed, through a blue cotton shirt below that, and down half a dozen inches of skin on my chest.

He was surprised and fed up that at first he hadn't succeeded, but he'd heard all about try try again. He crowded through my door after me with the knife already rising for another go. I backed through the tiny hall and into the sitting-room, unable to take my eyes off his intentions long enough to find any household object to fight him off with.

He came on with a feint and a slice at my middle regions and I got another rip in my jacket and a closer look at some narrowed and murderous eyes.

He tried next a sort of lunging jump, the point of the knife coming in fast and upward. I tried to leap away backwards, tripped on a rug, fell on my back and found my hand hitting the base of the standard lamp. One wild clutch and I'd pulled it over, knocking him off his aim just when he thought he finally had me. The lamp hit him with a crash, and while he was off balance I got both my hands on his knife arm; but it was then that I discovered the rock-like muscles. And also, unfortunately, that he was more or less ambidextrous.

He shifted the knife like lightning from his right hand to his left and I avoided the resulting stab only by a sort of swinging jump over an armchair, using his arm as a lever. The blade hit a cushion and feathers floated up like snowflakes.

I threw a cigarette box at him and missed, and after that a vase which hit but made no difference. As long as I kept the armchair between us he couldn't reach me, but neither did he give me much chance of getting past him to the still open door to the stairs.

Behind me on a wide shelf stood my portable television. I supposed it might stop him if I threw it at him, but on the other hand . . . I stretched out backwards without losing sight of his knife, found the on-off switch, and turned the volume up to maximum.

The din when it started took him totally by surprise and gave me a fractional chance. I pushed the armchair viciously forward at his knees and he overbalanced, twisting as he tried to get his feet under him. He went down as far as one knee, partially recovered, and toppled altogether when I shoved again with the chair. But it was nothing permanent. He was rolling back to his feet like a cat before I had time to get round the big chair and step on some of his tender bits.

Up until that point he had said not a word and now if he did I wouldn't hear; the television literally vibrated with the intense noise of some pop star or other's Special Spectacular; and if that didn't bring the U.S. cavalry, nothing would.

He came. Looking cross. Ready to blow like a geyser. And stood there in consternation in my open door.

'Fetch the police,' I yelled, but he didn't hear. I slapped the off-switch.

'Fetch the police,' I yelled again, and my voice bounced off the walls in the sudden silence.

The man with the knife turned to see, gave himself fresh instructions, and went for my friend from downstairs. I did a sort of sliding rugger tackle, throwing myself feet first at his legs. He stumbled over my shoes and ankles, and went down on his side. I swept one leg in an arc and by sheer good luck kicked him on the wrist. The knife flew out of his hand at least ten feet, and fell nearer to me than him, and only at that point did he think of giving up.

He scrambled to his feet, looked at me with the first sign of uncertainty, then made up his mind, turned on his heel, crashed past my neighbour and jumped down the stairs in two giant strides. The front door slammed behind him with force that shook the building, and from the window I saw him running like the Olympics under the street lamps.

I looked breathlessly at the mess in my sitting-room and at my man from downstairs. 'Thanks,' I said.

He took a tentative step into the sitting-room.

'You're bleeding,' he said.

'But not dying.' I picked up the standard lamp.

'Was he a burglar?' he asked.

'A murderer,' I said. 'Enter a murderer.'

We looked at each other in what was no doubt professional curiosity on both sides, because all he said next was, 'Sit down, you're suffering from shock.'

It was advice I'd given pretty often to others, and it made me smile. All the same there was a perceptible tremble somewhere around my knees, so I did as he said.

He looked around the room, looked at the knife still lying where it had fallen, and took it all quietly.

'Shall I carry out your instructions, or were they principally a diversion?'

'Hm?'

'Fetch the police.'

'Oh. . . . It can wait a bit.'

He nodded, considered a moment, and then said, 'If you'll excuse me asking, why was he trying to kill you?'

'He didn't say.'

My neighbour's name was Stirling. C. V. Stirling, according to the neat white card beside his bell push. He had grey patches neatly brushed back over his ears and nostrils pinched into an expression of distaste for bad smells. His hands looked excessively clean and well manicured, and even in these bizarre circumstances he wore a faint air of exasperated patience. A man used to being the brightest person around, I guessed, with the power to make it felt.

'Did he need to?'

'It would have been helpful,' I said.

He came a pace nearer.

'I could do something about that bleeding, if you like.'

I looked down at the front of my shirt, which had changed colour pretty thoroughly from blue to red.

'Could you?'

'I'm a surgeon,' he said. 'Ear, nose and throat actually. Other areas by arrangement.'

I laughed. 'Stitch away, then.'

He nodded, departed downstairs, and returned with a neat flat case containing the tools of his trade. He used clips, not needles. The slice through my skin was more gory than deep, bleeding away persistently like a shaving nick. When he'd finished, it was a thin red line under a sticking plaster.

'You were lucky,' he said.

'Yes, I was.'

'Do you do this sort of thing often? Fight for your life, I mean.'

'Very rarely.'

'My fee for professional services rendered is a little more chat.'

I smiled wryly. 'OK. I'm an investigator. I don't know why I was attacked unless there's someone around who particularly does not want to be investigated."

'Good God.' He stared at me curiously. 'A private eye? Philip Marlowe, and all that?'

'Nothing so fancy. I work in racing; for the Jockey Club. Looking into small frauds, most of the time.'

'This,' he waved at my chest and the knife and the scattered cushion feathers, 'Doesn't look like a small fraud.'

It didn't. It didn't look, either, even like a severe warning off.
It looked like a ruthless all-out push for a final solution.

I changed my clothes and took him round to the grill for the
overdue steak. His name was Charles, he said, and we walked
home as friends. When I let myself in upstairs and reviewed the
general untidiness it occurred to me that in the end I had never
called in the police. It seemed a little late to bother, so I didn't.

CHAPTER NINE

I CAUGHT THE ELEVEN TWENTY-FIVE to Norway the next
morning with the knife wrapped in polythene in my sponge-bag;
or rather the black zipped leather case which did that duty. It
was a hunter's knife, the sort of double sided blade used for
skinning and disjointing game. The cutting edges had been
sharpened like razors and the point would have been good as a
needle. A professional job: no amateur could have produced
that result with a few passes over a carborundum.

The handle was of horn of some sort, but workmanlike, not
tourist-trap stuff. Between handle and blade protruded a short
silver bar for extra leverage with fingers. There were no fingerprints on it anywhere, and no blood. Punched into the blade
near the hilt were the words *Norsk Stål*.

Its owner hadn't, of course, intended to leave it behind. Just
one dead body neatly disposed inside its own front door, out of
sight and undiscovered for a minimum of twenty-four hours.

He hadn't followed me into the house: he'd been there before
I came, waiting higher up the stairs for me to come home.

At breakfast time I'd knocked on the doors of the other three
tenants, the one in the basement, the one above me, and the one
above that, and asked them if they'd seen my visitor on the
stairs or let him in through the front door. I got negatives all
round, but as one of them said, we were hardly a matey lot, and if
the visitor entered boldly while one of the tenants was leaving,
no one would have stopped him. None of them remembered him,
but the basement man observed that as the laundry van had called
that day, a stranger could easily have walked in with the man who
collected and delivered the boxes from the hall.

There had been nothing suspicious or memorable about my
visitor's appearance. His face was a face: hair brown, skin sallow,
eyes dark. Age, about thirty. Clothes, dark grey trousers, navy

close-fitting sweater, neat shirt and tie showing at the neck. Entirely the right rig for the neighbourhood. Even a little formal.

B.E.A. landed on time at Fornebu and I took a taxi straight
out to the racecourse. Nothing much had changed in the two and
a half weeks I'd been away, not even the weather or the runners
in the races, and within the first half hour I had spotted all the
same faces, among them Gunnar Holth, Paddy O'Flaherty, Per
Bjørn Sandvik, Rolf Torp and Lars Baltzersen. Arne greeted me
with a beaming smile and an invitation to spend as much time
with Kari and himself as I could.

I walked around with him for most of the afternoon, partly
from choice, partly because Baltzersen was busy being Chairman.
Arne said that whereas he personally was pleased to see me, many
of the racecourse committee had opposed Baltzersen in the matter
of bringing me back.

'Lars told us at the Tuesday committee meeting that you were
definitely coming today, and that caused quite a row. You should
have heard it. Lars said that the racecourse would be paying your
fare and expenses like last time, and half of them said it was
unjustifiable to spend so much.'

He broke off rather suddenly as if he had decided not to repeat
what had actually been said.

'I could easily have been persuaded to stay at home,' I said. But
by words, I reflected. Not knives.

'Several of the committee said Lars had no right to act without
taking a vote.'

'And Lars?'

Arne shrugged. 'He wants Bob Sherman's death explained.
Most of them just want to forget.'

'And you?' I asked.

He blinked. 'Well,' he said, 'I would give up more easily than
Lars or you. Which is no doubt why,' he grinned, 'Lars is Chairman and you are the chief investigator, and I am only a security
officer who lets the racecourse takings be stolen from under his
nose.'

I smiled. 'No one blames you.'

'Perhaps they should.'

I thought in my intolerant way that they definitely should, but
I shook my head and changed the subject.

'Did Lars tell you all about the attack on Emma Sherman, and
about her losing her baby?'

'Yes,' he said. 'Poor girl.' There was more lip-service in his voice
than genuine regret. I supposed that no one who hadn't seen her

as I had could properly understand all that she'd suffered; and I knew that it was in great part because of Emma that I was back in Norway. No one should be allowed to inflict such hurt on another human being, and get away with it. The fact that the same agency had murdered Bob and tried to see me off was in a curious way secondary: it was possible future victims who had to be saved. If you don't dig ground elder out of the flower beds it can strangle the garden.

Rolf Torp was striding about in a bad temper. His horse, he said, had knocked itself that morning and his trainer had omitted to tell him it couldn't run. He had taken the afternoon off from his mining office, which he wouldn't have done if he'd known, on account of being indispensable and nothing constructive ever being achieved in his absence.

After he had delivered himself of that little lot he adjusted his sights more specially on me.

'I was against bringing you back. I'll tell you that myself. I told the committee. It is a waste of our money.'

His name was on the list Emma had given me of the contributors to the solidly worthwhile cheque the Norwegian owners had sent. If he thought that any available cash should only be spent on the living, perhaps it was a valid point of view; but he wasn't paying my expenses out of his own private pocket.

He was a man of less than average height and more than average aggressiveness: a little bull of a man with a large black moustache that was more a statement than an adornment. Difficult to please and difficult to like, I thought, but sharp of eye and brain as well as tongue.

His voice boomed as heavily as a bittern in the reed beds, and although his English was as comprehensive as most well-educated Norwegians', he spoke it unlovingly, as if he didn't care too much for the taste.

I said without heat, 'As a miner, you'll understand that surveys are a legitimate expense even when they don't strike ore.'

He gave me a hard look. 'As a miner I understand that I would not finance a survey to find slime.'

Klonk. One over the head for D. Cleveland. I grinned appreciatively, and slowly, unwillingly, the corners of his mouth twitched.

I made the most of it. 'May I come and see you in your office?' I asked. 'Just for a few questions. I might as well try my best to earn what you're paying me, now that I'm here.'

'Nothing I can tell you will be of any help,' he said, as if believing made it so.

'Still. . . .'

The vestiges of smile disappeared, but finally, grudgingly, he nodded.

'Very well. Tomorrow afternoon. Four o'clock.' And he went so far as to tell me how to find him.

As he walked away Arne said, 'What are you going to ask him?'

'Don't know yet. I just want to see his background. You can't tell what people are really like if you only meet them at the races.'

'But,' he said, blinking furiously, 'why Rolf Torp?'

'Not especially Rolf Torp,' I said. 'Everyone who knew Bob Sherman.'

'David!' He looked staggered. 'It will take you months.'

I shook my head. 'Several days, that's all. Bob didn't know as many people here as all that.'

'But he could have been killed by a total stranger. I mean, if he saw someone stealing the money and didn't know him. . . .'

'It's possible,' I said, and asked him if he had ever heard Bob talking about bringing any sort of package from England to Norway.

Arne wrinkled his forehead and darted a compulsive look over his shoulder. No one there, of course.

'Lars mentioned this mysterious package on Tuesday night. No one knew anything about it.'

'What did Lars actually ask?'

'Just said you wanted to know if anyone had received a package from Bob Sherman.'

'And no one had?'

'No one who was there, anyway.'

'Could you write me a list of those who were there?'

'Yes,' he said with surprise. 'If you want it. But I can't see what it could possibly have to do with Bob's death.'

'I'm a great one for collecting useless information,' I said smiling, and Arne gave me a look which said oh yeah, plain as plain.

The races proceeded the same as before, except that the watching crowd were a good deal thinner than on Grand National day. The birch trees had dropped most of their yellow leaves and looked silver, the daylight was colder and greyer than ever, and a sharp wind whipped around every corner. But this time I had come prepared with a ski-ing cap with ear flaps and only my nose, like everyone else's, was turning blue.

Gunnar Holth saddled two for the hurdle race, hurrying busily from one to the other and juggling both sets of owners with anxious dexterity. One of his runners was the dappled mare with the uncertain temper, whose owner, Sven Wangen, was on Emma's list. Arne confirmed that the big young man assiduously hopping out of the way every time the mare presented her heels was indeed Sven Wangen, and added that the brunette sneering at him from a safe distance was his wife.

The jockey mounted warily and the mare bucked and kicked every inch to the start. Arne said that like all mean, bad-tempered females she would get her own way in the end, and went off to invest a little something on the Tote.

Wise move. She won. Arne beamed and said what did I tell you, when she comes here bitching she always wins. Was she ever docile? I asked, and Arne said sure, but those were her off days. We watched her being unsaddled in the winner's enclosure, with Gunnar Holth and Sven Wangen both tangoing smartly out of her way.

I told Arne I would like to meet Sven Wangen because Bob had ridden a winner for him on that last day. Arne showed reservations, so I asked him why.

He pursed his mouth. 'I don't like him. That's why.'

'What's wrong with him?'

'Too much money,' Arne said reprovingly. 'He behaves as if everyone ought to go on their knees when they talk to him. He has done nothing himself. The money was his father's. His father was a rich man. Too rich.'

'In what way too rich?'

Arne raised his eyebrows at what evidently seemed to him a nonsensical question, because from the tone of his reply it seemed he held great wealth to be morally wrong.

'He was a millionaire.'

'Don't you have millionaires in Norway?'

'Very few. They are not popular.'

I persuaded him, however, to introduce me to the unpopular Sven Wangen, whose father had made a million out of ships: and I saw at once why Arne didn't like him.

Perhaps two inches taller than I, he looked down his nose as if from a great height; and it was clear that this was no accidental mannerism but the manifestation of deep self-importance. Still probably in his twenties, he was bulky to the point of fatness and used his weight for throwing about. I didn't take to his manner, his small mouth, or his unfriendly light amber eyes: nor, in fact, to his wife, who looked as if she could beat the difficult mare's temper by a couple of lengths.

Arne introduced me, and Sven Wangen saw no reason at all why I should call upon him at any time to ask him questions. He had heavy rust-brown hair growing long over his ears, and a small flat cap which made his big head look bigger.

I said I understood he was a member of the racecourse committee which had asked me to come.

'Lars Baltzersen asked you,' he said brusquely. 'I was against it. I said so on Tuesday.'

'The sooner I get the questions answered, the sooner I'll go home,' I said. 'But not until.'

He looked at me with intense disfavour. 'What do you want, then?'

'Half an hour in your house,' I said. 'Any time that would suit you except for tomorrow afternoon.'

He settled in irritation for Sunday morning. His elegantly thin wife manufactured a yawn and they turned away without any pretense of politeness.

'See what I mean?' Arne said.

'I do indeed. Very unusual, wouldn't you say?'

'Unusual?'

'The rich don't usually behave like that.'

'Do you know so many rich people?' Arne asked with a touch of sarcasm.

'Meet them every day of the week,' I said. 'They own racehorses.'

Arne conceded that the rich weren't necessarily all beastly and went off on some official tasks. I tracked down Paddy O'Flaherty and found him with five minutes to spare between races.

'Brown envelope of blue pictures?' he repeated. 'He never said a dicky bird to me, now, about any blue pictures.' He grinned, and then an uncertain memory floated back. 'Wait now, I tell a lie. Back in the summer, now, he told me he had a good little tickle going for him, do you see? Always one for a chance at easy money, so he was. And there was this day, he winked at me like, and showed me the corner of an envelope in his overnight bag, and he said it would make our hair curl, so it would. So then I asked him for a look, do you see, but he said it was sealed some way so he couldn't steam it. I remember that, sure now I do.'

'The last time he came, did he say anything about bringing an envelope?'

Paddy shook his head. 'Like I said. Not a word.'

I thought. 'Did he come straight to your stable from the airport? Did he arrive on time, for instance?'

'I'll tell you something now. No, he didn't.' He concentrated. 'He was that late I thought he'd missed the flight and would come in the morning. Then, sure, a taxi rolls up and out he hops, large as life. He'd bought a bottle of brandy on the plane and there wasn't much left of that, now, before we went to bed.'

'What did he talk about?'

'Bejasus, how do I know, after all this time?'

'You must have thought often about that night.'

'Well, so I have, then.' He sighed at my perseverance, but thought some more. 'Horses, of course. We talked about horses. I don't remember him saying why he was late, or anything like that. And sure now I'd have thought it was the flight that was late, that was all.'

'I'll check,' I said.

'Look now, there was only one thing he said . . . Late on, when we'd maybe had a skinful, he said "Paddy, I think I've been conned." That's what he said now. "Paddy, I think I've been conned." So I asked him what he meant, but he didn't tell me.'

'How insistently did you ask?'

'Insist . . ? Bejasus, of course I didn't. Uh . . . there he was putting his finger over his mouth and nodding . . . he was a bit tight, do you see? So I just put my finger over my mouth like him and I nodded just the same. Well now, it seemed sensible enough at the time do you see?'

I did see. It was a miracle Paddy remembered that evening at all.

The afternoon ambled on. Gunnar Holth won the steeplechase with Per Bjørn's Sandvik's Whitefire, which displeased Rolf Torp, who was second. Per Bjørn, it appeared, had not come to the meeting: he rarely did on Thursdays, because it showed a bad example to his staff.

It was Lars Baltzersen who told me, with warm approval in his voice. He himself, he said, had to leave his work only because he was Chairman, and all his employees understood. As one who had played lifelong truant at the drop of a starter's flag, I found such noble standards a bit stifling, but one had to admire them.

Lars and I crossed the track and climbed the tower and looked down at the pond below. With its surface ruffled by the breeze it was far less peaceful than when I'd first seen it and just as brownly muddy as the day it gave up its dead. The swans and the ducks had gone. 'It will freeze soon,' Lars said. 'And snow will cover the race-course for three or four months.'

'Bob Sherman is being buried today,' I said. 'In England.'

He nodded. 'We have sent a letter of regret to Mrs Sherman.'

'And a cheque,' I said: because his name too was on the list. He made a disclaiming movement with his hands but seemed genuinely pleased when I told him how much Emma had appreciated their kindness.

'I'm afraid we were all a little annoyed with her while she was here. She was so persistent. But perhaps it was partly because of her that we asked you to come. Anyway, I am glad she is not bitter about the way we tried to avoid her continual questions. She would have a right to be.'

'She isn't that sort of person.'

He turned his head to look at me. 'Do you know her well?'

'Only since all this started.'

'I regret the way we treated her,' he said. 'I think of it often. Giving her money does not buy us off.'

I agreed with him and offered no comfort. He looked away down the racecourse and I wondered if it was his guilty conscience that had driven him to persuade me back.

After the next race, a long distance flat, we walked across together to the weighing room.

I said, 'You were in the officials' room that day when Bob Sherman poked his head in and could have seen the money lying on the floor.'

'That's right,' Lars said.

'Well . . . what was the question?'

He was puzzled. 'What question?'

'Everyone's statement to the police was the same. You all said "Bob Sherman came to the door asking some question or other". So . . . what was the question?'

He looked deeply surprised. 'It can't have had anything to do with his disappearance.'

'What was it?'

'I can't remember. Nothing of the slightest importance, I assure you, or of course we would have told the police.'

We rejoined Arne, and Lars asked him if he by any chance remembered what Bob had wanted. Arne looked just as surprised and said he had no idea, he'd been busy anyway and probably hadn't even heard. The racecourse manager however knew that he had known once, because it was he who had answered.

'Let me think,' he said, frowning. 'He came in . . . not his feet, just his head and shoulders. He looked down at the money, which was lying in front of him. I remember that distinctly. I told the police. But the question . . . it was nothing.'

I shrugged. 'Tell me if you ever remember?'

He said he would as if he thought it unlikely, but an hour later he sought me out.

'Bob Sherman asked if Mikkael Sandvik had already gone home, and I said I didn't know.'

'Oh.'

He laughed. 'Well, we did tell you it was nothing important.'

'And you were right.' I sighed resignedly. 'It was just a chance.'

At the end of the afternoon Lars took me up to his Chairman's room to give me the copies the police had provided of their Bob Sherman file. He stood in front of the big stove, a neat substantial figure in his heavy dark blue overcoat and ear-flapped astrakhan hat, blowing on his fingers. 'Cold today,' he said.

I thought I probably knew him better than anyone I'd met in Norway, but all the same I said, 'May I call to see you in your office?'

He'd heard about my appointments and smiled wryly at being included. 'Saturday, if you like. I'll be there until noon.'

Declining a pressing invitation from Arne to dine with him and Kari, I ate early at the Grand and went upstairs to do my home-work. The police had been painstaking, but the net result, as Lars had said, was nil.

A long and immensely detailed autopsy report, filled with medical terms I only half understood, concluded that the deceased had died of three overlapping depressed fractures of the skull. Unconsciousness would have been immediate. Death followed a few minutes later: the exact interval could not be specified. Immersion was subsequent to death.

The nylon rope found on the deceased had been unravelled strand by strand, and an analysis had indicated it to be part of a batch manufactured the previous spring and distributed during the summer to countless shops and ships' chandlers throughout greater Oslo.

The nylon rope found embedded in a concrete block in the Øvrevoll pond was of identical composition.

The cement block itself was a sort of sandbag in widespread use for sea-walling. The type in the pond was very common, and none of the contractors currently using it could remember having one stolen. The writer of the report added his own personal opinion that no contractor would ever miss one single bag out of hundreds.

The properties of the bag were such that its ingredients were crumbly when dry, but solidified like rock under water. The nylon rope had been tied tightly round the cement bag while it had still been dry.

Extensive inquiries had dug up no one who had heard or seen any activity round the pond on either the night of the deceased's disappearance or the night he had been removed from the water. The night-watchman had proved a dead loss. There were lists of everything they had found in Bob Sherman's pockets and in his over-night bag. Clothes, watch, keys were all as they should be: it was papers I was interested in, and they, after a month submerged, were in a pretty pulpy state.

Passport and air ticket had been identified. Currency notes had been nearly all British: total value fifteen pounds sterling. There had been no Norwegian money to speak of, and certainly not five canvas bags of it.

The report made no mention of any papers or ruins of papers being found in the overnight bag. Nor of photographs: and photographic paper fared better than most under water.

I read everything through twice and drew no conclusions which the police hadn't. Bob Sherman had had his head bashed in, and later he'd been roped to a cement bag and dumped in the pond. By person or persons unknown.

By person or persons who were doing their damnedest, also, to remain unknown.

I lifted the polythene-wrapped knife from my sponge case and propped it against the reading lamp: and immediately the slice down my chest took up throbbing where it had left off that morning. Why was it, I wondered irritably, that cuts only throbbed at night?

It was as well though to have that to remind me not to walk trustingly into hotel rooms or hail the first taxi that offered. Business had been meant in London, and I saw no safety in Oslo. I smiled ruefully to myself. I was getting as bad as Arne at looking over my shoulder.

But there could be a lot more knives where that one came from.

CHAPTER TEN

IN THE MORNING I took the knife along to the police and told them how I'd come by it. The man in charge of the case, the same policeman who had been overseeing the dragging of the pond, looked at me in a sort of startled dismay.

'We will try to trace it, as you ask. But this knife is not rare. There are many knives of this kind. In English those words *Norsk Stål* on the blade merely mean Norwegian steel.'

His name was Lund. His air that of long-term policemen everywhere: cautious, watchful, friendly with reservations. It seemed to me that many policemen were only completely at ease with criminals; and certainly the ex-policemen who worked for the investigation branch of the Jockey Club always spoke of petty crooks more affectionately than of the general public.

Dedicated to catching them, policemen also admired criminals. They spoke the same language, used the same jargon. I knew from observation that if a crook and a detective who didn't know each other turned up at the same social gathering, they would unerringly seek each other out. Unless one of them happened to be chasing the other at that moment, they would get on well together; a fact which explained the apparently extraordinary shared holidays which occasionally scandalized the press.

Lund treated me with scrupulous fairness as a temporary colleague. I thanked him warmly for letting me use his files, and he offered help if I should need it.

I said at once that I needed a car with a driver I could trust, and could he recommend one.

He looked at the knife lying on his desk.

'I cannot lend you a police car.' He thought it over, then picked up a telephone, gave some Norwegian instructions, put down the receiver and waited.

'I will ask my brother to drive you,' he said. 'He is an author. His books make little money. He will be pleased to earn some for driving, because he like driving.'

The telephone buzzed and Lund evidently put forward his proposition. I gathered that it met with the author's approval because Lund asked when I would like him to start.

'Now,' I said. 'I'd like him to collect me here.'

Lund nodded, put down the receiver, and said 'He will be here in half an hour. You will find him helpful. He speaks English very well. He worked once in England.'

I spent the half hour looking through mug-shots, but my London assailant was nowhere to be seen.

Lund's brother Erik was a bonus in every way.

He met me in the front hall with a vague distracted grin as if he had been waiting for someone else. A tallish man of about fifty-five, he had sparse untidy blond hair, a shapeless old sports jacket, and an air of being totally disorganized: and he drove, I soon discovered, as if other cars were invisible.

He waved me from the police building to a small-sized cream Volvo waiting at the kerb. Dents and scratches of varying rust vintages bore witness to long and sturdy service, and the boot was held shut by string. Upon opening the passenger-side door I found that most of the interior was already occupied by a very large Great Dane.

'Lie down, Odin,' Erik said hopefully, but the huge dog understood no English, remained on his feet and slobbered gently down my neck.

'Where first?' Erik asked. His English, as his brother had said, was splendid. He settled himself in the driver's seat and looked at me expectantly.

'What did your brother tell you?' I asked.

'To drive you around and if possible make sure no one bumps you off.' He said it as casually as if he'd been entrusted to see me on to the right train.

'What are you good at?' I said curiously.

'Driving, boxing and telling tales out of school.'

He had a long face, deeply lined round the eyes, smoother round mouth and chin: evidence of a nature more at home with a laugh than a scowl. In the course of the next few days I learnt that if it hadn't been for his highly developed sense of the ludicrous, he would have been a dedicated communist. As it was he held good radical left wing views, but found himself in constant despair over the humourlessness of his fellow travellers. He had worked on the gossip pages of newspapers throughout his youth, and had spent two years in Fleet Street; and he told me more about the people he was driving me to visit than I would have dug out in six weeks.

'Per Bjørn Sandvik? he repeated, when I told him our first destination. 'The upright man of the oil fields?'

'I guess so,' I said.

He took off into the traffic without waiting for a gap. I opened my mouth and shut it again: after all, if his brother was trusting him to keep me alive, the least I could do was let him get on with it. We swung round some hair-raising corners on two wheels but pulled up unscathed outside the main offices of Norsk Oil Imports Ltd. The Great Dane licked his chops, totally unmoved.

'There you are,' Erik said, pointing to an imposing double door entrance into a courtyard. 'Through there, turn left, big entrance with pillars.'

'You know it?'

He nodded. 'I know most places in Oslo. And most people.'
And he told me about his years on the newspapers.

'Tell me about Per Bjørn, then.'

He smiled. 'He is stuffy, righteous, and has given himself to
big business. During the war he wasn't like that at all. When we
were all young, he was a great fighter against the Nazis, a great
planner and saboteur. But the years go by and he has solidified
into a dull lump, like the living core of a volcano pouring out and
dying to dry grey pummice.'

'He must have some fire left,' I objected. 'To be the head of
an oil company.'

He blew down his nostrils in amusement. 'All the oil companies
in Norway are tied hand and foot by government regulations,
which is as it should be. There is no room for private speculation.
Per Bjørn can only make decisions within a small area. For anything above ordering new ashtrays he has to have permission from
the government.'

'You approve of that?'

'Naturally.'

'What do you know about his family?' I asked.

His eyes glimmered. 'He married a thoroughly boring plain
girl called Ragnhild whose dad just happened at that time to be
the head man in Norsk Oil Imports.'

I grinned and climbed out of the car, and told him I would
be half an hour at least.

'I brought a book,' he said equably, and pulled a tattered paper-
back of *The Golden Notebook* out of his jacket pocket.

The courtyard, tidily paved, had a stone-edged bed of frost-
bitten flowers in the centre and distinguished pale yellow buildings all round the edge. The main entrance to the left was imposing, and opposite, to the right, stood a similar entrance on a
much smaller scale. The wall facing the entrance from the street
was pierced with tall windows and decorated with shutters, and
the whole opulent little square looked more like a stately home
than an oil company's office.

It was, I found, both.

Per Bjørn's secretary fielded me from the main entrance, shov-
elled me up one flight of carpeted stairs and into his office, told
me Mr Sandvik was still at a meeting but would not be long, and
went away.

Although the building was old the head man's room was modern, functional, and highly Scandinavian, with thickly double-

glazed windows looking down into the courtyard. On the wall hung a simple chart of a rock formation with layers labelled impermeable, source, permeable and reservoir; a list saying things like spudded Oct. '71, plugged and abandoned Jan. '72; and three brightly coloured maps of the North Sea, each of them showing a different aspect of the oil drilling operations going on there.

In each map the sea area was subdivided along lines of latitude and longitude into small squares which were labelled 'Shell', 'Esso', 'Conoco', and so on, but although I looked carefully, I could see none marked Norsk Oil Imports.

The door opened behind me and Per Bjørn Sandvik came in, as pleasant and easy as ever and giving every impression of having got to the top without pushing.

'David,' he said in his high clear voice, 'sorry to keep you waiting.'

'Just looking at your maps,' I said.

He nodded, crossing to join me. 'We're drilling there . . . and there.' He pointed to two areas which bore an entirely different name. I commented on it, and he explained.

'We are part of a consortium. There are no private oil companies in Norway.'

'What did Norsk Oil Imports do before anyone discovered oil under the North Sea?'

'Imported oil, of course.'

'Of course.' I smiled and sat down in the square armchair he indicated.

'Fire away,' he said, 'with the questions.'

'Did Bob Sherman bring you any papers or photographs from England?'

He shook his head. 'No. Lars asked us this on Tuesday. Sherman did not bring any papers for anyone.' He stretched out a hand towards his desk intercom. 'Would you like some coffee?'

'Very much.'

He nodded and asked his secretary to arrange it.

'All the same,' I said. 'He probably did bring a package of some sort with him, and he probably did pass it on. If anyone would admit to having received it we might be able to take it out of consideration altogether.'

He stared vaguely at his desk.

'For instance,' I said, 'if what he brought was straight pornography, it probably had nothing to do with his death.'

He looked up. 'I see,' he said. 'And because no one has said they received it, you think it did not contain pornography?'

'I don't know what it contained,' I said. 'I wish I did.'

The coffee arrived and he poured it carefully into dark brown crusty mugs.

'Have you discarded the idea that Bob Sherman was killed by whoever stole the money?'

'It's in abeyance,' I said, refusing the offered cream and sugar. 'Could you give me your impression of Bob Sherman as a man?'

He bunched his lips assessingly. 'Not over-intelligent,' he said. 'Honest, but easily influenced. A good rider, of course. He always rode well for me.'

'I gather Rolf Torp thought he rode a bad race for him that last day.'

Sandvik delicately shrugged. 'Rolf is sometimes hard to please.'

We drank the coffee and talked about Bob, and after a while I said I would very like very much to meet Per Bjørn's son Mikkel.

He frowned. 'To ask him questions?'

'Well . . . some. He knew Bob comparatively well, and he's the one good contact I've not yet met.'

He didn't like it. 'I can't stop you, of course. Or at least, I won't. But he has been very upset by the whole affair, first by thinking his friend was a thief, and now more since he knows he was murdered.'

'I'll try not to worry him too much. I've read his short statement to the police. I don't expect to do much more than cover the same ground.'

'Then why bother him at all?'

After a pause to consider it, I said, 'I think I need to see him, to get the picture of Bob's visits complete.'

He slowly sucked his lower lip but finally made no more objections. 'He's at boarding school now,' he said. 'But he'll be home here for the afternoon tomorrow. If you come at three, he'll be here.'

'Here . . . in your office?'

He shook his head. 'In my house. The other side of the courtyard.'

I stood up to go and thanked him for his time.

'I haven't been of much use,' he said. 'We've given you a pretty hopeless job.'

'Oh well . . .' I said, and told myself that things sometimes broke if one hammered on long enough. 'I'll do my best to earn your money.'

He saw me to the top of the stairs and shook hands.

'Let me know if there's anything I can do.'

'I will,' I said. 'And thank you.'

I walked down the quiet stairs to the large empty hall. The only sounds of life seemed to come from behind a door at the back of the hall, so I walked over and opened it.

It led, I found, straight into the next door building, one dedicated not to front offices but to getting the paper work done. Even there, however, things were going at a gentle pace without any feeling of pressure, and in the doorways of the row of small offices stretching away from me stood relaxed people in sweaters drinking coffee and smoking and generally giving no impression that commercial life was rushing by.

I retreated through the hall, through the courtyard, and back to Erik Lund. He withdrew his eyes from his Golden Notes as I climbed into his car and appeared to be wondering who I was.

Recognition of sorts awoke. 'Oh yes . . .' he said.

'Lunch, then?' I suggested.

He had few definite views on where to eat, but once we were installed in a decent restaurant he lost no time in ordering something he called *gravlaks*. The price made me wince on behalf of the racecourse, but I had some too, and it proved to be the most exquisite form of salmon, cured instead of smoked.

'Are you from Scotland Yard?' he asked after the last of the pink heaven had been despatched.

'No. From the Jockey Club.'

It surprised him, so I explained briefly why I was there.

'What's all this about being bumped off, then?'

'To stop me finding out what happened.'

He gazed past me in thought.

'Makes my brother Knut a dumb cluck, doesn't it? No one's tried to get rid of *him*.'

'Knock down one policeman and six more pop up,' I said.

'And there aren't six more of you?' he asked dryly.

'The racing cupboard's pretty bare.'

He drank coffee thoughtfully. 'Why don't you give it up while you're still whole?'

'Natural bloody obstinacy,' I said. 'What do you know about Rolf Torp?'

'Rolf Torp the terror of the ski slopes or Rolf Torp who designs glass houses for pygmies?'

'Rolf Torp who owns racehorses and does something in mines.'

'Oh. Him.' He frowned, sniffed, and grimaced. 'Another god-damn capitalist exploiting the country's natural resources for private gain.'

'Do you know anything about him personally?'

'Isn't that personal enough?'

'No.'

He laughed. 'You don't think money-grubbing says anything about a man's soul?'

'Everything any man does says something about his soul.'

'You wriggle out of things,' he said.

'And things out of people.'

'Well,' he said smiling. 'I can't actually tell you much about that Rolf Torp. For one thing I've never met him, and for another, capitalists make dull copy for gossip columns unless they're caught in bed with their secretaries and no pyjamas.'

Blue pictures for blackmail, I thought irrelevantly. Or black and white pictures for blackmail. Why not?

'Do you know anyone called Lars Baltzersen?' I asked.

'Sure. The Chairman of Øvrevoll? Every man's idea of a respectable pillar of society. Entertains ambassadors and presents prizes. Often a picture on the sports pages, always beside the man of the moment. Mind you, our Lars was a live wire once himself. Did a lot of motor racing, mostly in Sweden. That was before banking finally smothered him, of course.'

'Family?'

'Dutch wife, lots of solid children.'

I paid the bill and we strolled back to the car. Odin stared out of the front window and with his huge head close to the glass, his eyes unblinking. Some people who stopped to try 'isn't-he-a-nice-boy' noises got a big yawn and a view down a cavernous throat.

Erik opened his door, gave the dog a shove and said *'Fanden ta dig.'* The Dane shifted his bulk towards the back seat without taking offence, and the journey continued.

'What did Lars do in the war?'

'He wasn't here,' he said promptly. 'He was in London, reading the news in Norwegian on the radio.'

'He didn't tell me he'd lived in London.'

'He's quiet now. Another dead volcano. More pummice.'

Erik crossed some traffic lights three seconds after they turned red and genuinely didn't seem to hear six other motorists grinding their brake drums to screaming point. Odin gave him an affectionate nudge in the neck and Erik put out the hand he needed on the gear lever and fondled the huge wet nose.

He pulled up in front of a modern square-built glass and slab affair a mile out of the city centre, a far cry from Sandvik's architectural elegance.

'This is the address you gave me,' Erik said dubiously.

'Fine,' I said. 'Would you like to wait inside?'

He shook his head, though the afternoon was cold and rapidly growing dark. 'Odin gives off heat like a nuclear reactor and I don't like sitting in plastic lobbies being stared at.'

I left them to their companionship and rode a lift up to Rolf Torp's office, where again as I was early I was asked to wait. This time not in Torp's own office, but a small purpose-decorated room overflowing with useful handouts about 'Torp-Nord Associates'.

The walls here also were hung with diagrams of rock formations, charts of progress and maps showing areas being worked. These maps were not of the North Sea but of the mainland, with the thickest cluster of work-tags to the west of Oslo, in the mountains.

Someone had told me Rolf Torp's business was silver, but it wasn't or no longer chiefly. His associates had switched to titanium.

Before he finally turned up (at four twenty) for his four o'clock appointment I had learnt a good deal I didn't especially want to know about titanium. For example that it weighed only 0.163 lbs per cubic inch and in alloy form could reach a tensile strength of 200,000 lbs per square inch. Bully for titanium, I thought.

Rolf Torp was much like his product in tensile strength but couldn't match it for lightness. He made no effort to conceal that my visit was a nuisance, bursting into the waiting room saying, 'Come on, come on then. I can give you ten minutes, that's all,' and stomping off to his own office without waiting to see if I followed.

I did, of course. His office was much like Sandvik's: same type of furniture, fabrics and carpet, a reflection of prevailing style but no clue to the occupant. The walls here were dotted with framed photographs of various stages of metal production, and another large map with thumb tacks took pride of place.

'How do you mine titanium?' I asked, and sat in his visitors' chair without being invited. Irritably he took his own place behind half an acre of tidy desk and lit a cigarette.

'Like one?' he said belatedly, pushing a box towards me.

'No, thank you.'

He flicked a lighter and deeply inhaled the smoke.

'You don't find titanium lying around like coal,' he said. 'Are you sure you want to use your ten minutes on this?'

'Might as well.'

He gave me a puzzled look over the heavy black moustache, but seemed to find his own subject a lot less temper-disturbing than mine.

'Titanium is the ninth most common element on earth. It is found in ninety-eight per cent of rocks and also in oil, coal, water, plants, animals, and stars.'

'You can hardly dig it out of people.'

'No. It is mostly mined as a mineral called ilmenite . . . which is one-third titanium.'

'Does your firm do the actual mining?'

He shook his head. 'We survey, do first drillings, advise and establish.

I looked vaguely at the photographs on the walls.

'Apart from high speed aircraft, what's the stuff used for?'

He reeled off technical uses as if he'd been asked that one once or twice before. Towards the end, slowing down, he included paint, lipstick and smokescreens. There was little you couldn't do, it seemed, with the strength of the Titans.

'Did Bob Sherman bring you any photographs?'

I asked him casually without looking at him directly, but if it jerked him at all I couldn't tell, as he swept any involuntary movement into a quick gesture to flick off ash.

'No, he didn't.'

'Did he ask your advice about anything?'

'Why should he?'

'People do need advice sometimes,' I said.

He gave a laugh that was half a scowl. 'I gave him some. He didn't ask. I told him to ride races better or stay in England.'

'He didn't please you?'

'He should have won on my good horse. He went to sleep. He stopped trying to win, and he was beaten. Also he did not ride as I told him, all the way round.'

'Do you think someone bribed him to lose?'

He looked startled. For all his bad-tempered criticism it hadn't occurred to him, and to be fair, he didn't pounce on the idea. 'No,' he said heavily. 'He wanted to ride that horse in the Grand National. It started favourite and it won.'

I nodded. 'I saw the race.'

'That's right. Bob Sherman wanted to ride it, but I would have got someone else anyway. He rode it very badly.'

I imagined that any time Rolf Torp's jockey didn't win, he had automatically ridden badly. I stood up to go, which puzzled him again, and shook his hand.

'Coming here has been a waste of your time,' he said.

'Of course not. . . . I'll let myself out.'

He didn't stop me. I closed his door and did a brief exploration. More offices. More bustle than at Sandvik's. More impression of work being done, but nothing so earthy as a lump of ore.

Erik was not parked out front where I had left him. I went through the big glass entrance doors, peered briefly into the darkness, and ignominiously retreated. One thing I did not plan to do was walk around at night alone, making everything easy for assassins.

After ten minutes I began to wonder if he'd simply forgotten about me and gone home, but he hadn't. The small cream Volvo returned at high speed and stopped outside in its own length. Its owner extricated himself from the quivering metal and strolled towards the building.

'Hullo,' he said, as I met him. 'Hope you haven't been waiting. I had to get Odin's dinner. Forgot all about it.'

In the car, Odin loomed hungrily over my head, dribbling. Just as well, I thought, that he was about to be fed.

Erik returned us to the Grand at tar-melting speed and seemed disappointed that I hadn't wanted any longer journeys.

CHAPTER ELEVEN

THE RECEPTIONISTS of the Grand considered me totally mad because I was insisting on changing my room every day, but they would have thought me even madder if I'd told them the reason. I asked them just to allocate me the last empty room, or if there were several, to give me a random choice at bed time. They did it with politely glazed eyes while I thankfully put my trust in unpredictability.

When Erik dropped me at the door and took his big friend home I telephoned to Arne and Kari and asked them to dinner.

'Come here,' Kari demanded warmly, but I said it was time I repaid their kindness, and after much demur they agreed to the Grand. I sat in the bar and read a newspaper until they arrived, and thought about growing old.

It was strange, but away from her chosen setting, Kari looked a different person. Not so young, not so domesticated, not so tranquil. This Kari, walking with assurance into the bar in a long black skirt and white ruffled shirt was the woman who designed interiors as a business. This Kari, wearing perfect make-up, diamonds in her ears and hair smoothly pinned up, looked at once cooler and more mature than the casual home-girl. When she put a smooth sweet-smelling cheek forward for a kiss and gave me a pretty look from under her lashes I found I both liked her less and wanted her more; both of which reactions were disconcerting and no good.

Arne was Arne, the antithesis of a chameleon, his personality so concretely formed that it retained its own shape whatever the environment. He swept four-square into the bar and gave it a quick suspicious survey to make sure no one could listen at his shoulder. 'Hallo, David,' he said, shaking my hand vigorously. 'What have you been doing all day?'

'Wasting time,' I said smiling. 'And wondering what to do next.'

We sat in a comfortable corner and drank (as for once it was the right hour on the right day) whisky.

Arne wanted to know what progress I had made.

'Not much,' I said. 'You might say none.'

'It must be very difficult,' Kari said sympathetically, with Arne nodding in agreement. 'How do you know what to look for?'

'I don't often look for things. I look at what's there.'

'All detectives look for things. Look for clues and follow trails. Of course they do.'

'And trudge up dead ends and find red herrings,' I said.

'Herrings are not red,' Kari said in puzzlement.

Fifty-seven varieties of herring in Norway, and not one of them red.

'A red herring is something that doesn't exist,' Arne said, but had to explain it again to her in Norwegian.

She laughed, but returned to her questions. 'How do you solve a crime?'

'Um . . . you think what you might have done if you'd been the crook, and then you look to see if that's what he did. And sometimes it is.'

'No one else solves crimes like David,' Arne said.

'Believe me,' I said. 'They do.'

'What do you think the crook did this time?' Kari asked.

I looked at her clear grey eyes, asking the questions I couldn't answer without freezing the evening in its tracks.

'There's more than one,' I said neutrally. 'Emma Sherman saw two.'

We talked about Emma for a while. Arne met her grandfather during his brief visit, and knew he had not been able to identify either of the intruders.

'And nobody knows what they were looking for,' Kari said thoughtfully.

'The men knew,' I said.

Arne's eyes stretched suddenly wide, which made a change from blinking. 'So they did,' he said.

'Of course they did,' she said. 'I don't see the point.'

'It isn't really a point. Only that someone somewhere does know what is missing. Or what was missing, because it may have been found now.'

Kari thought it over. 'Why do you think they didn't search the Shermans' house at once, as soon as they'd killed Bob Sherman? Why wait a month?'

Arne went back to blinking fit to bust, but he left it to me to answer.

'I think,' I said, 'It was because Bob Sherman was found, and whatever it was that was missing wasn't found with him.' I paused. 'Say Mr X kills Bob and dumps him in the pond, for a reason as yet unknown. Suppose this was after Bob delivered a package he had been bringing with him. Suppose also that Bob had opened the package and taken out some of the contents, but that Mr X did not discover this until after he'd killed Bob and put him in the pond. O.K. so far? So then he has to guess whether Bob had the missing contents in his pockets or his overnight bag, in which case they too are safely in the pond, or whether he passed them on to someone else, or even posted them home to himself in England, before he was killed. Short of getting Bob out of the pond, Mr X can't find out for certain, but the longer the missing contents don't turn up, the surer Mr X becomes that they are with Bob. Right. But then Bob is found, and the missing contents are still missing. So a search party is sent out to find out if Bob took them out of the package at home before he even left England, and Emma was unfortunate enough to choose just that moment to go back for some fresh clothes.'

Kari's mouth had slowly opened. 'Wow,' she said. 'And it seemed such a simple little question.'

'I told you,' Arne said. 'Give him one fact and he guesses the rest.'

'And a guess is all it is.' I smiled. 'I don't know why they took a month to start searching. Do you?'

Kari said 'But you must be right. It sounds so reasonable.'

'Like the earth is flat.'

'What?'

'Sounds reasonable until you know different.'

We went in to dinner. There was an orchestra playing, and dancing, and later, with the coffee, a singer. It was all too much in the end for Arne who stood up abruptly, said he needed some air, and made a compulsive dash for the door.

We watched his retreating back.

'Has he always been like that?' I asked.

'Always since I've known him. Though lately, perhaps, it has been worse. He used not to worry about bugging machines.'

'He used not to know they existed.'

'Well . . . that's true.'

'How did it start? His persecution complex, I mean.'

'Oh . . . the war, I suppose. When he was a child. I wasn't born until after, but Arne was a child then. His grandfather was shot as a hostage, and his father was in the resistance. Arne says he was always frightened when he was a child, but he wasn't always sure what he was frightened of. Sometimes his father sent him to run with messages and told him to be sure not to be followed. Arne says he was always terrified those times that he would turn round and find a big man behind him.'

'Poor Arne,' I said.

'He has been to psychiatrists,' Kari said. 'He knows . . . but he still can't help it.' She looked away from me, at the couples slowly circling on the square polished floor. 'He can't bear dancing.'

After a few seconds I said 'Would you like to?'

She stood up without hesitation and danced with natural rhythm. She also knew quite well that I liked having her close: I could see it in her eyes. I wondered if she'd ever been unfaithful to Arne, or ever would be. I wondered about the age-old things. One can't help it, I find.

She smiled and moved forward until our bodies were touching at more points than not, and no woman ever did that unless she meant to. What we were engaged in from that moment on was an act of sex: upright, dancing, public and fully clothed, but an act of sex none the less. I knew theoretically that a woman could reach a vivid orgasm without actual intercourse, that in fact some could do it when all alone simply by thinking erotic thoughts, but I had never before seen it happen.

It happened to Kari because she wanted it to. Because she rubbed closely against me with every turn of the dance. Because I didn't expect it. Because I didn't push her off.

Her breathing grew slower and deeper and her eyes lost their brightness. Her mouth was closed, half smiling. Head up, neck straight, she looked more withdrawn and absent-minded than passionately aroused. Then quite suddenly her whole body flushed with heat, and behind her eyes and right through her very deep I was for almost twenty seconds aware of a gentle intense throbbing.

After that she took a great deep gulping breath as if her lungs had been cramped. Her mouth opened, the smile broadened, and she unplastered herself from my front.

Her eyes grew bright as stars, and she laughed into mine.

'Thank you,' she said.

She had finished with dancing. She broke away and walked back to the table, sitting down sociably as if nothing had happened. Oh thanks very much, I thought, and where does that leave me? Dealing with an unscratchable itch and without the later comfort of doing it on my own like she had, because I'd never found that much fun.

'More coffee?' I said. One had to say something, I supposed. How about 'Damn your eyes you selfish little pig'?

'Thank you,' she said.

The waiter brought more coffee. Civilisation won the day.

Arne returned looking windblown and a little happier. Kari put her hand on his with wifely warmth and understanding, and I remembered ironically that I had wondered if she were ever unfaithful to him. She was and she wasn't: the perfect recipe for having it both ways.

They left shortly afterwards, pressing me to spend another evening at their flat before I went home.

'See you on Sunday at Øvrevoll,' Arne said. 'If not before.'

When they had gone I collected my suitcase from the hall porter and took myself to the reception desk. There were five empty rooms to choose from, so I took a key at random and got myself a spacious double room with a balcony looking out towards the parliament building. I opened the well-closed double doors and let a blast from the Arctic play havoc with the central heating. Then I shut them again and went coldly to bed, and lay awake for a long time thinking about a lot of things but hardly at all about Kari.

Erik came to breakfast the next morning. He joined me with a grin, helped himself to half a ton of assorted pickled fish from the buffet, and ate as if there were no tomorrow.

'Where to?' he asked after two further bread rolls, four slices of cheese and several cups of coffee.

'Øvrevoll,' I said.

'But there's no racing today.'

'I know.'

'Well, if that's what you want, let's go.'

Odin, in a friendly mood, sat centrally with his rump wedged against the rear seat and his front paws and huge head burying the handbrake. When Erik gave him a nudge with his elbow the dog lifted his chin long enough for his master to release the wheels. A double act of long standing, it seemed.

The journey was a matter of staring death in the face, but we got there. The main gates of the racecourse stood open with various trade vans standing inside on the tarmac, so we simply drove in and stopped near the weighing room. Erik and Odin unfolded themselves and stretched their legs while I went on my short and abortive mission.

There were cleaners, a man and two women, in the weighing room building, and none of them spoke English. I went outside and cajoled Erik, the easiest task on earth, to do my talking.

He asked, listened, and passed on the bad news.

'They say Bob Sherman's saddle was here for a long time. In the changing room, on the peg nearest the corner.'

I had just looked all round the changing room. No saddles on any pegs and no trace of Bob Sherman's.

'They say it went at about the time the body was found in the pond. They don't know who took it.'

'That's that, then.'

We left the weighing room building and strolled the few yards to the racecourse rails. The morning was icy, the wind fresh, the trees sighing. Winter on the doorstep, snow on the way.

Down the sand track Gunnar Holth's string was starting a canter, and as we watched they came up fast towards us and swept past along to the winning post and round the top of the course where the pond lay. Paddy O'Flaherty in his brilliant woollen cap rode in front, giving a lead and setting the pace. With racing the next day, it was little more than a pipe-opener, and the string presently slowed to walk home.

'Next stop,' I said, 'is Gunnar Holth's stable.'

We drew up in the yard as the horses came back from the track steaming like kettles under their rugs. Gunnar Holth himself jumped down from Sandvik's Whitefire, patted him vigorously, and waited for me to open the game.

'Morning,' I said.

'Morning.'

'Can we talk?'

He nodded resignedly, led Whitefire off into the barn, returned, jerked his head towards his bungalow and opened his door. Erik this time chose to stay in the car for which Gunnar Holth, having spotted Odin, looked thankful.

'Coffee?'

Same orange pot on the stove. Same coffee, I dared say.

'I am looking for Bob Sherman's saddle,' I said.

'His saddle? Didn't he leave it behind? I heard he did. . . .'

'I wondered if you knew who had it. I want to find it . . . It belongs to his wife now.'

'And saddles are worth money,' he said, nodding. 'I haven't seen it. I don't know who has it.'

I asked him obliquely twice more in different ways but in the end was satisfied that he knew nothing helpful.

'I'll ask Paddy,' I said. But Paddy too had few ideas.

'It was there, so it was, until they pulled the poor devil out of the water. Sure I saw it there myself on Grand National day. Then the next meeting, on the Thursday, it was gone.'

'Are you sure of that?'

'As sure as I'm standing here.'

I said mildly, 'Why? Why are you so sure?'

His eyes flickered. 'Well . . . as to that, now. . . .'

'Paddy,' I said. 'Come clean.'

'Uh. . . .'

'Did you take it?'

'No,' he said positively. 'That I did not.' The idea apparently outraged him.

'What, then?'

'Well now then, do you see, he was after being a real mate of mine, Bob was . . . Well I was sure now, in my own mind, that he would want me to do it. . . .' He ran down and stopped.

'To do what?'

'Look now, it wasn't stealing or anything like that.'

'Paddy, what did you do?'

'Well . . . there was my helmet, see, and there was his helmet, hanging there with his saddle. Well now, my helmet had a strap broken, so it had, and Bob's was there, good as new, so I just swopped them over, do you see. . . .'

'And that was on Grand National day?'

'That's right. And the next race day, after Bob was found, his saddle was gone. And my helmet was gone with it, do you see.'

'So Bob's helmet is . . . here?'

'It is so. In my box, now, under my bunk.'

'Will you lend it to me for a while?'

'Lend it?' He was surprised. 'I thought you'd be taking it away altogether, now, as by rights it belongs to his missus.'

'I expect she'd be glad for you to keep it.'

'It's a good helmet, so it is.'

He went and fetched it and handed it over, an ordinary regulation jockey helmet with a chin strap. I thanked him, told him I'd let him have it back, waved goodbye to Gunnar Holth, and set off on the perilous passage back to central Oslo.

In between bounces I pulled out the padded lining of the helmet and looked underneath. No photographs, papers or other missing objects. Nothing but black regulation padding. I put it back into place.

'No good?' Erik said sympathetically, peering round Odin.

'All stones have to be turned.'

'Which stone next, then?'

'Lars Baltzersen.'

The route to his bank lay past the front door of the Grand, so I stopped off there and left Bob Sherman's helmet with the hall porter, who was already sheltering my newly re-packed suitcase. He told me he would take good care of anything I left with him. I left three 10-kroner notes with him, and with a smile he took good care of those.

Lars had almost given up.

'Thought you'd changed your mind,' he said, showing me into his office.

'Had to make a detour,' I said, apologizing.

'Well, now that you are here. . . .' He produced a bottle of red wine and two small glasses from a discreet cupboard, and poured for us both.

His room, like Sandvik's and Torp's, was standard Scandinavian, modern vintage. Commerce, I supposed, must be seen to be up to date, but as a source of personal information these interiors were a dead loss.

No maps on his walls. Pictures of houses, factories, office blocks, distant ports. When I asked him, he told me that his banking firm was chiefly concerned with financing of industrial projects.

'Merchant banking,' he said. 'Also we run a building scheme very like an English building society. Except that here, of course, we lend at a much lower interest rate, so that mortgages are cheaper.'

'Don't the investors complain?'

'They get almost the same return as British investors. It is just that Norwegian societies don't have to pay big taxes. It is the tax which puts up the British mortgage rate.'

He told me that there were many small private banks in Norway running building schemes, but that his own was one of the largest.

'There is a terrible shortage of building land around Oslo,' he said. 'Young couples find it very difficult to find a house. Yet far out in the country there are whole farms standing empty and derelict. The old people have died or are too weak to work the fields, and the young people have left the hard life and gone to the towns.'

'Same everywhere,' I said.

He liked wooden houses best, he said. 'They breathe.'

'How about fire?' I asked.

'It always used to be a fearful risk. Cities were burnt sometimes. But now our fire services are so fast, so expert, that I am told if you want to burn your house for the insurance, you have to hose it down with petrol. Otherwise the fire will be put out at the first puff of smoke.'

We drank the wine and Lars smoked a cigarette. I asked him about his years in London and about his motor racing in Sweden, but he seemed to have no interest left in them.

'The past is over,' he said. 'It is banking and Øvrevoll which I think about now.'

He asked me if I yet knew who killed Bob Sherman. Such faith in the way he put it.

'Not yet,' I said. 'What's my limit on expenses?'

I couldn't pin him to an amount. It seemed that if I succeeded there was no limit. If I failed, I had already overspent.

'Have you any ideas?' he asked.

'Ideas aren't enough.'

'You need proof as well, I suppose.'

'Mm . . . have to make like a poacher.'

'What do you mean?'

'Set traps,' I said. 'And keep my feet out of other poachers' snares.'

I stood up to go. He too said my visit had been a waste of time because he had told me nothing useful.

'You never know,' I said.

Erik and I had lunch in a café not far from his brother's headquarters because I wanted to call in afterwards to see him. He would be off duty at two o'clock, he said on the telephone; if that would do, he could see me before he went home.

Erik spent most of lunch explaining with chapter and verse why all revolutions ended in gloom because all revolutionaries were incapable of humour.

'If the activists knew how to be funny,' he said, 'the workers would have ruled the world long ago.'

'Jokes should be taught in school,' I suggested.

He looked at me suspiciously. 'Are you taking the micky?'

'I thought that was the point.'

'Oh God, yes.' He laughed. 'So it is. What makes you spend your life detecting?'

'Curiosity.'

'Killed the cat.'

'Shut up.'

'Sorry,' he said, grinning. 'Anyway, you're still alive. How did you train for it? Is there a school for detectives?'

'Don't think so. I went to university. Tried industry, didn't like it. Didn't want to teach. Liked going racing . . . so got a job going racing.'

'That's as smart a canter over the course as I've ever heard, and as a gossip columnist I've heard a lot. What did you read at which university?'

'Psychology at Cambridge.'

'Ah-hah,' he said. 'Ah absolutely *Hah*.'

He came with me up to Knut's office, leaving Odin in charge of the car. Knut was tired after an apparently frustrating spell of duty, yawning and rubbing his eyes when we walked in.

'I am sorry,' he said. 'But I have been awake since two o'clock this morning.' He shook his head to clear it. 'Never mind. How can I help you?'

'Not in detail today. Tell me if your terms of reference would let you catch a rabbit if I enticed one out of a hole.' I turned to Erik. 'Explain to him. If I set a trap, can he help me to spring it? Is he allowed to, and would he personally want to?'

The brothers consulted in their own language, Knut neat, restrained, over-tired, and Erik with undisciplined gestures, bohemian clothes and wild wispy hair. Erik was older, but in him the life force still flowed with generous vigour.

In the end they both nodded. Knut said, 'As long as it is not against the regulations, I will help.'

'I'm very grateful.'

He smiled faintly. 'You are doing my work.'

He collected his coat and cap and came down to the street with us. His car it appeared, was along with Erik's in the side road running down beside a small railed public garden. Erik's car was a centre of attention. About ten feet away from it, ranged round in a semi-circle, stood about a dozen children and one uncertain looking policeman. His face changed thankfully at the sight of Knut, and he saluted and began to shift his anxiety on to someone else.

Erik translated for me, looking puzzled. 'One of the children says a man told her not on any account to go near my car. He told her to run home as fast as she could.'

I looked at the car. Odin was not facing out of the front window as usual, but out of the back and he was looking down, not interestedly at the crowd. Something in the great dog's world seemed wrong to him. He was standing rigidly. Much too tense. And the boot was no longer tied up with string.

'Oh Christ,' I said. 'Get those children out of here. Make them run.' They simply stared at me and didn't move. But they hadn't been near the Old Bailey in London on 8th March 1973.

'It could be a bomb,' I said.

CHAPTER TWELVE

THE CHILDREN recognized the word but of course they didn't believe it. The people in London hadn't believed it until the flying glass ripped their faces.

'Tell them to run,' I said to Knut.

He decided to take it seriously, even if it were a false alarm. He said something unequivocal to the policeman, and he grabbed hold of Erik's arm.

He knew his brother. He must have loved him more than most. He grabbed him tight just as Erik took his first step towards the car, saying 'Odin,' half under his breath.

They more or less fought. Knut wouldn't let go and Erik grew frantic. Knut put a lock on Erik's arm which would have arrested a twenty stone boxer with a skinful, and Erik's face crumpled into despair. The two of them, step by contested step, retreated from the car.

The policeman had chased the children away to a safe distance and was yelling to approaching pedestrians to get behind cover. No one paid any attention to me, so I nipped smartly along the pavement, put my hand on the handle, wrenched the door open, and sprinted.

Even then the wretched dog didn't come at once. It took a
screeching whistle from Erik to get results, and Odin came
bounding after me down the pavement as if it were playtime.

The bomb went off just as he drew level, twenty feet from the
car. The blast slammed us both down in a heap, hitting like a
fierce blow in the back, knocking all breath out, leaving one limp,
weak, and shaken.

Not a big bomb by Irish standards. But this one had presumably
not been meant to destroy the neighbourhood. Just the occupants
of a car. Two men and a dog.

Knut helped me to my feet and Erik took hold of Odin's collar,
kneeling down and patting him solicitously. Odin slobbered all
over him, as good as new.

'That was stupid,' Knut said.

'Yes,' I said.

'Are you hurt?'

'No.'

'You deserve to be.'

'It might not have gone off for hours.'

'It might have gone off while you were beside it.'

Erik's car was gutted. Windows blown out, interior torn to
shreds, boot burst wide open. I picked splinters of glass out of the
hair on the back of my head and asked him if it was insured.

'I don't know,' he said vaguely. He rubbed his arm where Knut
had locked it. 'Knut wanted me to wait for an expert to come to
see if it was a bomb, and if it was, to dismantle it.'

'Knut was quite right.'

'He didn't stop you.'

'I'm not his brother. He had his hands full with you, and the
bomb probably had my name on it in the first place.'

'What a bloody awful way to die.' He stood up and grinned
suddenly, his whole face lighting up. 'Thanks anyway,' he said.
Which was pretty generous, considering the state of his Volvo.

Once the fireworks were over the children came back, staring
at the wreck with wide eyes. I asked Knut to find the little girl
who'd been told to run home, and he said he'd already sent his
policeman to bring her.

Apart from the car, there was little damage. The windows had
been broken in a severe looking building on the far side of the
road, but neither the railings nor the shivering bushes in the little
public garden nearest the Volvo seemed to have suffered. Cars
parked several yards away fore and aft were slightly scratched with
glass splinters but otherwise undamaged. If the bomb had gone off

while we had been driving along a busy street, there would have been a lot more mess.

The little girl was blonde, solemn, hooded and zipped into a red anorak, and accompanied now by a scolding older child of about thirteen who had fallen down on the job of looking after her and was busy justifying herself. Knut, as with the boy on the racecourse, won the smaller girl's confidence by squatting down to her level and chatting along quietly.

I leant against the railing and felt cold, and watched Erik smoothing Odin's sand-coloured skin over and over, seeing him dissipate an overwhelming build-up of tension and release in small self-controlled gestures. Odin himself seemed to be enjoying it.

Knut stood up, holding the little girl's hand.

'Her name is Liv. She is four. She lives about half a mile away and she was playing in the park with her big sister. She came out of the gate down there and walked up the road. Her sister had told her not to, but Liv says she doesn't do what her sister says.'

'The sister's too damn bossy,' Erik said unexpectedly. 'Little Fascist.'

'Liv says there was a man cutting some string at the back of the car and the big dog looking at him out of the window. She stopped to watch. She was behind the man. He didn't see her or hear her. She says he took something out of his coat and put it inside the boot, but she didn't see what shape it was. She says the man tried to shut the back of the car, but it wouldn't shut. Then he tried to tie the string where it had been before, but it was too short because he had cut it. He put the string in his pocket, and that was when he saw Liv. He told her to go away, but she seems to be a child who does the opposite of what she's told. She says she went up to the car and looked through the side window at the dog, but the dog went on looking out of the back. Then the man shook her and told her to run home at once and not to play near the car. Then he went away.'

Knut looked at the small crowd of children beginning to cluster around Liv.

'She is one of those children who draws others to her. Like now. They came out of the park to join her, and she told them about the man cutting the string and trying to tie the boot shut again. It was that which interested her most, it seemed. Then my policeman came along, on his way to start his afternoon duty, and he asked the children why they were standing there.'

'Then we came?'

'Right.'

'Has Liv said what the man looked like?'

'Big, she said. But all men are big to little girls.'

'Could she see his hair?'

Knut asked her. She answered. Knut said, 'He was wearing a woollen cap like a sailor.'

'What did his eyes look like?'

Knut asked. Her little voice rose clear, high, definite, and all the children looked interested.

'He had yellow eyes. Sharp, like a bird.'

'Did he have gloves?'

Knut asked. 'Yes,' he reported.

'What sort of shoes?'

Back came the answer: big soft squashy ones, like on a boat.

Children were the best witnesses on earth. Their eyes saw clearly, their memories were accurate, and their impressions weren't interpreted by probability or prejudice. So when Liv added something which made Knut and Erik and the older children laugh, I asked what she'd said.

'She must have been mistaken,' Knut said.

'What did she say?'

'She said he had a butterfly on his neck.'

'Ask her what sort of butterfly,' I said.

'It's too late for butterflies,' Knut said patiently. 'Too cold.'

'Ask her what it was like,' I urged.

He shrugged, but he asked. The reply surprised him, because Liv described it with sharp positive little nods. She knew she'd seen a butterfly.

Knut said, 'She says it was on the back of his neck. She saw it because his head was bent forward. It was between his woolly cap and his collar and it didn't move.'

'What colour?'

He consulted. 'Dark red.'

'Birth mark?'

'Could be,' he agreed. He asked her one or two more questions and nodded to me. 'I should think so,' he said. 'She says it had two wings lying open flat, but one was bigger than the other.'

'So all we need now is a big man with yellow eyes and a butterfly birthmark.'

'Or a small man,' Erik said, 'With the sun in his eyes and a dirty neck.'

'No sun,' I said. The iron grey sky pressed down like an army blanket, without warmth. The shivers in my gut, however, had little to do with the cold.

Knut sent his policeman to fetch experts in fingerprints and explosives and took the names and addresses of half the children. The crowd of watchers grew a bit, and Erik restively asked Knut when he could go home.

'What in?' said Knut pointedly, so we stamped around on the pavement for nearly another hour.

With darkness we returned to Knut's office. He took his coat and cap off and looked wearier than ever.

I borrowed his telephone and rang the Sandviks to apologize for my non-arrival. I spoke, in the event, to Mrs Per Bjørn, who explained that her husband was out.

'Mikkel did wait for you, Mr Cleveland,' she said in heavily accented English. 'But after one hour he went away with some friends.'

'Please tell him I'm very sorry.'

'I will tell him.'

'What school does he go to?'

'College of Gol,' she said, and then thought better of it. 'But I do not think that my husband would like. . . .'

I interrupted. 'I just wondered if I could see him this evening before he goes back.'

'Oh. . . . He is going straight back with the friends. They will have started by now.'

'Never mind, then.'

I put down the receiver. Knut was organizing coffee.

'Where is the College of Gol?' I asked.

'Gol is in the mountains, on the way to Bergen. It is a holiday ski town, in the winter. The college is a boarding school for rich boys. Are you going all the way out there to see Mikkel Sandvik? He knows nothing about Bob Sherman's death. When I saw him he was very upset about his friend dying like that. He would have helped me if he could.'

'How upset? Crying?'

'No, not crying. Pale. Very shocked. Trembling. *Upset*.'

'Angry?'

'No. Why should he be angry?'

'People are usually furious when their friends are murdered. They feel like strangling the murderer, don't they?'

'Oh, that,' he said, nodding. 'No, I don't remember that Mikkel was especially angry.'

'What is he like?' I asked.

'Just a boy. Sixteen. No, seventeen. Intelligent, but not out-standing. Average height, slim build, light brown hair, good manners. Nothing unusual about him. A nice boy. A little nervous, perhaps.'

We sat around and drank the coffee. Odin had some too, in a bowl, with a lot of sugar. Erik had recovered from the nearness of losing his companion and was beginning to think about his car.

'I'll need to hire one, I suppose,' he said. 'For driving David around.'

'You're not driving David any more,' Knut said positively.

'Of course I am.'

'No,' said Knut. 'It's too dangerous.'

There was a small meaningful silence. Anyone in future who drove me must be presumed to be at risk. Which put me high in the unpopularity stakes as a passenger.

'I'll manage,' I said.

Erik said, 'Where do you plan to go?'

'Tomorrow, to call on Sven Wangen, then to Øvrevoll. On Monday . . . I don't know yet.'

'I could do with another of those Grand breakfasts,' he said.

'No,' said Knut. They argued heatedly in private, and Knut lost. He turned a grim face and a compressed mouth to me. 'Erik says he never leaves a job unfinished.'

Erik grinned and rubbed a hand over his straggly blond hair. 'Only dull ones.'

Knut said crossly, 'I suppose you realize that one of these attempts will be successful? Two have failed, but. . . .'

'Three,' I said. 'Someone tried to drown me in the fjord the first day I came to Norway.'

I told them about the black speedboat. Knut frowned and said, 'But that could have been an accident.'

I nodded. 'At the time, I thought it was. I don't think so any longer.' I got up to pour myself some more hot strong black coffee. 'I do rather agree with you that they will succeed in the end, but I don't know what to do about it.'

'Give up and go back to England,' Knut said.

'Would you?'

He didn't answer. Nor did Erik. There wasn't an answer to give.

Knut sent me back in a police car to the Grand, where as the bar was again shut (Saturday) I ate an early dinner, collected my suitcases and Bob Sherman's helmet from the porter, picked a room at random from those available, and spent the evening upstairs alone, sitting in an armchair and contemplating several unpalatable facts.

Such as, there was a limit to luck and little girls.

Such as, next time they could use a rifle, because sniping was the surest way of killing.

Such as, tomorrow if I went to the races I would be scared to death the whole bloody day.

Not much comfort in the hope that old yellow-eyes with the birthmark might be a lousy shot.

There were various other thoughts, chiefly that somewhere there existed a particular way of discovering who had killed Bob Sherman, and why. There had to be such a way, for if there wasn't, no one would need to kill me. Knut hadn't found it. Maybe he had looked the solution in the face and not recognized it, which was easy enough to do. Maybe I had, also, but could be expected to understand later what I had heard or seen.

Yellow-eyes must have followed Erik's car, I thought. Erik's breakneck driving and red light jumping made it exceedingly unlikely that anything bar a fire engine could have tailed us to Øvrevoll: but then I'd considerately returned to the Grand to dump the helmet, and made it easy for a watcher to pick us up again.

I hadn't spotted a follower, nor had Erik. But our trip to Baltzersen's and from there to where we parked for lunch had been comparatively short and in retrospect almost legal. Anyone risking a couple of head-on crashes could have kept us in sight.

Yellow-eyes was the man who had attacked Emma; and it seemed likely that the man who kicked her grandfather was the man who'd tried to knife me. Both, it seemed to me, were mercenaries, paid to do a violent job but not the instigators. They hadn't the aura of principals.

To my mind there were at least two others, one of whom I knew, one or more I didn't. To bring out the unknown, I had to bamboozle the known. The big snag was that when it came to setting traps, the only bait at present available was myself, and this cheese could find itself eaten if it wasn't extremely careful.

It was easy to see that to bring out the big boys, yellow-eyes and brown-eyes would have to be decoyed away while at the same time a situation needing instant action was temptingly arranged elsewhere. How to do it was another matter. I stared at the carpet for ages and came up with nothing foolproof.

I wished there was a way of knowing what Bob Sherman had been bringing to Norway. Unlikely to be straight pornography, because Bob had told Paddy O'Flaherty that he, Bob, had been conned. If he had opened the packet and found that it did not contain ordinary pornography, he might well have thought that.

Suppose . . . he had opened the packet and reckoned he was not being paid enough for what he was carrying.

Suppose . . . he had removed something from the packet, meaning to use it to up the stakes.

But . . . he couldn't have used it, because, if he had, the enemy would have known he had taken it, and would not have killed him without getting it back.

So suppose . . . simply opening the packet and seeing the contents was in itself a death warrant.

Suppose . . . the enemy killed him for knowing the contents, and only discovered afterwards that he had removed some of them.

It came back to that every time.

So . . . what the *hell* was in that packet?

Start another way. When had he opened the packet?

Probably not at home. Emma had seen him put it in his overnight bag so as not to risk forgetting it. Yellow-eyes and friend had subsequently smashed the place up looking for things from it, and hadn't found any. So it seemed reasonable to suppose that he had set off from home with the envelope intact.

He had had all day at Kempton races. Time enough if he'd urgently wanted to open it: but if he'd felt like that, he'd already had it available all night.

Not much time at Heathrow between arriving from Kempton and boarding the aeroplane. Hardly the opportunity for an impulsive bit of snooping.

He had turned up at Gunnar Holth's an hour or so later than expected. So he could have done his lethal bit of nosey-parkering either on the flight or in the first hour after he'd landed.

On the flight, I thought, was most likely of all.

A couple of drinks under his belt, an hour or so to while away, and a packet of blue pictures temptingly to hand.

Open the packet and see . . . what?

Suppose he had had perhaps half an hour before landing to come up with the idea of demanding a larger freight fee. Suppose he took something out of the envelope and hid it . . . where had he hidden it?

Not in his pockets or his overnight bag. Perhaps in his saddle, but doubtful, because for one thing his racing saddle was tiny, and for another he'd ridden three races on it the following day.

Not in his helmet: no papers or photographs lurked inside the padded headband.

Which left one unaccounted-for hour, during which he could have left any object at the reception desk of any hotel in Oslo, with a request to keep it for him until he returned.

In one hour he could have hidden something anywhere.

I sighed. It was hopeless.

I stood up, stretched, unpacked a few things, undressed, brushed my teeth.

Bob's helmet lay on my bed. I picked it up and dangled it by the chin strap as I pulled back the quilt and pushed up the pillows as a back-rest for reading before sleep. Sitting between the sheets I turned the helmet idly over in my hands, scarcely looking at it, thinking about Bob and the last day he'd worn it.

I thought seriously about wearing it myself to Øvrevoll to protect my head, and buying a bullet-proof vest besides. I thought ungenerous thoughts about Emma's husband because I too could still die for what he'd done.

No papers. No photographs. I pulled the soft black padding out again. Nothing, still nothing tucked behind it.

In the crown there was just the small round centrepiece of black-covered padding suspended by straps fixed into the shell itself. A marvellous piece of engineering, designed to prevent a man falling on his nut at thirty miles an hour off a galloping horse from bashing his skull in. The central suspend piece of padding shielded the top of the head and stopped it crashing into the shell itself at concussion speed. Underneath the central piece of padding there was no room at all for any papers or photographs or anything out of magazine-sixed packets. I put my hand below it, just to make sure.

And there, in the roof of his helmet, Bob had left the key.

Literally, the key.

I felt it there with complete disbelief.

Fixed to the hard outer casing by two crossed strips of sellotape, unseen until one deliberately pushed the central piece of padding sideways out of position, was a key.

I unstuck it from the helmet and pulled off the sticky tape. It was a yale type key, but with a small black tag bonded on instead of the usual round metal thumb plate. A small white number, C_{14}, was stamped on the black plastic on the side which had been against the helmet's wall. The key itself, at first, second, third glance, had been unnoticeable: and Bob certainly could have ridden his races with it firmly and invisibly in place.

C_{14}.

It looked like a locker key. Very like those from the left-luggage lockers of any big airport or railway station in the world. Nothing at all to show to which city, country or continent it belonged.

I thought.

If the key had been in the package, one would have expected it to be of extreme importance. Vital enough to be worth dragging the pond for, when it was found to be missing. Or searching for at once in the house in England.

The men searching the house in England had specifically mentioned papers. They had been looking for papers, not a key. So suppose Bob had left the papers somewhere in a locker, and this was the key to it.

Much easier. It cut out New York, Nairobi and outer Mongolia and narrowed the search to most of southern England or anywhere in Oslo. The harmless looking little key promised to be everything I needed. I closed my hand over it, with an illogical instinct to hide it, to keep it safe.

Bob too must have felt like that. The care with which he'd hidden it revealed the strength of his instinct. And he hadn't known at the time how true that instinct had been.

Smiling at myself I nevertheless followed his example.

There was in my suitcase a fresh unopened dressing for the cut on my chest, thoughtfully provided by Charles Stirling in case I needed it: but since the intermittent throbbing had faded to an intermittent itch, I'd left his original handiwork undisturbed.

Laying the key on the bedside I pulled off the old dressing to take a look: and dark, dry and healthy, the slit was healing fast.

I fetched the new plaster and stuck it on, with Bob Sherman's precious key snug inside it against my skin.

CHAPTER THIRTEEN

ERIK CAME TO BREAKFAST looking almost as depressed as the freezing wet day outside. He brought two plates heaped like the Matterhorn over from the buffet, sat opposite me, and toyed with the foothills. 'Did you sleep well?' he asked.

'No.'

'Nor did I. Kept hearing the bang of that bloody bomb.' He looked at the smoked fish I had acquired before his arrival. 'Aren't you eating?'

'Not madly hungry.'

He raised a grin. 'The condemned man syndrome?'

'Thanks.'

He sighed, adjusted his mind to the task and began proving his stomach was as big as his eyes. When both plates were empty of all but a trace of oil and six dorsal fins he patted his mouth with a napkin and resurfaced to the dangerous Sunday.

'Are you seriously going to the races?' he said.

'Don't know yet.'

'I didn't bring Odin today. Left him with a neighbour.' He drank his coffee. 'I hired a bigger Volvo. A fast one. Here's the bill.' He dug in his pocket and produced a receipt.

I took out my wallet and paid him. He didn't say leave it until later.

A party of English racing people came into the restaurant in ones and twos and sat together at a table near the window. I knew most of them: a top amateur jump rider, a pro from the Flat, an assistant trainer, an owner and his wife. When they'd chosen their food and begun to eat I drifted over to them and pulled up a chair.

'Hi,' they said. 'How's things?'

Things, meaning mostly their chances that afternoon, were relaxedly discussed, and after a while I asked the question I had joined them for.

'Remember the week-end Bob Sherman disappeared? Did any of you happen to come over with him on the same flight?'

The top amateur rider had. Glory be.

'Did you sit next to each other?'

He explained delicately that he had travelled first class, Bob tourist.

'But,' he said, 'I gave him a lift into Oslo in my taxi.'

'Where did you drop him?'

'Oh . . . here. I was staying here, but he was going on to that trainer feller he rode for. He thanked me for the ride . . . and I think he said he would catch the Lijordet tram if there was one. Anyway, I remember him standing on the pavement with his bag and saddle and stuff. But does it matter? After all, he rode next day, all right.'

'Was the flight on time?'

'Don't remember that it wasn't.'

I asked a few more questions, but the amateur remembered nothing else of much significance.

'Thanks anyway,' I said.

'Hope you get whoever did it,' he said. He smiled. 'I expect you will.'

If he didn't get me, I thought with a twinge, and went back to collect Erik.

'Where first?'

'All the railway stations.'

'All the *what*?'

'The nearest railway station,' I amended.

'Whatever for?'

'I want a time-table.'

'They have them here at the hotel desk.'

I grinned at him. 'Which is the nearest station?'

He said doubtfully, 'The Østbanen, I suppose.'

'Off we go, then.'

He shook his head in exasperation, but off we went.

From the Østbanen, I discovered trains ran through Gol on the line to Bergen. Trains ran also to Lillehammer, Trondheim, and the Arctic circle. Østbanen was the main long-distance terminus in Oslo.

It had left-luggage lockers and it even had a C14. But the locker was empty, the key was in the open door, and the tag was different.

I took time-tables which included Gol, where Mikkel Sandvik's school was.

One never knew.

'What now?' Erik said.

'The other railway stations,' I said, and we went there, but without finding any matching black tags.

'Where else would you find lockers like those?'

'Besides railway stations? At the airport. In factories, offices, schools. Lots of places.'

'Available to a foreign traveller at eight thirty on a Saturday evening.'

'Ah . . . Fornebu. Where else?' Where else indeed. 'Shall we go there?'

'Later,' I said. 'After Sven Wangen.'

Erik objected. 'He lives in the opposite direction, farther out than the racecourse.'

'All the same,' I said. 'Sven Wangen first.'

'You're the boss.'

He looked carefully several times in the driving mirror as we set off, but said he was sure we were not being followed. I believed him. Nothing could have stayed with Erik when he was really trying.

'Tell me about Sven Wangen,' I said.

He pursed his mouth in much the same disapproving way that Arne had. 'His father was a collaborator,' he said.

'And no one forgets it?'

He sniffed. 'Officially, the past is past. But after the war, the collaborators didn't thrive. If some town wanted a bridge built or a school, for instance, it would happen that an architect or a builder who had worked well with the Nazis would just not be the one to get the contract.'

'But Sven Wangen's father was already rich . . . from shipping.'

He looked at me sideways while taking a sharp turn to the left and missed a lamp post by millimetres.

'Arne Kristiansen told me,' I said.

'Inherited wealth is immoral,' Erik said. 'All estates should be distributed among the masses.'

'Especially the estates of collaborators?'

He grinned. 'I suppose so.'

'Was the father like the son?' I asked.

Erik shook his head. 'A hard-headed greedy businessman. He made a lot of money out of the Nazis.'

'Surely that was patriotic of him?'

Erik wouldn't have it. 'He did nothing for his fellow-countrymen. He made money only for himself.'

'The father destroyed the son,' I said.

'Destroyed him?' He shook his head. 'Sven Wangen is an overpowering boor who always gets his way. He's nowhere near destroyed.'

'He's an empty person. Because of his father, I shouldn't think he ever had a chance to be normally liked, and people who are spurned for no fault of their own can become terribly aggressive.'

He thought it over. 'Guess you may be right. But I still don't like him.'

Sven Wangen lived in the style to which he had been born in a huge country house built mostly of wood, partly of stone. Even on a cold wet early winter morning it looked neat, clean and prosperous. Everything growing was sharply clipped into geometric precision, a regimentation totally uncongenial to Erik's casual, generous and untidy mind. He stared around in distaste, his give-everything-to-the-masses expression much in evidence.

'All this for two people,' he said. 'It's wrong.'

The place oppressed me as well, but for a different reason. There were too many windows all looking with black eyes towards the car. If I got out and stood away from its protection I would be a sitting target for anyone in that house with a gun.

Erik got out of the car. I had to force myself to follow him.

And of course, no one shot. If I'd really thought they would I wouldn't have gone. But it was one thing telling myself that Sven Wangen wasn't going to kill me on his own doorstep and another getting my nerves to believe it. Something, I thought grimly, was going to have to be done about those stupid nerves, or I'd never complete the course.

A middle-aged woman came to open the front door and show me down the hall to a small sitting-room with windows facing the drive. Through them I could see Erik pacing up and down in the rain radiating Marxist disapproval and stamping the undeserving bourgeoisie into the gravel with each crunch of his heel.

Sven Wangen strolled into the room eating a sugary pastry and staring with cold eyes down from a great height. 'I'd forgotten you were coming,' he said. 'Have you solved everything yet?' A slight sneer. No friendliness.

'Not everything.'

A small bad-tempered flash in the supercilious eyes.

'I've nothing to tell you. You are wasting your time.'

They'd all told me that, and they were all mistaken.

Without a hat, Sven Wangen was revealed as going prematurely bald, the russet hair as thick as ever round the back and sides, but almost as thin as Erik's on top. He took a large sticky bite, chewed, swallowed: added another fraction to his overweight.

'The last day Bob Sherman rode for you, did he say anything unexpected?'

'No, he did not.' He hadn't bothered to think about it.

'Did you take him for a drink to celebrate the winner he rode for you?'

'Certainly not.' He started another mouthful.

'Did you talk to him at all . . . either before or after the race?'

He chewed. Swallowed. Looked closely at the pastry, prospecting the next area. 'In the parade ring, I gave him his orders. I told him I expected better than he'd just done for Rolf Torp. He said he understood.'

Bite. Munch. Swallow.

'After the race, he unsaddled the horse and went to weigh in. I didn't see him again.'

'While he was unsaddling, did he tell you how the mare had run?'

'No. I was telling Holth she needed a good thrashing to quieten her down. Holth disagreed. I didn't speak to Sherman.'

'Didn't you congratulate him?' I asked curiously.

'No.'

'Do you wish you had?'

'Why should I?'

You might need to eat less, I thought, but refrained from saying so. His psychological hang-ups weren't in this instance my affair.

'Did he mention delivering a package which he had brought from England?'

'No.' He stuffed the rest of the gooey goody into his mouth and had difficulty closing his lips.

'Did you ask him to ride the mare next time he came?'

He stared, then spoke round the dough and currants. 'He didn't come again.'

'I mean, that last day, did you ask him to ride for you again?'

'Oh. No.' He shrugged. 'Holth always engages the jockeys. I just say who I want.'

'You never telephoned to Sherman in England personally to discuss his rides for you?'

'Certainly not.'

'Some owners do talk to their jockeys' I said.

'I pay Holth to do that sort of thing.'

What a lot you miss, I thought. Poor fat unloved deprived rich young man. I thanked him for his time and went back to Erik. Sven Wangen watched us through the window, licking the sugar off his fingers.

'Well?' Erik said.

'He might have issued the orders, but he never killed anyone himself.'

Erik grunted as he started the hired Volvo towards the gate. 'Where now?'

'You're wet,' I said. 'Why did you stay out in the rain?'

He was almost embarrassed. 'Oh . . . I thought I'd hear you better if you yelled.' We went in silence for five miles down the road and then he pulled up at a fork. 'You'll have to decide here,' he said. 'That way to Øvrevoll, and that way to the airport. The racecourse is much nearer.'

'The airport.'

'Right.'

He blasted off down the road to Fornebu as if trying to fly there.

'Mind we aren't followed,' I said.

'You're joking.'

The thirty mile journey, from one side of Oslo to the other, took just over half an hour.

No one followed.

C14 was locked and C13 next to it had a key in its door with a black tag, just the same. Both were large lockers in the bottom row of a three-high tier.

Erik, who had allotted himself full bodyguard status, stood at my elbow and peered at the ranks of metal doors.

'Are these the lot you're looking for?'

I nodded. 'I think so.'

'What do we do now, then?'

'We walk around for a bit to make sure there's no one here we know.'

'A sensible idea.'

We walked around and stood in corners to watch, but as far as I could see every person in the airport was a complete stranger. Drifting gently back to the lockers, Erik stood stalwartly with his back to C13 and looked ready to repel boarders while I inconspicuously fished out the hidden key and tried it in the C14 lock.

The right key, no mistake. The locker door swung open revealing a space big enough for two large suitcases: and on the scratched metal floor, looking lost and inappropriate, lay a folded piece of paper.

I bent down, picked it up, and tucked it into my inside jacket pocket. 'See anyone?' I asked Erik, straightening again.

'Not a soul we know.'

'Let's grab some coffee.'

'What about the locker?'

I looked down at C14 with its key in the lock and its door open. 'We don't need it any more.'

Erik steered us to the airport buffet and bought coffee for both of us and a couple of open sandwiches for himself. We sat at a plastic-topped table amid travellers with untidy hand luggage and children running about doing what they were told not to, and with an almost fluttery feeling of expectation I took out the paper Bob Sherman had left.

I had supposed it would prove to be a base for blackmail: incriminating letters or photographs no one dared show his wife. But it proved to be neither of those things. It proved to be something I didn't recognize at all.

For one thing, the paper was thinner than I had at first supposed, and only seemed to be thick because it was folded several times. Unfolded, it turned out to be a strip six inches across but nearly three feet long, and it was divided into three columns which were intended to be read downwards. One could not, however, actually read them, as each inch and a half wide column seemed to be composed of variously shaded blocks and squares, not letters or figures. Down the long left-hand edge of the paper were numbers at regular intervals, starting with 3 at the top and ending with 14 at the bottom. Across the top in hand-written capitals was a single heading: Data Summary.

I refolded the strip and put it back in my pocket.

'What is it?' Erik asked.

I shook my head. 'Don't know.'

He stirred his coffee. 'Knut will find out.'

I considered that and didn't especially like it.

'No,' I said. 'This paper came from England. I think I'll take it back there to find out what it is.'

'It's Knut's case,' he said with a certain amount of quiet obstinacy.

'Mine as well,' I hesitated. 'Tell Knut I found the paper if you must, but I'd rather you didn't mention it to anyone at all. I don't want it leaking out round Oslo, and if you tell Knut he will have to record it, and if he records it, you never know who will see it. I'd much rather tell him myself when I get back. We can't anyway make a useful plan of campaign until we know what we're dealing with, so nothing can really be gained by telling him now.'

He looked unconvinced, but after a while all he said was, 'Where did you find the key to the locker?'

'In Bob Sherman's helmet.'

His obstinacy slowly melted to resignation.

'All right,' he said. 'I won't tell Knut. He could have found the key first.'

As logic it hardly/stood up, but I was grateful. I looked at my watch and said, 'I can catch the two-five to Heathrow.'

'Right now?' He sounded surprised.

I nodded. 'Don't tell anyone I've gone. I don't want any friend of yellow-eyes waiting at the other end.'

He grinned. 'David Cleveland? Who's he?' He stood up and turned to go. 'I'll give your regards to Odin.'

I watched his untidy back depart forthwith through the scattered crowd towards the distant exit and felt unexpectedly vulnerable without him. But nothing dire happened. I caught the flight and landed safely at Heathrow, and after thought left my car where it was in the car park and took a train to Cambridge.

Sunday evenings in mid-term was as good a time as any to beard professors in their dens, but the first one I backed was a loser. He lectured in Computer Science: but my Data Summary, he said, had nothing to do with computers. Why didn't I try Economics? I tried Economics who said why didn't I try Geology.

Although it was by then getting on for ten o'clock I tried Geology, who took one brief glance at the paper and said 'Christ, where did you get this, they guard these things like gold dust.'

'What is it?' I asked.

'A core. A chart of a core. From a drilling. See those numbers down the left hand side? I'd say they refer to the depth of each section. Might be in hundreds of feet. Might be in thousands.'

'Can you tell where the drilling was done?'

He shook his head, a youngish earnest man with a mass of reddish hair merging into an undisciplined beard.

'Could be anywhere in the world. You'd need the key to the shadings even to guess what they were looking for.'

I said in depression, 'Isn't there any way of finding out where it came from?'

'Oh Lord yes,' he said cheerfully. 'Depends how important it is.'

'It's a long story,' I said doubtfully, with a look at his clock.

'Sleep is a waste of time,' he said like a true scholar, so I told him more or less exactly why I wanted to know.

'Have a beer?' he suggested, when I'd finished.

'Thanks.'

He found two cans under a heap of uncorrected essays and ripped off the rings.

'Cheers' he said, dispensing with a glass. 'All right. You convinced me. I'll pass you on to the people who drew that chart.'

I was astonished. 'How do you know who drew it?'

He laughed. 'It's like knowing a colleague's handwriting. Any research geologist could probably tell you where that chart came from. It's a research lab job. I'll give the managing director a ring in the morning and explain, and see if he'll help you. They're awfully touchy about these charts.' He eyed it thoughtfully. 'I shouldn't be surprised if there'll be an unholy row, because from what you've said I should think it was stolen.'

The seeds of the unholy row were plain to see, next day, on the face of Dr William Leeds, managing director of the Wessex-Wells Research Laboratory. An impressive man, small, calm and decisive, he looked deeply disturbed at what I'd brought him.

'Sit down, Mr Cleveland,' he said.

We sat one each side of his managerial desk.

'Tell me where you got this.'

I told him. He listened intently, without interrupting. At the end he said, 'What do you want to know?'

'What this chart is about. Who could benefit from getting hold of it, and how.'

He smiled. 'Fairly comprehensive.' He looked out of his big first floor office window for a while at a row of leaf-dropping willows across a stretch of lawn. Deep in the heart of Dorset the laboratory stood in ancient parkland, a Victorian country residence sitting easily beside new low flat-topped workaday workshops. Dr Leeds's window overlooked the main artery of pathways linking the complex, a neat finger on the pulse if ever I saw one.

'Almost anyone could benefit from getting hold of it,' he said. 'If they were unscrupulous. This chart cost perhaps half a million pounds.'

My mouth fell open. He laughed.

'Well . . . you have to remember that drill rigs are enormously sophisticated and expensive. You don't get a core by digging a hole with a spade. This one . . .' He tapped the paper, 'is only five inches in diameter but about fourteen thousand feet in depth. A fourteen thousand foot drilling costs a lot of money.'

'I can see,' I said, 'that it does.'

'Of course you couldn't sell it for that, but I should think this particular chart might be worth a hundred thousand, if you had a market.'

I asked if he would explain in more detail.

'A chart like this is information. You can always sell information illegally if you know someone ready to buy. Well . . . suppose this core showed a deposit of nickel, which it doesn't, incidentally, and you knew exactly from which particular drilling it came, you would know whether it was worth investing money in the drilling company, or not. For instance, during the Poseidon nickel boom in Australia, you'd have been able to make literally millions on the stock market through knowing infallibly in advance which of the dozens of prospecting companies had made the drilling that was richest in ore.'

'Good grief,' I said.

'It can work the other way too,' he said. 'If you know that a concession which has been expected to give a high yield is in fact not going to be good, you can sell while the share price is still high.'

'So it wouldn't only be people engaged in mining who would be ready to buy such a chart?'

'Certainly not. The people who make most out of the earth probably don't know what a drill looks like.'

I said, 'Why sell the chart to someone else? Why not make millions on the stock market yourself?'

He smiled. 'It's much safer to be paid a lump sum into a nice anonymous Swiss bank account than to start dealing in shares. Any geologist dealing much in significant shares would be detected at once.'

'Do people approach geologists, asking them to sell information?'

'They do. We try to protect our geologists here by not letting them know exactly where the material they're working on has come from. But obviously we have not been entirely successful.' He looked bleak. 'We know from past experience that a working geologist is usually approached by a middle man, an entrepreneur who buys information from the research source and then sells it to a bigger fish who operates in the world markets.'

'Am I dealing with the middle man or the big fish?'

He smiled and shook his head. 'Can't tell. But the middle man, I suspect, as you found the chart so close to source.'

'What exactly do these columns mean?' I asked.

He picked up the chart and showed me. 'The first column is lithology . . . the composition of the rock layers. The second is the original particle type . . . that means micro and macrofossils and micrite. The third . . .' He compressed his lips, clearly most upset by this one. 'The third is a fairly new and highly secret process, scanning electron microscopy. Our clients will be particularly furious that this finding has been leaked. They paid a mint for it. We can stay in business here only as long as every client remains convinced that the analysis he is paying for will never be seen by anyone except himself.'

I said, 'This chart wouldn't be much use, though, without the key to the various shadings.'

'No.' He thought. 'If I had to guess, I'd say this might be used as a sort of appetizer, or a proof that the middle man had the real goods to sell. We don't normally make up charts in this form. This is an abbreviation. A condensed, composite edition. Specially made.'

'But would the rest of Bob Sherman's package be worth anything without this chart?'

'Oh, sure. It depends what else was in it. A written analysis would be just as good as a chart. If they had a written analysis it wouldn't matter at all that much if they lost the chart.'

I thanked him for his help. 'Could you tell me where that drilling was made . . . and what for?'

He glanced at it. 'I can tell you in general just by looking at it. But do you want to know precisely, to the half mile?'

'Please,' I said.

'Then come with me.'

He led me along a wide passage, through some swing doors, and into a modern wing tacked on to the back of the original house. We were bound, it seemed, for the records department, but to get in there even the managing director had to announce himself to the inmates and get the door unlocked electronically from inside.

He smiled wryly at my surprise.

'We usually pride ourselves on our security. We're going to have a great upheaval sorting out which of our people sold the information on this chart.' A thought struck him. 'I suppose you wouldn't like to come back and work on it yourself?'

I wouldn't have minded, but explained about the Jockey Club. 'Pity,' he said.

He unerringly sorted out one particular folder from the thousands in the filing cupboards which lined the walls. He knew exactly which company had commissioned the analysis, and he knew roughly from where the core had been taken.

He turned a few pages, comparing the chart with the notes. 'There,' he said finally, pointing with his finger. 'Those are the co-ordinates you want.'

I looked over his arm. Read the co-ordinates.

Read the name of the company. I'd never heard of it.

'Thank you very much,' I said.

CHAPTER FOURTEEN

I CALLED to see Emma.

The cottage was warm and welcoming in the cold afternoon, alive with a glowing log fire and a huge vase of bronze chrysanthemums. None of the furniture had been replaced and the curtains were still at the cleaners, but Emma herself during the past week had made strides. There was at last a shade of colour in her cheeks and the faintest of sparkles in the eyes. The pretty girl had come back to life.

'David! How great to see you. Have a hot scone. They're just out of the oven.'

We sat in front of the fire eating the scones with butter and jam and concentration.

'Golly, you must have been hungry,' she said later, eyeing the almost empty dish. 'I really made them to take over to Grandfather.' She laughed. 'Guess I'd better make some more.'

'They were lovely.' What with bombs and general chasing around I had missed a lot of meals and picked at others. With Emma, for the first time in days, my stomach nerves felt safe enough to encourage intake.

'I don't know whether to ask,' she said, 'but have you found out anything about Bob?'

'Not enough.' I looked at my watch. 'May I use your telephone?'

'Of course.'

I called a stockbroker I knew who owned racehorses and asked him about the share movements of the company which had commissioned the analysis of the core.

'That's easy,' he said. 'About two months ago the share price started to soar. Someone had a hot tip, bought at the bottom and made a real packet.'

'Who?' I said.

'Impossible to tell, but probably a syndicate, considering the huge sums involved. All done through nominees, mostly on overseas markets.'

I thanked him and rang off; and after that I called S.A.S., who made warm noises and said sure there was a free seat on the six-thirty. A lot of my mind persisted in telling me that there was another flight in the morning and widows were meant for consoling: well, maybe, but not this one, not yet.

I kissed her good-bye.

'Come again,' she said, and I said 'I will.'

I handed in at Heathrow the car I'd hired that morning in Cambridge, and squeezed into the six-thirty at the last call. I didn't seem able to help the tension screwing up again as we began the descent into Oslo, but a harmless taxi took me uneventfully to the hotel, where the reception desk resignedly let me choose my own room.

I telephoned to Erik.

'Where are you?' he demanded.

'At the Grand.'

'For God's sake . . . didn't you go?'

'There and back.'

'Did you find out . . . ?'

'Up to a point. I know what it is, but not who it belongs to. Look . . . could you give me Knut's home number?'

He told me. 'Do you want any more driving done?'

'I'm afraid so, if you can face it.'

'Count,' he said, 'on me.'

I rang Knut who yawned and said he'd just come off duty and wouldn't be back until two o'clock the following afternoon.

'Do you know a place called Lillehammer?' I asked.

'*Ja.* Of course.'

'What's it like?'

'How do you mean? It is a big town. A tourist town in the summer, and a ski place in the winter. No visitors go there in October and November.'

'If you wanted to meet someone secretly in Lillehammer, within fairly easy walking distance of the railway station, where would you suggest?'

'Not in a public place?'

'No. Somewhere quiet.'

There was a pause. Then he said, 'It might be better to walk away from the town itself. Down towards the lake. There is a road going down to the bridge over the lake. It is the main road to Gjøvik, but there is not much traffic, and there are some small side roads down to the houses round the lakeside. Is that what you want?'

'Sounds perfect.'

'Who are you going to meet?'

I told him at considerable length. Somewhere along the way he shed his fatigue, because when he next spoke his voice was alert and even eager.

'*Ja.* I understand. I will arrange everything.'

'I'll see you in the morning, then.'

'*Ja.* Agreed. And . . . er . . . take good care, David.'

'You bet,' I said.

I rang Erik again, who said certainly he would come to breakfast, drive me to Knut's office, and get me to the station in time to catch the ten o'clock to Lillehammer.

'Is that all?'

'No. . . . Would you meet me again when I get back? Four thirty, I think.'

'All right.' He sounded almost disappointed.

'Bring knuckledusters,' I said, which cheered him.

Next, Lars Baltzersen.

'Of course I've heard of that company,' he said. 'Their shares are booming. I bought some myself a few weeks ago and already they show a good profit.

'Do you know anyone else who bought any while the price was still low?'

A pause, then he said, 'Rolf Torp did. I believe it was Rolf who told me about them, but I can't be sure.' He cleared his throat. 'I have heard worrying rumours, though, that the really big buyers were in the Middle East. One cannot be sure. There is much secrecy. But it seems likely.'

'Why would that be worrying?' I asked, and he told me.

Last of all I telephoned Arne. Kari answered, her voice warm, amused, and full of memory from our last meeting.

'Haven't seen you since Friday,' she said. 'Why don't you come to dinner here tomorrow?'

'Love to,' I said, 'but I don't think I can.'

'Oh. Well . . . how's the case going?'

'That's really what I wanted to talk about with Arne.'

She said she would fetch him, and he came on the line. He sounded glad that I'd called.

'David . . . haven't seen you for days,' he said. 'What have you been doing?'

'Ferreting,' I said. 'Look, Arne, I've had a piece of luck. Some man in a place called Lillehammer telephoned and said he could tell me something about Bob Sherman being killed. He said he almost saw it happen. He wouldn't say any more on the phone, but I'm going to meet him tomorrow. The thing is . . . I wondered if you'd like to come with me. I'd be glad of your company, if you could spare the time. And he didn't speak very good English . . . so you could interpret for me, if you would.'

'Tomorrow?'

'Yes. I'm catching the ten o'clock train in the morning.'

'Where in Lillehammer are you meeting this man?'

'On the road to Gjøvik, down near the bridge over the lake. He's going to be there at midday.'

He said doubtfully. 'I suppose I could. . . .'

'Please do come, Arne,' I said.

He made up his mind. '*Ja.* I'll come. Are you still staying at the Grand?'

'Yes,' I said. 'But you are nearer the station. I'll meet you there.'

'Right.' He hesitated again. 'I hope he isn't some lunatic, making up stories.'

'So do I,' I said.

*   *   *

I slept with my bed pushed right across the door, but nobody tried to get in.

Erik had brought Odin again to assist with the guard duty, athough I now knew from longer acquaintance that the Dane's fierce appearance was only a front. A right great softy lived inside the sandy skin.

Together nonetheless they conveyed me safely to the police station where Knut met us, keenly awake a good five hours before he was due on duty. Up in his office I gave him the geological chart, which he inspected curiously.

'Don't lose it,' I said.

He smiled. 'Better to lose my life, I suspect.'

'You'll get it photo-copied?'

He nodded. 'Straight away.'

'See you this evening, then.'

We shook hands.

'Be careful,' he said.

Erik and Odin stuck beside me while I bought my ticket and walked to the barrier. It was the worst morning yet for jumpy nerves, with me far outstripping Arne in the matter of looking over my shoulder. By this evening, I thought grimly, I'd either be safe or dead. It seemed an awful long time to the evening.

Arne, already waiting on the platform, greeted me with a big smile.

'What number is your ticket?' he asked.

I hadn't realized that each ticket bore a seat number on the train, but it was so.

'I'll see if I can change mine to be next to yours,' he said, and vanished on his errand at high speed. While he was gone I found my allotted number, a window seat facing forward, halfway up one of the large airy coaches. With only a few minutes to go to departure time about half the seats were filled with respectable-looking citizens, and I managed to look over my shoulder only twice.

Arne returned with an air of satisfaction and the ticket for the seat beside mine.

'That's better,' he said, and gave all the worthy fellow travellers a severe inspection before sitting down. 'I should have waited for you at the ticket office . . . didn't think of it in time.'

Erik, with Odin still beside him, suddenly appeared on the platform outside the window, rapping to attract my attention and vigorously beckoning me to talk to him. I pointed to the rear of the door to hear what Erik wanted to tell.

'I saw him,' he said, almost stuttering with urgency. 'Get off the train and come with me.'

'Who?'

'It'll go if you don't get off quickly. The man who planted the bomb. Big, with a butterfly birthmark. I saw it. He was buying a ticket . . . he dropped some change and bent to pick it up. I saw his neck . . . and I saw his eyes. They really are a sort of yellow. Very light and bright and odd. Do hurry David. There was another man with him. They got on this train, in the rear carriage. Three carriages back from here.'

A whistle blew. He practically danced with frustration.

'Get off. Get off. . . .'

I shook my head. 'I'll find a way of avoiding them.' The train began to move. 'Thanks a lot. See you this afternoon. Mind you come.'

'Of course I'll come.'

The train gathered speed, diminishing my protectors second by second until I could no longer see the bewilderment on Erik's face or the patient lack of comprehension on Odin's.

'Who was that?' Arne asked as I returned to my place.

'Someone I hired to drive me around.'

'Extraordinary looking chauffeur, isn't he?'

I smiled. 'His driving is pretty hair-raising as well.'

'Tell me about this man we're going to see.'

'I don't know much, really. He said his name was Johan Petersen. . . .'

Arne grunted. 'There are dozens of Johan Petersens.'

'He said he was at the races the day Bob Sherman disappeared. He said he would like to tell me something about that. He said he lived at Lillehammer and worked there in the timber yard. I asked him to come to Oslo, but he said he couldn't take the day off. He said he'd meet me during his lunch break today. It was very difficult to understand him clearly, as he spoke so little English. It'll be fine with you there.'

Arne nodded, blinking away as usual. The train took things easily, sliding quietly through the outer suburbs in a typically unhurried Norwegian fashion.

'How will you know him?'

'He said he would know me. All I have to do is walk down towards the bridge carrying an English newspaper.'

'Did you bring one?'

I nodded. 'In my coat pocket.'

The train was well heated. Coats were expected to be shed, and there was a rail at the rear equipped with hangers, where Arne's coat and mine hung side by side.

The line ran north through farmland and woods and alongside an extensive lake. On any other day I would have enjoyed the journey but it was extraordinary how a little fear could keep the mind focused close at hand. Old yellow-eyes and his pal were a sight too near for comfort, and I'd developed an even worse over-the-shoulder compulsion because of passengers walking up the centre aisle through the train. Every bang of the door from one carriage to the next had me looking to make sure.

A woman in a blue overall pushed a trolley into the carriage, selling from it hot drinks, biscuits and sweets. Arne bought me coffee. The trolley trundled away, and bang went the door behind her.

We stopped lengthily at a largish town, Hamar, a junction with masses of open windswept platforms and no air of shunting or bustle. Then on again, moving faster, on towards Lillehammer. Two and a half hours, altogether, on the train.

'I missed you at the races on Sunday,' Arne said.

'Yes. I meant to go, but it was so cold.'

He gave me a look of friendly contempt.

'I might be going home soon,' I said.

'Are you?' He was surprised. 'I thought . . . you'd never leave us without finding out. . . .'

'Well, after this trip today we should know a lot more. With a bit of luck. And then there's the key. . . .'

'What key?'

'I found a luggage-locker key stuck in Bob Sherman's riding helmet.'

'You didn't!'

I nodded and told him about the trail to Paddy O'Flaherty's. 'So you see, although I'll go home soon, we should have most of the answers.'

Arne was enthusiastic. 'That's great,' he said. 'All we have to do now is find what's in the locker which the key fits.' A thought struck him. 'Perhaps it's that money. In the canvas bags . . . you know, the money that was stolen.'

'It's a thought,' I said. I didn't launch into explaining what actually had been in the locker; time enough for that later, as from the way the other passengers were standing up and putting on their coats it was clear we had nearly arrived. The train ran beside Lake Mjøsa and in the distance I could see the timber yard, with acres of pine tree logs floating in the water.

Arne held my coat for me, and I his for him. He smiled a little sadly. 'Kari and I will miss you.'

'I'll be back one day. I like Norway every much.'

He nodded. The train passed the end of the bridge to Gjøvik, climbed a hill slowly, inched into Lillehammer station, and sighed to a stop. We stepped out into a stinging wind under a grey cloud-filled sky. So much, I thought, for all those happy holiday posters of sun and snow and people on skis showing their suntans and teeth. It was odd, too, how none of the far frozen north railway stations had sheltering roofs over the platforms. Perhaps no one ever stood waiting in the open air, so that roofs were redundant and there was some point in them all still looking like the last scene in Anna Karenina.

'Are you coming, David?' Arne said.

'Yeah.' I stopped looking around vaguely and followed him through the main doors into the booking hall. At the far end of the platform two men, by-passing the station buildings, had set off quickly in the general direction of the road to the bridge. One was big. The other, of the same build as my attacker in the flat. They were too far away for me to swear to it in court.

But I was sure, just the same.

The small booking hall was scattered with prospective travellers wearing limbo expressions, waiting for time to pass. There were seats round the walls, doors to washrooms, a window for buying tickets; all the amenities in one central area. Arne said he wanted to make a telephone call before we set off to the meeting with our informer down the road.

'Carry on,' I said amiably.

I watched him through the glass wall of the booth feeding money into the slot and talking earnestly into the mouthpiece. He talked for a good long time, and came out smiling.

'All done. Let's go,' he said.

'Arne . . .' I hesitated. 'I know this is going to sound silly, but I don't want to go.'

He looked dumbstruck. 'But why not? This man might have seen who killed Bob Sherman.'

'I know. But . . . I can't explain it. I have . . . the weirdest feeling of premonition. I've had it before . . . I can't . . . I can't ignore it. Something tells me not to go. So I'm not going.'

'But David,' he said. 'That's crazy.'

'I can't help it. I'm not going.'

'But what about the man?'

I said helplessly. 'I don't know.'

Arne grew impatient. He tried insults. He tried persuasion. I wouldn't budge. In the end he said, 'Give me the newspaper. I'll go and meet him myself.'

'But,' I objected, 'if my premonition means there is some danger down that road, it must be dangerous for you as well. I had a premonition about a street once before . . . I wouldn't go down it, and a few seconds later several tons of scaffolding collapsed on to where I would have been. Ever since then, when I've a strong feeling against doing something, I don't do it.'

He blinked at me earnestly. 'If I see any scaffolding, I'll keep away from it. But we must see this Johan Petersen and hear his story. Give me the newspaper.'

Reluctantly I handed him the previous day's *Express*.

'I'll wait for you here,' I said.

He nodded, still not pleased, and set off on his own. I chose a place to sit at one end of one of the bench seats, with solid wall at my back and on one side. On my other side sat a plump teenage girl in a shaggy sheepskin coat eating herring sandwiches noisily.

A few people came. A train arrived and took most of them away, including my neighbour. Time passed very slowly.

An hour and a half between our arrival and the train back to Oslo. An hour and a half to kill. Correction, I thought wryly. To stay alive. I wished I smoked or bit my nails or went in for yoga. I wished my heart wouldn't jump every time people walked past the window in pairs. I wished I knew what view yellow-eyes and brown-eyes held on murdering in public, because if only I was sure they wouldn't risk it I could save myself a lot of fretting. As it was I sat and waited and slowly sweated, hoping I'd judged their limit right.

When the passengers for the Oslo train started arriving and buying tickets I bought two myself for Arne and me. I asked particularly for the most public pair of seats in the carriage, as observed on the way up, and although I had difficulty explaining what I wanted as the ticket seller spoke little English, I got them.

Back in my careful corner I found myself flanked by an elderly man with an ear-flapped cap topping cream-coloured skin over an elongated skull. He had heard me speak English at the ticket window and was eager to tell me that he'd been in England the year before on holiday with his son and daughter-in-law. I encouraged him a bit, and got in return a minute by minute conducted tour from Tower Hill via Westminster Abbey to the National Gallery. By the time Arne came back, a quarter of an hour before train time, we were chatting away like old friends.

Arne was looking anxious. I stood up to meet him, gesturing to the elderly man and saying, 'We've been talking about London. . . .'

Arne glanced at the man without really seeing him and abruptly interrupted. 'He didn't come.'

'Oh no,' I said.

Arne shook his head. 'I waited. I walked down to the bridge twice. I showed the newspaper. No one spoke to me. No one even walked past looking as if they were looking for anyone.'

I made frustrated noises. 'What a boody nuisance. I'm so sorry, Arne, to have wasted a whole day for you . . . but he sounded so definite. Perhaps he was delayed and couldn't help it. Perhaps we could telephone the timber yard. . . .'

'I did,' he said. 'They haven't any Johan Petersen working there.'

We stared at each other. I said depressedly, 'I banked so much on his giving us some really vital information.'

He looked at me uncertainly.

'My premonition was all wrong then,' I said.

'I told you.'

'Yes, you did.'

He began to fish out his wallet.

'I've got the tickets,' I said, producing them. 'Two seats together.'

'Oh . . . good.'

The train arrived, dark red and silver, and we climbed aboard. The seats were all I'd hoped, right down at one end, with their backs to the wardrobe end but facing every other seat in the coach. By a stroke of luck my elderly friend of the London holiday took his place on the aisle three seats down. He had a clear view of Arne and me, and waved and smiled. I told Arne how friendly he had been. Like all Norwegians, I said.

Arne jerked a look over his shoulder. Only a row of hangers with coats; but he didn't look happy.

Two bright-eyed young girls came and sat in the two seats directly facing us. I moved my feet out of the way of theirs, and smiled at them. They smiled back and said something in their own language.

'I'm English,' I said, and they repeated 'English' and nodded and smiled again. 'And this is my friend Arne Kristiansen.' They put the introduction down to the eccentricity of foreigners, saying hello to him with giggles. Arne said hello back, but he was old enough to be their father and not interested in the girlish chat.

The train started back towards Oslo. We talked for a while about the non-appearance of Johan Petersen and I said we would just have to hope that he would telephone again.

'You'll let me know if he does?'

'Of course,' I said.

The lady in blue overalls arrived, pushing her comforts trolley down the aisle. I said it was my turn to buy the coffee, and despite Arne's protestations I did so. I also offered drinks to the two girls who thought it a great lark and went pink. They asked Arne to see if it was all right for them to have orangeade, as they didn't like coffee. The lady in blue overalls patiently attended to all Arne's translations and finally with a smile gave him my change.

Arne began to wear the hunted look he often did in crowds. 'Let's go somewhere quieter,' he said.

'You go,' I said. 'But I rather like it here.'

He shook his head, but he stayed.

To his relief and my regret the two young girls got off at Hamar, giggling goodbye with backward glances. No one embarked to take their empty places, but after the train had started again my elderly friend got to his feet and came inquiringly towards us.

'May I sit with you?' he said. 'It is so interesting to talk about England.'

Too much for Arne. He rose abruptly to his feet and dived through to the next carriage. The door banged behind him.

'Have I upset your friend?' asked the elderly man anxiously. 'I am sorry.'

'He has problems,' I said. 'But not of your making.'

Relieved, he launched into more reminiscences which bored me to death but quite likely kept me alive. He was still there, talking inexhaustibly, as we drew into Oslo. And on the platform, flanked by Odin, stood Erik anxiously looking out for me, just as promised.

There wasn't much time left. If they were going to make an attempt now they were going to have to do it in the open.

I stepped off the train and turned towards Erik. And there between us, looking sickeningly businesslike, stood the two men I least wanted to see.

CHAPTER FIFTEEN

BATTLE never commenced.

Erik saw them at the same moment I did, and yelled 'Police' at the top of his lungs.

Every person within earshot stopped to look.

'Police,' he yelled again, pointing at yellow-eyes and brown-eyes. 'These are thieves. Fetch the police.' And he repeated it in Norwegian, very loudly.

It broke their nerve. They looked round at the growing circle staring at them wide-eyed, and suddenly made a bolt for the exit. No one made much effort to stop them, and the chief expression on every beholder's face was astonishment.

Erik strode up to me and pumped my hand.

'Just putting your theory into practice,' he said. I looked blank.

He explained. 'Knut told me you didn't think they'd kill you while people were looking. So I just got a few people to look.'

'Thanks.'

'Call it quits,' he said with a grin, and patted Odin.

I discovered that the palms of my hands were wet and a lot of me was quietly shaking. 'I need a telephone,' I said.

'You need a good stiff drink.'

'That too.'

I rang Knut. 'I'm back at the terminus,' I said.

'Thank God for that.'

'Did it work?' I asked with some intensity, because I'd risked my skin for nearly seven shivery hours and no one could be entirely objective after that.

'Yes,' he said, but there was an odd note of reservation in his voice. 'At least . . . *ja*.'

'What's the matter?'

'You had better come here, to the police station. It will be easier to explain.'

'All right.'

I stepped outside the box and almost fell over Odin who was lying across the door like a medieval page. He gave me a reproachful look, stood nonchalantly up, and yawned.

I asked Erik, 'Did you see Arne Kristiansen anywhere?'

'Who?'

I scanned the crowd without success. 'Never mind. I expect he's gone home.'

In gathering dusk Erik drove sedately (only one near-miss) to the police building, where I went upstairs and found Knut sitting alone and chewing a pencil. He gestured me to the visitor's chair and produced only the vestige of a smile.

'Well . . . we did everything you suggested,' he said. 'We planted the chart in a locker at Fornebu and put the key loose in the helmet in your room at the Grand. We sprinkled anthracene dust over every surface an intruder would touch and we waited at Fornebu to see if anyone would come.'

He rattled the pencil along his teeth.

'Someone did come,' he said.

'Who?'

He sighed. 'You'd better come and see.'

He led the way out of his meagre office and down an uncarpeted corridor, and stopped outside a cream painted door. Bright light from inside shone through a small glass panel let into the wood at viewing height.

'Look,' Knut said.

I looked.

The room was small and bare, containing only a simple table and three chairs. One chair was occupied by a young uniformed policeman looking stolid. On another, smoking quietly and as calm as if he were back in his own boardroom, sat Per Bjørn Sandvik.

I pulled my head away from the glass and stared at Knut.

'Come back to my office,' he said.

We went back and sat down as before.

'He came to Fornebu and opened the locker,' Knut said. 'That was at . . .' he consulted a note-pad, ' . . . fourteen thirty-five hours precisely. He removed the chart from the locker and put it in an inside pocket. I myself and two other officers went up to him as he was walking away from the lockers and asked him to accompany us to this police station. He seemed surprised but not . . . not deeply disturbed. I have arrested many people . . . Per Bjørn Sandvik did not behave like a guilty man.'

He rubbed thumb and finger down his nose.

'I don't know what to make of him, David. He shrugged and said he would come with us if we liked, but he said almost nothing else until we got back here. He was completely calm. No sign of stress. None at all. He has been here now for about an hour and a half, and he has been calm and courteous the whole time.'

'What explanation did he give?'

'We went into that interview room and sat on the chairs, with a constable to take notes. Mr Sandvik offered me a cigarette. He said he had only been trying to help the investigation into Bob Sherman's death. He said Arne Kristiansen had telephoned to say that you had found a key which might lead to useful information, so he went to the Grand Hotel to fetch the key, which he recognized as having come from Fornebu, as he has often used those lockers in the past. So he went to the airport . . . to see what Bob Sherman had left there. He said he thought it might have been the missing money, but it was only a paper. He hadn't done more than glance at it when we stopped him.'

'Did he give any reason for doing all this himself and not waiting for Arne or me to get back or enlisting the help of the police?'

'*Ja.*' He smiled a small tight smile to mock me. 'He said Arne asked him to do it. Arne wanted to prove to the racecourse committee that he was worth his salary as an investigator, so he telephoned to Sandvik as a member of the racecourse committee to tell him about the key. Arne apparently said that if he and Mr. Sandvik helped with the case, the committee would not be able to give all the praise to you.'

'What do you think?'

He looked depressed. 'Per Bjørn Sandvik is a leader of industry. He is much respected. He is being very reasonable, but if we keep him here much longer he will be angry.'

'And your superiors will lean on you?'

'Er . . . *ja.*'

I thought.

'Don't worry, Knut,' I said. 'We've got the right man.'

'But he is so confident.'

I nodded. 'He's working on a false assumption.'

'What's that?'

'He thinks I'm dead.'

Per Bjørn Sandvik got a very nasty shock indeed when I walked into the interview room.

Muscles round his eyes and mouth contracted sharply, and his pale skin went perceptibly paler. But his resilience was extraordinary. Within three seconds he was smiling pleasantly with the deceptive lack of agitation which was so confusing Knut.

'David!' he said as if in welcome, yet I could almost hear and certainly sense the alarm bells going at panic strength.

'I'm afraid this isn't the happiest of meetings,' I said.

He was making such an urgent reappraisal that the muscles round his eyes were moving in tiny rhythmical spasms: which booted out of me any hint of complacency, because people who could think as quickly and intently as that in such adverse circumstances had brains to beware of.

Knut followed me into the room and told the young policeman to fetch another chair. While he went to get it I watched Per Bjørn finish reorganizing his thoughts. Infinitesimally, he relaxed. Too soon, I reckoned: and I couldn't afford to be wrong.

The extra chair came, and we all sat down round the bare table as if to a simple business discussion.

I said, 'It must have occurred to you by now that there was no Johan Petersen at Lillehammer.'

'I don't understand,' he said pleasantly in his high distinct diction. 'I thought we were talking about the locker key and Fornebu airport.'

'We're talking about Arne Kristiansen,' I said.

A pause. I waited. But he was too cautious now to take any step without prospecting for quicksand, and after some time, when he said nothing, I invited him a little further along the path.

'You shouldn't rely on Arne,' I said. 'Arne is deep in, up to the neck.'

No response.

'Come to think of it,' I said. 'Up to his neck and over his head, considering the amount of swimming he's done.'

No reaction.

'All that messing around in the fjord,' I said. 'There was me thinking Arne had drowned, while all the time he had a scuba suit on under his red anorak. Nice snug black rubber with yellow seams, fitting right up over his head to keep him warm.' I'd seen the black-and-yellow under his anorak. It had taken me days to realize it had been rubber. But then that chug down the fjord happened before I'd begun to be sure Arne was on the other side.

'A strong swimmer, Arne,' I said. 'A tough all-round sportsman. So there he is standing up in the dinghy waving his arms about as if to warn the speedboat not to run us down while all the time signalling to it that yes, this was the dinghy it was supposed to be sinking. This dinghy, not some other poor innocent slob out on a fishing trip. Arne swam ashore, reported an accident, reported me drowned.'

A pause.

'I don't know what you're talking about,' Per Bjørn said, and patiently sighed.

'I'm talking about Arne putting on his scuba suit and diving into the pond at Øvrevoll to get Bob Sherman out of it.'

Silence.

Arne had been sick when he saw the month-dead body. At night, when he'd fished Bob out and wrapped him in tarpaulin it couldn't have seemed so bad: but in the light of a drizzly day it had hit him a bull's-eye in the stomach.

'I'm talking about Arne being the one person who could be sure no one saw him putting bodies into ponds, taking them out again, and later putting them back again. Arne was security officer. He could come and go on that racecourse as he pleased. No one would think it odd if he were on the racecourse first, last, and during the night. But he could also make sure that the night-watchman saw nothing he shouldn't, because the night-watchman would carry out any attention-distracting task Arne gave him.'

Nothing.

'This is speculation,' he said.

Knut sat still and quiet, keeping his promise that he would make no comment whatever I said. The young policeman's pencil had made scarcely a mark on the page.

'Arne stole the money himself,' I said. 'To provide a reason for Bob Sherman's disappearance.'

'Nonsense.'

'The impression of most people in the official's room was that the money had been put in the safe. And so it had. Arne himself had put it there, as he usually does. He has keys to every gate, every building, every door on the place. He didn't take the money during the five minutes that the room happened be empty. He had all night to do it in.'

'I don't believe it. Arne Kristiansen is a respected servant of the racecourse.'

He sat there listening to me with long-suffering courtesy as if I were a rather boring guest he was stuck with.

'Bob Sherman brought a packet of papers with him from England,' I said.

'Yes, you've already asked about that. I couldn't help you.'

'Unfortunately for him, he was curious. He opened the package and saw what he had no business to see. He must have done this on the flight over, as he left some of the contents in a locker at Fornebu.'

Per Bjørn slowly turned his good-looking head until he was facing Knut, not me, and he spoke to him in Norwegian. Knut made gestures of regret and helplessness, and said nothing at all.

'Bob Sherman was too fond of schemes for getting rich quickly,' I said. 'He was being paid for bringing the envelope, but it seemed to him that he could push the price up a bit. Very much his mistake, of course. He got bonked on the head for his pains. And no one discovered until long after he was dead and in the pond that when he'd opened the envelope he'd taken something out.'

Per Bjørn sat impassively, waiting for the annoying gnat to stop buzzing around him.

I buzzed a bit more. 'Because what he took out was in a way a duplication of what he left in.'

That one hit home. His eye muscles jumped. He knew that I'd noticed. He smiled.

I said, 'Bob Sherman took the precaution of hiding the key to the Fornebu locker in his racing helmet. By the time he was brought out of the pond it had been discovered that he had removed a paper from the envelope, but a search of his waterlogged clothes and overnight bag failed to produce any sign of it. So did a search of his house in England. By the time I realized what must be going on, and came to wonder if Bob had somehow hidden the missing object in his racing saddle or helmet, others had had the same idea. His saddle, which had stayed on its peg in the changing room for a month after he disappeared, was suddenly nowhere to be found.'

He sat. Quiet.

'However, the helmet with the saddle was no longer Bob's but Paddy O'Flaherty's. I told Arne about the exchange. I told him I'd found the key.'

Per Bjørn crossed one leg over the other and took out his cigarettes. He offered them round, then when no one accepted, returned his case to his pocket and lit his own with a practised flick on a gas lighter. The hand which held the lighter was rock steady.

'I didn't tell him that we had already opened the locker and seen what it contained,' I said. 'We wanted to find out who else besides Arne was looking for the missing paper, so we gave that person an opportunity of finding it.'

'Ingenious,' he said. 'What a pity you had made the fundamental mistake of believing Arne Kristiansen to be connected with Bob Sherman's death. If he had been guilty of all you say, of course it would have been an excellent trap. As it is, of course . . .'

He delicately shrugged. Knut looked worried.

'There was the problem of the two men who searched Bob Sherman's house,' I said. 'If we didn't decoy them away they would be available to fetch the key and open the locker. So we provided an urgent reason for them to leave Oslo. We invented, in fact, a possible eye-witness to the killing of Bob Sherman. I told only Arne Kristiansen that I was going to Lillehammer to meet this man, and I asked Arne to come with me. On the train I told him about the key and said that as soon as I got back I was going to give it to the police. I told him that the police were expecting me to report to them at once on my return, to tell them what the man in Lillehammer had said. This meant to Arne that if I didn't return the hunt would be on immediately and there might be no later opportunity to get into my room for the key. It had to be done quickly. A risk had to be taken.'

I paused. 'You took it,' I said.

'No.'

'You believed no one knew of the existence of the key except Arne and myself. You were wrong. You believed there was a possible eye-witness to Bob's murder and you sent your two assassins to deal with him. You expected them also to kill me as well. They aren't very successful at that. You should sack them.'

'This is ridiculous,' he said.

I said, 'I asked the reception desk at the Grand not to worry if anyone asked for my room number or my door key.' And extremely odd they'd thought it, after all the hide and seek of the previous days. 'We made it as easy as we could.'

He said nothing.

Knut had sprinkled the room with anthracene dust, which clung invisibly to any clothes or flesh which touched it and showed up with fluorescence under a strong ultra violet light. Anyone denying he'd been in my room would have been proved to be lying. But Per Bjørn had out-thought that one and hadn't denied it. He must have done a great deal of fast figuring during his non-speaking ride from Fornebu to the police station. He couldn't have known about the anthracene, but he must have guessed that a trap so complicated in some respects wasn't likely to be naïve in others.

I said, 'The paper you were looking for is a chart of a core taken from area twenty-five/six of the North Sea.'

He absorbed that shock as if he were made throughout of expanded polystyrene.

I gave him some more. 'It was stolen from the Wessex-Wells Research Laboratory in Dorset, England, and the information it contains was the property of the Interpetro Oil Company. It is a chart showing exceptionally rich oil-bearing rock of high porosity and good permeability at a depth of thirteen thousand feet.'

It seemed to me that he had almost stopped breathing. He sat totally without movement, smoke from the cigarette between his fingers rising in a column as straight as honesty.

I said, 'The Interpetro Oil Company isn't part of the consortium to which your own company belongs, but it is or was mainly Norwegian owned, and the well in question is in the Norwegian area of the North Sea. Immediately after Bob Sherman brought his package to Norway, the Interpetro shares started an upward movement on the world stock markets. Although a great deal of secrecy surrounds the buying, I'm told that the most active purchasers were in the Middle East. You would know far better than I do whether it is to Norway's advantage to have one of her most promising oil fields largely bought up by oil-producing rivals.'

Not a flicker.

I said, 'Norway has never really forgiven the citizens who collaborated with the Nazis. How would they regard one of their most respected businessmen who sold advance news of their best oil field to the Middle East for his own personal gain?'

He uncrossed his legs and recrossed them the other way. He tapped the ash off his cigarette on to the floor, and inhaled a deep lungful of smoke.

'I wish,' he said, 'to telephone to my lawyer. And to my wife.'

CHAPTER SIXTEEN

KNUT AND I went back to his office and sat one each side of his desk.

'Can you prove it?' he said.

'We can prove he went to the Grand, fetched the key and opened the locker.'

'Anything else?'

I said gloomily, 'It's circumstantial. A good defence lawyer could turn everything inside out.'

Knut chewed his pencil. 'The scandal will ruin him,' he said.

I nodded. 'I'll bet he's got a fortune tucked away somewhere safe, though.'

'But,' Knut said, 'he must care more for his reputation than for just money, otherwise he would simply have left the country instead of having Bob Sherman killed.'

'Yes.'

We sat in silence.

'You are tired,' Knut said.

'Yeah. So are you.'

He grinned and looked suddenly very like Erik.

I said, 'Your brother told me Per Bjørn Sandvik was in the Resistance during the war.'

'*Ja*. He was.'

'Nothing wrong with his nerve,' I said. 'Nothing then, nothing now.'

'And we are not the Gestapo,' Knut said. 'He knows we will not torture him. We must seem feeble to him, after what he risked when he was young. He is not going to give in and confess. Not ever.'

I agreed.

'These two men,' I said. 'Yellow-eyes and brown-eyes. They're too young to have been in the Resistance themselves. But . . . is there a chance their fathers were? Arne's father was. Could you run a check on the group Per Bjørn belonged to, and see if any of them fathered yellow eyes?'

'You ask such impossible things.'

'And it's a very long shot indeed,' I sighed.

'I'll start tomorrow,' he said.

Some coffee arrived, very milky. I could have done with a treble scotch and a batch of Emma's scones.

'You know,' I said after another silence, 'There's something else. Some other way. . . . There has to be.'

'What do you mean?'

'I mean. . . . It was just luck finding that key. If Paddy hadn't swapped the helmets we would never have found the paper at Fornebu.' I drank the coffee. It wasn't strong enough to deal with anything but thirst. 'But . . . they tried to kill me before they knew the chart wasn't in the pond with Bob Sherman. So there must be something else which they couldn't afford for me to find.'

I put down the cup with a grimace.

'But what?' Knut asked.

'God knows.'

'Something I missed,' he said with gloom.

'Why would they think I would see it if you didn't?'

'Because you do,' he said. 'And Arne knows it.'

Arne. . . . My friend Arne.

'Why didn't he kill you himself, out on the fjord?' Knut asked. 'Why didn't he just bang you on the head and push you overboard?'

'It isn't that easy to bang someone on the head when you're

sitting at opposite ends of a small dinghy. And besides . . . leading a beast to the abattoir and slitting its neck are two different things.'

'I don't understand.'

'Arne was keen for me to die but wouldn't do it himself.'

'How do you know?'

'Because he didn't. Over the last few weeks he's had more chance than anybody, but he didn't do it.'

'You couldn't be sure he wouldn't.'

'He's a complex person but his attitudes are all fixed . . . if he didn't do it the first time he wouldn't do it afterwards.'

A few more minutes dawdled by while I tried to concentrate on what I hadn't discovered.

Useless, I thought.

Yesterday, I thought, I didn't know who had manipulated Interpetro Oil. Today I did. Did that make any difference?

'Oh my Christ,' I said, and nearly fell out of my chair.

'What is it?' Knut said.

'I'm bloody mad.'

'What do you mean?'

'You remember that bomb. . . .'

'Well, of course I do.'

'It was such a sloppy way to kill someone,' I said. 'It might have gone off before we got back to the car. . . . It didn't kill us, so we thought of it as a failure. But it didn't fail. Not a bit. It was a roaring success. It did just what it was meant to.'

'David. . . .'

'Do you remember where I was going that afternoon? I didn't go, because the bomb stopped me. I'm so damned stupid . . . it isn't *what* I haven't seen, it's *who*.'

He just stared.

'*It's Mikkel Sandvik.*'

I telephoned to the college of Gol and spoke to the headmaster.

'Oh, but Mikkel isn't here,' he said. 'His father telephoned on Sunday morning to say that Mikkel must go and visit his aunt, who was dying and asking for him.'

'Where does the aunt live?'

'I don't know. Mr Sandvik talked to Mikkel himself.'

There was some speaking in the background, and then he said, 'My wife says Mikkel told her his Aunt Berit was dying. He went to catch the Bergen train. We don't know where he went after that. . . . Why don't you ask his father?'

'Good idea,' I said.

'What now?' Knut said, when I told him.

'I think. . . . I'll go and see Mrs Sandvik, and see if she'll tell me where Mikkel is.'

'All right. And I will do what I must about keeping Mr Sandvik here all night.' He sighed. 'A man like that . . . it doesn't seem right to put him in a cell.'

'Don't let him go,' I said.

'Oh no.'

Erik had gone home long ago but Knut reckoned I was on police business and sent me to the Sandvik house in a police car. I walked through the arch into the courtyard, turned right, and rang the bell outside the well-lit imposing front door.

A heavy middle-aged woman opened it. She wore frumpy clothes and no make-up, and had a positive, slightly forbidding manner.

'*Ja!*' she said enquiringly.

I explained who I was and asked to see Mrs Sandvik.

'I am Mrs Sandvik. I spoke to you on the telephone a few days ago.'

'That's right.' I swallowed my surprise. I had thought she would already have known about her husband being at the police station, but apparently he hadn't yet made his two calls. When we had left him, Knut had said he would arrange for a telephone to be taken to the interview room and plugged into the socket there, which I supposed took time. No one was positively rushing to provide facilities for a suspect, not even for Per Bjørn Sandvik.

It made it easier, however, for me to ask questions.

'Come inside,' she said. 'It is cold with the door open.'

I stepped into the hall. She invited me no further.

'Mikkel?' she said in surprise. 'He is at school. I told you.'

I explained about his Aunt Berit.

'He has no Aunt Berit.'

Wow.

'Er. . . .' I said. 'Does he know anyone at all called Berit?'

She raised her eyebrows. 'Is this important?'

'I cannot go home until I have seen Mikkel. I am sorry.'

She shrugged. After a longish pause for thought she said, 'Berit is the name of an old nurse of my husband. I do not know if Mikkel knows any person called Berit. I expect so.'

'Where does your husband's old nurse live?'

'I don't know.'

She couldn't remember the old nurse's surname, and she wasn't sure if she was still alive. She said her husband would be able to tell me, when he came home. She opened the door with finality for me to leave, and with a distinct feeling of cowardice, I left. Per Bjørn had smashed up her secure world and he would have to tell her about it himself.

'He might be with his father's old nurse,' I told Knut. 'And he might not.'

He reflected. 'If he caught the Bergen train, perhaps the Gol ticket office would remember him.'

'Worth a try. But he could be anywhere by now. Anywhere in the world.'

'He's barely seventeen,' Knut said.

'That's old, these days.'

'How did Mrs Sandvik take the news of her husband's arrest?'

'I didn't tell her. I thought Per Bjørn should do that.'

'But he has!'

'She didn't know,' I said blankly.

'But,' Knut said, 'I am sure he made his two calls almost half an hour ago.'

'Bloody hell,' I said.

He steamed out of the office at twenty knots and yelled at several unfortunate subordinates. When he returned he was carrying a piece of paper and looking grim, worried and apologetic all at once.

'They find it difficult not to obey a man with such prestige,' he said. 'He told them to wait outside the door while he spoke to his wife and his lawyer, as both calls were of a private nature. They did what he said.' He looked at the paper in his hand. 'At least they had the sense to dial the numbers for him, and to write them down. They are both Oslo numbers.'

He handed the paper over for me to see. One of the numbers meant nothing. The other meant too much.

'He talked to Arne,' I said.

I pressed the bell outside Arne's flat and after a long interval Kari opened the door.

'David.' She seemed neither surprised nor pleased to see me. She seemed drained. 'Come in,' she said.

The flat seemed somehow colder, less colourful, much quieter than before.

'Where's Arne?' I said.

'He's gone.'

'Where to?'

'I don't know.'

'Tell me everything he did since he came home.'

She gave me an empty stare, then turned away and walked through to the sitting-room. I followed her. She sat on the cream coloured sofa and shivered. The stove no longer glowed with warmth and welcome and the stereo record player was switched off.

'He came home upset. Well . . . he's been upset ever since this Bob Sherman thing started. But today he was very worried and puzzled and disturbed. He played two long records and marched about . . . he couldn't keep still.'

Her voice had the calmness of shock. The reality of whatever had happened had not yet tipped her into anger or fear or despair: but tomorrow, I thought, she might suffer all three.

'He rang Per Bjørn Sandvik's house twice, but they said he wasn't in. It seemed to worry him very much.'

There was a tray on the coffee table in front of her laden with an untouched dish of open sandwiches. They made me feel frantically hungry as I hadn't eaten since a pin-sized breakfast, but she gave them an indifferent glance and said 'He left them. He said he couldn't. . . .'

Try me, I thought: but hostessing was far out of her mind.

'Then Per Bjørn Sandvik rang here. Only a little while ago . . . but it seems hours and hours . . . Arne was relieved at first, but then . . . he went so quiet . . . I knew something was wrong.'

'What did he say to Per Bjørn? Can you remember?'

'He said *Ja*, and No. He listened a long time. He said . . . I think he said . . . don't worry. I'll find him.'

'That was all?'

She nodded. 'Then he went into the bedroom and he was so quiet . . . I went to see what was the matter. He was sitting on the bed, looking at the floor. He looked up at me when I came. His eyes were . . . I don't know . . . dead.'

'And then?'

'He got up and began packing a suitcase. I asked him . . . he said don't worry me . . . so I just stood there. He packed . . . he threw things into the case . . . and he was muttering away, mostly about you.'

She looked at me intently but still with the numb lack of emotion.

'He said . . . "I told him, I told him David would beat him . . . I told him at the beginning . . . he still says David hasn't beaten him but he has, he has . . ." I asked Arne what he was talking about but I don't think he even heard me.' She pressed her fingers against her forehead, rubbing the smooth skin. 'Arne said . . . "David . . . David knew all day . . . he made the trap and put himself into it as bait . . . he knew all day." Then he said something about you using some girls and an old man, and something about orangeade . . . and a premonition you invented. He said he knew you would be the end of everything; he said so before you came.'

She looked at me with the sudden awakening of awareness and the beginnings of hostility. 'What did you do?' she asked.

'I'm sorry, Kari. I gave Arne and Per Bjørn Sandvik a chance to show they knew more than they ought about Bob Sherman's death, and they took it.'

'More than they ought . . . ?' she repeated vaguely: then overwhelmingly understood. 'Oh no. Oh no. Not Arne.' She stood up abruptly. 'I don't believe it.' But she already did.

'I still don't know who killed Bob Sherman,' I said. 'I think Arne does know. I want to talk to him.'

'He's not coming back. He said . . . he would write, and send for me. In a few weeks.' She looked forlorn. 'He took the car.' She paused. 'He kissed me.'

'I wish . . .' I said uselessly, and she caught the meaning in my voice though the words weren't spoken.

'Yes,' she said. 'In spite of everything . . . he likes you too.'

It was still not yet eight o'clock and Per Bjørn was still in the interview room when I got back to the police station.

'His lawyer is with him,' Knut said morosely. 'We won't get a word out of him now.'

'We haven't had so many already.'

'No.' He flicked the paper with the telephone numbers which was lying on his desk. 'This other number . . . it isn't the lawyer's.'

'Whose, then?'

'It's a big second class hotel near the docks. Dozens of incoming calls; they couldn't remember one more than any other. I have sent a policeman down there with a description of the man with yellow eyes.'

'Mm. Whoever he spoke to at the hotel then telephoned the lawyer.'

'*Ja,*' he said. 'It must be so. Unless Arne did.'

'I don't think so, from what his wife said.'

'He had gone?'

I nodded. 'In his car.'

He put his hand again on the telephone. 'We will find the number and put out an alert: and also check with the airport and the frontier posts with Sweden.'

'I know the number.' I told it to him. He looked surprised, but I said, 'I've been in his car . . . and I've a memory for numbers. Don't know why.'

He put out his alerts and sat tapping his pencil against his teeth. 'And now we wait,' he said.

We waited precisely five seconds before the first call came through. He scooped up the receiver with a speed which betrayed his inner pressure, and listened intently.

'*Ja*,' he said eventually. '*Ja . . . takk*, thank you.'

He put down the receiver and relayed the news.

'That was the policeman I sent to the hotel. He says the man with yellow eyes has been staying there for a week, but this evening he paid his bill and left. He gave no address. He was known to the hotel as L. Horgen. My policeman says that unfortunately the room has already been cleaned because the hotel is busy, but he has directed them to leave it empty until we've searched it and tried for fingerprints. Excuse me while I send a team to do that.'

He went out of the office and was gone a fair time, but when he came back he had more to tell.

'We've found Arne's car. It is parked not far from the quay of the Nansen shipping line, and one of their ships left for Copenhagen an hour ago. We are radioing to the ship and to Copenhagen to pick him up.'

'Don't let them relax at Fornebu,' I said.

He looked at me.

I grinned faintly. 'Well . . . If I wanted to slip out by air I'd leave my car beside a shipping line and take a taxi to the airport. And Arne and I once discussed quite a lot of things like that.'

'He'd know you'd guess, then.'

'I'd pin more hope on the ship if he'd left his car at the airport.'

He shook his head and sighed. 'A good thing you're not a crook,' he said.

A young policeman knocked, came in, and spoke to Knut.

He translated/for me. 'Mr Sandvik's lawyer wants to see me, with his client. I'll go along to the interview room. . . . Do you want to come?'

'Please,' I said.

With Per Bjørn, his lawyer, Knut, me, and a note-taking policeman all inside with the door shut, the small interview room looked overcrowded with dark suits and solemnity. The other four sat on the hard chairs round the plain table and I stood leaning against the door, listening to a long conversation of which I understood not a word.

Per Bjørn pushed back his chair, crossed his legs and set fire to a cigarette, much as before. His lawyer, a heavy self-possessed man of obvious worldly power, was speaking in an authoritative voice and making Knut perceptibly more nervous minute by minute. But Knut survived uncracked and although when he answered he sounded friendly and apologetic, the message he got across was 'No.'

It angered the lawyer more than the client. He stood up, towering over Knut, and delivered a severe caution. Knut looked worried, stood up in his turn, and shook his head. After that the young policeman was sent on an errand, presently returning with a sergeant and an escort.

Knut said 'Mr Sandvik . . .', and waited.

Per Bjørn stood up slowly and stubbed out his filter tip He looked impassively at the escort and walked calmly towards them. When he drew level with me at the doorway he stopped, turned his head, and stared very deliberately at my face.

But whatever he was thinking, nothing at all showed in his eyes, and he spoke not a word.

Knut went home, but I spent the night in his office sleeping on the floor on blankets and pillows borrowed from the cells; and I daresay I was less comfortable than the official guest downstairs.

'What's wrong with the Grand?' Knut said, when I asked him to let me stay.

'Yellow-eyes is on the loose,' I said. 'And who knows what instructions Per Bjørn gave him?'

Knut looked at me thoughtfully. 'You think there's more to come?'

'Per Bjørn is still fighting.'

'*Ja*,' he sighed. 'I think so too.'

He sent a policeman out to bring me a hot meal from a nearby restaurant, and in the morning at eight o'clock he came back with a razor. He himself, trim in his uniform, seemed to have shed yesterday like a skin and arrived bright eyed and awake to the new day. I shivered blearily in my crumpled clothes and felt like a reject from a doss house.

At eight forty-five the telephone rang. Knut picked up the receiver, listened, and seemed pleased with what he heard.

'*Ja. Ja. Takk,*' he said.

'**What is it?**'

He put the receiver back. 'We've had a message from Gol. The man who was on duty in the ticket office on Sunday remembers that a boy from the College bought a ticket to Finse.'

'Finse. . . .' I thought back to my timetables. 'On the Bergen line?'

Ja. Finse is the highest town on the line. Up in the mountains. I will find out if anyone has seen him in the streets or knows if he his staying.'

'How long will that take?'

'One can't tell.'

'No.' I thought it over. 'Look . . . the train for Bergen leaves at ten, if I remember right. I'll catch it. Then if you hear that Mikkel is or isn't at Finse, perhaps you could get a message to me at one of the stops up the line.'

'Have you forgotten yellow-eyes?'

'Unfortunately not,' I said.

He smiled. 'All right. I will send you to the station in a police car. Do you want a policeman to go with you?'

I thought. 'I might get further with Mikkel if I go alone.'

On the train I sat next to a total stranger, a cheerful young man with little English, and spent an uneventful journey looking out at peaceful fields and bright little dolls-houses scattered haphazardly on hillsides.

At Gol there was a written message.

'Young man disembarkation to Finse the Sunday. One knows not until where he gone. The questions is continue.'

'Thank you very much,' I said.

The train climbed slowly above the tree line into a landscape of blue-rock and green-grey water. Snow scattered the ground, at first in patches, then in profusion, and finally as a thin white rug over every sloping surface, with sharp rock edges like hatchets showing through.

'Is small snow,' said my companion. 'In winter in Finse is two metres.'

'Two metres deep?' I asked.

He nodded. '*Ja.* Is good for ski.'

The railway ran for a time alongside a fiercely cold-looking wind-ruffled grey-green lake and slowed with a sigh of relief into Finse.

'Is hot summer,' my friend said, looking around in surprise. 'Is snow gone.'

He might think so, but I didn't. Snow still covered everything worth mentioning, hot summer gone by or not; and icicles dangled from every roof like stiff glittering fringes. Once out of the warmth of the train the cold bit sharply and even in my ear-covering cap and padded jacket I wrapped my arms round my chest in a futile attempt to hold on to my body heat.

I was met by the bulk of the Finse police force in the shape of a broadly smiling officer of turnstile-blocking size.

'Mr Cleveland.' He shook my hand. 'We do not know where is this boy Mikkel Sandvik. We have not seen him in the village. There are not many strangers here now. In the summer, and in the winter, we have very many strangers. We have the big hotel, for the ski. But now, not many. We have look for an old woman who is called Berit. There are two. It is not one, because she is in bed in the house of her son and she is . . . er . . . she is . . . old.'

'Senile?' I suggested.

He didn't know the word. 'Very old,' he repeated.

'And the other Berit?'

'She lives in a house beside the lake. One and a half kilometres out of Finse. She goes away in the winter. Soon, now. She is a strong old woman. In the summer, she takes people who come to fish, but they have all gone now. Usually on Wednesdays she comes for food, so we have not gone to see her. But she is late today. She comes in the mornings.'

'I'll go there,' I said, and listened to directions.

The way to the house of Berit-by-the-lake turned out to be merely a path which ran between the railway line and the shore, more a matter of small stones and pebbles through an area of boulders than any recognizable beaten track. With its roughness still half covered with crusty ice, it was easy to imagine that once the new snows fell it would be entirely obliterated.

CHAPTER SEVENTEEN

I LOOKED BACK.

A bend had taken Finse out of sight.

I looked forward. Nothing but the sketchy path picking its uncertain way through the snow-strewn boulders. Only on my right could be seen any evidence of humanity, and that was the railway. And then that too ran straight ahead behind a hill while the shore curved to the left, so that in the end there was just me

and the stark unforgiving landscape, just me trudging through
an energetic wind on a cold, wild and lonely afternoon.

The path snaked its way round two small bays and two small
headlands, with the hillside on my right rising ever more steeply
the further I went, and then all of a sudden the house lay before
me, standing alone on a flat stony area spread out like an apron
into the lake.

The house was red. A strong crimson. Roof, walls, door, the lot.
The colour stood out sharply against the grey and white of the
shore and the darker grey-green of the water; and rising beyond
it at the head of the lake stood dark towering cliffs, thrown up
like a sudden mountain against the Northern sky.

Maybe it was a grand, extraordinary, awe-inspiring sight. Maybe it should have swelled my spirit, uplifted my soul. Actually it
inspired in me nothing more noble than a strong desire to retreat.

I stopped.

Surely Sandvik wouldn't have sent his son to this threatening
place, even if he did urgently want to hide him. Surely Mikkel
was half the world away by now, with Arne cantering post haste
in his wake to look after him.

Damned bloody silly place to build a house, I thought. Enough
to give anyone the creeps, living with a mountain on the doorstep.

I went on. The house had a landing stage with a motor boat
tied to a post like a hitched horse in a Western. It also had looped
up lace curtains and geraniums on the window sills. Red
geraniums. Naturally.

I looked in vain for smoke from the chimney, and no one stared
out at me as I approached.

I banged the knocker. The door was opened straight away by a
ramrod-backed old woman, five feet tall, sharp eyed, entirely self-
possessed. Far, very far, from dying.

'*Ja?*' she said inquiringly.

'I'd like to talk to Mikkel,' I said.

She took a very brief pause to change languages, and then in a
pure near-Scots accent said, 'Who are you?'

'I am looking for Mikkel.'

'Everyone is looking for Mikkel.' She inspected me from head
to foot. 'Come in. It is cold.'

She showed me into the living-room, where everything was in
process of being packed away in crates. She gestured round with
a fine-boned hand. 'I am leaving now for the winter. It is beautiful here in the summer, but not in winter.'

'I have a message from his father,' I said.

'Another one?'

'What do you mean?'

'Already one man came this morning. Then another. Both of them said they had a message from his father. And now you.' She looked at me straightly. 'That is very many messages.'

'Yes . . . I have to find him.'

She put her head on one side. 'I told the others. I cannot judge which of you I should not tell. So I will tell you. He is on the mountain.'

I looked through the window to the wall of rock and the end of the lake. 'Up there?'

'Ja. There is a cabin up there. I rent it to visitors in the summer, but in the winter the snow covers it. Mikkel went up their this morning to bring down the things I do not want to leave there. He is a kind boy.'

'Who were the other men who came?'

'I don't know. The first one said his name was Kristiansen. They both said they would go up and help Mikkel bring down the things, although I said it was not necessary, there are not many things and he took the sleigh.'

'The sleigh?'

'Ja. Very light. You can pull it.'

'Perhaps I had better go up there as well.'

'You have bad shoes.'

I looked down. City casuals, not built for snowy mountains, and already darkly wet round the edges.

'Can't be helped,' I said.

She shrugged. 'I will show you the path. It is better than the one round the lake.' She smiled faintly. 'I do not walk to Finse. I go in the boat.'

'The second man,' I said. 'Did he have extraordinary yellow eyes?'

'No.' She shook her head decisively. 'He was ordinary. Very polite. Like you.' She smiled and pointed through the window. 'The path starts over there behind that big rock. It is not steep. It winds away from the lake and then comes back. You will see it easily.'

I thanked her and set off, and found almost at once that she was right about the shoes. One might be able to see the path easily, but that was because it was a well-worn track through the snow, patterned widely on either side by the marks of skis, like a sort of mini highway.

I slithered along in the brisk wind, working round the hillside in a wide, ever-upward-sloping U: but it proved to be not so far as I'd feared, because long before I expected it I came to the top of a small rise and found below me, suddenly only a few yards away, a sturdy little log hut, built to the traditional Norwegian pattern like a roofed box standing on a slightly smaller plinth.

It was already too late to make a careful and inconspicuous approach. I stood there in full view of a small window: so I simply walked straight up and looked through it.

The cabin was dark inside and at first I thought it was empty. Then I saw him. Huddled in a corner, with his head bent over his knees, slowly rocking as if in pain.

There was only one small room. Only one door. I put my hands on its latch and opened it.

The movement galvanized the figure inside into action, and it was only something half seen, half instinctive, which had me leaping sideways away from the entrance with adrenalin scorching down to my toes. Blast from a shotgun roared through the doorway, and I pressed myself against the heavy log wall alongside and hoped to God it was impervious to pellets.

A voice shouted something hysterically from inside.

Not Arne's voice. Young. Stretched to breaking.

'Mikkel,' I said. 'I will not harm you. I am David Cleveland.' Silence. 'Mikkel. . . .'

'If you come in, I will shoot you.' His voice was naturally high pitched like his father's, and the tension in it had strung it up another octave.

'I only want to talk to you.'

'No. No. No.'

'Mikkel. . . . You can't stay here for ever.'

'If you come in, I'll shoot.'

'All right . . . I'll talk from here.' I shivered with cold and wholeheartedly cursed him.

'I will not talk to you. Go away. Go away.'

I didn't answer. Five minutes passed with no sound except the blustering wind. Then his voice from inside, tight and frightened. 'Are you still there?'

'Yes,' I said.

'Go away.'

'We have to talk sometime. Might as well be now.'

'No.'

'Where is Arne Kristiansen?' I asked.

His reply was a high keening wail which raised goosebumps up my spine. What followed it was a thoroughly normal sob.

I crouched down low and risked a quick look through the door.
The gun lay in one hand on the floor and with the other he was
trying to wipe away tears. He looked up and saw me, and again
immediately began to aim.

I retreated smartly and stood up outside against the wall, as
before. 'Why don't you tell me?' I said.

A long pause of several minutes.

'You can come in.'

I took another quick look. He was sitting straight legged on
the floor with the gun pointing at the door.

'Come in,' he said. 'I won't shoot.'

'Put the gun on the floor and slide it away.'

'No.'

More time passed.

'The only way I'll talk,' he said, 'is if you come in. But I will
keep the gun.'

I swallowed. 'All right.'

I stepped into the doorway. Looked down the double barrels.
He sat with his back against the wall, holding the gun steady. A
box of cartridges lay open beside him, with one or two scattered
around.

'Shut the door,' he said. 'Sit down opposite me, against the wall.
On the floor.'

I did as he said.

He was slight and not full grown. Brown hair, dark frightened
eyes. Cheeks still round from childhood; the jaw line of an adult.
Half boy, half man, with tear stains on his face and his finger on
the trigger.

Everything movable in the bare little cabin had been stacked in
a neat pile to one side. A heavy table and two solid chairs were
the total to be left. No curtains at the single small window. No
rugs on the bare wood floor. Two collapsible camp beds, folded
and strapped together for transport, leaned against a wall. A pair
of skis stood beside them.

No logs by the cold stove, and no visible food.

'It'll be dark soon,' I said. 'Within an hour.'

'I don't care.' He stared at me with burning eyes and unnerving
intensity.

'We should go down to Berit's house while we can still see the
way.'

'No.'

'We'll freeze up here.'

'I don't care.'

I believed him. Anyone as distracted as he was tended to blot even extreme discomforts out of his mind: and although he had allowed me into the hut he was far from coming down off the high wire. Little tremors of tension ran in his body and twitched his feet. Occasionally the gun shook in his hands. I tried not to think gloomy thoughts.

'We must go,' I said.

'Sit still,' he said fiercely, and the right forefinger curled convulsively. I looked at it. And I sat.

Daylight slowly faded and the cold crept in inexorably. The wind outside whined like a spoilt child, never giving up. I thought I might as well face it: the prospect of the night ahead made the fjord water seem in retrospect as cosy as a heated pool. I put my padded mitts inside my padded pockets and tried to kid myself that my fingers were warm. And it was a minor disaster that the jacket wasn't really long enough for sitting on.

'Mikkel,' I said. 'Just tell me. You'll explode if you don't talk to someone. And I'm here. So just . . . tell me. Whatever you like.'

He stared fixedly through the gathering dusk. I waited a long time.

'I killed him,' he said.

Oh God.

A long pause. Then on a rising note he said it again, 'I killed him.'

'Who?' I said.

Silence.

'How?' I said.

The question surprised him. He took his gaze for one moment off my face and glanced down at the gun.

'I . . . shot. . . .'

With an effort I said, 'Did you shoot . . . Arne?'

'Arne. . . .' The hysteria rose again. 'No. No. No. Not Arne. I didn't kill Arne. I didn't. I didn't.'

'All right,' I said. 'All right, Mikkel. Let's wait a bit . . . until you can tell me. Until you feel it is the right time to tell me.' I paused. 'Is that O.K.?'

After a while he said, '*Ja*. O.K.'

We waited.

It got darker until it seemed that the only light left was the reflection from the window in his eyes. I could see them long after the rest of him dissolved into one amorphous shadow, two live agonized signals of a mind desperately afraid of the help it desperately needed.

It must have occurred to him as to me that after total darkness I would be able to jump his gun, because he stirred restlessly on the floor and muttered something in Norwegian, and finally in a much more normal voice said 'There is a lamp in a box. On top of the things.'

'Shall I find it and light it?'

'*Ja.*'

I stood up stiffly, glad of the chance to move, but sensing him lift the gun to keep me where it mattered.

'I won't try to take the gun away,' I said.

No answer.

The heap of gear was to my right, near the window. I moved carefully, but with many small noises so that he should know where I was and not be alarmed, and felt around for the box on top. Nothing wrong with his memory: the box was there, and the lamp in it, and also a box of matches.

'I've found the lamp,' I said. 'Shall I strike a match?'

A pause. '*Ja.*'

It proved to be a small gas lamp. I lit it and put it on the table from where it cast a weak white light into every corner. He blinked twice as his irises adjusted, but his concentration never wavered.

'Is there any food?' I asked.

'I'm not hungry.'

'I am.'

'Sit down,' he said. 'Where you were.'

I sat. The gun barrels followed. In the new light I could see down them a lot too well.

Time passed. I lit the lamp at four-thirty in the afternoon and it was eight before he began to talk.

By then, if I was anything to go by, he had lost all feeling from the waist down. He wore no gloves and his hands had turned blue-white, but he still held the gun ready, with his finger inside the trigger guard. His eyes still watched. His face, his whole body, were still stiff with near unbearable tension.

He said suddenly, 'Arne Kristiansen told me that my father was arrested. He told me he was arrested because of you.'

His voice came out high and his breath condensed into a frosty plume.

Once started, he found it easier.

'He said . . . my father wanted us to go to Bergen . . . and on a boat to Stavanger . . . and fly. . . .' He stopped.

'And you didn't go,' I said. 'Why didn't you go?'

The gun shook. 'They came in. . . .' he said.

I waited.

He said, 'I was talking to him. Outside. About going away.' A pause. 'They came over the hill. On skis, with goggles.' Another pause. 'One of them told Arne to step away from me.' After a longer pause and with an even sharper burst of remembered terror he said, 'He had a knife.'

'Oh Mikkel,' I said.

He talked faster, tumbling it out.

'Arne said "You can't. You can't. He wouldn't send you to kill his own son. Not Mikkel." He pushed me behind him. He said "You're crazy. I talked to his father myself. He told me to come here to take Mikkel away." '

He stared across at me with stretched eyes, reliving it.

'They said . . . my father had changed his mind about Arne going. They said they were to take me themselves on a ship to Denmark and wait until my father sent money and instructions. Arne said it was not true. They said . . . it was true . . . and they said . . . Arne was going no further than right here. . . . He didn't believe it . . . he said not even my father would do that. He watched only the one with the knife and the other one swung a ski stick and hit him on the head. . . . He fell down in the snow . . . I tried to stop them . . . they just pushed me off . . . and they put him on the sleigh . . . they strapped him on . . . and pulled him up the path.'

The panic he had felt then came crowding back into his face. He said painfully, 'I remembered the gun in the cabin . . . I went inside and loaded it . . . and put on my skis and went after them . . . to stop them . . . but when I found them they were coming back . . . without the sleigh . . . and I thought . . . . I thought . . . they were going to . . . they were going to. . . .'

He took a deep shuddering breath. 'I fired the gun. The one with the knife . . . he fell down. . . .'

'I fired again,' he said. 'But the other one was still on his skis. . . . So I came back to the cabin because I thought he would come after me . . . I came back to reload the gun. But he didn't come. . . . He didn't come. . . .

'You came,' he said. 'I thought it was him.'

He stopped.

'Did you know the two men?' I asked. 'Had you ever seen them before?'

'No.'

'How long was it before I came?' I said.

'I don't know. A long time.'

'Hours?'

'I think so.'

I hadn't seen any of them on my way up.

'Killing is wrong,' he said jerkily.

'It depends.'

'No.'

'To defend your life, or someone else's life, it would be all right,' I said.

'I . . . I believe . . . I *know* it is wrong. And yet I . . . when I was so afraid. . . .' His high voice cracked. 'I have done it. I despise killing and I've done it. And I would have killed you too. I know I would. If you hadn't jumped.'

'Never mind,' I said: but the horrors were still there in his eyes. Making it deliberately an emotion-reducing question I asked, 'Have you known Arne Kristiansen long?'

'What. . . . ?' His own voice came down a bit. 'About three years, I suppose.'

'And how well do you know him?'

'Not very well. On the racecourse. That's all.'

'Has your father known him long?'

'I don't think so. . . . The same as me. At the races.'

'Are they close friends?'

He said with sudden extreme bitterness, 'My father has no close friends.'

'Will you put the gun down now?' I said.

He looked at it. 'All right.'

He put it beside him on the floor. A relief not to be looking down those two round holes.

The lamp chose that moment to give notice it was running out of gas. Mikkel switched his gaze from me to the table, but the message of fading light didn't seem to pierce through the inner turmoil.

'The lamp is going out,' I said. 'Is there a spare gas cylinder?'

He slowly shook his head.

'Mikkel,' I said. 'It is freezing and it will soon be dark. If we are to survive the night we must keep warm.'

No response.

'Are you listening?'

'What?'

'You are going to have to face life as it is.'

'I . . . can't. . . .'

'Are there any blankets?'

'There is one.'

I began to try to stand up and he reached immediately for the gun. 'Don't be silly,' I said. 'I won't hurt you. And you won't shoot me. So let's just both relax, huh?'

He said uncertainly. 'You had my father arrested.'

'Do you know why?'

'Not . . . not really.'

I told him about the oil transaction, playing down the disloyalty, to put it no higher, that Per Bjørn had shown to his country, but there was, it seemed, nothing basically wrong with Mikkel's brains. He was silent for some time after I'd finished and the muscles slowly relaxed limb by limb.

'Once he had been found out,' he said, 'he would lose his job. He would lose the respect of everyone. He wouldn't be able to live like that . . . not my father.'

His voice at last was sane and controlled; and almost too late. The lamp was going out.

'The blanket,' he said, 'is in the beds.'

He tried to stand up and found his legs were as numb and useless as mine, if not more so. It kicked him straight back to practical sense.

'I'm cold!'

'So am I.'

He looked across, seeing our predicament squarely for the first time. 'Stand up,' he said. 'Walk about.'

Easier said, but it had to be done.

'Can we light the stove?' I said. 'There are four more matches, the cardboard boxes, and the table and chairs, if we can break them up.'

We had both by then tottered to our feet. The lamp shone with one candle-power, sadly.

'There is no axe,' Mikkel said.

The lamp went out. 'I'm sorry,' he said.

'Never mind.'

We jumped up and down in total darkness. Funny if it hadn't been urgent. Blood started circulating again, though, to the places where it was needed, and after half an hour or so we were both warm enough to give it a rest.

'I can find the blanket,' Mikkel said, and did so. 'Shall we share it?'

'We certainly shall.'

We both wore warm jackets and he, when he remembered where he'd put them, had a cap and mitts like my own. We laid the folded canvas beds on an insulating foundation of cardboard boxes, and wrapped ourselves from the waist down in one cocoon in the single blanket, sitting close together to share every scrap of warmth. It was too dark to see what he was thinking, but there were faint tremors still, occasionally, through his body.

'I took the rest of the bedding down to Berit's house yesterday,' he said. 'On the sleigh.'

'Pity.'

The word switched his thoughts. He said abruptly 'Do you think Arne is dead?'

'I don't know,' I said. But I did think so.

'What will happen to me, for killing that man?'

'Nothing. Just tell it as you told me. No one will blame you.'

'Are you sure?'

'Yes.'

'I am as bad as anyone else who kills,' he said, but this time there was adult acceptance and despair in his voice, not hysteria. I wondered if it were possible for a boy to age ten years in one night, because it would be better for him if he could.

'Tell me about Bob Sherman,' I said; and felt the jolt that went through him at the name.

'I . . . can't. . . .'

'Mikkel . . . I know that Bob brought the stolen surveys from England to give to your father. . . .'

'No,' he interrupted.

'What, then?'

'He had to deliver them to Arne. I didn't know they were for my father when I. . . .' He stopped dead.

'When you what?'

'I musn't tell you. I can't.'

In the darkness I said calmly, almost sleepily, 'Did Bob tell you he had brought a package?'

He said unwillingly, 'Yes.'

I yawned. 'When?'

'When I met him in Oslo. The night he came.'

I wondered if he felt in his turn the thud with which that news hit me.

'Where in Oslo?' I said casually.

'He was outside the Grand with his saddle and his over-night bag. I was walking home from a friend's house, and I stopped. He said he might go and catch the tram. I asked him if he would like some coffee first, so we walked along to our house. I carried his saddle.' He paused. 'I liked Bob. We were friends.'

'I know,' I said.

'My father was out. He usually is. Mother was watching television. Bob and I went into the kitchen, and I made the coffee. We ate some cake my mother had made.'

'What did you talk about?'

'At first about the horses he was riding the next day. . . . Then he said he had brought a package from England, and he'd opened it, and it didn't contain what he'd been told. He said he had to give it to Arne Kristiansen at the races but he was going to ask a bit more money before he handed it over.'

His body trembled against mine within the blanket.

'He was laughing about it, really. He said they'd told him it was pornography, but it wasn't, and he didn't know what it was even though he'd seen it. Then he took the package out of his case and told me to look.' He stopped.

'And,' I said, 'when you saw what was in the package, you knew what it was?'

'I'd seen papers like that before . . . I mean . . . I knew it was an oil survey. Yes.'

'Did you tell Bob what it was?'

'Yes. I did. We talked about it a bit.'

'And then?'

'It was late. Too late for the tram. Bob took a taxi out to Gunnar Holth's stable, and I went to bed.'

'What happened the next day?'

'I promised . . . I promised I wouldn't tell anybody. I didn't tell the police. I mustn't tell you. Especially not you. I know that.'

'All right,' I said.

Time passed. It was almost too cold to think.

'I told my father about Bob Sherman's package on the way to the races,' he said. 'He took me in the car. I only told him for something to say. Because I thought he might be interested. But he didn't say much. He never does. I never know what he's thinking.'

'Nor do I,' I said.

'I have heard people say he looks kindest when he is being most cruel. When I was small, I heard it first.'

'Is he cruel to you?'

'No. Just . . . cold. But he is my father.'

'Yes.'

'I think I want to tell you . . . but I can't.'

'All right.'

A long time passed. His breath and body movements betrayed his wakefulness and the churning thoughts in his mind.

'Mr Cleveland? Are you awake?'

'David,' I said.

'David. . . . Do you think he meant those men to kill me?'

'No, I don't.'

'He told them where to come. He told me to come to Finse. He told Arne Kristiansen to come to Finse. And those men.'

'He did,' I said. 'But I should think they spoke the truth. I should think he meant them to take you out of the country, after they had dealt with Arne. I should think they were very clumsy to let you see them actually attack Arne, but then they have more strength than brains, those two. Arne is the only one who could go into court and give conclusive evidence against your father: and I do think that your father is ruthless enough to have him killed to prevent that.'

'Why . . . why do you think so?'

'Because he sent those two men after me, too.'

I told him about the boat in the fjord, the knife in Chelsea, the bomb in Erik's car.

'They're terrible men,' he said. 'They frightened me the instant I saw them.'

He relapsed into silence. I could almost feel him thinking, suffering, working it all out.

'David?'

'Yes?'

'It was my fault Bob died.'

'Certainly not.'

'But if I hadn't told my father that Bob knew he'd brought an oil survey. . . .'

'Arne would have told him,' I said flatly. 'You can go on saying if for ever. If Bob hadn't opened the package. If your father hadn't been ruthless enough to get rid of him. But all these things happened. They all happened because your father is both greedy and proud, which is always a pretty deadly combination. But also he learned how to live a secret life when he was young. Against the Nazis, it was good. Everyone admired him. I should think he's never lost the feeling that anything anti-authority is daring and therefore all right. I should think he put the police into the place of the Nazis, as the enemy to be outwitted. He thinks like lightning, he gives away nothing under questioning, he coolly takes tremendous risks, he arranges without mercy for people to die. He's still acting the way he did when he was twenty. He always will.'

Time passed.

'David. . . .'

'Yes?'

'I'll have to tell you,' he said.

I took a deep breath. It felt icy in my lungs. 'Go on,' I said.

He paused again. Then he said, 'I was talking to Bob at the races. He laughed and told me it was all fixed, Arne was going to drive him to the airport afterwards and pay him extra for the package.' He stopped.

I waited.

His voice went on, hesitant, but at last committed.

'By the end of the races it was dark. I went out to the car to wait for my father. He is often late because of being on the committee. I sat in the car and waited for him. I hadn't talked to him at all at the races. I usually don't see him much there. He's always busy.'

He stopped again. His breathing grew heavier, more disturbed.

'Most of the cars went. Then two people came past and in some passing headlights I saw they were Bob and Arne. I was going to call out to them . . . I wish I had . . . but I couldn't get the window down fast enough . . . and then they were over by Arne's car. They were talking face to face. I could only see them now and then, you see, when car lights pointed that way as people went home. But I saw another man walk up behind Bob and raise his arm. He held something shiny. . . . Then he brought it down. . . .'

He stopped. Gulped a bit. Went on, 'The next time I could see, there were only two people there. I thought . . . I couldn't *believe*. . . . And then one of them turned and came towards our car. I was scared. . . .'

He shuddered violently.

'But he just opened the boot and threw into it something which clinked, and then he got into the driving seat, and he was smiling.'

A long pause.

'Then he saw me sitting there, and he looked absolutely astonished. And he said . . . he said . . . "Mikkel! I'd forgotten you were at the races".'

His voice was full of pain.

'He'd forgotten me. Forgotten me.'

He was trying not to cry.

'My father,' he said. 'My father killed Bob Sherman.'

CHAPTER EIGHTEEN

WE WENT DOWN to Finse at first light, him sliding easily on his
skis, me scrunching and slipping in my city shoes. If I looked anything like he did I had blue-grey circles round my eyes, hollows at
the corners of my mouth, and a certain overall air of extreme
weariness.

He had said little more during the night. He had rolled his head
on to my shoulder at one point and fallen exhaustedly asleep, and
in the early morning, when he stirred, he had been calm and
apparently untroubled, as if the final unburdening of the horror
he'd lived with through eight long weeks had set him quietly free.

I left him with the warm comforting people of Finse, and went
up the mountain again with several local men. This time I went on
skis, shuffling along inexpertly up the slope. They waited for me,
making jokes. They had cheerful faces, carefree smiles. And the
sun came wanly through the clouds, the first time I'd seen it in
Norway.

We reached the hut and went on past it, up beyond where the
path petered out into a flat field of snow. Two of the men were
pulling a sleigh, a lightweight affair sliding easily on ski-like
runners; just like the one old Berit has, they said.

Brown-eyes was lying face down in the snow.

Dead.

But he hadn't died from gunshot wounds: or not primarily.
He'd died from exposure and cold.

The men from Finse looked in silence at the trail leading away
behind his body. He'd been pulling himself along, crawling. The
snow where he'd been was streaked black with his blood.

They wrapped him in canvas, put him on the sleigh, and
turned to go to Finse.

'I'll go that way,' I said, pointing to where brown-eyes had
come from.

They nodded, consulted, and sent a man with me, as they didn't
trust my rudimentary ability on skis.

We followed the blood-stained trail up a shallow slope and on
to a sort of plateau whose far edge was a smooth horizon against a
pale grey sky. The trail ended in a jumble of tracks which the man
from Finse rapidly interpreted.

'This is where he was shot. See the blood. There was another
man with him.' He pointed to a set of ski marks setting off at a

tangent across virgin snow. 'That man is an expert cross country skier. He went fast. He left the other man lying wounded in the snow. He did not come back with help. If he had, he could have followed the trail of blood.'

Yellow-eyes had just upped and left. But Knut would find him in the end.

'The two men came across to here ski-ing fast and easily,' my guide said, and pointed to tracks stretching across the plateau.

'There are other tracks over there,' he said, turning to his right and stretching out a well-gloved hand.

'Let's look,' I said.

'Two men,' he said. 'Pulling a loaded sleigh.'

Although I expected it, it hit in my gut.

'They came that way,' I said, pointing back towards the hut.

He nodded. We went back along the trail until we found the marks of Mikkel's skis beside it.

'The boy came to here. Stopped. Then he turned and went back. You can see from his tracks that he was disturbed when he came. And panic stricken when he left. Look at the depth and the sharpness and the small steps.'

'We might find the cartridges,' I said.

He nodded. We looked for a while and found both of them, bright orange cylinders on the snow.

'And now. . . .' I gestured ahead along the trail which Mikkel had been following: two men and a loaded sleigh.

The marks ran regularly across the plateau towards the horizon. We followed.

The horizon proved to be not the end of the world, but the brow of a hill. Down the other side the slope was steep, short, and sharp edged, and far beyond it, mile upon mile, lay a vista of snow-scattered peaks. We were standing at the top of the cliffs above the lake where Berit lived.

The marks of the two men on skis stopped at the brow of the hill and turned back.

The sleigh marks ran on straight and true to the edge.

'I want to go down there,' I said, and unclipped my skis.

My guide didn't like it, but produced a rope from round his waist. He tied me to it, and paid it out foot by foot, standing four square and solid at the top of the slope.

I went down slowly in my borrowed boots, finding the snow surprisingly glassy and having to be careful not to slide. Having to concentrate, too, on not feeling giddy, and finding it as difficult as ever. When I stood at length on the edge I could see all the lake stretching away, with Berit's house a crimson blob far down to the left.

Beside my feet the marks of the runners looked shallow and crisp, speaking of speed. And they ran on without pity, pointing straight out into space.

The drop in front was six hundred feet, perpendicular. The ruffled green water lay secretively below. Nothing else. Nothing to see.

Arne, I thought. Flying through the air on a sleigh, down to his death.

Arne . . . who didn't look over his shoulder the one time the enemy was really there.

Arne, my treacherous friend.

You would have sworn that round the snowy cliffs you could hear crashing chords of Beethoven echoing in the wind.

THE
SILVER MISTRESS

Peter O'Donnell

'The Silver Mistress' is published by
Souvenir Press Ltd

The Author

Peter O'Donnell is a prolific writer. He began at the age of sixteen and has lost count of the number of stories he has written since. His first full-length novel, *Modesty Blaise,* was such an immediate and tremendous success that he soon found he had been 'taken over' by this powerful female character. That first book was translated into more than a dozen languages, and his later books have proved equally successful. Modesty Blaise adventures are now awaited eagerly by readers all over the world.

CHAPTER ONE

QUINN WONDERED VAGUELY if he was going to die for the miserable reason that he had no particular wish to continue living. The thought produced a spurt of angry contempt in him which cleared his muzzy brain a little, and he muttered, 'Gutless bastard.'

Slowly he eased his thin wiry body to a sitting position on the broad ledge of rock, and lifted his good hand to push back a lump of hair which had fallen over his eyes.

His head throbbed, and he knew that he was concussed. The period of lucidity would not last long. Soon his mind would drift away from reality, as it had done half a dozen times in the hours since he had fallen, and he would again lie in a stupor, troubled by dreams and memories which made the sweat start from his body.

Six hundred feet below him, the waters of the Tarn whispered in the great gorge as the river wound its way west to join the Garonne. Not far above him was the top of the gorge. It was here that he had stood when the pale March sun was at its height, looking across at the scrub-dotted face of the canyon wall on the far side, looking down at the dark waters which had spent a million years cutting this valley through the French limestone, and trying to feel something, anything other than bleak despair. But the ancient majesty of all that lay before his eyes brought no touch of healing.

He remembered turning away, easing the small pack on his back. It was then that his foot must have skidded on a mossy piece of rock. He did not remember falling, only coming slowly to consciousness, with nausea tugging at his stomach and a hammer pounding ponderously in his head. That was three hours ago now. He had been able to measure the time by looking at his watch during moments when his head was clear. He had hurt his left wrist in the fall. It was swollen and shiny from the fingertips almost to the elbow. Broken perhaps. He had taken off his wristwatch because of the swelling.

Carefully he studied the hands of the watch, and absorbed the fact that it was now three-thirty. With an effort he got to his knees and made his eyes focus on the almost sheer stretch of rock which rose above him. Only eighteen feet, and there were a few niches and crevices. Absurd that he could not climb it. But his left hand was useless, and on the two occasions when he had made a fumbling attempt to climb he had been forced by dizziness to abandon it quickly and sit down to avoid another fall.

Quinn looked about him. The ledge was moon-shaped, twenty paces long and six feet wide at the point where he knelt, tapering away to nothing on each side of him. The only way out was up. Apart from the concussion, which made his co-ordination clumsy, he doubted that he could have made the climb without two good hands.

Once more he wondered if he was deceiving himself, if sub-consciously he lacked the will to try because he did not really care what happened to him.

His mind clouded again, and there was a time of dream-like confusion, shot through with flashes of the old nightmare. For the hundredth time he saw the grenade rolling along the aisle of the aircraft, bobbling from side to side like a grisly roulette ball choosing its slot. He heard the cries of fear as the passengers shrank away from its passing, huddling in their seats. He saw the white-faced man, sitting with his wife and the little girl, dive forward in what could only have been an attempt to smother the thing under his own body. But the black pineapple lurched under the seat, and was still rolling when it roared its frightful death-cry.

Quinn jerked to wakefulness, shuddering, his hands pressed over his ears. Sweat was dripping from his chin, but he ached with cold. He studied his watch. Four o'clock. Dusk would fall soon, and so would the temperature, close to zero. In his pack was a light showerproof top-coat, a bar of chocolate, and a flask which had held coffee but which had been punctured when he fell. Not much of a survival kit, he thought dully. One night of exposure might not kill him, but a second would do the trick.

It came to him that there would have been little point in climbing to the top, even if he had been able to do it, for he was on the wrong side of the gorge. Here there was no road above him, only a narrow path, which dipped and soared as it wound its tortuous way past the ravines slicing the canyon wall, a route to test a fit man. On the far side of this path, lay a stretch of broken rock and then the belt of firs he had come through earlier. Beyond the trees stretched the arid region of the Causse de Méjean, a depopulated area so waterless that the few sheep which grazed there had evolved a camel-like ability to go for long periods without drinking. There you could travel a dozen miles and find only an ancient shepherd and his wife living in a crumbling village which had once boasted a population of twenty.

The road which followed the gorge lay a thousand yards away, on the north side of the great gash which contained the Tarn. He could see a short stretch of it from where he sat, a hundred yards of sharply curving bend. He remembered now that during earlier periods of consciousness he had twice waved his handkerchief on seeing a car and a truck pass along that stretch, but they had been in view for no more than ten seconds, and the chances that anyone might spot him in so brief a time were scarcely worth reckoning.

'Up the creek, you are, Quinn,' he told himself, and grinned foolishly. 'Up a big, big creek without a paddle. Have some chocolate, son. Maybe you can keep it down this time. Full of energy, chocolate. Nearly as good as spinach . . .' It was as he fumbled in his pack that he saw, across the valley, a toy-like van, a Dormobile perhaps, creep slowly into the bend and come to a halt. After a moment, two penguins climbed out of the cab.

Quinn thought about this laboriously, then gave a nod of satisfaction, wincing as his head throbbed. 'Nuns,' he mumbled. 'Can't fool Quinn. No, sir. Sisters of mercy, God bless 'em. The hand of the Lord works a miracle for good old Quinn. Come on now, little sisters, look this way and see me waving.'

He could make out the white blobs of their faces surrounded by the black wimples as he began to wave his handkerchief, three short waves, three long. The penguins began to walk slowly round the curve of the bend. They stopped, seemed to speak together, and one of them pointed down the road. They moved on, halted for a few moments, then turned and walked back to the van. There they stood waiting, doing nothing, neither of them so much as glancing across the gorge.

Quinn's arm ached with the effort of waving, and his head was swimming again. He allowed his arm to fall. 'Today's miracle will not take place,' he thought. Raising his eyes to the sky, he shrugged and said without rancour, 'Please yourself, you bloody old tease.'

He ate some chocolate and sat watching the distant figures. His throat was parched and there was a taste of bile in his mouth. When his vision blurred and his mind began to slip stealthily away again he was unaware of it.

The younger of the two nuns, the one with the round pretty

face, stood by the line of once-white stones which rimmed the outer side of the bend and which had once been a low wall. Beyond them there was nothing, for here the side of the gorge was more than sheer, leaning out over the river a long six-second drop below.

Her companion stood by the Dormobile, a woman in her middle thirties with a fresh complexion and a face in which the strong bones were dominated by a large, proudly-bridged nose. The younger nun looked up the slope of the road, then at the seamed wall of rock which bordered its inner side.

She sniffed and said, 'About time we 'ad word from 'is nibs. Don't want to 'ang around 'ere all bleeding day.' Her voice held the adenoidal accent of Liverpool, faintly overlaid by an American twang.

The second nun looked at her sharply. 'I'll not tell you again, Angel dear.' Her voice rose and fell with the sing-song lilt of the Scottish Highlands. 'When we're wearing the habit it's as nuns we speak, even with each other. And besides, it's not becoming for a young lady to speak so coarsely.'

The girl laughed, her muddy eyes malicious. 'I s'pose it's becoming for a lady to run a cat-'ouse in New Orleans?'

'Och, you've a nasty tongue in your head today, Angel. If I once provided a particular service for gentlemen there, it was no more than a professional necessity. It wasn't I who made the world the way it is, and we all just have to do the best we can.'

'All right for Madam Clare. You should've tried some of them services they wanted.'

'We'll not discuss that, dear,' the older nun said stiffly. 'You were glad enough to take the job at the time, and it's long finished now anyway. You're very lucky that I chose you to bring along with me when I was offered such an excellent new position.'

'I was the only one with the guts for it. Can you see Maisie or Jacquie or any of 'em doing a good job with a razor or a bit of piano wire? Besides, sometimes I think you're a bloody old dike, and fancy little Angel a bit.' She grinned like a vicious child.

The lips beneath the handsomely hooked nose tightened. 'You're a very dirty-minded girl, Angelica. I think a word to Mr Sexton is called for.'

The younger nun's face grew wary. She knew she had gone too far. You could never make Clare lose her temper, she thought, but when the old bitch started calling you Angelica it meant she was angry. And Clare angry was Clare dangerous. The muddy eyes lost their sparkle of malice and became contrite, wheedling.

'No. I'm sorry, Clare, honest. I just get a bit excited when there's a job on, and say daft things. You know. Don't say anything to Mr Sexton. He put me through it something 'orrible last time——'

She broke off, and together they swung round at a faint sound. A man had dropped to the road from the twenty-foot high cliff which bordered it. He wore dark slacks and blazer, with a pale yellow shirt and a black cravat. Field glasses hung at his chest. Six feet tall, he was broad-shouldered and walked with a quick step of extraordinary lightness, as if his feet scarcely touched the ground. His square face was framed in a neat golden halo by thick curly hair and a beard. The eyes were pale blue. About him there was an air of bounding vitality and the impression of a man from another age, a throw-back. Dressed in armour and with a broadsword in his hand, he would have been the traditional image of Richard the Lionheart.

Clare said, 'Ah, there you are, Mr Sexton.' Nobody called him anything other than Mr Sexton, not even his employer. The man smiled and nodded. He had just covered a mile, moving fast over scrubby broken rock, but his rate of respiration was normal.

'And there *you* are, dear ladies. The car is on its way and should be here in less than five minutes. Are you ready?'

'Quite ready, Mr Sexton. There's no change in the arrangements?'

'None, Mrs McTurk. You and Angel will manage the initial stage. I shall remain out of sight and watch for approaching traffic until it's time for the kill.'

'Very well, Mr Sexton. But I'm sure Angel and I could handle the whole matter without difficulty. The lassie has her wire handy.'

'I've every faith in you both, Mrs McTurk.' The eyes glinted with laughter. 'But if you allow Angel to use her wire, I'll be very cross with you, and I'm sure you'd have little taste for my corrective treatment.'

Angel giggled. Clare's fresh cheeks lost some of their colour. 'Och now, there's no need to talk like that, Mr Sexton. I've never failed in my duty yet. It was a suggestion, just.'

'Then forget it, Mrs McTurk. This is a very important operation and we have precise instructions for it.' He moved to the side of the road where the rock wall of the cutting dipped to little more than eight feet, jumped and caught the edge, drew himself up so easily that he appeared to flow over the top, and vanished from their view.

Angel moved to the Dormobile. took out the jack and rested

it against a wheel. 'I 'ate that bastard,' she said idly. 'He can make you wish you was dead with no damage to show for it.'

A thousand yards away, beyond a dozen of the bends which contorted the serpentine road, the Peugeot 504 kept a steady pace. In the back, Sir Gerald Tarrant yawned. He was tired but happy. Tired because he had spent a wearisome week in Brussels chairing the Co-ordinating Committee for Nato Intelligence, and had now been travelling across France for the past eight hours. Happy because in another twenty minutes or so he would arrive at L'Auberge du Tarn, a small inn perched above the river below La Malène, and there Modesty Blaise would be waiting for him.

He would spend four days in her company, doing nothing except walking, fishing, and probably losing a few pounds to her at bezique of an evening. He could not remember looking forward to anything so much in years. She was the most restful of companions. He half-smiled at the thought, for it was a paradox. Those who knew only what she had done rather than what she was like would never have dreamt of applying the word restful to Modesty Blaise. He wondered if, with sufficient low cunning, he could coax her to talk about one or two of her exploits, but was not optimistic about his chances of success.

Both she and her remarkable friend and retainer, Willie Garvin, seemed to have a fixed aversion to giving any detailed account of their activities, either during the years when she had run the criminal organization known as *The Network*, with Willie as her right arm, or since their retirement, when Tarrant had been able to make use of them simply because they found that the spice of occasional danger had become an addiction.

A touch of melancholy pressed down on Tarrant. Sooner or later they would go on a job and not come back. It was inevitable, and even in the past year they had come within a whisker of it twice. There was a little comfort, though not much, in reflecting that the last and fatal job would not be one that he had instigated. For some time now he had refused to use them for any further operations. It would not even be a job of their own seeking, he admitted. They seemed born to trouble. It simply came to them.

Tarrant fingered his greying moustache and sighed. With an effort he pushed back the shadow of melancholy and watched the constant movement of the driver's shoulders with the turn of the wheel on the winding road.

'All clear on your instructions after you've dropped me off, Reilly?' he said.

'Yes, sir.' Reilly's dark red head nodded. 'I carry on to Millau, book into the *Moderne* there, and wait two days for Mr Clayton to make contact. If he hasn't shown up after two days, I ring the office for orders. March code, variation six.'

'Good.' Tarrant leaned back in his seat. Reilly had been his driver for two years now, and was an efficient man, well able to deal with a routine courier job. It occurred to him that Reilly had been unusually silent during the long drive. Normally he would make a little small-talk—not much, just an occasional five minutes of casual conversation in that soft Irish voice. Reilly could invariably tell when his master wanted to be quiet.

'Anything wrong?' Tarrant asked.

He saw Reilly give a little start. Then the man shook his head. 'No, sir. I'm fine. What makes you ask?'

'Oh, you seem rather quiet.'

'I thought you'd be having a lot to think of after the week in Brussels, sir. Didn't want to disturb you.'

Tarrant realized now that his own long silence, ever since Nevers, had probably given Reilly the impression that he wished to be left in peace. But he had not been thinking about Brussels. he had been thinking about his coming few days of holiday.

It was Willie Garvin who had suggested it two weeks ago, at Modesty's penthouse overlooking Hyde Park, when she had invited Tarrant to dinner and had remarked that he looked tired.

'Tell you what, Princess,' Willie had said in his gravelly voice as he refilled Tarrant's glass. 'You're spending a couple of weeks on the Tarn, so why not talk Sir G. into coming down for a few days? Do 'im good.'

Tarrant remembered the hopeful pleasure he had felt as she lifted an eyebrow and smiled at him.

She wore a long dress of dark blue silk that matched her eyes. Regrettably it covered her splendid shoulders, but it set off the long column of her throat admirably. Her black hair, piled in a chignon, was in what he always thought of as her grown-up style. When she wore it loose, either in bunches at her ears or tied back behind her neck, she looked far younger than her years. She said, 'It's a nice idea, Willie, but Sir Gerald's a VIP. He can't run off for a long week-end with a woman of doubtful reputation.'

'Will you be alone?' said Tarrant. 'Willie's not going with you? Or . . . anyone else?'

'Willie's going to be with his titled girl-friend on her farm in Bucks.'

'Lady Janet?'

'Yes. His faithful steady, and very nice to come home to. Much better than he deserves. What about it, Sir Gerald? I'll be staying at a little inn on the Tarn. Would you care to risk your reputation?'

'More to the point, what about your reputation with the patron?'

'Patronne. What will really shock Mme Martine is giving us separate rooms. She's very romantic.'

'She would surely take my advanced age into account?'

'A mature gentleman lover is an established tradition in France.'

Tarrant laughed. 'I'd better pretend to be your elderly uncle.'

'You really mean you'll join me? It won't be exciting. I just walk, and laze, and watch the river go by.'

Willie chuckled. 'Go careful, Sir G. When the Princess says "walk", she means she goes roaming out over the causse with nothing to eat or drink, no shoes, no blanket, like a perishing nomad. If you want to learn 'ow to stay alive finding berries and fungi, catching rabbits, milking a ewe, and eating things to make a hyena think twice, you'll 'ave a ball.' He looked at Modesty. 'You'd better not keep 'im out all night though Princess. I don't think 'e'd fancy curling up in a gully with dead leaves for a blanket. Oh, and don't give 'im snake to eat, like you gave me that time in New Mexico, remember?'

'I remember the fuss you made. And it was a garter snake, much nicer than the worm snakes I've eaten in the Zagros when I was small.'

Tarrant stared from one to the other and said, 'I expect you're pulling my leg?'

Modesty gave him an apologetic look. 'Not really. I like to revert to my childhood ways now and again. Like an aborigine going walk-about. It stiffens the sinews, and it's nice when I stop and come back to this.' Her little gesture took in the spacious dining-room, the gleam of silver and glass on the long table, and the sumptuous silken glow of the Shah Abbas carpet.

Tarrant said doubtfully, 'I'm sixty-one, my dear. Such activities might stiffen *my* sinews in a less metaphorical fashion.'

'That's where Willie's pulling your leg. He knows I wouldn't go walk-about with you there. You could have a nice rest and we'd just do whatever you feel like doing. There's good fishing to be had, so maybe you could teach me how to handle a rod?'

'It sounds like Paradise,' said Tarrant, and meant it. 'I'm more than grateful.'

Now he was within a quarter of an hour's drive from the Auberge du Tarn, looking forward to a bath, dinner with Modesty, and a leisurely cigar as they talked afterwards, perhaps by a window looking out over the river, with the cruel and devious world of his profession forgotten for a few blissful days.

It was extraordinarily kind of her, he thought, considering the sweat, toil and blood she had expended for him. Scars could be invisibly mended by surgery, but that did not cancel the reality of torn flesh and pain. He was responsible for at least two bad wounds her body had borne. How she could have any affection for a man who had put her at appalling risk on several occasions he could not fathom. But there was no doubt she was fond of him in some very real way. Perhaps he was a kind of father-figure to her, he thought. If so, he was well content with that, and had no inclination to ponder how intriguing it would now be if he were thirty years younger at this moment.

His thoughts were interrupted by a sudden slowing of the car, and he saw that they had entered a downhill bend where a Dormobile stood parked at the widest point, a jack standing by one wheel. There were two nuns, one studying an instruction manual; the other looking hopefully towards them.

Reilly brought the car to a halt ten paces away, switched off the engine and said without looking round, 'Shall I give them a hand, sir?'

'Yes, you'd better. They look rather lost.'

Reilly got out, then opened the rear door. 'Like to stretch your legs, Sir Gerald?'

'No just carry on. I don't feel like making laboured French conversation with the good sisters if it can be avoided.

'I thought you might fancy a breath of air, sir.'

Tarrant looked at the man curiously. His face was pale and there was a film of sweat on his brow.

'If I want to get out I'll make up my own mind, Reilly. Are you all *right*?'

Reilly's hand came into view. Absurdly, there was a revolver in it, pointed at Tarrant, a ·38 Smith and Wesson Bodyguard with a two-inch barrel. Tarrant blinked once, then caught at the slackening muscles of his face to prevent his jaw sagging in a foolish gape.

'Get out,' Reilly said in a low voice.

Tarrant looked down the barrel which could drive a piece of lead into his body at a velocity of 855 feet per second. So Reilly had sold out to the opposition. Or to somebody. The opposition did not usually go in for killing or kidnapping Heads of Intelligence these days. The profession had become much more sophisticated since the almost open warfare of the fifties.

Slowly he slid along the seat to the open door, and saw Reilly step back a pace, keeping the gun levelled. Tarrant was getting the first primitive reaction of shock and fear under control now, and said quietly, 'You know I'm carrying no documents, Reilly.'

'Just get out.'

Tarrant obeyed, wondering what he could do. 'I'm over sixty,' he thought. 'Reasonably fit, but the edge is long gone and I've no experience of this.' Ironic to remember that he had been responsible for the training of hundreds of men and women for this kind of situation. He had visited the big house in Surrey where they were sent for instruction, and watched them at work, but he had little idea how best to tackle Reilly.

He saw the two nuns moving forward. They were part of it, of course. Glancing along the road towards them he said, 'I take it the nuns are all part of the team? And the gendarme?'

Reilly's head twitched round, and in the same instant Tarrant took a pace forward and struck at the forearm with an outward sweeping motion, to carry the gun out of line. His body hit Reilly's chest, and his knee came up hard for the groin. It almost worked, but he was a fraction slow. Reilly had seen in a split-second glance that there was no gendarme, and had turned slightly so that the knee drove into his thigh. Then the gun looped over and hit Tarrant on the side of the head. It was only a glancing blow, but enough.

He staggered, sparks exploding before his eyes as his mind reeled, and would have fallen but for the car at his back. His limbs were rubber, and he half turned, clutching at the car to prevent himself going down. The nuns were there in front of him now. Something jabbed hard against his back, and from behind him Reilly's voice said in a husky whisper, 'Keep still!'

Hands gripped his arm, and he felt the sleeve of his jacket being pushed back. He tried to wrench his arm away, but the hands holding it were very strong. For a moment his vision cleared, and he saw the face of the taller nun. She locked his wrist under her arm-pit and said, 'The needle, Angel.' The face of the other nun swam into Tarrant's view, a young and pretty face, marred by the eyes. They were muddy brown, and the eyes of an evil child.

There came a sharp prick, followed by the small but longer pain as the injection coursed into him. Then nothing.

Reilly stepped back, lowering the gun, and wiped his brow as he watched the two women ease Tarrant to the ground. The younger one looked across the road, clamped her lower lip between her teeth and gave a sharp whistle. A bearded man in a black blazer appeared on top of the rock wall. He looked down, nodded, then dropped to the ground like a cat and crossed to where Tarrant lay.

'Very good, ladies,' he said, and smiled brightly. Bending, he lifted Tarrant's body as if it had been a truss of hay, and carried it down the road to the Dormobile. The older nun followed. The other remained near Reilly, her eyes fixed on him. Neither of them spoke. Reilly's face was haggard as he put the gun in his pocket. He watched as the man and the taller nun put Tarrant on some sort of bunk in the back of the Dormobile, strapped him down, then got out and closed the doors. The nun remained by the van, looking down the road. The man walked back to the Peugeot.

'Very good, Reilly,' he said, and took an envelope from inside his jacket. 'Five thousand dollars. The balance due.'

Reilly opened the envelope, pulled out a slip of blue paper and studied it. His hands were shaking. The younger nun walked a little way up the road to the next bend and stood there.

Reilly said, 'All right.' He put the envelope away and looked at the man in the black blazer. 'We stopped because he wanted to stretch his legs. He was standing by those stones on the bend there, near the edge. I was cleaning the windscreen. I heard him call, but when I looked round he'd gone. Must have felt dizzy and fallen.'

Mr Sexton nodded, merriment in his pale blue eyes. 'Keep it as simple as that,' he said. 'You'd better find the nearest phone now.'

Reilly turned to get into the car. As he did so, Mr Sexton moved. He glanced up and down the road. Neither of the two nuns gave any sign. He took a quick step forward. His right arm swung up and down with such sudden speed that to the normal eye it would have blurred like the spoke of a turning wheel. The edge of the stiffened hand struck Reilly on the back of the skull, exactly in the centre. There was a soft, deadened sound of impact.

Reilly sprawled forward across the front seat of the car. There was a three inch fracture in his skull, and pieces of shattered bone were embedded in his brain. He was not dead yet, but he was dying fast. Mr Sexton looked pleased as he transferred the gun and the envelope from Reilly's pocket to his own, took hold of the man's limp legs and pushed him fully into the car. He looked towards Angel, then Clare. They were watching the road as before.

The rear door of the car was still open. Mr Sexton wound down the window, looked at the set of the hinges, then bent and gripped the bottom of the door with one hand, the upper framework of the window with the other. His eyes half closed and he seemed to relax in this strange position, his hands moving just a little, very gently, as if seeking some esoteric communion with what he held. Then he drew a deep breath, his eyes opened wide, and he straightened up slowly but smoothly.

There came the sound of rending metal as the steel surrounding the riveted hinges gave way beneath the inexorable pressure. The door broke away from the lower hinge. Mr Sexton continued lifting and twisting. The metal round the upper hinge broke. He stepped back, hoisted the door on to the roof of the car, dusted his hands, pushed Reilly's body into a crumpled ball on the nearside of the front seat, and climbed in behind the wheel.

The engine came to life and the Peugeot moved forward. Mr Sexton slipped into third gear, then steered with one hand holding the door open. The car gathered speed. The line of stones protecting the outer curve of the bend made a frail barrier. One second before the wheels struck, Mr Sexton dived. He hit the road, rolling in a perfect break-fall, and came lightly to his feet, watching as the Peugeot reared up over the stones, hesitated, hovered, then lurched forward to plunge over the edge. It did not once touch the inward-leaning side of the great gorge. The first thing it struck was the river, six hundred feet below.

Angel and Clare walked to the Dormobile. Mr Sexton brushed dust from his jacket and said, 'One last look round, ladies.' He moved to the wall of the cutting and drew himself up.

Angel muttered, 'Bloody show-off.'

'Now, Angel.'

'Well, 'e is. Smashing the mick's head when it just needed a tap on the neck. And ripping that door off so they won't be surprised when they don't find the old bloke's body in the car. It'll be split open like a sardine can anyway, after that drop——' She broke off as Mr Sexton jumped down to the road again and walked towards them. He carried the field glasses and wore a thoughtful look.

'There's a man across the gorge,' he said. 'On a ledge a little way from the top. He was waving an SOS, but then he stopped and toppled over sideways. Passed out, I imagine.'

Clare gave him a startled look. 'D'you think he saw anything?'

The broad shoulders shrugged. 'He wouldn't be able to make out much detail without glasses. Anyway, he must be too badly hurt to climb up, so he's stuck there. A night in the open might well finish him off.'

'All the same, if he did see something, and if he's found before
he dies of exposure . . .' Clare peered across the valley. 'Perhaps we
should see to him, Mr Sexton?'

'We'd have to get across to the other side, then back up-river
from the bridge. And there's no road that side. It might take four
or five hours to find him, Mrs McTurk, especially after dark.' He
glanced at the Dormobile. 'And we can't roam around with that
cargo aboard.'

'You'll just leave him, then?'

'He'll keep for tonight.' Mr Sexton looked at his wrist-watch.
'We'll be back at base in four hours, then Colonel Jim can decide.
He might send me back, or put in one of the odd-job teams to fix
it.'

'Well . . . it's your decision, Mr Sexton.'

'Always remember that, Mrs McTurk. Colonel Jim is very hot
on chain-of-command. We don't want him sending you along to me
for disciplinary measures.' His eyes twinkled. He reached out
suddenly and pinched Angel's buttock, saying, 'Or do you think
she might enjoy it, Angel?'

The girl bit off a scream of pain and jumped back, teeth set in
her lip, face screwed up in agony. Foul abuse was on her tongue,
but with an effort she held it back. 'No,' she said, panting. 'I don't
reckon she'd enjoy it much, Mr Sexton.'

'There's the voice of experience.' Mr Sexton opened the back
doors of the Dormobile. 'We'll get started, then.' He climbed in
and sat down beside Tarrant's unconscious form. 'Drive carefully,
Mrs McTurk. We want no trouble. That's more important than
speed.' He closed the doors.

Clare and Angel moved to the cab, Angel limping a little and
rubbing her buttock. 'Bastard!' she hissed. 'I'd like to get be'ind
him one night with a bit of wire. Make 'is eyes pop clean out of
'is rotten 'ead, I would. He's just about made a bloody 'ole right
through my bum.'

'You're being *coarse* again, Angel.'

CHAPTER TWO

FOUR HOURS LATER, in the Auberge du Tarn, Modesty Blaise
stood by the big window which looked out over the river and
tried not to let her mind picture Tarrant's broken body.

Mme Martine stood with hands clasped beneath her large

bosom and said, moist-eyed, 'I am so sorry, mam'selle. So very sorry. Milord was an old friend?' Since she had known that Modesty's guest was called Sir Gerald Tarrant she had insisted on referring to him as milord.

Modesty said, 'Yes. I was very fond of him.' She wore slacks and a sweater, both damp with the same heavy night dew that lay on her hair. It was now three hours since a boatman passing down the Tarn had seen, in the last of the dying light, the wreckage of a car protruding from the shallows. On his report, two men from the Poste de Police at La Malène had taken a motorboat up-river to investigate. One of them had braved the chill waters to find a body in the car and two torn suitcases in the broken boot.

It was two hours since they had sent another man up to the heights from which the car had fallen; and there, even by torchlight, he had found evidence of the car's plunge to destruction in the metal-scrapes on the rocks bordering the curve. On his way back he had called at the auberge to drink a pastis and tell of the accident. It appeared that there had been two in the car, he said, and they were foreigners, English. A search would be made for the other body down-river by daylight. The clothes in one of the suit-cases had tailor's name-tabs. The name was different from that in the passport found on the dead man. Presumably it was the name of the other unfortunate, whose body was missing. A M'sieu Tarrant.

Mme Martine had clasped her hands to her head in shock, and run to tell Modesty. In the past two hours Modesty had been down to the Poste de Police to look at the body. She knew Reilly as Tarrant's driver, and had identified him. She had taken a large flash-lamp, driven up the road to the point where the car had gone over the edge, and spent twenty minutes there. A strange thing to do, Mme Martine thought, but then Mam'selle Blaise was an unusual young woman. Even now, as she stood looking down from the window upon the river where her milord friend had died, there were no tears. Except for her stillness and the quiet emptiness in her eyes, one would not have known that she grieved. The English were strange people.

The telephone rang. Mme Martine ran into the hall to answer it, and returned a few moments later. 'It is your call to London, mam'selle.'

Modesty went through to the phone, flinching from what she now had to do. This was going to hit Jack Fraser badly. He had spent fifteen years as an intelligence agent in the field before taking a desk job as Tarrant's number two, a man who had walked with death and dealt it out himself when occasion called. Under Tarrant he had sent men on missions from which they had not returned, and he had the case-hardened attitude his job demanded; but this would hurt him deeply. Fraser held no more than a handful of people in any esteem, but Tarrant was one of them.

She picked up the phone and said, 'Jack?'

'Fraser speaking, Miss Blaise.' The voice was humble and ingratiating, Fraser's habitual pose.

She said, 'I'm sorry to hit you with this, Jack, but it's bad news. About Tarrant.'

A pause, then : 'How bad?' The voice had changed.

'There's been an accident, and he's dead.'

Fraser said softly, 'Oh, God.'

She gave him the facts briefly and ended, 'They don't seem too certain about finding his body. Apparently it could get sucked into one of the under-surface caves before it reaches the Garonne, and then just . . . stay there. I've given them your number to call —not this one, the official one.'

Fraser said, 'Thank you.' After a long silence he went on, 'You don't think this might have been arranged?'

'I wondered, and I've had a quick look round, but it seems like a straight accident. Would any of the various oppositions make him a target today?'

'I doubt it.' Fraser's voice was flat. 'That's gone out, like gunboat diplomacy. It was only a thought.' Another long silence. 'This probably won't be published for a day or two, until the Minister's had a full report from the French. Do you want me to call Willie and tell him?'

'No, I'll call him myself tomorrow. There's nothing he can do, so I don't want to hand him this as a night-cap. I'm sorry, Jack. So damn sorry.'

Quinn lay huddled against the rock, teeth chattering, his thin coat wound tightly about him, and watched the early-morning sun lift over the canyon edge of the river bend. His head was clearer now, and did not throb so painfully, but the night had been a confused eternity of misery, and there seemed no strength left in his chilled, aching body.

Sometime during the night, between periods of sleep, half-sleep and stupor, he had eaten the last of his chocolate. He was desperately thirsty, and sucked dew from his coat to ease his parched throat. Perhaps the sun would begin to warm him soon. He ought to get up and stamp about, to stir his sluggish circulation. Wearily he pushed himself to a sitting position and sat nursing his hurt arm. A movement drew his eye, something on this side of the gorge, where the cliff-top jutted out in a point, only a hundred yards away. He screwed up his eyes and opened them again.

A woman. Gleam of brown legs below a dark green skirt. Black hair. Something like a small sack hanging from one shoulder. She stood on the edge, looking across the valley.

Quinn's heart pounded. He drew in a breath and called. But only a croaking sound came from his lips. He seized the coat in his good hand and began to flap it about wildly as he scrambled to his knees. She turned towards him . . . but continued turning. Christ, she was going away! Her head came back, and he saw the white of her face under the black hair. For a moment she was still, then one arm lifted in a wave, and she moved away from the cliff-edge at a run, vanishing from his sight.

Quinn found that he was panting, trembling. He did not dare stand up for fear of falling, An age seemed to pass, and then he saw her above him, on one knee on the cliff edge, looking down. Surprise tinged the relief that swept him, for the face above the charcoal sweater was not a peasant-girl's face. Wide mouth, broad forehead, handsome bone-structure under the firm tanned flesh, raven hair tied back at the neck, large calm eyes.

'Vous êtes blessé?' Her voice was pleasantly mellow. Quinn groped for words from his meagre stock of French. 'Oui. Je tombe. Mon bras.' He held up his swollen wrist.

She said, 'You sound English. Is it just the arm?'

'God, you're English too!' He shook his head to clear it. 'That's a help. No, on top of the arm I gave my head a hell of a crack. Been here since yesterday afternoon. Can you go and get some-body to haul me up? I'm a bit groggy.'

She nodded and stood up. He saw that a small duffle-bag hung from her shoulder and that simple monk sandals were hooked to the draw-string of the bag. She said, 'I won't be long. You'd better lie down and rest, your colour's battleship grey.' Then she was gone.

Quinn sank back on his haunches, bemused. What the hell was an English girl doing, wandering about on the edge of nowhere? Any girl other than a peasant, in fact, and she wasn't that. No weird hippie, either. Quinn had an eye for quality, and was cer-tain her sweater had been of fine cashmere. A thirty guinea job at least.

She hadn't wasted time on questions. He liked that. But if she thought she wouldn't be gone long, then she wasn't too bright. Quinn visualized what he knew of the causse. No inhabited village for miles. She would have to follow the tortuous river track all the way to La Malène. He would be lucky to see a rescue party in under four hours. He shivered. God, he was cold. He had not felt so cold since that long trip through Lancaster Hole two years ago. He sat down with his back to the wall and began to exercise, bending and stretching one leg, then the other, then his sound arm, trying to drive the blood through his veins a little faster.

Ten minutes later a sound made him look up. The girl was climbing down. She wore the sandals now, and carried a coil of rope like a bandolier. The duffle-bag hanging from her shoulder bulged squatly. She moved with certainty, finding toe and finger-holds with little groping. He saw the full length of one down-reaching leg, right up to the black pants, and noted the smooth play of lean muscles in the elegant curves.

'A dancer,' he thought. 'With those legs, a quid says she's a dancer. But why the hell——?' Anger exploded in him as she dropped the last few feet to the ledge and turned to face him. 'Very clever, ducky,' he said spitefully. 'And now what? If you think you can haul me up on your own, you're out of your tiny mind.'

She showed no sign of resentment, but put down the coil of rope, pushed back a wisp of hair, and began to open the duffle-bag. She said, 'My car's in the woods only a quarter of a mile away. I just went back to collect some stuff from it. Don't worry about climbing up, we'll manage.' She took a first-aid box from the duffle-bag and knelt beside him. Her hand rested on his brow for a few seconds, then she picked up his wrist, her long fingers on the pulse. 'Did you hit your head very hard?'

The anger drained out of him. Her quietness made him confused. He muttered, 'Hard enough. Knocked myself out. And afterwards I kept fainting or something. It's all a bit muddled now.'

She took his head in her hands, turned it to look in each of his ears, tilted it back to look into his nostrils, then pulled down his lower lip, and examined his teeth.

He said sourly, 'What's all that in aid of?'

'No bleeding from your ears, nose or mouth. That's good. With any luck you haven't cracked your skull. Now turn round a little and lie back. No, so your head's on my lap. That's right, now just lie still.'

He felt her fingers exploring his scalp. They found the lump above his right ear and rested there for a while, probing gently, then moved on. It was an extraordinarily pleasant sensation. Quinn felt the knots within him loosening. There was something about the touch of her hands that gave him a foolish sense of well-being.

'All right, sit up now.' She helped him, then knelt in front of him and held up one finger. 'Look at my fingertip as I move it from side to side.' She watched his eyes follow her moving finger. After a few seconds she reached out her other hand to cover his left eye. 'Good. Now again. No, don't look at *me*, watch the finger. That's better. Let's try the other eye.' Her hand moved slowly from right to left and back again. 'Good.'

She sat back on her haunches and drew the duffle-bag towards her. 'You'll need an X-ray, but I don't think there's much damage apart from concussion. I expect your arm took the main fall and your head hit the rock afterwards.' She took out a long section of French loaf wrapped in greaseproof paper, a packet of raisins and a quarter-bottle of brandy. The loaf had been split and buttered, with slices of ham between.

She said, 'You're lucky I'm travelling first-class today. Start eating while I see to your arm, and then you can take a little brandy.'

Quinn bit hungrily into the bread, watching her as she poured a colourless liquid on to a piece of lint. She rested his hand on her knee, wrapped the lint about his swollen wrist and forearm, and began to bandage.

He swallowed and said, 'Are you a doctor or something?'

'No. I've done some casualty work.' She spoke almost absently, and he felt a little nettled by her manner.

'My name's Quinn,' he said.

'Hallo, Mr Quinn.'

'Christ, is this going to be formal?'

'What do your friends call you?'

'My enemies call me Henry. My friends just call me Quinn.'

'Hallo, Quinn. I'm called Modesty Blaise. What are you doing here?'

'I was just walking. Misjudged time and distance, so instead of heading back to the hotel at St Chély I thought I'd carry on to La Malène for the night.' He glanced up. 'Took a look at the river and bloody well slipped.'

She knotted the bandage and looked across the gorge. 'You must have been here when the car went over the edge yesterday. A grey Peugeot. Did you see it happen?'

He stared. 'Went over the edge? God, no. I didn't see it go over.' He wolfed the last of the bread and ham, and picked up the packet of raisins. 'I kept passing out then coming round again. Must have missed that bit.' He looked acrosss the gorge and grimaced? 'How many?'

'In the car? Two.'

Quinn shook his head. 'Poor devils,' he said soberly. 'You'd have a long time to think on a drop that deep. I mean, it would seem a long time. You get through a lot in a few seconds when you can see your number coming up.'

'Yes.' She picked up the bottle and poured a measure of brandy into the cap. 'You can get this down you, now there's something in your stomach. Then we'll see about moving.'

His hand was shaking so much that she had to hold the cap to his lips for him to sip the brandy. He could feel it spreading warmth through his chest. Between sips he said, 'You came in a car? How did you get it up here?'

'If you cut south from La Malène there's a rough track that loops round into the causse. You can make seven or eight miles an hour on it. The last mile's rough going, when you turn off the track to reach the woods. You have to move at a slow walk, but it means you can tuck the car away in the trees, out of sight.'

He looked at her, puzzled. 'And then what?'

'I go for a walk. Usually over the causse. Today I came to have a look at the river first. I was just going when I saw you.'

'You walk over the causse?' He looked at her light clothing and the sandals which were no more than soles and leather thongs. 'You're mad, ducky.'

She gave a little shrug, evidently not interested in his opinion. He realized now that almost from the first moment it had been as if her thoughts were elsewhere, even while she talked and tended his hurts. And she had not smiled. Not once. He had a sudden urgent wish to see her smile.

He chewed on another handful of raisins, and swallowed. 'Modesty Blaise, you said?'

'Yes.'

'Nice name. I like it. What happens now?'

'I'll fix a sling for your arm, then walk you up and down a bit to get the stiffness out of your muscles.' She glanced up the eighteen-foot stretch of wall. 'It's not far, and there are some fair holds. I brought a cross-peen hammer from the car, so I can chip them deeper for you before we start. I'll be at the top, holding you on the rope.'

'You're competent, ducky. I'll give you that. But I don't fancy another fall.'

She looked at him from eyes of midnight blue, and there was no morsel of doubt in them as she said. 'You needn't worry, Quinn. I won't let you fall.'

Ten minutes later, with the rope looped in a bowline about his chest, Quinn began the short climb. His one-handedness unbalanced him, but the rope helped to counteract this. She stood braced on the crest above him, the rope belayed round her body, not merely keeping it taut, but taking a good part of his weight as he hung on the rock face and groped for one of the foot-holds she had chipped for him.

Halfway up, one of his legs began to shake uncontrollably. He gasped and swore as he felt himself sag to one side, but the rope held him. He looked up. He could see only the line of the rope and then the line of one arm with her face looking down over the point of her shoulder as she took almost the whole of his weight. The eyes seemed black now, and coldly ferocious, but her voice was quite neutral as she said, 'Take your time, Quinn. I've got you.'

He set his teeth, flexed the treacherous leg several times to gain control of it, then moved another few inches higher. Two minutes later he heaved his trunk over the edge. She helped him crawl clear and he lay panting as she slipped the rope from his body and began to coil it. He saw that there was blood on one of her hands. She was breathing deeply and sweat shone on her face, but she did not seem distressed. She glanced across to the far side of the valley and her brow creased in a small frown, as if something was puzzling her.

Quinn said breathlessly, 'I'm . . . giving you . . . quite a bit of trouble.'

'Don't worry about it. Do you want to rest before we make for the car?'

He shook his head, and managed a grin. 'The old blood's crawling around a bit faster now, and the Quinn body begins to feel as if it might belong to Quinn again. Sorry if I've been a bit terse.'

'That was nothing. You've done well.'

'There's no need to be bloody patronizing, ducky.'

She almost smiled then, and said, 'Are you Irish?'

He glared indignantly. 'Do you *mind*?'

'No offence.'

'Just because the name's Quinn, I don't have to be bloody Irish, do I?'

'I was thinking of the temperament. Never mind. Let's get moving. You'll have to lean on me.'

'I can manage.'

But he could not manage, and after fifty unsteady paces he was glad when she looped his sound arm over her shoulders, and held him at the waist. Now he could feel the sinewy power in her as she moved, steadying him and acting as a prop to ease the burden of his weight.

'Look,' he panted when she made him sit and rest for a few minutes in the belt of firs, 'I forgot to say thanks, right? Sorry about that. The fact is, I don't often get my life saved by a beautiful girl, so I'm not used to the routine, but you've been a cracker, ducky, a real de luxe cracker, and I'm bloody grateful, I really am.'

'Good. You don't think you could stop calling me ducky?'

Quinn's teeth showed and he made a sweeping gesture. 'Consider it done. Nice to get a reaction at last. Tell me, what were you wearing on your feet *before* you put those sandals on?'

'On my feet? Nothing.'

He stared at them. They were not small feet, but shapely and strong. 'Are you crazy, or doing some kind of penance?'

'No. I've got peasant feet. Soles like leather. But the sandals help on broken rock if I'm moving fast.'

'I *see*. Yes, I see now. Some people might think you an unusual lady, Miss Blaise—oh, is that right?' His eyelids fell shut and he jerked them open again with a little start. 'I mean, Miss?'

'Yes. Come on, Quinn, before you fall asleep. Last lap.'

As she helped him up he said vaguely, 'A spinster . . . saved by a spinster.'

The Renault stood in a clearing amid the trees, a dozen paces from the open causse. Quinn was leaning on her heavily by the time they reached it. She eased him into the passenger seat and fastened the seat-belt. He slumped back with a sigh of relief. Her hand rested on his brow as she said, 'How's your head?'

'Muzzy, but not too bad. Better than last night. I thought it was going to come apart then. I'm just tired now, I think.'

'I'm not surprised. Last night could have killed you.'

'I'm very thirsty.'

'All right, but you'd better not drink too much.' She gave him water from a bottle, put the first-aid box on the floor in the back, and moved away to put the rope and duffle-bag in the boot. When she returned, Quinn sat leaning back with his eyes closed. As she took off the sandals for driving she found herself studying him.

Until now he had been an anonymous character who needed help, a man of no particular interest to her, with a few quirks which might have been either amusing or annoying at any other time, when her mind was not troubled by sorrow. His face was drawn and haggard now, but she placed him at twenty-five or six. No older. His hair was dark brown, long but not too long, brushed back and reaching to the middle of his neck in a few tousled curls. His eyes were grey-green, she remembered, set nicely wide above a rather large mouth and a longish nose. The chin was good and he had excellent teeth.

As she got behind the wheel she frowned again, trying to think what he could have said or done that was itching somewhere in the back of her mind. There had been something not quite right in a word or phrase or look, but she could not pin it down. She put the nagging question from her mind as she eased the car slowly out of the trees and began to crawl across the just-possible route she had found leading from the track which wound through the causse.

The bad stretch took twenty minutes, but once on the track she was sometimes able to push the speed up to eight miles an hour. The track looped away from the Tarn, through undulating terrain, eventually joining a small road which led west to La Malène. She wondered what to do about Quinn. She could take him straight to Millau, to the hospital there. That was only an hour's drive once she was on the N.107. Alternatively she could go to Toulouse, where Dr Georges Durand's excellent and expensive clinic stood in its own splendid grounds two miles out of town.

She had financed the setting-up of the Durand Clinic several years ago. Georges Durand was brilliant and discreet and could call on the finest specialists. In the old days her men of *The Network* had been mended there when need arose. So had Willie Garvin, and so had she, both more recently than *The Network* days. Plastic surgery had eliminated scars from her body on two occasions, and dental surgery replaced broken teeth after she had been brutalized during the *Sabre-Tooth* business in Afghanistan.

Quinn needed no discreet treatment—at least as far as she knew. But if she took him to Durand he would get the best, and on the house. She spared a glance at him. He was very young and would probably find the costs of a stay in a French hospital alarming. Better make it Toulouse, then. She felt a flicker of irritation with herself for weakly taking on a three-hour drive when she had no responsibility for the boy beside her, but then shrugged mentally. What the hell did it cost her to drive a few extra miles, anyway? She had nothing else in particular to do.

She wondered why she had thought of Quinn as a boy. He was probably no more than two years younger than she was. That was if you counted in calendar years, of course. She glanced at him again, half-smiling as she remembered his flashes of petulance and the youthful male arrogance, and she thought wryly: I was nearly as old as God when you were first starting to shave, Quinn.

She first saw the car a mile away, moving slowly along the track to nowhere. It was a big black car, a Citroen perhaps, and they would meet in less than five minutes, down in the long shallow basin which lay between them, where a stand of straggly trees bordered the track.

She braked to a gentle halt, took field glasses from under the dashboard, and focused them. The black car was a Citroen, and it had stopped. One man in a dark suit had got out and was looking towards her, also through glasses. She thought she could make out two others in the car.

A small early-warning light flashed on in her head. Thoughtfully she put the glasses back and shook Quinn gently by the shoulder. His eyes opened at once, and she realized that he had not been asleep, only dozing.

She said, 'Have you got any friends in the district, Quinn?'

'Eh? No. I'm on my own here.'

'Any enemies?'

He stared. 'For God's sake, what are you talking about?'

She pointed. The black car was moving again. 'There are some men in that car, and I fancy they're looking for you. I can't think of any other reason for them to be up here.'

'There could be a dozen reasons. *You* were here.'

'And you said I was crazy. Never mind, we'll soon find out.' She let in the clutch and drove on. The gap between the two cars grew smaller. When the Citroen reached the stand of trees and halted she was still two hundred yards away. The trees squeezed the track at that point, the one place where she could not pass the other car. The warning light in her head grew stronger.

Three men got out and stood looking towards the Renault. They all wore dark suits, and two of them wore hats. She could not see their faces yet, but she knew these men were trouble, knew it without knowing or caring how she knew. Perhaps it was something in their stance, or in the leisurely way they had positioned themselves, one beside the bonnet of the Citroen, the other two well forward and on each side of the track.

She slowed a little, but kept going and said, 'Listen Quinn, and don't argue. Those men mean trouble. Maybe you know what it's about, maybe not, but that doesn't matter now. You're in no shape for trouble, so whatever happens you sit tight and do nothing. Understand?'

He gave a huff of incredulous laughter. 'Look, ducky, have you suddenly developed a feverish imagination? Do you think they've driven up here to find someone they can roll for a wallet?'

'No. I'd put it a bit higher than that. The one with folded arms has got his hand on a gun under his jacket.' She reached under the dash and put something in the pocket of her skirt. He glimpsed a spindle of wood with a rounded knob at each end, like a miniature dumbell. 'Sit tight, Quinn,' she said. 'Just sit tight, that's all.'

She had not raised her voice, and her expression had not changed, but there was a new quality about her which made the derisive protest die on Quinn's lips. This was no nervous female, he had proof enough of that. He looked ahead at the figures of the waiting men, and a cold finger touched his spine. There *was* something about them . . .

The track improved slightly and she pushed the speed up to ten miles an hour. Reaching across him, she unlatched the door, then unlatched her own offside door. They rattled, but the forward speed prevented them from swinging open.

'Just hold your door to, with your fingertips, very lightly,' she said, and as he obeyed her he saw that she was using her left hand to keep the offside door pulled to. His tired, muddled brain tried to imagine what her purpose could be.

Fifty yards now. Another ten seconds and they would have to stop, nose-to-nose against the Citroen. Quinn saw the men's faces clearly. They were impassive, almost bored. His mind still could not accept her certain conviction, but some deep instinct brought a cold sweat to his face.

'Look,' he muttered, 'for Christ's sake stop and make a run for it.'

'Shut up. Keep still. Hold that door lightly.'

The two nearer men stood one on each side of the track, so that she would pass between them with half an arm's length to spare on each side. The third man, the only one without a hat, leaned against the side of the Citroen's bonnet and seemed to be cleaning his nails with a knife. He looked up, and waved a languid hand in a signal to halt.

Modesty began to slow down, and then, as the bonnet of the Renault passed between the two men, she stamped hard on the brake. The wheels locked in a short straight skid. Quinn was flung forward against his seat-belt. Both doors swung open hard, with the stored energy of their forward motion suddenly released by the abrupt halt.

The man with folded arms, on Quinn's side, had turned a little. The impact of the swinging door took him on his left arm and shoulder, the metal corner of its top edge gashing the side of his face as he stumbled and went down. Quinn heard him cry out. The other man had taken the blow partly on one hand, and had probably broken a finger or two, for he was clutching at his hand as he staggered, struggling to hold his balance.

Modesty Blaise was out of the car. Dazedly Quinn realized that she must have virtually gone out with the swinging door. He groped for the clasp of his seat-belt, heart pounding, but could not tear his eyes from her as he watched her take one stride and swing a long brown leg. The ball of her bare foot made precise and explosive contact with the man's jaw. Before he hit the ground she had swung round, put a hand on the bonnet and vaulted across it with a fluency which made the preceding kick-and-turn an integral preliminary of the whole movement.

The man with the gashed face had rolled away from the car and come to his knees. There was a gun in his hand now, but before he could lift it she had kicked again. He squealed as her foot smashed against his elbow, and the gun flew up in a loop to land five paces away. Her right hand swung smoothly, not very hard, and again the flowing movement seemed all of one piece with the rest.

In her fist was the little wooden dumb-bell. One knob of it rapped sharply against the side of the man's head, below and behind the ear. He fell limply sideways and lay still. Her head came round instantly to sight the third man. His reactions were quick, for already he had covered half the distance towards her, running hard, the short-bladed knife held low and angled upwards.

To Quinn it seemed that she relaxed a fraction, almost with relief. Then she raised the little dumb-bell as if in readiness to strike, took two running paces forward, and dived. It was totally unexpected and impeccably timed. She hit the ground in a long rolling somersault which brought her in under the oncoming man's knife-hand, and her legs flashed up in a two-footed kick which drove into his middle just below the rib-cage.

Even in the car, Quinn heard the agonized whoop of the breath being driven from his body. His feet came clear of the ground as he was flung back, a boneless puppet tossed through the air to land in a crumpled, unmoving sprawl.

She was on her feet again, her head moving quickly to sight the first two men. They both lay still.

Quinn called in a croaking voice, 'Hey . . . ! ' He did not know what he would have said next, but if she heard him she ignored it, knelt over the hatless man and fumbled under his jacket, then at his hip. When she stood up there was a wallet in her hands. She flicked quickly through the contents, dropped the wallet and moved to the man who had drawn a gun.

Quinn watched dazedly. She repeated the procedure, picked up the gun and moved to the unconscious man on the off-side. Her quick search produced another gun, a revolver. She walked to the Citroen, got in behind the wheel, started the engine and backed the car quickly to where the track widened. Quinn saw her get out, lift the bonnet and reach down into the engine.

She straightened, walked back to the Renault, put the Citroen's distributor-arm and the revolver into the cubby-hole under the dash, slipped the magazine from the automatic, worked the slide to eject a cartridge from the breech, clipped the magazine into the butt again, and put it in the cubby-hole as she got in behind the wheel.

Quinn saw that she was frowning, in annoyance now rather than puzzlement. He found that his heart was still thumping, and made a great effort to keep his voice cool and steady as he said, 'Well . . . congratulations.'

She gave a small angry shake of her head, started the engine and let in the clutch. 'I kicked that gun too damn far. Out of reach. If the last man had pulled a gun I might have been in trouble.'

After a long silence Quinn said, 'Never mind. We all make mistakes.' He was furious to find that he was shaking and had difficulty in speaking without a stammer. Irrationally, his fury focused in the girl beside him. Drawing a deep breath, he said savagely, 'I do hope they weren't cops of some kind.'

She shook her head. 'They weren't cops.'

'You can tell these things, of course?' She nodded absently, and his restraint broke. 'Jesus Christ, who *are* you?'

'What do you mean?'

He jerked a thumb over his shoulder. 'That! It was——' He rubbed a hand along his brow angrily. 'It reeked of long practice, and you didn't bloody well learn it in the Girl Guides.'

She said, 'Gaston Bourget, Jacques Garat, and the third one had no identification on him. You know the names?'

He stared blankly. 'Why the hell should I know them?'

'If they came up here to do you some mischief there's a connection somewhere.'

'If they did, I haven't the faintest idea why. After what I've just seen it seems a lot more likely they came after you. Are you a Mafia chief or a secret agent or something?'

She almost smiled. 'I run a hat-shop in Kensington, Quinn. I'm sure they weren't looking for me.'

His red-rimmed eyes glared with exasperation. 'All right then, they must have been after a spot of rape. Not me. You. They saw you come up here and thought, "That's a nice rapable bit of crumpet, let's follow her up on the lonely causse and—wham, bang, thank you ma'am.".'

She said slowly, 'Could be, I suppose, but I doubt it.'

He began to laugh, feebly and rather painfully in his weakness. 'Jesus, they picked the wrong bird today,' he stuttered, hiccuping. 'Wh-wham, bang, th-thank *you* ma'am for that kick in the gut . . .' The laughter went wrong, and tears ran down his cheeks. He felt shame and rage, but could not stop the shaking and the tears. She brought the car to a halt, and he felt her cool hand on his neck. He tried to push her away, croaking, 'I'm all right! I'm *fine*, ducky—just for God's sake leave me alone.'

But the comforting hand remained, and her voice held a warmth and gentleness he had not heard in it till now as she said, 'Poor old Quinn with his rotten head. Come on now, stop being tough and just let go. You're going to swallow a couple of tablets, and go to sleep, and when you wake up you'll be in a nice comfortable bed and you'll feel a new man.'

With an enormous effort Quinn took hold of himself. Through bleary eyes he saw that she had lifted the first-aid box from the back and was taking a bottle of tablets from it. When she turned towards him she smiled. It was a friendly smile, and a wave of self-loathing rose within him.

'Sorry . . . about calling you ducky,' he said shakily. 'Trouble with me, I'm a nasty bastard.'

CHAPTER THREE

THERE WAS A CONGREGATION of fifty in the small Norman church of St Mary's, Wixford, two miles south of the Thames, in the county of Berkshire.

Lady Janet Gillam sat at the end of the third pew, hymn-book resting on her trousered knees, her jaws aching with the long strain of suppressing the explosive giggles which kept threatening to burst from her. The stern Presbyterian upbringing of her childhood in the Scottish Highlands was proving a feeble barrier against irreverence as the tall young vicar announced the last hymn.

At the organ, his brown and weatherbeaten face emerging from a white surplice, his thick fair hair well-greased to make it less unruly than usual, Willie Garvin turned his head towards her and rolled up his eyes. Then with grave dignity he began to play the introductory bars of the hymn.

This was the fourth time he had played the same tune during the morning service. Lady Janet's chest hurt, and her eyes brimmed with tears. She ducked her head of short chestnut hair low over the hymn-book and moved her lips slightly, but did not dare to relax her control sufficiently to sing.

She could still conjure up the look on Willie's face two days earlier, in his pub, *The Treadmill*, when she had asked him to help.

'*Me?* Ah, come off it, Janet. You're putting me on.'

'No, Willie. The organist's sick and they have a man coming for the evening service, but Mr Peake can't find anyone to play for the morning service, so I said I was sure you'd do it. He's an awful nice man, the vicar, and with such a wee congregation it'll be just pathetic without music for the hymns. I didn't like to say no when he asked if I could find somebody.'

'Why ask you? You're not exactly a regular member of 'is flock.'

'No, but I'm the nearest thing he can find to a Lady of the Manor, and I knew you could play.'

'Play? That was at the orphanage, Jan. I never learnt any music, all I did was learn what notes to press for one 'ymn. Just one.'

'I know, but you told me it was a tune you could sing several different hymns to. What tune was it?'

'St Flavian. But——'

'How does it go, Willie?'

'Oh, blimey. Dee-dee-dah-dee-dah . . . With *weary feet and saddened 'eart from toil and care we flee*——'

'Just right for Mr Peake's congregation. I told him he'd have to find four hymns to fit whatever your tune was.'

Willie looked at the earl's daughter dazedly. 'You crazy Scotch nit!'

'That's no way for a man to talk to his mistress, is it now?'

'I 'aven't been to a church since I was seventeen,' Willie said reminiscently. 'And then it was to pinch some lead off the roof.'

'You must have been a very nasty boy.'

'I was, Jan. 'Orrible. And I got caught, so I was stupid, too.'

'Well now's your chance to make up for it a little bit. And think what a good story it'll give you to tell Her Highness.'

That was how Lady Janet usually referred to Modesty Blaise. There had once been a hostile undercurrent in it, but no longer. She had learned that the strange, dark-haired girl did nothing to bind Willie Garvin to her. The fact that a part of him would always belong to her was something neither she nor Willie could help, for it derived from the years past, when Willie had worked for her and become another man through her; when shared danger forged bonds woven from a thousand threads of steel.

Lady Janet had come to terms with this. She knew she possessed a part of Willie which would never belong to Modesty. It was not so much that he and Modesty denied themselves the ultimate physical union but that neither of them had ever seemed to regard it as a possible part of their relationship. The pattern had been set from the beginning, and it would not change now.

Lady Janet did not know if her mention of the good story it would make for Her Highness had swayed Willie's decision about playing the organ. If so, she did not care. It was enough that he had agreed. The hymn ended. Willie played the Amen, sat back with a smug, pontifical air and folded his hands. When the final blessing had been given and the congregation began to shuffle slowly along the aisles to the door, he played them out with the same tune. Some of them were looking a little bewildered.

In Willie's car, driving back to her farm which lay a mile from *The Treadmill*, Lady Janet let her laughter have free rein at last, dabbing at her eyes, choking. 'Lord, Willie, you—you looked such a clown in the s-surplice. I thought I'd never get through.'

'I could see you were moved, Jan. I got a lovely ecclesiastical touch, eh? And I'll tell you something else. I nearly got paid for it. Seventy-five pence, 'e said was the rate.'

'Willie! What did you do?'

'Told 'im it was all fixed and you were going to pay me in kind.'

'You——? Oh, you liar!'

He turned a hurt face towards her. 'You mean you're not?'

She laughed and slipped a hand through his arm. 'That depends. I don't do short-times. Can you stay the night?'

'Got me nightshirt and toothbrush packed.'

'There's a clever little organist.'

At one o'clock the next morning Lady Janet lay with her head on Willie's shoulder, her good leg resting across his thighs. It was an hour since they had gone to bed, but they had not made love. The phone call from Modesty, from her flat in Montmartre, had cast a shadow over the day.

A man called Tarrant, a friend of Modesty's and Willie's, had been killed in a car accident. Sir Gerald Tarrant. Lady Janet had met him once at *The Treadmill*, a courteous man with a rather Edwardian style of dress and manner. She had liked him.

Willie said softly, 'You awake, Jan?'

'M'mm. My damn leg's itching.'

'Want me to give it a massage?'

'Maybe, if it doesn't stop soon. Tarrant was a big Intelligence chief, wasn't he?'

'Yes, but you're not supposed to know that.'

'Lord, Willie, I've eyes and ears, and I've learned a few things about you and Modesty these past two or three years.' Her fingers found the puckered scar on his thigh. 'Sometimes I've guessed when you were going on a job, or whatever you call it. Was that for Tarrant?'

'Once or twice.'

'I know you don't have to, so what makes you do it? Why look for trouble?'

'We don't look for it, Jan. Something comes along, and you just can't turn round and walk away from it.'

'Why not?'

'There's always some reason.'

She was silent, remembering. Here she lay, Lady Janet Gillam, daughter of an earl, with her head on the shoulder of a Cockney who had walked into her life three years ago. That was after her jet-set, hell-raising days; after her stupid, defiant marriage to Walter Gillam, the drunken playboy who had killed himself in the same car-crash which had deprived her of her left leg from just below the knee.

She had limped out of hospital months later on a steel half-leg, a different person. Rejecting all help from her father, she had set to work running the farm Walter had bought on a whim and in which he had lost almost all his money. After four years of ferocious work the corner was turned. By then she was twenty-eight, and it was then that the three cold-eyed men had appeared on the scene, offering protection against all the disasters which could so easily ruin a farm. Protection at a price.

She had never known how Willie Garvin, the mainly absentee landlord of *The Treadmill*, found out what was happening. But he appeared at the farm one day, told her he knew of her difficulties, and smilingly assured her that she need worry about them no longer. She would not be troubled again.

His promise was good. Later she learned something of how he had dealt with the problem, and realized that he had put himself into considerable danger for her, though he seemed to think quite genuinely that it had been a very minor exercise. She did not take him to her bed from gratitude, but simply because she wanted to. And that was strange, for she had thought she could never again bring herself to lie freely with a man, exposing the ugliness of her injury. But some deep-seated instinct had told her that this, her missing half-leg, would make no difference to Willie Garvin, and her instinct had been sound.

With Willie she felt no shame or embarrassment at her deformity. He did not ignore it, but accepted it. And the quality of his acceptance was so complete that she could now let him strap the steel leg on for her, or massage the itching stump, without a moment's fear that he would feel any distaste.

By unspoken agreement there were no strings to their relationship. Willie was often away. She knew there were sometimes other girls. When he came back, she was always glad. By the same token, he did not take her for granted. There was always the tacit but unmistakable agreement that if ever she wanted to be finished with him he would accept it without question or rancour.

Her thoughts shifted suddenly to the nagging worry she had been tempted to speak of several times over the past two months. She was not quite sure what had held her back. Pride, perhaps. Reluctance to break a confidence. Even an element of fear as to what the outcome might be if Willie decided to involve himself.

In the darkness he said, 'What is it, Jan?'

'What do you mean?'

'Something's been bugging you. I don't want to be nosey. I thought for a bit that maybe you wanted to call time on me, but it doesn't seem like that now. So if I can 'elp you at all, just say.'

She propped herself on an elbow, turned on the bedside lamp and looked down at him, trying to make up her mind. He touched her hair and said, 'Just up to you, love.'

Without making any conscious decision, she said, 'What does a person do about blackmail, Willie?'

He stared. 'You?'

'No.' She hesitated, then went on. 'Fiona, my young sister. She's married to a tycoon in New York, and she was over here on a flying visit a few weeks ago. You weren't around at the time.'

'Someone putting the screws on her?'

'For two years now. She broke down and told me, but I think she was sorry afterwards.'

'What's the lever?'

'She had an affair with some man three years ago. It's long finished and I don't know the details, but somebody does.'

'Best thing she can do is tell 'er tycoon and say sorry.'

'You don't know Tommy Langford. He'd be for crucifying her. And there are the two children.'

'Does she know who's doing it?'

Lady Janet shook her head. 'It's not the ex-boyfriend. He died of a coronary.'

'Does the blackmailer 'ave proof?'

'She doesn't think so. But it's not really needed. They *know*. Where and when and who. She could never out-face Tommy on it if they gave him the word.'

'They?'

'The one who put the squeeze on her was a nun. A Scottish nun. But Fiona's sure there's somebody behind her.'

'A *nun*? You mean a phoney one?'

'I suppose so. You'd not be likely to find a real one mixed up in it.'

'No blackmail note? They just sent in the nun?'

'I couldn't say about a note, Willie. I didn't really know what questions to ask.'

He took her hand. ' 'Course you wouldn't. Did Fiona tell you 'ow much she's paid so far?'

'I'm not sure of the total, but it's one thousand dollars a month.'

'*What*? Just that? Regular? How's it handed over?'

'By transfer from her account to the account of some charity relief fund at a bank in Macao.'

'D'you know the name of the bank?'

'Fiona did tell me, but all I remember is that it started with *novo* and a word like provident came into it.'

'*The Novo Banco Previdente e Comercial de Macau?*

She stared down at him. 'Yes, I'm sure that's what she said. Willie, how did you know?'

'We used to do business in Macao and Hong Kong.' He spoke absently, busy with his thoughts. 'The New Provident, eh? Well there's a thing. And the charity angle means it's done all nice and legal, through Exchange Control.' He thought for a few moments, then frowned. 'But it's too small, Jan. A thousand dollars a month doesn't fit.'

'Doesn't fit what?'

'The caper. The organisation's too fancy for the turnover.'

'What do you know about any organization?'

'I know something about The Provident.'

'Well, I can only tell you what Fiona told me. I asked why she didn't get on to this bank and try to find out who was behind the charity account, and she almost flew into a panic. She said there wasn't any point in finding out, because it wouldn't make any difference. She'd rather go on paying than risk Tommy being told.'

'It'll come to that in the end, Jan. They'll bleed 'er till she cracks.'

There was a silence, then Lady Janet said slowly, 'It doesn't seem like that, Willie. I mean, they haven't demanded any increase, and she can *afford* twelve thousand dollars a year. She has an income of her own. She said it bites hard, but it's not a back-breaker.'

'She'll just go on paying, then?'

'I think so. I believe she only told me about it because she had to tell someone. It wasn't that she thought I could do anything.' She gave a little shrug. 'But it seems an awful thing, Willie. I thought maybe you could . . . well, advise me. They say the police in this country are very discreet in dealing with blackmail, but I don't know about America and I don't know about Interpol. Maybe that's silly. Do Interpol deal with such things?'

Willie shook his head. 'They'd only work on requests from member police forces, and it doesn't sound as if Fiona would play ball on that.' He was silent for a full minute, eyes thoughtful, idly stroking the crisp chestnut curls above her ear. 'This is a funny one, Jan. Very off-beat. Mind if I talk to The Princess about it?'

She smiled. 'That was nice, Willie. I didn't think you had any secrets from Modesty.'

'None of me own, I suppose. But this is yours. I won't speak if you say so, but this caper makes no sense, and she's red 'ot at work-ing out that kind of thing.'

'And if she works it out?'

'There might be something we could do. Privately.'

She put her head down on his chest and said gently, 'Willie, I wouldn't want to be under any sort of obligation to her.'

'You wouldn't be, Jan. It's the other way round.'

'You mean because I took my father's plane and flew you up to Glasgow that night when those men had her in Castle Glencroft?'

'She was a goner if we 'adn't got there in time. It was you commandeering Daddy Earl's plane that turned the trick. She's not the sort to fall on your neck, Jan, but any time you've got trouble she'll come running.'

'All right. If you think it might help, speak to her, Willie.'

He nodded. 'She'll be back in a few days.'

At nine o'clock in the morning, Dr Georges Durand telephoned Modesty at her flat in Montmarte. He said, 'Your Mr Quinn is not what I would call an ideal patient, Modesty.'

She was standing by an easel, oils and brushes set out, trying to put on the small canvas an arrangement of fruit in a bowl. She had no talent whatsoever for painting, and always destroyed a picture as soon as she had gone as far as she could go with it, but she found the constant striving and constant failure oddly therapeutic.

She said, 'I'm not going to bleed for you, Georges. Most of your patients are rich and cantankerous. Quinn's poor and cantankerous, that's all. Have the tests shown any damage?'

'No. The wrist is unbroken and we are giving it intensive treatment. The young man is fortunate to have a thick skull, but the concussion was quite severe, and I have said he must stay here and rest for three more days.'

'He knows he won't have to pay?'

'Yes. And he keeps demanding to be told where you have gone and how he can get in touch with you.'

'Don't tell him, Georges. Hide his clothes if need be, to keep him there for three days, then just let him go.'

'As you wish, Modesty. I think a little sedation will help. Your Mr Quinn seems to have—what is it you say in English? A monkey on his back?'

'So I noticed. There's a lot of it about these days, Georges.'

'Truly. My psychiatric section thrives increasingly. A great success.'

'For the patients?'

He laughed. 'Well . . . occasionally. How is the good Willie Garvin?'

'He's all right. We're both a little down at the moment.'

'Ah, your friend who was killed. Again I express my sympathy.'

'Thank you, Georges. And thank you for ringing.'

She put down the phone and eyed the canvas with wry contempt. A mess. A ludicrous mess. She squeezed more paint on to the palette and began to mix it thoughtfully. She still could not pinpoint the thing about Quinn which had left a smudgy question-mark in her mind. The fact that it continued to irritate her, like a piece of grit in a shoe, was in itself irritating, for she knew it could be of no importance to her. No importance whatever.

Deep beneath the layers of conscious thought, in the dark wells where memories lie dormant and logic has no meaning, some tiny threadworm of instinct struggled doggedly to reach the light of her awareness and tell her that she was wrong.

Mr Sexton said, 'It was unfortunate, of course. If we'd known Modesty Blaise of all people would stumble on him at such an early hour, I'd have dealt with the matter myself. These sub-contractors are only to be trusted for run-of-the-mill work.'

On the other side of the long dining table Angel shifted her weight to favour the left buttock, where the bruise made by Mr Sexton's finger and thumb still hurt. She pulled up her short skirt a little more, so that da Cruz, beside her, could get a better view of her legs. Da Cruz was the only one in this godforsaken old castle she fancied at all. He wasn't exactly chatty, but there was something a bit exciting about him. Maybe it was being a mixture of three-quarters Portuguese and a quarter Chinese.

Mellish, on the other side of the table, with the light gleaming on his balding head through the fuzz of sandy hair, was a miserable sort of bugger, and she hated his posh drawling accent. The three Japs or Chinks or whatever they were who did the work and the cooking didn't appeal. Too foreign. As for Mr Sexton . . . she winced inwardly. Gawd, not him!

Her review did not include the man who sat at the top of the table, wearing a bright yellow woollen shirt with a red necker-chief held in a gold ring, chewing ponderously on a piece of cheese as he considered Mr Sexton's remark. You didn't even begin to think about Colonel Jim like that. He was a heavy man, over fifty, pear-shaped, with a big chest sloping out to a bigger belly, massive chin set under a wide loose mouth, crew-cut grey hair and shaggy eyebrows. Sometimes Angel thought she was even more afraid of Colonel Jim than of Mr Sexton.

You wouldn't flash your legs at Colonel Jim anyway, but especially you wouldn't do it with his wife sitting there on his right, between you. Pop-eyed Lucy with the blonde curls, curvy figure and wheedling voice.

Colonel Jim. Angel gave a mental snort of contempt. Everybody had to call him that. Except Lucy of course. Anyone would think he was running an old soldiers' club or something. Still, he was clever. Christ he was clever to have worked up this lark. He'd got it running good in the States, and now he was breaking new ground. Angel hoped he'd send her out on plenty of work. Sticking around in the chateau was enough to send you up the wall, and he'd taken this place for a year.

She hitched her skirt another fraction higher and shot a sideways glance at da Cruz.

Clare, wearing a sensible jumper and skirt with a single row of pearls, sat between Mellish and Mr Sexton, finishing her crème caramel, transferring small portions on the tip of her spoon to her prim mouth. She put down the spoon and was on the verge of speaking, but stopped short. Lucy Straik was about to utter words, once she could formulate whatever vague concept was drifting in the wide empty reaches of her mind, and Lucy Straik did not like to be interrupted. Neither did Colonel Jim Straik like Lucy to be interrupted.

She put a hand on her husband's forearm and said, 'Poppa, I been *thinking*.' Her voice had the heavy twang of the Deep South.

Colonel Jim nodded fondly. 'Good girl. What you been thinking, Momma?'

She pursed short fat lips and absently smoothed the white sweater over her large bosoms. Her complexion was smooth, creamy and natural. The bright brown eyes, whose protuberance hinted at thyroid imbalance and sexual appetite, were thoughtful. 'We-e-e-ll, I been thinking we don't *know* if this man saw anything across that gorge place. But we oughta find him and find out——'

'Sure, Momma. But it's counter-productive to worry about finding out *if* he saw anything. Wastes time. Efficiency-wise, the right answer is you just find him and make him redundant.'

'I hadn't *finished*, Poppa.'

'Aw, sorry, honey.' He chuckled and patted her cheek. 'You go right ahead.'

'We-e-ell, if this woman Mr Sexton said about, if she took care of them *stupid* men, and took this man away, the one across that gorge place, so they didn't get to kill him after all, then sure as hell she'd take him to a doctor or a hospital, wouldn't she? So there can't be *many* doctors and hospitals just around there, can there? So why not have Clare and Angel put on them nuns' clothes and go look?'

Mellish blinked once then looked away, his face completely

neutral. Clare smiled and nodded, and only Angel knew her well enough to detect the flicker of contempt in her eyes. Da Cruz drank some wine. Mr Sexton, eating fresh fruit, nuts and honey, drinking water, was the only one who made no attempt to hide his reaction. With open amusement he said, 'But Mrs Straik, that's exactly what the dear girls were doing from noon till midnight yesterday. Colonel Jim sent them out as soon as Bourget phoned in to report their miserable failure.'

Lucy Straik's eyebrows rose in two high curves. 'Aw, gee. Is that right, Poppa?'

'Sure, Momma. You were here when I sent 'em.'

'I was? I musta been thinking about something else.'

He leaned towards her with a loose-lipped grin and rested a large hand on her thigh. 'I know the kinda things Momma thinks about mostly.'

'Poppa! You'll *embarrass* me.' She wriggled shyly.

'Don't you worry your beautiful head about business, honey. I'll take care of that.' He turned to Mr Sexton, still smiling, but there was suddenly a new quality in the smile, a million miles removed from the maudlin fondness of a moment before. 'You know this Blaise girl, Mr Sexton?'

'By reputation. It must have been her. We know Tarrant was joining her at the Auberge du Tarn. Reilly told us so, and Bourget's description fits. I don't know of any other woman who could have walked over Bourget and his colleagues like that. Not even Angel and Clare together.'

'Does Blaise know you by reputation?'

'I think not. I only came into the business a couple of years ago. As you know.'

'I think maybe we'd better take out a little insurance, Mr Sexton.'

'I'll put it in hand tonight.' Sexton paused, then added politely, 'How long will you let Tarrant sweat before we work on him?'

'I'm going to give it another twenty-four hours. Then a general chat, so I can lay it out for him. Then you rough him up. Then Mellish makes with the pentothal.' Colonel Jim stripped the band from a cigar. 'Clare treats him nice but talks ugly to make him sweat. Angel give him a lay to loosen him up. Another civilized chat . . .' He shrugged. 'Maybe we'll switch it around a little. I like to play these deals ear-wise.' He looked up from the cigar, smiling, but the eyes were slits of grey granite. 'Don't overdo the hard treatment, Mr Sexton. He's no chicken, and a stiff's no good to me.'

Mr Sexton nodded. 'I'll exercise careful judgement, you can be sure of that.'

Lucy Straik said, 'You're sure as hell right Poppa can be sure of that, if he says so.'

Mr Sexton grinned and inclined his head. 'His wish is my command, Mrs Straik.'

'His wish is . . .? Hey, that's *cute*!'

Colonel Jim chuckled and put away his unlit cigar. 'So are you, honey. So are you.' He got to his feet, taking her by the arm. 'C'mon now, let's go bye-byes.'

She giggled. 'You're a tiger, Poppa.'

He walked her to the door, an arm about her waist, his gait rather lumbering. The belly did not sag when he stood. The heaviness was of muscle rather than fat. He said, ' 'Night, boys and girls,' without looking back, and the door closed on a murmur of polite response from the company.

Clare got up briskly and said, 'Would anyone care for a rubber of bridge?' She knew da Cruz was usually willing. Angel would have preferred poker, but she would play bridge, badly of course, if the Portuguese did. Mr Sexton never played. Clare looked at the thin sandy Englishman beside her and said hopefully, 'Mr Mellish?'

He shrugged agreement, but still sat holding his brandy, watching the door. After a moment he shook his head and said softly, 'Extraordinary. I'll never get it.'

Mr Sexton said, 'Get what?'

'Colonel Jim and her. Little Lucy.'

Mr Sexton put down his napkin and stood up, his bright clear eyes amused. 'It's simple enough.' Moving round the table he tapped Mellish on the shoulder with a finger, and the sandy man jumped nervously. 'You're the technical expert, Mellish, so you ought to be able to figure out the pattern. She fills a need in him. Colonel Jim dotes on that idiot lump of forked meat—mainly because she *is* an idiot. She's nicely put together, of course, but that's a secondary attraction. You can add that she's spiteful and selfish, and he enjoys indulging her.'

Angel said, 'Sounds bloody kinky to me.'

'Aren't we all, Angel?' Mr Sexton turned his smile upon her. 'You ought to know.' The smile lost its amusement and became empty. 'But I hope none of you will ever mistake Colonel Jim's indulgence of Lucy for weakness. If it became a necessary business requirement, he'd tell me to snap her pretty neck and wouldn't feel a qualm. He can easily find another just like her.'

Setting chairs round a card-table, Clare said, 'Och, that's not a nice thing to say, Mr Sexton. You've no romance in you.'

'We're not in a romantic business, Mrs McTurk.'

'Business is something else, Mr Sexton. It shouldn't mean there can be no romance in our *personal* lives.'

'Ah, you have a tender heart, dear lady. Do you still carry a torch for the good sailor McTurk, who wedded and bedded and left you?'

Angel giggled and said, 'She carried a razor for 'im. Followed 'im all the way to Santiago and cut 'is rotten throat while 'e was asleep.'

'It's no matter for humour, Angel,' Clare said stiffly. 'We reap as we have sown. McTurk should have remembered that.'

'Christ, you're a corker, Clare. A right corker.'

Da Cruz said slowly, in accented English. 'May I ask you a question, Mr Sexton?'

'Yes?'

'Are you . . . afraid of Colonel Jim?' There was a sudden silence. Mellish plucked at his lower lip. Angel froze in the act of rising, eyes flickering with alarm.

Mr Sexton said calmly, 'No. I'm not afraid of him, da Cruz. The rest of you are, and should be. But it's my unique satisfaction and delight to be afraid of nobody in this world.'

Da Cruz hesitated, then said, 'I work for him for money, but mostly because I would be afraid not to. I think that is so with the others here. But I do not know your reason, Mr Sexton.'

He threw back his golden head and laughed. Angel, Clare and Mellish relaxed. 'My reason? That's very simple. He provides clients for me, da Cruz. Or perhaps patients would be a better word.' Mr Sexton rested his hands on the end of the table, looking down the length of it and far beyond the faces turned towards him, the blue eyes focused on some point immeasurably distant. With no hint of vanity, and like a man uttering an article of faith, he said lightly, 'I am the greatest combat-man in the world. You know that, all of you. You've watched me at practice with Tokuda and his friends downstairs. Those three are among the best. And I handle them like a man stropping a razor. I've devoted my life to it, studied under the greatest masters of Japan, Korea, Thailand . . . and the west, for what that's worth. And I've gone far beyond them all.'

He paused. His eyes focused and he straightened up, smiling again. 'But it wasn't enough, dear friends. When a man spends his life acquiring a huge skill, he must find means to exercise that skill in its ultimate function. And Colonel Jim provides that for me.'

He stood with hands in the pockets of his blazer, and gave da Cruz a measured look. 'There. You're answered, da Cruz. But do think twice about asking personal questions in future, won't you? I might not be in so expansive a mood next time.' With an amiable nod he turned and went from the room, walking with the lazy, feline walk of a strolling leopard.

Angel let out a sigh of relief and hungrily lit a cigarette. Except for Colonel Jim, nobody smoked at meals until Mr Sexton had left the room. He did not like tobacco smoke. She rested a hand on da Cruz's shoulder so that her knuckles touched his neck, and said, 'You want to watch it a bit, Ramon. You never know with 'im. Mind you, I still don't see why 'e plumped for coming in with Colonel Jim. I mean, If 'e likes a bit of killing now and then there's much more of it about in the States with the Mafia, say, or some of the new darkie mobs.'

'I sometimes wonder if you've any sense at all, Angel,' Clare said impatiently, opening two packs of cards. 'Mr Sexton's a gentleman, and a Colonial gentleman too, so naturally he'd not wish to work for any riff-raff. Our turn to be partners, I think, Mr Mellish?'

As they settled at the card-table and cut for deal Mellish looked at his watch. 'I've only time for a quick rubber. I want to run over my notes on Tarrant for an hour before I go to bed.' He stroked his thin nose. 'If I were Colonel Jim I'd try the degradation technique first. Stick him in the oubliette and let him stew in his own muck for a few days, till he hates himself.'

Angel grinned. 'It's not all that sweet in the cell. Besides, you'd disappoint Mr Sexton. He likes to do 'is little bit.' She picked up her cards and began to sort them, shifting uncomfortably on her chair. 'Honest to God, my arse is killing me. And you ought to see this lot of bus tickets. No bid.'

CHAPTER FOUR

SIR GERALD TARRANT finished reciting to himself as much of Mark Antony's part as he could remember from the long-ago University days when he had belonged to an amateur dramatic society, and opened his eyes.

He supposed another hour had passed. He threw off the blanket, rose a little stiffly from the hard wooden bunk, and began to walk up and down. The cell was dry but cold. He could move only four paces each way. The bunk was set against the wall opposite the door, which was of solid oak and had no peep-hole that he had been able to discover. At one end of the cell stood a small table, bearing the remains of a loaf of stale bread and a half-empty flask of water. At the other end was a large bucket with a wooden lid. Light came from a low-wattage bulb hanging by two inches of flex from an ancient beam in the ceiling. There was nothing in his pockets, not even a handkerchief, and his wrist-watch had been taken away.

This was where he had woken from a drugged sleep . . . twenty hours ago? Thirty? Forty? It was hard to judge. No window allowed him to tell night from day. He had seen nobody, heard no sound. Rasping a grimy hand across his cheek and chin, he judged that he had a two-day stubble of beard, and decided that they would probably show themselves within the next twelve hours.

Who were They? One of the official opposition groups, or one of the independents, like Salamander Four, who had taken on the job under contract? Not important. The ultimate aim would be the same—to scoop out the information in his brain like the yolk from an egg. A surprising move, this kidnapping. It broke a pattern of international Intelligence which had been established for a good many years. But that, too, was of no importance now. It had happened.

This was the softening-up period, of course, designed to work on his nerves. Interrogation would come later. It might be crude, but would more probably follow a slower but surer technique, the hard-soft play, the man of brutal menace alternating with the sympathetic type who offered cigarettes and coffee. And they would probably use drugs, thiopental combined with methamphetamine. He decided that later it would pass some time usefully if he set about recalling all the reports he had read on that procedure.

He looked at the bread and water. He was a little hungry and very dry, but it might be unwise to drink again for a while yet. Impossible to be sure how long this first stage would last. Tarrant continued pacing. He felt the crawling of nerves in his stomach, and acknowledged to himself that he was afraid. This was natural and reasonable, and did not matter, he told himself. The only thing that mattered was his degree of resistance to interrogation when the time came. His own agents were trained to withstand a considerable level of mental and physical torture. Some had known the grim need to call upon that training. Of those, some had died before talking, others perhaps had talked before dying. He would never know who had done which.

He wondered which category he would be in, and very soberly considered whether or not it was his proper duty now to destroy himself. If he left it until the moment when he could endure no longer, he might well lack the will to do it. Perhaps it would be premature now, he knew too little of the situation to be able to judge. But it would be wise to give thought to the matter early on, for it would not be easy to find the means, here in the cell, if and when the time came. The flask was soft plastic. No hope of cutting an artery with that. Hang himself with strips torn from the blanket? There was nowhere to secure the blasted rope high enough above the stone floor. A head-first dive against the wall? Or from the bunk to the floor? Not promising. Unless you did the trick at first attempt you'd simply knock yourself silly.

He felt exasperated by his own inadequacy, and found himself wondering what Modesty Blaise or Willie Garvin would have done. Immediately he knew that self-destruction would not have entered their minds. Their entire energy would have focused upon finding a way out. Tarrant's shoulders moved in a rueful shrug. It was different for them. They did not carry in their heads the same mass of information. They were a generation younger, had rare skills, and would probably have been prepared for trouble to some extent—a hidden pick-lock or other ingenious small devices.

All the same, it was working thinking about Modesty. At best it might bring a useful idea, and at worst it helped pass the long hours. So what would she do now, assuming she could find no way past the cell door? Tarrant concentrated, drawing on snippets of memory from the rare occasions when she or Willie had let slip a word about their philosophy of response when a caper went sour.

It came down to opportunism. Sooner or later the opposition must make some sort of move, and her mind would be tuned to recognize opportunity, or the chance of creating it. This might come in a dozen different ways, and would usually be unexpected, easy to miss. But it would come.

Tarrant sighed. It would come for her, perhaps. Willie had told him of the time when Mike Delgado, the mercenary killer, had held a gun on her at point-blank range. He had relaxed for no more than a mocking word, and in that instant she had drawn and fired across the small of her back, a trick shot, killing him with the smile still on his lips. She had been armed then, of course, but she had not been armed that day in Kalimba when . . .

He shrugged irritably. All well and good, but you needed the capacity for such opportunism, and Tarrant knew that he did not possess it. Another thing. While waiting for the next move she would have put herself to sleep, for days if need be, husbanding her resources. This was a faculty verging on the mystical, acquired in the harsh days of her childhood and later brought to a higher pitch of control under the guidance of an impossibly ancient *yogarudha* in the Thar desert north of Jodhpur.

Willie Garvin also possessed it to a lesser degree. Soon after she had taken him into *The Network* she had sent him to spend two months with Sivaji. It was, according to Willie, an eerie experience. The skeletal old man said little and explained nothing. He just sat. And you sat with him, living on a few dates. After a while you didn't need to lie down to sleep, you weren't even sure of the difference between sleeping and waking. You simply sat. But at the end of it all, something had been imparted. You couldn't name or describe it.

Tarrant sat down on the bunk and rubbed his eyes wearily. No use wishing that he had the abilities of Modesty Blaise. Whatever was coming would have to be met from his own meagre resources.

Play for time, he thought. Resist up to a point, then feed them a little false information. Make it hard stuff to check, mix in a little truth where it's unimportant. Plan your role and get into the skin of it. Stiff upper-lip type, high resistance to pain (oh, God!), but susceptible to dialectic argument. Fascist leanings—always good material for conversion to the other extreme.

All right. Now, what do you hang on to when it gets bad? You're playing for time. Time for what? There has to be a spark of hope. Modesty. She was there at the Auberge du Tarn, no distance from where Reilly held a gun on you while the nuns gave you the needle. Did they fake an accident? Presumably. So Reilly will have a prepared story to tell. And Modesty won't swallow it. She won't. She'll talk to Reilly, that's certain. She'll spot something. Hunch. Instinct. She *won't* swallow it. She'll come looking for you. That's right. Just give her time. Play for time . . .

In a small part of his mind he knew that he was deceiving himself. The opposition would have covered his disappearance in a way that was water-tight, and there was no real hope at all. But a false hope was better than nothing.

'I once knew a girl who was a dactyliomancist,' said Willie Garvin. He sat on a high stool in the big kitchen of the penthouse, eating raisins from a jar at his elbow.

Modesty, in a white blouse and tartan skirt, was making a batch of quiche lorraine for the deep-freeze, with constant reference to a cookery book. Her moderate-to-good culinary results were gained more by application than flair.

It was nine of a March evening, two days after her phone-call from Montmartre to tell of Tarrant's death. Willie had picked her up at London Airport a few hours ago. Little had been said between them about Tarrant. His passing had saddened them, but it did not lie in their natures to mourn.

Modesty looked up from the book and said, 'A what?'

'A dactyliomancist. This girl I knew.'

She gave a casual nod. 'Oh, was she?'

'M'mm.' Willie ate some more raisins. 'She used a ring about two inches across, made of iron, with a little 'ole on one edge and a spike opposite.'

'Not a bad idea. Willie, why tell me that mixed grill snack we had was enough, and then sit eating all my raisins?'

'Oh, I'm not 'ungry, Princess. I just like eating raisins.'

'I know. I seem to keep that jar filled just for you.'

'Saves 'em going stale. You 'ardly ever use 'em for cooking.'

'I'll be lucky to get the chance. Just a minute.'

She went out of the kitchen. Willie pricked up his ears, listening for her footsteps and the opening and closing of doors. Yes, she had gone into the little study adjoining her lapidary workshop, to have a quick look at the dictionary. He grinned. She wouldn't find the word in the Concise Oxford Dictionary there.

He ate a few more raisins. It was good to see her back. He never felt quite complete without her—not necessarily there with him in the same room or house or even county, but in the same country at least. She came back into the kitchen, frowning a little, and began measuring flour on the scales. Willie chuckled inwardly. He'd got her with dactyliomancist all right.

She said idly, 'How did this girl make out with her predictions? I wouldn't have thought a suspended ring could tell you much.'

He stared indignantly. 'You've got a new dictionary!'

She turned her head and grinned at him with urchin triumph. 'The complete O.E.D. You'll have to sweat for obscure words now, Willie love. How does this suspended ring work for fortune-telling, or were you just making it up?'

'I never make it up, Princess. It was when I was a kid, on the run from Borstal, and Doreen was an Irish scrubber I shacked up with in Liverpool for a few weeks. Thick as a brick, she was, but quite a looker, and like a demented anaconda in bed.'

'That's good?'

'No. But at seventeen you're not all that discriminating, so it seems not bad. Trouble was, it was murder *getting* 'er to bed. Full of guilt and doubt. Doreen was. Spent hours arguing aloud with 'erself about whether she would or wouldn't. I'd sometimes drop off to sleep on the couch listening to 'er.'

'What about the ring?'

'She used to 'ang it on a fine wire, 'old it up over a little table with a cross chalked on the top, so the spike on the ring nearly touched the cross, and ask it questions. It swung one way for yes, and the other way for no.'

'That's not prediction.'

'I know, but Doreen thought it was. She'd ask it about 'er job and 'er love-life and which stuff to use for dry 'air, and what picture to go and see. Everything.'

'And trusted the answers?'

'Like 'oly writ. After the first week I rigged a big magnet on a swivel bar under the table, and I'd sit opposite 'er, working the answers with the magnet.'

She gave a splutter of laughter. 'You mean the should-she shouldn't-she answers?'

'Especially that. Saved 'er a lot of agonizing and guilt.'

'Golden-hearted Willie.'

'They don't make 'em like me any more.'

'Look, let me finish this, then I want to talk about Janet. Why don't you make yourself comfortable in the sitting room while you're waiting? There's a new Frank Zappa album on the stereo.'

'I'd rather stay and watch, Princess.'

'All right, but shut up while I concentrate, or I'll make a mess of this.'

He sat contentedly, watching her move, think, frown, turn, bend, straighten, pour and mix. Her legs were a marvel, he thought without any shred of longing. But most of all he liked looking at the column of her throat. Even after so many years were still moments when he felt amazed that it should be Willie Garvin, gutter-bred roughneck, to whom she had given her total trust and friendship.

Half an hour later she sat with her legs tucked beneath her at one end of the big chesterfield, holding a cup of coffee. Willie, in a deep armchair on the other side of the coffee-table, said thoughtfully, 'I still can't make much sense of it. The New Provident and Commercial Bank of Macao means Mr Wu Smith, and 'e's the biggest villain in South-East Asia.'

'Too big to bother with the handling percentage on a thousand dollars a month, that's certain. So it has to be more.'

' 'ow can it be more, Princess?'

She stirred her coffee. 'I don't know. But we do know Wu Smith, so there's more in it somewhere along the line.'

They were silent for a while, thinking about the man in Macao. Wu Smith did not initiate crime. He was a backer and a handler, and he dealt in any commodity, no matter how dirty. His bank would finance any project Wu Smith deemed sound, and he was a skilled judge. He financed those who operated in drugs, vice, gold-smuggling, currency coups, and whatever else he thought sufficiently profitable. His backing was expensive but reliable. He also handled stolen goods on a huge scale, and his bank was available to those who needed absolute secrecy concerning whatever passed through their accounts. The New Provident was even more secure than a Swiss bank, for it had the advantage of being immune to official inquiry on the grounds of suspected criminal activities by its clients.

Macao made this possible because it was small, a miniature Hong Kong, six square miles of Portuguese territory lying eight thousand miles from Lisbon, hemmed against the South China Sea by the great brooding mass of the Chinese mainland. In this colonial speck of ground the law had always been flexible, yielding to the corrupt systems of the old China. Here Mr Wu Smith was too big to be touched as long as he did not directly provoke Lisbon.

Five minutes after she had last spoken Modesty said, 'You don't go into the plastic gnome business with only one plastic gnome to sell. So Janet's sister can't be the only one on the hook. Wu Smith's handling the take for somebody with a lot of clients to squeeze.'

Willie looked mildly surprised. 'A blackmail job's usually a one-off thing. Mr X knows Mr Y did something nasty to Mrs Z in the woodshed, and puts the screws on. I mean, you can't exactly advertise for customers, so where do you pick up the dirt on a whole block of 'em?'

'I've never thought about it before, but I fancy someone has now, so let's do the same. Go on Willie, where do you dig dirt by the shovel-load?'

Another five minutes passed, and Willie said slowly, 'The Americans use psychiatrists like we use dentists. Regular sessions. A shrink would collect dirt wholesale, wouldn't 'e?'

She gave him the rare smile that lit her face from within and always brought him a special pleasure. 'Willie the Wonderboy does it again. Yours may not be the right answer, but that doesn't matter a damn. It's an answer. Anyone with access to the tapes and records of the right kind of shrink could get himself a list of clients. You might ask Janet if her sister has a psychiatrist.'

'I'll do that. It's somewhere to start from.'

After another long silence she said, 'It's beginning to take a little shape, Willie. Suppose they've given a switcheroo to the old technique. You don't squeeze your clients dry, you make a careful assessment of what they can afford to pay on a regular basis, without becoming so desperate that they cut their throats or break down and blow the whole thing.'

'A steady income and all risks cut to minimum?' He blinked. 'Jesus. If it's a phoney charity account, like Janet said, they probably get tax relief on what they pay.'

She half laughed. 'It's smooth. But it's still blackmail. We'd better go out to Macao and see Wu Smith.'

Willie rubbed his chin uneasily. 'Look, you don't 'ave to mix in on this, Princess. Janet said————'

'I can guess what she said, Willie love. Did you put her right?'

'I said you'd jump at a chance to square things a bit.'

'Good.'

'What do we do about Wu Smith, though? We put a load of stolen bullion through 'im once, back in *The Network* days, but we're not exactly dear old mates. We want whoever's be'ind the blackmail account. Wu Smith won't give it away and won't sell it, that's for sure. Maybe we could snatch 'im, but it'd be quite a trick.' He frowned. 'Even then you'd need a blow-lamp to make 'im talk, and that's not our form.'

'We'll just have to think of something.'

Her Indo-Chinese houseboy, Weng, came into the sitting room and said, 'Have you finished with the coffee, Miss Blaise?'

'No more for me. Willie? All right, you can clear away, Weng. And when you've done that, get on the phone and book three seats on the earliest flight you can get to Hong Kong.'

'Three seats, Miss Blaise?'

'Yes. You'll be coming with us.'

Weng's dark face above the while jacket broke into a smile. 'It will be very enjoyable for me to see Hong Kong again.' Modesty had put him through University there, and it had been his home for four years.

She said, 'You're still in contact with your old friends?'

'Yes. I am an industrious correspondent, Miss Blaise.'

'Good. When you've fixed the flight, book two calls to Hong Kong. The first to Li Feng. Do you think he'll rent us that house he owns on Lantau for a few days?'

'For the right price, certainly. Better to let me negotiate for you, Miss Blaise.'

'All right. Then I want to speak to Charlie Wan. Or Susie if he's not in.' She looked at her watch. 'He should be, it's three a.m. there now, and it'll probably only be six when you get the call through.'

Willie said, 'Charlie Wan?'

She gave a small shrug. 'Nothing specific yet. I just think he might be helpful.'

'You could 'ave Charlie's right arm after what you did for 'is wife.'

When Weng had picked up the tray and gone, Willie said, 'Look, are you sure you want to dive into this right away, Princess?'

'I'm glad of something to do.' She got up, went to the sideboard, and returned with a board and chess set. 'Let's play for a while, Willie.'

'Sure. You got any ideas?'

'It's my turn for white, and if you play your usual Indian Defence against a Queen's Pawn opening I've thought of a variation on the seventh move that's going to devastate you.'

He smiled. 'I meant about Mr Wu Smith.'

She began to set out the pieces. 'I've got a germ, Willie. A very small germ. It'll grow better if I leave it alone and don't keep prodding it about.' She moved her queen's pawn forward two squares. 'Come on, take your thrashing like a man.'

At noon the next day Lady Janet Gillam received a phone call from Willie Garvin. He said, ''Allo, Jan. Just thought I'd let you know I've talked to Modesty and we'll be away for a bit. Maybe a week, maybe less. It depends 'ow things go.'

She felt sudden anxiety. 'You mean about my sister?'

'That's right. It's only the first step, but if it comes off we'll know who's be'ind that account, and we can take it from there.'

'Willie, I want to come with you.'

'Eh?' His voice was incredulous. 'Don't talk wet, Jan. There's nothing you could do.'

'I know. I won't get in the way, but I want to . . . to be somewhere near, anyway.'

'But there's no point, love.'

He heard her impatient exhalation. 'Willie, this isn't easy to explain, but there's a big piece of you that's just—oh, I don't know—a sort of blank to me. For God's sake, I don't want to own you, I only want to get a wee glimpse inside that blank.'

'Better not, Jan,' he said gently. 'It gets a bit dark in there sometimes.'

'Ah, you stupid . . . *man*! Let me speak to Modesty, she'll know what I mean.'

'I expect she would, but it's just not on, Jan. Not this time. We're flying out to Hong Kong in a couple of hours.' There was a long silence. 'You still there, Janet?'

'Aye, I'm here. And you'll be going on from Hong Kong to Macao? Is that it?'

'Something like that.'

'All right, Willie. I'm too late this time, but I wish . . . well, tell her what I said, anyway.' She gave a dry little laugh. 'And please take care. We one-legged girls find fellows hard to come by.'

'I'll probably 'ave to carve me way through a seething 'orde of 'em by the time I get back.'

'Please call me as soon as you do, Willie. My best to Modesty, and thank her.'

'I'll do that. 'Bye, Jan.'

Mr Sexton said in French, 'So you believe she checked your wallets for identity?'

Gaston Bourget fingered the plaster on his jaw, and thought that this man's accent was even more horribly English than that of the English Prime Minister, Mr Heet, whom he had once heard speaking in French on television. He said, 'She checked for identity, yes.' Hunching his shoulders he pushed his hands deeper into the pockets of his top-coat. 'Why bring us to this godforsaken hole to talk?'

The four men stood within the thick walls of a dry-stone hut set on the slope of a thinly grassed valley amid the foothills of the Pyrenees. The floor was of beaten earth, the roof timbers had rotted at the ends and fallen in years ago. The heavy door had survived its hinges and lay on the ground. There had never been a window.

Mr Sexton eased the rucksack from his back and set it down. It gave the sound of iron clanking on iron as he did so. He said, 'It is a convenient place. You took a taxi from the station to Miellet, then walked over the hills as instructed?'

The biggest of the three Frenchmen, the leader, said sourly, 'Eight kilometers. It was unnecessary.'

'I think not. This woman Blaise has important friends in high places here in France. They could well be looking for you.'

Jacques Garat, who had two fingers in a splint, said, 'They will not find us. And if they did we would tell them nothing, you can rest assured.'

Mr Sexton smiled. 'I shall do that.'

The leader said, 'There remains the question of payment. That is why we have made the journey today, m'sieu.'

'Payment, Servalle? But you failed to carry out the work. You fumbled the job, and now you must disappear. I don't want you questioned by the police.'

'You failed to warn us that Modesty Blaise was involved.'

'That was a chance matter. Such contingencies are your affair.'

'We do not agree with you, M'sieu Sexton. You expect us to disappear without payment?'

The three men moved a little, making a half-circle about the Englishman, and abruptly the atmosphere was ugly. Mr Sexton gave a genial chuckle. 'I certainly expect you to disappear,' he said, and on the last word, with no apparent preliminary movement, he rose clear of the ground in a twisting jump, his left foot driving forward like a piston. It took Gaston Bourget in the throat, smashing his larynx.

Mr Sexton landed on his right foot, lightly poised and spinning, the heel of the left striking the back of Servalle's knee as he lunged at the place where Mr Sexton had been an instant before. Servalle cried out in pain as his legs were swept from under him, the cry changing to a gasp as his back hit the ground.

Garat had a gun half-drawn when his arm was paralysed by the grasp of fingers which felt like rods of iron driving into flesh and muscle. The scream was still in his throat when Mr Sexton, with a sharp exhalation of breath, struck a hand-edge blow which stove in a section of Garat's skull above one ear.

Servalle was coming unsteadily to his feet. Mr Sexton turned briskly, drove a stiff thumb into his midriff, took him in a curious grip of the head, turned again and flipped him almost casually over in a somersault, retaining the grip on the head so that the neck snapped abruptly in midthrow.

When the dead body hit the ground, Mr Sexton looked about him, white teeth showing in a grin of delight. With sprightly enthusiasm he moved to his rucksack and opened it. Inside was a considerable length of steel chain. Five minutes later he had passed an end of the chain through a small gap in the wall opposite the doorway, and secured it round the door which he had carried out and propped against the outside of the wall at that point.

He put on thick gloves, took the other end of the chain, moved back through the doorway, found a projecting ridge of rock against which to set his feet, passed the chain round his waist, took a grip on it like the anchor-man in a tug-of-war team, and braced himself.

For half a minute he breathed deeply, concentrating, then suddenly poured his strength into a steadily increasing pull. The ancient door pressed hard against the outside of the wall, its timbers groaning. The chain quivered, then grew still, rigid as a bar. A big stone fell from the top of the wall, then another. The wall itself teetered, leaned slowly inwards, and fell.

Mr Sexton straightened up and nodded approval, then moved to release the chain and draw it from under the pile of stones. The two end walls, unsupported by the rear wall now, offered less resistance when he came to topple them inwards by the same method. And the front wall, pierced by the doorway, came down easily in two sections.

At the end of ten minutes there was nothing to be seen but a great mound of rough-hewn grey stones. The three bodies lay buried beneath it. Mr Sexton surveyed his handiwork, packed the chain into his rucksack, put the heavy rucksack on his back, and set off cheerfully on the fifteen kilometre walk to the small village where he had left his car that morning.

It was satisfying to feel he could now report to Colonel Jim that he had taken out a little insurance, as instructed.

CHAPTER FIVE

MR WU SMITH yawned contentedly as he made his way up the gangway of the hundred-ton motor cruiser, *Dama Infeliz*, anchored at his private mooring in Taipa harbour, the green and red flag of Portugal fluttering at the mast in the moonlight.

He had just won a thousand dollars at the one form of gambling he permitted himself. His cricket, Silver Dragon, had defeated the much-favoured cricket of his old friend Chung in a twenty-minute battle. Wu Smith leaned on the gleaming brass rail with no fear of soiling his beautifully tailored white suit, and recalled the event with pleasure.

Victory had involved careful training. Silver Dragon came from a graveyard, as did all the best fighting crickets. But Silver Dragon had come from an English graveyard in Hong Kong, perhaps where the dust of one of Wu Smith's own ancestors lay. He had fed it a special diet of lotus seed with rice which had been soaked in milk before being cooked with frogs' legs. And he had allowed it union with a female cricket once a week, to maintain the Essential Harmony of yin and yang. Tonight Silver Dragon had won, despite old Chung's brushing at his cricket's antennae with a hair before the fight to make it angry.

Yes, it had been a good evening, thought Mr Wu Smith. In fact it had been a good year, with his various enterprises prospering handsomely. Not for the first time, he reflected how fortunate it was that a Chinese mandarin had granted this scrap of land to the Portuguese more than four centuries ago, in recognition of their work in suppressing piracy.

It was good to be a citizen of this tiny European province which clung to the great bulk of China like a flea on an elephant, to be one of the quarter-million human beings packed into the mainland peninsula and the two islands of Taipa and Coloane, which together made up the colony. The whole area was smaller than Kennedy Airport, which he had once passed through, but there were advantages in smallness.

Because Macao was small, Red China did not covet her. Like Hong Kong, little more than an hour's run eastward on the hydrofoil, she provided a commercial pore through which the giant could breathe. Mr Wu Smith approved the government of the colony. Those responsible to Lisbon did not allow Macao to degenerate into a cess-pit of vice and crime, though this was a myth that died hard in the West. At the same time, they were prudent and understanding men in a commercial sense, who knew the value and necessity of invisible exports. Free trade in gold. Twenty-two tons imported annually. None officially exported. It went out all over the Far East in small packets, to people who would never trust in paper, and who paid a high premium for the yellow metal to store away in secret places.

The New Provident and Commercial Bank of Macao prospered. The network of various agency operations prospered. Through Mr Wu Smith you could buy a woman in Aleppo and sell her in Monte Video. There were packets of heroin passing through Marseilles now which had originated as raw opium in the Golden Triangle where Burma met Thailand and Laos; on this Wu Smith had received commission, though the produce of the poppy had never come within five hundred miles of Macao.

Even the cross-border commerce with the Communists was thriving. There were commodities Mao's children needed which Wu Smith could supply. His relationship with General Ching Po, the authority in the Kwangtung area beyond the Barrier Gate, was excellent according to the agents who handled these matters. Mr Wu Smith himself would not have dreamed of crossing the border, even if the Chinese permitted it. He considered them too unpredictable. In a business sense you could trust them, but their political suspicions were so violent and illogical as to make them dangerous. Never mind. He could deal with them without exposing himself to personal risk.

Mr Wu Smith was a man who had spent most of his life being careful not to expose himself to personal risk. He was well aware that he had enemies, both within the law and within its opposite extreme, the underworld. He moved nowhere without his personal bodyguard, the silent Thailander who stood two paces away now. His house was a stronghold, and when he slept on the motor cruiser, which he much preferred when the weather was fair, it always lay at anchor half a mile off-shore. There were five other guards aboard, all armed, and two of them took shifts in watching the radar screen once the vessel had anchored for the night, to give warning of any approach.

Wu Smith wondered whether to send for a girl to round off the evening, and decided against it. The pleasure of the cricket fight was enough. Only a foolish man made the mistake of crowding one pleasure upon another.

He turned to the Thailander and said in Chinese, 'Cast off and move out to the anchorage. I shall sleep now.'

As he entered his cabin he felt the engines murmur gently, easing *Dama Infeliz* away from her mooring.

Under the hull, where the keel knifed down, two scuba-suited figures clung to magnetic limpets clamped to the steel plates. They were large limpets. If the cruiser accelerated suddenly it would be the grasp of human hands that broke before the grip of the limpets. But *Dama Infeliz* was merely moving out to anchor for the night, and idled gently on her way, as expected.

Ten minutes later the guard on radar-duty switched on the screen and settled down to his four-hour vigil. Close under the rake of the stern, Modesty Blaise and Willie Garvin surfaced quietly. They had already unstrapped their aqualungs and weight-belts, allowing them to sink. A waterproof bag was attached to Willie's leg. He inflated a rubber ring, so that they could float easily without treading water, and attached it to the stern by a large rubber suction disc on the end of a cord. Together they waited in the darkness. The water was cool but not cold, and their wet-suits provided insulation, but at intervals they exercised for five minutes, hand against hand in a session of controlled and silent Indian wrestling, to forestall stiffness.

One hour after midnight the guard on the radar screen in the wheelhouse felt a current of cool air, though he had not heard the door open. As he turned, the light went out. That was the last thing he remembered for some hours. The two patrolling deck-guards had each suffered a comparable experience already. One had a stiff neck and the other a lump over one ear as mementoes, but neither remembered when the blow had been struck. Soon the three off-duty men, including Wu Smith's personal bodyguard, passed from sleep to deeper unconsciousness as a result of inhaling ether sprayed from an aerosol container. So did Mr Wu Smith, lying asleep in his luxurious cabin.

Ten minutes later the beam of a flash-lamp flickered twice from the deck, and in response two men in a dinghy with an outboard motor began to row steadily towards the *Dama Infeliz* from the point half a mile away, where they had been waiting. Weng was at the tiller.

The dinghy came alongside the motor cruiser, and left almost at once with three extra passengers, one of them unconscious and wrapped in a blanket.

Mr Wu Smith woke to find himself lying on a canvas bed in a room with peeling white-washed walls. The shock was considerable. A single naked electric lamp of high wattage hung from the ceiling, its dazzle making him wince. One large window was heavily curtained with blanket material.

Wu Smith lifted himself on one elbow. How could this be? he wondered dazedly. He had gone to sleep in his cabin on *Dama Infeliz*, securely guarded, and woken here in this . . . this place. Bare boards, trestle-table, filing cabinets against the wall, cheap wooden chairs. It was like a room in army barracks.

His stomach turned over as he brought the figure sitting behind the table into focus. Chinese. Forty or fifty years old. Black cropped hair. Drab greenish-brown uniform with red tabs on the collar. Cap with a five-pointed red star resting on the table at his elbow as he sat with head bent over an open file, one of several stacked in a neat pile.

Wu Smith sat up slowly, feeling sick. A soldier stood at the door. Slung on his shoulder was a Type 56 assault rifle, the Chinese Communist version of the Russian 7·62 mm. AK-47. Another soldier sat at a radio in the corner, earphones on his head, writing on a message-pad. Wu Smith looked again at the man behind the table. There would be no insignia of rank, he knew. The Party had abolished such bourgeois displays of class since 1965, dividing the People's Liberation Army into two groups only, commanders and fighters. The man's uniform was of better quality cloth than the uniforms of the other two soldiers, but Wu Smith did not need this to tell him who was in which category.

The man looked up. 'So you are awake,' he said in Chinese, and lit a cigarette. Wu Smith recognized the packet. The cigarettes were manufactured in Canton.

Wu Smith said shakily, 'What has happened?'

The man behind the table exhaled smoke and studied Wu Smith with cold, uninterested eyes. 'I am General Wang Shi-Chen. You have entered the People's Republic secretly, without permission, and will now be interrogated.'

Wu Smith gulped and waggled a protesting hand. His head throbbed and his mind was fuzzy. 'I did not enter secretly—I mean, of my own wish I did not enter at all!'

General Wang Shi-Chen closed the file and said to the soldier at the door. 'Take him away and bring him back one week from today in a more co-operative frame of mind.'

Wu Smith said frantically. 'No! If you please, General, I simply wished to say that I am here by . . . by mischance. That my offence was not—was not deliberate. I should be greatly obliged if you would call General Ching Po on the telephone. He will vouch for my . . . my goodwill towards the People's Republic.'

'Ching Po has been arrested,' the man at the table said, his cold eyes flaring with sudden anger. 'It was Chairman Mao himself who discovered that Ching Po was no true comrade but a capitalist spy and an enemy of the party.'

Wu Smith felt as if he had been hit with a hammer. After a long silence he said with a ghastly attempt to smile, 'Thank heaven for Chairman Mao's perception. I was completely deceived.'

'Chairman Mao's abilities are not to be attributed to a non-existent heaven.'

'Of course, of course. A thoughtless phrase, General.' Wu Smith ransacked his mind for safe words, and said hopefully, 'I shall be very glad to answer whatever you wish to ask me.'

General Wang Shi-Chen drew a pad towards him and stubbed out his cigarette. 'You will bear in mind that we know a great deal concerning your operations, Wu Smith. If what you tell me fails to conform with what we know, you will have cause to regret it.'

Sweat broke out on Wu Smith's face. 'There is no question of that, General.'

'Sit there.' The pencil pointed to a chair facing the table. Wu Smith got unsteadily to his feet and almost fell into the chair. The man behind the table looked at the watch on his wrist and said, 'Let us begin with an account of your commerce with the traitor Ching Po.'

An hour later Mr Wu Smith's throat, already dry from fear, was becoming sore from talking. It was a horrible thing to find himself pouring out secrets of professional contacts and activities he had nursed to himself for so many years, but he no longer cared. Given total co-operation, these maniacs might, just might decide to set him free. For Wu Smith at this moment nothing else counted. He had always made the protection of his clients a firm principle, even at financial expense to himself, but he saw no virtue in doing so with his own well-loved skin at the mercy of fanatics.

He talked of gold and drugs, diamonds and wheat shipments, foreign exchange manipulation and casino operations. He named officials amenable to bribery, and men who aided the flow of escapees across the channel from Lapa Island. He was able to deny indignantly and truthfully that he gave any aid to traitors escaping from the happy paradise of The People's Republic, or that he passed secrets of the peace-loving army and navy to the imperialist powers.

It was somewhere towards the end of the first hour that General Wang Shi-Chen turned a page of the pad and said, 'Your bank, The New Provident and Commercial Bank of Macao, has the account of . . .' He referred to a thick notebook. 'The South-East Asia Refugee Children's Relief Fund?'

Mr Wu Smith shook his head dully, 'No.'

The black eyes hardened, and the pencil tapped warningly on the table. 'Think carefully, Wu Smith. We know what we know.'

Anxiety pierced the lethargy which had settled upon Wu Smith. His hands fluttered. 'I assure you, General. I handle no account of that name.'

'Think again. It is a cover account. A false charity.'

'Ah!' Relief spread through Wu Smith. 'We have only one such account. You must mean The Orient Society for the Disabled.'

'Possibly.' There was suspicion in Wang Shi-Chen's look. 'Who is the principal?'

'I have not met him. My dealings have been with a man called da Cruz, a white Portuguese. Almost white.'

'I ask again, who is the principal?' Wang Shi-Chen glanced at his notebook, then looked up again with the manner of a man awaiting confirmation.

Wu Smith said, 'All cheques, drafts and authorities must bear the signature J. Straik.'

'The spelling?' Wang Shi-Chen jotted the name down. Then, 'A foreign name. English perhaps. In Hong Kong?'

'No. Until a few weeks ago the address for correspondence was in New York. I—I cannot remember the details. Since then the bank has been given a new address. In France.' Wu Smith rubbed his forehead in an effort to concentrate. 'A castle. Chateau Lancieux. I do not remember the town or village, but it lies in the department of Ariège. I can of course look it up in our records, and would be very glad to send you all details——'

'It is quite unimportant, Wu Smith.' The man at the table tore the page from his pad and crumpled it. 'A number of my questions are designed to ascertain whether or not you are telling the truth.'

'I assure you——'

'I am assuring myself, Wu Smith. Now let us move to another matter. You have a financial interest in a group which distributes dirty films.'

'*Dirty, General?*' Wu Smith was horrified. 'I understood they were instructional. I have not seen any myself, of course . . .'

Wu Smith did not know how much later it was when his tormentor at last put down the pencil, sat back and made a curt gesture towards the soldier at the door, who came forward with a glass of water. Wu Smith took the glass in unsteady hands and drank greedily.

'Thank you, General,' he croaked, bobbing his head and trying to smile. 'Most kind of you. I trust I have been of some assistance . . .' The glass was taken from him. 'And that my—my mischance in entering The People's Republic without permission will be excused?'

General Wang Shi-Chen permitted himself a shrug which seemed to hold some degree of approval. 'That is yet to be decided. But it lies in your favour that you have behaved wisely throughout this interrogation.'

Wu Smith barely heard the last words. A great darkness was engulfing his mind. He felt himself toppling sideways, and then there was no more. The soldier caught him and nodded to the radio operator, who got to his feet. Together they carried Wu Smith to the bunk.

General Wang Shi-Chen blew out a long breath and stood up. In excellent but slightly accented English he said, 'My God, I'm a damn sight more tired than when I last played Hamlet.'

The door opened. Modesty Blaise and Willie Garvin came in. They both wore slacks and sweaters. Behind them came Weng, grinning. Modesty went to General Wang Shi-Chen, put her arms round his neck and pressed her cheek against his. 'You should win an Oscar for that, Charlie. We got everything on tape. I couldn't follow it all, but enough to know you were marvellous. And you had only twenty-four hours to rehearse.'

Charlie Wan, who had graduated from Pembroke College, Cambridge, sixteen years ago, smiled and said, 'It was a good brief you gave me, and I've always liked improvising.'

'You're sure he'll never recognize you again?'

'Not without the cheek-pads, and when my hair's grown again. He rarely comes to Hong Kong anyway, and I'm too busy direct-ing for the University to appear onstage myself. You got the main thing? Straik?'

'Yes. Chateau Lancieux. You buried it beautifully in a mass of other stuff.'

'Susie says I'm to bring you and Willie home for dinner. Young Weng and his friends too, of course.'

'We might just make it before we fly out tonight. I'll call you at home, Charlie. Can you and Weng's boys get this studio of Li Feng's back in shape?'

'No trouble.' Charlie Wan, President of the Drama Society at Hong Kong University, looked across at the unconscious form of Wu Smith. 'What about that?'

'He'll wake up soon after dark in a boat tied up near the Hydrofoil Pier on Macao.'

Willie Garvin said speculatively, 'Wonder what 'e'll make of it all?'

'He'll probably think it was real, until he finds that General Ching Po still runs Kwangtung.' Laughter sparkled in her eyes. 'After that . . . well, I suppose it'll give him something to sweat about for the next few months, wondering who made him sing and why.'

Willie grinned. ' *"For they that led us away captive required of us then a song."* Psalm 'undred and thirty-seven, verse three.'

Tarrant sank down on to the bunk and stretched out his legs. His mouth felt coated with bile, and throughout his body the nerves twitched and shrilled their message of pain. His clothes were rumpled and grubby, the jacket ripped. He felt like a living scarecrow.

His mind was a little clearer than it had been since the session with Mellish and Colonel Jim earlier. No doubt the more recent treatment from Mr Sexton had helped to clear some of the drug-induced sluggishness.

Tarrant looked at the tiny marks made by his thumbnail on the wooden head of the bunk. Six days now, if his calculations were correct. They were taking things slowly and carefully, thank God. It made sense, of course. You could break a man in hours with violent torture, but you were almost certain to produce severe mental confusion in him. This could reduce the output of his memory by as much as fifty per cent, and rendered what he did tell you unreliable.

They weren't using large doses of the barbiturate/stimulant, he thought. That could be self-defeating, too. The so-called truth drugs didn't make anybody tell the truth. They relaxed tension and made you expansive, then put you very quickly to sleep. So the trick was to blend in a stimulant like methamphetamine, which produced a sense of alertness and well-being. So you talked, and garrulously. But with great effort you could just keep ahead of your words and steer them into half-truths or lies or nonsense.

He closed his eyes and made a conscious effort to relax his weary body. Six days now. It might soon be time to pretend collapse and start feeding out a little of the false information he had been concocting. That might give him a few days respite.

It wasn't the kind of information he had expected them to squeeze out of him. This much had emerged at the extraordinary first interview, after the bearded man had come to take him from the cell. Mr Sexton. Tarrant knew all their names now, even knew that this was the Chateau Lancieux, a small and lonely castle standing amid the foothills of the Pyrenees. Only one part of it was in use, but from what he had seen he judged it to be of the sixteenth century, restored in the nineteenth. Today it would be a white elephant, of interest only to a recluse ... or to some-body like Colonel Jim.

Tarrant remembered his first sight of Colonel Jim, sitting at the desk in what had probably once been a sewing room and was now a study. The brainless blonde woman, astonishingly his wife, was lolling in an armchair to one side of the big desk, painting her nails, when Mr Sexton ushered him in. The hook-nosed Scotswoman, called Clare by everyone except Mr Sexton, who called her Mrs McTurk, was about to leave.

Colonel Jim was watching his wife fondly, but swivelled his chair to face them as the two men entered. Mr Sexton said, 'Sir Gerald Tarrant, Colonel Jim.'

The big head nodded and a big hand gestured ponderously. 'Sit down, Mr Tarrant. I guess we don't worry too much about titles here. Okay, Clare, you run along.'

Tarrant sat down in a chair facing the desk, weighing up the American and coming to the unhappy conclusion that he was formidable. Mr Sexton moved away and leaned against the wall. Colonel Jim smiled a toothy, saurian smile and said, 'Let's get down to the nitty-gritty, Mr Tarrant. You're in charge of the Special Intelligence Section of the British Foreign Office. You've had quite a lot of time to think about things the last day or so, and you're pretty damn sure that you're in the hands of somebody who's going to dig a lot of important secrets out of you.'

The blonde giggled. 'Like secret formulas, Poppa, and the plans of the new carburettor for a submarine, I bet that's what he thinks.'

'Now hush up, Momma,' Colonel Jim said amiably. 'I'm talking business with this guy.' He looked at Tarrant. 'Well, you can stop sweating, Mister. We don't want your crummy secrets. Just lemme tell you about my kind of business.' He opened a humidor on the desk. 'Cigar?'

Tarrant said crisply. 'No, thank you.'

Colonel Jim lit one for himself and leaned back, looking at the glowing end. 'I'm in blackmail. You could say I'm doing for blackmail what Ford did for automobiles. Lemme ask you a question, Mr Tarrant. Where's the big dough these days? The big tax-free dough?'

Tarrant said, 'I'd rather you told me.'

'It's in crime, Mister. But there's a hell of a lotta competition, on the trading side and the service side both. Drugs, flesh, heists, gambling, whatever you do you gotta fight cops and competitors. Blackmail's different.' He leaned forward and jabbed the air impressively with his cigar. 'Blackmail's the *only* crime where the losers co-operate with you. Right? And they're more scared of the cops coming in than you are. Right?'

His wife said, 'Right, Poppa.' She waved her hand in the air, fingers spread. 'You like this colour?'

'Suits you fine, Momma. Just fine. I like 'em good and red. You know anything about business, Mr Tarrant?'

Tarrant fought down a sense of unreality and said, 'Not a great deal. But more than you, if you seriously imagine I'm likely to be a profitable blackmail client.'

Colonel Jim chuckled, and the slatey eyes gleamed. 'You're not a client, Mr Tarrant. You're more like virgin ground where there's raw material waiting to be dug out. In a business like this we need material to work on. Now over in the States I got a big stake in six very ritzy private nursing homes. All legitimate. Right? The only thing is, I get to see the records. A lotta folk have break-downs, a lotta folk have sex problems, drink problems, kink problems. So we help 'em. We use deep analysis, hypnosis, modern drugs, all ways to crack 'em wide open and get at what's screwing 'em up. You beginning to see the shape of the picture, Mr Tarrant?'

With carefully judged distaste Tarrant said, 'I assume a propor-tion of the material you extract in this way is suitable for black-mail.'

'Right on the nose. So now I'm moving into Europe and I need raw material here, but we can't work the same set-up. They won't have me start any nursing-homes here. Same in Germany, Spain, Italy and the goddam UK.'

His wife looked up. 'They said *we* were foreigners! Imagine it. Who do they think they are, calling you an' me foreign, Poppa?'

'I guess the way they look at it, we could be kinda foreign to *them,* Momma,' Colonel Jim said reasonably. Then, to Tarrant, 'So you can see where we're at, Mister. You're our starter for raw material. I figured we'd cover UK first.'

Tarrant frowned. 'I don't follow you,' he lied.

Colonel Jim spread a hand. 'Security. Screening. I had a real expert assessment made on the number of files that pass through your hands in a year. Some of 'em have to carry a lotta dirt. I figure if you really got down to remembering hard, you could come up with maybe fifty or sixty names to make suitable clients for this operation.'

'Absurd.'

'Man in your position, right at the top, he needs a real good memory, Mr Tarrant. He's the one with the overall picture. You see a little thing here and a little thing there, and they click with a little thing you read in a file last year someplace. Then you set your boys to check up. Right? So we can use that kinda memory. You know the dirt and the names that go with it, so all you got to do is tell us.' Colonel Jim smiled the toothy smile that formed a horizontally curving slit almost to his back teeth. 'And you don't even have any trouble conscience-wise. Right? Like I said, I don't want to know about bombs or torpedoes and all that crud. Just the dirt.'

He lifted a hand as Tarrant started to speak. 'One more thing. A real rich client's fine. But revenue-wise we're very happy to service the little guys. Lemme put you in the picture. We run an inquiry on a client, and we *don't* squeeze him till the pips squeak.' He curled his big spatulate fingers gently, as if holding an imaginary orange. 'We just pressure him to twenty-five per cent below the safety line, and that's where we fix the retainer he pays for our goodwill. You get me?'

'A retainer? You mean they keep paying?'

'Ninety-eight per cent, so far. We've had only three clients who got dissatisfied and went to the cops. Only line of inquiry they got is through our receiving agency. Soon as that happens, we get word. Then Mr Sexton here takes over.'

'He reveals the dirt?'

'Hell no. Never that. He kills 'em, Mister. Makes it look accidental. He's the greatest at that. You should know.'

'But meanwhile your receiving agency has been pin-pointed.'

'Foreign-based institution. No easy way of bringing action against it. Besides, we got a nice routine. Say the F.B.I. or Interpol make inquiries. Our agent says what the hell is this all about? He says he's had payments from the client totalling so much over a period so long, for a charity relief fund that this agent operates. So the guy wants it *back* now? He's telling some crazy *story*? So here's a draft for the dough. All of it. And we want no further subscriptions from this person.'

Colonel Jim waved a hand in a conclusive gesture, then smiled again. 'By this time he's dead. Or she is. Right? So the cops think they have been taken for a ride by some kinda nut. What black-mailer gives the dough back? What blackmailer doesn't spill the dirt when a guy turns stubborn?' He drew on his cigar and shook his head sagely. 'Cops get confused easy. Mind you, if it hap-pened ten, fifteen times, maybe they'd get to wondering a little. But it won't, Mr Tarrant. I'm a good marketing man, and I fix just the price the market can carry.'

Tarrant hoped he was hiding what he felt. Danger lay in this sense of relief welling from the knowledge that if secrets were torn from him they would be secrets of little importance to security. The danger was that once you began to talk it was hard to stop, and he had no way of knowing whether Colonel Jim's plausible account of his business activities was true. This might be a subtle psychological move, to open him up readily in one area so that it would then be easy to probe him in other areas. There was the more positive personal danger that when he had been sucked dry, regardless of the purpose, he would be killed. He said stiffly, 'I have no information to give.'

Colonel Jim nodded. 'I figured you'd feel that way. Well, we're not gonna hurry you, Mr Tarrant. You just think it over for a few days.' He heaved his bulk from the chair and moved to where his wife sat. 'Get your pretty li'l butt off there and sit on Poppa's lap, Momma.'

She giggled, and Tarrant watched them settle themselves in the armchair. An arm round the woman, Colonel Jim said, 'Make it just two minutes, Mr Sexton.'

The man in the black blazer, who looked like a Viking or a Crusader, stepped forward briskly and took Tarrant's arm. Next moment Tarrant gasped with shock as he was plucked from his chair. He had never dreamt that such strength could exist in a man. He was on his feet for no more than a second, then a finger jabbed at him twice, in the shoulder and thigh-joint. It was like being jabbed by a steel bar, and each finger-blow hit precisely upon a nerve-centre. Paralysing pain exploded through his arm and left leg. He crumpled to the floor and Mr Sexton flicked a foot at the side of his knee, striking with the toe.

Somehow Tarrant prevented himself from screaming, and the sound he uttered was a quivering grunt of agony. He was lifted to his feet like a child, felt his arm seized and wrenched sharply, and reeled back against the chair as he was released. New pain swept him like a wave, and he thought his arm was broken.

The rest was a blurred nightmare of agony and humiliation. Mr Sexton worked briskly and clinically, like a man operating a machine he understood perfectly, probing the nerve-centres, knowing the precise degree of stress that sinew and bone could take without permanent damage.

Sometimes Tarrant was on the floor, sometimes on his knees, and sometimes, when he was lifted by those terrible hands, on his feet briefly. Once, as he swayed on all fours, his vision cleared for a few seconds when Mr Sexton stepped back to consider his next move, and then he saw the stupid, excited face of Colonel Jim's wife as she sat on his lap in the armchair, eyes sparkling, body wriggling with pleasure.

The humiliation of being so helplessly punished before her was as bitter in its way as the pain was searing. When it ended, when he lay curled on the floor and Mr Sexton stepped back for the last time, Tarrant could hear his own sobbing grunts, could feel tears running from his eyes, and knew a shame more crushing than anything his imagination could have conceived.

Later, in his cell, he lay making a conscious effort to repair the breaches that shock had made in his defences, enlisting pride, anger, hope, hatred, any emotion to help seal the cracks.

'Now you know,' he told himself contemptuously. 'Now you know, to just a small extent. This is what lies at the end of it for some of the men and women you've sent out. Remember Pirie? Remember him when you got him back by swapping the Hungarian? They'd broken Pirie, but it took them six weeks. There's a target for you to hang on to . . . Stiffen the sinews, you chairborne bastard, summon up the blood. Are you going to sing for creatures like these? Dear God, that ghastly woman . . . wriggling on that fat-bellied ape's lap, watching. And Mr Universe Sexton with his clever tricks. Modesty would take the smile off his face. Or Willie. But it's going to take time for them to find you, so you're on your own for a while. Like Pirie. Six-weeks Pirie. Relax . . . it's only pain. Let it wash through you. Don't fight it. Watch yourself, watch your reactions, keep a mental initiative . . .'

It was then that the Scottish woman, Clare, came into the cell. He thought fleetingly of trying to knock her unconscious, but abandoned the idea almost at once. His limbs were like lead, and she looked very strong. Also, he was quite certain that somebody, probably Mr Sexton, was outside the door.

Clare sat down on a folding chair she had brought with her and began to work on a piece of crochet she carried, fingers flashing nimbly. As she worked she talked in her ladylike, sing-song accent. The content of what she said was all the more horrible by contrast with her manner, for she spoke of torture as if discussing cake-making at a vicarage tea-party.

'I'm sure I hope it won't come to the worst, not for a gentleman like yourself, Sir Gerald. You'll not mind me calling you Sir Gerald? Oh, whatever am I thinking of—that's quite formal, isn't it now? What else should a body call you? And speaking of bodies, I remember another man Mr Sexton had to deal with a few months back. In September, I think it was—och, no, it must have been late October, for I mind it was turning a wee bit chilly. Some sort of electrical thing it was that Mr Sexton used in the end. A transformer, would it be? I've no head for such mechanical things, I'm afraid. I always say men have a more *natural* grasp of mechanics and suchlike, wouldn't you agree with me now, Sir Gerald? Well, whatever it was, it did awful severe damage to the poor wee man. His genitals, you know. I well mind saying to Angel at the time—but you've not really met Angel yet, have you? A nice girl, though maybe too kind-hearted for her own good in some ways, I often think. Well, I said to Angel at the time, "That's one poor man who'll not be copulating again, mark my words," I said. Of course that didn't arise in the end, for he completely lost his reason. I felt it was a happy release when Mr Sexton finally did that bone-breaking-by-numbers performance of his, to put him to rest. . . .'

And so it went on, the obscene menace clothed in tones of conversational gossip. Tarrant knew the purpose was carefully calculated, as everything that lay ahead of him would be calculated. This was to weaken him by anticipatory fear, and the fact that he realized the intention did very little to diminish its effect, for there was small cause to believe that the threat was a bluff.

The following day he was taken to the study again where a sandy man with sparse hair injected a drug into his arm and began to question him. Colonel Jim and his wife, Lucy, sat watching. The woman was eating chocolates fed her by Colonel Jim, who kept popping one between her full pouting lips every few minutes.

Tarrant was cautiously pleased with his control throughout this session. He could not help talking under the power of the drug, but he found himself able to anticipate the flow of what he was about to say, and to modify the truth so that it became either meaningless or harmless. Later, sitting in his cell with a mind still clouded, he warned himself against giving into a feeling of euphoric confidence. That would be a classic symptom presaging breakdown.

The same evening he suffered another session of pain and humiliation at Mr Sexton's hands. It took place this time in a large room with a gallery round it. The room had been converted into something of a gymnasium, and reminded him a little of the long windowless building behind Willie Garvin's pub, which enclosed the work-out room where he and Modesty Blaise practised their skills.

There was no questioning, either before or after this beating by Sexton. It seemed to be more of a demonstration for the audience looking on from the gallery, Colonel Jim and his company. With them was a man Tarrant had not seen before, a dark man with a touch of Chinese in him, whose name he had since learnt was da Cruz. The session went on longer than before, to the accompaniment of excited little whoops and cries from Lucy Straik. 'Hey, go man, go! Give him the finger job, Mr Sexton! Wow! Hear that squeal!' But strangely, Tarrant found himself better able to endure this time. Perhaps anticipation had reduced the shock of the assault, he thought later. Perhaps one adapted to humiliation, and even to pain. Certainly he had not cared about the beastliness of the gloating Straik woman this time. He had simply let himself go limp, knowing that any attempt at protection would be useless, and tried to withdraw mind from body, not attempting to quell the sounds of agony that burst from him.

That night Angel came to him in the cell, whispering sympathy, glancing fearfully at the door, telling him what bastards they all were, and in the end trying to edge on to the bunk with him and offer the use of her body in consolation. He knew that this was their angle for the soft play; but even knowing it, he found to his horror that for a moment or two he was roused to crude desire. It was primitive reaction following the fear and the beating, the subconscious urge of the aching body and shaken mind for any form of reassurance, and he killed it quickly, with self-disgust, turning away from the half-naked girl with the muddy, evil-child eyes.

Next day he was provided with bread and cold soup, and left completely alone. Today, the sixth day he believed, there had been another session with Mellish and the needle. Some hours later Sexton had taken him to a well-appointed bathroom suite, provided him with an electric razor, and allowed him to make a complete toilet. Tarrant tried to remain impassive and avoid showing how thankfully he seized the opportunity to be clean and shaven. It was with distaste that he put on his grubby and rumpled clothes again.

When he was dressed he was taken to the dining-room, where Colonel Jim and his companions were being served dinner by two silent Japanese, broad-shouldered men, above average height for their race, who moved lightly on their feet. Noting their hands, the flesh thickened to hard corn along the edges, Tarrant knew them for karate men.

Dinner was a curious experience. The conversation was dull, dominated mainly by Lucy Straik, who rambled on with aimless enthusiasm and almost complete inconsequence about any subject that her husband or Mr Sexton brought up. Tarrant was neither excluded from the conversation nor brought into it. He sat at the table with a sense of disassociation, accepting everything offered him to eat, but restricting himself to two glasses of the rather poor wine.

When dinner ended, the company moved to the gymnasium as if adjourning for entertainment in a drawing-room, and Tarrant was beaten again. This time, because of the sudden contrast, the shock hit deeply before he could brace himself against it.

He lay in his cell now, struggling to recover his mental balance. It would be Mellish with the hypodermic again tomorrow in all probability. Or a soft-sell interview in the study with Colonel Jim. Or one of Clare's talks followed by sympathy from Angel. Or something new. If he was going to feed out a little false information, better not to do it under the drug; he might too easily slip up. Squeeze out something reluctantly under Colonel Jim's questioning, perhaps. A show of wavering to begin with.

Tarrant considered his body for a moment. One eye half-closed. Plenty of bruises, and a swollen knee and elbow. Any number of minor twinges. But no broken bones yet, and no permanent damage. Sexton knew his job. They wanted him left with memory unimpaired when finally they broke him. A tricky business, to destroy the will without damaging other areas of the mind.

Six days now. Well, he could keep going for a while yet. Until Modesty came. (She won't and you know it—*stop thinking like that, fool.*) He could keep going till Modesty came. A few days? A week? Best not to look too far ahead.

Tarrant turned painfully on to his side. Like an alcoholic withstanding his devil in measures of twenty-four hours, he told himself that he would not break in the coming day.

CHAPTER SIX

WILLIE GARVIN said, 'No, I'll do it.'

He took Modesty's empty plate and fork from her, and put them on top of his own. 'A nice dish of spaghetti that was, Princess. Lovely sauce.'

'It's all in the way I open the tin, Willie.'

As he carried the plates out to the kitchen, Modesty refilled their glasses with red wine. Willie returned, sat down in the armchair by the coffee-table and picked up his glass. They had come into Heathrow that morning, and slept for most of the day. This would not prevent them going to bed in another two or three hours and sleeping the night through. Both possessed the knack of storing sleep or of going without for long periods. Modesty had put on a dark blue shirt and a grey skirt with a gold mesh belt. Willie wore a black sweater in fine jersey.

He said, 'What's next then, Princess?'

'Well, it looks as if we've found the baddies.' She thought for a few moments. 'I suppose we ought to check with Janet before we make another move. Have you rung her?'

'I phoned from the airport while you were in the loo, but just to say we were back safe. I'd promised.'

'We could go down and see her tomorrow.'

'That's the day she usually comes up to town. I'll give 'er a ring and ask 'er to look in sometime during the afternoon, if that's all right.'

'Fine.' Modesty looked down into her glass. 'She's going to want to come on this jaunt, if we go ahead.'

'I only told you what she said about that because she asked me to. But she can't, Princess. I mean, taking Janet on a caper with us is crazy.'

'Not exactly on it. But she'll want to be around. We could make a base twenty miles away, where she'd be all right. We'll get the map out again later.'

Willie looked baffled. 'I thought you'd just reckon it was a nonsense. We can't take 'er on a conducted tour up the sharp end of a caper, and she won't get much out of sitting around in the middle distance.'

'It's something. She'll get a peek into the area of Willie Garvin that's a blank to her.'

'Well . . . if you say so, Princess. I don't really get it.'

'That's because you're male and dense, Willie love.' The phone at her elbow rang. She picked it up, listened, and said, 'Thank you. Ask him to come up.' Then, to Willie, 'Jack Fraser's here.'

A private lift from the reception area served the penthouse. When the gates slid open and Fraser stepped out on to the tiled floor of the wide foyer, Modesty was waiting to greet him. He was a rather small and very unimportant-looking man in a dark suit, carrying a bowler hat and the rolled umbrella. To the world in general he presented a nervous and humble aspect. This was as deceptive as his appearance. Before his promotion to a desk job, Fraser had fought in the great underground spy-war that erupted in Berlin during the fifties. He was clever, ruthless and experienced.

Tonight he did not wear his ingratiating manner, but put down his hat and umbrella on the drum table and said, 'Hallo Modesty. Where the hell have you been hiding? Got any of that brandy left?'

'Large and neat?'

'That would be fine. Hallo, Willie.' He moved down the three steps which pierced the low wrought-iron balustrade separating the foyer from the long sitting room with its ivory tiles, golden cedar-strip walls and Isfahan rugs.

Willie was at the small bar set in an alcove. He said, 'Hallo, Jack. I'm sorry about Tarrant.'

Fraser took the glass of brandy, murmured his thanks, and moved to the chesterfield, waiting for Modesty to seat herself before he sat down at the other end. 'Something pretty rum came up,' he said. 'I'm buggered if I know whether it means anything or not, but I just want to throw it at you.' He sipped the brandy, exhaled a little sigh of wonder and raised the glass to Modesty. 'You must have robbed Olympus for this.'

'Not Olympus. A German steel tycoon, some years back now. It came with the sundries, and I've only six bottles left.'

'You're mad to offer it. Look, this morning I found out that Reilly had gone bent.'

'Tarrant's driver?'

'That Reilly. I had a routine report from F. Section and there was a bit in it about Reilly.'

'F. Section's the Far East?'

'Yes. We sent Reilly out to Hong Kong six weeks ago.'

'That's odd. We're just back from there. Why did you send him?'

'Partly for experience. I'd had in mind to recommend him for promotion to regular courier work, so I found a few small jobs for him to do. I was also testing him, so I had him covered.'

'What happened?'

'A woman happened.'

'Couriers go to bed with women like other people, Jack.'

'This woman is suspect. A free-lance go-between. We've made use of her ourselves.'

'If somebody paid her to pick up Reilly, how would they identify him for her?'

Fraser grimaced. 'Look, I know Tarrant's position was supposed to be secret in this country, but half the Press knew and all the foreign opposition. Hundreds of people could have fingered Reilly as Tarrant's driver.'

'All right, she picked him up. Then what happened?'

'We've no idea. But about two weeks later somebody paid three thousand pounds into an account Reilly had opened a few days before at a bank in Dublin. Transferred from The New Provident and Commercial Bank of Macao. That's Mr Wu Smith, so we've no hope of tracing the payment to source.'

He saw the glance exchanged by Willie and Modesty. 'What's wrong?'

Willie said, 'Nothing. It's just the flux.'

'The what?'

'Willie calls it the flux,' said Modesty. He doesn't believe that coincidences are coincidences. He says there's a magnetic flux about the earth which causes like events to occur simultaneously or in sequence. Open *The Times Literary Supplement* and you find three different people have written books about Queen Victoria's third cousin twice removed who was Governor of Honduras or somewhere. All published in the same month. And nobody ever heard of him before. It's the flux.'

'What the hell's it got to do with this?'

'We were talking about Wu Smith's bank half an hour ago. Something quite different. But go on. How did you pick up the Dublin account?'

'Just luck. The Treasury undercover boys have been twisting a few arms for us, to find out about I.R.A. money coming in from abroad. Reilly's name popped up under the heading of New Deposits. The Hong Kong report came in the same day. Some fool had held over the thing about Reilly and this woman for the monthly summary, instead of sending through a special. When we checked back hard, we found Reilly broke his journey home to spend two days somewhere in France. Falsified his time of departure from Hong Kong to cover it in his report.'

Fraser rolled some brandy round his mouth. Modesty said slowly, 'You think Reilly was paid to arrange the accident?'

'No. That doesn't quite fit with the fact that Reilly died too. I think he was paid to set Tarrant up for somebody else to do the job, or paid half in advance more probably, and that whoever did it knocked Reilly off at the same time, as a safety-play.' Fraser paused, looking down into his glass. Then he looked up, his thin features suddenly haggard. 'I'm not so sure Tarrant's dead. There's still no body.'

Willie Garvin sat up straight. 'A snatch? With the car accident to cover it?'

Fraser shrugged. 'It makes more sense. Action against Intelligence top brass hasn't been trendy for a while now. But if somebody's coming back with it, they'd do themselves more good by snatching Tarrant and scraping information out of him than by a straight killing.'

Both men looked at Modesty. She sat with her hands folded in her lap, eyes blank, looking at nothing. After a few moments she said very softly, 'Oh, my God. That's what I've been trying to remember.' She stood up and began to pace slowly, holding her elbows, eyes half closed in concentration.

Fraser said, 'Remember what?'

'Tell him about Quinn, Willie. I want to play it back in my mind, just what he said.'

In a few short sentences Willie gave Fraser the story Modesty had told him of the injured man she found on the heights above the Tarn, and of their way-laying by the three men on the deserted causse.

Fraser said, 'Christ, you mean he could have *seen* something?'

Modesty stopped pacing, took a cigarette from an ivory box and lit it. She said, 'He was concussed, and he'd been passing out on and off, so he was pretty confused. I said to him——and these are the exact words: "You must have been here when the car went over the edge yesterday. A grey Peugeot. Did you see it happen?" Now listen carefully. He said, *"Went over the edge? God, no, I didn't see it go over."* '

Willie frowned. 'There's something . . . a bit wrong with it.'

'I know, and it's been nagging me. But I've got it now. If he'd said, "God, no, I didn't see it," full-stop——that's fine. But the last two words make all the difference. There's an implication. He saw the car, but didn't see it go over.'

Fraser said doubtfully, 'It's a bit subtle.'

'I heard the words, the intonation, Jack. And if he saw the car but didn't see it go over, then it *must* have been parked there for a while, on that bend.'

Fraser rubbed the heel of his hand across a damp brow. Willie said, 'Suppose Reilly set it up at that spot for the opposition, by arrangement. And suppose some'ow they spotted Quinn across the gorge. Then you've got a good reason why them three villains turned up. They were sent to do Quinn.' He looked at Modesty. 'We'd better get 'old of him, Princess. Quinn maybe doesn't realize it, but 'e knows something.'

She bit her lip. 'That's the hell of it. He'll have left Georges Durand's clinic now, and he could be anywhere. God, I'm a fool.'

Willie grinned faintly. 'I often wonder 'ow you get by.' He looked at Fraser. 'You can trace 'im, Jack. The Princess got the names of two of the villains she clobbered. René Vaubois of SDECE will 'elp.'

Fraser nodded. He looked very tired. 'He'll help quicker if Modesty asks him. He owes you for that Montmartre business. His life.'

Willie leaned forward. 'Look, all of a sudden we think Tarrant's alive, right? So why sit there looking like an undertaker's mute with the belly-ache?'

Fraser drained his glass and put it down. 'Because I like the old bastard,' he said bleakly. 'Because if we're right, he could be in a mental home in Moscow now, or somewhere similar. Because they're going to pull him to pieces very slowly, and then kill him.'

Modesty said, 'Then we must get him back in a hurry.' Her face was calm, her voice mellow, but about her there was an emanation so intense that Fraser felt he could almost see it as a luminosity. He had known this experience with her once before, and remembered comparing the impact of it with the tingling frisson of apprehension he had felt when de-fusing a booby-trap with a three-way detonator.

He suppressed a flare of hope and said dourly, 'Get him back? From Moscow?'

She looked at him. 'From anywhere, Jack. If it came to that, I've still got two lines into The Centre from the old days. Besides, it may not be Moscow. And in spite of Hong Kong, I don't think it's Peking. They don't work that way. This could be an independent group, in which case Tarrant might still be in Europe. Who's running your section at the moment?'

'I am. With limited authority, pending the appointment in a few days of whoever replaces Tarrant. If you're wondering whether I can mount a big operation to find him, the answer's no. I'm just minding the shop, and it's no use going to the Minister with a hunch based on a few shreds of information.'

'You must have some idea who the new man will be.'

'Yes. Corder. The Minister's pet.'

'What's he like?'

'A brontosaurus.'

'What?'

'That prehistoric monster with a brain the size of a walnut located somewhere in its arse.'

She half smiled. 'I thought it was in the tail, and that it was a myth anyway.'

'Corder hasn't got a tail.' Fraser shrugged. 'I could be flattering him there, maybe he just keeps it hidden.'

Willie said, 'I don't reckon a big operation, Princess. It's bound to leak.'

She nodded. 'I was only worried that a new man looking at what Jack's dug up about Reilly might make the same kind of guess and start something.'

'He won't get to see what I dug up if that's how you want to play it,' Fraser said.

Willie stood up and took Fraser's glass. 'Finding Quinn's the first move. Let's 'ope it doesn't take long.'

'We can try phoning Georges Durand,' Modesty said. 'He might have some idea where Quinn was going when he left the clinic.'

Fraser lifted a hand reluctantly. 'No refill, Willie. I want to make those six bottles last." He looked at Modesty. 'What do you hope Quinn can give you?'

'A lead, perhaps.'

'He wouldn't have seen much detail at that distance.'

'If the opposition sent a party to sign him off, they must have been worried about whatever he might have seen.'

Fraser's eyes narrowed and a hard smile touched his lips. 'Maybe they're still worried. Still looking for him. He might be useful bait if we can get hold of him.'

'I'd thought of that too.' She moved to the huge floor-to-ceiling window that looked out over Hyde Park. 'See if you can raise Georges now, please Willie.'

The phone rang a second before Willie picked it up. He said 'Yes. Albert?' His eyebrows lifted suddenly. '*Who?*' He shot a startled glance at Modesty. Then, 'All right, can you pour 'im into the lift or shall I come down?' A pause. 'Fine.'

He put down the phone and ran a hand through his hair. 'It's the flux,' he said. 'There's a bloke down in reception wants to see you, Princess. Albert says he's stoned to the eyeballs. And 'is name's Quinn.'

Fraser stared, then stood up and grinned wolfishly. 'We've got our bait, by God.'

Two minutes later the lift doors slid open. Quinn walked out carefully into the foyer and looked down the great sitting room to where three figures stood. He wore rumpled corduroy trousers and a bulky sheepskin jacket. One hand held a battered travelling case. His face was pallid and shiny, eyes bright but wandering, as if he had difficulty in making them focus. He put down the case, stumbled slightly as he straightened up, then moved forward to the low iron balustrade.

Modesty said, 'Help him down the steps, Willie. Hallo, Quinn.'

Quinn took the steps warily, then shook off Willie's hand. 'I can manage, my good fellow.' He put his hands in his pockets and looked about him, then made a breathy attempt to whistle. 'Oh, my word. A nice little pad. And you run a hat-shop in Kensington, eh?'

She smiled and moved towards him. 'Come and sit down, Quinn.'

He allowed her to lead him to the chesterfield, and slumped down heavily. 'Who are all these men?'

'All friends of mine. Would you like some coffee?'

'Aha! You're a coffee-maker to boot, eh?' He grinned and pointed a faltering finger at her. 'First I thought you were a dancer. The legs, see? Jesus, they're good. Then I thought you were a doctor. Then the hat-shop bit, and then . . . what was it? Oh, I know. A secret agent.' He giggled. 'Wham, bam, thank you ma'am, and another Redskin bit the dust.'

Modesty said, 'How's your head now?'

'The head? Marvellous. A bit muzzy just at this moment, but that's from drinking black velvet. And the arm. Look.' He held up his left hand and waved it about. 'Good as new. Intensive treatment from the good Dr Durran. What a pad he's got there. And all free. I asked him about that. "I'm a philanthropist," he says, "Bollocks," I told him, not knowing the French, "it's little old Modesty the Mystery who's picking up the tab, and just why would she do that?" So he said, "She must have fallen under the spell of that tremendous charm you have, Mr Quinn." '

Quinn glowered about him. 'Sarcastic French sod.'

Modesty sat down beside him and said, 'Where are you staying?'

'Staying?' He gazed at her blearily. 'I don't know. Find a hotel somewhere. I only got in this morning.' He screwed up half his face in a laboured wink. 'But old Quinn's been pretty cunning. Got a mate in Fleet Street, see? Crime bloke. In the know. Drinks black velvet. So I routed him out and poured the stuff down him while I chatted him up. Down me, too.' He wiped sweat from his clammy face. 'I asked him, "You know anything about a girl called Modesty Blaise? Got a hell of a straight-left with her foot," I told him. "Christ," he says, "I can give you a million rumours, boy, but all I can tell you for sure is she's loaded, and she's been mixed up in at least three cloak-and-dagger stories we've never been allowed to print." So I kept pumping him, see? And he told me . . .'

Quinn stopped short, catching his breath. A greenish tinge came into his face. He tried to rise, fell against Modesty, muttered, 'Oh God, I'm going to be sick.' And was.

Fifteen minutes later, Willie Garvin pulled him from under a warm shower where Quinn had been cursing and struggling feebly in his grasp, picked him up, laid him on a massage table, and rubbed him dry vigorously with a rough towel.

Thirty minutes later Willie came out of the penthouse guest-room and joined Modesty. She had changed into an emerald green silk wrap-over robe, let her hair down ready for bed, and was standing by the window, looking out over the darkness of the park. Fraser had gone, after one searing comment on Quinn.

Willie said, 'He's asleep, Princess. Right out. Weng's taken 'is clothes down to the all-night cleaners. Yours too.'

She turned. 'Thanks, Willie love.'

'Looks like we got two jobs on the go. D'you want to see Janet tomorrow anyway?'

'Yes. Even if it's only to explain that we may have to hold fire on her thing until we've got something else cleared up. I'll talk to Quinn in the morning, then we can decide the next move.' She thought for a moment. 'You might plug in the intercom in his room. I'll switch mine on so I can hear him—just in case he wakes up and starts blundering around, wondering where he is.'

'I'll do that. What do you reckon about old Tarrant?'

'We still can't be sure he's alive, Willie . . . but I hope so.'

'Me too. I don't think they'll do a crash job on 'im. They'll take it slow. Get more information that way.'

'All the same, we'd better find him fast.'

He saw her eyes swim, and was startled for a moment. Sometimes he had known her weep briefly after a caper, in his presence only, from strain and pain and reaction. But never otherwise. For the past half hour he had been too occupied with Quinn to register the anxiety that was gnawing within him or to realize how strongly it would be reflected in her. He liked Tarrant very much, but knew that Modesty's affection for him was deeper, perhaps in a way only possible for a woman. Not that it was sexual. Simply filial.

She blinked and managed a smile. 'Sorry. It's just that . . . he's not young, Willie. You know the sort of things they'll do to him. And he isn't used to—I don't know—not so much the pain, the indignity if you like. There's little new anyone could do to us, but it's different for him.'

Willie looked at the great S-shaped scar on the back of his right hand, made by a hot iron, the initial of a man now dead. He looked at Modesty, knowing the splendid body beneath the silk robe, knowing it had suffered rape and wounds, knowing it because he had three times nursed it back to health. She was right. They were neither of them new to the shattering impact brutality has upon the inner self. They had learned how to absorb it, and later forget it. But it would be different for Tarrant.

He said, 'Just so long as we find 'im. He's the kind that's got a lot of gristle.'

'Yes. I'm sure he has. Goodnight, Willie.'

She touched his arm and moved away to her bedroom.

The lever flew off the Mills grenade as the barrel-shaped handful of destruction hit the deck of the aircraft. Quinn sprawled across the half-conscious Arab, head twisted to look back over his shoulder, a silent scream of horror erupting in his mind as the ugly black pomegranate rolled lurchingly down the aisle.

Futile fragments of hope flared and died in him during the eternal seconds of watching. It was the good old-fashioned Mills. Could have been made years ago. Perhaps the spring would be weak, the striker fail, or the percussion cap fail to ignite the five second safety-fuse, or . . . something fail.

The white-faced man in the aisle-seat on the port side dived forward. The rolling grenade swerved neatly to evade him, as if governed by some malevolent intelligence. It vanished under the seat where the man's wife and child huddled, and then came the frightful roar.

Nothing had failed. Except Quinn. . . .

Over the intercom, Modesty heard Quinn's gasping moans and mumblings. She slid quickly out of bed and was halfway to the guest-room before she had the robe belted about her naked body. Willie met her in the passage. The tortured groaning faded a little, then broke out anew.

'Some nightmare, Princess. Didn't need an intercom to 'ear it.'

'Yes. I'll see to him, Willie. You go back to sleep.'

'Sure?'

She nodded, and turned to the half open door of Quinn's room. Putting on the light, she closed the door and moved to sit on the edge of the bed, reaching out to put her hands on his shoulders as he writhed and uttered strangled incoherencies.

'Wake up, Quinn,' she said quietly, 'you're having a bad dream.'

His eyes opened wide, and he jerked to a sitting position.

'Oh God . . . !' He clung to her, panting, and she patted his back gently, saying, 'Poor old Quinn. That was a bad one. I don't think black velvet's your tipple.'

He let her go suddenly and drew back, blinking at her, then looking about the room. She saw bewilderment slowly fade as he tacked a few fragments of drunken memory together. At last he drew a long breath, looked at her with self-disgust dawning in his eyes, and said, 'Did I make an absolutely titanic fool of myself?'

'Anyone can have a nightmare.'

'I meant before that.'

'Well, if you could run an action replay for yourself, I don't think you'd be too happy about it. You were stoned.'

'I'm sorry.' He rubbed his eyes and shivered. 'Some bloody giant stripped me and held me under a shower—or did I imagine that?'

'No, that was Willie Garvin.'

He thought for a moment. 'Ah, yes. Duggan said about him.'

'Duggan being your Fleet Street friend?'

'Yes.'

'Lie down and cover up. You've got the shivers. Would you like a cigarette?'

'Please.'

She took two from the box on the bedside table, lit them both, put one in his hand, then set an ash-tray on the bed between them.

Quinn said wearily, 'I don't know why I always do things wrong. I wanted to find you so I could come and thank you. Bring you some flowers or something. Then I got smashed and behaved like ... what did I behave like?'

'Sort of cocky and hostile. More in the manner than the words.'

'Cocky and hostile. Yes, that would be about right. You tell it straight, don't you?'

'You asked me.' She smiled. 'At least you didn't call me ducky.'

'I'm glad about that.' He smiled back at her, and it was a good smile without the usual hint of acid mockery. 'Look, will you take it that I'm very grateful for all you did for me?'

'You're welcome. Can I get you anything? Not from the bar, but a sandwich or something if you're hungry?'

'Nothing, thanks.' He hesitated. 'If you'll let me loose in the kitchen I could make myself some coffee.'

'Coffee at two a.m.? It'll keep you awake.'

'That's the main idea.' He tried to speak lightly, but his voice was uneven and she saw that his hand holding the cigarette was trembling.

She said, 'Does it happen often, this nightmare?'

'Often enough.' His mouth worked, and he had difficulty in drawing on the cigarette.

'Would telling about it help?'

'I thought you might have guessed. Thought the name might have rung a bell. Henry Quinn, Second Officer on the good air-craft Delta Bravo, hi-jacked on the Rome flight last September.'

'There've been a lot of hi-jackings. And I was out of touch with newspapers and radio for a couple of weeks in September.'

He stared up into nothingness. 'Two Arabs. They took over as we were coming into Rome. A Trident of Corsair Airlines. When we landed they demanded the release of those three terrorists the Italians held after the shoot-up at Milan last year. Or they'd blow up the plane and everyone in it, including themselves. It went on for about eighteen hours, negotiations with Italian officials, the Red Cross, all that stuff.'

He tried to stub out his cigarette, but his hand was shaking so violently that she took the stub from him and crushed it in the ash-tray. 'I killed three people,' he said, and closed his eyes. 'One was a child.'

'What do you mean?'

He had found her hand and was holding it tightly, though she was sure he was unaware of it. He said, 'It was all going on, you see. Twelve hours, fourteen, sixteen. On and on. Oh Christ, I hated those bastards so much. I kept trying to feel afraid, but I couldn't. I was too mad. The passengers were bloody marvellous. This seems feeble, but I kept thinking. *How dare you! How dare you threaten all these men and women and kids, you mindless maniacs!*'

He rubbed a hand across his mouth. 'You can't get nearer to it in words, but the feeling was . . . huge. Towering.' He was silent for long moments, then went on, 'We played it according to the rules. The crew, I mean. Safety of passengers the prime considera-tion. So what does that mean? Does it mean you sit tight and hope they won't blow us all up? But suppose you're wrong, and they do? I still don't know. But there came a time when one of them was outside, arguing with the Minister or whoever. And the other one was standing at the end of the aisle, holding a grenade. A Mills bomb. He hadn't pulled the pin.' His eyes flickered to Modesty. 'They're safe until the pin's drawn, you see.'

'Yes.'

'Well . . . I'd been giving one of the hostesses a spell, serving food, and I saw a chance. This Arab's s.m.g. was slung on his shoulder. He just held the grenade. I was carrying a tray, and I'd managed to wriggle a bit of steel bar out of a rack in the galley. I'd been sweating cobs for hours, trying to make up my mind whether to have a go. Mike Charnely, the Captain, he was play-ing it cool and I think he was worried about me, because he kept muttering, "Don't do anything bloody stupid, Quinn." But then I saw this chance. I'd got the bar hidden under the tray, and when I was just a couple of steps from the Arab I dropped the tray and took a bloody great swipe at his wrist.'

Quinn's eyes were blank, and though his voice was low his speech became faster and more feverish. 'It should have been all right. If I made him drop the grenade he was sunk. But I missed. I mean, I hit him but didn't get it quite right. He hung on to the grenade, and he jumped back, pulling at the pin, and it came free just as I smashed him on the head with the bar. I went down on top of him when he fell, and I heard the thing hit the deck, and looked round, and it was rolling, rolling, wobbling about, and this poor devil with his wife and kid dived at it. He couldn't have stopped it or got rid of it, but he was going to smother it with his body. Christ, he was brave. But it swung away under the seats and rolled on, and then came that awful bloody bellow and blast, and then the screaming——'

His teeth were chattering too violently for speech. He turned his head from side to side, struggling for control. Modesty held his hand and waited. After a few moments he stopped moving and looked up at her very intently for a full two minutes with a wondering air. His defences had fallen completely now, and though grief aged his eyes he seemed to Modesty very young and helpless.

At last he spoke again, quietly and with little expression. 'It was one of those freakish things. Most of the blast went through the side of the aircraft. The man who dived wasn't hurt, neither was his wife. But the little girl and the two people in the seat behind were killed. Somebody outside was quick enough to nail the Arab there before he could do anything. Afterwards there was an inquiry. They said I was to blame for taking reckless action, and of course they were right.'

He lay breathing deeply as if he had run a race, and slowly something of the old hostility crept into his face. He said, 'Come on, you're supposed to say I wasn't to blame, it was just bad luck. All my friends tell me that. At least, to my face.'

She said quietly, 'What they think or what I think doesn't matter. It's your load, Quinn, so pick it up and carry it. Nobody else can do it for you.'

He was startled. 'Jesus. There speaks a hard lady. Just for the record, what *do* you think?'

'I'll tell you what I know, not think. If you'd made it, you'd have been a hero. Daring rescue by gallant pilot. Not many people stop to remember that "daring" means there was a risk, and that it could come out either way.'

'It came out the wrong way.'

'Too bad. I'm a hard-liner on this, Quinn. You let people see that the hostage game works and it spreads like a plague. It's done so.'

'I killed two men and a child.'

'They're dying every day, under cars or bombs or in Calcutta gutters with empty bellies.'

'And one or two more make no difference? That's great.'

'One or two more can save one or two hundred more if it stops the plague.'

'Peachy. If you don't happen to be one of the unfortunate.'

She nodded. 'That comes out the way it's written.'

'Kismet? A fatalist?'

She smiled. 'Of a sort. But not the passive sort.'

His good smile came back. 'I can bear witness to that. Wham, bam, etcetera.' He exhaled a long breath. 'Thanks for letting me slobber it all out. And for telling me to pick up my own load. That's better than soft words. I manage all right most of the time, it's just the nightmares that get me. Once you're asleep, you've got no armour. Look, would you like to know why I've been such a particularly unpleasant bastard to you?'

'Tell me.'

'Well . . . the truth is, you rather over-awe me. You did right from the start. And I suppose I resent it.'

'Over-awe you? Oh come on, Quinn.'

'It's true. You're a bit bloody marvellous, you know. I don't just mean looks and legs and all that, but . . . oh, I don't know. The way you keep *coping* all the time. Not failing. When a chap's not all that sure of himself, it's a bit much.'

She said apologetically, 'Sorry. But please try not to resent me. Are you going to be good and go to sleep now?'

He shook his head, forcing a smile. 'Not without my teddy bear. Too scared. Once it starts, I sometimes get a sequence of them. You go back to bed. Never mind about the coffee, I'm not sleepy now, but can I help myself to the fags?'

'Of course.' She stood up, turned, hesitated, then looked back at him. 'Would it help if I stayed?'

He stared uncertainly. 'You mean . . . with me? Here?' He looked round. There was no couch in the room. 'In bed?'

'If it would help keep the nightmares away.'

She saw swift yearning touch his face, and knew he was making an effort to speak lightly as he said, 'Is lucky old Quinn about to be seduced?'

'Lucky old Quinn can take his choice. He doesn't have to rise to an occasion. If he just wants a bit of warm friendly female flesh to keep him company, that's all right. It can be a great comfort.' She untied the robe and let it fall. 'Move over a bit.'

She slid in beside him, slipped an arm under his neck, drew his head down to rest on the warm slope between breast and shoulder, and reached up to the cord-switch hanging above. 'Light out?'

'Not yet.' He had gasped at the first contact of their bodies, and now held her close, a hand moving wonderingly over her smooth flesh. After a little while, when she felt him awakening, she tilted his head to kiss him, and whispered, 'You don't have to prove anything, Quinn. Just be happy.'

Later she was surprised by his gentleness as he used her, and by his concern for her own response, a concern that she sensed sprang not from male pride but from the wish to give as well as receive. She let slip her role as a comforter, joining with him gladly in the play and counterplay of making love.

Much later, just before they slept, Quinn with his arm thrown across her, he gave a warm, dreamy little chuckle, pressed her breast gently and murmured, 'Better than teddy bears. Thank you, ma'am . . .'

CHAPTER SEVEN

RENE VAUBOIS, head of Direction de la Surveillance due Territoire, looked at his watch and said, 'This has gone more quickly than I expected.'

Modesty spread the three photographs on the table. 'We've been lucky. If Bourget and Garat had been carrying false identification I could have spent all day here.'

'And this fellow Servalle.' Vaubois tapped one of the photographs. 'He was the third man?'

'Yes.' She turned from Vaubois to the Sûreté man. 'Can you say if there is a connection, m'sieu?'

'No question of it, mam'selle.' The Inspector passed a record card to Vaubois. 'They work together, these three. Marseilles based.'

'Union Corse?' Vaubois asked.

'No. Independent.'

'Good. Please put out an immediate call to have them picked up, Inspector. Priority red.'

'For interrogation by your department?'

'Yes.'

'Very well, m'sieu. One hopes for quick results, but if they have gone into hiding . . .' He gestured.

Vaubois nodded sombrely. It was now noon. Modesty Blaise had telephoned him at eight o'clock, Paris time, and he had picked her up from Orly Airport at ten. He said, 'Let us hope for good fortune.'

Five minutes later, sitting beside Modesty in the back of his car as it swept along Boulevard Haussmann, Vaubois said, 'You truly believe my colleague Sir Gerald may be alive?'

'I'm not satisfied that he's dead, René.'

'Assuming your hope is correct, it will be very . . . difficult to recover him. Perhaps impossible.'

'I'll think about that when I know where he is.'

'You know that the D.S.T. will give all possible help.' Vaubois made a regretful grimace. 'The aims of my department have occasionally conflicted with those of Sir Gerald's department, but he and I always had a pleasant understanding.'

'I know, René. If you can pick up those men and find out who sent them to deal with Quinn, will you call me at once?'

'Of course. Now, can I offer you an early lunch before taking you to Orly?'

'Thank you, René, but I must get back to London, and there's a flight at twelve forty-five. I've another possible lead to follow up.'

'This man Quinn?'

'Yes. He's at my place now. I think he must have seen something significant, otherwise they wouldn't have bothered about him.'

'Modesty, listen please. If we find cause to believe that Sir Gerald is no longer in the west, but held . . . say, in Moscow, then you must count him as lost. There is nothing to be done.'

'Just let them take him to pieces?'

'I'm sorry. Yes.'

'All right, René.'

Vaubois looked at her, then swore softly. 'I waste my breath.'

An hour earlier, while Modesty had been looking at photographs and dossiers in the *Renseignments Généraux* section of the Sûreté Nationale, Quinn was woken from sleep by a big man with untidy fair hair who told him that there was a bathroom en suite he could use; that his clothes, cleaned and pressed, were hanging on the clothes-valet; and that somebody called Weng would be putting up a late breakfast for him in the dining-room in half an hour.

Quinn, still half asleep, said, 'Where's Modesty?'

'Paris. She'll be back later today.'

The big man had gone before Quinn could collect his wits to frame another question. He got slowly out of bed. She had been there, with him, only a few hours ago. The memory of her was clear and marvellous. Paris? She was in Paris now? What the hell was going on? He'd have to ask that big bastard—what was his name? Willie Garvin. That's what Duggan had said in the boozer. Quinn decided, without quite knowing why, that he did not like Willie Garvin much.

Half an hour later, when he entered the dining-room, he found Willie Garvin sitting at the end of the table reading a newspaper, while a young Indo-Chinese set a place at one side. There was coffee, cream and milk, a rack of toast, and a chafing dish with eggs, bacon and kidneys.

Willie put down the paper and said, 'Bring another cup please, Weng. I'll 'ave some coffee too. This is Mr Quinn.'

Weng bowed slightly and smiled. 'Good morning, Mr Quinn.'

'Hallow.' Quinn sat down. He felt suddenly ravenous.

When Weng had left, Willie Garvin said, 'That black velvet's 'eavy stuff. Feeling a bit better now?'

'Very fair.' Quinn served himself and began to eat. 'When did Modesty go to Paris?'

'Caught the eight o'clock flight. She said to let you 'ave a good sleep.'

'I did. Where did *you* sleep last night?'

'I got me own room 'ere.'

'I see. No, I don't see. But never mind. Why did she suddenly shoot off to Paris?'

'To see a friend. She wants to get a line on those three blokes who came after you on the causse.'

'After *me*?'

'It begins to look that way.'

'Why?'

'She'll explain when she gets back. She wants to ask you a few things.'

Quinn felt a flare of anger. God knew what she thought he could tell her, but was this the reason for last night? Be nice to Quinn and give him a tumble because he can tell you something you want to know?

He said, 'Well, it's all been great fun. I'll just finish this and then be on my way.'

Willie Garvin said, 'No, you'll 'ave to 'ang on. I told you, the Princess wants to talk to you.'

'*Who* does?'

'Modesty.'

'Ah, your pet name for her. Very touching. But who's going to make me hang on, Garvin?'

'It's partly for your own good. We think somebody could still be looking for you, to finish what they tried to start that day when she clobbered 'em.'

'Looking for me? Balls. Who's going to make me hang on?'

Willie Garvin sighed. 'Let's not get to a confrontation. They upset me.'

Quinn began to butter another piece of toast, feeling savage. He surved his lips in a false smile and said, 'Modesty came to bed with me last night.'

Willie nodded. 'M'mm. After that nightmare. She said she'd stayed.'

'A very good screw.' Even as he said the words Quinn hated himself. They spoiled something good. But he kept smiling.

Willie picked up his paper. He might not have heard. Quinn said confidingly, 'The thing is old man, how much should I leave on the mantelpiece. I mean, what's the usual? Would a quid be all right?'

Willie Garvin thought for a moment, then got up and patted Quinn on the shoulder. 'You 'aven't quite got the idea,' he said. The big hand gripped suddenly. The other hand swung, open and slightly cupped. It smacked across Quinn's cheek with a sound like a paper-bag bursting, rattling his teeth and splintering his mind with shock. But for the hand holding his shoulder, he would have fallen out of the chair. After a few seconds his reeling head steadied. He tried to stand up, but could not move. The hand was like a clamp.

Willie Garvin said patiently, 'It's just a question of manners, Quinn. Look, I don't give a monkey's what you think about Modesty Blaise. I don't even care what you say about 'er. But when you've walked into 'er 'ome drunk, and been sick down 'er, when you've slept in 'er bed and she's stayed with you to help drive the nightmares away, when you're under 'er roof, sitting at 'er table . . . then don't say anything out of line about 'er to *me*. Because I'm a bit old-fashioned about manners, see?'

He let Quinn go, gave him a friendly nod, then sat down again and poured himself another cup of coffee. Quinn sat shaking. After a while he put his hands to his face and drew them slowly down his cheeks.

'Was I . . . really sick down her?' he asked in a low voice.

Willie waved a hand. 'Compre'ensively. But don't worry. She's not what you'd call squeamish.'

'Oh, Christ. Look, what I said just now . . . I didn't mean it. I wanted to needle you. But I didn't mean it by a million miles. I think she's . . . great. Marvellous. But I got knotted up with thinking she'd only done it because she can use me. And that hurt the stinking old Quinn ego, and started the stinking old Quinn viper-tongue going. Sorry. I really am bloody sorry.'

Willie said, 'She thinks you can 'elp us. But whatever she's done for you, all along the line, she'd 've done anyway.'

Quinn managed a smile. 'A sucker for lame dogs?'

'Sometimes. Some lame dogs. I could tell you about me, but I won't.' He pushed back his chair. 'We've got a few hours to kill, and the Princess said not to go out in case anyone's getting close to you. But there's a pool downstairs, and squash-courts, if you fancy working off your 'angover.'

'I haven't got one.' He looked at Willie tentatively. 'If I say she did my hangover a lot more than an Alka-Seltzer, you won't take that amiss?'

Willie smiled and shook his head. 'If you don't fancy exercise, there's the best collection of jazz records in London, and a pretty good selection of classics.'

'I haven't played squash for three years, but let's give it a whirl. And a swim after.'

'Right. I'll get some gear out.'

When Modesty arrived at two o'clock they had just finished changing after a leisurely half-hour in the residents pool. She sniffed the atmosphere, found it friendly, and was glad.

Quinn said, 'You've missed a hilarious sight. Me wearing Willie's shorts for squash. I looked like Amelia Bloomer.'

She patted his arm and said, 'Have you been behaving yourself, Quinn?'

'After a slightly false start, yes.'

'Willie?'

'Good as gold. You eaten, Princess?'

'I had something on the plane.' She sat on the chesterfield. 'Any luck with René Vaubois?'

'He's put out a red priority call to pick up those three men, but God knows how long it will take. Are you sitting comfortably, Quinn? I want to talk to you.'

'So Willie said. I've been floating in the pool, trying to recap on everything that happened while I was lying on the ledge. I kept coming and going, you know, and there wasn't much anyway, but at least I've been dredging for what there was.'

'Good. Now you were lying there, and for some of the time you watched that bit of road across the gorge, hoping you might signal somebody?'

'I wasn't hoping much. It only took a few seconds for a vehicle to cover that stretch, and it was on a bend, so anyone driving would have their eyes on the road. Well, anyone sane. I couldn't speak for French truck drivers.'

'When I asked about a grey Peugeot, you said you didn't see it go over. But did you see it all?'

'I don't know whether it was a Peugeot, but I saw a grey car parked there for a bit.'

'Parked? You're sure?'

'Of course I'm bloody sure, darling.' He smiled his nice smile. 'I'm only making bold to call you that because it bolsters my ego and stops me being overawed, and hence resenting you. See?'

'Keep it up, then. How long was the car there?'

He shook his head. 'Don't know. Too whoozy. But first the Dormobile thing arrived, then the car came later. They were there together for a bit.'

'A Dormobile?'

'Well, something of the sort. I'm not a student of vans. Two nuns got out of it.'

Modesty and Willie said together: 'Nuns?'

'That's right. Why not? Nuns drive that sort of thing all over the place these days. I can't think why. But haven't you noticed?'

Modesty said slowly to Willie: 'You did say the squeeze was put on Janet's sister by a nun?'

He nodded. Quinn was about to speak, but saw that they were both distant with thought. He had an odd feeling that some almost telepathic exchange was taking place between them. At last Willie said, 'Maybe it's the flux again. Or maybe we 'aven't got two jobs going after all.'

She said, 'But——' then broke off. 'No, let's get the whole story first.' She turned to Quinn, and now it seemed to him that her midnight-blue eyes were almost black. 'Could you start from the van arriving and take it from there?'

'All right. Well, it parked on the bend and two nuns got out. I was a bit loose in the head and thought they were penguins at first. They didn't do anything, just walked about a bit and waited. I tried to signal them, but they didn't see me. Or I suppose they didn't. Then I drifted off again. Do you mind if I have a cigarette?'

'In the box there.'

He lit one and said thoughtfully, 'I've just no idea how much time passed before I came round. The van and the nuns were still there, but now there was this grey car parked a little way behind. And there was a man beside it. He bent down and . . . well, sort of lifted the door off its hinges and put it on top of the car.'

Modesty said, 'Hold on a minute. Car doors don't just lift off.'

'I know. I've been thinking about it in the pool. But that's what he *seemed* to do. He bent down and took hold of the door, and after a bit he just seemed to stand up with it in his hands and put it on top of the car.'

Modesty glanced at Willie, who shook his head. She returned to Quinn. 'All right, then what?'

'Nothing. I mean, there's a bit of a blank. I just have this little snap-shot in my head of the chap with the door. I believe I started looking round for my coat, so I could wave it about, and flaked out again—ah, *that's* right! But I must have come round a few minutes later, because I remember waving then. The nuns were still there, by the van, but the chap had disappeared. No he hadn't. My God, just talking seems to bring it back. There was a kind of bluff bordering the road there, and he was up on top of it. I remember now, he looked like a cross.'

Modesty said, 'You mean he had his arms stretched out? Like this?'

'Don't push that lovely bosom at me, I'm trying to concentrate. No, it must have been like this.' He raised his arms horizontally, then bent them at the elbows to bring his hands close to his face.

Willie said, 'Jesus, he was looking through glasses.'

Quinn blinked, then lifted his hands a little. 'Hey, you're right! So the bastard did see me, but didn't do a thing about it.'

Modesty said, 'He did something about it all right, he sent the muscle in next morning, to make sure of you.'

Quinn looked at her, then at Willie, and finally at his cigarette. 'My God,' he said soberly, 'I'd better start believing it.'

Willie said, 'You were signalling? Waving the coat?'

'Like mad.'

'You said the nuns were still there by the van. And the bloke was on top of the bluff. What about the grey car?'

Quinn closed his eyes and sat very still for a long time. At last he opened them and shook his head apologetically. 'I don't know. I can't *see* it there now, but I'm not sure.'

Modesty said, 'If you saw them drive off, you'd have noticed if the grey car was left.'

'I didn't see any of that. After waving the coat for about two minutes I ran right out of juice and just flopped. I don't mean I passed out. I just lay there.' He grimaced. 'I rather fancy I snivelled a bit. I'm pretty hot on self-pity. By the time I'd dragged myself up to have another go, the road was empty. I didn't hear the engine or anything. They'd just gone.'

It was silent in the big room for a long time. Quinn watched the two faces curiously. They were blank-eyed, and he could almost hear the intensity of thinking behind those eyes.

Willie said, 'Take the door off to account for the body missing.'

Modesty's dark head moved in assent. 'That makes it a snatch.'

'Using nuns, too.'

'There doesn't *have* to be a connection with the squeeze nun.'

'But . . .'

'Yes. Phoney nun and phoney nuns. A bit strong, even for your flux, Willie.'

Quinn said, 'I wouldn't at all mind knowing what you're talking about.'

She looked through him, caught her breath, and pounded a clenched fist gently on her knee in rhythm with her words as she said softly, 'Willie, Willie, Willie . . . of *course.*'

Willie sat up a little, eyes bright. 'You got a connection?'

'We've been assuming Tarrant was taken by an opposition group to be scoured of security information.'

'Not?'

'Listen, when we were theorizing about Janet's trouble we said a psychiatrist's records would be a good source for large-scale blackmail. *So what about all the stuff Tarrant's got in his head?*'

Willie said in a quiet, awed voice, 'Jesus wept.' He got to his feet, picked up Modesty's hand and touched the back of it to his cheek. Smiling, he straightened up and looked at his watch. 'J. Straik, Chateau Lancieux.'

Quinn said, 'What?'

Modesty expelled a long breath of relief, then focused on him. She said, 'Oh, I'm sorry. We were thinking.'

'I guessed that. I'm pretty sharp.'

She stood up, moved behind his chair and rested her hands on his shoulders, kneading the muscles gently. 'Look, Willie and I have to go away for a few days. Did you have any plans?'

'I'm a gentleman of leisure, living on capital at the moment. Not much capital, mind. I've no family left, so I'm just sort of bumming around. The only plan I've got at the moment is to have you tell me what the hell's going on.'

'Would you like to stay here for a bit? Or I've a nice cottage in Wiltshire. We'll arrange cover for you until this is over.'

'Cover? Oh yes, I'm the man who knows too much, aren't I? Are you going to tell me what it is I've spilled that seems so important to you?'

'I can't, Quinn. It's very hush.'

He stood up and turned to face her. 'Don't talk a lot of cock, darling,' he said pleasantly. 'I've already guessed half of it. My Fleet Street mate mentioned Tarrant when he was talking about cloak-and-dagger stuff. Tarrant was in the grey car that went over, wasn't he? Well, no he wasn't, because you now think he was snatched. Something to do with blackmail information. And you're to go galloping off to the rescue. That may not be a hundred percent right, but I do get a bronze medal for trying? Next time don't forget I'm around when you're thinking aloud?'

Modesty studied him a little worriedly. Willie said, 'Better tell 'im, Princess. If 'e knows it all there's less chance of 'im chatting up the Fleet Street bloke again. That could put Tarrant down before we get to 'im.'

Quinn said to her quietly, 'I've got three lives on my conscience, and I don't want another one. You really can rely on me.'

'I know. Come and sit down with me.'

Three minutes later Quinn said, 'So you're going to this Chateau Lancieux, in the Pyrenees, to get him out?'

'Yes.'

'Why can't the French do it? I gather you have influence there.'

She looked at Willie, who lifted his shoulders and made a face, then back at Quinn. 'We think we can do it better. I mean, in actually getting Tarrant out. The French would have to operate within legal limits, and that would mean an official raid on the chateau. It's not quick enough against people ready for trouble. Tarrant would end up dead.'

'So what do you aim to do? Get into the chateau, shoot-up all the opposition, and pull Tarrant out?'

'No. If we can get in, and get Tarrant out without any rumpus, that's fine. The French can see to the rest of it, once he's safe.'

'All right. Now, you said I could stay here or at your cottage.' He looked at her blandly. 'But maybe somebody's still trying to kill me. I'd be much safer under your protection, so hadn't you better take me along?'

She shook her head and stood up. 'No, I'm sorry, but that's out.'

'I might be useful. I could dress up as a nun and go to the chateau begging for alms. You know, casing the joint.'

She gave him a puzzled look. He waved a hand and said, 'Never mind. How do you aim to make this stealthy break-in?'

She shrugged. 'I don't know yet. We'll have to get out there and take a good look at the situation first. Then we'll work something out.'

'Meanwhile Tarrant's being questioned with a lighted match under his toes, or something of that sort?'

Willie said, 'Leave it, Quinn. We'll move as fast as we can.' He turned to Modesty. 'Shall I slip along to Whitehall and put Jack Fraser in the picture?'

'Yes. Do that, Willie.'

He looked at his watch. 'Janet's coming at three, but I ought to be back by then. What do we tell 'er, Princess?'

Modesty made a small helpless gesture. 'The same as we've just told Quinn, I suppose. We'll be holding a Press Conference next. But she's met Tarrant, and you said she knows who he is.'

'Knows 'ow to keep 'er mouth buttoned, too.'

'I don't doubt that. All right. You go and see Fraser. I'll get the large-scale maps out, and the Michelin Guide.'

Lucy Straik said, 'You should just take a look at that crack in the ceiling, Poppa. Some old chatto this is. I bet it must be a hundred *years* old.'

Colonel Jim, sprawled above the soft moist body, lifted his head to look down at her. 'Goddamit, Momma. Can't you pay a little attention?'

She giggled rather breathlessly under his weight. 'I *was* payin' attention, Poppa, but honest to God, you go on so long. Must be half an *hour* ago I hit tops. You're just too greedy all the time. Maybe you should save it up a bit at your age.'

'Poppa don't like that kinda talk, Momma. You start fancying something younger on the hoof, and ——'

'Gee, I never meant *that*. You're great.' She wrapped her arms around him. 'C'mon, now, let's go. Give Momma the old one-two.'

'If Momma's gonna watch cracks in the ceiling she better close her eyes or turn around someway.'

'*Okay.* So let me up a little. There. You're real mean today, Poppa.'

'I can be, honey. If I figure you're finding Poppa a kinda chore. I'll have to liven you up some.'

'You *wouldn't* let that Mr Sexton do anything!'

'Don't count on it. Hey, just the idea's put a squib under you, huh? Right, now . . .'

There was a tap on the door. Colonel Jim swore, then lifted his voice. 'Yeah? What the hell is it?'

'Sorry if you were resting,' Mr Sexton called cheerfully. 'An interesting communication from London.'

'I'll be in the study in five minutes, Mr Sexton. No, make it ten.'

Mr Sexton said, 'Right.'

Lucy giggled. 'Five, I betcha. You know Momma when she puts her mind to it.'

Mr Sexton was standing by the window when Colonel Jim came into the study, wearing a dressing gown over pyjamas, and sat down at the desk.

'You said interesting, Mr Sexton.'

'Yes. For insurance purposes I told your man in London to keep an eye on Modesty Blaise.'

'Good thinking. So?'

A stroke of luck. He made one or two calls to the apartment block where she lives, on various pretexts, and he happened to be in reception last night when a young man arrived drunk and told the porter he wanted to see Modesty Blaise. He gave his name as Quinn, and then Stenmore heard him say, "If that doesn't ring a bell, tell her I'm the bastard she hauled out of the gorge".'

Colonel Jim rested a big hand on the desk, fingers tapping slowly. 'Reckon there's anything he could tell her?'

Mr Sexton shrugged. 'Who knows? But we were going to put him away before, to make sure.'

'Yeah. Even if this Quinn guy saw something and told her, I don't see any way she could locate us. But contingency-wise, we better cover ourselves. Have Stenmore watch her place real close. I want tabs on her. If she makes a move, I want to know where she's headed.'

'I've told him exactly that, Colonel Jim. I also called Ferrand, in Toulouse, and told him to have some eyes standing by so that we can locate her if she heads this way. She'll have Garvin with her, of course.' Mr Sexton chuckled. 'Ferrand said not call on him for any soldiers, because he wouldn't tangle with Modesty Blaise or Willie Garvin under any circumstances. But he'll finger them for us if they come into the area.'

'I don't figure we need any strong-arm help, Mr Sexton.'

'Neither do I.' Mr Sexton smiled happily. 'As a matter of fact, I'm very much hoping they'll come. I believe they're really very good, and it's time I had something to stretch me a little.'

CHAPTER EIGHT

IT WAS TWO HOURS since Quinn had told his tale.

Willie Garvin knelt over a map spread on the floor, measuring with a pair of dividers. Modesty was speaking in French on the telephone.

Quinn sat smoking, unobtrusively studying the woman who was watching Willie. She had arrived an hour ago, a woman as tall as Modesty and perhaps a year or so older, fresh and cool with short chestnut hair, a superb complexion, and light hazel eyes set in strong features. She wore a camel trouser-suit and walked with a slight limp. Her voice and turn of phrase held a flavour of Scotland, but no more than that.

Lady Janet Gillam. Quinn had been a little taken aback by the title; quite impressed, to his annoyance, when he gathered that she was in fact the daughter of the Earl of Strathlan and Inverdall; and delightedly incredulous when he realized that she was Willie Garvin's girl-friend. In many ways Quinn was enjoying himself as he had not enjoyed himself for a long time now. To enter the world of Modesty Blaise and Willie Garvin was, he found, an experience of unceasing interest and one which roused new curiosity in him from hour to hour. It was only marred by the thought of a man who was no more than a name to him. Tarrant.

Quinn had a lively and sensitive imagination. The concept of torture, repugnant enough to any normal mind, produced in him a reaction of physical nausea. He remembered, as a child, running from the Chamber of Horrors at Madame Tussauds because the sight of rack and thumb-screw filled his mind with sickening images and his heart with a sense of wild, unbelieving hatred.

He was keeping all thought of the man Tarrant shut carefully away. This was not too difficult, for the centre of his attention was occupied by something else; an urgent, almost desperate longing. And he was waiting for the right moment to speak.

At the moment Modesty was talking on the phone to a man who, Quinn gathered, had carried out certain illegal activities for her in the Pyrenean border area during years when she ran an organization called *The Network,* of which Duggan had spoken that night in Fleet Street.

She put down the phone and said, 'According to Viret, the Chateau Lancieux lies three kilometres from the nearest village, which is just a cluster of half-a-dozen cottages. Then you've got

Niaux at eight kilometres and Lousset at fifteen. Look up the Michelin for Lousset, Willie, and I'll get Janet booked in there.'

Lady Janet said, 'You'll not be there yourselves, Modesty?'

'No. We'll drop you there, then take to the hills. But you'll be our emergency line of communication. We'll give you two phone numbers, one in France and one here in London.

Lady Janet's smile was a little rueful, and Modesty said, 'It's not a mock-up job, honestly.'

'You'll hardly be able to get in touch with me from the hills. What sort of emergency were you thinking of?'

'If we're not back before a deadline we'll give you, then you'll know something's gone wrong.'

'Oh.' Lady Janet looked down thoughtfully at her hands.

'Or it's just possible we might ring you from the chateau, depending on how things work out there.'

Willie looked up. 'There's a phone-line?'

'So Viret said. The Germans used the chateau as their head-quarters for patrolling the escape routes to Spain during the war. Apparently it's changed hands several times since then, and dirt cheap because it's a white elephant. He doesn't know who's there now.'

Quinn said, 'Lady Janet, how did you persuade these two to take you along on this?'

'Janet, please.'

'Thank you. How did you persuade them?'

She looked at Modesty. 'I'm not at all sure.'

Willie, a finger on the Michelin Guide, said, 'There's *Le Lion Rouge*. Twelve rooms, central-'eating, bidet, bath and parking. Plain but adequate. Fairly comfortable restaurant. That do you, Jan?'

'Anywhere I don't have to get up at five and milk cows is five-star for me.'

Quinn said, 'Make it two rooms, Modesty.'

She looked at him with suppressed impatience and said, 'We've been into all that.'

'Ah, but we haven't, my little wham-bam sweetheart. There are matters you wot not of. For example, have you ever done any caving? Pot-holing?' He lifted a hand. 'No, don't shoot me down. I'm serious.'

She looked at him suspiciously. 'All right. We've done very little. Carlswark Cave in the Peak District and Eastwater Swallet in the Mendips. Just to see what it was like. It didn't have much appeal for either of us, so that was all.'

'It's just what happens to grab you. I liked it. Haven't done much this year, but it was my only hobby for about four years.'

Janet said, 'What does it have to do with the situation, Mr Quinn?'

'Just Quinn, please. I'm glad you asked me that.' He looked at Modesty. 'What it has to do with the situation is that you want to find a sneaky way of getting into the Chateau Lancieux. And good old pot-holer Quinn can show you the way.'

Willie got up from the floor. Modesty took a cigarette and sat down on the arm of the chesterfield, watching Quinn. 'I knew you had something brewing up,' she said. 'A cave?'

'Verily a cave. If you don't know it already, that area's stiff with caves. It's a calcareous region. You've got the tourist caves at Mas d'Azil, at Labouiche, and at Niaux. But there are dozens of caves and grottos all around the Ariège. I spent three weeks there with a club one summer, and we had a French instructor who took us into half a dozen different holes that few people in the area even knew existed. There was one he called the Lancieux Cave.'

Modesty said, 'You mean it actually leads into the chateau?'

'No, it's a bit trickier than that. As a cave, it would be classified as moderate. That means a few tough patches here and there. We covered about a mile. I don't remember the details, except that there's one place where an underground river widens out into a small lake, and you need a rubber dinghy. But the main point is this. There were all sorts of passages leading off the main run, and about half a mile in there was a kind of water-slide on one side. Fairly broad, like a chute leading up, and with a few inches of water running down the middle of it. The instructor said he'd climbed it once, and it led to the chateau. I'm not sure which part, but I suppose it would be the kitchens or the dungeons if they still exist.'

Willie said, 'A sort of garbage chute from the kitchens?'

Quinn rubbed his chin. 'I've just remembered what made me mention dungeons. He said some old skeleton had been found at the bottom of the chute. I mean, very old. They reckoned it could only have come down from above, and was probably the remains of somebody who'd been quietly got rid of, back in whatever century. But if the corpse did come down the chute, it implies a hole at the top big enough to bung a body through.'

Willie said, 'There could be a grille at the top now.' He looked at Modesty. 'All the same, it's a bloody marvellous chance, Princess. With tools, we could lever a grille out.'

Modesty said to Quinn, 'Where's the entrance to the cave?'

He laughed, and spread a hand. 'Have a heart, darling. How the hell does anyone describe how to find a crack in the side of a valley in the Pyrenees? I know I didn't even *see* the chateau while we were above ground, so it must be on the other side of a ridge. But I don't know which ridge, or which crack. I can take you there. I remember the road and the track, and the lie of the land when we left the track. But I can't tell it.'

Modesty stood up and inhaled on her cigarette. 'Could you find it after dark?'

He shook his head positively. 'No. Much too confusing. I'd want to reach the valley with half an hour of light to spare. And I'll have to come into the cave with you, to show you where the chute lies, or you could miss it.'

Modesty looked at Willie. 'It's tempting,' she said quietly. 'But it's too close, Willie. We've no right to put him in the firing line.'

Quinn hit the arm of his chair with a fist. 'Don't be bloody stupid!' he said furiously. 'Look, I'm not an idiot. I'm not going to come charging in with you and start leaping about, kicking people in the jaw. I know very well that's not my line, for God's sake.' He leaned forward, and she saw the gleam of damp on his brow. 'There's a man being . . . being tortured, perhaps as we're sitting here. Is that so? If somebody doesn't get to him, he's finished. Now look, I've killed three innocent souls. That's good old Quinn's record. And this is probably the only chance I'll ever have to help *save* anyone. So don't stand there like a bloody pudding and tell me I mustn't!'

There was a startled silence. Lady Janet looked curiously at Modesty. She stood with eyebrows raised high and startled amusement in her face as she spoke. 'Well, I'll say one thing for you, Quinn. You're original. I've never been called a pudding before.'

The humour faded She was silent for a little while, then went on slowly. 'I think they'll be taking their time about breaking Tarrant. But even so, you're right, he could be getting badly hurt at this moment.' She moved to the phone. 'You know, there are times when I like you quite a bit, Quinn. All right, two rooms.'

With a hand on the phone, she paused and looked at Willie. 'Have you got all the gear we might need, down at *The Tread-mill*? I mean, for the caving bit.'

He thought for a few moments, then nodded. 'I reckon so. I'll go over it with Quinn, then run down and pick it up.'

'Take Janet, so she can pack a case and get her passport. When I've booked the rooms I'll call Dave Craythorpe and see if he can fly us over to Toulouse tonight. There's an airfield there at

Blagnat. If we leave by eleven, we could check the cave at first light, do a recce of the area round the castle by day, and be all set to go in tomorrow night.'

Quinn said diffidently, 'Couldn't you go straight in?'

'By day? No, it's too risky for Tarrant. If there's trouble, he could get hurt, so we don't want trouble. Just quietly in and quietly out. We also don't want to bring him out by the cave. He's not young and he won't be in good shape. So we have to know our getaway route by dark, and that means a long and careful day's work.'

Ten minutes later, at the wheel of his Jensen heading for the M4, Willie said, 'What's up, Jan?'

She gave a strained little laugh. 'It's all going so fast!'

'It's got to, love. If you feel you'd rather pull out——'

'No,' she said sharply. Then, very quietly, 'I felt like a bloody little mouse sitting there. I've never seen that aspect of Her Highness before, and it's a bit frightening.'

Willie grinned. 'She's on our side, remember.'

'I didn't mean that. She was so damn good it was overpowering. When you feel your personality being swamped, you don't like it, and I was beginning not to like her one bit.'

'You swamped? With six 'undred years of noble Scottish blood behind you? Come off it, Jan. Head waiters cringe when you walk in, even before they know who you are.'

'They bow and scrape for you too, Willie, even with that Bow Bells accent. You know why? Confidence. You're a reflection of her.' He glanced at her, but she did not look annoyed, only puzzled and perhaps wryly amused as she said, 'I was just starting to hate her when Quinn called her a pudding. I thought she'd flay him, but no. She was damn near giggling inside, I could tell. She really liked him for it. And *I* liked her for that.'

'Well, she's got a sense of 'umour, Jan. Like a kid she is sometimes.'

'Aye. I should think she's like all kinds of different things sometimes, Willie.'

At eight the next morning, Lady Janet Gillam woke in a small room with flower-pattern paper on the walls and home-woven rugs scattered on a well-polished if creaking floor, six hundred miles from London.

She had not expected to sleep, but had done so as soon as her head touched the pillow, three hours ago. She lay trying to dispel the strange feeling that she was in a world not quite real.

The Cessna had taken off only a few minutes after ten. She remembered feeling taut with a blend of excitement and apprehension. Before they gained cruising height, Modesty and Willie were asleep, slumped in their back-tilted seats. Quinn caught her eye, jerked his head at them and said, 'Makes you sick, doesn't it? I'm tired as hell, but I'd need a couple of sleeping pills to do that right now.'

Her rueful smile showed fellow-feeling. 'It's an enviable gift. I have some pills if you want one.'

'Thanks, but I'll probably be blundering about the Pyrenees by dawn, and I don't want to be in a stupor.' He indicated Willie. 'I've only spent a few hours with him, but I'd say you've got quite a character there.'

'Yes. So have you.'

'Modesty? I don't think I've exactly got her. But while it lasts I'm finding her a unique experience. Half the time she treats me as if she was my mum.'

'But the other half?'

'That's quite a bit different. Mind you, there hasn't really been a great deal of time overall, but she does pack it in. Do you have the feeling that you're not really here, and that you'll wake up at home any minute?'

'You too? Thank God for that, Quinn.'

'Join the club.' He reached out politely and shook her hand. 'I've got a pocket chess set. Do you play?'

'Badly. Willie murders me.' She looked at the sleeping figures. 'You know what those two do? Play chess in their heads.'

'Pair of bastards. You sound as if you're in my league though. How about it?'

'All right.'

She played two games with Quinn, then spent an hour sitting with the pilot, Dave Craythorpe, a lanky man of about forty with thinning hair. Uncommunicative at first, his manner changed when he learned that she held a Private Pilot's Licence with an Instrument Rating, and after talking technicalities for a while he allowed her to take the controls for half an hour.

Soon after two a.m. they landed at Blagnat. Two cars were waiting for them there, delivered by a car-hire firm in Toulouse. They completed formalities, picked up the car-keys at the airfield office, and drove off south. At four they stopped a mile short of Lousset, a small village by a tributary of the Ariège. Quinn took over the wheel of Willie's car and drove on with Janet to *Le Lion Rouge*.

The patron was expecting them, but Janet felt that he would have been undisturbed by their arrival at this early hour anyway. Her French was limited but sufficient, and her ear did not have to cope with a local patois since the patron had come from Rouen twenty years earlier. She learned that since it was so late in the year only two other rooms in the inn were occupied, each by an elderly French gentleman. Both were residents, and it was their habit to quarrel continually. The patron hoped that madame and m'sieu would not find this annoying, and would understand that it was not serious.

Janet explained that her brother, Mr Quinn, had unfortunately left his brief-case at the garage in Toulouse where they had hired the car. It contained important notes for the book he was writing, and he intended to drive back there at once.

The patron clucked his sympathy, showed them their rooms, hoped that madame would sleep well after her tiring journey, and saw m'sieu off, promising he would try to ensure that the French gentlemen quarrelled quietly in the morning so that m'sieu could sleep soundly on his return.

Lying in the warm bed, and looking out through the latticed window on the new day, Janet wondered what the others were doing at this moment. A frisson of unease touched her. Apart from one occasion she had never known when Willie Garvin was engaged in something of this kind. He did not tell her, though sometimes she guessed on his return. She knew little but fragmentary details of anything he had done with Modesty. But this was happening now, and very close. Close enough for her to feel a part of it. Her mouth twitched in a dry smile. Well, this was what she had wanted.

There was a soft tap on the door. She sat up and called, 'Entrez.'

The door opened and Quinn put his head round it. He was unshaven and looked tired but content. 'Good morning, Sister Janet. Did I wake you?'

'No, I came round five minutes ago. Lord, it's good to see you, Quinn.'

'All right if I come in?'

'Vanity says no, but curiosity says yes. I must look a gummy-eyed mess, but you've seen me now, anyway.'

Quinn pushed the door to, moved to an upright chair by the window and sat down. 'To be honest,' he said, 'I was just thinking how bloody marvellous you look. It's grossly unfair. You're one of those people who always seem to have just stepped out of a bath even when they haven't. It must be the complexion.'

She was pleased, and let her smile show it. 'Country wench.'

'No, you don't give that impression at all. It's a child's complexion.'

'I can give you five years, Quinn.'

'Really? I seem to be having a phase for older women.' His grin was engaging. 'You've no idea what a kick I'm getting out of chatting with the daughter of a belted earl in her boudoir. I must have a servile streak in me somewhere.'

She looked at him curiously. 'Willie said you could be a bit savage, but I haven't noticed it yet.'

'Oh, I can, Janet. I can. I'm all bitter and twisted inside. But . . .'

'But what?'

'Well, I don't really know. Modesty was uncommonly kind to me after I'd behaved like a pig, and then Willie gave me a thundering great clout over the ear'ole, and I've felt better ever since. Do you want breakfast now?'

'I want to know what happened this morning.'

'Well . . . nothing special, but it was exciting in a weird kind of way. We hid the cars about three miles from the cave entrance, and went across country on foot. Willie and Modesty were humping a great load of gear apiece, but they wouldn't let me help and it didn't seem to bother them. Do you mind if I smoke?'

When he had lit the cigarette, he said, 'They were working from a blow-up of some map. I said I only knew the way by the track, but they said we'd strike that later, and they were right, even though it was still half-dark for the first two miles. Anyway, we sighted the track, I got my bearings, and we were in this valley at first light.'

'And you found the cave?'

'It only took me twenty minutes. I remembered better than I thought. And inside it was much the way I'd been trying to recollect during the flight out. There's a twisty bit at first, and a long steep descent, then a fifteen-foot pot and a traverse along a stream until you come to the stalactite chamber. That's quite a sight. It's crossed by another stream, or maybe the same one, except it's not a stream any more, but a lake. We used the little inflatable boat for that, one at a time.'

'It's deep?'

'God, yes. A freak thing. When I first did the cave, our instructor lowered a weight on forty-feet of cord, and didn't find bottom. It's like a water-filled pot-hole. But we'd have used the boat anyway, rather than wade. You always stay dry as long as you can when you're caving. Too much loss of body-heat once you're wet.'

He half closed his eyes, remembering. 'Well, then there's a squeeze through a bedding plane. That was a bit tight for Willie, but he made it. After that you have to get up a ten foot pitch, and the rest is straightforward. I showed them the water-chute, the slide leading up to the chateau, and then we came out.'

Lady Janet stared out through the window at the bright sunshine, trying to feel the dank iciness, to see the ancient blackness yielding to the gleam of lamplight. The cave was like some huge sprawling animal, she thought, which had lain underground for a million years. She said, 'They didn't go up the slide to see if there was a grille at the top?'

'No. They'll do that tonight. They've left all the gear there, and they seem pretty sure they'll cope with a grille if there is one.'

'Where are they now?'

'Heading back to the castle to have a good look at it.'

'Back?'

'Oh, yes. When we came out of the cave, they saw me safely to where we'd left the cars. That's when it got weird. We were crossing a series of valleys. We'd lie flat, just looking for about five minutes. Then Willie would move down and up to the next ridge. He didn't seem to hurry, but God he was covering ground fast. He'd disappear, sort of fade into the ground, and we'd watch for another couple of minutes before Modesty and I moved. They'd each got an automatic rifle, an M16 she called it. So they were covering each other at every move.'

'Why was it weird?'

'Well . . . you don't exactly think of them as a cautious pair, but they were concentrating like hell and taking no chances at all.'

'I find that comforting.'

'So do I. And it's weird seeing them work together. They hardly talk at all, but they operate like one pair of hands.'

'Yes.' Lady Janet stubbed out her cigarette. 'Well, I suppose that's comforting too.' Quinn looked at her quickly but said nothing. After a moment she smiled and said, 'I'll get up and have a bath now. You'd better catch up on some sleep, Quinn.'

He suppressed a yawn. 'Will you wake me at noon?'

'Yes. When are Modesty and Willie going to get any sleep?'

'Between dusk and when they aim to enter the chateau, about three a.m. They'll sleep in the cave. We left food and gear there.'

She closed her eyes for a moment, then opened them again. 'I'm glad you brought your pocket chess, Quinn. I don't fancy you or I will be sleeping much tonight.'

*   *   *

Lying prone on a table pushed against the window, Mr Sexton lowered the field-glasses and murmured, 'They're as good as their reputation, which is very good indeed.'

Colonel Jim said, 'You still can't spot 'em?'

'Not a sign.' Mr Sexton slid back off the table and moved away from the window. 'And I've been scanning from different positions for a couple of hours now.'

Mellish looked up from the notes he was studying. 'They may not be out there.'

'They're out there all right.' Mr Sexton smiled. 'They're making a very careful reconnaissance to find the best way in and the best way out. The only thing that puzzles me is why they've brought in that pair at *Le Lion Rouge*. Blaise and Garvin always work alone.'

Colonel Jim rubbed a big hand aganst a heavy jowl. 'When d'you figure they'll try it?'

'Oh, tonight. They know Tarrant's on the griddle, so they're up against time.'

'That's my thinking, too. Question is, how they'll try it.'

Mr Sexton shrugged. 'There are various possibilities, none very good, and we'll be ready for them all.' He looked at his watch. 'Clare and Angel should be back soon, and we might learn something useful then.'

'Yeah.' Colonel Jim mixed himself a drink, frowning. 'What's bugging me is how they homed-in on us here. Maybe this Quinn saw something when you picked up Tarrant, but that wouldn't give 'em the chateau. So where's the leak?'

'It's certainly a question that needs answering,' agreed Mr Sexton cheerfully. 'But once we've got Blaise and Garvin we'll soon find out.'

Lady Janet and Quinn sat in the small lounge of *Le Lion Rouge*. They had finished lunch an hour ago, a lunch made entertaining by the energetic quarrelling of the two elderly Frenchmen the patron had spoken of. These two had now retired to an enclosed sun terrace at the back of the inn and were playing an acrimonious game of cards.

Lady Janet said, 'Will you take another flying job?'

'I don't know.' Quinn looked at the dregs in his coffee cup. 'I haven't thought much about it. Airlines don't like pilots who get their passengers killed off. Would *you* like to fly with a chap who'd done that?'

'It wouldn't worry me. I think you had awful bad luck. But if the airlines feel that way, there are other flying jobs. I've a brother-in-law in the States who might help. He owns an air-freight company, among other things.'

'You're very kind.' He looked at her in silence for a while, his young face curious. 'It must be a bit rotten for you. About Modesty and Willie. I don't mean now, I mean generally.'

For a moment she stared him down, the cold pride of generations of Covenanters in her eyes. 'I've no wish for sympathy, Quinn.'

'I'm sorry——'

She raised a hand to stop him, her expression changing. 'No, I didn't mean to snap at you. I'm a wee bit over-touchy on that point, maybe. All right, it's something I've learned to live with. When I first met her and saw what she was to Willie, I had a bad attack of the hates. I think any woman would have. But that's long over now.'

'You like her?'

Lady Janet lifted an eyebrow at him, then gave a small shrug. 'I respect her. She never competes, never patronises, never uses her influence over Willie or so much as lets it show. I value her goodwill. It comes to me through Willie, but it's no less real for that, and it's a very positive thing. But we'll never be cosy intimates, having long sessions of girl-talk together.'

She paused, thinking, then went on slowly. 'There's another thing. I like Willie better than any man I've known. He's very intelligent, and kind, and he has a great gift for understanding a woman.' She half-smiled. 'Above all, he cheers you up, and there aren't too many you can say that about these days. But he wasn't always the way he is now, Quinn. He says he used to be a very nasty character indeed until Modesty came along and bought him out of gaol somewhere out East, years ago.'

'That's when he started working for her?'

'Yes. As far as I can make out, it was something like being reborn for Willie. So whatever he is now, she made him that way, and I've her to thank for it.'

Quinn eyed her with respect and said thoughtfully, 'Not many women would, though.' He looked about him and lowered his voice. 'This waiting's a hell of a business, isn't it?'

'Awful.' She looked at her watch. Tomorrow at noon, if there had been no word from Modesty and Willie, she was to make two phone-calls. Both were restricted numbers, one for a man called Vaubois in Paris, another for a man called Fraser in London. She was simply to say that Modesty and Willie had gone into the Chateau Lancieux to find their friend, and had not returned.

Lady Janet felt slightly sick, imagining how it would be next day, as the morning wore on, if no word came.

Quinn said, 'Have you hurt your foot? I noticed you limping a bit.'

'I've half a leg missing. This one. I lost it in a car smash a few years back.'

'Oh, Lord.' He rubbed his eyes with finger and thumb. 'Sorry, love. Old Quinn isn't exactly a master of tact.'

'It was a natural question. Old Quinn worries too much, probably because he's still pretty young.'

'I'm going to put on about ten years in the next twenty hours.'

'And I'll be a hag by midnight. Do you know exactly what they aim to do, once they get in?'

'Not exactly. But I gather the general aim is to locate the baddies and immobilize them, then find Tarrant at leisure, phone us here to stop worrying, and bring him away.'

'How does the immobilizing bit work?'

'Quietly, they hope. They have an interesting range of equipment, including ether sprays and suchlike, but if they run into anyone on the hoof I suppose they'll be rather brusque with them.' He reflected for a moment or two. 'I've actually seen Modesty flatten three men in about five seconds. If Willie's as good, which I don't doubt, then we've reason to feel encouraged, haven't we.'

She patted his hand. 'Keep telling me that every hour on the hour.'

The patron entered the lounge. 'Excuse me, madame. An English lady has come. She speaks no French and I do not understand what she desires. Would you have the kindness to speak to her?'

At the first mention of an English lady, Quinn and Janet had stood up, excitement leaping between them. Now they exchanged a wry look, and Quinn said, 'It couldn't have been Modesty anyway. Much too soon.'

'We'd better go and see what she wants.'

A woman was waiting in the small courtyard. She wore a light motoring coat and a head-scarf. The hair peeping from beneath the scarf was sandy-gold. The features were strong, but the thin high-bridged nose gave a slightly predatory impression.

Lady Janet said, 'Can we help you? I speak a little French.'

The wide-set eyes lit up with relief. 'Lord above, you're Scottish, surely?'

Lady Janet smiled politely. 'We seem to get everywhere, don't we? What's the trouble?'

'I'm travelling with my niece, and we've broken down a few hundred yards along the road. It's my own silly fault, I'm afraid. They told me at the garage where we hired the car that the needle on the fuel-gauge was reading proud, but I forgot.'

Quinn said, 'It's just petrol?'

'Aye, I'm sure it is. I had a spare can, and put that in, but the battery ran flat before enough petrol came through to the carburettor—at least that's what Angelica said. I'm a fool with such things.'

'There's a little garage here,' said Lady Janet. 'They'll give you a tow-start.'

'My dear, I've been there. The wee man's out and his wife says he'll not be back for two hours.'

Quinn said, 'Never mind. We'll drive you back and give you a tow.'

'Och, that's awfully kind of you.'

Five minutes later, where the road dipped in a long hollow, Quinn pulled in front of a blue estate car, a Citroen Safari, and backed up to it. A pretty girl in a short white dress stood on the verge beside the car. Quinn opened his door to get out, then heard a little gasp. He turned his head and froze. In the passenger seat beside him, Janet sat with her head tilted awkwardly back, her face draining of colour. The Scotswoman sitting behind her said, 'Stay where you are please, Mr Quinn.' She was holding Janet by the hair with one hand, pulling her head back. In the other hand was a slim knife, its point pricking the side of Janet's neck. The woman said, 'I've only to push it in just a wee half inch and she's dead, Mr Quinn.'

The girl in the white dress stood by Quinn's door now. She giggled and said, 'She'll bleeding well do it, too, you can bet your balls on that, whacker.'

'We'll have no smut, thank you, Angel,' the Scotswoman said severely. 'Get back in the car and don't drive too fast, Mr Quinn, you'll follow her. I wouldn't advise any foolishness, like braking suddenly. It just needs a quick jab in this big artery here, you understand? We'll be stopping in a mile or two, to leave your car and change to ours, and you'll be given no chance for heroics, Mr Quinn. Angel has a silenced gun in that handbag. Now, have I made everything quite clear?'

White-faced, hands shaking on the wheel, Quinn nodded slowly. Angel slammed the door, and from the corner of his eye he saw Janet wince as the knife pricked her neck with the shudder of the car. He watched the Citroen pull out past him, then switched on and moved off carefully. His limbs felt leaden, and his mind was in chaos.

Fifty minutes later, lying face to face with Janet on a thick car rug spread on the Safari floor, their arms passed about each other's body and their wrists manacled, Quinn glimpsed the chateau through the off-side window. It stood halfway up the long slope they were now mounting by a dusty track which zig-zagged up from the valley. The Scotswoman was driving, unbelievably delivering a monologue about a crochet pattern to the girl beside her, Angel, who seemed from her lack of response to be not even mildly interested.

It came to Quinn that from somewhere in the valley, Modesty Blaise and Willie Garvin would be watching at this moment. They would have seen the Citroen leave the chateau, and were now marking its return. If they were using glasses, if they spotted him in the car . . .

Hampered by Janet's weight on his arm, he tried to lift his head and shoulders. Without turning round Angel said, 'You want to know what I'll do if you don't keep your bleedin' 'ead down, Quinnie?' He twisted his head and saw her eyes in the mirror. She had adjusted it so that she could watch them in the back. To Quinn those eyes were an outrage in the pretty young face. They held glints of childish pleasure in things unspeakable, the amusement of a small devil in hell.

She said, 'What I'll do is 'op over there and twist me piano wire round that toffee-nosed bird's neck. Then you can watch 'er tongue turn black, Quinnie. You ever seen that? It's a real giggle.' She sniggered and nudged the woman beside her. 'Go on, let's 'ave a bit of fun anyway, Clare. We can always say she started yelling or something.'

'You'll do no such thing, Angel dear,' Clare said firmly. 'I'll not tell lies to Colonel Jim for you. He said to fetch them back in prime condition, and in prime condition we'll fetch them back, young lady.'

'Ah, bollocks,' Angel said sulkily.

Quinn rested his head, dazed with horror. Janet's face was only a few inches from his. She was still pale, but there was a dour set to her mouth, and though her eyes held no hope they were calm. She moved to touch his cheek with her lips briefly, then drew back her head again and whispered, 'Hang on, Quinn.'

It was the voice of the aristocrat in the tumbril. There was nothing left to cling to, except pride.

CHAPTER NINE

MODESTY BLAISE WOKE UP and lay quietly in her sleeping-bag for a few seconds in the total darkness. Beside her Willie stirred and said, 'Two o'clock, Princess?'

'It should be. Just a moment.' She flashed the beam of a pencil-torch on her watch. 'Five minutes to. Light the lamp, Willie.'

He sat up, and she held the beam on the pressure lamp for him while he lit it. They were fifty yards from the cave entrance, on a broad stretch of dry rock and with a sharp dog-leg of tunnel between them and the opening in the valley-side. Under their denim shirts and slacks they both wore woollen tights and string vests. Even so it was cold when they emerged from the warmth of the sleeping-bags.

They put on light quilted jackets, combat boots, and nylon overalls, then rolled up the sleeping-bags and set them in a vertical crevice. Willie rested a hand on a long canvas bag with shoulder-straps attached, and said, 'We taking the rifles?'

She thought for a moment, then shook her head. 'They're a damn nuisance to carry on a sneak-job, and if it does come to a shoot-out we'll be in the close-quarter business.' A Colt .32 was holstered on her thigh, beneath the jacket and overalls which she would be taking off once they were inside the chateau.

Willie carried two throwing-knives. Usually he wore them in twin sheaths strapped in echelon on his left breast. Tonight, because there was an awkward squeeze to face, he carried one knife at each hip under the overalls. They were from a range of knives he made with his own hands. These two had a modified Bowie-style tip with a straight back-edge. The blade was diamond-shaped in cross-section for strength, carried a quarter-inch brass strip on the back, and was blued to cut reflection at night. The full tang was set in a haft of Gerber Armorhide, a metal alloy with a finish like sharkskin, moulded with a concave sweep between the butt and the brass face where the tang entered the haft. Both knives had been carefully balanced to make a full revolution in twelve feet with a normal throw, but this could be varied by wrist-action at the moment of release. His accuracy with them was incomparable.

Modesty put a bulging haversack in the crevice with the rifles and sleeping-bags, looked at her watch and said, 'Two-fifteen, Willie.'

'Right.' He swung a rucksack on to his back, and together they began the journey into the Lancieux Cave. Electric lamps were clipped to the front of their plastic helmets. Willie had put out the pressure lamp and was carrying it as a reserve. The cold grew more penetrating as they moved on, but they registered it only on their exposed hands and faces.

Modesty led the way. There was no obvious main route, but the way Quinn had taken was fixed in her mind. Sometimes they moved through narrow passages, sometimes the walls fell back. Underfoot the rock was wrinkled and pitted, demanding wariness. The convoluted maze was no man-made thing with level floors and vertical walls to serve the two small creatures now violating its ancient privacy. It had been shaped by Nature's freakish hand over infinite millenia and many an Ice-Age.

Yet when they had descended the fifteen-foot pot and traversed the sloping wall that leaned outwards from a shallow stream, they reached a huge stalactite chamber which seemed to echo man's architecture, though it had been shaped eons before man's fore-bears used the first primitive tool. The roof rose in a vast dome seventy feet high. The stalactites that hung from it were small, few more than an arm's length, but they were tightly clustered and glinted like great silver needles in the lamplight. There were no stalagmites rising from the floor. The walls were wrinkled like curtains. Around the perimeter shimmered white patches of the calcite deposit called moonmilk.

The floor of the chamber was split by what might have been a wide stream but was in fact a pool of unknown depth. Twenty-three feet wide, it extended from wall to wall. The banks of rock did not slope gently into the pool, but dropped abruptly from eighteen inches above the surface. Whatever the source of the waters that fed it, and whatever the outlet, both were hidden. On the surface, no current was perceptible.

The miniature rubber dinghy had been left inflated and tucked out of sight in a hollow close to the wall of the chamber. Willie set it on the water. Modesty got in very carefully, facing the way they had come, then paddled with her hands to send the little craft drifting across to the far side. Willie held the end of a thin nylon rope attached to the stern. When Modesty had climbed out he drew the rope in, made the crossing himself, and set the dinghy behind a low outcrop of rock. Beyond the pool lay a stretch of flat ground giving way to a slope of irregular dripstone steps which rose to the far wall of the chamber.

Three rifts pierced this wall. Modesty led the way into the

smallest, which lay on the right and offered a narrow triangular passage through which they crawled for eighty yards on hands and knees. It ended in a grotto with a slot-like, almost horizontal opening between two layers of rock. This bedding-plane squeeze extended for fifteen yards, and five minutes passed while Willie edged his bulk through inch by inch. Beyond the squeeze the going was easy, apart from the ascent of a ten-foot pitch. Here a short electron ladder had been set up during their trip with Quinn, using a maypole of heavy-duty aluminium alloy.

A hundred yards beyond the pitch lay the point where the slide from the chateau pierced the passage at an angle. The floor of the slide was five feet broad. Down its centre ran a trough or depression carrying a rapid flow of water a foot deep. The water debouched into the passage where Modesty and Willie stood, spreading to fill a shallow stream-bed at their feet as it crossed the passage diagonally, to vanish into a swallet some distance from them on the far side.

They had left ropes, pitons and a copper-headed hammer beneath an undercut in the rock when Quinn had brought them to this point twenty hours earlier. He had not been able to tell them the length of the slide, but after studying it they had assumed that it ran fairly straight and at a rising angle of no more than forty degrees overall.

Willie put the pressure lamp in a crevice to one side of the chute, set down his rucksack and looked at Modesty. She nodded, and bent to pick up a coil of rope and the canvas bag containing the pitons and hammer. Willie eased himself carefully into a face-down position to the left of the tumbling water, where there was a slightly greater width than was offered on the other side of the trough, and began seeking niches in the slimy rock for fingertips and boot-tips.

After a few moments he began to edge up the slope like some monstrous crawling insect. When he had gained a few yards, Modesty started after him. One end of a long rope was looped round her elbow. The other end was tied to the rucksack and to the bag with the pitons and hammer. The hope was that the pitons would not be needed. If they were, the soft copperhead of the hammer would cut noise to a minimum.

After thirty feet Willie paused for a while, then turned on his back. In the light of her helmet-lamp Modesty saw that for a few feet the floor of the slide rose steeply; but the roof was low here, and stippled with nodules, making it possible to use hands and feet for edging up the slope with a chimneying technique.

Beyond the steep incline the slide resumed its forty degree gradient, and after another twenty feet Willie stopped again. The floor was wider here. He edged over and beckoned. Modesty came up beside him. Four feet ahead of them was a vertical wall of rock, the height of a man. The lower part of it was natural, the stream emerging from a submerged opening at the base of the wall. At a height of three feet the wall became man-made, of rough-hewn stone blocks bonded by mortar. Centred above the stream at this point was a slot like a giant letterbox, four feet wide and half as deep. There was no grille, but set in the thickness of the wall were three stubs of rusting iron, the bases of heavy bars which had once guarded the aperture.

Modesty wriggled forward, hooked a hand over the edge of the slot, and stood up, straddling the gushing water. Slipping the loop of rope from her arm, she hooked it over one of the iron stubs, unclipped the lamp from her helmet, and bent forward across the two-foot thickness of the wall. The beam of the lamp showed a cobwebbed cellar. Dust lay thickly on the flagstones. To one side was a short flight of stone steps leading to a heavy wooden door. The cellar was vaulted, and the light of her lamp could not penetrate the full extent of it, but this section seemed to have been used as a workshop at some time, probably during the German occupation. Along one wall stood a massive wooden bench with a vice bolted to the front of it. On the wall above it were racks for tools, empty now. Under the bench stood a cluster of rusting jerricans, bottles, cans of paint and grease, and a variety of screw-top containers. Two large and grimy high-voltage bulbs hung from flex above the bench.

She drew back, nodded to Willie, then threw one leg over the edge of the slit and wriggled through, swivelling on her belly to lower her feet to the cellar floor. She stood up, moved the beam slowly round, then bent and beckoned to Willie.

He was halfway through the slot, and swivelling to bring his legs round, when the lights in the cellar went on. Head twisted awkwardly, he saw in the limited area of vision offered by the slot that a man had moved out from behind the nearest pillar, a fair, bearded, smiling man in a black blazer. Modesty had dropped the lamp and was moving fast. She had already covered half the distance that lay between her and the smiling man. The instant surge of alarm in Willie eased a little. The man was empty-handed and alone. She would have him before he could draw breath to shout.

Swinging round, he slithered backwards through the slot, and as his feet touched the floor he heard the sound of a soft impact, a gasp, and the scuffling thud of a body crumpling to the floor.

He straightened up and turned, whispering, 'Blimey, Princess, d'you reckon they——?' Shock hit him, a series of shocks compressed into high frequency. She lay huddled limply on the dusty floor, her helmet rolling away. The bearded man was in mid-air, hurtling at him in a huge leap, poised to perfection, one foot driving out like a piston to strike under the heart.

There was no time for thought. Instinct twitched his body in an awkward, unbalanced evasion. The foot scored across his ribs in a glancing blow, and he stumbled sideways, fighting for control, desperately aware that the bulky clothing hampered his speed and that he faced an opponent of dazzling skill. The bearded man landed perfectly, and rose again as if from a trampoline. He touched down just out of arm's reach, swayed sideways, moved in with the speed of a darting lizard, then struck almost casually with the edge of his right hand.

Still off balance, Willie Garvin caught the wrist and kicked for the knee. In one fluid movement the bearded man broke the hold, moved his leg to evade the kick and swung the same leg incredibly high to take Willie on the side of the head with the sole of the foot. Lights exploding before his eyes, Willie reeled back. The strength shown by the breaking of the wrist-grip piled new shock upon all that had gone before. He let himself go, falling so that he would hit the floor in a backward breakfall and could then try for an upward kick as the man came in. But the head-blow had confused his sense of direction. The bench was behind him now, and he fell back obliquely on to the pointed anvil of the vice.

Pain exploded in his shoulder with paralysing effect. He lurched sideways, clawing for a hold on the bench, and lunging feebly with one foot at the blurred figure that swam into his vision. The man in the black blazer brushed the kick aside, then chopped with carefully controlled force between the hinge of the jaw and the ear.

Willie Garvin slithered to the ground and lay still.

Mr Sexton peered into the depths of the cellar where the light failed to penetrate, and said, 'All over, Colonel Jim.'

Colonel Jim moved out of the shadows. Da Cruz was beside him, carrying a machine pistol, a 9mm Stechkin with a 20-round staggered-row box magazine. Mr Sexton bent over Modesty Blaise, lifted an eyelid with his thumb, then straightened up. Colonel Jim said, 'They better be alive, like I told you, Mr Sexton.'

'Prime condition,' Mr Sexton said cheerfully. He glanced across at Willie Garvin. 'Well, not quite. I'm afraid Garvin's damaged a little. He fell against that vice.'

Colonel Jim's shark-like mouth opened in a chuckle. 'That don't bother me none.'

'It's annoying for me, though.' Mr Sexton fingered his short beard. 'I was looking forward to a really interesting bout later.'

'Didn't look like they could give you much trouble, Mr Sexton.'

The fair man's eyes twinkled. 'It's all relative, but they're extremely good, you know.' He glanced at Modesty. 'She had no chance, of course. The element of surprise. She was scarcely expecting anyone at my level.' He smiled. 'There isn't anyone else at my level. But she's very fast and moved beautifully, especially so when you consider she's bundled up in a wad of clothes.'

His gaze turned to Willie Garvin. 'He had a fraction of a second to realize what he was up against, and I must say he reacted extraordinarily well. I'm stronger, of course. I tested that. But he has great qualities. It's very annoying about that shoulder. Even if he hasn't broken anything he'll be as stiff as a board on that side for a week or two.'

Colonel Jim took a cigar from his jacket pocket and considered. 'Maybe we'll be able to give you a week or two, Mr Sexton. Depends what insurance they took out. If it was only Quinn and that Mrs Gillam, we got no worries.'

'That's excellent,' Mr Sexton said heartily. 'It's stimulating to have a good store of practice material in hand.'

The door creaked open and Mellish appeared at the top of the steps. Relief touched his face as he took in the scene. He said, 'Everything all right?'

Colonel Jim held a match to his cigar. 'What else? Got your needle and dope, Mellish? Good. Now here's what you do.' He pointed with the cigar. 'Right now you give these two a shot to keep 'em quiet for a few hours. Then Mr Sexton carries 'em upstairs. I want 'em searched. Every stitch. The word is, they're pretty sneaky. Get Angel in on the search, Mr Sexton. She's sneaky too.'

Mellish said, 'Where shall we put them when we're finished? We've only got two cells with sound doors and locks.' He knelt over Modesty and opened a flat box containing disposable syringes and ampoules.

Colonel Jim said, 'I want these two kept apart. Let's see now, how long have we had Tarrant in the stink-hole?'

Mellish looked up. 'Over thirty hours.'

'Okay. Get him out, clean him up, and find something decent

for him to wear. Then, when you've finished with these two, you put Garvin in with Quinn and the Gillam girl. Blaise in with Tarrant.' He paused, considering. 'Yeah, do it like that. It'll work good for us, I reckon. And we'll leave 'em sweat a while. See what time and twitchy nerves can do before we start making anyone redundant.'

Mellish got up and moved to Willie Garvin. Mr Sexton said, 'It's Tarrant we want to talk. The rest are expendable.'

'That's right.' Colonel Jim watched the needle slide in. 'I figure if we take it slow and make the others redundant one at a time, he'll crack. He's tough, but kinda sensitive.'

Mr Sexton sighed contentedly. 'They'll all have to go eventually, of course. Who would you like me to discharge first, Colonel Jim? I mean, when the time comes to begin.'

The big man rested his cigar hand on the slope of his belly and pondered. Slowly his mouth stretched, and an indulgent twinkle came into the granity eyes. 'We'll let Momma choose,' he said. 'She'll like that.'

An hour later, in the big bedroom she shared with Clare, Angel sat on the edge of her bed and idly swung the two-foot length of fine wire, holding one of the two wooden toggles attached to the ends. The wire touched the carved top of the thick wooden bedpost, curving round it under the centrifugal pull of the heavier toggle at the far end, and as this swung towards her, Angel caught it deftly in her free hand.

'I fancy that Garvin,' she said. 'He's a big 'un.'

Clare looked up from her crochet and nodded towards the wire Angel now held taut round the bedpost. 'Fancy him for that, you mean?'

'No, daft. Fancy a good grind with 'im.' Angel gave the thin wire a jerk, then giggled. 'I like big 'uns for this too, though. There's more of a kick when they're twice your size and squirming about like a live winkle on a pin. Don't matter 'ow big they are, once you get your knee in their back, they're cooked. Remember that bloke at Point Clair, the big darkie——'

'I've no wish to be reminded, Angel.' Clare's nose twitched with distaste. 'We all have unpleasant duties to perform from time to time, but discussion of them is coarse and unladylike.'

Angel swung the wire again. 'I don't see anything unpleasant about 'em.'

'You lack breeding, dear, but we won't argue the matter. Do you know what plans Colonel Jim has for our visitors?'

Angel looked sulky. 'Well, he's going to cater for Mister bleeding Sexton, we can guess that. Teacher's pet, 'e is. I bet all I'll get is that gimpy red'eaded bird to see off.' A malicious glint touched her muddy eyes. 'Still, I can pretend it's you Clare, eh? After all, she's Scotch too.'

'I wish you'd not say *Scotch*, Angel. Scottish. And I wasn't asking about disposal, I was asking how Colonel Jim proposed to make use of them.'

'Going to use 'em for squeezing Tarrant of course.'

'Aye, but how?'

'Let 'em sweat a bit, then 'ave Mr Sexton knock one of 'em off in front of the rest, just to show we mean business. Let 'em sweat again, then pick another of 'em and put the screws on slow, with Tarrant there. And so on, I suppose.'

Clare nodded, lips pursed judiciously. 'Sir Gerald is a gentleman,' she said. 'I'd imagine he would react best to sight of one of the ladies under treatment by Mr Sexton. I must confess to a wee hope that it'll not be Lady Janet. As a compatriot, I'm bound to prefer that she has a nice quick end.' She smiled archly. 'Sir Gerald Tarrant and Lady Janet Gillam. My word, but we've such distinguished company just now.'

She held out the crochet-work at arm's length and studied it with her head a little to one side. 'D'you not think this a pretty pattern, Angel dear?'

CHAPTER TEN

WILLIE GARVIN'S FIRST AWARENESS was of pain. The whole of his left shoulder and back throbbed. He kept his rate of breathing unchanged and lay still.

The cellar. Modesty unconscious. The brief frantic fight against the smiling man with the golden beard. A master. Unbelievable. Then falling back . . . against something. Paralysing pain.

And now. Lying on what felt like a thin straw palliasse. Hard floor beneath.

Alone? No. Faint sound of clothes rustling in movement. Breathing. A voice said dully, 'What time is it?'

Quinn's voice.

As Willie opened his eyes Janet said, 'I don't know, they took my watch with everything else. About noon, I think.' She sat beside him on another palliasse, her back to the wall, looking away towards Quinn, who sat facing her across the corner of the long narrow cell, arms wrapped about his knees. She looked down at Willie and gave a little start. His right arm moved quickly to touch his fingers to her mouth, warning her to silence. She flinched, and he saw dried blood on her swollen lower lip.

Painfully he sat up, flapping a hand at Quinn to prevent him speaking. The nylon overall and quilted jacket were gone. So were the knives. His shirt hung loose, his combat boots were unlaced, his belt unbuckled. He knew he had been carefully and expertly searched.

Janet and Quinn, here in the Chateau Lancieux. So that was it. Keeping shock from his face, he gave a reassuring nod and got to his feet, buckling his belt. Carefully he moved his left arm, up, forward, back. Stiff. The shoulder-blade badly bruised. Plenty of pain but fair mobility. Nothing broken.

The light was bright, and came from a single large bulb hanging from six inches of flex. He began to move slowly round the cell, eyes probing every inch of wall and ceiling. When he was satisfied he examined the floor and the door. The door was very solid and had one large keyhole. The stops were on this side, so the door opened outwards. He wondered if there was a drop-bar on the other side.

At least the cell wasn't bugged, unless there was a pick-up clamped outside the door, but that wouldn't yield much providing they spoke in whispers. His examination had taken ten minutes. Janet and Quinn had not moved, had simply watched.

He sat down beside Janet again, took her hand, and beckoned Quinn to join them. Quinn rose from his palliasse. His eyes were feverish and his pale face twitched uncontrollably.

Willie said, 'No bugs, but talk soft.' He looked at Janet. 'About noon, you reckon?'

'Yes.' Her hand was shaking as it gripped his. 'They brought you in hours ago.'

'Modesty?'

'In another cell. With Tarrant, I think. We heard them say something like that when they were carrying you in.'

Relief eased the tightness in Willie's chest, and he let out a slow breath. 'When did they get you, Jan?'

'Yesterday, at *Le Lion Rouge*, just after lunch. A woman came, a Scotswoman . . .' She told him what had happened, and though her low voice did not falter he could feel the tension quivering in the sinews of her hand. 'I'm sorry, Willie. We just walked into it. We're not very . . . experienced in this sort of thing.'

He said gently, 'Breathe deep and slow, and try to unwind, love. You're burning up too much juice. You too, Quinn. Push the air right down deep, and it'll relax your belly.'

Quinn had not uttered a word yet. While Janet spoke he had knelt upright on the palliasse, arms hanging by his sides, never taking his over-bright eyes from Willie's face. Now he said very distinctly, 'I told them, Willie. They knew you were coming, but not how. I told them.'

Willie turned his head to look at Janet, lifting her hand and touching it to his lips. 'They give you a bad time, Jan?'

Before she could answer Quinn said, 'There's a man named Sexton. Mr Sexton, they all call him. They asked what you were planning to do, and we pretended we didn't know. Then Sexton stood behind Janet and reached in front of her. He smiled all the time. She didn't make a sound, but she was . . . writhing. She bit through her lip. And then, just as she passed out . . . there was this awful sound. I thought he'd killed her. But after a minute or two she came round, and he was going to do it again. So I told them.'

Willie nodded. 'I'd 'ave told 'em sooner.'

'What?' Quinn blinked and shook his head as if trying to clear it.

'You got no choice, Quinn, not when they just want one simple answer. They can always rip it out of you. It's different with Tarrant, they daren't do a crash job on 'im.' He felt sorry for Quinn. The boy must have been suffering agonies since yesterday, seeing himself as a betrayer. No point now in saying that he should have babbled a false story, should have told them the plan was for a spot-landing by parachute on the roof an hour before dawn. That might have done. But Quinn could never have concocted a convincing lie under pressure.

Willie feigned a little start of surprise and said, 'Christ, 'ave you been *blaming* yourself, Quinn?'

'What the hell do you think?' Quinn's voice was a savage whisper, but there was a small, desperate note of hope in it.

'I think you ought to kick me and the Princess right in the teeth,' Willie said. And that was true enough he thought bleakly. As they stared at him he went on, 'We're the only ones to blame. The clever pair. We know it all. Except we slipped up right from the start. Before the start.'

Janet said, 'I don't see what you mean.'

'We knew they'd tried to knock Quinn off, and we knew they might still be after 'im, just in case 'e'd seen anything that day they nabbed Tarrant. And they were, Jan. Someone tailed Quinn to Modesty's place. Or maybe they were watching it anyway. Those three she clobbered on the causse must've twigged who she was. So Quinn arrives, and within twenty-four hours we all go rushing off to a private airfield, never even looking over our shoulders. It'd take a smart bloke about ten minutes to find out what flight-plan Dave Craythorpe filed. Then this smart bloke gets on the blower and says, "They're landing at Blagnat." ' Willie exhaled disgustedly. 'They've 'ad tabs on us all the way.'

There was a long silence, then Quinn said slowly, 'Well . . . that makes me feel a bit better.'

'Don't get over the moon about it.' Willie rotated his shoulder. 'There's a lot of aggravation ahead, and we start from 'ere. Who's to blame makes no difference.' He looked at Janet. 'Is Sexton the fair bloke with a beard?'

'Yes, that's him, Willie.'

'He's the only one I've seen. Fastest thing on two feet I've ever seen, too.' He massaged the shoulder, clamping down on the sense of shock that came with remembering those brief moments in the cellar. 'He caught us on the 'op, and took us out in five seconds flat. Is Sexton the bossman?'

Janet shook her head. 'No, that's an American. They call him Colonel Jim. We don't know his other name.'

'I expect it's Straik. J. Straik. You seen anyone else?'

'There's his wife. He calls her Momma. She's a sort of B-picture southern belle. And two women, Clare and Angel. I think they may have been the nun-women, Willie. There's an Englishman, middle-aged and rather jumpy, but I didn't hear his name spoken. And a half Chinesey looking man called da Cruz. Portuguese, I suppose. There may be others. I don't know.'

Quinn said, 'When Sexton brought us down here he talked to Angel about someone being on guard. It sounded like Ee-tow.'

'Ito? Japanese?'

Quinn shrugged. 'Maybe. We haven't seen him.'

Janet said in a low voice, 'Willie, you were saying just now we have to start from here. Is there really any chance?'

'There's always chances, Jan. Things don't often go right all the way, and then you 'ave to improvise a bit.' He brought his right foot up to lie across his left thigh and began to probe with sinewy fingers at the welt of the sole. 'It's a pity I didn't let you come on the Macao thing instead of this one. That was a beauty.' He glanced at the door. 'It's a mortice lock, and pretty new, but I can fix it if——'

He broke off as the composition sole separated and peeled away. Within the half-thickness of the sole were several curiously contoured hollows, empty. Willie grimaced. 'I 'ad some pick-locks in there.' He matched the studs and sockets which clipped the two layers of the sole together, then stood up and put his weight on the foot to clip them together.

Janet and Quinn watched as he fingered the cuffs of his shirt, the collar, then unbuckled his belt and checked the waistband of his slacks. He shook his head and said, 'They didn't even miss the sling in me waistband. The Princess was carrying a few things, but they'll 'ave done a strip job on 'er, too.'

Quinn said, 'Well . . . that's it, then.'

Willie glowered at him. 'Just keep up the deep breathing and don't get morbid. Go on, I bloody mean it, Quinn. Stand up. Breathe right out, nice and slow. Now suck it in. Slower. That's right. Shove it in till your lungs creak. Good. Out again. Now keep that up for ten minutes and don't talk. Come on, Jan, you too.' He reached down to help her to her feet. She began an effortful smile, then saw that he was serious and stood with her back to the wall, watching Quinn and trying to match her breathing with his.

Willie moved to the door, knelt to peer closely at the lock, shook his head regretfully, and moved back to the corner where Quinn and Janet stood. They looked at him with wide bewildered eyes, breathing obediently, like children performing some baffling adult ritual which would make everything come right because a grown-up had said so.

'Just carry on and listen,' Willie said softly. 'You got to understand the set-up, then we'll all 'ave a better chance when it comes to the crunch. They aim to knock us off in the end. Can't afford to do anything else. We're only alive now because they can use us in some way, probably to lever stuff out of Tarrant. At a guess I'd say they'll get us altogether some time early on, to see 'ow we react with one another. You two stay quiet. That means you watch your tongue, Quinn. Don't be surprised if the Princess starts a cat-and-dog fight with me, blaming each other for getting nailed. It's a good principle, letting the opposition think you're cracking a bit. Another thing, maybe they won't feed us, but if they do, eat while you've got the chance.'

He paused, gathering his thoughts. There was a filthy taste in his mouth, he was very dry, and his shoulder throbbed. When he had time to sit quietly and concentrate he would abate the pain, setting it at a distance so that it seemed not to be a part of him.

He smiled and said, 'Somewhere along the line we'll get a chance. I got no idea what shape it'll be, or 'ow good. It might be pretty thin, but it'll come. If it's while we're together, I'll get the sign from Modesty. I'll be getting signals from 'er any time we're together, telling me what line to play. Now listen. Don't live on your nerves waiting for it. Try and relax. If ever you 'ear me say, *"I could do with a beer,"* you'll know something's going to pop any second. Don't move till we've started it. Then if there's anyone near enough, kick 'em in the slats. If not, duck for the nearest cover and leave it to me and the Princess.'

He paused again, aware that there were a hundred varieties of opportunity which might occur under different circumstances, and that none of the circumstances could be even guessed at yet. But at least he had done his best to lay down a basic guide-line, and it would help Janet and Quinn to have a positive sense of hope, however slender. He said, 'All right, you can ease up on the breathing.'

Janet moved forward, put her arms round him and rested her head on his shoulder. Quinn leaned back against the wall. After a moment or two he said gently, 'I think you're talking a lot of balls, Willie, but I could be wrong. I thought the same about the deep breathing, but it seems to have worked.' He forced a tired smile. 'I'm not exactly happy, you understand, but at least I don't feel that my guts are turning to vinegar.'

'It's a panic-killer, the breathing. Sovereign remedy. We'll 'ave ten minutes in every hour. Now let's sit down. Jan, I want you to go over the opposition again, one at a time. What they look like and act like, what impression they make on you. And Quinn can chip in with 'is own ideas as we go along.'

Janet said, 'We haven't seen much of them, Willie.'

'Never mind. Let's 'ave all you can remember. I want to get the feel of 'em.'

Tarrant looked at the faint outlines of the sketch he had made with a wet finger on the surface of the table.

'That's about all,' he said. 'There's a lot of the chateau I haven't seen, of course.'

'Never mind, this is quite a bit.' Modesty's hand moved over the crude sketch, touching the table lightly. 'We're in this section, a corridor with cells on one side, most of them without doors. A kind of open hall here, in the middle of the run, and you think Willie and the others are locked up in the end cell, here, where the corridor dead-ends?'

'That's right. I heard movement along there soon after Sexton carried you in.'

'All right, we'll assume it. At the other end, a door and steps leading up to the ground floor. Kitchen on the left, here, and you think the access to the cellar is by steps down on the far side of the kitchen.'

'That's my impression, Modesty. I'm not quite sure why.'

'Something you've seen or heard without quite registering it at the time. Now, the dining-room here, and a big sitting-room on the north side. Staircase to a sort of mezzanine, where this gallery looks down on Sexton's gym.'

'He calls it his consulting room when I'm taken there for treatment.'

She turned her head to look at Tarrant. He wore a garment which was like a one-piece track suit of thick navy blue blanket-material. His greying moustache straggled a little, untrimmed. His cheeks were hollow, the eyes deep-sunk, his movements slow and careful like those of a man plagued by rheumatism. He was freshly bathed, but she knew that for thirty hours he had been huddled in an oubliette, a tiny airless chamber, left to suffer hunger and thirst in his own stench.

She slipped her hand under his arm and pressed it gently, then looked at the sketch again. 'You haven't been higher than the mezzanine?'

'No. I imagine they're using only some of the bedrooms.'

'When did you know they'd got Lady Janet and Quinn?'

'Sometime yesterday. Soon after it happened, I suppose. Sexton came in and called to me down in the stink-hole. He said you were coming in through some cave, and he'd be waiting for you.'

'Did they know about the cave before?'

'Vaguely, from what Clare said. She came and talked at me later. One of her well-bred horror sessions. The agent showed them the disposal chute in the cellar when they first rented the place. Sexton went down to have a look yesterday evening. He got as far as some sort of pool. Said he didn't fancy a cold swim unless it was necessary.'

She thought for a moment. 'Did that surprise you?'

'Surprise me? I'm not sure. I was too . . . dismayed to know you were walking into a trap to think of much else. Perhaps it surprises me a little now. I tend to think of Sexton as a machine. Invulnerable.'

'Do you know where he comes from?'

'No. But I gather most of his life was spent in the Far East.'

'I see.'

Tarrant wondered why the point interested her. He was very tired, yet his mind was crystal clear as if from a stimulant drug.

It was seven hours since Sexton had carried her into the cell, Angel following with a palliasse. Her clothes were in disarray, as if she had been stripped and clumsily dressed again while unconscious. Sexton laid her on the palliasse, straightened up and looked down at her with interest. 'She came well prepared,' he said. 'You'd be surprised what we found on her.' He made Tarrant get off the bunk and examined it closely, then the table.

'No nails,' he said. 'Good solid jointing. I can't believe the ingenious lady will find much help here.'

When they had gone, Tarrant buttoned her clothes and arranged her in what seemed a comfortable position. He knew he had not the strength to lift her to the bunk. Sadness was like a cold lump in his chest. Foolishly he found himself wishing that he had not hoped for her to come.

When she woke at last from the drugged sleep, Tarrant had been given more than enough time to bury his despair and rehearse the demeanour of a man still of good spirit and cautiously hopeful. Although he did not know it, the pattern of her awakening followed the same pattern as Willie Garvin's. She did not open her eyes until she was fully conscious, and then quickly motioned him to silence. She sat up, taking brief stock of her surroundings and studying him for what seemed a long time. He saw pity and anger in her gaze when she knelt up and rested her hand on his shoulder for a moment, and he realized that he must look far worse than he had imagined.

She touched fingers to his lips for continued silence, then all feeling vanished from her face to be replaced by a cold, almost brutal speculation as she began to search herself, feeling in her pockets, in the various hems of her shirt, in the loosened club of hair held by thick rubber bands at the nape of her neck, and finally sitting down to remove the sole from one of her boots. The search produced nothing, but if she was disappointed she gave no sign. She stood up and began to move slowly round the cell. It was not until she had examined it minutely that she spoke at last. Sitting on the bunk beside him, her voice a low whisper, she began a series of questions.

As one who had de-briefed many agents in his time, Tarrant saw her purpose and shaped his answers to it. Over and above the cold facts of their situation, she was seeking the intangibles of impression and insight. Carefully Tarrant described Colonel Jim and each one of his company, adding as much as he had been able to gather concerning inter-relationships between them.

Then came an account of his treatment at their hands, and finally she had asked him to sketch as much of the layout of the chateau as he had been able to see. She stood gazing absently down at the barely visible wet-finger sketch now, and said, 'Have you noticed any kind of alarm system?'

'I believe all outer doors and windows are wired,' he said. 'Da Cruz and one of the Japanese were testing recently when I was being brought back after a session with Mellish and Colonel Jim. Da Cruz spoke of "trying the stairs", so possibly there's an internal alarm on the main staircase at least.'

She rubbed a palm across the table, then drew him to the bunk to sit down again and said, 'This man Sexton. I only glimpsed him for a couple of seconds, and I underrated him badly. He put me out with a counter very few experts could bring off. Have you had any chance to watch him in action?'

'Yes, before a painful session in the gym, two days ago. He was working-out with the three Japanese.'

'We obviously didn't extend him much in the cellar, but he had one or two advantages then, and a little goes a long way in top-class competition. How good is he?'

Tarrant considered grimly. 'I think few men can be as strong. But he's more than strong. Unarmed combat is his religion.'

'Comparisons. You've seen me work out with Willie.'

'I think he must be faster. He has beautiful fluency. I would say his technique was complete. He claims, and not boastfully, to be the best in the world. I think it may be true.'

She nodded. There were few men whose judgment in such a matter she would have relied on, but Tarrant was one of them, and for a particular reason. He was a skilled fencer, who in his twenties had fenced for England. No other sport is so demanding upon the eye of the watcher. To the layman, a long engagement is little more than blur. Only the fencer can follow and itemize the sequence of blade on blade. And this faculty would make Tarrant a reliable judge of Sexton's skill in combat.

He said, 'Why do you ask?'

She gave a little shrug. 'A man like that craves to prove himself against the best opposition. I just have a feeling Willie or I might be on the list.'

'God forbid,' Tarrant said fervently.

'I'll go along with that.' She smiled briefly. 'Willie and I don't want to prove anything.'

Tarrant said, 'There's something I haven't yet told you. I'm afraid Willie's hurt.'

She did not move, but he was watching her eyes and saw shock hit her. Then she had absorbed it, and it was gone.

'Badly?'

'I don't know. It's his shoulder. Apparently there was a brief battle with Sexton, and Willie fell against a bench or something.'

'That wouldn't—oh, there was a big vice on it.'

'Sexton seemed mildly annoyed by the incident.'

'Yes . . . that fits, if he wants competition. Still, it sounds as if Willie has only one arm out of action.'

Tarrant stared. The hint of relief in her eyes seemed quite genuine. He said, 'You find it comforting?'

'I'd rather have Willie around with one arm than anyone else with two,' she said almost idly, as if thinking of something else. Tarrant sat watching her with growing fascination. In the past he had often wondered exactly how she would appear at the crunch of a mission which had gone wrong. It had long been a source of irritation to him that his French colleague, Vaubois, had once seen her in action. Tarrant had never done so, except at practice with Willie. Now he was seeing her, if not in action then in the toils of a disastrous mission which would probably be fatal, and he found it difficult to describe her manner. "Absorbed" was the only word that came to his mind, but it was inadequate. Negatives were easier. Not defiant, not optimistic, not pessimistic, not grim. Just totally absorbed by the problem. He remembered watching the pole-vault in the Olympics, remembered the long minutes of concentration before the vaulter at last began his run. It was something like that.

She said, 'They're bound to have covered the situation at *Le Lion Rouge*.'

'Yes. That was included in Clare's monologue. A couple of hours after she got back here with Lady Janet and Quinn she phoned the inn and spoke to the patron as Lady Janet. I suppose they'd have a rather similar French accent, both being Scottish. She said Mr Quinn had been taken ill while getting the other car going, that he had a heart condition and she'd driven him straight to hospital in Toulouse. An English friend would be calling to settle the bill and pick up their bags. Mellish drove down in the Simca during the evening and did just that.'

'They're thorough.'

'Very.' He looked at her. 'Does Fraser know you were coming here to the Chateau Lancieux?'

'Yes. When he doesn't get a call from us today he'll start worrying, but he won't take any action for a while.'

Tarrant nodded ruefully. Fraser was a cool man who knew well enough how easily a mission could be delayed by small factors. If you panicked and interfered with an operation too early, you could blow the whole thing. So Fraser would hold his hand until he was certain something had gone seriously wrong. And then? A call to Réné Vaubois, who would send in a team. Tarrant shrugged mentally. At the first hint of trouble Colonel Jim would kill off his captives. The labyrinth of caves would make an ideal place for Mr Sexton to dispose of the bodies.

He said slowly, 'My dear . . . I've no personal experience of this kind of situation. Will you tell me honestly what you think our chances are?'

She looked at him a little puzzled. 'I can't, Sir Gerald. I won't know what they are until it's all over. I only know there'll be chances. But there are so many variables, depending on how the opposition handle us, it's impossible even to imagine them. At the moment there's no point in trying to plan in any specific sense. We just have to be quick enough to see the chance that's worth taking.'

'I'm afraid,' he said slowly, 'that's something which is to your address and Willie's, rather than mine.' He had hoped for something more, and was trying to conceal his disappointment.

'We might do very well,' she said, 'if only we could get our hands on a little piece of stiff wire.'

'The lock? But there's a drop-bar on the outside.'

'Then we'd need at least ten inches of wire for that.' She looked about the cell. 'There's nothing here, and I expect Willie's having not better luck. What do they give you when they feed you?'

'Soup and bread.'

'I meant utensils.'

'Oh. A plastic bowl and spoon. Taken away after five minutes.'

'That doesn't offer much, then. But bear the thought in mind any time they take you out of the cell. I know they're not likely to leave convenient bits of wire about, but if you spot anything that might remotely be useful, try to get hold of it. The others will be doing the same. Willie will tell them.'

She stopped speaking and sat for a minute in silence. Then the look of concentration cleared from her face and she gave him the same sort of smile she might have given across the table if they had been dining in her apartment.

'Would you like to sleep now? Or talk? Or play a little chess?'

For a moment Tarrant wondered if he were dreaming. He fought against the sense of unreality and said, 'I don't think I could sleep just now, I feel rather over-stimulated.'

'That won't do. You'll get adrenalin fatigue. We'll play a little therapeutic chess to damp you down. How far can you go in your head?'

Tarrant said apologetically, 'About two moves, I imagine. It's something I haven't tried.'

'Never mind. We'll start by using the flag-stones as a board, and set up an end-game with two or three pawns and . . . say a rook and a bishop each.' She stood up and began to move across the cell, counting the flags.

Tarrant watched her dully. She meant well, of course, but if she thought to drag his mind from the enclosed world of dread and despair in which he had lived these many days past, then she was wildly mistaken.

Yet twenty minutes later, as he sat with narrowed eyes fixed on the flags, struggling to hold his visualization of the imaginary chess pieces and their relative positions, the most important thing in the world for him was to find some way to prevent the threat of Modesty queening one of her pawns.

CHAPTER ELEVEN

TARRANT ROUSED FROM SLEEP at the touch of Modesty's hand on his shoulder. Something was going on in the passage outside the cell. He sat up painfully and put his feet to the floor.

Willie's voice was suddenly raised in fury, '*Watch* it Quinn, you stupid bastard—that shoulder's bust! You jog me again and I'll kick your nuts off!' A laugh, and a half-heard voice which Tarrant knew was Sexton's. The sound of movement faded along the passage.

'That was Willie acting up for my benefit,' Modesty whispered. 'Nuts was a negative. He's playing his shoulder as worse than it is. Sounds as if they're all being taken upstairs.'

Tarrant rubbed his eyes, realizing with a sense of oppressive shame that this was the first time he had thought about Lady Janet. He remembered meeting her, and taking an immediate liking to the tall Scottish girl. There was the man with her, too, the young man who had brought Modesty and Willie in through the cave. They were innocents who had strayed into the battleground, but that would not save them. He said, 'Lady Janet . . . and this man Quinn. Poor devils.'

'I know. And they complicate the situation.'

'So do I, my dear. I'm half a cripple just now. You're carrying too many passengers.'

She tilted her head, listening. 'Someone's coming back.'

Thirty seconds later they heard the key thrust in the lock and turned. The drop-bar was lifted and the door swung open. A Japanese holding a machine-pistol stood well back across the passage. Mr Sexton's head appeared round the edge of the door. He gestured to the pistol and said, 'I deplore this needless precaution, but Colonel Jim insisted. Just remain seated, please.' He moved into the cell, then took a step to one side, leaving a clear field of fire.

Modesty studied him carefully, noting the thick deltoid muscles which lifted the shoulders of the blazer. She guessed that the whole of his body was similarly muscled, and the way he moved confirmed Tarrant's description of him.

He was studying her with equal and more open interest, and began to smile happily as he said, 'Let me put you in the picture. Your friends are above now, making a much needed toilet—under supervision of course. As Tarrant will have noticed, we've removed his soil-bucket. Colonel Jim, being a product of the Bible Belt, retains one or two old-fashioned notions about ladies and gentlemen confined together. Some things strike him as not being fittin' or decent, to use his own words. Apart from scatological matters, however, he's contrived to shed all other inhibitions of his upbringing. So if you, Miss Blaise make a foolish move, Ito will shoot.'

Mr Sexton chuckled, and pointed to the ceiling. 'On hearing this, his compatriot, Muro, will at once gun down your friends upstairs. The reverse applies should *they* make any foolish move. Tarrant will be preserved, of course. We have need of him. Now, do you feel you've grasped the situation clearly?'

Modesty said, 'Yes. Did you ever train under Saragam?'

Mr Sexton's eyes widened with pleasure. 'You know him? Splendid. Yes indeed, I spent a year under him in Bangkok, until there was no more he could teach me. But that was in my youth. What made you ask?'

She rubbed the side of her neck, where a yellowing bruise showed. 'That counter you used in the cellar. It had Saragam's style.'

'Perhaps so. Of course, you could scarcely name a master of any system of combat I haven't trained under. But I flatter myself I've gone some way beyond them all. Very perceptive of you to have noticed a hint of Saragam, particularly in such a brief encounter.' Mr Sexton looked at his watch. 'What an interesting chat we could have. But Colonel Jim is waiting, and I don't doubt you'd be glad to enjoy the pleasures of the powder-room before we begin the evening's entertainment.'

Tarrant felt his stomach clench in a tight ball, and said, 'What have you in mind?'

Mr Sexton gave him an innocent look. 'Nothing very exciting, I'm afraid. We have to make our own entertainment here. But I thought Miss Blaise and her friends might be interested to watch me give a little demonstration in the gym before we all dine together.

Tarrant relaxed a little. 'Am I to take part in the entertainment?'

Mr Sexton smiled and shook his head. 'Not this time.'

Willie Garvin followed Quinn and Janet along one side of the gallery which looked down on the brightly lit hall below. His left hand was tucked into his shirt-front, and he shuffled along slowly, as if the slightest movement sent spears of agony through his shoulder.

Colonel Jim and his wife stood at one end of the gallery. She held a tall drink in her hand. Willie knew them at once from Janet's description. He studied Colonel Jim, and felt a little chill touch his spine. The eyes were bad. Bad in a different way from Angel's, the kid who walked behind them now with the machine-pistol, keeping a safe distance. Angel's eyes were bad because she was a warped human. Colonel Jim's because he was a creature in whom the concept of humanity did not exist, whose mind held no place for it. Willie had seen one or two like him before. Just one or two, but enough to recognize the species. He glanced at Quinn and Janet. They were holding up well, Quinn dourly calm, Janet aloofly so.

There was movement on the far gallery. Modesty and Tarrant were being shepherded in by another gun-carrying woman and a thin sandy-haired man. That would be Clare and Mellish. Willie studied Tarrant for a moment. He looked gaunt and sallow, and though he tried to move steadily he could not hide his weakness. Hammering down the spurt of anxiety that started to rise within him Willie thought bleakly, 'God Almighty, we're a bunch of cripples.'

Modesty tilted her head a fraction to one side. Willie rubbed his slung arm slowly, then touched his right eye with three fingers, telling her that his arm was only thirty per cent out of action.

She rested her hands on the rail and studied the gym below. Willie did the same.

Da Cruz entered the gallery through a door behind Colonel Jim and said, 'They're just about ready.'

Lucy Straik said plaintively, 'You mean it's only a demo? Gee, I thought you were gonna have Mr Sexton knock one of 'em off, Poppa.'

'Just take it easy, Momma.' He slipped an arm round her plump waist. 'You're always in too much hurry with everything.'

'But you *said* so.'

'I said you could take your pick, Momma, and so you can. But Jesus, you didn't hardly even get to take a look at the field yet.'

Lucy Straik looked along the gallery, to one side then the other. She sipped her drink. '*I'm* not crazy about knocking folks off,' she announced virtuously. 'It's just *anything* makes a change in this dump, that's all. I mean, anyone gets fed up with being bored, don't they? Why can't we go and see Paris or somewhere?'

'You just stop talking dumb, Momma,' Colonel Jim said amiably. 'Once I got this project running we'll take a real nice vacation.'

A door opened in the hall below, and Mr Sexton walked in. Three Japanese followed. They were big men, only two or three inches shorter than the Englishman. All wore singlets, loose slacks ending well above the ankle, and plimsolls. Within a few moments the gym was full of movement. Mr Sexton began a routine on the horizontal bar. One of the Japanese took the parallel bars, and the other two the vaulting horse. It was a dazzling display, worthy of professional acrobats. The four men interchanged, switching from one piece of apparatus to another, never still, throwing handsprings and somersaults, forward and reverse, spinning and bounding tirelessly.

After five minutes they stopped and removed their singlets and plimsolls.

Mr Sexton took the thick rope which was hanging from the centre-beam of the high ceiling and looped it to one side behind the vaulting horse, leaving the big mat in the centre clear. He returned to the mat and stood waiting. His body was golden and the muscles moved beneath the skin like rounded steel plates and flexible cables, perfectly machined, gliding in oil.

One of the Japanese handed him an iron bar. He held it in front of him, concentrating for a full thirty seconds. Then the great deltoid muscles leapt up, biceps and triceps bunched smoothly. The bar yielded, and was bent steadily into a U-shape.

Quinn gazed down with tired, red-rimmed eyes, and thought drearily, 'I was right . . . he just tore the door off Tarrant's car that day. Oh God, they're going to throw Modesty to him, I know they are.'

Lucy Straik sipped her drink and sniffed. She had seen it all before.

Lady Janet dragged her eyes from the terrible golden man below and glanced at Willie. She could read nothing in his face, but his eyes roved the whole area of the gym constantly, and every few seconds he looked sharply across at Modesty on the far gallery. Following his gaze, Janet felt an inward lurch of new despair as she saw that Modesty's calm had begun to give way. Her hands were moving nervously, fingers fluttering a little. She tapped the rail, brushed her cheek, linked her hands and separated them again, fidgeting as if unable to control her nerves.

Mr Sexton's performance continued. He broke a two-inch plank with the edge of his hand, and another by a bare-foot kick. He smashed bricks and a stack of tiles. One of the Japanese swept the surface of the mat with a soft broom, and Mr Sexton took up his position again. A Japanese advanced to face him and the first combat began.

It was a demonstration match. The kicks, chops and punches were pulled at the last instant, the throws and holds performed without that final savagery which would have crippled or killed. But even to the inexperienced eye Mr Sexton's superiority was clear. His opponent submitted after sixty seconds, and the second Japanese took his place.

The style was slightly different this time, though only Modesty and Willie among the spectators could have analysed the difference of technique. The result was the same, and so it was again with the third of Mr Sexton's sparring partners.

Finally the three came at him together, and it was only then that Mr Sexton really exerted himself. Watching the scene, Quinn had the odd sensation he had known that day on the causse, when Modesty had gone into action against the three men. It seemed to him that the Japanese were moving at great speed and Mr Sexton unhurriedly; yet his flowing, seemingly leisured movements outpaced those of his opponents. It was an eerie and chilling demonstration of mastery.

Quinn was unable to judge what was deemed to be a disabling blow or throw, but after two minutes one Japanese retired, followed quickly by another, and the third submitted in Mr Sexton's grasp. The bearded man stepped back, smiled, and looked up to where Modesty stood.

'I hope you found it interesting, Miss Blaise. A long way beyond Saragam, wouldn't you say?'

She was still again now, but did not speak. Lucy Straik said, 'I'm hungry, Poppa. When the hell we gonna eat?'

Colonel Jim said, 'Momma's hungry, Mr Sexton. Have your boys hustle things along.'

Mr Sexton grinned. 'Ten minutes, Colonel Jim. Just time for a shower. Dinner's ready to serve.' He glanced to each side of the balcony. 'Clare, Angel, take our guests along and make sure you keep them in two separate groups, one in the dining room, one in the sitting room until we're all ready for table.'

Angel muttered under her breath. 'Big-'ead.' Then to Willie, 'Go on, Gorgeous. That way.' She nodded her head. 'Young Pink-eyes beside you, and Lil the limp be'ind. I'll shoot 'er first if there's any funny business.'

Willie eyed her with interest and said quietly, 'Just so long as you don't shoot *me*, love. Waste of a good 'ot-blooded lad, that'd be. Maybe I'll get to show you sometime.'

Angel gave a snort of laughter, tinged with regret. 'You should live so long.'

Dinner was almost at an end. Colonel Jim and his company sat at one end of the long table, with Lady Janet among them. At the other end, Modesty and Tarrant sat facing Willie and Quinn. The Japanese called Ito stood three paces behind Modesty, holding a machine-pistol. It was at Lucy Straik's demand that Janet had been separated from the others. Her reasons became apparent only when she began to ply Janet in a querulous manner with questions about what she called the British Nobility, questions which Janet answered briefly and in a neutral voice. On first entering the room Willie Garvin had glared bitterly at Modesty, called her a stupid bitch and begun blasphemously to enumerate her failings. Colonel Jim had stopped the flow of vituperation, informing him coldly that a lady was present, and indicating Lucy Straik. Modesty had not spoken at all, and both Tarrant and Quinn had followed her lead. The dinner was simple but good, with steak as the main course, and they had all eaten everything offered.

Lucy Straik was saying to Janet, 'You mean you just *inherit* being a lord and all that?'

'Yes. Unless a new title's created.'

'What's that other thing, then? An earl. How does anyone get to be an earl?'

'He can be created an earl by the sovereign. Usually he inherits it.'

'Some people! Fancy just being a nobility as easy as that, Poppa.'

'Don't cut any ice with me, Momma.'

'Well, I'd like if it was *me*, I guess.' To Janet, 'If your pop's an earl, do *you* get his title when he kicks off?'

'No. But in the absence of male issue it passes down through the female line.'

Angel giggled. 'It won't pass down your line, ducky.'

Janet said without expression, 'Then it will continue through my sister. Or failing her, a more distant relative.'

'Hey!' Lucy Straik's eyes were round. 'My folks came from England, like maybe a hundred years ago. So *I* could be some sorta long lost cousin of some old duke or earl, couldn't I, Poppa? I read about that in a book once.'

Twenty generations of high-born Scots stared from Lady Janet Gillam's eyes as she said, 'You?'

Willie Garvin winced, inwardly cursing the momentary rising of the proud blood. Lucy Straik scowled and said venomously, 'You don't wanna talk to me like that, honey. Not the spot *you're* in.'

Willie said loudly, 'Look, 'aven't you got any Garibaldi biscuits in the 'ouse?'

There was a baffled silence, then Colonel Jim said, 'What biscuits?'

'Garibaldi,' Willie repeated peevishly. 'Little oblong ones, with currants in. I know it's funny, but I always like to finish up with Garibaldi biscuits.' He leaned forward, head turned to look confidingly at the blank faces. 'As a matter of fact I've liked 'em ever since I was a kid. I remember when I was a little boy I used to say, "Mummy, I 'ope they 'ave Garibaldi biscuits in Heaven." ' He sat back. 'So I just wondered if you'd got any, see?'

Angel sniggered suddenly. Colonel Jim looked at Mr Sexton and said, 'Is he some kinda nut? What the hell's he talking about?'

Mr Sexton smiled. 'It's humour of a sort, Colonel Jim. I've no doubt we can cure him.'

'Yeah. You're the doctor.' What passed for Colonel Jim's lips stretched in a smile, and he made the strange clucking sound which was his chuckle.

Tarrant saw Modesty's hand move slightly as it rested on the table, the index finger crossing the thumb. Willie had drawn breath to speak again, but flickered a glance at the hand and subsided. It dawned on Tarrant that she had just told Willie not to draw the fire from Janet any further, or at least not to draw it upon himself.

Tarrant ate slowly, forcing the food down. This meal presaged something bad; that was in the text of Colonel Jim's policy, part of the soft/hard technique. The captives would be used as levers to make him talk, but he knew that to talk would save nobody. He also knew with dreadful certainty, and had told Modesty, that somebody was due to die before ever the leverage began. Colonel Jim believed in demonstration, and had sufficient hostages to play with.

At the far end of the table Lucy Straik sulked. Colonel Jim brooded. Clare began to inflict her own long and inaccurate explanation of the system of Scottish nobility on an uninterested da Cruz. Mellish fidgeted. Angel's eyes darted from face to face with malicious glee. Lady Janet ate mechanically, like an unwilling automaton under orders, looking blankly ahead of her. And Mr Sexton leaned back, smiling absently as he toyed with a glass of water.

Across the table from Tarrant, Quinn ate with trembling hands, eyes blinking every few seconds in a dead-white face. Tarrant had the impression that it was fury rather than fear which shook him. Modesty behaved as if she were sitting at table alone, and Willie was doing the same now.

Five minutes later Colonel Jim pushed aside his coffee-cup and said, 'Well, Momma. Who's it going to be?'

Lucy Straik's bulging eyes glinted, and her full mouth thinned. 'Her,' she said, and nodded at Janet. 'Give her to Angel.'

'Me?' Angel grinned with pleased surprise. 'Coo, that's ever so nice of you, Mrs Straik. I'll pop and get me wire.'

It was as Angel started to rise that Modesty spoke for the first time. Looking across at Willie, speaking as if nobody else were present, she said conversationally but very clearly, 'I knew that fat cow would pick your Scotch bit of tail. It's a pity in one way. I was hoping for a chance to show that muscle-bound bastard how much he doesn't know.'

The whole table froze, except for Willie, who said in a sour voice. 'You bloody well messed it when you 'ad the chance.'

She put a last morsel of cheese in her mouth and said contemptuously. 'On equal terms I'd kill him. For God's sake, you saw him prancing about in his Jacques Tatti trousers. He's too limited.'

Grudgingly Willie said, 'I know that, but——'

Lucy Straik was on her feet, face crimson, shouting. 'You heard what she *called* me, Poppa? Fat, she said! I'm changing my mind and I'll have *her*. You tell Mr Sexton to fix her, right *now*!'

Mr Sexton put down his glass very carefully. For once he was not smiling. He shot one blazing glance down the table, then looked at Colonel Jim. Little flecks of gold glinted in the blue of his eyes as he said quietly, 'I second that motion, Colonel Jim. But not tonight. She's had an exacting twenty-four hours and I don't want her to be at the slightest disadvantage . . . even against my limited skills.'

Colonel Jim rubbed his big jaw and gazed down the table with empty grey eyes. 'Momma wants it now.'

Mr Sexton's smile came back, but there was a tightness about it. 'Mrs Straik has all the sweet impulsiveness of a child,' he said. 'But I'm sure you can persuade her that there's much pleasure in anticipation.'

'Yeah.' Colonel Jim nodded slowly. 'Yeah, that's right about anticipation, Mr Sexton.' He reached out and squeezed his wife's thigh, leering at her like an impassioned crocodile. 'We'll make it tomorrow morning, Momma. Say about ten, so you don't have to hurry up outa bed.'

She pouted sulkily. 'That's not what you said.'

'It's what I'm saying now, Momma, so hush-up and don't argue. I wanna go to bed.'

He took her wrist and rose to his feet. 'Ten o'clock, Mr Sexton.' He nodded to the table. ' 'Night, folks.'

CHAPTER TWELVE

QUINN SAT CLASPING HIS KNEES and said absently, 'I tried to pinch a fork, but that Jap was watching every second.'

Janet sat beside him, legs outstretched, her back against the wall. There were dark smudges of strain under her closed eyes. She said slowly, 'What did that girl mean . . . about going to get her wire?'

Willie, pacing the cell and exercising his stiff shoulder, shot a warning glance at Quinn and said, 'Forget it, Jan. We got more important things to think about now.'

Quinn sighed. He seemed to have passed through fear and anger, out into a calm void, like a ship in the eye of a hurricane. He said, 'We're not idiots, Willie. We know why she needled Sexton. Just tell us one thing without wrapping it up. Does Modesty have any chance at all against him?'

Willie sat down cross-legged, facing them. Janet opened her eyes. He said very softly, 'I'm not going to wrap anything up, so listen. Number one, you don't know the big reason why she needled Sexton, you only know why she picked that moment to do it.'

Janet said, 'The girl was going to strangle me, wasn't she?'

'Shut up and listen, Jan. Number two, you want to know what chance she's got, so I'll tell you the form. Sexton's a fanatic. He's a natural to start with, and 'e's spent a life-time training to make 'imself the best ever. He's not muscle-bound. The Princess threw that in because she knew it'd make 'im mad. He's about ten per cent faster than she is, and a mile stronger. He moves like a Swiss watch, and 'is timing's the best I've ever seen.'

Quinn whispered, 'Dear Christ. . . .'

'That's 'alf the picture. Now I'll give you the other 'alf. First, when it comes to the real thing, I don't reckon Sexton's ever 'ad to fight against odds for 'is life, it's always been a walkover. Modesty's been up against odds since she was a kid, and she knows all about it. When she fights going away on the back-pedal it's like trying to nail a ghost. She's got . . . reserves, resources. And when it comes to making use of terrain and externals she's so bloody sneaky you'd never believe it.'

Quinn said, 'I don't know what you mean by externals. Are you saying she can beat him?'

Willie half closed his eyes, gazing at the blank wall. 'I don't know,' he said at last. 'On form, and fighting on Sexton's 'ome ground in that gym, the odds are too big. But it's academic any-way. If she did break Sexton, she wouldn't last ten seconds. They'd gun 'er down.'

A trickle of sweat ran down the side of Janet's face. 'You mean she was just . . . buying time?'

'A bit more than that.' Willie edged closer and lowered his voice to a bare whisper. 'We fixed this up while we were watching the demo. She signalled me. It's a thin chance, but we've ridden out of trouble on thin chances before, so you needn't think it's a

non-starter. She could only flash me the main points, but I know
'ow she works so I can fill in the rest. Now look. . . .'

His finger traced imaginary lines on the palliasse. 'This is the
gym, and we can reckon the same situation as today. We'll be
'ere on the gallery. Angel covering us. Tarrant on the other side,
Clare covering 'im. Colonel Jim and 'is good lady 'ere.' His finger
moved again. 'Probably da Cruz and Mellish somewhere around,
but that doesn't matter. The key things are the two Stechkins,
the machine-pistols Angel and Clare carry. All right so far?'

He looked up. Janet and Quinn nodded. Their eyes were very
wide.

'Good. Now I can't say just what's going to 'appen when the
fight starts. Maybe the Princess will catch 'im on the 'op and shake
'im a bit. The main thing is that early on, maybe after a minute,
she'll break and run.'

'Run?' Quinn whispered. '*Where?*'

'For the vaulting 'orse.' Willie pointed. 'She wants a diversion
just before that, so this is where you come in, Jan. She'll throw
me a signal. You watch *me*, not the fight. When I shake my 'ead
like this, you start screaming like you've gone into 'ysterics. Loud,
Jan, a proper screech. And keep it up. You got no idea what a
sudden terrific screaming noise can do when it's unexpected. It
gets to the nerves and freezes 'em for 'alf a second or so.'

His finger moved on the palliasse. 'That's when the Princess
jumps for the 'orse, takes off from that to grab the gallery rail
'ere right by Clare and Tarrant, and comes swinging over the top.
With any luck she'll be close enough to turn the rail-vault into
a drop-kick, and nail Clare while she's still frozen. That's when I
go for Angel, and you two keep out of the way. Drop flat.'

There was a long silence.

Then Quinn said softly, 'You're both mad. Raving bloody mad.
It's Hollywood stuff.'

Willie shook his head. 'The mechanics are right. The 'orse is
placed in just the best position, so she'll be out of Clare's sight
until she comes whistling over the gallery rail. And Modesty's as
good a gymnast as Sexton. It'll all be quick as a whip, Quinn, so
don't 'ang about on dropping flat. There's another thing working
for us, too. I doubt if Angel and Clare 'ave ever fired those
Stechkins, and they're buggers for accuracy without a shoulder-
stock on 'em. You got to 'old 'em down 'ard, or you find you're
blasting 'oles in the ceiling. So even if one of 'em gets to squeezing
the trigger we still got a good chance. And once we've got the
pistols it's a new story. Modesty's a crack-shot. She'll knock Sexton

off first go. And I'll 'ave mine shoved up Colonel Jim's nose before 'e knows what's 'appening.'

Again there was a long silence. Quinn began to breathe deeply. After a while he said, 'You make it sound feasible, Willie. But there are about a thousand "ifs", and any one of them could bitch the whole thing.'

Willie shrugged. 'Not a thousand. About ten. I'm not pretending it's rosy, but it's the best chance we're going to get.'

Janet felt Quinn's hand find hers and grasp it. She returned the pressure, watching Willie, who sat staring down at the palliasse as if visualizing once again the set-up in the gym. With a flicker of pallid humour she remembered that she had wanted to know what it was like for him and Modesty in this strange dark area of their lives. Now she had found out. She did not think she would have much time left in which to reflect on her discovery.

Fifty yards away at the other end of the corridor, Tarrant lay on his bunk, eyes closed against the light. Modesty was asleep on the palliasse. He had wanted her to take the bunk, but she had assured him with a smile that the floor would do very well for her and she wanted him to get as much rest as possible for to-morrow.

She had explained the plan carefully, and now Tarrant felt the cold relief of a man who knows the worst at last. He did not believe that any of them would live, but it was something to feel that a term had been set to this nightmare. He opened his eyes, turning his head to look down at her. She was breathing evenly. Sleep had smoothed the hardness from her face, restoring it to the face of the young woman he knew at home. It was unlined except for little crow's-feet at the corners of the eyes. She laughed rarely, but had a habit of crinkling her eyes when she smiled, and this had left its mark. A mark Tarrant found oddly moving at this moment.

He thought of her facing Sexton's quick and dreadful hands tomorrow, and he shuddered. If she left it too late to break and run. . . .

He closed his eyes again, and sweat broke out on his body.

Willie Garvin found himself awake, which he had not intended. His internal clock, which was very accurate, told him that it was no later than two-thirty. He lifted his head. Quinn lay awake. Janet was sitting up, lower lip caught between her teeth, rubbing her knee.

Willie said, 'The leg playing up, love?'

She nodded. 'I haven't had it off for two days, and——'

'Bloody fool!' The words broke from Willie in a shocked whisper. He came bolt upright and clasped his hands to the sides of his head. 'I ought to be *shot*!'

Quinn pushed himself up on one elbow and said wearily, 'You probably will be in a few hours. But why especially?'

'The leg.' Willie looked at Janet, excitement flaring in his eyes. 'Is it the new one, Jan? With the articulated foot?'

'Yes——'

'It's got two wire braces running down to the pivot. *Wire,* Jan.' He closed his eyes briefly and gave an angry shake of his head. 'Wire. We've 'ad it with us all the time. Get it off, love. Quick.'

She said uncertainly, 'Willie, I . . . I can't walk without it, I'm helpless.'

'You're going to ride out of 'ere with any luck. Tonight.'

She looked at him, then leaned forward and drew up the trouser-leg. Quinn was sitting up now. He looked away quickly. Irrational though it was, he knew that being so crippled must bring a sense of humiliation, perhaps especially to a woman.

When he looked again Willie held the contraption in his hands and Janet sat with the trouser-leg lying flat and empty below the knee, watching. The leg was not solid but made from several broad strips of thick sheet metal, varying in width, skilfully curved for shape and added strength. The false foot was solid, and free to pivot through a few degrees at the ankle.

Willie said, 'It's steel wire and a bit thick, but it'll do for the lock, once I can work it out of these 'oles in the reinforced section 'ere. I'll 'ave to break it up though, Jan. I'll need a strip of the alloy for lifting that drop-bar. The wire won't be long enough.'

Janet said in a low voice, 'Is it a better chance than tomorrow, Willie?'

'About ten times better.'

'Thank God for that. Go ahead.'

It took him half an hour to work the rivet-head ends of the two wires through the holes in the tough metal. Another full hour passed in shaping the end of one into a carefully judged double-hook, like an elongated letter F. This was achieved partly by using as pliers a narrow crevice between two of the stone blocks forming the wall, and partly by gently hammering with the solid foot, now detached.

In the second wire Willie made a simple half-inch right-angle at one end, then turned to the main part of the leg and began to crush lengthwise the section of sheet-metal forming the shin, using his heel and the stone flags as the jaws of a vice. His fingers were bleeding now. Janet and Quinn sat watching in silence, holding hands but scarcely aware of it. After what seemed an age, Willie held a thin flat strip of metal in his hands, half an inch wide and ten inches long, one edge smooth, the other rough where he had broken it by constant bending. He wiped sweat from his brow and moved to crouch by the door, setting down the strip of metal and picking up the probes.

Quinn whispered, 'What time is it, Willie?'

'About four-thirty. Sunrise at around seven. Don't talk for a bit.' Holding a probe in each hand, he inserted them in the keyhole very gently. Five seconds later he was snatching up the strip of metal and darting across the cell. *Something's 'appening along the passage. Lie down and get that chunk of leg out of sight.'*

He thrust the probes and metal strip into Quinn's hands, then moved quickly back to crouch by the door, an ear pressed against it, eyes closed. After two minutes he exhaled a long breath and stood up, frowning.

Janet whispered. 'What was it, Willie?'

'Not sure. They came to the other cell, and I 'eard Sexton's voice. Then they went away. I can't figure it.'

'Maybe . . .' Quinn hesitated.

'Go on.'

'Well, it's basically Tarrant they're working on. They've been . . . interrogating him. Maybe Sexton's taken him away for a session. You know, in the early hours, when you're at a low ebb. That's a favourite time, isn't it?'

Willie nodded slowly. 'I 'aven't got a better idea, so let's gamble on that and reckon they won't look in on us. I'll get the lock open and give 'em 'alf an hour before I start on the bar.'

Twenty-five minutes later, crouched by the door, he heard renewed sounds of activity along the passage. Then silence again. The lock was open now, the probes in his pocket. He picked up the metal strip. The problem was to force one end of the strip round the right-angle formed by the top of the door-frame, so that it would protrude sufficiently to catch under the drop-bar when the strip was eased upwards. Fortunately there was a good half-inch of play in the door, now that the tongue of the lock had been withdrawn, and this offered room for manœuvre.

Twice he forced the strip partly through the right-angled gap, only to have the end gouge into the wood of the frame and jam there. He withdrew the metal and spent five minutes rubbing the corners on stone, to round them a little, then tried again. The strip bent, slid through, jammed, came free, and moved again as Willie thrust hard.

Very cautiously he slid the strip upwards, felt the metal catch the drop-bar, and lifted slowly. He pushed. The door opened an inch or two. He snaked a hand round the edge, gripped the drop-bar and lowered it to the bottom of its retaining bracket without a sound. Relief swept through him.

He turned and grinned. Quinn was kneeling up, still holding Janet's hand. They were both staring solemnly, like children watching their first puppet show and trying to associate it with reality. Willie moved across the cell and squatted close to them.

'We're off,' he breathed. 'Quinn, you'll 'ave to carry Janet till we get outside. Keep a few steps be'ind me and tread soft.' Quinn nodded and stood up, turning. Willie took Janet under the arms, lifted her, kissed her quickly on the cheek, and put her on Quinn's back.

The passage was dimly lit by a single bulb at the far end. Half-way along, the walls fell back for a short distance to form a square chamber four times the width of the passage. Willie glanced back, received a nod from Quinn, and moved silently on. He had taken only two steps across the chamber when a brighter light blazed suddenly from a centre bulb. The Japanese called Ito, dressed in slacks and a sweater, was rising from a camp-bed against the wall, his hand on a dangling cord-switch. He was on his feet instantly, dropping into a defensive crouch, eyes fixed on Willie, his hand leaving the switch to seek a large round bell-push screwed to the wall. And in that moment Willie drew himself loosely to attention and bowed from the waist.

The hand reaching for the bell-push was still. Ito cocked his head curiously. His eyes flickered past Willie to where Quinn stood just within the passage, Janet on his back. Then he looked at Willie again, and grinned, shuffling forward with spread legs bent slightly, perfectly balanced.

In the split seconds of the confrontation, of sighting the Japanese, of knowing there was no time to reach and silence him, and of seizing the one hope that remained, Willie Garvin had at the same time made an instant appraisal. This was the man who had favoured aikido rather than karate or one of the other systems in the demonstration with Sexton. He would go for disabling throws and holds rather than blows.

Willie said softly, 'Stand still, Quinn.'

Quinn obeyed, leaning against the corner of the wall to ease the weight of his burden a little. He felt weak with shock, and could feel the trembling in Janet's arms clasped across his chest. He understood vaguely that Willie had contrived to silence the Japanese by a challenge, and that some peculiar notion of pride had made the man accept.

Willie's left arm dangled uselessly. He turned his right side to Ito and inched forward. The Japanese seemed to flow at him with a smooth, undulating movement. Willie struck for the throat, lunging with stiff fingers. It seemed incredibly fast to Quinn, but the blow missed by a fraction and Ito's hands caught the arm at wrist and elbow. A foot swung to Willie's armpit, then Ito fell sideways with a rolling motion and Willie was flung up and over as if he weighed no more than a sack of hay.

Quinn heard Janet draw a sobbing breath, saw Willie arch his back to take the impact of the fall with his feet before hitting the flags with his back. Ito still held the arm. He rolled, locking the arm with his leg, hands flashing out for a neck-lock with Willie beneath him.

Willie's legs lifted, bent, then snapped out and down. His body lifted six inches in a abortive shoulder-spring, taking the weight of the Japanese with him. And then, as he fell back, Willie's head flashed forward in a butt which cracked home savagely on the bridge of Ito's nose.

The neck-lock broke. Ito rolled and came to his feet like a cat, blood pouring down over his mouth. Willie rolled sideways and rose more slowly, left arm still dangling. To Quinn's horror he seemed dazed from the butt, for his back was towards the Japanese as he straightened. Ito sprang, one arm snaking about Willie's neck from behind, the other hand clamping on his own wrist in a curious way, with the thumb extended and probing into the neck.

It was then, as he stood half-crouched with Ito clamped against his back, that Willie's left arm came to life. It curved up and back, reaching over to catch Ito with hooked fingers under the base of the skull, and in the same instant Willie flexed his legs and somersaulted forward.

It was not a complete somersault, it could not be with the weight of another man to carry. For one fearful moment Quinn and Janet saw the two locked bodies seeming to hang in the air, heads down, bent in a kind of jack-knife position. Then they fell, and as they fell Willie straightened his legs and brought head and shoulders forward.

Alone, he would have hit the floor with his shoulders. As it was, Ito's head struck the stone with Willie's full weight on top of him. There came a dull, ugly impact. Willie gave a hiss of pain. For a moment all was still, then Willie rolled painfully away from the man beneath him and rose slowly to his feet, working his shoulders. One of Ito's legs twitched, and then he was still again.

Janet whispered, 'Is he . . . dead?'

Willie bent and felt for the throb of the carotid artery in the neck. 'It's a good description,' he said a little breathlessly. 'That's what 'appens when you're too academic. I tried 'im bar-room style, and 'e couldn't adjust quick enough.'

He moved to Quinn, put a hand on his shoulder, the other hand to Janet's cheek.

'You two all right?'

A ghost of a smile twitched Quinn's pallid lips. 'We feel a bloody sight better than we did half a minute ago. I just wish it had been Sexton.'

Willie said soberly, 'I'm glad it wasn't. Come on.'

Janet stopped him with a quick gesture. 'Just a minute, Willie. There's a key hanging on the wall there. It might save time.'

He looked, then smiled. 'Good for you, love.'

Tarrant lay on his bunk exhausted. His body felt as if it had been broken in bits and put clumsily together again. It was the worst session he had experienced with Sexton, and once again he had been taken by surprise, unready for it. He wondered if he would ever again be able to get up and walk. It was hard enough to breathe. His chest felt as if were in clamps.

Modesty was bent above him, her hands firmly massaging his diaphragm. He croaked, 'Please, my dear. It doesn't matter. You must rest. You've got to rest . . .'

She smiled briefly. 'I'm all right. And you'll feel better soon. He's been at your nerve-centres, but I'm using *katsu*. It's a restorative technique——' She broke off and her head came up sharply, listening. The key was turning in the lock. Somebody tapped very softly and in rhythm. Two taps, three taps, one tap. Her eyes widened, and as she heard the small sound of the drop-bar being lifted she whispered, 'My God, it's Willie.'

The door swung open with a faint creak. Willie stood there. Beyond him, Quinn was supporting Janet as she stood on her one good leg, leaning back against the wall, the trouser of her other leg hanging empty.

Modesty stared, then looked at Willie. 'The leg,' she said softly, and shook her head. 'I'd better take up ludo. Why in God's name didn't I think of it?'

Willie rolled up his eyes in sympathy. 'I know 'ow you feel,' he whispered. 'Which way do we play it, Princess? They 'ad a Jap on guard but I've done 'im. Reckon we can clean 'em up while they're all in bed?'

'Did he have a gun?'

'No.'

She stared blankly through him for long seconds, then said, 'We won't try cleaning them up. It's tempting, but there's an internal alarm on the main stairs somewhere, and probably others. We don't know the layout upstairs. And if it came to a fight through the chateau . . .'

Willie nodded. As a group they would have no mobility. Tarrant, Quinn and Janet would be passengers in a running battle. He said, 'The kitchen window, then?'

She mentally re-ran their long study of the chateau from outside. 'Yes. It's ground level and they keep the cars in the courtyard there. No gates. Go and kill the alarm on that window, Willie, then check the cars. I'll follow with Quinn and Janet. You and I can come back for Sir Gerald.'

Willie moved off quickly. Modesty turned back to Tarrant. 'Just lie quietly. We'll be back soon.' He nodded weakly, and she went out to Quinn and Janet. 'Time to go home. What's the easiest way for you, Janet? Piggy-back, or holding you up between us?'

'I'll ride Quinn if he doesn't mind.' She managed a smile. 'Sorry to be a drag.'

Quinn whispered fiercely, 'Don't ever bloody well say that again! *Ever*. Give a hand to get her up, Modesty.'

They made their way along the passage, through the door and up a flight of steps, then turned left to enter the big kitchen. The window which looked out on to the courtyard stood ajar. Thin wires, bare ends twisted together, hung from the lintel. Quinn, panting now, was about to lower Janet to a chair, but Modesty said, 'No, we'll get you both outside. You first Quinn. I'll pass Janet to you.'

Quinn stood Janet down and Modesty supported her while he climbed out through the window. The sill was six feet from the ground below. Janet said, 'Oh Christ, I feel so helpless. I hate myself.'

Modesty pressed her arm gently. 'Stop feeling like that. You upset Quinn badly just now. Come on, he's ready.' She put an arm round Janet's waist, hooked the other arm under her good knee, and with astonishing strength lifted her and slid her through the window. Quinn made a step for her with one hand, then caught her round the loins and let her slither down until she was able to stand with her back to the wall.

Modesty stood at the window, staring into the darkness. It was an almost moonless night. Willie would be working by touch alone. Once she heard the muffled sound of a bonnet being lifted. Five minutes passed, then Willie loomed out of the darkness and looked up at her with bleak eyes.

"There's only the van and the Simca,' he whispered. 'Both immobilized. No distributor arms. No sign of the Safari.'

She had half expected the cars to be immobilized, and shrugged in the darkness. 'You'll have to do it on foot, Willie love. Can you carry Janet with that shoulder?'

'Sure.'

Quinn said, 'I can carry her.'

Modesty glanced down at him. 'You'd be knocked out after a couple of hundred yards,' she said gently. 'You can't use the road. It'll be light in an hour, and they could be scouring the area for you ten minutes later. You have to go across country, and that's hell. But Willie can make better than a mile an hour even with Janet on his back.'

She looked a question at Willie, her face just visible in the light that filtered into the kitchen from the passage.

Willie thought for a moment, then nodded. 'Quinn leads. I tell 'im which way to go. He clobbers 'imself on any rocks, or trips in any ruts. I can't risk a fall with Janet.'

'Right. Which way will you head?'

'North. The other way's too steep. Besides, we can make for where we 'id the car if we go north.'

'All right.' She visualized the terrain. 'You'll have three valleys to cross. Then you hit the stretch of road with a long drop on the far side. You'll have to move half a mile along it before you can get down into the last valley and swing east for the car. That road's going to be the danger if they come after you on wheels, so watch it, Willie.'

Quinn whispered, 'What the hell's all this "you" stuff? Why don't we get going?'

Willie said in a flat voice, 'She's got to 'ang on for Tarrant.'

'Hang on?'

'He's just had a twenty-minute session with Sexton,' Modesty said, and though she whispered her voice held the edge of Toledo steel. 'Ask Janet what one minute's like. He can't move.'

Quinn sagged against the wall, pushing back the hair from his sweating forehead. Willie said, 'How long before you can get 'im mobile, Princess?'

'An hour. Not less. Then he'll only be able to creep.'

'It'll be getting on for sun-up by then.'

'I know. Probably safer to take him out through the cave. I'll see.' She reached down and touched Janet's shoulder. You'll be all right with Willie. Just do whatever he says. You too, Quinn.'

Then she was gone. Willie turned his back, crouched and picked up Janet. 'I'll lead till we turn off the track,' he whispered. 'That'll be when we come to a gully after about a minute. Then you take over as front legs, Quinn. It's going to be rough, so go careful. I don't want to end up carrying you as well.'

'All right,' Quinn said in a low, tired voice. 'All right.' He did not speak again until they had passed through the open gates and were moving down the track. Then, 'You know she's going to get killed, don't you. She'll never try to take Tarrant through that cave, she knows the cold will kill him in his condition.'

'Not if she gets 'im through pretty quick. Tarrant's a gutsy old bugger. And anyway, 'e won't dare die on 'er, not the mood she's in now.'

'Oh, for God's sake,' Quinn muttered bitterly.

As they moved on into the blackness, Willie felt something warm splash on his neck. He whispered very softly, 'Don't cry, love. Last lap now.'

He could barely hear her voice as she said, 'That poor old man, Willie . . . and Modesty. It's awful leaving them. Awful.'

'Try not to worry, Jan. We won a break and she's got the bit between 'er teeth. I've seen 'er like that before.' Willie nodded to himself, remembering. 'She'll bring 'im out. And Christ 'elp anyone who gets in 'er way now. Anyone.'

CHAPTER THIRTEEN

FRASER SAID HUMBLY, 'Forgive me for telephoning you at this hour, m'sieu, but I felt I should inform you without delay.'

Réné Vaubois, sitting up in bed with the telephone to his ear, said frostily, 'Let me understand you clearly, Mr Fraser. You suspected that she was on Tarrant's trail. You decided to question her house-boy, and learned that she and Willie Garvin left with two others for Chateau Lancieux three nights ago.'

'Exactly so, M'sieu Vaubois. Weng says that he expected them to have telephoned at least twenty-four hours ago. I very much fear that something has gone amiss.'

'You knew nothing until you questioned the house-boy, presumably at about five o'clock this morning, Mr Fraser?'

'Nothing, m'sieu. Of course.' Fraser sounded hurt.

Vaubois thought, 'Liar.' He knew something of the man's record. Aloud he said, 'A curious hour to decide upon questioning him.'

'I am on night duty, m'sieu.'

'I see. The Chateau Lancieux, you say?'

'Yes.'

'Very well. You realize that I consider such unauthorized activity on French soil to be gross interference?'

'You are right to be angry, M'sieu Vaubois,' Fraser said virtuously. 'And I hope very much you will have the opportunity to take action against Miss Blaise and Mr Garvin. It's not the first time they have offended in this way. You may recall that occasion in Montmartre when—oh, but you were there yourself, of course. It was you the assassins were trying to kill.'

Vaubois sighed and said, 'I take your point, Mr Fraser. Thank you for calling me. Goodbye for the present.' He put down the telephone and picked up a green one beside it.

In an office in Whitehall, Fraser sat back and began to clean his spectacles gloomily. He hoped he hadn't jumped the gun. Vaubois sending his men in might be the worst thing that could happen. But it looked bad. The silence had gone on too long now. It was the old story of agonizing alternatives. You could only make a choice and hope to God it was the right one.

Colonel Jim looked down at the map and rolled an unlit cigar between his fingers. Grey bristle covered his unshaven jowls. It was six-thirty, and fifteen minutes since Muro had gone to relieve Ito and found him dead.

Mr Sexton, Clare and Angel were in the study with Colonel Jim.

Mr Sexton said, 'They got out of the kitchen window. I'd say they headed across country.'

Colonel Jim nodded ponderously. If he was shaken by the escape he showed no sign of it. 'That figures. But Tarrant and that gimpy Mrs Gillam are going to slow 'em down. They can't take 'em south. That's for goats. So they go north, this-away. If they don't hole up somewhere, we'll get 'em on this stretch of road. And we got plenty of time. So you strike direct after 'em on foot, Mr Sexton.' His hand moved on the map. 'The rest of us 'll cover the roads way out to here and here, closing in.'

Mellish came into the study, sweating. He said, 'The only car left is the Citroen. That was parked at the back. They tore the high tension leads out of the other two.'

Colonel Jim stared at him unmoved and said, 'Right. You and da Cruz start getting everything packed up. Could be we gotta make an emergency move.' He waited till Mellish had left, then turned to survey Sexton and the two women. 'Could be they split up,' he said. 'Blaise or Garvin going solo to get to a phone fast. You follow me? So organizationwise we have to figure on temporary suspension of operations, and dispersal of executives with a view to reconstruction later, Right?'

Clare said, 'Whatever you think best, Colonel Jim.'

'We got contingency plans for dispersal. Passports. Identities. The full works. But from a corporate point of view you just can't avoid the redundancy element in this kinda situation.'

Colonel Jim rolled the cigar back and forth, and shook his head. 'What I gotta say now is sad. Very sad. I want you all to know I feel it real deep. But you can't run a business on sentiment, so here it is. Momma's gotta go redundant. She's been a great kid and I'm crazy about her, but she's gonna be bad medicine on the run. Unacceptable risk. She's dumb, and she's gonna be complaining all the time, and she'll talk out of turn. That could blow us all. You understand?'

Clare said, 'Of *course* we understand, Colonel Jim. And I'd like to offer you my very sincere sympathy.'

'You're a real person, Clare. I appreciate that.' Colonel Jim turned his head to look at Angel. 'Go fix her, Angel. Make it nice and quick, honey.'

Angel smiled and ran her tongue round her lips. 'It won't take a jiffy,' she said.

The door closed behind her. Mr Sexton said slowly, 'Are you quite sure one redundancy is sufficient, Colonel Jim? Clare here is sound as a bell. We need Mellish and da Cruz, and they'll follow the contingency arrangements anyway, for their own sakes. But Angel has . . . a rebellious streak. There's a touch of spite——'

Colonel Jim waved a hand. 'I'm ahead of you, Mr Sexton. Angel needs good supervision, and that's out, once we scatter.' He tapped a finger to his temple solemnly. 'She's kinda kinky up here. I sometimes wonder if that kid knows right from wrong. So she's gotta go. I hate firing folks, but it's just part of the job and I'm not gonna duck it.'

He paused and blinked wrinkled eyelids. 'I just do the best I can for the whole team. That's how come I chose Angel to fix Momma. It'll give the kid a little kick before she goes.' He glanced at the door. 'She'll be pretty well through with it by the time you get upstairs, Mr Sexton, so you better run along and sign her off. Make it fast.' He returned to the map. 'I want both them stiffs down the chute in five minutes.'

Mr Sexton smiled and moved briskly to the door.

A stone's-throw away Tarrant lay on his belly, clinging to the rope that hung down the water-slide. In the moving beam of Modesty's helmet-lamp he could see the stream to his right, racing down the trough to the depths below. His feet rested on her shoulders, and she was taking most of the weight from his chilled and feeble hands as she moved steadily down.

It was over an hour since she had returned to the cell and told him that the cars were immobilized. Willie was on his way with Janet and Quinn. On foot, but they would be all right. Now she was going to give him some more restorative *katsu*, and in a little while he'd be able to move. She just wanted him to relax, close his eyes and imagine himself floating weightless, in darkness, not seeing, hearing or feeling. Not even thinking. Nothing.

He looked up at her and said, 'Modesty, it's no use. I beg you to go now.'

The midnight-blue eyes became black and cold as she said, 'Don't you dare. Don't you *dare* let me down. Just stop talking and turn over so I can get at your spine.'

She whispered to him as she worked, gently compelling him into a quiet dark void. Gradually pain ebbed from his joints and muscles. Gradually the numbed nerve-centres began to re-establish communication with the areas of the body they controlled. It could not be said that he fell asleep, or woke up, but he lost all sense of time, and it was as if he had slept soundly when she said, 'That's all there's time for. We have to go now.'

To his astonishment he could stand. His body still knew pain, but it was distant. His muscles were still slow and feeble, but they obeyed him, and he was able to follow her out of the cell and along the passage.

They reached the cellar on the far side of the kitchen only three minutes before the alarm was raised. Tarrant felt sick with shock as the distant clamour reached them, but she said quietly, 'We were just in time. They're not going to look in here. I left the kitchen window open.' She had been into the depths of the cellar seeking old sacks, cardboard, newspapers, anything to pad out the garment he wore, but without result. Now she was on one knee by the bench, peering at the cans, bottles and containers there, and said, 'What are you wearing under that track suit?'

'They gave me somebody's underwear when they took me out of the stink-hole.'

'All right.' She stood up with an open can of car-grease and set it down on the bench where one of the caving helmets lay. The other had disappeared. 'Strip off and smother yourself in grease, then dress again. It's cold down there.' She moved to the chute and reached inside. Her rope was still looped over the stub of iron, as she had left it. Not trusting the rusted iron to hold against the double weight when they went down, she drew the rope across the cellar to the bench, secured the end round the big vice, and hauled with her full weight. The bench did not move.

She unclipped the lamp from the helmet. It was the larger helmet, Willie's. Tarrant could wear that. She would carry the lamp, in her teeth if need be—no, she could make a headband with a strip torn from her shirt-tail. Two minutes later it was done. She turned to Tarrant. His movements were laboured but controlled, and he seemed very calm. His body was thickly greased from head to foot, and he was just tucking the vest into some coloured shorts.

She whispered, 'You're not claustrophobic?' He shook his head. 'That's good. But a cave can be a little scary, first time. Especially the squeezes. Try not to waste energy on what you can see coming next. Try not to think about time, or cold, or anything except whatever we're doing at that moment.'

'I once climbed a few mountains. I think I know what you mean.'

'Fine.' She gave him a quick smile as he finished buttoning his track suit. 'Sorry to act the bossy bitch. I only do it because I'm the bossy-bitch type.'

'You inspire confidence. What next?'

'I'll help you through the slot, then I'll pass you and go down first. It's a forty-degree slope, and slippery, but you can use my shoulders for foot-rests.' She picked up the can of grease, eased the hook of the wire handle out of the hole on one side, and attached it to the back of her belt. 'We'll take the grease along. You won't be feeling too flexible just now, and it might help when we reach the tight squeeze. Ready?'

The descent of the slide took little more than four minutes. As they went down Tarrant became increasingly aware of the penetrating cold on his hands and face, but it was not yet chilling his body. He tried to shut his mind to hope and fear, to anxiety and speculation, focusing entirely on her whispered instructions and hoarding the remnants of his mental and physical energy. He was in her hands, and his greatest fear was that he might fail her.

When they reached level rock she said, 'Wait. Don't move.' He saw the beam of her lamp swing away and down, saw her dim shape crouch, and heard a faint sound. A match flared, a light flickered. Rapidly the light became a brilliant incandescent glow which threw back the blackness, and he saw that she had lit a pressure lamp.

'That's better,' she whispered. 'I was hoping Sexton hadn't found it. He's taken our gear from the end of the rope, but that doesn't matter now.' She turned. 'Follow me over this stretch, and keep close. It's fairly easy, but watch where you step. We can do without a sprained ankle.'

Tarrant began to follow slowly at her heels, watching the rocky floor in the light of the pressure-lamp which she held to one side as she moved.

Lucy Straik was sitting at her dressing table when Angel tapped on the door and entered. Angel's hands were behind her back. Lucy glared at her sulkily in the mirror.

'So what's he want *now*?' she said irritably. 'First he says we can sleep late, then he's awake early with the hots, knocking for me to spread, and *then* there's all this ruckus about goddam Tarrant and the others.'

'Well, it's serious, Mrs Straik,' Angel said apologetically, moving forward to stand behind her. 'Ever so serious. We've got to be ready to move out fast, Colonel Jim says.'

'Fast? When do I get to *eat*? When do I get to *pack*?'

'Oh, you needn't worry, Mrs. Straik.' Angel giggled suddenly. 'You'll be staying.'

Lucy Straik stared at the girl's reflection. 'Staying? What the hell's that supposed to mean?'

'What it bleeding well means is this, ducky.' Angel's right hand came out from behind her back. The thin glistening wire whirled through the air, coiling about the white neck. Her left hand caught the flying toggle. There was a choking gasp and a thump as Lucy Straik was dragged backwards off the dressing-table stool.

A minute later Angel took her knee from the back of the dead woman and stood up, releasing the toggles. 'Soppy fat bitch,' she said contentedly, and turned Lucy Straik over with her foot. A sound made her glance round.

Mr Sexton stood in the doorway.

Angel sniggered, and jerked her head at the body. 'Pop-eye the Sailorwoman, eh?'

'A nice job, Angel,' Mr Sexton said approvingly. He moved forward and smiled into her eyes. 'It's rather a pity, but Colonel Jim told me to make this quick, so——' His arm flashed up, scythed down.

The edge of his hand hit her skull like an axe. She was dead before the knowledge that she was about to die could register.

Mr Sexton left the bedroom walking briskly, carrying a body over each shoulder.

Three minutes later, in the study, Clare was saying diffidently, 'You didn't mention it, Colonel Jim, but I was wondering if you wished to look upon Mrs Straik for the last time before . . .' She gestured delicately.

Colonel Jim looked up from the map and said, 'Who?'

'Mrs Straik. I wondered——'

'No, Clare. I guess not.' Colonel Jim shook his head and sighed. 'I want to remember Momma just the way she was.'

'I think you're wise, Colonel Jim. I feel the same about Angel. A dear girl, but——'

She broke off as Mr Sexton came in quickly. There was a taut eagerness in his manner but his voice was cool as he said, 'It wasn't quite the way we thought, Colonel Jim.'

'How's that.'

'I've just taken the late Mrs Straik and Angel down to the cellar. The light was on and the rope from the chute had been fixed to the bench. Some of them went out that way.'

Colonel Jim said slowly, 'Some of them?'

'It's not the best way to go, except for anyone too crippled to walk far—or who couldn't get out before sunrise, like the rest.'

Colonel Jim flapped a hand. 'Hold it. Let me figure this.'

After a little silence the big head nodded. 'Yeah. Ito must've been dead a good hour before first light, Mellish reckoned. Could Tarrant make it with 'em then?'

'No. I'd just been treating him. I'm surprised he's been able to move at all.'

'He couldn't take the cave on his own?'

'Not a chance. Somebody stayed with him until he could make a move, and that can't have been long ago.'

'Blaise. She took him down.'

'I have the same feeling, but I'm not sure why.'

'The Scotch woman, Mrs Gillam, she can't walk. That thing you found in the cell was a false leg, or what was left of it. Right? So

Garvin carries her. Blaise waits with Tarrant. Quinn could have gone with either of 'em.'

Colonel Jim blinked at the ceiling. 'Right. We got only the one car, and we need that for Garvin's party, so we can't cover where the cave comes out. Hell, we don't *know* where it comes out. How long you reckon Blaise and Tarrant been gone, Mr Sexton?'

'I think they were in the cellar when Muro raised the alarm,' Mr Sexton said softly. 'She couldn't have got him mobile any earlier. I think they've been gone no more than ten or fifteen minutes.'

'You can catch 'em?'

'Oh, yes.' Mr Sexton smiled. 'They'll have to move at Tarrant's pace. I can catch them all right.'

'Do it. I'll take care of Garvin's party.' Colonel Jim glanced out of the window, looked at his watch, then tapped the map. 'We'll catch 'em on this piece of road.' He rubbed his chin with a thumb. 'It's looking good. If we can pick 'em all up we're in the clear.'

He shook his head, frowning. 'Maybe I acted a little hasty over Momma.'

The sobbing, rasping sound of his own breathing beat at Tarrant's ears, magnified in this tiny capillary of the earth's skin along which he crawled. There seemed to be no oxygen in the air, and his heart was thudding in an effort to compensate.

The ten-foot pitch had taxed his strength, even with Modesty's help. The long squeeze through the bedding plane had taxed his nerves. He had claimed not to be claustrophobic, but this was something new. He had felt that the great mass of rock was moving, pressing down upon him.

The narrow triangular passage in which he crawled widened a little, and the silhouette of Modesty ahead of him stood up. His effort to copy her failed, and he crept on. Then the walls fell away and he stared drunkenly about him. They were in the great cathedral of the stalactite chamber, a crystal hall with the light darting and winking flamboyantly from the long, fairy-like needles which clothed the roof. She turned to help him to his feet, but his legs would not respond. He shook his head, clutching her arms, and wheezed, 'A moment, my dear . . . please, just a few moments . . . I'm trying, but my wretched body won't obey.'

She crouched, holding him, and said, 'We'll take two minutes. Just breathe deeply and——' Her voice snapped off and she drew back a little, head tilted, staring at the rift from which they had just emerged. He saw her mouth go hard, nostrils flare.

She moved away and into the mouth of the fissure, then crouched with a hand cupped to her ear. There it was again. As if in a whispering gallery the faraway sound was brought to her along the labyrinth, the faint rustling scrabble of a shoe on rock. She could pin-point it, a sole-edge scraping as someone inched through the bedding plane.

She turned away from the fissure and said in a flat voice, 'Somebody's coming after us.' A pause. 'It's Sexton.' She knew with utter certainty that it would be Sexton. Vaguely she heard Tarrant croak, 'Oh dear God. . . .'

Before his voice faded to silence she had made a dozen calculations and knew what lay inescapably ahead for her to do. There was the lake and the hidden boat. They would have time to cross, but Sexton would not be stopped by the water. He would swim. The best place to deal with him would be on the far side, as he tried to climb out. But if he had a gun he could shoot them both down as she waited for him across that thirty-foot stretch. And if they went on he would surely catch them long before they reached the cave's end where the rifles lay.

She said quietly, 'We've got about four minutes. You have to make one big effort. Come on, hang on to me.'

Together they stumbled down the step-like ridges of rock, her arm about his waist, his arm across her shoulders. Then came the flat stretch and the brink of the small lake. She let Tarrant sink to his knees, ran to fetch the little dinghy from behind the outcrop, stood the pressure lamp on the flat surface of a hummock of rock, returned with the dinghy, set it down on the water, and took off her headlamp. Tarrant watched her without a shred of hope. Sexton was coming, and that must be the end. He wished she would leave him and go on alone, but knew it was a waste of breath to urge her.

What was she doing now? He blinked at her bemusedly, and wondered if she had gone mad. Fingers flying, she had whipped off her shirt and the string vest beneath. Now the plain black bra. The boots came off. She was unbuckling her belt, setting down the can of grease in front of him. She hooked thumbs in the long woollen tights and the nylon briefs beneath, and stripped them off together with her slacks in one bundle.

She stood up naked, holding her shirt and wrapping it about both her hands, then said sharply, 'Grease me. I can't do it myself, I've got to keep my hands dry. Grease me all over. Hurry.'

He pulled himself together, scooped two handfuls of grease from the can, stood up, and began to smear her neck and shoulders.

In a shaking whisper he said, 'But you can't . . . you can't *fight* him.'

'Oh yes.' Her eyes were huge, and ebony. 'This is the place. Not his gym. No smooth mat for fancy footwork. Hard stone, and un-even. He's a warm-weather man. Didn't want to swim that pool unless he had to. Likes a warm-up. I start better than most from cold, so he's lost his edge on speed down here.' She moved her arm. 'No—leave a strip clear round that right elbow.'

While she spoke, Tarrant had greased the front of her body from brow to groin, and her arms. She half turned for him to grease her back, and after a few seconds said, 'Now the legs. All the way. This isn't a surface for fancy kicks and chops, so he'll want to get hold of me, and I need an edge there. He's too strong.'

Tarrant knelt and obeyed. Buttocks, thighs, calves, ankles—his hands moved over her firm flesh, and he was dimly surprised at its warmth. No other emotion moved in him, no embarrassment or sensual stirring. There was only sadness. He felt like some ancient priest of Egypt performing a funeral-rite, oiling a beautiful young body too soon, before death had finally struck.

A gleam of bright light showed at the point where the rift entered the chamber. Modesty said, 'All right. Get in the boat, quickly. Face this way, paddle with your hands, and be careful climbing out, you mustn't get wet.' She crouched and held the dinghy steady while he obeyed, then threw in the tow rope, her bundle of clothes and the headlamp.

Tarrant looked into her face from only a few feet away, and scarcely recognized her. The features might have been cast in bronze, and in the eyes there was a dark intensity. Cold, brooding, primordial.

She said, 'As soon as you're across, take the headlamp and go on. You can't miss the way from here. There's a pot to climb, but it's not high and you'll find a rope-ladder there ready. I'll catch you up.'

She gave the boat a gentle push, and in the same moment her expression changed. She smiled, the corners of her eyes crinkling in the way he knew so well, and gave a little reassuring nod. 'Don't worry, old love,' she said gently. 'We're going to win this one now.'

Then she stood up, turned her back on him, moved away to the centre of the flat stretch of rock, and stood waiting, her arms hanging by her sides. As he began to paddle, Tarrant knew that from this moment she had forgotten him completely.

CHAPTER FOURTEEN

SEXTON WAS COMING. He moved steadily down the stepped ramp from the rift, emerging into the great sphere of light thrown by the pressure lamp. In his hands were a large flash-lamp and a machine-pistol. Tarrant dragged himself out on the pool's edge, head twisted to look back, unable to tear his eyes from the scene. It was like looking upon a well-lit stage.

She had moved across a little and turned, so that she was in semi-profile to him, watching Sexton as he moved at an angle down the slope, the light catching his golden hair and beard. She stood with feet apart, her head thrown slightly back. By some trick of the reflected light which shone down from the glittering mass of needles in the dome, her body was turned to silver. Her hair, drawn tightly back, gleamed like a black helm. But for the rise and fall of the breasts under her steady breathing, she might have been an heraldic figure; woman rampant, silver, crowned sable.

Blood pounded in Tarrant's brain, and he felt his sense of reality slipping. Here, in this timeless womb of earth, the weight of ages bore down upon him, and as he gazed spellbound across the black lake she seemed a myth made flesh, a daughter of Mars, supreme mistress of the warrior arts, carrying an aura taut, lusty, bracing. In his tired wavering mind he seemed to hear the brassy voice of trumpets against a swelling background of martial music. Now was the moment when all finer shades of choice were wiped away, leaving only a diamond-hard simplicity . . . a time to kill or a time to die. She stood ready for either.

For the space of a few heart-beats Tarrant felt the heady splendour of her challenge so strongly that it swamped the dark ugliness he knew must come. Then he saw Sexton moving down upon the silvery figure, sure-stepping, poised, incomparably skilled, unimaginably strong, unique in his mastery; and the blood chilled in Tarrant's veins as he remembered that she was no indestructible creature of myth, but a young woman of flesh and bone. Flesh to be torn and bone to be broken by the iron lightning of this man's frightful power. Not even the silver mistress could withstand the golden master.

Mr Sexton stopped, surveyed the situation, then chuckled. He was wearing a roll-neck sweater instead of his usual blazer. He bent to put down his pistol and torch in a crevice of rock, then moved on down to the flat stretch of rock.

She had known, Tarrant thought. She had known Sexton would want to do this with his bare hands, given the slightest chance. The man came on and halted six paces from Modesty. 'I hope you're not expecting to seduce me,' he said. 'Aren't you rather cold like that?'

She stood like a statue, not answering. Sexton glided a step nearer, testing the footing carefully. Then suddenly, moving very lightly and with that deceptive fluency which concealed speed, he came at her.

Tarrant could never afterwards remember the sequence of that dreadful battle. He knew after the first few seconds that she was matching Sexton for speed, but even with his analytical fencing brain he could not follow the moves and counter-moves. He remembered only a general impression of the two figures weaving, closing, parting as if in some eerie dance. He saw the flash of striking hands, of lashing feet. Once Sexton tried a leaping karate kick, but almost lost balance on take-off and had to twist cat-like away from a whip-lash counter with the ball of her foot.

Mostly what Tarrant remembered was Modesty's body, silver-gleaming in the light, firm-breasted and long-limbed, always circling back, back, gliding and turning in a darting counterpoint of movement that seemed to unite in a pre-arranged harmony with Sexton's attack. There was blood on her side now, where a glancing kick had torn skin from the ribs, but she seemed unaffected by it. The grease had helped the deflection, and was serving her well. Twice Sexton caught her briefly, once by the forearm and once by the ankle as he evaded a kick. Tarrant's scalp crawled with fear, but each time she twisted the greasy limb free as the awful fingers closed.

They were moving nearer to the lake now. Sexton's back was to Tarrant. He was crouched a little, arms slightly spread, edging towards her. It was then that she moved forward for the first time, suddenly flowing at him with bewildering speed, into the iron arms. The move was so wildly insane that it took Sexton unawares. But it caused him no flicker of concern. Her face was against his chest, her arms round his waist, and she was encircled by his grasp, too close to drive knee into groin. Her greased body would not help her now. With a flicker of surprise Sexton felt her lift his weight, so that his feet came an inch or two clear of the ground.

He laughed, knowing that from this position there was no way she could throw him, no way she could escape. Hooking his hands together behind her back, he prepared to crush her slowly. But she was still moving, carrying him back . . . back. In the instant of shock, when he realized her purpose, it was already too late. They were falling, locked together. He snatched a frantic breath as his back hit the water, then the ferocious cold enfolded him, striking into his bones. He was unready for it, mentally and physically, and there were seconds of almost total paralysis. His grip slackened as they sank down, and then he had lost her, the slippery body writhing from his enfeebled grasp.

Fighting sudden panic, he kicked out hard for the surface, but she was behind him now. A forearm slid under his chin, clamping tightly against his throat as the hand found a grip on her other arm, at the crook of the elbow; and the hand of that other arm was spread against the back of his head in a lock that could have broken his neck but for his abnormal strength. Her legs coiled about his waist, putting pressure on his ribs.

On firm ground he could have dislodged the hold in one of five ways, or by sheer strength alone. But here there was no purchase for his feet, and the paralysis of cold had sapped power from the great muscles. He fought for mental balance, then reached back for her upper arm, seeking a nerve-centre to probe. His fingers slipped over the greasy flesh, and she hammered with her heel at his groin with one foot, using her other leg as a flail-like paddle to turn their locked bodies in a slow backward roll.

Water rushed up Sexton's nose. He snorted it out, losing precious air from his lungs, then suddenly went mad, groping for thigh, arm, shoulder, face, anything he could reach, anything he could savage to make her loose the hold.

Somehow he caught her foot at his waist, and tried to summon strength to snap the ankle. There was thunder in his head, agony in his chest. The grip across his throat slackened. Hope roared in him . . . then vanished utterly, for he knew that even in the easing of the hold she had tricked him. His diaphragm, seeking relief for the tortured lungs, responded before he could control it.

He breathed—and breathed water.

Then the neck-lock snapped tight again and his spirit broke. His obsessed mind cried out with bitter agony that he had been tricked, not defeated. The last thing he knew was a surge of corrosive hatred that swamped all else, even the fear of death.

Modesty felt him go limp. It was not enough; not with Sexton. Her own body was clamouring for oxygen now, but she subdued it. Dredging up the last reserves of her strength she poured them all into a sudden leverage against the massive but unresisting neck.

Tarrant knelt by the lake's edge, staring fixedly. The ripples were dying. He had seen one slight upheaval when her leg broke the surface briefly, but that had been a full minute ago. His nerves, flayed with the tension of waiting, became suddenly slack. It was over. A few minutes before, when he had paddled across the pool in the dinghy, he had felt the icy water snap venomously at his hands like a living thing. Such cold was a killer. She had gone, taking Sexton with her. They were both dead.

Something splashed in the water ten feet to the left of the point at which he had been staring. His head snapped round. He saw the gleam of her body against the blackness of the water, heard the great sobbing inhalation as she dragged air into her lungs. Her hair had come loose and covered her face. She threw it back with a jerk of her head, and swam three slow strokes to reach the edge of the lake on Tarrant's side.

By the time he had unlocked his creaking joints and stumbled towards her she had dragged herself out and lay face down on the rock.

'Aaaah-huhh ... Aaaah-huhh ... Aaaah-huh.' The racking sound of her breathing echoed through the great chamber. He crouched beside her, patting her shoulder futilely, and croaked, 'My dear, my dear ... you must get dressed. The cold ...'

She lifted her head, looked up at him blankly for long seconds, then panted, 'Clothes ...'

When he brought her the bundle of clothes she was already kneeling up, sitting on her heels. She took the string vest and began to dab herself with it. The water rolled easily away from the grease covering her body, the grease which had saved her from the grip of Sexton's hands, and had given a vital measure of insulation against the numbing iciness of the pool.

She stood up, gave Tarrant the vest and turned. As he dabbed her back he saw that her right arm had been savaged from shoulder to elbow, and was bleeding. She took the vest again, but it was sodden. Throwing it aside she made a bundle of her pants and bra to dry her legs.

Her breathing was steadier now. She pulled on the woollen tights and denim slacks, then put on her shirt. He saw that her hands were shaking and could hear her teeth chattering, but sensed that this was only partly a result of the cold. He had glimpsed something in her eyes, in that first moment when she looked at him, and had recognized it as fear. Fear in retrospect, released within her only when it no longer mattered. She had veiled it instantly, but he knew he had not been mistaken, and in that moment of revelation his respect for her soared to the ultimate plane.

She buckled her belt with trembling hands, looking at him balefully, and said in an uneven voice, 'Why the hell are you still *here*? I told you to go on.'

'My dear,' he said simply, 'I couldn't.'

'Couldn't?' Her eyes flared, and she stuttered slightly. 'Of c-course you could! Christ, you m-men are all the same! It t-took me two *years* to make Willie get on with his own bit and leave me to do mine!'

Tarrant felt a wave of feeble, idiotic laughter rise in him, and held it down. 'I'll try to beat Willie's time,' he said meekly.

Her anger fell away and she looked at him with something like a smile. 'Wait here, I'm just going to get the lamp.' She paddled across in the dinghy, secured the pressure-lamp and paddled back. As she climbed out beside him the surface of the pool rippled suddenly, disturbed from below. Something rose slowly from the dark waters, a sweatered arm, then a mop of sopping fair hair. Sexton's sightless white face emerged. His body rolled, and slowly sank again. Before it vanished Tarrant saw that the head lolled at an impossible angle from the great shoulders.

He said shakily, 'You made sure.'

She nodded, and bent to wring out her hair. 'You don't get a second chance with a man like Sexton. He was the best I've ever seen. I could never have taken him on his own ground.'

'On his own ground,' Tarrant repeated slowly. She was no doubt right about that. But the ground and the situation were all a part of the battle, any battle. A point Sexton had missed and she had not. She had been interested in his aversion to severe cold even in the cell, because she had sought to know her enemy. She had used the grease, the terrain, and the pool.

Tarrant said, 'He wasn't the best. He lacked your resource in seizing exterior advantages.'

'Maybe. But I wouldn't like it to do over again. How are you feeling?' She straightened up.

'A little tottery.' He smiled. 'But immensely confident now.'

'Good. There's only one tough bit left. A fifteen-foot climb. In twenty minutes we'll be home and dry.'

In fact it was seventeen minutes later when she picked up the bed-rolls, haversack and two rifles, and led the way on for another fifty paces to where the cave broke surface in a little hollow set amid bushes on the valley-side. The sun was up and hung in a clear blue sky, shining along the length of the valley. Close to total exhaustion though he was, Tarrant felt his spirit lift as he looked upon the new day.

She made him take off his shoes and get into one of the sleeping-bags, then opened the haversack and fed him chocolate, raisins and glucose tablets, followed by a stiff measure of brandy from a flask.

Pushing back a thick tress of damp hair from her face she said, 'I'm sorry I bit your head off back there. I seem to get a bit edgy after something like that.'

Tarrant said, 'Please.' He was too tired to laugh.

'It was stupid. You've been so good. Now lie down and sleep.' She patted the rifle she held. 'Nothing to worry about any longer. If we haven't seen any signs of life by noon, we'll start moving.'

He lay back, the sleeping-bag warm about him, the brandy glowing within him. 'We must take turns,' he said laboriously. Finding words seemed suddenly a great effort. 'You need to rest too, and I can . . .' His words slurred, then faded into silence, and he slept.

The ill-kept little road clung to the slope of the winding valley, a rock wall on one side, a fall of fifty or sixty feet on the other, almost vertical. At one point the rising face was pierced by a gully which angled into the road from above. It was one of those rare days of early April, when the air is dry from first light and the sun gives a foretaste of its summer heat.

Willie Garvin stood at the edge of the road where the gully debouched into it, listening. Lady Janet stood on her one leg, Quinn's arm round her waist for support. Her hair was limp and dusty, plastered to her head. Her trousers were black at the thighs from the sweat of Willie's back. Quinn's shoes were scuffed and cut by rock, his trousers torn at both knees. He looked a scarecrow. Distress haunted his eyes as he said through dry lips, 'They'll guess. They'll realize we couldn't have carried Tarrant as well. They'll guess she took him down the chute. That American bastard's a maniac, but he's got an instinct.'

Willie said absently, 'Shut up, I'm listening. There was nothing but the deep silence of the Pyrenean valleys. No sound of a car. He relaxed only a little, not relishing the next fifteen minutes when they would be exposed on the road moving along it for half a mile before they came to the point where the sharp drop became a slope and they could move down to cross the next valley. Off the road there was at least a certain amount of dead ground to provide cover. Once on it, they were committed to fifteen minutes of exposure.

He turned to Quinn and Janet. 'Right. All aboard. We'll make this next bit as quick as we can.'

Quinn said with nervous anger, 'Don't you bloody well care?'

'Eh? About what?'

'About Modesty, for God's sake. I just said, they'll guess and they'll go after her.'

Willie turned his back to Janet so that she could put her arms round his neck, and picked her up. His bruised shoulder was one huge ache, and he was very tired. He said patiently, 'You're always aggravating yourself, Quinn old mate. You keep unpacking your troubles from your old kitbag and 'aving a good brood over 'em. I'll start worrying about Modesty when I can *do* something about it. Now belt up.'

Lady Janet said wearily, 'Don't go on at him, Willie. I keep thinking of her, too. And that poor old man. It . . . it's all right for us now, but——'

'Let's 'ope you're right, love. Off we go.'

They moved on to the road and started down it, Willie setting a pace that was almost a lope.

Half a mile away, on a high mound of rock, Tokuda lay with field glasses to his eyes. He lowered them and began to slither down a long slope to where the Citroen stood. Colonel Jim sat at the wheel, Clare beside him, da Cruz and Muro in the back. Clare and da Cruz carried machine pistols, Colonel Jim a heavy Colt .45 holstered on his hip. Only Mellish had remained at the chateau to watch and wait.

It was Janet who first heard the distant sound. They had just passed a point where the narrow road widened in a bulge to form a lay-by on the open side, so that vehicles could pass. There had once been a barbed wire fence edging the drop here, but this had long since been broken down, and all that remained were half-a-dozen rusting angle-iron supports.

Janet said, 'Willie, I heard a car.'

They stopped moving and listened. She shook her head. 'It's gone now, the valley plays tricks with sound, but I know I heard it. From somewhere behind.'

Willie looked about him. He did not doubt her. Colonel Jim or Sexton was coming, probably with company, and there was no way off the road now, no time to go back to the gully.

Despair came very close. He shut his eyes for a moment, then opened them and turned, sweeping the whole scene in search of any factor which could be turned to advantage. The face of the rising rock was bare of the slightest crevice for concealment. The drop on the other side was sheer, a killer. He heard the distant note of the car's engine himself now, and said hoarsely, 'Take 'er,

Quinn. Quick, Look, there's a sort of bulge in the rock face about fifty paces on. Tuck in be'ind that.'

As Quinn took Janet on his back he said hopelessly, 'It won't hide us, Willie——'

'I know.' Willie's voice was surprisingly gentle. 'Just do what I say though, and make it fast.' Then he turned and began to run back up the road, towards the bend they had just passed. The lay-by was sixty paces short of the bend. He gripped one of the tall angle-iron supports and began to work it back and forth in the hard ground, thrusting and pulling with furious strength.

Quinn staggered to the bulge of rock, turned, and set Janet down. She stood leaning against it, gripping his arm, looking up the road towards Willie. Quinn whispered, 'What's he doing?'

'I don't know.' Her voice shook. 'He's got something in mind.'

'They always have. But I don't see . . .' The words trailed away.

They saw Willie crouch, grip the loosened support and drag it slowly from the ground. He stood up holding a seven-foot length of rusted angle-iron, cut obliquely to a point at one end. Then he moved out into the middle of the road, holding the angle-iron across one shoulder in his right hand, hefting it, finding the balance he wanted.

The sound of the car was louder now. It was moving in third gear for the bends, but not slowly. Willie cocked his head, listening, judging. They saw him lift the angle-iron, poising it like a spear. The noise of the high-revving engine warned that the car was on the straight stretch approaching the bend. Five seconds passed, and Willie began to run forward. After a pace or two his gait changed to a curious stiff-legged sideways run. Quinn recognized it. He had seen it once at an international athletics meeting. It was the run-up of the javelin thrower, though the poise of the iron shaft was not the same, for the vital need was for accuracy rather than distance.

The car whipped round the bend smoothly, and even as it straightened up Willie made his judgment and his throw, putting all the trained co-ordination of nerve and muscle behind it. His skills were wide, but this was his special gift, to throw a missile, any missile, with an instinctive understanding of its properties in flight, and a faculty for judging distance and power to produce superb accuracy. The crude spear flew on a very low trajectory. The car was thirty yards from Willie when the length of angle-iron left his hand, and twenty when the point shivered the windscreen. In that second of time he glimpsed Colonel Jim and Clare in front, others in the back.

Sixteen pounds of hurtling sharp-pointed iron hit Colonel Jim high up in the chest, its speed combining with that of the on-coming car at the moment of impact. It drove through him, through the back of the seat and ended with its point buried under da Cruz's ribs.

The windscreen was opaque, crumbling under the weight of the iron shaft now. The car came straight on. Willie watched it, crouched, waiting for the swerve. It was a gradual swerve, inwards towards the rock face, and the nearside wheel would catch him. He jumped, a diving roll, his body curving over the corner of the front wing. As he came to his feet, gasping with the renewed pain in his shoulder, he heard the crash and the shriek of metal against the wall. The car bounced off, raced for the edge and flew out into space.

The clangour of its fall echoed through the valley. It was still bouncing and rolling when Willie reached the edge. Then it erupted in flame. He stood watching for a few seconds, drained of all emotion. The wreck lay upside-down. Nobody had been thrown clear.

He looked up the road, remembering some flicker of movement his eye had caught as the car raced down upon him. One of the Stechkin machine-pistols lay on the ground. Clare, or somebody, must have been riding with it at the ready, hand resting on the ledge of the open window.

He walked a few paces and picked it up, then began to trudge down the road to where Quinn stood supporting Janet. They had managed to move to the edge now and were looking at the furnace of the blazing car. As he came up their heads turned to look at him, relief mingling with shock in their eyes. Quinn said hoarsely, 'Did you see who . . . ?'

'Colonel Jim and Clare. Two others in the back, maybe three.'

Quinn made a shaky sound that was not very much like a laugh. 'You're not bad, Garvin. Not too bloody bad at all. She said we'd be all right with you.'

Willie looked at Janet. 'You okay, love?'

She looked down at the fiery wreck, eyes hard in the damp, dust-smeared face. 'If you mean that, I'll not be sending any flowers, Willie. I just hope Sexton was in it.'

Willie grinned tiredly. 'You Scotch women are a hard lot, Mrs Gillam. Come on. Time for piggy-backs again.'

Twenty minutes later, when they were halfway across the valley, the clatter of a helicopter broke suddenly upon them as the machine lifted above the ridge ahead. It was an Alouette-3, and passed to their left at three hundred feet before tilting to swing in a tight circle.

Willie looked quickly up and down the valley floor, spotted the flat area where the helicopter was most likely to land, and nodded to a huddle of boulders a stone's-throw to his right. They reached cover at a stumbling run and he stood Janet down.

Quinn's face was drawn. He said, 'Do you think . . . ?'

'No.' Willie shook his head and checked the machine-pistol. 'I think a bloke called Fraser got windy and started something. But just in case Colonel Jim whistled up reinforcements, we'll be a bit careful. They won't reckon we're armed, and we've got good cover 'ere. I'm not much cop with handguns, but once I see the whites of their eyes they'll get a nasty surprise.'

The helicopter swayed down, raising a thin cloud of dust. Its skids touched the ground two hundred yards away and the sound dropped to a gentle clatter as the rotor idled. Two men got out. One wore a combat jacket and carried a sub-machine gun slung. The other was in a dark business suit.

As they approached Willie laughed, moved a pace or two out of cover and waved. 'It was Fraser getting windy,' he said. 'That's René Vaubois.'

Janet wiped sweat from her face with a dirty hand. 'Is it . . . is it really all over then, Willie?'

'Just got to pick up Modesty and Tarrant.'

'I hope it's just that for them.' She drew in a long slow breath and went on almost absently, 'Well . . . I wanted to know. I wanted to know how it was for you with her. Now I've found out in a big way. And I'll tell you one thing, Willie. God forbid you do anything like this again, but if you do I'll not be jealous. She can have this bit of you and welcome.'

Quinn, supporting her with an arm about her waist, said, 'That gets my vote too.' He put up a hand, turned her face towards him and kissed her briefly on the cheek. 'If anyone wants' to know, I think you're an extremely smashing lady. So whenever he buggers off with Modesty, you just give a whistle. I'll fill in for him.'

She looked at Quinn, smiling with wry affection. 'Now if only you were a bit older, Quinn. And if only I were a bit more promiscuous. . . .'

Vaubois picked his way over the rough ground and halted facing Willie. His manner was stiff and unfriendly. He said in his excellent English, 'You do realize that you are on French soil?'

Willie eyed him with frowning admonition, and turned to Janet. 'Lady Janet,' he said, 'may I present M'sieu Vaubois, a very old friend. M'sieu Vaubois, I present Lady Janet Gillam and Mr Henry Quinn.'

Vaubois gave him a glare, then bowed to Janet and Quinn. 'Lady Janet, Mr Quinn—a great pleasure.'

Before he could speak again Willie said aggressively, 'We know we're on French soil all right. Is this 'ow you welcome tourists? It's a bloody disgrace. We come 'ere to do a bit of caving and next minute we find ourselves in some chateau being knocked about by a bunch of real frighteners. I nearly 'ad one of my bad turns. Honest, Réné, you ought to——'

'And you happened to find our mutual friend Tarrant in the chateau?'

Willie looked surprised, then nodded with eager innocence. 'I can't think 'ow you guessed, but you're right. It was a very rum coincidence, that was.'

'All right, Willie. I've already had some of Fraser's double-talk today. But this was *my* job, and I am very angry with you.'

Willie grinned. 'No you're not. You're steamed up because you're worried about Modesty. That's why.'

'Nonsense!'

Lady Janet said politely in an arctic voice, 'You seem not unfamiliar with this kind of affair, M'sieu Vaubois. Tell me, if you had been in Sir Gerald Tarrant's position, who would you have wished to come and get you out?'

Vaubois sighed, and met her gaze with a good-humoured smile. 'Forgive me if I do not answer you, Lady Janet.'

Willie said, 'You got men watching the chateau, Réné?'

'Yes. Very discreetly.'

'You can tell 'em to move in now.' Willie looked along the valley to the pall of smoke rising above the burnt-out car. 'I don't reckon they'll find much left there, though.'

'I'll get on the radio,' Vaubois said. Then, impatiently, 'Now, where *is* she? And Tarrant?'

'I'll show you where they ought to be. Can you take the three of us in that chopper?'

Tarrant opened his eyes. The sun had filled the valley with warmth, and the glare had roused him. His body was sore and his joints ached, but his mind was quiet for the first time in many days. He turned his head.

Modesty knelt less than two paces away, gazing out above him at the valley through a gap in the low bushes. The rifle was held loosely in one hand, resting across her knees. She held a stalk of long grass in her teeth, nibbling it absently. The freakish heat was such that she had rolled up the sleeves of her shirt. The front hung unbuttoned. He studied her with quiet wonder, for she was not simply keeping watch. Her face held a look of absorbed pleasure, as if she were drinking in all that met her gaze as she slowly turned her head. After a few moment she took the stalk of grass from her lips and touched it to a rock just beside her. Tarrant was able to make out a large beetle on the rock, examining the proffered stem.

He raised himself on an elbow and said, 'Good morning.'

She looked at him, at little surprised, smiling, making no attempt to hide what the open shirt revealed of her body. He knew she was not deliberately displaying herself. It simply did not occur to her that it mattered, not here and now, after so much.

'Hallo,' she said. 'You're not supposed to wake up yet. You've only been asleep for an hour.'

Her right arm was blue and yellow with the bruises raised by Sexton's probing fingers, and the sight made him wince. He said, 'You haven't slept at all, my dear.'

'That's all right.' She gestured vaguely about her. 'I'm enjoying it.'

He wriggled stiffly out of the sleeping-bag and stood up, puzzled, rubbing a hand over his bristly chin. As he looked about him, at the valley and the sky, something stirred in the depths of his being, and next moment a great wave of exhilaration surged through him, so sudden and strong that he caught his breath. Then he understood what she had meant, and reached out to take her hand as she stood up beside him.

It was as if his blood had turned to champagne, by no means wiping out the weariness of his aching body, but making it of no importance. The impact of this totally unexpected sensation caused his head to swim, but he heard himself laugh with joy.

It was over. The long agony was behind him, and he lived again. The cell, the drugs, the probing, the filth, the slimy horror of Clare's monologues, the mounting dread of torment under Sexton's pitiless hands . . . all were past.

Bemusedly, he looked upon the outside world again. It was not a pretty valley, with its semi-barren slopes falling to a broad, rock-strewn bottom. But spring had begun, new grass was thrusting from the scanty soil and crevices. The scrubby bushes were wearing green again. Insects darted busily in the air. And above the line of the ridge was a canopy of bright blue sky holding a golden sun.

Modesty said, 'It's good, isn't it?'

He nodded. She stood gazing out over the valley as if seeing it for the first time, and despite the dark circles under her eyes her face seemed very young. Tarrant knew that in this moment he was at one with her. The moment would pass, but he felt that he had been born anew from the cave's womb and been granted the gift of seeing the world with new eyes. It was a feeling incomparable with any he had ever experienced, and he knew that he would never be quite the same man again.

With extraordinary happiness singing in his blood he said, 'Yes. It's very very good.'

The sudden sound of the helicopter as it appeared over the ridge did not startle them. When Modesty touched his arm and dropped to one knee he followed suit. She reached for the haversack and changed the magazine of the M16, watching the helicopter as it tilted and swung along the slope of the valley below them at little more than a hundred feet.

She said, 'That just could be reinforcements Colonel Jim's called up, but——'

She stopped. The unmistakable figure of Willie Garvin sat in the open doorway of the helicopter, one arm waving slowly back and forth. Tarrant heard the note of relief in her voice as she said, 'They made it, then. And there's our Willie making sure we see him. He knows I've got a magazine of incendiaries here.' They stood up again and she linked her arm through Tarrant's, waving the rifle above her head. 'Good for Willie. After me, there's nobody more cautious.'

Tarrant looked at her and saw that she had spoken with sober approval. He took her hand and began to laugh.

CHAPTER FIFTEEN

IN A WHITEHALL OFFICE on a morning in early May, a few minutes after five-thirty, Tarrant unplugged the shaver, put it away in his desk, smoothed a hand over his chin, put on his jacket, and straightened his tie.

Ten minutes later his driver dropped him at Curzon Gate and he began to walk briskly through Hyde Park. The sun had not long risen, and the day was crisp but not cold. He was conscious of a sense of well-being, and looked forward to the thirty-minute walk which would bring him to his flat.

A month had passed since the day when Modesty brought him

out of Chateau Lancieux. Of that time, he had spent ten days at
Dr Georges Durand's clinic, undergoing a variety of tests and
remedial treatment, and two weeks of convalescence at Modesty's
house west of Tangier, the house where she had lived in *The Net-*
work days, set on The Mountain and looking out across the straits.
There he had been sumptuously cared for by her steward, Moulay.

She had sent flowers to him at the clinic, and flown out once to
Tangier to spend a day with him. At first he had thought it strange
that she and Willie made no contact with him, but later he understood and was grateful. Reaction had left him less than himself,
and he was glad they had not seen him in his weakness, given to
inexplicable bouts of shakiness and emotion which brought tears
to his eyes for no reason he could recognize. But this was past and
done with. He felt now as he had felt that morning outside the
cave, seeing the world with new eyes and marvelling at it, but
without the pain and exhaustion he had known then.

During his time at the clinic he had three times laboriously
composed and then destroyed a letter of thanks to her, finding the
written words stilted and inadequate. He wanted her to be with
him, so that she would read in his face some small measure of his
feeling, and he remembered now his delight at seeing her that day
in Tangier, when his weakness had passed.

When the moment came, she did not stop him or brush his
thanks aside, but listened with solemn face and a twinkle in her
eyes as he spoke the simple words, then said when he had finished,
'There. That's got it off your chest. And now I've some messages
for you——'

'Please.' He lifted a hand, then felt in his pocket. 'It's not quite
all off my chest yet. I have a small present for you, my dear. It's
quite impossible to find anything adequate of course, particularly
for a girl who has everything, so this is just a little memento.'

In the padded box he handed her was a charm bracelet with a
single gold charm on a heavy chain. Moulay had taken him to a
goldsmith who had made the charm to order in three days.
Modesty lifted it from the box. 'Why, this is lovely. It's a tiny
drum, isn't it? I don't quite see why . . . no, wait a moment, there's
a lid on it and a little handle—oh!' Her face lit up with delight.
'It's a can! A can of grease!'

'Not with contents. I trust the need won't arise again.'

She stood up and moved to the window, studying the charm in
the light. Round the squat cylinder were engraved the words, *With*
love and gratitude—G. T. Aglow with almost childish pleasure,
she came back to the armchair where he sat, slipped an arm round

his neck and bent to kiss him on the cheek. 'What a nice man you
are, Sir Gerald. Thank you for a lovely present.'

'It's just what you've always wanted?'

'But of course.'

'Good. Now, you said something about messages?'

'Oh, yes. First, Fraser and Réné Vaubois set their Portuguese
colleagues to cleaning up Mr Wu Smith's end of the blackmail
racket we told you about on the way to the clinic.' She sat down.
'It just means a notice going out to all contributors that no further
payments are to be made to that account. Wu Smith protested his
shocked horror to learn that his bank had been used in this way,
and he's making all speed to co-operate—so that's that bit. Quinn
asked me to thank you for the letter you wrote him, and to say he
didn't do a damn thing and was more of a hindrance than a help.
That's not true, but I'm just passing the message. And Lady Janet
sends you her regards.'

'Don't tell me there's nothing from Willie?'

'Willie hates you. You saw the bit with Sexton in the cave, and
he says it was wasted on you. He can't be consoled for having
missed it.'

Tarrant fingered his chin. 'It's all very well when you know how
it came out. But he'd have died a thousand deaths at the time, as
I did.'

'The funny thing is, Lady Janet and Quinn wish they'd been
there too. Not for technical reasons, like Willie. They just wish
they'd seen Sexton get his come-uppance. I'd no idea how blood-
thirsty nice people can be.'

'He was an evil man. But their desire is theoretical, I fancy.
There's no pleasure in the reality. Not even satisfaction. Just . . .
I don't know. Relief?'

'That's all. Oh, Willie did send a message. He tells me that for
a healthy male in the later stages of convalescence there's nothing
to beat a nice enthusiastic hunk of warm woman——'

'Oh really, Modesty!'

'Yes, he said you'd say that, and I was to tell you not to talk
nonsense about "at my age" and soon. He suggests a mature
Frenchwoman in your case, and if you'd like him to arrange it he
can recommend the very one.'

'He's a blasted pimp.'

Remembering as he walked through the empty park, Tarrant
chuckled. The odd thing was that Willie's prognosis had been
accurate. During the last few days of his convalescence he sometimes wished he had taken the suggestion less lightly.

He walked on, enjoying himself. Tarrant, the new man. There was no doubt he felt ten years younger than he had done six weeks ago, at the Nato Intelligence meeting. By the end of his convalescence he had been itching to get back to work, and had returned to tackle it with a zest which astonished Fraser. There had been a minor crisis in J Section yesterday, and he had remained at the office to deal with it, snatching a few hours sleep on the camp-bed he kept there. But he did not feel jaded.

A bench stood beside the path where it dipped and curved slightly. Tarrant sat down and took out his cigar case. He had not indulged all night, and could not remember when he had last smoked a cigar at six in the morning, but he intended to do so now. He lit the Punch-Punch claro carefully. The fragrance of it blended splendidly with the clear morning air.

From beyond the rising curve of the path came the sound of a voice raised in exhortation. 'Come on, Quinn, you can shove 'arder than that. Loosen your truss and get your 'ead down.'

Another voice, breathless. 'You . . . weigh a bloody ton, Garvin. Either that or she's got a lead backside.'

Something appeared at the top of the gentle slope. It consisted of two or three planks set on four wheels, with a rope attached like reins to the axle of the two front wheels for steering. Tarrant had seen children in the slums riding pram-wheel carts of this kind, but not for many years.

Modesty sat in front, Willie close behind her, his legs extended each side of her so that his feet rested near the front wheels. Her own legs were drawn up, the long white-and-gold dress she wore rucked back to her thighs. A mink cape covered her shoulders. Quinn was pushing. He and Willie wore dinner jackets. As Quinn straightened up and the cart began to roll down the slope, Lady Janet Gillam appeared beside him. She wore an evening trouser-suit in apple-green velvet which set off marvellously her chestnut hair.

Tarrant stood up, raised his hat and saluted with his umbrella as the cart rolled towards them. Willie jammed a foot against one wheel.

The cart swerved and slowed to a halt in front of Tarrant.

Modesty looked up at him with pleased surprise and said, 'What on earth are you doing here at this hour?'

'Some of us work, my dear. Did you trade in the Rolls for this?'

'No. Weng's waiting with the Rolls at Queen's Gate. We saw a boy with this when we were driving to the Old Vic, and Willie haggled with him.'

'I 'ad to go up to two quid,' Willie said. 'He was a big kid, about eight.'

Lady Janet and Quinn came down the slope arm in arm, and Tarrant greeted them, bowing over her hand. 'Is this a celebration?' he asked.

'It's the end of one, Sir Gerald.' Janet smiled and inclined her head towards Quinn. 'He's off to a flying job in the States tomorrow.'

Tarrant would scarcely have recognized Quinn as the pallid, red-eyed young man he had seen at Chateau Lancieux. He was very slightly drunk, but looked older and steadier, and was grinning as he said, still rather breathlessly, 'How are you, Sir Gerald?'

'Astonishingly fit, thank you. The best of luck in your new venture.'

'Give me a couple of years and I'll probably get the American Colonies back. We've been doing the town. First night of the new Stoppard, dinner at Le Gavroche, and a club-crawl. Have you ever been to a casino with those two crooks?' He nodded to Modesty and Willie on the cart.

'Well, I have to be careful of the company I keep. Is that how you wound up the celebration?'

'Quinn's Benefit,' they called it. 'A going-away present. Started with a tenner and worked the blackjack table as a syndicate.' He laughed. 'It was an eye-opener, wasn't it, Jan?'

She smiled. 'We came away with three hundred and eighty-seven pounds, and Willie says they weren't cheating, you just have to understand about the odds.'

'You can't cheat at blackjack, Lady Janet,' Tarrant observed. 'so we must credit him with telling the truth for once.' He turned to look down at Modesty and said severely, 'I'm bound to point out to you that you're showing your knickers.'

Willie said in a shocked voice, 'Language, Sir G! I'm surprised at you.'

Modesty shook her head. 'He stops at nothing, Willie love. If you knew the scandalous things he gets up to with a handful of grease and a naked girl, you'd blush for him.'

There was a time when Tarrant would have coloured with embarrassment, but no longer. He was another man now. 'You missed a rather interesting occasion there, Willie,' he said smugly. Reaching out past Modesty with his umbrella he tapped Willie on the shoulder. 'All right, get off. It's my turn now.'

Willie looked astonished for a moment, then grinned and edged himself off the cart.

Tarrant handed him the umbrella, cigar and hat, and took his place.

'Rest your 'eels 'ere, Sir G, ready to brake——'

'Kindly save your breath for pushing us up yonder slope, my good man,' Tarrant said briskly. 'And the next one. I intend to see this young lady to her carriage.'

Quinn gave a crow of triumph. 'Loosen your truss, Willie old mate.'

The cart began to roll. Tarrant reached past Modesty and gripped the rope, steering carefully, peering forward over her shoulder. Willie trotted behind.

Quinn took Janet's arm again and they walked on companionably down the slope. After a little while Quinn said, 'I'm excited and grateful about the job, but I'm sorry to be going.'

'I know. But after a year or two you'll be able to pick up again here, if you want to. And anyway . . .' she pressed his arm, 'you know you'd never be permanent for her. Only Willie's permanent.'

'Yes. I can't help wondering how permanent either of them's going to be.

'Please, Quinn. Don't.'

'Sorry, love. It was an idiotic thing to say. No reason why they should get involved in anything like that again.'

'No reason at all.'

She thought, 'Until one comes along.' But she did not speak the thought aloud. Perhaps Quinn's hopeful assertion would prove true, and they would not go away again. Or if they did, surely they would come back . . ? Time enough to be afraid when the moment came. And it might not come.

She said, 'Have you had any good nightmares lately?'

He half laughed. 'Just one. More of a bad dream, and that was about Sexton.'

'Not so bad as the other kind?'

'Nothing like it. I wouldn't say I'm purged of guilt, but I'm purged of wallowing in it, and that's a hell of a big step.'

'Good.'

'Are you coming to see me off, Jan?'

'Of course. You and I are the sole members of the Chateau Lancieux Old Comrades Association.'

'Well, I seem to remember there were others present.'

'Oh, we can't accept that lot.' She nodded ahead. 'They haven't got our amateur status.'

On the gently rising slope, Willie was using the brolly to pull the cart now, wearing Tarrant's hat and smoking his cigar.

Modesty said, 'We're all going to my place to sleep, Sir Gerald. Would you like to join us for an egg-and-bacon breakfast? Weng can run you home afterwards.'

'I'd be delighted.' Tarrant lifted his voice. 'Pull a bit harder, my man. Nearly at the top now.'

'Very good your honour.' Willie dragged the cart over the low crest, stood aside and touched his borrowed hat humbly.

The cart rolled on, Tarrant steering happily as it gathered speed. Modesty lifted a hand and waggled it in front of his face. He was absurdly pleased to see that she wore the charm bracelet on her wrist.

A REPORT
FROM GROUP 17

Robert C. O'Brien

*'A Report from Group 17' is published
by Victor Gollancz Ltd*

The Author

Robert C. O'Brien was born in New York City in 1922; his parents had both, at some time, been school teachers, and he was educated mainly in New York, as the family moved to various suburbs of the city. He intended becoming a professional musician, and studied pianoforte at the Juillard School. In addition, he took several courses of study at Columbia University including biology, philosophy and English literature. Later he held various jobs: in a bookstore, a mail room, an advertising agency, and as a newspaper reporter and staff writer on a couple of magazines. During this time he began freelance writing—stories, poems and essays. In 1972 he won the Newbery Award for his book, *Mrs Frisby and the Rats of NIMH*.

Robert C. O'Brien died in 1973.

To Sarah

In the ultimate chess game, the pieces are too big and heavy to move. The players may only sit and stare, wondering what would happen *if* . . . ? Eventually one of the players falls over, dead, and so the game is won by default. Time thus becomes the only considerable factor, and it is to the advantage of each player to hasten the ageing process of the other.

From the Notebooks of Marshal Dubrev Vasilovsky,
Leningrad, 1951

Between the two superpowers, any serious overt attack one against the other, whatever its form, will bring total nuclear retaliation. Thus, in effect, all normal implements of war are negated: rifles, cannon, tanks, ships, planes, men. Only biological attack remains, which need never be overt. Indeed, the victim of such an attack, though he may suspect, can never be sure he has been attacked.

Ibid.

There is a theory, current among some historians, and encouraged by certain archaeological evidence, that the fall of Rome was not attributable to the Huns and Goths with their primitive military techniques, but to a subtle alteration in the chemistry of the Tiber, from which the city drew its drinking water.

Ibid.

CHAPTER ONE

HE GOT SICK three days before he died. At first he only twitched, not all the time but now and then, and she could tell by watching him that he did not know when the twitches were coming, because he would drop things he had tried to pick up, and sometimes, if he was standing and his leg twitched, he would fall down.

As he got worse he did this more than before, and more violently, and began to drink great quantities of water, gulping enormously, then quitting, then starting again as if no matter how much he drank he remained as thirsty as before. She thought that drinking so much must be bad for him, and so, apparently, did the keepers, for after a while they stopped giving Abel (that was the name she had given him, Abel) any more water when he had drained his pail.

He was an ape, a big chimpanzee. His keepers were two men with hypodermic needles and bottles and jars of powders and liquids (chemicals?—she was not sure) and machines with pipes and hoses. One of the men was older and one was young. The older one, who had stringy grey hair and thick glasses, was in charge.

From her watching place, on the top of the wall where the branches and leaves kept her hidden, she could not see the machines very well. They were inside the concrete building near the cage; it had only one window on her side, and that one barred. Still, when the lights were on she could see a little. Besides the machines, there were more cages inside the building. There was also a stairway leading down, and what was in the basement she had no idea at all.

Sticking out from behind the building was one end of the swimming pool, also made of concrete, that nobody ever swam in. They did dip water out of it sometimes in odd-shaped glass bottles, and other times they poured stuff into it from their jars.

Today Abel was dying. She was sure of that. His twitching never stopped; he lay on the floor of the cage, whimpering; his long arms and legs were knotted around his body in such a way that she could no longer tell his front from his back. His neck was the worst. It was bent backward, so that his head seemed to be put on upside down. The keepers made no attempt to help him, but only watched. One of them was writing notes in a book.

Then, in one great spasm of twitching, under the terrible pull of the muscles, a bone broke, and then another. She heard the two snaps clearly, and the sound made her feel sick. She could watch no longer. She jumped, almost fell, down from the high wall.

She should not have jumped: that made noise. Having made it, she made more: instead of creeping silently away as usual, she ran, sending the stones rattling on the dry gravel road. She looked over her shoulder. But if the keepers had heard, they were not following. No head appeared over the wall to shout after her, and in a minute she had reached the bicycle hidden in the bushes across the road.

As she rode home, the road at first paralleled the massive stone wall, which was (so they said) seven feet tall, not counting the spiked iron fence that rose from the top of it. It was also (so they said) more than a mile long, surrounding the riverfront and enclosing a castle as well as the animal place. The castle had been built in the preceding century by a Russian duke and had (so they said) a hundred rooms. She had never seen it: it was not visible from the wall. In any case, she was more interested in animals than in Russians.

She wondered what the next one would be. Poor Abel. So far, except for one dog, they had all been monkeys, though of different sizes. The chimpanzee had been the biggest. None of them ever lived more than two or three weeks.

At the bottom of the hill the wall turned a corner and went left; the road went straight. Here, as they parted, the wall offered a break in its hard stone face: a pair of solid iron gates, painted black, as big as barn doors. She had never seen them open. It was customary, when she dismounted her bike for the push up the hill, at least to peer through the crack between them; not that there was ever anything to be seen but the empty driveway beyond. Today she did not bother. She was still unnerved by Abel's unpleasant death, and more, by her leap and run. The more she thought about it, the dumber it seemed she had been.

At the top of the hill stood her house, her home for as long as she could remember, a white, neatly kept oblong of frame and cinder block. There was no car in the driveway, which meant her mother was not yet home from work, which meant it was not yet five-thirty, which meant that if she started immediately she might get her homework done in time to watch the eight o'clock movie on television. Or was it her night to do the dishes? No, it was John's, because her mother had done them last night, and it went down by age.

She went to her room, got out her books and started on her geometry. Her younger brother, Willis, appeared in her doorway. He was five, and attended kindergarten.

'Allie?'

'What?'

'Where did you go?'

'No place. Down the hill.'

'But I wanted to go.'

'You weren't here.'

'I was so.'

'Not when I went.'

'Well, the bus was late.'

'Anyway, you don't have to go every time.'

'Did you go to'—he shut the door, since this was private between them—'the animal place?'

'Maybe.' She found that she did not particularly want to talk about it.

'*Did* you?'

'Yes.'

'Did you see Abel?'

'Never mind.'

'What happened?'

'He died.'

'Died! Oh, Allie. Did he bleed?'

'No. Anyway, I didn't want to watch.'

'Why not? I would have.'

'How do you know? You never even saw him. You've never seen any of them.'

That was true. Though Willis had been with her when the animal place was first discovered, he was unable to climb the tree that led to the top of the wall—climbing the tree was, of course, how she had discovered the place—and so he had, in return for sworn secrecy, received only verbal accounts of what went on there. While she watched, he waited. Furthermore, he waited in abject silence, not permitted to play, as that would make noise.

The two keepers, when they talked, spoke in a language she could not understand at all. But without being able to grasp even a word, she was nonetheless absolutely certain about one thing: they were working in secret. If they should discover that she was watching them, they would put a stop to it one way or another. On the other hand, if her mother knew she was watching something that was supposed to be private she would call it prying, and would undoubtedly forbid her to continue.

Therefore, threatened from both sides, she said nothing about the animals to anyone, and strictly instructed Willis to do the same. He would follow orders. He liked secrets, and was loyal about keeping them. And he admired his sister, who was seven years his senior, with an intensity that amounted to fanaticism.

Dr. Helmuth Schutz, the head keeper, studying his dying chimpanzee, had, in fact, heard the noise Allie made as she jumped from the wall. Intent only on what the animal was doing, he pressed the sound instantly into his memory, from which it emerged disturbingly fifteen minutes later. By that time the chimpanzee had lost respiration eight minutes ago and must be assumed dead despite two last, large injections of atropine. Another failure, another example of stupidity.

Not his failure nor his stupidity. The stupidity of officialdom, of bureaucratic regulations applied to science by ill-educated laymen who did not understand even vaguely the biological processes involved in the experiments. Petty, puffed-up clerks who could not grasp the simple fact that it was impossible to determine the stamina and resistance of a smuggled, black-market ape, age unknown, health background unknown.

He thought of Kublitz, the slight, sickly faced supervisor to whom he must make application (always in quadruplicate, always on the same proper forms, always with all of the fifty-eight blanks filled in) for equipment, supplies, research animals, chemicals, nutrients. Not so much as a pipette could be acquired without bowing to Kublitz.

To men like Kublitz, biological research was simple: an ape resembles a man, therefore it will react like a man. Stupidity. In most cases the reaction of a rat was more reliable, and rats were available by the dozen. But even assuming an abundance of research animals—rats or chimpanzees, healthy ones—what was the use? He could, perhaps, determine eventually the likely rate of spread of a viral infection through a group of chimpanzees. But this information would be of dubious value, or, at best, preliminary value, to his employers. Eventually, to obtain meaningful statistics pertaining to men, human subjects must be used in the research. He had demonstrated this point—he had proved it—in Silesia in 1943. His present employers had not forgotten that, or him. If they had, would he be here?

Why, then, could he not convince his employers that his present research would produce results which could only be, at best, inconclusive and might be, at less than best, misleading? Why indeed? Because of Kublitz. It was as simple as that. In the bureaucracy, Kublitz was the next step up. Except through Kublitz, he had no contact with his superiors.

Dr Schutz's assistant, a methodical but surly young man named Georg Wolter, came out of the laboratory carrying a zipper bag of grey plastic.

'We will have the autopsy now?' He spoke, as always, in German.

'It is necessary,' Dr Schutz replied in the same language. 'How else can we prepare the report?'

'Of what use are such reports?' Georg at least agreed with Dr Schutz as to the value of chimpanzees as research animals.

They placed the body in the plastic bag. It was as he closed the zipper that Dr Schutz remembered that someone or something, over behind the wall, had, a few minutes ago, made a loud noise.

CHAPTER TWO

FERGUS O'NEIL, aged thirty-six, Ph.D., F.N.B.S., sat at his desk in his dismal office and stared out the window at the dirty snow, the murky sky, the bedraggled bushes, the bare birch trees standing like skeletons holding hands. There was a pile of aged correspondence, unopened, on his desk. He was suffering from a hangover. Still he mustered his thoughts in a logical manner.

Problem: what do you do when you solve a problem?

Solution: you find a new problem.

Problem: what new problem?

Solution:

But there, each time, he went blank. How do you summon the energy after three years of hard work, night and day, to start all over again? He recognized his ailment, one peculiar to research scientists, who call it PTS, Post Terminal Slump. For two years he had worked on the b-virus, he and Jerome and John, the Midnight Squad, and finally they had isolated it. Then another year, as John said, training it, getting it to do what it was supposed to do, and finally, wildly, succeeding.

And now the PTS.

Problem: how to regenerate enthusiasm?

Solution: take a vacation. They had husbanded the research grant, which was nonaccountable; there was still a little money left. Take time off to think about the unpleasant alternatives. A steady job. In a corporation laboratory? Teaching? Endless papers to correct. Seas of bright undergraduate faces at eight in the morning, and him with a hangover. Tricky questions from show-off junior Phi Beta Kappas. He knew. He had been one himself.

At age twelve it was discovered that Fergus O'Neil, then attending junior high school in Massapequa, Long Island, had an I.Q. that ran off the chart. This fact was supposed to be concealed from him; intelligence ratings were confidential, to avoid odious comparisons. But it filtered through, from school psychologist to teachers to his parents to Fergus. It did not make him conceited. Instead, he regarded it with the same mild sense of good fortune as he did having good vision, an ear for music, and the ability to swim the 100-metre free-style fast enough to make the team. They were endowments, not achievements.

In high school, Fergus got 'A' in all subjects except biology, where, to everyone's astonishment except his own, he got only a poor 'C-minus.' He himself was more annoyed than surprised. Biology was a subject with which he could not come to grips, and he was reasonably sure that the fault lay not in him but in the subject itself. As taught in the Massapequa schools, at least, biology was a mixture of folklore and tradition, inexact description, arbitrary classification and nomenclature, and endless memorization. It was not a science at all in the sense that physics was, or even chemistry. From Pliny to Linnaeus, biologists were mere journalists of the obvious, notekeepers, prosy lecturers, bird watchers. Not until Darwin and Mendel was there even the beginning of an analytical approach, the asking of how and why, rather than merely what and where.

Yet it was potentially a true science. He had the feeling, even in high school, that it was on the edge of revolution.

In college, Fergus argued with himself for almost three years as to whether his major study should be history or physics. Late one night in the middle of his junior year he decided against both in favour of biology. He thought: it is, in the end, the basic subject, without which there could be neither of the others. He also thought that if there was a revolution coming, he might help it along.

There was a knock on his office door, and Miss Penfield entered. Miss Penfield, whose first name was Adele, was secretary to Fergus and two other faculty members at the Institute for Advanced Biological Studies in Cambridge, Massachusetts. She had been hired not for her looks, nor even for her speed at shorthand, but because she had a background in biology and knew how to spell ribonucleic, cytidine, and glycoside. She was plain of face and destined for spinsterhood, a fact she accepted calmly; she was devoted to all three of her masters, but especially to Fergus, since he alone remained a bachelor. She had never seen his rooms, but she was sure they were not properly dusted. Since she was older than he was, she called him by his first name, a liberty she did not take with her two professors, both of whom were in their sixties.

'Miss Penfield,' said Fergus, still staring out the window, 'do you know why I prefer the laboratory to the office? Because it has no windows. A window on Cambridge in April is an offence. You're seeing last October's snow, and it's turned rotten.'

Miss Penfield was familiar with PTS.

'You could pull down the shade.'

'That would be escapism. The laboratory is windowless for a purpose. Whether the shade is up or down, that decayed snow is out there. So are all the dead trees and bushes. In April they should be alive again. The fact is, Cambridge is unfit for human habitation.'

'I've lived here all my life,' said Miss Penfield. 'Fergus, you feel bad because you're finished with the b-virus.'

'I know it. But looking out the window helps.'

'Helps how? If it's so ugly.'

'Helps me to make up my mind.'

'You're not thinking about leaving?' She sounded distressed.

'I'm thinking about never seeing another winter in New England.'

'But you've never seen one, locked up in that laboratory. Sometimes it's beautiful. People come here from all over——' She stopped, remembering what she had come in for. 'That man who called——'

'What man?'

'The man from Washington. The colonel. He called you three times yesterday. I told you.'

'Starting with lunchtime,' Fergus said, 'I don't remember yesterday very well.'

'I suppose not. Anyway, he's coming in to see you.'

'About what?'

'He wouldn't say. But I can make a guess.'

'Make it.'

'He's a colonel. He's from Washington. He wants to offer you a job. He's one of them.' She put the word 'them' in italics.

'Miss Penfield, you forget. There is no more "them." Germ warfare has been abolished.'

'That's what they say. They didn't abolish the generals who ran it.'

'And you committed me anyway?'

'Well, I couldn't be sure. And he sounded pleasant enough, so I didn't want to be rude.'

Only a few minutes after the visitor arrived, Fergus could recall that Miss Penfield's intuition had been, as usual, accurate. He wore civilian clothes, a dark blue suit; he had dark grey hair and a calm face. He handed Fergus a card which said:

JAMES ATTENBOROUGH

COLONEL

UNITED STATES ARMY

In the lower left-hand corner was the additional information, 'Research and Development.'

'Have a chair, Colonel. What is it that you research and develop?'

'For the past several days, the research has centred on you, your published papers, your current work with the b-virus, which is, I believe, just completed but not yet published. As to what will develop'—he smiled—'that's up to you.' He spoke as if he had an unmilitary sense of humour; as Miss Penfield had said, pleasant enough.

'And before that?'

'I was in charge of a section of Fort Detrick. Biological weapons. Specifically, microbiology and virology.'

'And now find yourself unemployed.'

'Not quite. I'm Regular Army, so the most I'd get would be a transfer. As it turns out, it isn't even much of a transfer. For the moment, at least.'

'But we've banned biological weapons.'

'We have. They haven't. Nearly half of our work at Fort Detrick was figuring out what the opposition was working on, and how to counteract it.'

'In other words, you go on just as before.'

'There are those who think we should. I'm not one of them. I don't like germs. You can't aim them accurately.'

'But you're still at Fort Detrick.'

'In and out. Right now I'm on a special project, rather an odd one. It's what brings me here.'

'Why here?'

'Because I want to ask your help. In fact, I'm offering you a job.'

Score two for Miss Penfield. 'What's the nature of the project?'

'Biological weapons.'

'Defensive, of course.'

'Of course.'

'I'm sorry, Colonel. You know as well as I do that in biology—my branch of it, at least—you can't separate offence from defence. If it's at Fort Detrick, if it's for the Army, it's military. The potential is there, tied up in the knowledge. I won't touch it. Now or ever.'

The Colonel smiled again. He looked as if he had heard exactly what he expected to hear. He said, 'The project in which I'm involved is not at Fort Detrick, and it's not for the Army. It's civilian—the Department of State. I'd like to explain it, if I may.'

Fergus was only mildly curious. 'If you like. But I repeat, if it has anything to do with germ warfare, I'm not interested.'

The Colonel seemed to be changing the subject. He asked, 'Have you ever heard the name Helmuth Schutz?'

CHAPTER THREE

THE ODD THING about the household was that it worked. Improbable as it had seemed, at first. even to her; impossible and annoyingly perverse to her friends, relatives, and especially her in-laws. There were disadvantages, she would admit, to a widow's living alone in the woods with her three children. But there were disadvantages to being a widow wherever you lived.

After Andrew died in the crash, his parents, who were well-to-do, had invited her to come and live with them in their big house in Washington. Temporarily, of course, but to stay as long as she liked, until she found a nice apartment and, if she wanted it, a job. As it turned out, she found the job first, and it was not in the city but out in the country where they lived, in the new medical clinic the county had built. Dr Lewis, who treated her for shock after her husband's death, had remembered her and told her about it. She kept track of appointments and mailed out bills. The pay was not high but the work was easy and the commuting only ten minutes over a pretty country road. Most of all, she had been unable to face the thought of being cheerful (for the children's sake) in a cheerless place, a strange house, a new apartment. The job made it possible to stay in the place Andrew and she had loved together.

She saw, as she came in, that John had split the wood for the fireplace and stacked it neatly on the back porch. Poor John; his conscientiousness at fourteen nearly always made her feel like crying. Allison's bicycle was sprawled where she had leaped off it. Willis was at the door to meet her.

'How was school?'

'It was good. Miss Davis read us a book, only she didn't finish it.'

She went to the kitchen, saw that someone, almost certainly John again, had put away the breakfast dishes she had left in the rack. She decided on veal chops for dinner; veal chops, rice, and broccoli. There was cake for dessert.

'That's nice. What was the book?'

'I forget. It's about a girl that lived in the mountains, but I forget her name.'

'Heidi?'

'That's *right!*' Willis was astonished. 'How did you guess?'

'I read the book once myself. It's a very famous book.'

'Did Allie read it?'

'I expect so. I think she has a copy on her bookshelf.'

'Can I borrow it?'

'Ask her. But not now. Let her do her homework.'

There was a letter for her, addressed in blue ink, 'Mrs Jennifer Adam, RFD # 2 . . .' in a familiar hand, from Mrs George Adam, in Washington. Her mother-in-law phoned once a week and wrote once a month. It could wait until after dinner.

The household had worked at first, or so she thought then, because they had been forced together, like people after a shipwreck, all bereft by the loss, needing each other's presence. So short a time ago it seemed; yet it was fourteen months now, and she realized that the pervading sadness had dissipated almost entirely. The empty chair, the empty bed were always present and they were aware of them, yet there was as much joy, no more and no less, in the house and in the barn and the pasture as there had been before. It was not her doing; she wondered at it at first but no more; it was his. The staunchness of spirit, the unvarying independence which had prompted him to buy this house in the woods in the first place, had been inherited (or otherwise acquired or learned—how could one tell?) by his children and from them, somehow, by her. Disaster had submerged them only momentarily; like corks they had bobbed up again immediately to the same buoyancy as before. The household was—was there a better word for it?—stalwart.

The house was not really in the woods, but near the edge of it. They had bought it along with sixty acres of land which would, they hoped, increase in value; yet they bought it not as an investment but because it had the quality of remoteness that Andrew sought. From its windows no other habitation could be seen, and since the road came to an end in mud and river not far beyond them, scarcely ever did a car drive by. Of the acres about ten were cleared, and on these they had kept, over the past fourteen years, a jumble of animals: horses, ponies, dogs, cats, a lamb, rabbits, chickens. A nearby farmer had even once given them a baby pig, which became a pet and at maturity would still come running, along with the dogs, when whistled for. It squealed as it came, and it was John's theory at age eight that it thought it was a dog, and that the squeals were barks.

The veal chops, salted, were in the pan; the rice and broccoli were boiling. She called to John and Allison to set the table and then to eat. Willis asked Allison if he might borrow her book.

'What book?'

'*Hiding.*'

His mother said: 'Willis, it's *Heidi.*'

'High *Dee.*'

'What do you want it for?'

'To read.'

'You can't read.'

'I can read *Work and Play.*'

'Yes, but *Heidi*'s harder.'

'Let him borrow it for a little while to look at the pictures.'

'Okay. But don't colour in it.'

John changed the subject. 'Big Henry came to call.'

She sighed. 'What did he bring this time?'

'Nothing. Only an offer of his services.'

'Oh? What kind?'

'He wanted to know if you'd like him to plough the garden again.'

'What did you say?'

'I told him you would be delighted—that your gratitude would be unbounded.'

'And what did he say to that?'

'He said he'd be around early evenin' one day this week when she's dried up some.'

'I'd have more gratitude if he'd let me pay him.'

'A smile is all the pay he asks.'

It was true. Big Henry, whose last name was Carpenter, was a slightly retarded member of a rambling local family. Some of the Carpenters were on relief, some were small farmers, some worked on the roads; one, the most prosperous, was a building contractor. Henry, nearly forty, had never been married; the sight of a pretty widow could set him dancing, though he was, in fact, too shy ever to look directly at her, but stared always at the sky over her shoulder, letting his peripheral vision do its best. He brought her presents of fresh corn, and venison, bass, quail in season. He was at present her only male admirer, and that was one of the disadvantages of living in a house in the woods.

After the autopsy on the chimpanzee was finished, Dr Schutz left his assistant to complete the cremation, and walked alone over to the part of the wall where the noise had come from. There was nothing to be seen on his side, and the wall itself was too high to scale or see over without a ladder. Standing back, however, he observed that a good-sized young tree, an aspen, had grown up close to the wall on the other side; some of its branches, newly green with spring leaves, passed through the ironwork on top. That should not be, he thought. A tree could serve as a ladder, and the purpose of this wall was to keep intruders out. He should complain to Kublitz, who would have the tree removed. At such things Kublitz, who had a passion for security, would be efficient.

Then he had a second thought. It would perhaps be better to find out first who or what had been in the tree. It might have been just an animal—there was a large animal, native to these woods, that climbed trees. *Beutelratte*. What was the English? Opossum. But if it was a person, that would be much more interesting. Someone watching—someone spying? Interesting, but not alarming. Nothing that he and Georg Wolter were doing, seen from such a vantage point, would provide even a clue to the nature of their research. Especially to an ordinary observer, and especially to one who could not possibly have any idea who he, Helmuth Schutz, was.

He thought a moment, and then set out along the wall, walking parallel to it. There was the faint remainder of a path, though this part of the grounds was at present almost entirely unused. He went quickly, for the daylight was fading and he would not be able to see much longer.

There it was, ahead, as he had thought: an iron gate, double, heavily barred and hooked with a chain, but not locked—again, to keep intruders out rather than the occupants in. A driveway with a thin coating of grey pebbly gravel led back from the gate into the woods, off to his left in the direction of the big house. From the house itself, on the other side of the grounds, he had seen it emerge from the woods; it led to the back door—perhaps originally a service entrance. He did not know. He slid the bar back and unhooked the chain. The gate opened inward; though disused, it swung easily and silently on its hinges. He pulled it in only a foot, enough to slip through.

Outside he found himself on a rough gravel road, to the left leading steeply uphill, to his right running parallel to the wall, in the direction he had just come from. He could see the aspen tree, and beyond it where the road deteriorated into a delta of muddy ruts as it reached the low marshy land that bordered the river; the Potomac. It was wide here, flowing sluggishly towards Washington, the capital of this country in which he, a stranger, an alien—a double alien—did not belong at all.

At the base of the tree he studied the ground. Because of shade from the wall and the foliage it was only sparsely grown up in weeds, and it was soft. Even in twilight it took no skill to see that what had made the noise was human. There were a confusion of footprints, but one pair, between the wall and the tree trunk, were deeply impressed. They were clearly made by someone who had landed hard, someone wearing tennis shoes, for there was no heel. More interesting, they were narrow, almost certainly those of a woman or a girl who, for some reason had been watching him from the top of the wall.

Still thinking, he found a dead branch lying near the roadside and scraped the ground, obliterating the deep prints and leaving that patch of earth softer than the rest. He decided against saying anything to Kublitz for the time being.

CHAPTER FOUR

'HELMUTH SCHUTZ,' Fergus O'Neil said. 'Yes. He was a student of Genini's in Italy, a German. He ran a four-year series of experiments and wrote a paper—a book really. What was it? "Virus and Heredity". I read it.'

'Almost,' said Colonel Attenborough. 'It was "Genetics and Virology".'

'Right. The experiments were ingenious—brilliant, I guess. But he made some pretty wild claims. Growing feathers on rabbits, something like that.'

'Not quite. By altering genetic cells with injections of virus into the nucleus, he induced changes in bone structure, hair, pigmentation. He claimed these mutations were passed on through ten, twelve generations. He offered pictures to prove it, but some of his more conservative colleagues still didn't believe it. Now, they probably would. But that was in 1937, before anybody ever heard of DNA.'

Fergus said, 'He was—if he really did it—altering the DNA without even knowing it existed.'

'Don't be too sure he didn't know. I re-read his book the other day. He had an uncanny intuition. He described how the DNA works almost perfectly. He just didn't know what it looked like.

'Anyway, they laughed at him—they got pretty sarcastic in some of the scientific journals. He turned sour. Just then the Nazis came along. They picked him up. Made him their boy. They wanted him to breed supersoldiers.'

'They're not the only ones to have that idea,' said Fergus dryly.

'No, but as far as we know, they're the only ones who ever did anything about it. They put Dr Schutz in a fancy laboratory in Munich and gave him everything he asked for. And for rabbits, they substituted people. At first Jews, then Polish prisoners of war, mostly women.'

'I'd forgotten,' said Fergus. 'He wrote another paper about that.'

'Not a very scientific one. "Experimental Use of the *Untermensch*".'

'I've read that one, too, or excerpts from it. An almost ranting defence of the idea of using human beings as laboratory animals. Sacrifice the weak to make the human race stronger. The Poles were the weak, the *Untermenschen*. The Germans were the human race.'

'You have a good memory.'

'That's about all I remember. Except that he died at the end of the war, somewhere in East Germany.'

'It was in Silesia. He was running a laboratory next to a concentration camp. There were rumours: he was producing zombies —making his own submen. And he didn't exactly die. The Russians overran Silesia, blew up his lab. He disappeared, and was presumed dead. The presumption was wrong.'

'Are you saying he's still alive? He can't be still working. He hasn't published anything in twenty-five years.'

'Not under his own name. And not for circulation to a very wide audience. Does the name Vasilovsky mean anything to you?'

'Not a thing. Sounds like a Russian.'

'Marshal Dubrev Vasilovsky is, nominally at least, in charge of biological warfare for the Soviet Union. I say nominally because we think his appointment may have been just a sop for the Red Army. You see, in Russia the army doesn't control germ warfare, not this branch of it at least. It's under the KGB—the Ministry of Intelligence.

'In any case, that doesn't really matter. Russian research on biological warfare, when reported, appears under Vasilovsky's signature. The individual scientists or teams who did the work are identified only by numbers. Perhaps they prefer that. The reports are top secret, and, as I said, don't reach a very large audience. Most of the work is done in a group of laboratories at a place called Novokuznetsk, in southern Siberia. It's not a place that one can visit freely.'

'And Dr Schutz is there.'

'He was there. He isn't any more.'

Fergus O'Neil, still sitting behind his desk, tilted his chair back. He opened a drawer, took out a paper clip, turned it in his fingers, put it back, and shut the drawer.

'Colonel Attenborough, I will admit that the conversation has been interesting so far. But it doesn't seem to be getting anywhere, does it? Can you tell me, straight out, what all this has to do with me?'

'It has this to do with you: Dr Schutz is here, in this country. He's working in a laboratory near Washington, D.C. We want to find out why, and what he's doing. To do that we need your help.'

'Surely he's not here legally? A known Nazi—wouldn't he be a war criminal? At least an undesirable alien.'

'He is not here legally. In fact, officially he's not here at all.'

'Then why not just arrest him? Ask him what he's doing. Then kick him out.'

'There's nothing I'd like better. But as I said, it's a State Department thing, and they say we can't touch him.'

'Why not?'

'It takes some telling. Do you know the city of Washington?'

'I've been there a few times, looking for money.'

'Have you ever been up the Potomac River?'

'No. Wait. Yes. Some friends took me sight-seeing once—up to a waterfall. About ten miles upstream.'

'The Great Falls of the Potomac. Above that, the river broadens out, then narrows again, and then backs up into a good-sized lake —Seneca Lake, they call it. Most of the land on both sides is in woods, and the plan is to keep it that way as a national park. But one big stretch, just at the lower neck of the lake, has a history of its own.'

'Is that where Dr Schutz is supposed to be?'

'It is. About 1910, the Russian government sent a new ambassador to Washington. He was a cousin of the Czar, a Count Alexander Orlov or Orloff, something like that. He was rich, of course, and he couldn't stand Washington—it was too hot for him. So he bought several hundred acres of river-front land about twenty miles out of town, laid a private road into it, and built an enormous house—a castle. He called it Villa Petrograd; it even has onion domes like the Kremlin. He lived there, and came to town, to the embassy, only when ceremony required it. He built a high stone wall around the place—it's as secure as a fort—and when the revolution came, he just stayed on. He was smart. He had his money in a Swiss bank.

'Count Alexander died in 1938, and left no heirs. His wife was dead. He had had two sons, but both were in school in Russia when the revolution came. They never got out. After his death, for several years the castle just sat there empty.

'Then an unusual thing happened. A few years earlier, the United States government had officially recognized Communist Soviet Russia for the first time. A new Russian embassy opened in Washington. The new ambassador, a communist named Grushenkyn, claimed Villa Petrograd for Red Russia. He said since it had been built and used by the former ambassador it was Russian government property.

'It was an odd claim, and wouldn't have stood up five minutes in court. But it never got to court. What Grushenkyn wanted, it turned out, was a country place where he and other iron curtain embassy people could go on weekends. As it happened, our embassy in Moscow was looking for the same kind of place. So a deal was worked out. We acquired an estate on a lake thirty miles out of Moscow; they got Villa Petrograd. It's got something like a hundred and twenty rooms.

'Part of the deal was that both places have the status of an embassy—foreign soil. American police, FBI, you name it, can't stick a toe inside the grounds of Villa Petrograd without violating diplomatic immunity.'

'I get it,' said Fergus O'Neil. 'Even if you know Dr Schutz is in there, you can't get at him.'

'Not unless he strays outside the grounds. Presumably he knows that, and so far as we know, he hasn't strayed. In fact, no American—State Department, FBI, nobody—has actually seen him.'

'Then what makes you think he's there at all?'

'Because of some extremely reliable information from Novokuznetsk. And because of some odd things that have beeen happening at Villa Petrograd. The odd things have to be considered in the light of one overriding fact. Just downstream from the Villa, the city of Washington taps the Potomac. That's where all the drinking water comes from.'

Giving as an excuse a non-existent headache, Dr Schutz left Georg Wolter in charge of the afternoon's duties in the laboratory. The work was routine in any case: renewing the nutrient for the cultures, recording their condition, checking temperatures in the incubators. Then analysing today's water samples from the river for chemical and biological variations; checking the thermograph and hydrometer for temperature and rate of flow of the water. Endless and boring work, but essential, more valuable than the stupid tests on the apes.

He started from the laboratory as if he were heading for the big house, the Villa, where he had his quarters. No need for Georg to know where he was going. Then, as soon as he was out of sight of the building, he left the small asphalt walkway and turned right through the woods. It was a beautifully kept forest; he would give his Russian hosts and their groundskeeepers credit for that; lofty, widespreading oaks, shadowy, well cleared of underbrush, like the *Wälder* at home in Germany. He enjoyed the walk to the gate.

Opening it, again just enough to slip through, he scanned the road in both directions. No one. He pulled the heavy gate shut behind him. Unless someone pushed it hard, there was no way to tell, from outside, that it was unlocked. He turned right and walked down the road a short distance towards the aspen tree. About halfway between the gate and the tree he turned left off the road, up the small embankment, through some dusty bushes and into the rather scrubby woods across from the wall. He picked a spot from which he was unlikely to be seen, but from which he could see the gate, the aspen tree, the wall, and most of the road. He sat down, waited, and watched.

In approximately half an hour—which was, on the doctor's Russian-made stainless steel watch, five minutes past four—he saw a bicycle come coasting down the hill, bumping over the rough road. On it rode a girl (he had been right) with light-brown hair hanging straight around her shoulders, age (he would guess) twelve or thirteen. She wore blue jeans neatly patched at one knee, and on her feet narrow white sneakers. She drove the bicycle past where he sat. She stopped, dismounted, and concealed it behind a bush. Then, walking softly, she went to the aspen tree.

She climbed it as easily as a ladder, disappearing into the foliage, then reappearing near the top, her head and hair level with the edge of the wall. Cautiously she inched higher, until she was looking down at where the laboratory must be. Dr Schutz thought she would not continue looking very long, since today there would be nothing to see but the buildings; Georg would be in the main laboratory, underground. He also thought, from the extreme caution with which she moved, that she was aware she might have been overheard on her last visit.

He was right on the first point at least. In fewer than five minutes her head disappeared among the leaves, and she climbed back down the tree. Somewhat less stealthily than before, she took her bicycle from the bushes and rode off. He was ready to stand up when he saw that she had stopped at the gate. Had she somehow perceived that it was unlocked? But no; she merely walked close to it, laying her bicycle down, and peered for a long moment through the crack between the two doors. Still, of all her actions, to Dr Schutz this last was the most interesting.

CHAPTER FIVE

'FOR ONE THING,' the Colonel said, 'they've built themselves a zoo. That wouldn't seem surprising, at first glance. I mean, the Villa is for recreation, and the Russians are great animal watchers. They love circuses. And yet, when you think about it, why bother? They have the Washington National Zoo, one of the world's best, only a mile from Embassy Row. They can be there in minutes.'

Fergus said, 'Maybe. Still, people do keep pets. What do they have in their zoo? Or do we know?'

'We know. By "we" I mean one of the US government agencies. The term, I believe, is infiltrated. We have an informant in the Russian Embassy, as we may assume they have one in ours. He goes out to the Villa. He tells us they have two rather mangy leopards, a small brown bear, a wild boar, and a smattering of monkeys and apes. Not a very impressive collection. There seems to be a turnover among the simians. They keep dying.'

'What's the connection between Helmuth Schutz and the zoo?'

'Not clear.' The Colonel opened his briefcase and took from it a folder containing a sheaf of papers. He handed one of the papers to Fergus. 'Here's a list of equipment recently purchased by the Russian Embassy. We're reasonably sure it's at Villa Petrograd. In the zoo.'

The list was a typed order form on the stationery of a laboratory supply firm in Baltimore: Bio-Physics Equipment, Inc. Fergus scanned it, disinterestedly at first, then curiously, finally with incredulity.

'This equipment at a zoo?' he said. 'The idea is ridiculous.'

'So we thought.'

'What would a zoo want with an X-ray spectrometer? Or a Bailey centrifuge? And all those Martel reduction jars and Petri dishes? That's all microbiology. That's the same equipment we've been using here with the b-virus.'

'I know,' said the Colonel. 'But stop a minute. Consider it the other way around. What would a microbiologist want with a zoo?'

'Of course,' said Fergus. 'Test animals.'

'Of course.'

'But there's another question. How could the Russian Embassy order this stuff? Wouldn't they realize——'

'How odd it looks?' The Colonel considered, and then gave away another secret. 'The fact is, they didn't order it directly. They bought it through a friend, an American. They have quite a few of those. Not traitors, really. Not even necessarily communists. Just people who like Russians, get to know them, and see no harm in doing their friends an innocent favour.'

'This one might not be so innocent.'

'There was a plausible story. The equipment was to be sent to the University of Moscow, for use in the Soviet Academy of Medicine.'

'But it wasn't?'

'Why should it be? Half the stuff on the list is German manufacture. It doesn't show, but it is. Why buy it here to ship to Moscow?'

Fergus studied the list again.

'It's a wonder they didn't buy an electron microscope while they were at it.'

'I can even guess at that. They're very expensive, as you know. My guess is that they'd completed that phase of the work at Novokuznetsk before they packed Dr Schutz up and sent him over here.'

'Do you know what that phase was?'

'No. There's the trouble. If it's been published it would be ultra-top secret. We get some of those papers eventually, but not all, and sometimes not until two years later.'

'Do you have papers on any of Schutz's recent work?'

'Yes. In General Vasilovsky's reports, Schutz appears as "Group 17". Four years ago, he was still working on genetics—basically the same problem that attracted the Nazis, but with better methods, modern tools. In short, controlled alteration of the genetic code—the DNA—by means of a virus, by radiation, by transplanting nuclei, by chemical mutagens.'

'Our b-virus project,' said Fergus. 'Could I see his reports?'

'For obvious reasons,' said the Colonel, 'I can't carry copies around with me. But you can see them if you'll come to Washington.'

'Colonel, I'm not going to Washington.' Fergus stopped, hesitated, and was lost. 'But if I should, what would I be expected to do?'

'Nothing hard, nothing dangerous. All we want from you is an educated guess. For that, we can offer quite a generous per diem, a consultant's fee. Say for a month, maybe two months—your option.

'First, you talk to some people from State. Second, talk to a man from CIA who knows quite a lot about Dr Schutz and his papers. Third, take a vacation. Rent a cabin near the river. We've got the cabin lined up, and it's cheap. In fact, free. Then go fishing.'

'Fishing? In this weather?' Fergus looked out the window at the grey-brown snow.

'In Washington, right now, the dogwood is blooming and the bass are biting. They're biting particularly well along the shore of Villa Petrograd.'

Allie and Willis followed behind Big Henry's tractor, gathering worms. Allie carried a used coffee can, into which she had crumbled some dirt. They had to stay close behind the tractor because most of the worms exposed by the big plough blade slid quickly back into the damp earth and disappeared. The engine was noisy and they talked little, but each time Willis extricated an unusually large worm he would hold it up joyously for Allie to admire. Finally she said, shouting over the clatter: 'Willis, don't *hold* them, just put them in the can. I know they're big.' He looked up at her and thought that her light hair, shining loose around her head, looked like a cloud in the sun. He liked everything Allie did, but he particularly liked her hair.

And her room. When the coffee can was full, or full enough, they took the worms to her room. It had a secret doorway. Allie said, 'Willis, it's not secret. Everybody can see it.' Still, none of the other bedrooms had one; it was there because Allie's room, on the ground floor (the other bedrooms were upstairs), had once been a screened porch, with a screen door leading out. When their father, John helping, had enclosed it, he replaced the screen door with a door of glass. It looked out on a narrow sweep of lawn and, beyond that, the woods. Willis thought it must be like sleeping outdoors. Also, one could leave and enter without anyone else knowing.

Through this door they took the worms.

'When can we go?'

'Saturday.'

'Oh, Allie. Why can't we go today?'

'You know the rule. We can't go to the river by ourselves.'

'Then let's get John.'

'John can't go. He's studying for Finals.'

'I'll ask him,' cried Willis, running for the stairs, for John's room.

'It's no use,' Allie called after him. 'I already did.' She put the can of worms under her bed. Willis came back.

'But the worms will all die.'

'No they won't. It's only two days.'

'Maybe we can go tomorrow.'

'John says Saturday. Anyway, Mother will be home, so she can go, too. But I'll tell you what.'

'What?'

'Tomorrow, right after school, we'll go and see if they have a new animal. I looked yesterday, and they didn't. But they might tomorrow.'

Kublitz's office, in the basement of the enormous spired and domed stone structure that was the centre of Villa Petrograd, stood entirely underground and had no windows. As Dr Schutz entered, he sniffed with distaste the faintly rancid smell exuded by the stone walls and the bare cement floor, a smell which clung to Kublitz wherever he went. It was a sour place, shadowy despite the fluorescent lights in the ceiling; a suitable habitat for the sharp-faced KGB agent behind the steel desk.

Four heavy safes stood along the wall behind Kublitz's desk, each with two dials on its door. Dr Schutz had seen many such safes in Siberia, in Novokuznetsk. No one person was permitted to know the combinations for both dials; thus two must always be present when a safe was opened. The safes were vented, and at the push of a button a gasoline geyser in each would turn it into an incinerator.

Without greeting, Dr Schutz handed his autopsy report to Kublitz and requested removal of another chimpanzee from the zoo to the laboratory. Kublitz, who was under orders to supply him with apes as needed, was nonetheless surly.

'They are not free, you know,' he said. 'They are expensive. You have already killed nine.' Kublitz, half Polish and half Russian, spoke no German. Since Dr Schutz spoke no Russian, they addressed one another in English. Kublitz's English was imperfect; Dr Schutz's was excellent.

'The animal was in ill health when I received it,' he said.

'So you have said before.'

'So it has been before. In any case, that phase of my research is complete. The mortality rate will now decline.'

'So? Complete and with what result?'

'That will be made clear in my report to Comrade General Vasilovsky.'

'Your report to the General is submitted through me,' Kublitz reminded him.

'The preliminary experimentation'—Dr. Schutz spoke rapidly, so that Kublitz would be unable to follow—'has been to determine variables and constants pertaining to survival ratios in viruses and streptococci of known virulence and resistance when subjected to standard procedures used in water-purification processes. These parameters have now been ascertained within viable limits—maximum variability plus or minus two-point-five per cent.' He paused, then added: 'In simple terms, Comrade Kublitz, we have learned how many germs, and what types, you must add to the water supply to be sure some of them come out the tap at the other end of the pipe.'

He was pleased to see that Kublitz looked shocked at so open a declaration of objectives, and that he looked quickly at the office door to make certain that it was tightly closed, which it was. The Americans, Dr Schutz thought, had a word that described Kublitz well: weasel. It matched both his face and his manner of speaking.

'Tell Wolter to apply at the zoo gate at six o'clock,' Kublitz said 'We will provide another ape.'

'I don't suppose there is a possibility of obtaining a dozen rats.'

'I have said before, there are no orders pertaining to rats. One does not keep rats in a zoo.' Kublitz added nastily: 'Nor humans.'

'My preliminary report to the General will be completed next week,' said Dr Schutz. 'In it I will point out that completion of this research, as well as any possible implementation, will be impossible unless results can be tested on a human subject. However carefully done, the work will be inconclusive. The genetic controllers are different—the cell structure is different. The chromosome number is also different.'

'Point out what you like,' Kublitz shrugged. 'Moscow has ruled against it.' He smiled, the smile of a weasel. 'Unless General Vasilovsky would care to make a suggestion that occurs to me.'

'What is that?' Was it possible that Kublitz had a useful idea?

'That perhaps you could test the results of your experimentation on yourself. Or possible, in the interest of science, young Georg Wolter would volunteer.'

Dr Schutz felt his neck stiffen with anger, and a pulse hammered in his right temple. In the long years in Siberia he had learned in such circumstances to remain absolutely still until it subsided. When it had done so he said, pleasantly, 'Perhaps, after all, that will not be necessary. We will see. Please have the ape ready. It is especially important.'

CHAPTER SIX

WILLIS, sitting under the aspen, leaning his shoulders against the wall and the soles of his shoes against the trunk of the tree, dreamed of being bigger. He wished he were big enough to climb the tree. He could not quite reach the lowest branch, and, as Allie had pointed out, even if she boosted him to that one he could not reach the next one above it. So he sat on the ground, and noted idly that the dirt under his knees looked as if somebody had been digging it or raking it; it was softer than usual and he could see in it the footprints of Allie's sneakers.

Now he wished she would come down again and tell him what she was looking at. There must be a new animal; otherwise she would not be staying up so long. When there were leaves on the tree, as now, he could not see her at all, and sometimes she stayed so long he grew afraid that she was not really there any more, that she had somehow gone away without his knowing.

To his delight, she did come down. A sneaker appeared, then a leg of her blue slacks, and then her face, a finger over her lips as she slid silently to the ground. She took his hand and he went with her, walking as quietly as she did, across the road to the bushes where the bicycle was hidden. Here one was permitted to whisper, and he did.

'Have they got one?'

'Yes. A big one, the biggest one yet.'

'A chimpanzee?'

'Yes. He's darker than Abel, but his eyes are lighter. And he's got a hole in one ear.'

'A hole?'

'Sort of a notch. Something must have bitten him when he was young.'

'What's his name?'

'I don't know. Victor, I guess. He's so big.'

'What's Victor?'

'It means he'd win if he got in a fight. He's smart, too.'

'How do you know?'

'I can tell by the way he looks at things. He picked up his water bucket, smelled the water, looked at the handle; then he held it up and looked at the bottom, but he didn't spill the water. That's smart.'

'Are they giving him shots?'

'No. The old keeper gives the shots, and he left.'

'Where did he go?' Willis always wanted detail.

'How do I know? He just walked away. The young one's doing something with the water in the pool. I'm going back up now.'

Willis resumed his vigil under the tree, but it was short. Allie came down almost immediately.

Across the road she said, 'He was just taking him inside.'

'Who?'

'The young one, taking Victor.'

She got her bicycle from the bushes and mounted it, pedalling slowly. Willis trotted to keep up, watching the blurred motion of her rear wheel spokes. Then he looked up and stopped. His whisper was barely audible: 'Allie, *look*!'

He pointed. For the first time he had ever known it to happen, the gate in the wall was open. Not wide; only a few inches, but visibly open.

Allie swung noiselessly down from her bike and stared. They were still perhaps sixty feet away from it. He looked at her, awaiting her decision.

Holding her bicycle by the handlebars she moved forward, choosing her footsteps carefully. Willis crept beside her, watching her. As they came close she laid the bicycle gently on its side. 'I'm going in.'

Since she continued to whisper, so did he. 'Me, too.'

'No.'

'Oh, Allie, please.'

'No.'

'Why not?'

'It's—trespassing.'

'But you're going.'

'I'm only going two steps, to look. Then I'll come out again.'

'Then will you tell me what you saw?'

'Of *course*. But don't you tell. Not anybody.'

'Oh, I *won't*.'

'Look, you go on up the hill. Just keep going home. I'll catch up with you in a few minutes.'

He looked backwards as he walked up, going slowly; she waved him on, an impatient gesture, so he turned and walked faster. When he looked back again she had pushed the gate open an additional few inches and was stepping through. Unexpectedly, and quickly, it closed behind her. Because the wall was so high and thick and dark, with such big spikes on top, Willis suddenly felt scared. He was glad, this time, that she had not let him go with her. He ran farther up the hill leaving the wall behind. When he turned again, the gate was still closed. Her bicycle, shining in the late afternoon sun, lay near it.

The cabin, made of logs, stood on a thirty-foot-high bluff overlooking a meadow which bordered the river. Fergus was grateful for the choice of the site, for the sun that was setting into the hills, for the mild wind that blew across the porch where he sat. He was surrounded by living trees with leaves the pale new green of spring, by blossoms of dogwood and redbud, by the smell of pine and wild cherry. Cardinals flashed in the branches, sparrows sang, and near the river blackbirds dazzled one another with diadems of crimson. It was a spot designed to heal one suffering from PTS. Fergus felt sorry for the people of Cambridge whom he had left behind in the chill morning plodding through the grey snow. He felt grateful to Colonel Attenborough, albeit wary; he mistrusted the disarming simplicity of the task he had been asked to do; he was prepared to jump backwards if it burgeoned, to pack up and leave, but he hoped it would not be soon.

He heard amidst the sylvan quiet the sound of a car, its tyres rasping softly on the dirt and gravel drive that led to the cabin from the entrance to the estate, a journey of some three-quarters of a mile. Fergus looked at his watch. The car would contain Colonel Attenborough and a companion. The man from State, who had met him at the airport and provided him with a car, had told him they would arrive at five. It was five.

The companion's name was Samuel Bayles. He was plump, wore rimless glasses, had a throaty voice with a New England accent, and looked, as all CIA agents should, like anything but a CIA agent. He carried an attaché case made of stainless steel, and this was fastened to his wrist by a chain.

The interior of the cabin they entered was a very large single room, some forty feet by twenty, roughly finished of logs chinked with mortar. A small bathroom with a stall shower cut out one corner, a storage closet another, and between these two, filling the rest of one end of the room, gaped a deep stone fireplace. A fire of split oak logs had been laid in it.

The other end of the room contained, in a row, stove, refrigerator, sink, and cabinets for food and utensils. Before these stood a long trestle table, and on that Mr Bayles set his case. He unlocked the chain from around his wrist.

'Foolishness,' he said, 'but it's the rule.'

Next he unlocked the case itself and removed the contents, a substantial sheaf of papers which he divided into three piles.

'These two,' he said, 'can stay. This pile has to go back on the chain with me, so you might want to look at it first.'

Fergus sat on a bench beside the table and examined the pile. The top paper, half a dozen sheets stapled together, was in Russian, printed in Cyrillic letters, which he could recognize but not read. It carried a broad stripe of bright green across the top of the first page. There were a half-dozen similar papers beneath it, each with a green stripe, each bearing a paper clip. 'There's a translation clipped to each one,' Mr Bayles said. 'Those are what we have of Dr Schutz's reports.'

Fergus removed the clip and looked at the translation of the top paper. There were some meaningless routing and identification numbers, and below those the words:

WARNING
GREEN CLEARANCE ONLY
HIGHEST SECURITY CLASSIFICATION
ILLEGAL POSSESSION CARRIES SEVERE PENALTIES

Below that came the title:

Report N5 17a-4. Alteration in chromosome structure of
bacteria *clostridium botulinum* (type E) by nuclear cloning.

Fergus skipped to the end of the report, which filled six pages
with type, tables, and diagrams, and looked at the signature. It
said merely:

Novokuznetsk, April, 1966.
Group 17.

'You needn't read the report itself now,' said Mr Bayles. 'I'll
explain what we've done. This pile'—he placed his palm on
the pile of papers in the centre of the three—'contains duplicate
translations of the texts of all six reports, but with names, titles,
dates, and numbers removed. Without those, there's nothing to
connect them to us, or to the Russians, and I can leave them here.
Still, please don't leave them lying around, and when you're
through with them we'll want them back.'

He turned to the third pile. 'These you may find useful.' He
handed Fergus what looked like a group of colour photographs,
each a foot square, and with them a handful of long, clear plastic
clips.

'Aerial photographs,' he said, 'made from a thousand feet. Slip
them into the clips so the numbers match, and you have a
sixteen-square-foot picture of the whole area.' He demonstrated,
assembling the picture on the flat table top. 'Quite good definition
—you can almost see the pebbles on the river bank. North is on
top.' He pointed to a brown-and-green oblong near the left side
of the picture. 'The roof of the cabin we're in. Over here is Villa
Petrograd.'

Fergus bent over the photograph. It was remarkably sharp. It
had been taken, apparently, in earliest spring, when the leaf-buds
were only a greenish haze on the trees and did not hide the
ground. The Potomac River, the same section he saw from the
porch, ran through it from left to right, roughly west to east. It
looked surprisingly clear and blue.

The Villa itself was near the lower right corner of the picture.
Seen from above it was a random sprawl of overlapping grey
rectangles on which were superimposed, puzzlingly, three large
greenish circles—of course, thought Fergus, the onion domes.
The structure was surrounded by wide-branched trees; in summer it would stand in a well-shaded park. Despite the Byzantine

domes it looked, in the picture at least, like a pleasantly imposing Victorian mansion.

Around the castle, the wall and its shadow combined to form a double thickness, a dark barrier more suited to a penal institution than a weekend resort. On three sides it ran nearly rectilinear —at a guess, fixing a scale from the trees and the river, a half-mile on each side. The fourth side was longer and followed the curve of the river.

'That part of the wall,' Mr Bayles said, watching where Fergus watched, 'runs along a bluff just above the high water mark. Right here'—he indicated an irregularity, a thinning in the line —'is a gate. There are four altogether, one in each side of the wall, all double, heavy-gauge iron. This one, you can see, opens on to the river front, and right in front of it there's a natural rock peninsula.' He pointed to a fingertip of grey projecting into the water. 'If you look closely, you'll see that the end is square.'

'I see it.'

'There they've built what looks like a concrete dock, but isn't. Oh, they could use it for a dock, maybe they do, but it's hollow, and below the surface there are openings on both sides to let the water in. Inside there are instruments.'

'Instruments? What kind?'

'Hard to be sure. You see, even that dock is diplomatic territory. We sent a scuba diver to look, but it had to be at night, and we didn't dare use much light. Also, the openings are barred. But there's at least a hydrometer—to measure rate of flow— and a depth gauge, a float to measure rise and fall. Both are wired so the readings are recorded elsewhere, inside the wall, probably here.' He pointed now to a complex of smaller buildings near a corner of the wall, close to the river but quite far removed from the Villa itself.

'What's all that?'

'This long one, here, with the square C-shape, is the zoo—a dozen big cages in a cinder-block building. The small one here is a summerhouse. The Russians sit there and play chess.

'And this one here, set back by itself, with a fence around it, is the animal hospital. At least that's what they tell the visiting Russians. In fact, it's a laboratory. That's where our friend Schutz operates. It's a lot bigger than it looks, because most of it's underground.'

When Willis got to the house his mother was already there, in the kitchen, starting to get the supper.

'Is Allie with you?' she asked. 'I need her to help.'

'Yes. She's coming in a few minutes.'

'Where did you go?'

'We . . .' He paused. 'Down the hill.' That was not a secret.

She looked at him. 'Not by the river?'

'Oh, no.' He welcomed a new subject. 'But tomorrow we're going fishing. We saved the worms.'

'We'll see. I hope I'll have time.'

'John says the bass are biting. Henry told him.'

'I know. Willis, run back and tell Allie to hurry, please. It's getting late.'

From the top of the hill he called her name, though not loudly.

'Allie.'

When no answer came, he ran down. At the sight of the wall he stopped.

'Allie?'

He saw the gate, still closed. But her bicycle was gone. She must have come out. She must have gone up the hill, and somehow he had missed her. He thought, she's home already. He ran back to the house. The sun had set, and it was getting dark.

CHAPTER SEVEN

ALLIE TRIED TO CALL OUT, but could not. Something thick and black had been drawn over her head, and a strong hand held it hard against her face. A sharp, hot pain stabbed her shoulder and sent its fire down her arm and up her neck to her head. She heard a thud and recognized the sound of the gate closing behind her. Then she turned freezing cold and went to sleep.

When she awoke she was lying on her back on a hard surface, and faces were moving above her in circles and looking down at her. For a long time her eyes would not work right, and when they did the faces swam together into one face and stopped moving. It was the animal keeper, the old one with the thick, round glasses and the wispy grey hair. He was watching her eyes, and at length he spoke.

'I think you are waking up now.'

She tried to answer but all that came from her throat was a blurred sigh; she could not make her mouth work. She tried to sit up but her muscles would not respond.

'I have given you some medicine. You will be all right. The medicine will make you feel nice.' That was true; she did feel nice, though she did not know where she was. All she could see was the face and the ceiling straight overhead, which looked like cement painted white and made her think of a basement. She could hear some noises, however. One was a faint whirring, as of a small motor running quietly—like a refrigerator. Another was a scuffling sound that stopped and started; she could not identify it, though it was familiar.

She forgot it almost at once, tried again to speak, and failed again. She wanted to ask the animal keeper where she was. Then she remembered the gate—she must be somewhere inside the wall. She thought of her mother. Her mother would be home now, and expecting her because it was getting late. A twinge of worry flickered in her mind and then died out. She went back to sleep.

A little later, still not quite awake, not quite able to come awake she had the sensation of being carried; an arm beneath her shoulders, her own arm dangling, her wrist brushing something cold, a stone floor. Then she was lying on her back again. She strained at her eyelids and they opened for a moment. She looked at the same white ceiling, but there was a pattern of curlicues before it, grey lines. She recognized them, from having looked down at the animal place. They were wire. She was in a cage. The scuffling noise was closer now.

The bass were striking the May Waxwing, a fact which made Fergus O'Neil happier at his employment than he had anticipated —happy enough to ignore, at least momentarily, a nagging increase in his misgivings. He was fond of fishing, and though he did not scorn spinning tackle, the flatfish, the Rapala minnow or even the earthworm, he preferred the purer art of fly casting. He realized with almost a sense of shock that his fly rod had not been out of its case in more than three years. Working on the b-virus he had excluded most other things from his mind. There was an involuntary asceticism characteristic of such research, at least in the case of Fergus; among things excluded, not deliberately but merely not thought about, were parties, dates, and holidays, and fishing went with them. He flicked his line over the river and watched a small bass lunge for the fly and miss it. The bigger ones would be in closer to the bank.

The increase in his misgivings had come about in the course of acquiring the aluminium canoe in which he sat, clad in pullover and corduroy slacks, his tackle box at his feet. It was a simple enough revelation, casually made, but it came at the end of a series of bits of information, which, like a column of ones and twos, insisted on being added together. He flicked his line again and added:

A remark by Colonel Attenborough: the cabin he occupied stood on an estate which belonged to a Mr Nunneley Wilcox. The name was puzzlingly familiar. Then Fergus placed it. Nunneley Wilcox had been for some years Undersecretary of State; he was rich, quietly famous, retired, and still served as an occasional presidential adviser.

A remark by Mr Bayles: the aerial photograph he had left with Fergus, of which Mr Bayles was very proud, had been made with equipment developed for U-2's and orbiting satellites. Spy equipment, rare, secret, and enormously expensive.

A remark by Colonel Attenborough: an aluminium canoe, rented from a commercial boathouse downriver, had been placed in the estate boathouse for Fergus's use. But when he went to the boathouse he found not one but three canoes, two of which belonged to the estate. Why rent one? He was not sure, but a thought occurred to him. A rental canoe was anonymous. Did they expect, then, that he would be watched?

A conversation with Mr Nunneley Wilcox himself: Fergus had gone to the estate house to get a key to the boathouse. It was a handsome Georgian mansion overlooking a lake on which white geese swam. At the door a maid in uniform answered his ring, asked him in and informed him that Mr Wilcox would like to see him. Mr Wilcox was in his study, a polished wood-and-leather chamber with a view of the geese; he was white-haired, tall, hawk-nosed, and cordial. He inquired politely as to whether all in the log cabin had been prepared to Fergus's satisfaction.

Then he added, 'I hope it's not too uncomfortable. My sons and I built that cabin ourselves, sort of an exercise in pioneering. We don't ordinarily let it—in fact, you're the first tenant we've had. I got a phone call from Jake Ewers, and he sounded quite urgent, so I didn't argue. He's an old friend.' Again a famous name. Dr Jacob Ewers was the director of the Agency for which Mr Bayles worked.

The subject had changed to fishing, and it was Mr Wilcox, as he handed Fergus the boathouse key, who advised him that the bass should, at this season, be taking May Waxwings. Throughout the interview he was noticeably uncurious as to why Fergus was present at all.

Taken singly, none of these things was cause for concern. Put together—a steel case chained to a wrist, a chartered plane, a million-dollar spy camera, a phone call from a director to a presidential adviser, a camouflaged canoe—they gave Fergus the uneasy feeling that he was caught up in a conflict bigger and more urgently menacing than Colonel Attenborough was willing to admit. His reassurance was, of course, that he was not really caught up in it. He could, and would, bow politely and walk away when he wanted to.

He had launched the canoe at the dock in front of the Wilcox boathouse. The river here resembled a wide and placid lake; Fergus drifted gently downstream, aided by a mild breeze, the spring sunshine pleasantly warm on the back of his neck. Except for a solitary fisherman in a red punt near the opposite bank, there was no one in sight. He tried to remember that his objective was not a string of bass but the Villa Petrograd. Mr Bayles had cautioned him: 'You won't be able to see much, but at least you'll get an idea of the physical appearance of the river front, how close the wall is to it, where the dock is. I wouldn't try climbing the wall. Then, after you've seen it, read the reports and see what you make of them.'

He saw the wall after floating a half-mile downstream, catching three large bass and throwing back half a dozen small ones. One might as well make the cover authentic. He would give two to Mr Wilcox and cook one for his supper. He fished close to the bank, which most of the way was flat and grassy—the meadow his log cabin looked down on. It would be flooded in high water, and soggy underfoot near the edge. But as the lake narrowed to turn back into a river, the steep bluffs closed in on it from either side. Here the wall loomed up unexpectedly; one did not see it from a distance because it was shadowed by large trees, already in leaf, that grew along its inner side.

He paddled closer and stared up at it. It was an almost painful incongruity in this sylvan valley. It rose from the stone palisade, and a cornice had been blasted or drilled away to accommodate its base. The cornice was itself fully ten feet above water level, and to this the wall and its spiked top added another ten. The effect was not that of a rich man's estate, but an insane bastion built by a xenophobe.

He let the canoe drift until he faced approximately the middle of its span. The current grew swifter here where the wide lake narrowed; farther downstream it must grow narrower still, for he could hear the rush of a rapids. He lowered the canoe's small anchor, flicked his May Waxwing towards shore, and stared beyond it into the shadows.

Directly in front of him lay the small peninsula, perhaps thirty feet long, the only place in the length of the wall where dry land extended a useful distance beyond it. At this spot the river's bank rose more gently, and rough steps had been cut into it leading to the iron gate visible in the deep shadow only as a darker square in the wall. At the end of the peninsula, near where his bass fly drifted, stood the square cement block. He watched the May Waxwing float to within a foot of it, accelerate suddenly, and then, to his astonishment, sink from sight.

He thought at first of a fish, but there was no swirl, no splash, no strike. He lifted his rod and the top bent solidly, motionlessly. It was snagged. Somehow, inexplicably, a surface fly on the end of a floating fly line had sunk and snagged itself underwater.

Fergus weighed anchor and paddled forward, stopping every few strokes to reel in line. The dock he approached was plain, rather an ugly grey; it merely squared off the end of the stone peninsula, rising perhaps a foot out of the water and measuring eight or nine feet on a side. It looked solid enough. He wondered what had led Mr Bayles to suspect it. Easily answered: in Mr Bayles's profession one must attempt to suspect everything, even a block of cement.

The side of the canoe scraped against it. Fergus put down his rod and paddle, pushed off a foot and took hold of his line, staring down to see where the end had gone. A small green leaf, floating lightly on the surface, swirled in a circle and sank gently into a miniature whirlpool. His line was just in its vortex. His fly had not simply sunk. It had been sucked under.

Tracing the line, he put his hand into the water and felt the small current pulling downward past his fingers. Rolling up his sleeve, he leaned over and nearly capsized the canoe. He swore mildly, straightened, and considered. The dock was unusual, as docks go, in that there was nothing to tie up to. At length, holding the anchor in his hand, he climbed on to it and found himself standing on a sign stencilled in the cement: 'No Trespassing'.

He placed the anchor on the sign and lay chest down beside it. He reached as far into the water as he could.

It was cold, barely above freezing, and made his arm ache. About a foot below the surface, following his line down, he found the barred opening. He leaned his head over and could see it, but not well; the water was murky and the angle bad. The bars were round metal pipes set two inches apart. The opening itself looked about two feet square. He could see nothing inside it but blackness.

His line had passed between two of the bars. Thrusting his hand after it, he learned where it had gone: just beside the square opening he felt the round mouth of a two-inch pipe, into which river water was flowing briskly. His May Waxwing had been sucked in with the current. He wrapped the line twice around his hand, keeping it close to the pipe's end, and tugged hard. It came free. The fly, now hopelessly soaked and bedraggled, had gone up the pipe about three feet and caught on something—perhaps a bend, an elbow?

More interesting was the question of the flow itself. Mr Bayles had said nothing of pipes or pumps, but only instruments. Since the intake was set off to the side of the barred opening, it was possible that his scuba diver had simply missed it—especially if the pump, wherever it might be, had not been running at the time. And where *was* the pump? Definitely not here, for there was no sound of machinery running. Somewhere inside the wall—but why? What need would the Russians in Villa Petrograd have for so much water?

Struck by a thought, Fergus crossed to the other side of the dock and lay down again. There, a foot below the surface, was a duplicate barred opening precisely opposite the first one. Reaching down, he found the matching pipe. From this one the water flowed out.

He had just risen from this discovery and was contemplating it when the gate opened and a man descended the stone steps. He was dressed in work clothes and the heavy shoes of a groundskeeper. When he reached Fergus he spoke in a heavy Russian accent: 'Is private. Keep out.'

'Sorry,' said Fergus, and added a near-truth, 'A fish ran with my line and it got snagged on your dock. I was just freeing it.'

The man looked at him with stony incomprehension and repeated, 'Is private. Keep out.' It was seemingly the extent of his English.

Fergus picked up his rod and line; he lifted his string of bass from the canoe. 'Fish,' he said, holding them up to make his mission clear.

The other made an equally clear gesture. He pointed at Fergus, at the canoe, and at the opposite bank of the river. He said again, 'Is private. Keep out.'

As he paddled away, Fergus thought, I have had my first skirmish with the enemy and have emerged with the advantage. I have learned something; he has not. At least he was fairly sure that the Russian had taken him for an ordinary fisherman. From the nature of the encounter. Fergus could guess that others had come before him; he had been chased by rote.

The flow of water in and out was curious. It was obviously being pumped to a point some distance away from the dock, being used for something, and then piped back to the river. It might mean nothing; it might have no connection with Dr Schutz. It could be used to cool an air conditioner, for instance. They would hardly need air conditioning today, but they could be testing it. He should have paid more attention to the outflow: had it been warmer than the river? Not much, or he would have noticed. It would be interesting to fill a small bottle with it. He had none with him, but surely the Colonel could provide one.

Near the bank across from the Villa he made a few more casts, having replaced his soggy Waxwing with a fresh one. But it was past midmorning, moving towards noon, and the bass had ceased to rise. They would start again at dusk. He turned upstream, back into the wide lake, heading for the cabin but staying close to the far shore and scouting for sites to fish in the evening. The red punt had gone.

Across the river he observed a small drama, not quite comprehensible to him because he could not hear the dialogue. At the edge of the meadow that began where the wall ended, a police car stood, identifiable by its domed roof light. Beside it two men in grey uniforms and tan hats, obviously state or county police, stood talking to a woman and a boy. The boy was holding the woman's hand. She wore light brown slacks and a green sweater. From a distance at least she looked rather pretty and appealing, seemingly in distress, for when she turned towards the river he thought he could see, even so far away, that her face looked sad.

CHAPTER EIGHT

MRS ADAM heard her son Willis come in and mount the stairs to his room. Allison, with her bicycle to push, would be following in a minute. However, she did not, and after a few minutes her mother called, 'Willis, did you tell Allie to come home?'

'No.'

'Why not?'

'She was already gone.'

'Gone where?'

'Gone home.'

'Willis, she's not home.'

'Yes she is. Isn't she?' He called, 'Allie? Allie?' There was no answer. 'Well, her bike was gone.'

'Gone from where?'

'Gone from the road. By the wall.'

'You didn't see her at all?'

John, who was studying for a history examination, had come from his room. He was tall, thin, with lank brown hair, one curving lock down his forehead, pale of complexion, serious of mien, with dark blue eyes.

'I'll get her,' he said, and set out down the road at a brisk walk.

In fifteen minutes he was back at a dog trot, looking paler than before. 'Mother, I can't find her.' He was panting; he had run all the way up the hill. 'I found the bike, but she's not there. I called. She didn't answer at all.'

'Where?'

'Well——' He dreaded to say it. 'At the river.'

'At the river!'

'That's where the bike is.'

'*Where* at the river?' She went to the closet and put on a light coat, a raincoat. From a desk drawer she took a flashlight. It had grown quite dark outside.

'Just at the end of the road. Right on the bank. The bike is lying in the mud.'

'Come on.' She started for the door and then stopped. 'Willis, you come too.' The thought of leaving Willis in the house alone had suddenly become intolerable; she did not stop to think why.

They called as they walked down the road, slowing their footsteps to listen for an answer that did not come. In the dark by the beam of the flashlight they found the bicycle next to the swirl of the water. They called again. The biycle had fallen with one handlebar extended over the bank like a thin arm, its handgrip pointing towards the water in a gesture both horrifying and inescapable. The ground was wet underfoot and sucked at the soles of their shoes. They looked for footprints but the flashlight created only contorted black shadows in the bog.

'Willis, did you and Allie come to the river today?'

'No. We never come to the river.' He was starting to cry; he tried not to. Why had Allie, when she came out the gate and got on her bike, then ridden the wrong way? She must have stayed inside too long, and then been mixed up by the dark.

Mrs Adam stood facing the river, staring into the water, unable to see anything. She looked to her right: there rose the stone wall that surrounded the Russian villa, visible in the night only as a darker shadow. Allie could not have wandered that way. There remained the meadow, to her left. She could have gone that way. But why? They had, on occasion, walked the riverbank to fish; sometimes they found Indian arrowheads there. Allie might have found one and looked for more. She said to the children, 'She might be in the field.'

But as soon as they started to look they knew it was futile. The flashlight beam dwindled to nothing thirty feet away. The meadow went on for a mile or more. In any case, Allie would not have kept going after dark; it was impossible to believe she would have done that.

She turned the flashlight out and led them back. 'It's no use,' she said. She wanted to give up, to slump down in the mud, to weep, but for the sake of the children she could not. She was sure that Allison had drowned; had somehow by mistake driven her bicycle to the riverbank, turned too sharply at the last minute and fallen. She could not dispel this picture from her mind, though she knew it was premature. Allison might be at home, waiting, wondering where they were, with a simple explanation of what had happened: someone had stolen her bicycle.

John said, 'Mother, we'd better go home and call the police.'

'I know.' They started up the hill. Willis was now crying openly. 'Mother, is she drowned? Where is she?' She put an arm around his shoulder, feeling its thinness shaking under her hand.

'Poor Willis, I don't know. Maybe the police will find her. We have to wait and see.'

The police came three times—twice that night, and again the next morning. It took them half an hour to arrive the first time, and while she waited she tried to get the children to eat some supper, and to eat some herself; she was able only to drink some coffee.

When they arrived, big, polite men in grey uniforms with pistols strapped to their sides, they asked questions: Allie's age, height, weight, colour of hair, clothing, any recent photographs? Their names, printed on small plates on their uniform jackets, were Officer Simon and Officer Davis.

Then they went in their police car, taking Mrs Adam with them, down to the riverbank where the bicycle still lay forlornly in the mud. She told them, as well as she knew, the events of the evening, pointing out the bottom of the hill where Willis had last seen Allison. The police car had a searchlight, and they trained it over the water, its beam shining all the way to the other bank, but revealing only trees, earth, and water flowing. It traced the near bank, stopping where something glinted. 'Beer can,' muttered Officer Simon. It reached the wall where it met the river, and followed its stony side up the hill until it disappeared into the trees. The light circled on, stabbing through the scrub growth on the bluff. It found something white and her heart leaped. 'Dogwood,' Officer Simon said. It swept the meadow for half its length, revealing nothing.

At last they took her home. Officer Simon put the bicycle in the back of the police car. 'No reason to leave it lying here,' he said. When they reached her house he took it out and left it carefully propped against the porch. There was finality in the act.

The second time they came was near midnight. Officer Simon, who had kind grey eyes in a face tanned bronze, whose voice had a soft Virginia accent, said, 'We went back down there, Mrs Adam, and looked some more. We called headquarters and put out a description, what we call an APB. We contacted the state police, and they'll put a launch in the water as soon as it's light. . . .'

'Not until morning.'

'Ma'am, there's a rapids just a little way down, and that's where they've got to look. They can't get down there in the dark. They'll use a helicopter, too, but it's no good at night. I'm sorry, Mrs Adam, but if she's in the river it isn't going to make any difference.'

The third time they came was midmorning. The state police launch had found nothing (they reported); the helicopter had seen nothing. Such reports, they cautioned, must be regarded only as inconclusive, not optimistic.

'Most often it's a week or more before they show up,' Officer Davis explained.

'They?'

'We get two or three drownings a year along there. It's the rapids.'

At the river front once more, the officers showed Mrs Adam and John what they had found by daylight—merely the confirming tyre marks of the bicycle leading over the mud to the water's edge. Of footprints there were a confusion, including their own from the night before. Willis stayed in the car, huddled in the corner of the back seat. He did not want to see.

'It's pretty clear what happened, Ma'am. She stayed around too late, got mixed up in the dark, rode in the wrong direction. Maybe something scared her. There are possums, raccoons, pretty big animals.'

'Allie wasn't scared of animals.' John spoke flatly. 'She liked animals better than anybody.'

Officer Davis said: 'Things look different at night, son.'

Officer Simon changed the subject. 'We checked the whole field, and the woods beyond it. There's a house up there on the bluff, a log house. Do you know who lives there?'

'I've seen the house,' Mrs Adam said. 'It belongs to Mr Wilcox. I believe he and his sons built it. But nobody lives there.'

The two officers looked at one another. 'Somebody's living there now,' said Officer Simon. 'There's smoke coming out the chimney.'

'We'll check it out,' Officer Davis said. 'It's just possible she went in there and fell asleep. If she got cold, she might have lit a fire. Kids do funny things.'

'No,' said Mrs Adam. 'It isn't possible. Allison wouldn't have done that. She was . . . ' She started to tell the two strangers what Allison was like; she realized there was no use trying; yet the recollection came clearly, too clearly, and for the first time the tears streamed over her face. John, looking frightened, came to her side and caught her hand but said nothing. She was glad Willis was not there to see. He was still huddled in the car, and as they drove back Officer Simon spoke to him.

'Show me where your sister was when you left her.'

'It was here.'

They stopped the car and got out again. They were near the corner of the wall, near the iron gate.

'You went home and she stayed here?'

'Yes. She told me to. And she would come in a minute.'

Officer Simon, followed by Officer Davis, walked to the gate, pushed it, then pulled it. It remained immovable.

'Locked.'

'That's the Russian place.'

John said: 'It's always locked. They don't use this gate.'

Officer Simon, his grey eyes speculative, said, 'Still, I'd like to have a look in there.'

Willis remained silent. He did not betray Allison, even though she was drowned. They returned to the car, and to the house. The officers left.

Fergus, having cleaned his three bass and put them in the refrigerator, was cooking his lunch, a hamburger, when the police car drove up. Through the cabin window he saw two men in uniform emerge from the car, and realized they must be the same two he had seen earlier near the riverbank. He recalled again the sad face of the woman who had been with them. They knocked and he opened the door, stepping out on the small flagstone terrace on the uphill side of the cabin.

They explained their visit. A girl had drowned in the river the preceding night. They had spoken to Mr Wilcox and learned that he, Dr Fergus O'Neil, was a guest in the cabin, here for the fishing. The cabin was the nearest habitation to the place where the girl had drowned. Had he heard or seen anything unusual?

'Nothing at all,' said Fergus. 'It's been perfectly quiet. Won't you come inside? Where and when did she drown?'

They came in, glanced quickly around the big, orderly, rustic room, noted the hamburger cooking, looked at the porch and admired the view, and left. Mr Wilcox, a famous and important man, had indicated strongly that Dr O'Neil's credentials were impeccable, and all the appearances confirmed this.

When Allie woke up again she could move, but only very slowly and very quietly, and she could not speak above a whisper. She had lost her voice, but she did not care. She felt nice. She knew all those things immediately on awaking, because she remembered them from her sleep. It was like a dream, but it was not a dream. The animal keeper, who was a doctor (he had told her he was a doctor, but not his name), said that when she woke up she would remember it all, and so she did. He had given her a shot. He told her the needle would not hurt, and it did not. His glasses were very shiny, and so thick she could not see his eyes. He told her that everything he said was true, and she would believe it whether she was asleep or awake, and she did. That was how she knew she could not speak, but only whisper. And she felt nice.

She looked up and was not at all frightened when she saw the brown, bearded face staring at her. Its ears stood straight up, and one of them had a hole in it. It was Victor, the new chimpanzee, in the cage next to hers. In the room with them there was a bench, a table, a big grey laundry tub with faucets, three doors leading out, and not much else.

CHAPTER NINE

IN THE MORNING in his room at Villa Petrograd, Dr Schutz sat in an armchair and considered Georg Wolter. He was uncertain about Georg. As an assistant in the laboratory, he was a competent though unimaginative biologist, thorough and careful. Moreover, he had a mechanical aptitude which had proved invaluable on this particular series of experiments, with so much equipment to keep in order.

But Georg was a literal-minded Bavarian, with a stolid respect for orders and regulations. Theoretically, he took orders from Dr Schutz. But Georg was also aware that they both took orders from a higher authority, and that they had been forbidden a human subject for their experiment.

A more delicate point. Georg, like himself, had worked in the secret laboratories in Novokuznetsk, where they had used human subjects extensively and without qualms—where, indeed, one of Dr Schutz's main interests was in using human subjects most effectively, keeping them docile and co-operative in delicate experiments where the subject's own help, even enthusiasm, was essential.

Georg would not be squeamish about using the girl as a subject, and as a biologist (unlike Kublitz) would recognize the value of doing so—since in the end, their research was to be applied to humans, not monkeys.

But value was one thing. Absolute necessity was another. Georg might be frightened. Value, yes—but what about the risk? What if they were caught? They themselves were also prisoners, though this was never discussed, nor openly admitted—Dr Schutz was an ex-Nazi, Georg a refugee from West Germany, where, if deported home, he would face trial for some offence unknown to Dr Schutz.

If Georg refused to co-operate, if Georg insisted on letting the girl go, or told Kublitz—what then?

That must not be permitted to happen.

It would then be up to him to convince Georg that the girl was not merely valuable to the experiment, but absolutely essential. To do that he would have to let Georg into his confidence and tell him of the plan he had told to no one else. That was a step he was loath to take. He did not want to trust Georg. Over the years he had learned to avoid, when possible, trusting anyone.

Actually, he thought, the risk to them was minimal, virtually non-existent. A girl had disappeared—at night, on the bank of a river, just above a dangerous rapids. How could anyone, even the most suspicious of police. connect this event with two biologists and a laboratory of whose existence they were completely unaware? It was this fact that he must stress when he talked to Georg. If that proved ineffective, there would still be time to consider alternatives.

He rose from his chair and looked out of the window. His rooms, an office-living room, bedroom, and bath, were in the rear of the Villa Petrograd on the third floor. They were small but comfortable, originally designed, he had been told, for the secretary of the old Russian duke, Orlov, who had built the place. His window overlooked a handsomely landscaped lawn and garden, behind which were two tennis courts and a field where, on weekends, younger members of the Red diplomatic corps played soccer.

Off to the right, obscured from his window by trees, stood the small zoo of which he was—or so the diplomats were encouraged to believe—the curator. Actually, the work in the zoo itself, the feeding and the cleaning of cages, was done by a member of the groundskeeping staff, a stupid and quite ill-natured peasant named Nikolai, who spoke only Russian and took orders from Kublitz.

He walked down the hall to Georg Wolter's room and knocked. He carried with him a copy of a German newspaper, the *Münchener Tageblatt*. Their newspapers, grudgingly provided by Kublitz, came through the Embassy in Washington, where they were read first and where some items were clipped for filing, so that they arrived tattered and averaged a month late. Still Dr Schutz always read them carefully, noting with particular interest certain names in the political news.

Georg was seated in a chair by the window, staring out, waiting. He took the bedraggled newspaper without enthusiasm, glanced at it, tossed it on his bed.

'We go now?' He spoke in German.

'In a moment. There is a matter to discuss.' Dr Schutz shut the door and came abruptly to the point: 'We have obtained a human experimental subject in the laboratory.'

'Ah, so!' Wolter was startled. 'But Kublitz has said . . .'

'Kublitz knows nothing. I obtained the subject myself.'

'You! But how was it possible?'

'Someone was spying on us, watching us over the wall. . . .'

'Over the wall? But that cannot be.'

'There is a small tree outside the wall behind the laboratory. I heard someone climbing in it while we were working. I found footprints under it. Yesterday I opened the gate—just a bit— and as I hoped, the spy came through. I was waiting inside. I had with me a hypodermic of pentothal and curare.'

'But that is dangerous. He will be missed. There will be a search and Kublitz will hear of it.'

'I think not. The intruder turned out to be quite insignificant— a girl.'

'A girl?' A small change of expression passed over Wolter's face. 'Who is she?'

'A girl of twelve years—perhaps thirteen. One may assume she lives in the neighbourhood. Fortunately she was riding a bicycle. I took the liberty of moving it to the bank of the river, placing it in such a position that it is obvious that she fell into the water. The girl has drowned.'

'We were instructed to stay within the walls at all times.' Wolter seemed, however, no longer to be seriously protesting.

'It took only a few minutes. By doing so, I removed any possibility of a serious investigation. If the police think the girl has drowned, they will wait for her body to rise and be found. They will search along the river, but they will know that it may be weeks before this happens.'

'And when it does not?'

'They will never be sure, of course. In drowning, as you know, the victims are not always found. But in any case, in two weeks we will no longer have need of her. If the police inquire then, and Kublitz suspects, there will no longer be evidence.'

Georg Wolter shrugged: 'It is your responsibility. You have given her sedation?'

'Hypnotics. The di-phenylitol series.'

'They are not always entirely dependable.'

'With her they have worked perfectly. I stayed with her for the whole series—all night. She is highly retentive. She memorized the entire set of instructions verbatim the first time; nonetheless I taped them and played them back three times, with each new injection. She will not forget them now until she is reinstructed. In any case, if necessary I can change to selinoids.'

Dr Schutz opened the door, and they set out for the laboratory. Wolter had yielded more easily than he had expected. He felt elation, for the first time in many years. His plan, so long dreamed, remained his own private possession.

This time both of the animal keepers came in. They talked to each other for a little while in the language Allie could not understand. The young one kept staring at her through the cage wall in a funny way. Then the old keeper, the Doctor, opened her cage door and spoke to her.

'You will come out.' He said it in English. She stepped out of the cage, which was just high enough so that she could stand upright.

'You will walk to the end of the room, open the door, and enter the bathroom. You will close the door. You will use the bathroom as before. You will open the door and return to the cage.'

Everything he said was true; thus it all happened as he said. When she returned to the cage door the young keeper stared at her again. She went in and they closed the door and locked it with a key. They had put some sandwiches and water in the cage, on the floor.

'You are hungry,' said the Doctor. 'You are thirsty. You will eat the sandwiches and drink the water.' The sandwiches were toast-and-butter, wrapped in a paper napkin. They were cold and greasy, but she ate them anyway because she was hungry.

The two men had begun a discussion in the other language. In a few minutes, still talking, they opened a door across from her cage and went into another room. They closed the door behind them but while it was open she saw that the room they were entering was a small hallway leading to a third room, much larger than the one she was in. It had no cages but was full of machines and instruments she did not recognize at all—things of shining steel and glass, with switches and tubes and dials. On the wall were shelves covered with jars, bottles, and glass dishes.

They closed the door, and a moment later she heard a motor running quietly, and the throbbing sound of a pump.

Mrs Adam found the can of worms under Allie's bed and carried them out to the garden. She turned the can upside down, tapped the bottom, lifted it, and watched the wriggling mass begin the slow process of untangling itself and finding the way back into the darkness of the fresh-ploughed earth. The garden was ready to plant. She had bought the seeds weeks ago: peas, beans, greens, lettuce, and the rest. She stood up and looked at the ground. She could not do it. The idea had no meaning; no impulse accompanied it. Like Allie, it was dead. And yet maybe she could, maybe she must. Things that had been done with purpose, with trouble, with joy, must now be done mechanically, the motivation replaced by the dry knowledge that they had been done before and therefore should be done again, like old religious rituals. Possibly if she did them the meaning would return, but she did not believe that. The household had been stalwart; the family had been strong enough to withstand another blow but not this one because this one removed the centre from the family so that it tilted and fell inward and was no more.

John came out. She thought he was coming to her but he did not; he walked down the drive to the road and turned right, down the hill toward the river. His face looked calm enough, but he did not speak, and so she worried and called after him, 'John, be careful, please.' She did not know what else to do. He was still young enough to believe what he needed to believe, which was that Allie was not dead but alive, somewhere, waiting to be found. She thought, he must be going to the rapids to look. He was strong, he was a skilful swimmer, but the rapids was a dangerous place for anyone. For the moment his delusion was his good fortune. He remained undaunted while she despaired, while Willis stayed desolate in his room. But she dreaded the time surely coming when fact in the form of his sister's found body would strike his youthfulness a wound all the more grievous for being delayed and resisted.

Willis, alone in his room on his bed, had stopped crying and was looking at the pictures in *Heidi*, the last thing Allie had given him. Not given, lent. He would put it back on her shelf later, maybe tomorrow. She would not mind if he kept it another day. He saw a picture of the gate in front of Heidi's grandfather's house, and it made him think of the gate Allie had gone through that he had not told about, and would not. She had only gone two steps in, to look. Still, she must have seen something to watch, or she would not have stayed inside until it got dark. He wished she had let him wait for her. Then, when she came out, he could have told her she was going the wrong way. He put his head on the book and presently fell asleep.

He was still asleep half an hour later, and so did not hear the soft sound of Allie's bicycle wheels rolling down the drive, nor see John, who had come back to get the bicycle, putting on the brakes as he turned right down the hill.

CHAPTER TEN

THE CHURCH BELLS rang gently across the woods to Fergus's cabin, reminding him that it was Sunday. In the cabin it was easy to lose track of days, with only the noises of the wind and the songbirds to break the flow of time. The morning sun shone horizontally through the cabin window, striking the log wall next to his cot, turning the dark wood to lustrous grey.

Fergus rose, made coffee, scrambled an egg, and packed his fishing box, placing in it beside his tackle three small plastic bottles. They were stoppered and, Colonel Attenborough had assured him, sterile. It occurred to him that on Sunday the river might be busy with fishermen, which would make it a bad day to try to sample the outflow from the Russian dock. That could, if necessary, wait over until Monday.

The bottles had been obtained after a telephone call made late Saturday from Mr. Wilcox's house (the cabin itself had no telephone), which led, an hour later, to another meeting with the Colonel and Mr. Bayles. That, in turn, had followed an afternoon of hard study.

After the police left, Fergus had eaten his hamburger and then taken from his suitcase, which he kept locked, the file of translated reports Mr. Bayles had given him. He sat at the trestle table and read them, first with curiosity, then with intense interest, but in the end with a feeling close to bewilderment. In a most peculiar way, they were unlike any scientific papers he had ever read.

Drifting downstream in the canoe, he cast out his Waxwing and went over the puzzle again, hoping for a bass to interrupt him. The morning was cooler than the preceding days, and he was grateful for a heavy rope-knit sweater he had brought from Cambridge. Perhaps it was due to the cold, too, that his dry fly drew no response from the water. There were three other boats in sight, each containing two fishermen. From what he could see, they were doing no better than he. Ahead of him, on his right in the distance, he saw a boy attempting to ride a bicycle along the riverbank. He seemed to be having difficulty staying upright, as if the wheels were bogged in the soft ground. An odd place, Fergus thought, to ride a bicycle. When he looked again he realized that it was the same boy he had seen before, with the woman and the two policemen.

His mind turned back to the Schutz reports. Fergus was used to reading scientific papers; from long practice even the most abstruse of them were usually quickly graspable; there was a sameness about them as to format, even as to style, with their determinedly impersonal use of the passive voice. But there was something wrong with Dr Schutz's papers. At first it had eluded him; he had decided that the author was merely bungling—perhaps senile?—and was taking an oddly oblique approach to the problem at hand.

The problem itself was direct, straightforward, and predictably horrifying. It was biological warfare, b-w to its practitioners; in a word, murder—mass murder in a style to make atomic warfare look like mercy killing. Fergus was sufficiently familiar with the allied worlds of war and science, the human means and the ends ape-chosen, to know that there were men in secret laboratories toiling at programmes like these: the slow delicate work of creating the irresistible disease, the plague that could wipe out the population of a city, a country, a continent.

On occasion, nature herself had shown that it could be done —had shown *how* it might be done. Breed a new germ in the dark slum sewers of Benares, send a camel caravan across the Asian steppes laden with spices and infection, and watch the Black Death explode across Europe—irresistible because it is new. When Columbus lands in the West Indies bearing guns, beads, and smallpox, there are perhaps a half-million Caribs living there. Half a century later there are none. During World War I, influenza, an old, familiar virus, produces a mutant strain and kills twenty million noncombatants. Nature can sneer at the guns and gases of men, which have murdered only a fifth as many.

And Dr Schutz knew, as Fergus knew, how to improve on nature, how to speed it up and nudge it in the desired direction. No longer does one wait for a mutation which may be years in coming. The modern biologist makes his own. By X-ray bombardment, by nuclear transplant, by alteration of the DNA, by removal with highly sophisticated submicroscopic surgery of an individual gene—so a whole new army of infections can be created against which man has no natural resistance, against which his antibiotics are ineffective.

This was the work Dr Schutz's paper described. He was chiefly concerned, at the time he wrote them, with two bacteria, one of a type called *coryna*, the other *anthracis*. Fergus was familiar with both. The *coryna* Dr Schutz was breeding caused a kind of diphtheria known in medieval literature as redspittle, highly contagious and invariably fatal. The word *anthracis*, in the original Greek, referred to glowing coals (hence *anthracite*), but in medicine described the shining red pustules that covered victims of the disease before they died. Modern b-w men knew the disease itself as anthrax.

In the sanitized Western world both bacteria were so rare as to be almost unknown, but Dr Schutz had, with the help of his military sponsors, obtained cultures of both—*anthracis* from the Sudan, where it was endemic among cattle, and *coryna* from a mosquito-ridden jungle in Malaysia. The germs in hand, he set about beefing them up. His problem was not virulence; both types possessed it in abundance. He worked instead on survivability and means of transport and distribution—how to deliver them to the consumer in lively condition. Judging by his own reports he had succeeded brilliantly.

In Report N5-17a-7 he told of work on *coryna*. By a series of gene-manipulations he had produced a strain which had, for b-w purposes, everything. First, it multiplied itself with explosive rapidity. Second, it was unaffected by pressures eight to ten times that of normal atmosphere. Third and most important, it could stand exposure to cold down to minus sixty degrees for indefinite periods. (In such conditions it seemed simply to encyst and hibernate; when warmed up it came vigorously to life again in seconds.) Obviously *coryna* was to be delivered to its target compressed in aerosol containers, making the flight in intercontinental missiles at very high, very cold altitudes. At a signal, at the right height over the right target—Atlanta? Boston? Cleveland? (and on down the alphabet)—the aerosols would discharge their billions of microscopic passengers into the gentle morning air to float down to victory.

Anthracis was to arrive, less glamorously, by water. Here the research concentrated on breeding into the bacteria a resistance to certain chemicals, notably the halogens, fluorine and chlorine, both increasingly used in municipal water systems. Again, Dr Schutz had succeeded brilliantly, and when the highly toxic drinking water had been consumed, after normal purification, by Laboratory Subject RS 22, the subject had died in thirty hours despite intensive therapy.

It seemed likely that this latter research had led to Dr Schutz's sudden appearance on the Potomac just upstream from Washington's water supply. Fergus, gliding down its gentle surface in a canoe, looked ahead into the shadows where the river narrowed. Was Dr Schutz, in his laboratory under those trees, even now preparing a culture of *anthracis* to insert into Washington's water supply? Mr Bayles and Colonel Attenborough both thought not. Dr Schutz's duties would be limited to perfecting the means; he might, indeed, prepare a sample culture. But they thought it unlikely that responsibility for an actual attack would rest with him. Still they could not be sure, and it was not theirs to take chances, which was why Fergus, the outside expert, had been brought in. Dr Schutz's presence so close to Washington must be regarded as automatically menacing.

All in all, Fergus thought, the Group 17 reports, as they pertained to germ warfare, were eminently sensible. The work described was businesslike, made use of the most modern tools and the newest microbiological techniques. Obviously Dr Schutz had kept up. There were gaps in the series, missing chapters, and sometimes annoying references to other papers not present, but in a general way they were understandable.

What did not make sense at all, what remained totally baffling, were the strange digressions. They were scattered throughout the papers, as out-of-place as playing-cards bound in a prayer book. They were concerned not with germ warfare but with the people Dr Schutz worked with. For example, all of the papers dealing with *anthracis* were interrupted by a detailed and continuing history of Laboratory Subject RS 22, who had helped prepare the culture and then poisoned himself by drinking it.

RS 22, male, weight on admission 74 kilograms, height 183 centimetres (Fergus had learned), had arrived in the Novokuznetsk laboratory on August 15, 1961, a volunteer recruited from a penal labour camp near the Siberian city of Vilyuisk, to which he had been sentenced for crimes against the State. He was one of fourteen subjects delivered to Dr Schutz—to Group 17—on that date. He had undergone a standard series of the Steinkopf Treatments, but with certain modifications. The modifications were identified only by code numbers which looked to Fergus like specific-gravity ratios.

Here, again, there was a footnote reference to another paper, this one particularly frustrating because Fergus sensed that the treatment was significant, yet the name 'Steinkopf' conveyed nothing. He had made a note of the listing given for this paper, AMB-6412-B. It was apparently part of a different series from the Reports, all of which began with the code letter N. He would ask Bayles-Attenborough about it.

All fourteen of the laboratory subjects had undergone the same treatments. Subject RS 22 had, before his death, been paired with Subject RF 7, a female; the pair had mated and produced offspring, born in the laboratory clinic on July 2, 1962, female, weight 2.6 kilograms. . . .

There followed a detailed history of the female progeny of RS 22 and RF 7. Fergus had read this part of the paper with growing bafflement. It was not merely an odd minor digression. It was as crazily ungermane as if pages from two entirely different reports had somehow become shuffled together and published by mistake —except, of course, that that should have been apparent through a break in continuity, an unfinished sentence or paragraph, and there was no such break. It was, rather, as if a cancer researcher at the NIH, working with rats, had suddenly lost all interest in cancer and become fascinated with the rats themselves.

Fergus's thoughts were broken by a shout, stifled as it began, a splash, a flurry of water in the sunlight. Twenty yards from his canoe the boy he had seen, still astride his bicycle, was disappearing beneath the surface of the water. The scene had an odd, slow-motion appearance; the bicycle tilted sluggishly to one side as it sank, and the boy, as if trying to steer, clung to the handlebars. Not until his head went under did he let go and claw the air with one hand; then the surface closed and there was nothing.

Fergus paddled hard forward. Over the side, straight below, he could see the boy struggling. His left leg was caught beneath the frame of the bicycle, which rested on the bottom; his right hand, outstretched, groping, was six inches below the surface. Trying not to capsize, Fergus reached down, caught the wrist and pulled. The bicycle turned in a swirl of mud and yielded. The boy had been under for perhaps a minute. His head emerged, his eyes open, staring, devoid of expression, for the moment not a human face but that of a saved animal. Then intelligence returned; the hand Fergus was not holding clawed upward and caught the side of the canoe, which now tipped perilously.

'Easy,' Fergus said. 'Hang on.' He paddled three more strokes and the bow scraped the bank. He jumped ashore, pulling the canoe after him, then reached a hand to the boy. They scrambled up the mud bank and sat side by side, gasping on the wet grass. Then the boy retched and lay back.

'I feel sick.'

'Rest and breathe,' said Fergus. 'You'll be all right. You ran out of air down there.' The boy closed his eyes; his face, which had turned blue-white, slowly regained colour. 'My leg was caught,' he said. 'You pulled me up. I remember it now.'

'You were riding too close to the edge,' Fergus said. 'That's dangerous. You might have drowned.'

'I know.' The boy added contritely: 'I'm sorry. I was trying to . . .' He stopped.

'Trying to what?'

The boy sat up abruptly. 'Where's the bike?'

'In the river—right out there on the bottom. I expect you can retrieve it later. . . .'

'But don't you see? That shows . . .' But now his face turned blue again, and he shivered violently.

'Lie down,' Fergus commanded. He pulled off his heavy sweater. 'Put this on. You're still in shock.'

The boy obeyed. When his shivering subsided he asked: 'What does that mean?'

'In shock? It means you don't have enough oxygen in your brain. It wears off in a while. Lying down helps.'

The boy lay still, his eyes closed, and seemed to fall asleep. Then he spoke again. 'I feel better now. The sun's getting warmer.'

'It is,' said Fergus. 'But lie where you are a while longer. Then try sitting up again. When you can walk, we've got to get you some dry clothes. Where do you live?'

'Just up the hill, not far.' He opened his eyes. His face looked better. 'If I hadn't got my leg caught, I could have swum ashore. Easily.'

'I expect you could. It was only a few feet.'

'Allie can swim like a fish.'

Fergus looked at him, puzzled. 'Allie?'

'I forgot. I guess I'm still dizzy. You don't know her. She's my sister. They say she drowned, but she didn't.'

CHAPTER ELEVEN

HE HEARD the wishful story from the boy, then the sad, true story from the mother, and Fergus, the detached, lost his detachment. In so personal a conflict of beliefs over so grave an event it was impossible not to take interest and eventually sides. At first he was inclined to believe the boy, whose faith in his own logic and whose need for an adult convert were compelling. But in the end Fergus joined the grown-ups; against John's hopeful arguments the solid facts stood like ugly ramparts. The bicycle *had* been in its position on the riverbank, the girl *was* totally gone, had been gone now for three days. He would like to have seen the bicycle there for himself; but no matter, he heard the mother for himself.

He had wandered by accident into the privacy of her grief and would have sprung back instantly but could not; he was held within it by the simple physical presence of her pale, wet, shivering son clad in his loaned sweater. When she saw him (emerging, by chance, from the front door just as they reached the house) she cried out as if playing: 'John. Oh my God.' Then she saw Fergus, a stranger, and controlled herself. 'I'm sorry. I've been upset.' 'He's all right,' Fergus had said, grasping the connection she had made between one drowned child and another nearly drowned. 'He rode his bicycle into the river.'

'Allie's bicycle,' John said. 'Mother, I was trying——'

She interrupted, looking at his pallor and his shivering. 'Go and change clothes, John, and get under a blanket. You'll be sick. You can tell me later.'

When John, after lying beside the river, had recovered enough to stand and walk up the hill, he had begun to talk rapidly, almost giddily.

'The police said she got on her bike up there by the wall and rode the wrong way by mistake. They think an animal scared her and she got mixed up. How could she get mixed up? One way is uphill, the other way is down. You can't ride up the hill.'

'When was this?' Fergus was inclined to agree with him.

'Friday night.'

'**Night.**'

'They keep saying, "It's easy to get lost in the woods at night." But can't they see? If she rode the wrong way, she wouldn't be in the woods. She'd know right away.'

'But if she was frightened . . .'

'By an animal? Allie wasn't scared of animals. Not ever. When she was a little kid, if we went to town, all she wanted to do was to go to the zoo. She'd stay all day if you'd let her.'

'Maybe it wasn't an animal.'

'Then what?'

'A person, a noise—who knows?'

'Well,' John said, 'maybe. I thought of that. But she didn't go the wrong way by mistake. And she didn't ride up to the edge and fall off. They're wrong about that. The ground is too soft. If you ride hard enough to reach the edge, the bike goes over.'

'As you did.'

'Yes. You can't turn, not the way they say she did. I tried it twenty times.'

'Then what did happen to her? Why hasn't she come home?'

'I don't know.' John's voice rose. 'I don't *know*. That's the trouble. And nobody's trying to find out.'

'Have you told your parents about—what you think?'

'I told my mother. She believes what the police say. My father is dead.'

So she was a widow. She left him in the living room, a room with a brick fireplace, a white mantel, a sofa, an upholstered chair, a hassock, an old but still handsome Oriental rug, a quietly pleasant room with sunshine in the windows and green leaves outside.

She came back carrying his sweater, and there was a new, perplexed expression on her face. 'It's too wet to wear,' she said, 'I'm sorry. I can put it on the clothesline in the sun.'

'It doesn't matter,' he said. 'It's warmer now. I'll carry it.'

She shook her head, and took the sweater out the back door. When she returned she said, 'I'll take it to you when it's dry if you'll tell me where. I don't know your name.'

'O'Neil. Fergus O'Neil.'

'John told me what happened, Mr O'Neil. I hadn't understood. You saved him. He would have drowned.'

Thus it fell to Fergus to explain what he had done, and what John had told him. 'He wasn't just being careless or foolish. You can't blame him too much. He was trying to find out what happened to his sister.'

'If he had drowned,' she said, 'I would have—' She stopped and sat down on the sofa, hands folded on her knees, like a schoolchild on a bench. 'I don't know what I would have done. I don't know what to do now. It's too much for him to stand, too hard, at his age. You see, his father died only last year. After that, the children seemed able to help each other. They stayed together so much. But now they can't. They need Allison. John thinks he's got to find her.'

Fergus thought: too much to stand at any age. Was it worse to lose a father than a husband? A sister than a daughter?

She went on. 'He won't believe, he won't grasp the idea that she drowned. What should I do? Pretend to believe him? Or try to persuade him that she's dead? Either one is bad.'

'I don't know,' Fergus said. 'Tell me what really happened.'

She told him, starting with Willis's coming home alone and ending with their trip to the river in the dark, three of them and the small flashlight, looking for Allie and finding only her bicycle in the mud. She told it in a quiet monologue as if, since he had asked her, and since he had saved her son's life, it was her duty to do so. He marvelled that she could tell it at all; he thought he had never met anyone in such despair, no one, at least, who could confess her own anguish with such grave self-control. When the confession was over he wanted to grant absolution, to put a hand on her shoulder and say, 'It will be all right.' But he could not.

'You see,' she said in the end, 'the point is that John went to the river only a few minutes after Willis came back. Then we all went. That's what the policemen finally realized. There wasn't time for anything else to happen to her.'

*　　　*　　　*

It was noon by the time Fergus reached the dock at the end of the stone peninsula under the wall. That, at least, was as he had planned it. He had no reason to believe that Villa Petrograd's —Dr Schutz's?—water pumping operation ran all day, whatever its purpose. But he hoped it might run at the same time each day; it had been about noon when he first discovered it.

This time, not wanting to risk again the attention of the Russian watchman, he did not climb on to the dock itself. Instead, as it came in sight he set down his paddle and took from his fishing box the three small plastic bottles, which he had marked with the numerals one, two, and three. Bottle number one would be for intake, the river water as it entered the pipe.

The canoe drifted downstream and scraped the dock. His left hand held the concrete edge; his right arm, sleeve rolled up, bottle in hand, the loosened plastic cork between thumb and index finger, plunged into the frigid water, found the barred opening, and felt the suction of the intake. The pump was running. The bottle, opened, gave off a small bubble; full, recorked, was in the fishing box.

On the other side, the outflow, he was more careful. He took two samples, each time pushing his hand as far as it would go up the iron throat, corking hard and tight before removing the bottle. Done, he let go and the canoe spun away, downstream towards the rapids. He watched the gate in the wall high overhead for a sign of activity. When he saw there was none he picked up the paddle.

On the way upstream he did not stop to fish, but paddled steadily; he had an errand to perform in the afternoon. He passed the corner of the wall, saw it leading up the hill, and thought of the house above, a house, one could tell, peculiarly chosen for joy and stricken instead by disaster, filled with sorrow through no fault of its own. He thought: it was no concern of his; but the thought disturbed him; it seemed wrong.

He had a momentary feeling, very powerful, of *déjà vu*, and then he remembered another day on another river when he was fourteen years old, fishing in a blunt-ended wooden rowboat anchored close to shore above a rapids. He had watched with curiosity the frantic activity of a pair of thrushes or thrashers—he was never sure which was which—a hundred feet upstream. They were diving at something in the water, attacking it, driving it away with a ferocity he had never seen songbirds exhibit before, all accompanied by a shrill, angry twittering. A snake, a snapping turtle, a water rat? Something that raided nests, broke eggs, or ate baby birds. It drifted or swam downstream towards him; it was going to pass close to his boat.

It did, gliding between him and the shore. He stared down at it and saw that he had been mistaken. It was a baby bird, a small water-soaked big-headed thing, struggling weakly, unable to rise, its head drooping under water half the time. One of the parent birds swooped past his head, so close he could feel the flutter from its wings; he pulled back startled and the baby slid past the end of the boat, speeding with the narrowing current until it reached the rapids and went under. Not until then did it occur to him that he could, by reaching out a hand, have lifted it from the water, put it on an oar blade and placed it gently ashore. He should have done it instinctively, and the instinct had been too weak, too slow. For the next several days the thought had worried him, returning so disturbingly that he had practised forcing it out of his mind; but it had never really gone.

As he paddled the canoe up to Mr Wilcox's boathouse he remembered his sweater. In the telling and hearing of Allison's story both he and Mrs Adam had forgotten it entirely. It was still on her clothesline.

CHAPTER TWELVE

ALLIE DID NOT KNOW how long she had been in the cage. That was because there were no real nights and days, no windows at all, and no way to see what was happening outdoors. When they turned the lights dim she slept, most of the time at least, and when they turned them bright—when they were there—she stayed awake. She thought that must be day-time. Sometimes they brought her food, but she could not tell if it was breakfast, lunch, or dinner, since it was nearly always the same, bread or toast with butter, wrapped in a paper napkin. Once they brought her an apple and once an orange which she peeled with her teeth and fingers. The doctor now gave her her drinking water at each meal in a kind of jar instead of a glass, a jar with straight white lines on the side and numbers written next to them. He always stayed and watched to make sure she drank it all.

She did not go outside, but saw only the room her cage stood in, and no one except the doctor, the young animal keeper, and Victor. She liked Victor the best, and had found a way of making friends with him. She had discovered that the square openings in the wire wall of her cage were large enough so that if she pushed hard she could get her hand through, and most of her wrist as well, though it scratched a little. When she first did this it was in the direction of Victor's cage, and he came over and stared, pressing his flat nose against the wire so hard she thought it must hurt. His eyes were dark brown and serious, his forehead furrowed and sad. When she pulled her hand back into the cage he continued to stare, and then tried to push his own hand out in the same way. He could not; it was far too big, but he did put two fingers through. They were the longest fingers Allie had ever seen, and reached more than half the distance between the two cages, so that when she put her own hand out again she found, unexpectedly, that she was touching him.

The first time she did this he gave a sort of a bark, snatched his fingers back, and leaped all the way to the far side of his cage, where he clung to the wall as if he were afraid. But two minutes later he was back, and this time when they touched, though he pulled his fingers away he merely examined them, as if her touch might have left a mark. Then he put his hand back, and left his fingertips gently touching hers. It became something like a game; each time one of them reached out, the other did, too. Allie thought of it as "holding fingers". Victor was getting to be her friend. She was glad of that, because although she continued to feel nice, she also felt, at times, lonely.

Fergus ate lunch—ham sandwich, glass of beer, cup of coffee —then took his three bottles of water, set them in a brief-case along with a notebook and a ball-point pen, and climbed into the State Department's car. He had donned a jacket, and in its pocket carried two letters of introduction and accreditation, one from Mr Bayles, one from Colonel Attenborough.

Half an hour later he arrived at the huge white building where Mr Bayles worked. He entered, as advised, through Gate 5. A red-and-white barricade blocked the asphalt roadway leading in; a guard in grey uniform, blank of face, ostentatiously unarmed, stepped from a sentry box. He spoke not a word but examined the letter from Mr Bayles, handed it back, returned to the sentry box, and pressed a button which raised the barricade. 'Mum's the word,' called Fergus, and drove in. He parked his car, as advised, in Area D.

Two guards later he faced a receptionist in, as advised, Room 2036. She wore a white coat and sat behind a counter. She had black hair and she looked young, pretty, and intelligent. Behind her an opaque glass wall blocked the rest of the room from view, but it had the familiar smell of a laboratory. The receptionist was expecting Fergus. She glanced at his letter from Mr Bayles, accepted his three little bottles, and affixed a paper tag to the neck of each.

He asked, 'Do you know when the report will be ready?'

She stared at him, then said, 'You're from outside.'

'Does that make a diffence?'

'Not really. Except if you weren't, you'd know I can't tell you that. I can tell only the department requesting the report.'

'Mr. Bayles.'

'I'm sorry. I can't tell you that, either.'

Since she was so pretty, Fergus smiled. 'Can you tell me your name?'

'Of course.' She smiled back. 'Mary Smith.'

Fergus left, following the blank wall that led to the exit, passing the wordless guards into the exterior daylight. Still, it was the only smile he had seen that day. It made him think of Mrs Adam; he recalled her gravely composed face as she had talked to him, and wondered how it would look if she should smile. There was probably nothing in the world, at this point in time, that could make her do so. He wondered how long it would be before she might be able to smile again, or laugh. The thought oppressed him. He wished he could have met her in some other way, at some other time.

By mid afternoon he had driven another fifteen miles, through downtown Washington and out the other side. He parked the car in a tree-shaded lot next to a low, graceful white building set in a green park. Its roof was fanciful; resting on a circle of glass, it resembled a pagoda ready to fly away. The roof sheltered the world's largest collection of biomedical writings, the National Library of Medicine.

If the Steinkopf Treatment was described in medical literature, it should be here.

Fergus could not have explained quite rationally his interest in the Steinkopf Treatment. A hunch, perhaps. He had had such intuitions before and had learned to respect them. In Dr Schutz's papers, the phrase was conspicuous not only by its irrelevance, but also by the fact that it was mentioned, almost deliberately, only in passing and only once. It would not attract attention, more than a fleeting question mark, of the reader whose interest was in the germs. But Fergus had lost interest in the germs— as had, he suspected, Dr Schutz.

He went first to a domed room in the centre of the building. From the ceiling, the apex of the dome, hung a multi-coloured spiral of beads that he knew instantly. It was a model based on a drawing he himself had made three years ago: a DNA molecule, from the nucleus of a frog's egg, the first ever drawn from life rather than mathematical theory. It had been a breakthrough and had won him the three-year grant that had, in turn, produced the b-virus experiment, still a month from publication but already recognizable as a bigger breakthrough.

The model, two feet in diameter, fifteen feet long, depicted only a part of the DNA molecule. A sign below it informed him that if reproduced in its entirety on this scale, the molecule would extend 142 miles. It might have added—but did not—that it would require approximately thirty million beads, each in precise, symmetrical apposition to its neighbour-bead in the next molecule. Alter a single bead and you had a new animal, a mutant monster unknown and unpredictable. In the seed of a multicelled animal, such a change in the DNA would affect every individual cell.

Below the dome the room spread wide; its brightly muralled walls enclosed depressingly endless ranks of filing cabinets—a card index. A sign informed him that the cards referred to books, tracts, theses, tape recordings, and motion picture films.

Fergus tried first the direct approach. He went to the cabinet labelled SORG-SZYM, pulled out drawer STEI-1, pushed it back, pulled out STEI-2, and scored a zero. There was no card bearing the name Steinkopf. That meant that there was nothing in the stacks, three acres of them, in print or on tape, by or about anyone called Steinkopf. Disappointing. Also puzzling: how could there be a Steinkopf Treatment without a Steinkopf? But not final. There was still the *Index Medicus,* and beyond that, the computers, the MEDLAR system.

Ten years of *Index Medicus,* forty volumes thick, occupied a bookcase of its own in the main reading room. Cumulated annually, it listed by author, subject, and title more than two million medical and biological articles from technical journals. But again, though there were papers a-plenty listed under Steiner, Steinholtz, Steinkirk, and Steinmetz—no Steinkopf.

All of this took perhaps twenty minutes and left him with MEDLARS, the world's largest computerized medical data bank. The acronym stood for Medical Literature Analysis and Retrieval System. Connected to a high-speed printer, MEDLARS could spew out biological information at the rate of 3,600 words a minute.

It was housed in the rear of the library in a soundproof, dust-proof, vibration-proof room. A grey-green door bore a sign that said 'Authorized Personnel Only'. At the desk near the door sat a pale, studious-looking young man, who read Colonel Atten-borough's letter carefully and then shook hands.

'Dr O'Neil. It is an honour. We know your work, of course. We process many inquiries about it. I myself am studying your endocrine-enzyme programme.'

'You're a biologist?'

'Biochemist. I have a two-year internship here with Dr Barclay.'

'David Barclay? You're lucky. You can't do better than that. What're you on?'

'Calcitonin.'

'In what?'

'So far, in fish, the ultimobranchial glands. Eventually, in sheep thyroid, I expect.'

'Give David my best wishes. We've met a few times. Are you working with the computer?'

'Part-time. Today I handle demand searches. I gather that's what you have?'

'A pretty vague one, I'm afraid.' And Fergus explained, volun-teeering only the barest outline: in studying a series of medical tracts he had found references to a treatment identified only by the name Steinkopf. The papers were foreign, the author not avail-able. He needed to know what the treatments were; also, who or what was Steinkopf?

'You've tried *Index Medicus*?'

'And the card file.'

The young man looked doubtful. 'There's a possibility,' he said, 'but generally all the proper names do go in the *Index*. Still, we can try.' He rose and led Fergus through the grey-green door to the computer room. Here, along the wall, joined part-to-part by cables like hoses, stood MEDLARS, a rank of dull grey metal boxes like heavy storage cabinets. In front of them a machine resembling an oversized electric typewriter whirred faintly when he pressed a switch beside its console of keys. Above it a square screen of grey glass flickered and came alight. From a box beside the console the young man selected three punched cards; he placed these in a slot behind the keyboard. Then seating himself on a stool, he typed on its keys the word STEINKOPF, which appeared in illuminated letters on the screen. He pushed a green button marked 'Retrieve'. There was a five-second pause. Then, directly below STEINKOPF appeared the words NO REFERENCE.

The young man said, 'I'm sorry. There's nothing on Steinkopf.'
He pressed a key and the words were erased, but he left the console whirring and the screen lit. 'If you could give me a little more
information—another name? Who published the papers that mentioned the treatment?'

'They haven't been published.'

'You're sure?'

'Quite sure.'

'Another approach—what was the treatment used for? Any
specific disease?'

'I don't know,' Fergus said. 'In a way, that's what I'm looking
for.'

'Not even symptoms? We're programming symptoms. We
haven't got it complete yet, but what we have is retrievable.'

'There are associated symptoms.' Fergus thought of Laboratory
Subject RS 22. He said aloud, but as if talking to himself: 'Loss
of identity. Morbid lack of anxiety, as in hypnosis. Perhaps an
induced euphoria.' Why else would RS 22 have continued an
experiment he knew was sure to cause his own agonizing death?
'Possibly, eventually, a suicidal tendency.'

The young man was expressing regret. 'All psychiatric,' he said.
'Those symptoms are of a mental illness, surely.'

'Yes. I suppose they are.'

'I'm sorry. We haven't the psychiatric symptomatology yet.' He
considered a minute, tapping a finger gently on the console. 'Another idea.' Fergus was scarcely listening. He was thinking about
RS 22. Of course. An induced mental state, a directed schizo-
phrenia. 'Most of that research comes from Germany or Austria,'
the young man continued. 'Were your papers in German?'

'No. Wait. Yes. Originally they must have been.' Schutz would
have written in German. 'I read a translation.'

'We might just try——' The young man sat on the stool again.
He typed at the keyboard, and two words appeared on the screen:

HEADSTONE   STONEHEAD

'Steinkopf might be translated either way,' he said, and pressed
the green button. They watched the screen. Again the five-second
wait. Under HEADSTONE appeared once more the words NO REFER-
ENCE. But beneath STONEHEAD the computer printed in small
glowing letters:

REFERENCE HIS MED CATALOGUE 69-3159 STONE HEAD VILLAGE
COMMUNITY. VON BULOW, H.

'You may,' said the young man, 'have struck oil.'

CHAPTER THIRTEEN

IN THE LIBRARY'S History of Medicine room, Fergus, at first scarcely glancing at the title, author, date, or binding of the book, scanned the table of contents and opened immediately to Chapter Seven, which was entitled 'The Stone Head Syndrome: A Diagnostic Puzzle.' The chapter itself was a section from a journal, beginning with a place-name and date:

Ayucalpa, Peru, September 15, 1936.

We had resolved, if time permitted, to make from this village, population 81, altitude 3,850 metres, a side excursion to the so-called Stone Head Community described by Cesar Diaz-Rodriguez in his account of his expedition of 1840. This portion of his book has been, as we noted earlier, largely discredited, since it was to this area that he claimed to have traced the Inca Ptoldec treasure. Having raised funds from associates to retrieve it, he absconded with the money.

Yet sections of his account (those having nothing to do with treasure) are told in convincingly vivid detail, and these details are of such a nature as to make at least a quick investigation seem germane to our medical research.

In Ayucalpa, therefore, we inquired of the local citizenry the whereabouts of the statue, the stone mansion, the huts and the waterfall described by Diaz-Rodriguez . . .'

Fergus, in disappointment, stopped reading. He had been excited to find any medical reference at all to Steinkopf, or Stone Head. Now he realized that it had been too much to expect. What could this book—apparently about medical research in Peru—have to do with Dr Schutz? He looked at the title page.

'A survey of Medical and Biological Aspects of High-Altitude Environment in the Peruvian Andes.

'Volume II. Expedition of 1935-1936. A continuing investigation into effects of prolonged hypoxia on human respiratory and neurological systems at elevations exceeding 3,000 metres.

'By Heinrich von Bülow, Professor of Medical Studies, University of Göttingen.'

Fergus thought: a typically Teutonic title, thorough and forbidding. The second and third pages of the book, solid with fine, dull print, were entitled 'Acknowledgments'. He glanced at them, spotted the name Diaz-Rodriguez again, and read:

We were frequently dependent on the work of the Peruvian explorer César Diaz-Rodriguez, whose maps, sketches, and geographical records we found generally reliable. In many cases they constituted the only information available on these remote, inaccessible, and inhospitable Andean valleys.

And then, from a paragraph two inches farther down the page, the name leaped out at him:

Acknowledgment and appreciation are also due to the Laboratory of Applied Biological Sciences in Berlin, and especially to Dr Bernhard Volrath and Dr Helmuth Schutz for their prompt and painstaking analytical studies and evaluation of material brought back from the field, including tissue sections, viral and bacteriological cultures, soil and water samples, and others. Such analyses in a fully equipped laboratory were, as always, essential to confirm and correct findings made with necessarily cruder equipment in the field. They are continuing as this account of the field work is written.

We wish to express thanks to the clerical and secretarial staffs of the School of Medicine, University of Göttingen, for their assistance in preparing . . .

Fergus returned to Chapter Seven, his opinion abruptly reversed. That there could be two Steinkopfs was a plausible coincidence. That there could be two Steinkopfs, both connected with Dr Helmuth Schutz, was not. He read on.

To our surprise we found the natives of Ayucalpa, Indians speaking a dialect of Quechua and very little Spanish, totally —one might even say determinedly—uninformed about the objects described. They seemed unaware of the existence of another valley to the west of their own. When we asked about a stone head, the village chief at first looked blank, then, with two other men, led us east (the wrong direction) to a hilltop where there stood a stone statue of Christ, arms outstretched over the valley, not at all similar to what Diaz-Rodriguez had described.

For the benefit of those not familiar with what he did describe, it would perhaps be permissible to quote briefly from that portion of his book. The book, his second published work, entitled *Exploration of the Peruvian Andes,* was kept in the form of a log. The entries in question cover two days, June 28-29, 1849.

At this point Diaz-Rodriguez was apparently travelling alone, one of his Indian bearers having died, the other deserted. He had been seven months in the field. The weather had turned cold. He could not record temperatures, his thermometer having been broken earlier, but he told of keeping his water canteen near the fire to prevent its freezing at night.

He wrote:

'I awoke at sunrise near the village of Ayucalpa, where I purchased food and replenished my water supply. Here I heard again about the valley I was seeking. After many disappointments I have learned not to trust the stories told by the natives in these high mountain villages, for they are all illiterate, superstitious, and, because of the thinness of the air, they are given to hallucinations and visions which they believe are real.

'Accounts of the valley, however, were peculiarly consistent, almost always involving the word "stone". Its people were ruled by a chief known as the Stone King, or sometimes King of Stones. Their god was a Stone God of fearsome proportions. The king, who was also the Priest of the Stone God, lived in a great palace made entirely of shining white stones. The king himself was immortal, a descendant of immortals; he possessed magical powers over his subjects, so that they obeyed his commands before they were even spoken. He could also, when he chose, make the earth tremble and move under foot, and cause waterfalls to appear where none had been before—powers, it may be noted, also often attributed to the Incas.

'In the past when I had asked where this valley might be found, the reply had always been indefinite—most often a gesture, a waving of the arm toward higher peaks to the west. But in Ayucalpa, for the first time, I was offered what seemed to be specific knowledge. The valley, I was told, lay straight towards the sunset, behind a ridge of snowpeaks plainly visible from the village.

' "How far?" I asked the head man.

' "Half a day," he said. "A day."

' "Two will come with me as guides. It will be faster."

'The head man looked away. "It cannot be done today," he said. Other men of the village who had been crowded close, listening, drew back. "There is the manioc to harvest. Too much work."

'By no amount of arguing, threatening, or bribery (though indeed I had little left to bribe with) could I persuade any of them to accompany me. The headman appeared increasingly uneasy at the discussion. As for the others, they had all disappeared into the dark doorway of their windowless huts.

' "Do you fear the people of this valley?' I asked finally.

' "No," said the head man. "Once we feared them, but no more. They do not come out. No one sees them. Still we do not go to their valley."

' "If no one sees them," I asked, "how do you know they are there at all?" I began to suspect another fantasy.

' "They are there," he replied. "They do not come out, but they are there." That was all the assurance I could get from him.'

In the end [Professor Von Bülow's text continued] Diaz-Rodriguez went alone; thus there was no witness to confirm the strange sights and bizarre events he claimed to have seen.

The countryside he crossed was typical of the bleak terrain of the high Andes, the cold desert called the Altiplano: grey-brown, dry, rocky, uneven; difficult to walk on. The only flora is a coarse, mosslike lichen that grows thickly on the stones, making them appear twice or even ten times as large as they are. In high wind its fibres ripple like grasses, giving the bleak plain the look of a lake in a squall. The inner layers of these lichens turn dense and fibrous, like dry sponge or peat. The natives burn them as fuel, chopping off brick-sized chunks with their machetes, or use them as building material to chink their stone huts.

Uncertain of his route, forced to detour twice by deep crevasses in the cracked and convoluted terrain, Diaz-Rodriguez spent most of the day reaching the ridge of mountains behind which the valley lay, a distance he estimated at eight to ten miles. It was almost sunset before he found a pass leading in, and came on the first of a series of astonishing sights.

The pass was narrow, between sheer walls of rock that rose on either side to two hundred feet or more. The effect was that of a tunnel, its stone floor leading downwards into the mountain. After ten minutes (estimated—his watch, too, was broken) he found his progress blocked by a very large round boulder. He thought he would have to go back, but then, in the dim light, he saw that there was a narrow opening on one side, a mere ten inches, so close that he had to squeeze against the stone. When he did he was astonished to find that it was polished as smooth as glass. It was not a natural boulder, but a carved stone sphere. The cleft curved around it, and when he had squeezed forwards a few feet he saw, ahead of him, shining in his eyes, a brilliant orange light. It was the setting sun—he had come through the heart of the mountain into the valley. In his own words:

'I gazed now upon a most astounding spectacle, which lay both before and behind me. Ahead was the valley, green and fair by contrast with the grim rock-desert I had left outside. It was well watered by two streams, which flowed from the snow peaks above. Directly ahead of me on the far side of the valley one of them hurled itself from a clifftop to form a tall waterfall of silver and white. On the same hillside as the waterfall, but farther to my left, stood the castle.

'It was square of shape, massive, of simple yet elegant architecture, its roof straight except at the centre, where a tower rose like a four-sided steeple. It looked large enough to house a hundred people, yet exquisite despite its size, for it was made (as the Indians had said) of white stone. It was surrounded by a wall of the same stone, and from a gate in this wall a road led down into the valley; along the road stood a score of smaller houses, also of stone but with thatch roofs.

'All this I observed from the niche where I stood beside the stone sphere. Then I walked forward a few paces, looked back (to assure that I would be able to find my way out)—and I was gazing on the Stone God. The boulder I had walked around, lit by the setting sun, was magnificently carved in the shape of a human face twenty feet from chin to brow; a sombre face, with a strangely Oriental look.'

There is no need [Von Bülow's account continued] to quote further from Diaz-Rodriguez's increasingly excited and detailed descriptions of the sights he saw as he made his way down the hillside into the valley. What we have already quoted is sufficient to identify the site: the large carved stone head, two streams, a waterfall, and a substantial structure of white stone. More important to us as medical researchers was his discovery as he entered the small community of stone houses. The entire population, with a single exception, was dead.

There were 112 bodies. A few of them, infants, small children, and very old people, he found in the houses, each of which he entered (and all of which, he noted, were uniformly clean and orderly). But most of them—he counted 91—had died in a group, seated in rows as if at a theatre or attending a religious ceremony, all facing the gate in the wall surrounding the great white castle. The area where they sat was a grassy semi-circle, a small park which looked as if it had been designed for such an assembly. Just outside the gate, awaiting a speaker or a priest, stood a podium of stone. The gate itself, of heavy, dark wood, was shut.

Diaz-Rodriguez, though not trained in medicine, was nonetheless curious as to what could have caused the disaster. He suspected some swift and deadly disease, which had struck them as they sat, so sudden in its action that they had no chance to arise; even those bodies that had fallen on their sides still remained bent at the hips and knees as if seated. He did not—for fear of contagion—examine them closely; but from a distance of a few feet no sign of any disease was visible. Their faces were without exception calm and in repose, almost as if they had died in sleep. Two thing he did notice: they looked extremely emaciated, as if they had not eaten for a long period, and their lips and mouths were grey and cracked, as if they had had no water to drink.

This was puzzling in the extreme, for on the way down the mountainside Diaz-Rodriguez had marvelled at the richness and abundance of the crops awaiting harvest in the terraced gardens: maize, potatoes, squash, beans, peas, and more. As for water, one of the mountain streams, as is customary in Andes villages, had been diverted in a stone aqueduct so that it gushed through the centre of town. How could the people have lacked plenty, both of food and of water?

Diaz-Rodriguez, by his own admission, felt increasingly oppressed and frightened by the presence of death, the silence broken only by the sound of the waterfall, a sense of danger. Whatever sinister agent had struck these people down might, at any moment, also strike him. Yet he could not bring himself to leave without entering the castle. It was there that he found the valley's only living inhabitant.

We may omit here his awestruck description of the castle's interior, the magnificent proportions of its chambers, the massive austerity of its stone-and-wood furnishings, contrasting with rugs of softest vicuña. He entered without difficulty; neither gate nor doors were locked.

'After I had explored the third room,' he wrote, 'still marvelling as I went, I heard a sound, a faint, sighing call. I was filled with fear, for I had believed all to be dead, and myself alone. It came again. It was a voice, barely audible, calling in Spanish, summoning me to come. Ahead a small stone stairway, four steps only, led to a door; the sound came from behind it. Cautiously I climbed the stair; carefully I opened the door, ready to leap back and run.

'Inside, on a very large wooden bed (but in great disorder) lay an old man. He was as frail as a skeleton, his hair only a few long strands of white, his face and hands dark and wrinkled. He seemed unable to rise, but his eyes were bright.

' "You are a stranger," he said. "You come from outside." He spoke as if he had been expecting me. His language was the Spanish of an educated man.

' "Yes," I said. "Only an hour ago."

' "You must speak to the people," he said. "I can no longer walk to the gate."

' "They are all dead."

'His eyes closed, and he lay a long time silent. Finally he spoke again.

' "All dead? Are they at the gate?" He did not wait for me to answer. "It is what I had feared. You have come too late, too late."

' "Is it a plague?"

' "No plague," he said. "They have starved." He opened his eyes again. "You need not fear a plague. Only do not drink the water from their stream." '

Fergus paused. He opened his briefcase and took from it the notebook and the ball-point pen. Then he read on, taking notes as he turned the pages.

CHAPTER FOURTEEN

VICTOR did not like the young animal keeper. That was because of the prod. Allie knew it was a prod because she had once seen a programme on television about cattle yards, and she recognized the stick with the battery on one end and the electric shock thing on the other. When they went to take Victor out (as they had taken the other animals out, to put them beside the pool, she did not know exactly why) they brought a smaller cage, one mounted on wheels, up beside his cage. Then they opened the doors to both cages, and Victor had to go through. Since he had learned that once inside the small cage he would be wheeled away and stabbed with a needle, he did not want to go, and that was when the young keeper used the prod. When Victor saw it coming at him through the side of his cage he ran away and went through the door quickly, but the young keeper was usually too fast for him, and prodded him anyway. When he did that Victor would leap, catch his breath with a gasping sound and then whimper, so that Allie could tell it must really hurt.

Once, when the Doctor was not in the room, the young keeper had kept prodding Victor even after he had gone into the small cage and the door had been shut, as if he were punishing him for something; yet, as far as she knew, Victor had not done anything wrong. When the young keeper had seen that she was watching he did a strange thing. He came over and stood by her cage, staring at her, as if he might prod her, too; but just then the Doctor had come in and they had wheeled Victor's cage away. Now whenever the young keeper came into the room Victor tried to hide: that is, he crept into the corner of his cage and curled up into the smallest ball he could make.

When Victor was out and she was by herself for a long time she usually slept even though the lights were on. Then she would dream about things that she did not think about while she was awake. One thing was that her shirt was too dirty. It was a cotton flannel shirt that she had put on when she came home from school. That seemed so long ago she could hardly remember it when she was awake, but when she was asleep it became clearer.

The shirt was pale blue, but somehow, before she woke up in the cage for the first time, it had got a big brown-and-green stain on the front, and two of the blue buttons were gone from one cuff, leaving only one button to hold it shut. It was also wrinkled from being slept in so much. In her dream this worried her; she knew her mother would not like her to be wearing such a dirty shirt, and she resolved to wash it, but she could never find a sink, or soap or water no matter where she searched.

Her hair needed washing, too, and was badly tangled. In her dream she found, in the pocket of her slacks, a yellow comb. She tried to pull it through her hair but the knots were so bad that during the second pull the comb slipped from her fingers and fell somewhere out of sight. She tried to turn her head to see where it had gone, but she could not.

When she was awake she remembered her family only dimly, but when she slept she dreamed about them and missed them. She had one dream: her mother and John and Willis were fishing along the river front, using the can of worms she and Willis had caught. In the dream she was watching them from somewhere—she could not quite tell where—and she wanted to run to them and join them but could not; she tried to call to them but she could only whisper, and they were too far away to hear. Then she looked aside, and still dreaming, saw the heavy wire walls around her—she was still in her cage.

For the first time it came to her, with a sense of shock and distress so strong she wanted to weep, that it was *wrong*, that it was unjust and bad, for the Doctor to have locked her in here, even if she had trespassed through the gate. By what right had he put her in a cage? Kept her from running to fish with John and Willis? From going home to her mother? In her sleep the indignity was clear: she had been captured. Her mother did not know where she was. If she did she would come and get her, she would call the police. Allie tried again to shout, but when she looked, her mother, John, and Willis had disappeared; she could no longer see the river.

So instead she dreamed a plan: when they opened the cage door she would not go to the bathroom. She would run to the door that led out, up the stairs and into the woods. She could run faster than they could.

But the wall! The gate would be locked. No matter. She would climb a tree—there were plenty of trees along the inside of the wall and she could climb, John once said, like a monkey. The idea made her feel giddy with longing. To go home! Why had she not thought of it before?

But when Dr Schutz came to open the cage door, the lock clicked sharply, the light glinted on his thick glasses, she woke up, shook her head to clear it, and the dream glimmered and slipped away. She felt nice.

It was Monday, a school day, but the children could not be asked to go back to school quite so soon. Instead, they were, despite everything, planting the garden. It was the only activity available close at hand, and could take place in the sun, out of the house, not joyful but at least familiar. Willis continued to cry silently, but only sporadically, as he knelt planting seeds in the rows she cut with the hoe. In the far corner of the ploughed ground John shaped hills for the melons.

Both the crying and the activity had become necessary to relieve the silence left behind, the depression finally rendered complete, by a visit from Mrs George Adam, the other Mrs Adam, who drove out from town in her big car to remind them, not unkindly and not in so many words, that someone must remain practical even during the cataclysm; it was, after all, her cataclysm as well, albeit a generation removed. Andrew had been her own son; these were her own dear grandchildren. Jennifer could not ignore a guilty feeling that her mother-in-law might now regard her with mistrust, as if she had turned out to be of bad blood, hag-ridden, attracting disaster of a kind not heretofore known in the Adam family.

In their living room the elder Mrs Adam spoke quietly but firmly about things they did not want to hear. When Allison would be legally termed dead there must be ceremonial recognition of the fact. Though there could be no interment there should be a service, and a stone marker to her memory, poor little girl, in the Adam family burial plot. She had talked to Dr Elsley, pastor of the Georgetown Episcopal church she attended, who had told her that it was customary in cases like Allison's—that is, disappeared and believed dead—to wait two weeks before holding a service, which was then virtually the same as a regular funeral, without a coffin but with flowers. Members of the immediate family customarily proceeded from the church to the graveyard to see and place a wreath on the memorial stone.

Willis listened at first, sitting at the top of the stairs, and then crept back to his room and closed the door. John sat in the living room with them. She was afraid that he was going to argue, but he did not. Faced again with adult authority, this time the austerity of his grandmother and the official finality of Dr Elsley and a church service, he seemed to crumble and lose hope; he only stared with dismayed eyes and did not speak at all.

When the big car drove away she had called John and Willis to help her plant the seeds, and together they tried to pretend that it was a normal and useful thing to do.

Fergus walked across the meadow from his cabin. He had finished Von Bülow's book and was in urgent need to talk to Mr Bayles and Colonel Attenborough, which he would do in the afternoon. But now he was going to get his sweater, and if it proved possible he was going to do more than that. He thought that he would find Mrs Adam and her two children still in a condition of distress. He hoped it might be less acute than during his last visit; in any case, though he had no clear idea how, he thought he would try to help them.

Inexplicably, though the prospect should have been depressing, it was not; he walked briskly and felt cheerful. Immediately he mistrusted his own altruism. He thought, if they were a different family—stupid, ugly, diseased, in a dirty house—would he have decided to help them? Impossible to be sure. He might, and merely not have felt cheerful about it. Surely there was nothing wrong, at least, in liking someone you had an opportunity to help.

He decided that his best chance would be Willis, only for the simplest of reasons: he was five. If Willis could be beguiled, even momentarily, the other two would be pleased and therefore also helped. He had met Willis just briefly at the end of his last visit, looking up as Mrs Adam talked and seeing the small figure sitting on the stairs, shaking hands when they were introduced. Willis looked astonishingly like his mother, bearing even the same grave expression. Yet Fergus thought he, at least, might be made to smile.

The meadow led along the river front to the small scrub woods that hid the road and the wall of Villa Petrograd. Here the ground sloped upwards and the grass gave way to thorny underbrush, honeysuckle and scraggly pines, cedars and beech, locust and dogwood trees.

As he neared the top of this bluff Fergus heard voices ahead of him: men talking, not very loudly and not in English. He paused. From the closeness of the sound he thought they must be outside the wall; the language sounded like Russian. Fergus decided to see before being seen. He moved forward cautiously and silently. Another noise began: the rasp of a saw.

At length, through a hole between a scrub pine and a small cedar, he could see them. There were two men, and one he recognized: it was the groundskeeper who had chased him from the dock. Fergus was glad he had been cautious. The man might think it odd if, having chased him off by water, he now found him approaching by land.

They were wielding a two-handled crosscut saw, cutting up a tree they had evidently just felled. Fergus could see the stump, cut off low to the ground, where it had grown near the wall. From its leaves and bark he recognized it as an aspen; he wondered why they had cut it and then realized that a tree of any size growing near the wall would provide an easy entry to anyone who wanted to pry into what went on on the other side. It also occurred to him, recalling the aerial photograph, that Dr Schutz's laboratory must lie fairly close to this corner of the estate. Interesting. Could it be they suspected others were curious about the laboratory? Again he was glad he had not been seen.

The two men, having cut the aspen into movable sections, ex-

changed a few more phrases in Russian and gestured in his direction. Each grasped a section and started across the narrow gravel
road: they were going to dispose of the tree in the woods where
he lay. Fergus swore silently and retreated down the bluff. His
foot slipped: he slid and found himself lying face down behind a
hummock of moss and honeysuckle. Had the Russians heard? No.
They were making noise of their own, dragging branches through
underbrush. They stopped short of the top of the bluff, released
their burdens, and went back for more. After two trips they were
done.

Fergus raised his head and stared after them as they picked up
their saw and walked up the road beside the wall. Halfway up the
hill, almost out of his range of vision, they stopped at a gate,
pushed it open, went in, and closed it behind them.

It was then that he looked down and saw the chipmunks. When
he had slid, his foot had dug away a rut in the dead leaves and
soft earth of the bluff exposing, from its side, their small warren.
Sitting on its floor, upright on her haunches, regarding him with
shining black eyes, was the mother, brown-striped and unafraid.
Behind her, new fur barely hiding their pink skin, crouched her
four babies. He had found Willis's diversion.

He walked out to the road and turned right. When he reached
the gate through which the two men had disappeared he paused,
then pushed tentatively with his hand against its iron face. It did
not yield. He continued up the hill.

Willis watched the chipmunks for an hour, lying on his stomach,
elbows in the dirt; Fergus sat beside him in the honeysuckle enjoying his enjoyment. By the time they had returned to the bluff the
mother chipmunk had been joined by the father, and together the
two small animals were working to repair their damaged home.
They did this with astonishing speed and skill, digging horizontally deeper into the bank and piling the earth thus removed to
close the hole Fergus's heel had opened.

Willis, grasping the engineering involved, said, 'Should I help
them?'

'Better not,' Fergus said. 'They're scared enough already.'

'They don't look scared. They didn't run away.'

'That's because they have babies. The babies can't run.'

Fergus had found the Adam family in the garden, and from
Willis's tear-stained face had guessed their situation, though he
had no way of knowing of the arrival and departure of Mrs George
Adam. When he had mentioned finding the chipmunks' nest

Willis had glanced up quickly, and Mrs Adam had given Fergus a look of gratitude which he recalled again now, sitting beside Willis. The look had made clear that she understood why he had come; it also made clear how much in need of help she was, and knew she was. So, he thought, he must try to help her, help them, further. He did not know how. He considered inviting them all to visit him in his cabin, to get them away, even briefly, from their sad house. But the cabin had a view of the river, which led back to the drowned sister Allison again. He would try to think of something else.

'Look now,' said Willis, his face so close to the ground that his words were muffled. Fergus leaned down beside him. As the father chipmunk continued work on the barricade, slowly closing their viewing aperture, the mother was moving her children. Taking them gently with her teeth by the scruff of the neck, she half-dragged, half-carried them back to the new, deeper, darker chamber they had excavated.

'Like a cat,' Willis said. 'Why is she doing that?'

'To get them back into the dark, I expect. Baby chipmunks don't go out of the ground until they're older. Maybe the light hurts their eyes.'

'You know a lot about chipmunks.'

'I studied animals in school.'

'Do you know about chimpanzees? Allie likes chimpanzees.'

'A little. They're a lot like people.'

'That's what Allie says!'

Fergus noticed his use of the present tense. He changed the subject.

'There, he's got the hole closed. I think we'd better go back. It will be time for your lunch.'

They walked through the trees and over the bluff, emerging at the road as Fergus had done earlier. For the first time Willis looked across at the wall. He stood still, and stared in indignation.

'Look,' he cried. 'Somebody cut the animal tree.'

'Animal tree?'

'Well, it's the tree to the animal place. Where Allie and I watch . . .' He stopped, and an expression of dismay came to his face.

'I don't understand.'

Willis said, rather forlornly, 'We used to play here sometimes.'

Fergus, not knowing there was a secret and a promise, assumed that Willis had forgotten, and now remembered that his sister was dead. He took him by the hand and they walked up the hill.

CHAPTER FIFTEEN

'THE TROUBLE WITH BIOLOGY,' said Mr Bayles, 'is that it doesn't go boom and it doesn't look good on television. It lacks glamour. So the boys at the EAC get half the research money; NASA puts on a TV show from the moon and gets the other half, and Fort Detrick gets closed down.'

They sat in Fergus's cabin around the long trestle table; the sun above had passed high noon; Mr Bayles had taken an assortment of papers from his steel briefcase. Beside them Colonel Attenborough placed three books, one in English, one in German, one in Spanish.

'You're opposed to that?' said Fergus.

'In a way, yes,' said Mr Bayles. 'I know all the arguments. But there are counter-arguments, too. They just don't get listened to —and it's partly because of that lack of glamour. Biology, right now, is the hottest, fastest-moving science there is. It's stupid to neglect it. It's about where physics was just before the war—on the brink of almost everything. Life from a test tube. What kind of life? Any kind you can name. But more important, kinds you can't name. Fergus knows all about that—there never was a b-virus until he made it.'

'And there isn't one now,' said Fergus.

'You didn't let it out. But now that you've shown how, there will be others. And who knows what they'll be used for? It's a frightening idea—but unlike the H-bomb it doesn't make you gasp. It's merely loathsome, and it makes you crawl.

'Take our own simple example. If the Russians built a missile launcher at Villa Petrograd, we'd publish the aerial photographs, or threaten to, and they'd have to tear it down. But what can we do with an invisible biologist working with invisible bacteria?'

'If that's what he's doing,' said Fergus.

Colonel Attenborough looked startled. 'You have doubts?'

'I have a lot of questions. First, about the water samples from the river. Your messenger brought the analyses last night. Nothing very startling. However, on my way back from the medical libary, I stopped at the Washington Sanitary Engineer's office and got this.' He handed a mimeographed sheet of paper to Colonel Attenborough, who looked at it and passed it to Mr Bayles. 'It took me all of three minutes to get it, and nobody asked me who I was or why I wanted it.'

Mr Bayles studied the sheet with a puzzled expression.

'It looks familiar, doesn't it?' said Fergus.

'It does. Let me see those analyses again.'

'I'll save you the trouble. That's a profile of the water that comes out of every faucet in Washington—every drinking fountain in the Pentagon, all the taps and sinks in the White House and the Mayflower. It's printed up twice a week and is available to the public. It has the bacteria count, halogen content, trace percentages of sodium, iron, calcium, all the rest. Perfectly normal city drinking water, taken from a mildly polluted river and run through a purification plant.

'The water in the bottle I filled from Dr Schutz's intake pipe is, of course, that polluted river water. But the samples from his outflow match exactly the water from the Washington city system. He isn't putting germs into the water. He's taking them out.'

'You think,' Colonel Attenborough said, 'that for some reason he's built a purification system.'

'Not just *a* system, but a miniature model of Washington's own system. It isn't hard to see why—that is, if you don't look too closely. His papers, the ones we've read, tell us he's working with waterborne bacteria, *anthracis* and others. So it's logical to try out his various strains on the system where they're to be applied— that is, if things get to that stage. He needs to find out which of his mutants will survive to come out the tap. But of course he doesn't want (or his employers don't want, and he's got strict orders) to put any real germs in the real water supply. Not yet. So he's built a duplicate system.'

Mr Bayles said, 'But our analyses found no exotic bacteria.'

'No. What we got was some overflow. He runs the system regularly, but of course he uses only a fraction of the water for actual experimentation. The rest he just pumps back into the river. But any water he contaminates he'll keep. First, because they told him to. Second, because he wants to test it. You can be sure he's got some kind of a retaining tank at the laboratory.'

'He has,' said Mr Bayles. 'It shows in the aerial photographs. It looks like a small swimming pool. We wondered what that tank was for.'

'So,' said Colonel Attenborough, 'he can practise wiping out Washington twice a day and work it up to peak efficiency. A nice arrangement.'

'So it would seem'—Fergus took back the mimeographed sheet —'if, as I said, you don't look at it too closely. But if you do, to me at least, it seems to fall apart. Think about this sheet of paper.

Also, consider the fact that the Russian Embassy is in downtown Washington, and that Villa Petrograd is where it is. And all that was true before Dr Schutz ever came here.'

'I'm not sure I follow you.'

'I mentioned that I got that paper from the Engineer's office. Anybody can get one, including anybody from the Russian Embassy. If they should want to check it for accuracy, they can fill a bottle from their kitchen sink in Washington and analyse it—any commercial laboratory can do it. Or they can fly it to Moscow and run it through their own lab.

'In the same way, if they want a sample of the untreated river water—again, they can pick it up at any time from just outside their gate at Villa Petrograd. Those two samples—the before and the after—are all they need.'

Colonel Attenborough looked merely puzzled, but Mr Bayles looked as if he were comprehending something he could not quite believe. 'Are you implying——'

'I'm implying that there's no reason at all for Dr Schutz to be here. I'm not even implying; I'm sure of it—*if* he is doing what all his reports have led us to assume he's doing. That is, experimenting with bacteriological warfare in a nice, sane, sensible way.

'This came to me suddenly after I had done quite a lot of reading then quite a lot of thinking—and then put myself in his place. I'm a biologist. So is he.'

'Suppose I went to work for you'—he looked at Colonel Attenborough—'and you assigned me to figure out how to start an epidemic in Moscow through its water supply. Not to start it, mind you, but just to figure out how. Would I work in some basement laboratory in Russia—where I might get shot if I stuck my head out? The idea is ridiculous. I'd do the research right at home in Fort Detrick, where I'd have unlimited facilities, all the staff I need, and where I could go for a walk when I felt like it.'

Mr Bayles said: 'But what about details on their water system?'

'If I needed details like that I'd rely on your people to get them for me. Whether I worked at Fort Detrick or in Moscow. I don't think for a minute that Dr Schutz has gone poking around the Washington water plant. And if somebody else did, some Russian KGB man, and gave him the information—couldn't they have sent it just as well to Novokuznetsk?'

'The fact remains.' said Mr Bayles, looking more perplexed than sceptical, 'that he *is* here. We've confirmed that beyond doubt. We even know what room he has in the Villa. And that he has an assistant—a rather nasty character named Georg Wolter.'

'Sure we know he's here,' agreed Fergus. 'What we don't know is why. But I can guess.'

'And that is?'

'He's here because he wanted to get out of Siberia.'

'You know,' said Mr Bayles, 'I've been thinking the same thing.'

Colonel Attenborough said, 'You don't think he's planning to defect?'

'With his record?' asked Mr Bayles. 'Defect to whom? Not to us. We'd try him and clap him in jail. At best he'd get a life term.'

'I agree. He's better off with the Russians than he would be with us. They can keep him under wraps; we couldn't. And I suppose he knows it.'

'Then what?'

'I think he's up to something else entirely. I think he sold the Russians—General What's-his-name——'

'Vasilovsky.'

'—Vasilovsky—a bill of goods. The General's a military man, not a scientist. The outfit running the show is the KGB, Russian intelligence, also not scientists. Schutz made his proposal sound plausible—it *does* sound plausible: come to Washington, set up a small laboratory, and check out his new germs *in situ*, in the very water where they're to be used. I expect the Russians had a few committee meetings about it and decided it was a good idea. Maybe they even gave Schutz extra points for zeal. Also, of course, it's not a very expensive project, considering the objective.'

'Assuming you're right,' said Mr Bayles, 'what have we got? Dr Schutz is here. He connived to get here, talked the Russians into sending him. He's working on a plan to cripple Washington with a deadly epidemic, but that's not the real reason he's here. Then what is?'

Fergus asked, 'Did you read the Von Bülow book?'

Mr Bayles said, 'We've both read the chapters on the Stone Head adventure. There wasn't time for more. Interesting, but pretty much a fairy tale.'

'So I thought at first. I don't any more. I think Dr Schutz has been working for years on something the Russians don't know anything about. It shows in his papers, in a strange sort of way. And it has something to do with that book.'

'You mean all the digressions—the footnotes and the personnel reports?'

'Yes. But the fact is, I think to Dr Schutz they aren't digressions at all. They're his main line of research. To him the germ-warfare experiments are the digressions.'

'Interesting idea,' said Mr Bayles. 'Have you figured out where it leads?'

'Not very precisely. One thing that puzzles me is why he used that odd method of writing his work up—inserting the material into his b-w reports. If he was running a side experiment of his own, why didn't he just keep private notes?'

Colonel Attenborough looked at Mr Bayles and smiled faintly. 'The academic background,' he said. 'Lovely. Shall I explain?' Without waiting for an answer he said to Fergus, 'If you had ever worked at Fort Detrick you'd know. Keeping private notes is absolutely forbidden. Every scrap of paper is classified, subject to inspection—and believe me, it *is* inspected. Even the wastebaskets are top secret. And when you leave your laboratory you leave your work clothes behind to be sterilized. In the decontamination chamber, minus your clothes, you yourself get sterilized. There's just no way you can smuggle out any notes, drawings, anything. And I'm sure the Russians are at least as careful.'

'So you see,' said Mr. Bayles, 'if your theory is right—and I admit it's one we hadn't thought of—and if Dr Schutz wanted to keep any records of his side experiments, whatever they were, there's only one way he could have done it. And that's just what you're saying he did: insert them in his reports.'

Colonel Attenborough, still looking puzzled, got up and walked to the window, staring out at the meadow and the river beyond. 'Your theory has logic,' he said. 'Dr Schutz may have been fooling the Russians, and if he was, he fooled us, too. You say there's nothing he can do here that he couldn't do better at Novokuznetsk. That seems reasonable enough, now that you've pointed it out.

'But there's something else. Quite a few of us have read all of those reports from Novokuznetsk. We've been puzzled by those digressions. Our biologists have studied them. And the fact is, if they aren't just meandering little sidelights, they aren't anything at all. They don't mean a thing.'

'You bet they don't,' Fergus said cheerfully. 'They aren't meant to. Schutz was keeping records, but records of what and for what purpose he was careful to conceal. In a way it's like listening to someone counting in the next room. You could listen to the numbers forever, and it would be meaningless. But once he lets slip the word "dollars"—or "sheep" or "peanuts"—then suddenly it all makes sense.'

Mr Bayles went straight to the core of the apple. 'And what's the word that Dr Schutz hasn't let slip?'

'Steinkopf. And he did let it slip—just once, just for the record. He knew the Russian generals wouldn't—probably couldn't—look it up. He counted on that.'

Mr Bayles sighed. He said, 'That's an awfully long leap.'

'I know it is,' said Fergus rather humbly, 'and it's a leap backwards. But I had to make it. All the way back to an expedition that ended in 1936, and to a concentration-camp laboratory in Silesia the Russians blew up in 1945. Back to the job Schutz was assigned by the Nazis in the first place. He's never quit.'

'Breeding the *Ubermensch*,' said Colonel Attenborough. 'The super race.'

'In a sense. But eventually he came up with a new approach. He learned to breed, instead, the *Untermensch*. It was easier. And you see, he realized that in the long run it doesn't make any difference.'

Colonel Attenborough murmured, 'The zombies. The sub-men in Silesia.'

'A crude beginning,' Fergus said. 'He's had twenty-five years to perfect it since then.' To Mr Bayles he added, 'A long leap, as you said. But what's worse, at the end of it I've landed in a pothole.'

'Which is?'

'I had a few nightmares last night after I figured this out. In one of them I kept giving injections to a chimpanzee. Then I'd ask it how it felt, and it didn't answer, because it couldn't talk. It just sat there. For some reason this irritated me greatly, and I woke up feeling distressed. When I did I realized what the dream meant.

'If Dr Schutz is doing what I think he's doing, the animals in his zoo aren't any use to him. Did you notice that in all his so-called digressions there's never a mention of a test animal? In this, his own private line of work, he's got to have a human subject.'

'Pothole indeed,' said Mr Bayles. 'As I said, we're really quite well informed now on Dr Schutz's activities, output, requests, receipts, and supplies. A human laboratory subject is something he doesn't have. That is, not unless he smuggled one in somehow through a hole in the wall.'

CHAPTER SIXTEEN

DR SCHUTZ felt like a card player who has been dealt a perfect hand. That is, he felt elated and lucky, and he knew the importance of showing no trace of this elation in his face or behaviour. He also knew that his luck was the result of patience as much as chance. If one played long enough, it was inevitable that one would get the right cards eventually, just as, if one tossed a coin long enough, it would land 'heads' fifty or even one hundred times in a row; a German mathematics professor he had known in the old days once calculated how many tosses it would require for this to happen dependably, on the average—an astronomical figure, but finite.

Dr Schutz had been playing the game for a long time—since January 14, 1945, to be precise, when his laboratory in Silesia had been surrounded by heavy-booted Russian soldiers in long brown outercoats, who burst open his locked door while he was deep in his greatest piece of biological research. They had 'liberated' all five of his current experimental subjects, three men, two women (thereby ensuring all of their deaths within a few days); but the Russian commanding officer, a loud-voiced Party member with a crude knowledge of German, had had a dossier and instructions on him, Helmuth Schutz, had interrogated him and shipped him east to Moscow with a box-carload of other elite political prisoners.

In the years since that time he had kept the experiment going, refining the techniques, working the fine specific-gravity ratios to precise perfection, regulating the gradations of their effect from null to mild to intense to acute with infinite variations in between.

All of this he had done under the noses of his Russian masters; all of it he had carefully recorded in their own military research reports, its true meaning unsuspected and incomprehensible to them. No doubt they regarded him as slightly mad; no matter: their own military research he had finished always on schedule, and it was clearly reported. They were satisfied. And his private research was not for the benefit of the Russians.

It was, rather, to benefit a German scientist named Hans von Bruckner, a biologist, who lived in Edelburg, a town in the Lüneburger Heide not very far from Hamburg and also not very far (but far enough) from where Dr Schutz had spent his boyhood, the only contented period of his life.

Sitting tonight in his chair in his room in the Villa Petrograd, Dr Schutz dreamed about Dr Von Bruckner not for the first time nor even the hundredth. He lived in a comfortable house, large but not ostentatious, with a touch of Gothic in its architecture; his own well-equipped laboratory stood a suitable distance away in a separate building on the same spacious grounds. He lectured once a week to a respectful group of graduate students at the University of Hamburg, and then shared a glass of wine in the *Stube* with two or three of the students, answering questions about genetics.

Once a month Dr Von Bruckner paid a visit to his old and close friend Friedrich Kassel, now Minister of Defence of the German Republic, whom he had known so well in the old days, the days before the Third Reich was crushed. There, in the minister's own living room, they talked about the state of science in Germany, and particularly about progress in some biological work related to the defence of the Fatherland. It was, of course, progressing well.

Dr Von Bruckner, in summary, led a quiet, useful, prestigious and prosperous life in an ever-more-prosperous Germany, which owed its prosperity, as well as its unquestioned leadership among nations of the world, to him.

Dr Schutz was particularly pleased with the name Hans von Bruckner—one of his better inventions—because it had a pure Germanic sound, as did the music of the composer from whom he had adapted it.

The dream was the end product of his plan. Like the rest of the plan it was flexible, amenable to change as all good plans must be. At present, for example, he was still deciding what to do with the girl. His original idea had been to complete the experiment, make the last refinements, go through the delicate process of administering the Steinkopf Syndrome for the first time in an open-flow water-treatment system, record the results, and then dispose of her by means of the same cremating equipment they used for the apes.

Now, instead, he was considering taking her with him. It was not essential; yet the idea had an elegance, a flair, like the flourish at the end of a signature. After the explanations of theory, the supporting statistics, the drawings and equations he would mark on the blackboards, they would be convinced—at least enough to let him prove what he claimed. But how much more effective to bring the proof forward then and there: the girl herself, the first walking victim of the infallible weapon he had developed.

He thought there would be no difficulty in taking her with him; or if there was, that it would occur at the very beginning of his trip, perhaps an added problem in arranging a passport. But the man who was going to get the passport, the man who headed the organization that would also provide him with air tickets and money—that man would know, and if it was impossible to take the girl, Dr Schutz would simply abandon her in Washington. She would not tell anyone where she had been; she would betray no secrets.

He had the name and the street address of the man firmly fixed in his memory (but not committed to paper); it had been given to him, along with other essential information, in Novokuznetsk by Laboratory Subject TM 9 in return for a few more days of life. It was subject TM 9 who had first told him of the existence and location of the Villa Petrograd. TM 9 had, in fact, worked at the Soviet Washington Embassy and stayed at the Villa frequently; that was before he had fallen on evil times and corrupt imperialist companionship, before he had been tried, convicted of conspiracy against the state, and sent to Siberia. It was he who gave Dr Schutz the specific information he had needed to complete the plan he had nurtured for so long. In return, Dr Schutz, after postponing his death as long as he safely could, allowed him to die by accidental narcotization rather than by *Clostridium botulinum,* the bacillus under study at the time.

In subsequent reports Dr Schutz had begun subtly to stress the advisability (slowly, slowly, making it sound like a necessity) of trying out his mutant water-borne bacteria on an actual open-flow water purification system. He stressed the differences in water sources, varying as they did in temperature as well as in mineral, chemical, and bacterial content. Obviously it would be most practical to test—indeed to breed—the bacteria in water where they might some day actually be used. He did not mention Villa Petrograd, but merely described, as precisely as he dared, what he required in the way of a test site. It was for the KGB's decision makers to scratch their heads, discuss the proposal in council, and come up with the proper location.

Dr Schutz's proposal—Group 17's proposal, made through Marshal Vasilovsky—was rejected at first on the grounds that it involved a danger of precipitating, by accident, a bacteriological 'incident'—a premature epidemic which would put the enemy on guard. This was expected, since Dr Schutz, in his first memorandum, did not suggest construction of a model water-purification system to simulate the enemy's. This was the essence of his plan; it went into the second memorandum, thereby refuting the only argument the decision makers had raised against his first proposal. They did not—again as expected—perceive the extremely dubious value of the idea as a whole. In the end they approved the proposal, and chose the Villa Petrograd as the test site. He had not underestimated their wisdom.

He considered the possibility that they might accept the proposal but send a Russian biologist instead of himself. He thought they would not: the record of Russian biologists sent to work in Western countries was deplorable; they defected with monotonous regularity. Dr Schutz, they knew, could not defect. In that they were correct. They did not know about Dr Von Bruckner.

The creation of Dr Von Bruckner, the papers, the birth certificate, the quiet but distinguished (and rather shadowy) early years of his career—all of these he would leave to his old friend Friedrich Kassel, whose rise to political power he had first heard about in Novokuznetsk through the *Gerüchtsnetz*, the Party grapevine whose efficiency seemed to increase rather than decline over the years since the end of the Third Reich (it was as if a sense of togetherness grew as survival was extended).

When German newspapers were finally permitted him he saw Friedrich Kassel's name more and more frequently and prominently in their columns until, only a year ago, he reached the lofty position of Minister of Defence. At first Dr Schutz wondered why certain of Friedrich Kassel's activities in the old days, particularly in the business of purging the Reich of undesirable citizens, remained unmentioned in the give-and-take of political campaigning. Dr Schutz knew of at least three or four people still in Germany, alive and free to speak publicly, who knew the facts and could corroborate them. Then he began to see their names, too, rising in prominence and he understood. Certain things were best left unmentioned.

This situation, plus the possession of his weapon, assured the safety and prosperity of Dr Hans von Bruckner when he reached Germany. *Bestechung und Erpressung,* or, as the English called it, the carrot and the stick.

Dr Schutz rose from his chair and walked through the door into his bedroom. He looked out of the window into the darkness: a cloudy night, no moon, no stars. He closed the Venetian blind carefully, turned on the lamp by his bed, and closed the door. It had no lock, but in the months since he had arrived at the Villa no one had yet disturbed his evening privacy. That was one of the benefits that accompanied the loneliness of being an exile, a captive enemy, and a spy.

He opened a bureau drawer and took from it a square simulated leather box containing a collection of personal articles: nail file, scissors, a bottle of aspirin tablets, a shoehorn. It also contained an envelope of brown paper, unsealed. He removed the envelope and emptied its contents on to the bed: American money, mostly silver, but including two one-dollar bills, all collected since he had reached the Villa.

It represented an indignity, the drab underside of espionage, not at all, at its working frontiers, a glamorous profession but one of scrabbling improvisation and mean living. One aspect, in his case, was that although the Russians provided him with comfortable quarters he received no money at all. He counted what lay on his bed; it had been scrounged and filched (an occasional visitor left a tip in the dining room; some left small change in their coat pockets in the Villa's cloak room; the dollar bills, a stroke of luck, he had found in a chair in the lounge): in all, six dollars and twenty cents.

He was not familiar with American money, but he thought that surely this would be enough for two people on the first leg of his journey. TM 9 had told him how this was done: a two-mile walk up the road that ran beside the Villa's rear wall; at the end he would find a highway where buses, silver and blue in colour, ran into the city of Washington at regular intervals—most frequently in the morning, which was when he would go, making the walk up the road just before daylight.

He made up his mind. He would take the girl. If the money proved insufficient for the bus fare he would simply leave her at the roadside. He would tell her to wave good-bye and walk away.

That left two imponderables, both, he thought, minor. One was Georg Wolter. There was no question of taking Georg with him. It was unlikely that the organization in Washington—which was part of a much more widespread organization—would be interested in helping Georg, who was not, one might say, a member of the club. But in any case he was sure Georg, if asked, would refuse to go back to Germany. He was also sure that Georg would not talk, that is, say anything about the girl, since to do so would implicate himself. Georg, in short, was not important. They would simply ship him back to Novokuznetsk.

The other unknown was the Russians, including Kublitz. Their reaction was harder to predict, but one thing was obvious: there could be no immediate hue and cry. Since he was not officially present in America, he could not officially disappear, nor be officially sought. His identity was unknown even to the Embassy staff: he was simply a zoo keeper, presumably a veterinarian. That was one reason, of course, that his departure was feasible. One does not put guards around a zoo. The KGB had counted on the fact that his life was forfeit if he should be caught by the Americans.

He expected them to do one of two things, both, by necessity, requiring time to set in motion. One, they—the KGB—could let it be known through channels not remotely connected with themselves or even the Kremlin that he, Dr Schutz, believed to be dead these many years, was in fact alive and at large in America. They could leak out a description and credible proof, even photographs. This would set in motion the American intelligence and police, and also probably that of the British, French, and the Germans; certainly the Israelis. But by the time this happened he should be safely in hiding, his new identity already close to creation.

The other possibility was that the KGB would hunt him down themselves. This was a calculated risk; he could not avoid it. But, again, it would take time to get the search going; and once Dr Von Bruckner came into existence, he did not mind if they searched for Helmuth Schutz. In fact it was likely that after an appropriate interval Helmuth Schutz, or a reasonable facsimile, might be found somewhere in Europe, already dead.

He would take the girl as far as he conveniently could. Since Dr Schutz was known to be travelling alone, she would be a useful part of his disguise; she would go along as his daughter, thereby reducing the chance of his detection.

It remained only to decide on timing.

CHAPTER SEVENTEEN

THE DOCTOR brought her a raincoat, a dark blue one with a letter in the pocket. He opened the door of her cage, handed her the coat, and told her to put it on. She wondered if they were going outside, but they did not. He told her to button it up and walk across the room, towards the door to the bathroom, and then back again. He watched; then he said, 'I think it fits well enough. Do you think so?'

Allie whispered, 'I think it fits well enough.'

Now would they go out? Instead, he asked her to take the coat off again. It was then that the letter fell from the pocket to the floor of the cage. It was in a pink envelope. The Doctor picked it up, glanced at it, crumpled it into a ball, and put it in his pocket. He took the coat and hung it on a hook on the wall across the room; then he thought a moment, took it down again, folded it up neatly, and carried it into the next room. The young keeper was not there.

Next the Doctor weighed her on the scale, as he did every day now, and wrote a number in a notebook. After that he closed her cage and left.

As soon as he was gone she went to the side of her cage and called to Victor in a whisper. He pressed his mournful brown face against the wire wall, and extended his long fingers through it. Holding them gently in her hand she fell asleep.

Instantly she was dreaming. She had received a letter. On the pink envelope her name was written clearly: Miss Allison Adam. It was in her mother's handwriting! Then her mother did know where she was. She tore it open, her hands shaking. The envelope was empty; there was no letter. Her mother had written to her and then forgotten to put it in. She looked at the envelope again. She was sure it was her mother's writing, but there was only her name —no address. Then how had it got here?

John had brought it! The thought flashed in her mind like a light. But why John? Because John was the one who would know how to find her; John could climb the animal tree and come down over the wall. But John did not know about the animal tree. Yet perhaps he did. Surely Willis, when she did not come home, would have told him. As if she were praying, she wished for Willis to tell; she thought, oh, *let* Willis tell John. She looked at the empty envelope and again she felt like crying.

Her dream became happier. John *was* looking for her. Willis had told him after all. She saw him, as from above, walking outside the wall, his pale face looking up, looking for a way over and in. He found the tree! She saw him climb it easily, incredibly fast. He grasped the spikes on top of the wall, swung over them, hung, and dropped, landing lightly with his knees bent. The scene shifted. She heard a door open—it was John coming into the room, approaching her cage. He had found her? She could not speak, but no matter, he saw her.

Then the cage door clicked and swung open and she awoke. It was not John at all. It was the young animal keeper. He was in her cage with the strange look on his face, even stranger than before, and the prod was in his hand. She sat up, and remained sitting quietly in the corner of her cage, the side near Victor. There was nothing else to do. She heard Victor gasp, a sort of a hissing sound, and felt him pull his finger away. The young man said something to her, but she could not understand the language he spoke.

After Mr Bayles and Colonel Attenborough left his cabin, somewhat past mid-afternoon, Fergus turned to the books and papers they had left behind. He had, before he left the medical library the preceding day, read to its completion the story of the Stone Head (or Steinkopf) village—both the account of the Peruvian,

Diaz-Rodriguez, and of the German medical expedition that followed him nearly a century later. Now he read them again, referring at times from the English translation to the original Spanish by Diaz-Rodriguez and the original German by Von Bülow. Mr Bayles had somehow procured all three, along with two bilingual dictionaries, in a matter of hours. He had had less success, so far, in identifying the missing paper Fergus wanted, 'AMB-6412-B', the oddly coded cross-reference mentioned in Dr Schutz's papers. Both he and Colonel Attenborough were sure it was not one of the Group 17 reports. Fergus hoped they were right.

The story Diaz-Rodriguez told grew stranger, more unbelievable as it progressed. Unbelievable? Yet the evidence of its truth surrounded him, and even the sceptical German scientists, somewhat to their own distress, were forced to corroborate at least parts of it.

The old man Diaz-Rodriguez had found in the white stone castle was dying. Moreover he wanted to die. His disease, probably (judging from Diaz-Rodriguez's description) intestinal cancer, attacked him with spasms of unendurable pain. He underwent two of these as he talked, and after the second his voice sank so low as to be almost inaudible. Yet he was determined to tell the story.

He had been born in the valley, as had his father and his grandfather and his great-grandfather—here his sure genealogy ended —and all had lived as absolute monarchs in a nation of slaves. His own family had once been numerous, but since they did not intermarry with the slaves, had dwindled away; he was the last surviving member. The slavery was not by force but was, rather, inescapable. As to how this situation had come about he was, by necessity, at the same time explicit and vague. At least four generations ago, perhaps more, a malady had struck the village and divided it as implacably as a wall—there had been no wall then, nor any stone castle—into two classes. Those who lived in the lower part of the valley and had their houses along the narrow road where the stream gushed—all of those were afflicted. The people who lived higher up, where the castle now stood, were not. These last were members of two families who eventually, through intermarriage, merged into one family, forming the dynasty from which the old man was descended.

The malady? It was not a sickness. Its victims remained healthy, but they underwent a curious spiritual and mental alteration. They became, as the old man put it, *como ovejas*—like sheep. This did not happen all at once, but gradually, over a period of years. The people in the higher part of the valley noticed, in the beginning, only that their neighbours (with whom they had been entirely co-equal) had become strangely listless. They neglected their crops—not completely, at first, but more each year; their houses and their terraces fell into disrepair; they seemed to forget to do the work essential to their own survival. Yet they were not merely lazy, because when they were urged to do these things they would do them, and they would work hard.

So the relationship of slave and master grew until, in the end, the valley people became completely obedient—but obedient to the point of helplessness. At birth, and as very small children, they seemed normal enough, but starting at about age three or four— as soon as they were old enough to understand simple commands —the ailment settled upon them, until by mid-childhood they would do nothing except upon command.

'As you have seen,' the old man told Diaz-Rodriguez, 'they would not even eat or drink, but only waited for me to come out to give them their day's orders. When I could no longer go, they starved, even with food all around them, waiting to be picked.'

There were legends (in a sense, Fergus realized, theories) as to what caused the malady. The old man's great-grandfather, a religious man, had claimed that he could remember how it began: God had struck the earth in anger, causing it to shake and a waterfall to spring from deep within the mountain. This waterfall was the source of the stream that ran through the village; those who drank its water were afflicted. The people higher up—his own family—drank from a different stream.

Realizing this, and deciding that the waterfall must contain some evil influence, the great-grandfather had eventually banned drinking its water. For ten years all drinking water had been taken only from the higher stream. But if the waterfall had been the cause, it was too late; the damage had been done, and the people did not recover. Their children, too, seemed to inherit the affliction no matter which water they used.

It was the great-grandfather who had started the work of building the massive white stone temple and carving the Stone Head. Both were offerings to his mountain god in the hope that he would withdraw the curse he had put on the valley. Both were built with slave labour, and both in vain.

To Diaz-Rodriguez this was again reminiscent of the Incas, and he wondered whether some similar event might have provided them, too, with the armies of slave labour they must have needed to build their cities, pyramids, stone works, and temples. But when he asked the old man, he found that the Incas—even the word 'Inca'—were unknown to him.

The last thing the old man said to Diaz-Rodriguez before he died was a repetition of his earlier warning: not to drink the water that flowed from the waterfall. 'And indeed I did not,' Diaz-Rodriguez wrote. 'Though I was in need of fresh water, I took none from either stream in that valley, but made my way back thirsty to the Indian village eight miles away. There the inhabitants, seeing me returning, had, to a man, fled and hidden, and I could find no one.'

Fergus turned to the German expedition. They, like Diaz-Rodriguez, had tried without success to hire a guide from among the Indians of Ayucalpa. Eventually, like him, they set forth without one. They were sceptical as to what they would find.

To their astonishment, they found that Diaz-Rodriguez had been accurate in every detail still possible to confirm a century later. The narrow pass leading in, the great Stone Head blocking the entry, the castle-temple, the waterfall, even the native houses, though crumbled, were still there. The valley was verdantly green, though weeds and vines had replaced the crops, and the terraces had eroded into rounded slopes. The wooden gate leading to the castle had rotted and fallen, but the stone podium still stood just outside the wall; nearby they found scattered fragments of human bones. The castle itself was roofless but still a formidable edifice.

The Germans had, by their own account, taken many photographs. Fergus wondered why they had never been publicized. It was possible, of course, that they had; more likely, he thought, they had been overshadowed by world events of the time, for in 1936-37 the early rumblings of World War II were beginning to crowd most other news off the front pages—especially news from Germany.

More important than the photographs was the fact, duly noted in Dr Von Bülow's log, that they had brought back samples of water from both of the valley's streams. On their return to Germany these had been turned over to the Laboratory of Applied Biological Sciences in Berlin, to Dr Helmuth Schutz.

The book, an account only of the field expedition, did not tell what tests, if any, had been made of the water samples in Berlin, nor with what results.

Fergus read on, taking notes, turning eventually from the books back to the Reports from Group 17. At length he searched and in a drawer found a long-bladed scissors, for which he was grateful to Mr Wilcox. When the sun set he rested, cooked two chops, two potatoes, a can of peas, and mixed himself a dry Martini from a full bottle of Gilbey's gin he had found on the shelf beside the refrigerator, along with other full bottles of Scotch, bourbon, vermouth, and cognac. After dinner he worked for another hour. By the time he was ready for bed he had reached some further conclusions. It was perhaps these conclusions that led him to his second nightmare in as many nights.

He dreamed of a tree by a wall. In its topmost branches a wounded bird struggled hopelessly, unable to fly. The reason for its distress was plain. At the base of the tree two men were at work with a saw; in a moment it would fall. Watching all this from far off, from a road leading up a hill, stood a small boy. Fergus could not distinguish his face, but he knew that the boy was Willis. As the tree leaned, slowly at first, gathering speed to crash, the boy turned, ran up the hill, and disappeared. Then the bird cried out in a human voice, and was no bird at all, but a girl. As the treetop struck the stony ground Fergus leaped forward and awoke, sitting upright in his bed in the dark.

He knew instantly that the dream was an emergence to the surface of his brain of an idea that had been struggling upwards for the past twenty-four hours. A missing girl. A laboratory experiment that cried out for—*required*—a living human being. An approximate coincidence in time was plausible. But add a precise coincidence in place and plausibility vanished. He looked at the lighted dial of his wristwatch. It was five forty-five. He got up and dressed quickly.

CHAPTER EIGHTEEN

THE MORNING was depressing, but Fergus was not depressed. He was out before the sun rose; he stood on his porch overlooking the black river, inhaling the chill air, testing the temperature. It had turned cold, of a kind not likely to change as the daylight advanced. A sharp wind scudded small broken clouds upriver towards the mountains. It was a day of setback for spring. Fergus felt joyful.

Should he walk or take the canoe? He decided on the canoe. Why not? It would give him access to the fourth wall if need be. The other three he could assay on foot. Not, he thought, that he was likely to try to scale any wall this morning, though he did not rule out the possibility. Now that he knew (as he was still thinking to himself at this hour: he *knew*) that there was a girl held captive behind the wall, he must examine the whole rock-sided, spike-studded monstrosity from a different point of view. It was no longer a hundred thousand tons of inert stone. It was an enemy. It was bigger and stronger than he, but he had the advantage, he could move. More, he could think. And as he stalked it, that was what he must do, for there were those on the inside, on its side, who could also think.

He wore the heavy rope-knit sweater Mrs Adam had dried for him. As he pulled it over his head, waiting now for the bacon and scrambled eggs to finish, the coffee to stop percolating, he thought of her and the feeling of comfort that descended over his shoulders was warmer than the wool, yet not dissimilar, a quiet joy: to be able to tell her that her daughter did, after all, live; was, after all, less than a mile away. He could not, he realized, yet tell her any such thing, nor even hint, because it would set her hoping, make her smile, make her unguard her face and her brain to too cruel a disappointment if he should prove wrong. This was one of the things to think about as he walked. What to say to her. What to say to John. Whom to talk to about the whole overwhelming intuition that had slid into his mind, a dart propelled from the soft, deep-lunged blowgun of a nightmare.

Bayles? He would seem the first choice. Or Attenborough? The thing was his project. But what had he said? 'We can't stick so much as a toe in there, you see, because it's diplomatic territory.' If only they were not so hopelessly, immovably official. Or were they? Could Bayles exchange his CIA suit for a sweater and a pair of sneakers?

After he had pocketed the key to the boathouse and pulled on a pair of leather gloves, a rainproof nylon jacket, and a wool hat against the cold, he started down the zigzag path to the river, and he thought, those are candidates for dialogue Number Three. There was only one candidate for Number One, and that was Willis, and for Number Two, and that was his mother. Willis knew more than he had told, and Fergus meant to find out what. What was the 'animal tree?' He thought he had guessed the answer, but there was more. He eased the canoe silently out of the boathouse; as an afterthought he tossed into its ribbed bottom a coil of heavy rope, one of many hanging from the boathouse wall, as always from all boathouse walls, and also a length of chain with a padlock on the end and a key in the padlock. His plan in this earliest stage was so simple as to be primitive—yet it was a necessary start, it was action. He would take the canoe downriver past Villa Petrograd, down near the start of the rapids, pull it to shore, chain it up to a tree, and set out on foot. He would then circumambulate the entire wall, with no more definite purpose than to see if it was all as formidable as the parts he had seen, or if there were scalable spots, places of crumbled rock and handholds; also if there were tall trees which might provide vantage points—to watch what? To watch what went on on the other side, as general or specific as might be.

The air was greying, but the water still wrinkled black around his paddle. On the ridgetop one hoarse-voiced bird caught a glimmer of dawn and hailed it without spirit, a raspy salute to a frigid morning, but enough—it woke the others, and the chorus grew. The canoe slid downstream alone. Here came the sudden corner of the wall; this time Fergus did not pretend to fish, had not brought his rod or box; he glanced up the road as he floated past it and was startled to see—or to think he saw—a man moving furtively uphill along the wall. The man, if it had been a man, wore dark green clothing, mottled like camouflage; it had been the gleam of his light eyes in a dark-tanned face, full on, looking over his shoulder, that had caught Fergus's eye. Which meant, possibly, that the man also had seen him.

The canoe by this time had passed the road on its way towards the Villa's dock, the wall's end, and the rapids beyond. He skirted the dock and kept going, farther downstream than he had been before. The wall stopped, or, rather, turned abruptly right, after about three hundred yards. Here he back-paddled, hanging still while he looked for a place to tie up. The bank was bluff, but there was a landing place, a great grey sycamore undercut by the current so that it leaned out over the river at a frightening angle; it would crash into the water within a decade or two but not today. Fergus found a stalwart limb, looped his chain around it, clicked his padlock and climbed ashore, tossing his paddle ahead of him, leaving the canoe afloat in the lee of the great grey trunk. As he concealed the paddle under a bush he surveyed the woods before him and the state of the wall.

It was instantly apparent that the Russians did not want anyone climbing inwards from outside the wall. The ground peripheral to it for a distance of some twenty feet had been kept clear; nothing grew—along this stretch at least—larger than weeds and blackberry thorns, which were abundant and forbidding. Obviously the Villa's property included ground outside the wall as well as inside, and the proprietors discouraged visitors. That was understandable. Small boys in the neighbourhood would inevitably be curious, and in the autumn there would be hunters. Villa Petrograd's grounds must contain hundreds of acres of prime hunting woodland.

Fergus hurried. He wanted to study the two unknown sides of the square enclosure (where, for instance, was the front gate?) and still reach Willis's house by seven-thirty. He recalled that he had heard of a school bus that left before eight, and Willis must not take it. He now tried to formulate a conversation, but could not. Let it formulate itself when the time came. *There:* an enormous oak tree. Beyond it, a hundred and fifty yards, what must be the front gate. Halfway up that tree one should be able to look down on the whole layout, entrance, house, zoo, and all.

The first branch was the hardest, ten feet above ground, and he was glad he had brought the rope. He tossed it over, knotted it, and pulled himself up. Fifty feet from the ground, with the tree still rising above him should he care to go higher, he stopped, secured his position, and looked. It was high enough. He had a fair view of the Villa, shadowy in the dim morning, its windows dark except for two or three lit on the ground floor rear—probably the kitchen.

The gate: it was obviously the main entrance. A black asphalt driveway led to it from outside; this narrow road appeared out of the woods and for its last quarter-mile was landscaped; cedars and flowering shrubs alternated and some—forsythia, jasmine—were already in bloom. It led to the gate, impressively square-pillared, where the asphalt ended. As it passed through the gate, the drive changed abruptly and prettily to white pebbles. The landscaping on the inside, from what he could see, was more elaborate, with the accent on roses, azaleas, camellias, and hydrangeas. Perhaps a hundred yards from the gate the meticulous white gravel curved in a graceful 'S' to deposit the visitors under an old-fashioned, shingle-walled, window-boxed *porte cochère*. It all looked elegantly Victorian, opulent, and rather comfortable. And at this hour, peaceful with sleep. Surely no one inside this charming, slumberous castle was dreaming of cold war.

And yet someone was. The coldest war of all, with one child as its first victim. And ultimately? He did not know yet how Dr Schutz planned to use his weapon, on whom deploy it, for whose benefit and to whose detriment. Except, so far, the girl, for test and demonstration. But demonstration to whom?

She would not be in the building before him, but almost a half-mile beyond (Fergus strained to recall the aerial photographs), a bit to the right, past what looked like tennis courts, a swimming pool, a soccer field. The light was improving—he could distinguish the goal net. Behind those a wood of formidable size, height, and blackness. He scrambled another twenty feet upward in his tree, and was rewarded. The zoo building itself was not to be seen, but at this altitude patches of the far wall were visible, the wall that must parallel the rocky road to the river.

And now, for a moment, Fergus thought he must be a victim of self-delusion. Then he knew he was not; he saw it in fact: just inside that far wall, the same dark-clad figure he had glimpsed from the canoe. It was moving in the stealthiest of walks, in the direction of the small zoo and the underground laboratory, where, if Fergus was right, Allison Adam was captive.

Fergus climbed quickly down, staying quiet, not wanting to be seen from the Villa, where two upstairs lights had turned on. He glanced at his watch: quarter to seven, and time enough yet for a look at the last wall. If the stealthy huntsman had disappeared around the corner of this last quadrant on the outside and had reappeared on the inside, he must have scaled the wall here. Perhaps not an important point. With a stout rope and a strong arm, Fergus now realized, the wall should be vulnerable anywhere one chose except along the waterfront.

Then why choose the fourth quadrant rather than one of the others? One groped stupidly for a reason and was, quite properly, thumped on the head: to avoid being seen, either entering or departing. A second lump of knowledge followed: the pale-eyed hunter had done it before, knew who and what were where, and how to avoid them.

Fergus was jogging now, cutting wide of the main gate; having crossed the blacktop road, cutting back to the final stretch of wall. Here the woods grew thickest of all; this stretch of the wall, the fourth side of the square, ran parallel to the river but half a mile back from it. Even here the Russians had cleared back all but the densest thorny undergrowth. Combined with the wall itself it did not form an impregnable barrier, but merely a steep, prickly, and hideously discouraging one, not to be climbed on picnic outings, nor, indeed, by any but the most determined and experienced woodsman.

And there, directly in front of Fergus, was where he had done it. Inconspicuous but not invisible, the track minimally hacked through the brambles ended in a one-man-sized clearing. At the top of the wall directly above, circling one black spike of the crowning fence, he saw one slim brown loop of hemp. Astraddle the top, the invader had pulled up his rope after him and lowered it inside to ease his way down, and to climb, when the time came, up and out again.

With no sure reason to do so, Fergus assumed that it belonged to the man he had seen near the wall. He considered and abandoned another assumption: that the rope and the man had nothing to do with him, or with Allison, or Dr Schutz. He thought again: beware of coincidences. It is too much. There is a link between this prying stranger and me. He considered his own rope, wound at his waist. Easy enough to loop it next to the stranger's and follow him over the wall. He looked at his wristwatch, whose hands were pushing towards seven-thirty.

Find Willis first.

That was easily done. When Fergus reached the drive Willis was coming down it wearing a shiny black raincoat and rainhat. Behind him his white house, his mother's white house, gave smoke from a single chimney and looked, in the drizzling rain on the edge of the wood, brighter and more cheerful than most houses could do in the sunshine. The cheerfulness was partly in the eye of the beholder, he knew; yet it would not be restrained.

Willis said, 'Hello, it's Mr O'Neil.' He seemed pleased and only slightly puzzled to see him so early. 'You going to see Mother?'

'No. I came to see you.'

'But you can't. The bus is coming.'

'I want you not to go on the bus this morning.'

'But I have to. It goes to school.'

'Let's go back and ask your mother.'

'John's already gone. His bus is early.'

'That doesn't matter.'

Not unwillingly, Willis turned around and plodded back through the rain to his front door. He waited while Fergus knocked.

She answered as if she had been expecting them. 'Mr O'Neil. So wet! Come inside. Willis, run or you'll miss your bus.'

'But he said——'

'I wondered if Willis could go on an errand with me this morning. I could take him to school later.'

'An errand. What kind of an errand?'

'A serious one.'

'Come inside. All right, Willis, you don't have to catch the bus.'

'Can I go then?'

'I don't know yet. Go to the kitchen and take off the wet coat.'
She led Fergus into the living room and sat down. She wore a blue
straight-up-and-down house dress, and her pale hair hung loose
over her shoulders. She tried to keep her expression uncommitted.
'So early an errand must be serious. Where will you go?'

'Not far.' This was the conversation he had not formulated. 'I
don't know how to tell you. In fact, I know it would be best, if you
can agree, not to tell you at all, but only promise to be back in an
hour or less.'

She shook her head. 'I'm sorry,' she said. 'That frightens me.'

'Believe me: I'm only looking for some information Willis
might have. If he doesn't, no one is any worse off, and I'll bring
him back. Or take him on to school.'

'And if he does?'

'Then I'll tell you more. There will be more to tell.'

'Does this have something to do with Allison?'

'I don't know how to answer that. If you mean, have I learned
anything about her, no. It has to do with something quite different, a programme I'm working on. But if I can talk to Willis, I
might be able to say more.' He added lamely, 'I know that's not
very good.'

She said, 'I don't know who you are. You came fishing up the
river, and you saved John's life. I made enough of that, but still
I wondered. You must be a friend of Mr. Wilcox, I thought, so
you must be someone important. And why you're here is not my
affair.' She reached a decision, and called out, 'Willis? Are you
ready to go with Mr O'Neil?'

Willis appeared, dragging the shining coat. 'Where?'

Fergus said, 'Down the hill. Not far.'

They put their coats on and set forth side by side, the tall and
the short, in the rain, while Mrs Adam watched them through
the front window. She was barely aware that the grey day seemed
somewhat less cheerless than it had been. She tried to refrain
from puzzling over this. from trying to explain it and the strange,
sudden visit; she turned instead to clearing the breakfast table.

Fergus sat on the white top of the newly cut stump, which felt
damp instantly through the seat of his trousers. Willis stood near
the wall.

'Tell about the animal tree,' Fergus said, 'and the chimpanzees.'

'It's gone,' said Willis. 'I told you, they cut it down. Besides,
it was a secret. Allie said not to tell.'

'Tell about it anyway,' suggested Fergus. 'Now that it's gone, it won't matter.'

Willis thought about all the times he had sat here under the tree waiting for Allie. How did Mr O'Neil know about the chimpanzees? He thought about how long ago the secret had been promised, and it became clear to him that Mr O'Neil was right, he ought to tell. It was all right, Allie wouldn't mind; it was all over now.

And so he told. He told how they had wondered what lay on the other side of the high wall, how they found—Allie found—the tree that grew near it, the only one that did.

'I couldn't climb it, but Allie could. The first time she did, she came rushing down, and we went to the woods across the road and she told me what she saw——'

'What was that?'

'A chimpanzee.'

'All by itself?'

'There were two men. Keepers. One old one and one young one. But after that she didn't rush. She came down quietly, like a cat, so they wouldn't hear her, because then they wouldn't let us watch.'

'What did the men do?'

'They gave shots with needles.'

'To the chimpanzee.'

'Yes, and it died. They got another one and it died, too. They all got sick and died, all except Victor. Abel was the worst.' Allie had, in the end, confided this to him. 'His bones broke, and that made Allie sick, so she fell out of the tree.'

'I see. And what about Victor?'

'Victor is still there.' Willis looked at the stump and then at the wall. 'He came after—I *guess* he's still there.'

'But there's no way to tell.' He slid the next question in. 'Did Allie ever climb down inside of the wall?'

Willis looked shocked.

'Oh, no. They'd see her if she did.'

'But there wasn't always someone there. Not even any chimpanzees. Why couldn't she go down then?'

'Well, because then there wouldn't be anything to see. Anyway, she didn't.'

Fergus felt his theory, his reconstruction of the action, slipping away. It had seemed so obvious: the girl had simply got in the habit of climbing the tree to watch, and occasionally, when all was quiet, climbing down the other side. Gradually, somehow, the enemy became aware of her presence, and one day they were waiting. But Willis was firm about this; she had not done it. Or not to his knowledge.

'So she never went inside the wall at all? You're sure?'

Willis, for the first time, looked evasive.

'Well, not from the tree.' He paused and then, looking beaten, handed over the final secret. 'She only went two steps, to look.'

'Two steps? I don't understand.'

'They left the gate open. She went through the gate, but only two steps.'

He had betrayed Allie, but it was too late, it did not matter. He recalled the whole frightening thing again. The way the gate bumped shut behind her, and her bike lying alone there in the slanted sunlight. He was glad now to tell it to Mr O'Neil. Yet for some reason, standing there in the rain, he began to cry, the tears mixing with the rain on his cheeks.

CHAPTER NINETEEN

THE KNOCKER on her front door sounded again, and they were back in only half the hour Mr O'Neil had asked for. She did not know what that meant beyond the fact that there was time still to get Willis to school, and that was what she should do; it would be better for him than staying home again on this wet day. Mr O'Neil's car was at his cabin, it was still raining, so they took hers, down the muddy driveway, left on the narrow lane out to the highway. They were silent during the ride to school, which lasted fifteen minutes.

After she had turned the car around and headed back through the rain, she asked, though she did not want to, what he had learned from Willis. She saw that he had been thinking about how to answer the question, and had made up his mind.

'I learned,' he said, 'that Willis has been fooling us all.'

She kept driving, but slowly, her eyes on the wet windshield.

'Fooling us.'

'He and his sister Allie had a game they kept a secret. It was a dangerous game. It involved, eventually, her going inside the wall of the Villa Petrograd.'

'*Did* she go inside?'

'Yes.'

'How often?'

'At least once. According to Willis, only once.'

'I don't know what that means.' Her voice sounded tired.

'So far, it's just a fact we didn't know before.'

'What made you suspect it in the first place?'

'Some things Willis said.' He told her what Willis had said, casually at first, about the animal tree, about chimpanzees. And then later, this rainy morning, about the two men, the keepers, and about the gate.

'It was clever of you. But I don't know where it leads. Unless you're saying that Allie is inside the Villa Petrograd now. And if that's what you're saying, I don't believe it.'

'No. I'm not saying that. Not quite so definitely. But I think it's a possibility that didn't get considered before. And one fact can't be ignored. The night she disappeared was, as far as Willis knows, the only time she ever went in there—the only time they ever found the gate open.'

She slowed the car still farther; she no longer trusted her driving, yet she did not want to stop and look at him. She trusted her face still less.

'Mr O'Neil, I'm trying to think, but I can't, I'm too confused. I'm in the middle of some kind of senseless nightmare, and now you've joined it, too. This morning when you came I was glad. I felt—relieved. I thought maybe I could ask you——'

She stopped talking and stared hard at the road.

'Ask me what?'

'For help. To stay calm. To let me know what to think. At first they said Allie was drowned, and I knew it was true—I found the bicycle myself, remember. That was awful, but it was done, it was over. Except that John never believed it. I didn't blame him. But then, suddenly, it wasn't just John. Next came Henry——'

'Henry?'

'He helps with the gardening. John talked him into believing that Allie wasn't drowned. That didn't surprise me—Henry's not very bright.

'But then that policeman, Officer Simon, came around. He *is* bright, or seems to be. He did this on his own. He didn't talk much, but he asked a few questions. What I gathered was that he, too, couldn't quite believe the drowning theory. Also, that it annoyed him—right at the spot where Allie disappeared was a big tract of land where they couldn't look for her at all, and it was the most sensible place *to* look. I believe they made a formal request, and were refused. I think what he planned to do was look anyway, unofficially. Some of the neighbourhood boys, when they were younger, made a game out of climbing that wall. Officer Simon was one of the boys. Henry was another.

'Officer Simon came, and left, and came again. The second time he wanted me to recheck exactly what Allie was wearing when she disappeared. Of course, she comes home from school in the afternoon and changes while I'm still at work. Still I did recheck.

'I spent two hours in her empty room, going through her things. Not that there are so many, but it was a hard thing to do. From what's missing I know: blue flannel shirt, blue jeans, white sneakers. The usual undergarments. The blue shirt: did it have buttons? Yes, of course. What colour buttons? Blue, I suppose, though they might have been white.

'I like Officer Simon. He'd been gentle and considerate from the beginning, and he still is. I suppose that's his trouble. He got to thinking: suppose we're wrong? And he couldn't sleep nights. Now he's turned private detective——'

'And you wish he wouldn't.'

'It's worse than that. Don't you see?' She stopped the car finally, pulling off the wet black country road and leaning her forehead on the steering wheel. 'There's a question none of them asks. Suppose Allie *did* wander into the Russians' property. She shouldn't have done it, I know. Still it's not such a terrible crime, especially if they left the gate open.

'But if she did—why didn't she walk out again? Or suppose she decided to explore, and they shut the gate, not knowing she was there. Wouldn't they let her out if she asked? *Why hasn't she come home?*

'If you think, that's all you get—that same question, *why?* There isn't any answer. I don't believe those people are fiends. If a twelve-year-old girl came trespassing on their land, would they lock her up? Shoot her? The idea is ridiculous. And would they then take her bicycle down to the river?

'You know they wouldn't. They'd simply turn her out and tell her to stay out. At worst they might call the police, or even the State Department, and make a formal complaint about trespassing. But they wouldn't keep her. It's not a military camp. It's a vacation place, a resort, or so they've always told us.'

Having told what she had to tell, she looked at him finally, not knowing what to expect. His expression was gentle. He said, 'I wish I could say something to make you feel better. I hope I can eventually. But all I can say now is that I think there is a chance that Allison really is in the Villa Petrograd. The odds are small enough so that I can't encourage you to feel hopeful. And yet, you see, I couldn't just ignore it. I had to talk to Willis, and to do that I had to upset you. And now——'

'And now what?'

'And now I don't know. There are some other people I have to talk to, and to do that I need a telephone.'

She started the car. 'Mr O'Neil, if you knew—if you suspected this about Allie, why couldn't you have told me before now?'

'Why? Because the idea didn't occur to me until five-thirty this morning. I haven't thought about anything else since.'

Having learned what he needed to know, having trodden on eggs, Fergus went back to his canoe, back to his cabin. On the way he thought hard, and felt his cheerfulness rising again, now that he was no longer obliged to conceal it from Mrs Adam. As he paddled hard upstream past the wall, past Dr Schutz's laboratory, he resolved to act on his own two convictions as if they were proven facts: One, that Dr Schutz (and his assistant—what share had he in the plan?) had physical possession of Allison Adam. Two, that he, Fergus, had surmised correctly the reason for this possession, and that the Russian owners of Villa Petrograd knew nothing about it.

He had a daydream fixed in his mind. He had the girl, Allison, by the hand, and was walking with her to the door of the white house to present her to her mother, perhaps to watch her smile. The dream was marred by two flaws, the first small: he had never seen Allison, so the girl at his side was faceless. The second was more fearful, a factor still unknown. He had studied Dr Schutz's experiments with the Steinkopf Syndrome. The girl had been in his hands for a week. Thus the smile remained uncertain.

He manœuvred the canoe through the boathouse door, scraping neither side, locked the river door behind him, replaced his coil of rope, his chain and padlock, and racked his paddle in its place on the wall. Having locked the land-side door as well, he set out at a trot for the cabin. It was uphill all the way, and he was pleased to note that he was not entirely winded when he reached the porch. It was not lunchtime, but almost, so he carried a handful of graham crackers to the State Department car, noting as he extracted them from the box that it was empty; he had nearly run through Mr Wilcox's cabin supplies and would have to find a grocery store to replenish them.

But first he had to find a telephone, and wished, not for the first time, that the cabin had one. The lack was deliberate; it added to the sense of rustic isolation, a pleasant feeling in ordinary circumstances but distressing now that his sense of urgency had grown overwhelming.

He had to contact Mr Bayles and Colonel Attenborough. On an impulse, he wanted first to talk to Officer Simon. Before he left Mrs Adam he had learned from her two things about him: his home telephone number, and the fact that he had remarkably pale grey eyes in a dark-tanned face. He was reasonably sure that Officer Simon owned a length of manila rope.

For a telephone, again on an impulse he could not explain, he did not go to Mr Wilcox's house. At the corner where the small road met the highway there was a gas station. This morning, riding with Mrs Adam, he had noticed near it a glass-walled telephone booth. He had a pocket full of change.

The rain continued, and water ran in small streams of dust and grease down the sides of the booth as Fergus dialled. He wondered why the telephone company made them of glass—breakable, hideously hot in summer, cold in winter, and ugly with dirt at all seasons. Officer Simon did not answer the telephone himself but was summoned by the female voice that did. He sounded hurried, but slowed down immediately when he heard the subject matter to be discussed.

'Did you know the girl?'

'No, not personally.'

'Then what's your interest?' A flagging of Officer Simon's own interest.

'I know her family slightly. Also, I'm living nearby. You may remember—the log cabin just up the river.'

'You mean on the Wilcox place?'

'Yes.'

'Your name's O'Neil.'

'That's right.'

'From Boston. We talked to you, we checked Boston, everything cleared okay.'

'Officer Simon, I've just been talking with Mrs Adam. Also with her son Willis. She says you're still looking for the girl.'

'The case is still open, if that's what you mean.' Officer Simon was cautious.

'Not exactly. Mrs Adam says you don't believe she drowned.'

'In an open case, Dr O'Neil, we don't *believe* anything except that the girl is gone, and we don't know where. So sure, we keep looking.'

'If you're looking in the Villa Petrograd, the Russian place, I have some information you ought to hear.'

There was a pause. When Officer Simon spoke again he was more cautious than ever. 'The Russian place—that's diplomatic territory, you know, outside our jurisdiction.'

'But the girl was in there.'

'You know that?'

'I know it.'

'You can prove it?'

'I can't prove it. But when you hear it, you'll believe it. When can I talk to you?'

There was another pause. When Officer Simon spoke his voice had become urgent again. 'Look, I'm on duty now. I'm already late. I can get off in six—maybe five hours——'

'But isn't this duty?'

'What you don't understand—the Lieutenant took me off this case.'

'But why, if it's still open?'

'Because *he* thinks the girl drowned. We got into a—Look, I'll see you at your cabin about five o'clock. On my own time. Okay?'

'Five o'clock. I'll be there.'

Five o'clock. That would be roughly six hours from now, time enough to break the news to Mr Bayles and Colonel Attenborough. It occurred to him what an extremely odd piece of news it would seem to them, with a personal aspect that they would be unlikely, at first, to comprehend.

He had seen no reason to mention to them at all any of the events connected with the Adam family. The boy on the bicycle, the two policemen, the missing girl—when he had last talked to Bayles and Attenborough those had all seemed unrelated to the project at hand. Now the two had sprung together like the jaws of a trap. And caught in the jaws, along with the girl, Allison Adam, was the biologist, Fergus O'Neil. He had lost his non-involvement. He now hated Dr Schutz.

In the rain-spattered telephone booth, as he dialled Mr Bayles's number, he had a disturbing thought: the surprising thing was not that the two groups of events had come together, but that it had taken him so long to put them together. He had the feeling that if he had mentioned the girl's disappearance, Mr Bayles, trained in the science of perpetual suspicion, would have spotted the connection instantly.

On the other end of the line Mr Bayles was cheerful.

'We finally found your missing paper—AMB-what-is-it—the one in the footnote—you remember?'

'Of course I remember. Do you have it?'

'There's a copy on my desk. It cost sixty German marks, about fifteen dollars, to have it Xeroxed. Another sixty to have it translated to English. You know why we couldn't find it? Because it wasn't classified. That's the trouble with working too long in this place.'

'Where was it?'

'Berlin. Archives of Medicine. Hence the A-M-B. Open to the public. Somebody here thought he recognized the style of classification from having done some research there just after the war. It's a pretty old paper, by the way.'

'I thought it would be.'

'But interesting. It's signed by our friend the doctor. And it ties in, in an odd sort of way, with your Steinkopf theory.'

'Look,' said Fergus, not trying to keep the urgency out of his voice. 'could we have another meeting? Can you get hold of Attenborough?'

'He's with me now. We were going to suggest the same thing. A couple of new things have come up. I'll bring the paper along.'

'Good,' said Fergus. 'But before you come, there's another line of investigation you might get started.'

It took him roughly five minutes to explain to Mr Bayles the kind of information he needed. After listening carefully, Mr Bayles's voice sounded more cheerful than before. 'It's our bread and butter,' he said. 'We'll see you in half an hour.'

CHAPTER TWENTY

THE ASSISTANT GROUNDSKEEPER, Nikolai, who took care of the zoo, had requested an urgent audience with Kublitz. Immediately after lunch he was admitted to the dank-smelling basement office with its steel desk, its safes, its shadowy lighting. Kublitz sat behind the desk, a ball-point pen held tightly in his hand, filling in forms. There were always forms.

Nikolai, in his rough clothes and heavy boots, stood until he was bidden to sit in the straight-backed grey chair facing the desk. Then he said, 'About the tree.'

'Yes?' Both spoke in Russian.

'The tree of which Schutz complained.'

'I knew of which tree you spoke.'

'It has been removed as ordered.'

'So I assumed. Is this all you have come to report?'

'No. But please understand, Comrade Kublitz, and make clear in your report, that the tree is the Embassy's responsibility.' Like Kublitz, who was his superior officer, Nikolai was not a member of the Embassy staff; they, along with Dr Schutz and Georg Wolter, were the only ones in the Villa Petrograd who were not. They were a group apart. Only grudgingly, on instructions from Moscow, had the Ambassador allowed this small company from the KGB to occupy one corner of his rest-and-recreation estate.

Nikolai was continuing: 'The Embassy grounds staff are under orders to keep clear the land five metres outside the wall. Because of the proximity of the road, that side of the wall had been neglected. It should not have happened.'

'It is a small matter,' Kublitz said, reaching for another form. 'The tree has been removed. In any case, Dr Schutz is unnecessarily nervous about such things.'

Nikolai leaned forward in his chair. He had now come to the point of his visit.

'So I, too, believed at first. But no more. I am convinced that someone is, in fact, spying on Dr Schutz and his work.'

'That is impossible. No one knows, excepting ourselves, of Dr Schutz's presence here. Unless, of course, you are implying carelessness in Moscow. The Ambassador himself had no knowledge of the nature of our research.'

'That may be. But one of the Embassy grounds staff, a man named Josef, has twice seen a stranger, obviously an outsider, in the woods near the laboratory.'

'How do you know this?'

'He told some of the other groundskeepers. I was present.'

'And he did nothing?'

'Josef is a dolt. He has worked here fifteen years, raking, shovelling, pruning. He thought it not important. There have been intruders in the past, he says, young boys, hunters, who have scaled the wall. It is difficult to do but not impossible. I myself might have thought this intruder innocent, perhaps merely curious, except for two things.'

'The two things?' Kublitz spoke impatiently. He thought that Nikolai, normally taciturn, was spinning out his tale for effect.

'Josef described the man's clothing. It amused him that the intruder was wearing an odd-coloured suit, covered with spots of green and brown. From his description I recognized it immediately: it is a camouflage uniform of the American military. Such a suit is, I believe, not obtainable except from official supply depots.

'Also, Josef was sure that it was the same man twice, on two different days, both times near dawn. Surely that sounds like more than idle curiosity.'

'The second thing?' Kublitz had now pushed his pile of forms away, and was paying full attention.

'The second thing I saw for myself. It was a man examining the dock in the river, the dock containing Dr Schutz's instruments and his water valves.'

'Examining? In what way?'

'As you know, there is an observation slot in the river gate. I looked through it, by chance, just in time to see the man climb from a canoe on to the dock. I continued to watch. He had been fishing, it is true. But he looked under the dock, and then reached with his arm into the water. Finally he extracted a hook which had become caught on the dock below the surface.'

'That means nothing. Fishermen are always entangling their hooks.'

'Perhaps. But this one, after freeing his hook, crossed the dock and examined the other side of it as well. Having discovered the intake valve, he was obviously looking for the outflow. I am reasonably sure he found it.'

'What did you do?'

'I opened the gate, walked to the dock, and told him to leave. He showed me the fish he had caught, said something in English which I could not understand, and left.'

'He may have been an ordinary fisherman. There are many on the river.' But Kublitz was obviously concerned.

'It is possible. But an American agent would know that, too. It is an easy disguise. Also—it is difficult to say why—he did not look like an ordinary fisherman, but like an intellectual.'

'Describe him.' Nikolai described Fergus with reasonable accuracy while Kublitz took notes on a plain lined pad.

He laid down his pen. 'Comrade Nikolai, none of the things you have told is in itself important. It is possible to obtain a camouflage suit. It is possible for a fisherman to be curious. But since there are three separate events, it may be that they are significant. I will consider the matter. Meanwhile, keep the zoo area under surveillance.'

Nikolai stood up. 'I will do what I can,' he said. 'But you are aware that I have other duties.' It was known that Nikolai did not enjoy his role as cage-cleaner.

'I am aware. It is possible we may require additional help.' He rose. The audience was ended.

As soon as Nikolai had left, Kublitz turned to the telephone on his desk and dialled an unlisted number in Washington.

'It complicates things,' said Mr Bayles. 'In fact, it's a pretty awful mess.'

'It is,' Fergus agreed, 'and a lot grimmer than the old one.'

'But is it really?' Colonel Attenborough questioned. 'Can you get much grimmer than *anthracis* and *coryna*? Two of the worst contagions known to medicine?'

'Medicine doesn't know the Steinkopf Syndrome. Is sudden death worse than a lifetime of idiocy? It's not a question you can argue sensibly, I suppose.

'In any case, we have the girl to consider. She's not a Russian political prisoner in Siberia. She's a twelve-year-old American child from just up the road. It makes a difference.'

They sat in Fergus's cabin; on this chill day they had left his trestle table spread with papers and sat at the other end of the room, where logs blazed in the fieldstone fireplace. Outside, the grey wind rattled gusts of rain against the windows, and cold rivulets ran through the trees down to the river.

'It makes a difference all right,' said Mr Bayles, 'if she's really there. There's our first problem: so far it's just conjecture.' He saw Fergus's face and added quickly: 'Fergus, I grant you it's convincing. It's even credible, as you say, that the Russians don't know anything about it. From what we hear, the KGB agent in charge, a man named Kublitz, stays away from the laboratory. He doesn't like germs. But we need to be surer than we are before we take any drastic action about it. And believe me, the action might have to be drastic.'

'Also,' the Colonel added, 'if she is there—or *was* there—we ought to know what's happened to her. It's an unpleasant possibility, but a real one, that Dr Schutz has finished his experiment and disposed of her. He'd have no qualms about that, and we know he has a crematorium for his champanzees. There's no assurance she's still alive, or that any trace of her still exists.'

'No assurance,' agreed Fergus, 'except that that's the whole point of Schutz's research. There's no need to kill anybody.'

'We need to get a clearer explanation of that,' Mr Bayles said, 'for ourselves and for others we may have to convince.'

'You will,' said Fergus grimly. 'First, that other business I phoned you about. It could turn out to be the key to the whole thing. Did you get it started?'

'I did,' Mr Bayles said. 'We should have the answer by tomorrow. Maybe tonight. I can even give you a partial answer now. Of actual Nazi party members—members you'd call quite ardent in Dr Schutz's day, but young and therefore not very prominent—there are probably a couple of hundred holding important jobs in Germany today. "Important" and "ardent" are variables, of course, and so the number depends on your definition. We have excellent dossiers on all of these. Most are in banking, business, and industry. Some are in science—mostly academic—some in the military, a few in politics. A very few in journalism and communications.

'Which ones Schutz would have known, and how well—that will take a little time, but not as long as you might think. The Colonel's division has a good file on Schutz himself up to his disappearance in 1945. It's a matter of matching them up.'

'I'd look for a public figure,' Fergus said. 'Somebody pretty high up who doesn't want a spotlight on his past.'

'There are some of those. They all have spotlights, but refrain from shining them on one another. A sort of a mutual let's-keep-our-mouth-shut society.'

'Also,' Fergus added, 'someone who can keep him under wraps. Because the German public isn't going to welcome Schutz back, no matter what. He's got to have a new identity.'

'So you think he's going to defect after all,' Mr Bayles said. 'A week ago we decided he couldn't.'

'A week ago I didn't know about the Steinkopf Syndrome. Also, remember, we were talking about defecting to us. We hadn't considered the other possibility: going home to Germany. Right now, it's the only sensible conclusion I can think of to what he's been doing.'

'Start at the beginning—which you just brought with you: that paper from the Berlin Medical Archive.'

'It doesn't tell you much,' said the Colonel.

'True,' said Fergus, 'and by not telling much, it gets the story started.' He walked to the trestle table and came back with a bulky sheaf of typed pages.

'A preliminary report—forty-eight sheets double-spaced, that's German for preliminary—on materials received March 12, 1937, at the Berlin Laboratory of Applied Biological Sciences from the Von Bülow medical expedition to the Andes. Signed by Dr

Helmuth Schutz. We know about the expedition—we've read the field report. Helmuth Schutz had read it, too, remember.

'Everything is here and accounted for, labelled, weighed, measured, described in tedious detail. Lung tissue, capillary cross sections, autopsy reports, haemoglobin measurements, dietary analysis, statistics on incidence of pulmonary disease, field micro-photographs of tubercules, even human foetuses in formaldehyde.

'But what about our water samples from the Steinkopf valley? Both in rubber-stoppered sterile glass containers. Containers carried in lined metal boxes. Container labelled 4-D-17, water from upper stream, intact. Preliminary analysis: ordinary pure mountain water, trace minerals listed.

'But container labelled 4-D-18, water from lower stream— empty on arrival. Explanation: container insufficiently filled at source, large air content of bottle causing implosion of rubber stopper at surface atmospheric pressure.

' "Explanation" my foot. Of all the items brought back—more than two thousand—this one alone failed to make it, *according to Dr Schutz*. Was anybody else there when he opened this particular crateful of samples? We don't know—but I'll bet there wasn't.

'It's easy to see how young Schutz (he was still in his late twenties then) would have been intrigued by the Steinkopf village story, both the original adventure of Diaz-Rodriguez and the follow-up visit by his German colleagues. He'd be curious about the water. Just as we were. But I'm betting he was a lot more excited than that. Because he spotted it right away as *just possibly* the very thing he'd been working on, getting red-hot on. A genetic change, a subtle but pervasive one, caused by some mutagen in the water.

'It might have been nothing. He knew that. It could have been a fairy tale contrived by Diaz-Rodriguez, or more likely, a bit of folklore he had picked up. Or it might have been an example of communal hereditary degeneration brought on by any of a hundred causes. Such phenomena are common in isolated moun-tain communities where there's a lot of inbreeding. Remember the Jukes and the Kallikaks.

'But two things would have fascinated Schutz: First, the sharp division of the village into two groups along the two waterways. Group A, water-source A, remain normal. Group B, water-source B, all deteriorate.

'Second, the nature of the deterioration: no physical debility, but a kind of a spiritual decline, a docility, a passive submissive-ness. A willingness, and eventually a need to take orders.

'Schutz knew it was a wild dream, but he was a dreamer. I can see him now, opening the crate containing that particular group of specimens. He finds the box labelled 4-D-18, opens it, and decants the water—there were 500 c.c.s of it—into a sterile bottle of his own, labels it, hides it away. Then he forces the rubber stopper into the empty bottle, where it will be found the next day, rattling around dry as a bone. The loss caused no great stir—it was, after all, a side expedition.

'He's got what he wants. Now, how to test it? He may have tried it on animals first, but I doubt it. How do you check subtle changes in the psyche of a dog or an ape? But just about this time the Nazis solved this particular problem with their own happy invention, the concentration camp. They liked Schutz, and they were, as we all remember, fascinated with genetics to the point of mania.

'They gave him a laboratory just outside Berlin, all the human guinea pigs he wanted, and a free hand. They had several broad objectives: they wanted to prove that Aryans, that is, *pure* Aryans, meaning Germans, were genetically different and superior. And that Jews were just the reverse. But they also wanted to learn about what we now call "genetic engineering". Breeding, yes, for super-Aryans, but more than that, actual gene manipulation.

'Schutz went to work on this. He had a staff, he had money, he had equipment. But he kept his little water bottle to himself. We don't know on whom he first tried it, or how. Did he administer it by mouth? By injection? However he did it, he got results. They must have been dramatic. At least they were convincing enough so that he kept working on it—*has* kept working on it ever since, and still is.

'Why didn't he tell his Nazi leaders about his discovery? I can guess at several reasons. Although he was top dog in his own laboratory, he wasn't very high up in the hierarchy—not even in the science end of it. If he came up with anything really hot, they'd have taken it over. Oh, they'd have let him work on it, probably given him a promotion—but it wouldn't be *his*.

'Also, he had problems: he didn't really know what he had. What was in that water? Was it a virus? A bacteria? A new chemical mutagen of some kind? Let's say he tried it on one or two human subjects. Let's say, since we don't know otherwise, that he gave them small doses, orally. And that the effects matched Diaz-Rodriguez's (or the old man's) description, at least well enough so he knew he was on to something. The victims changed; they lost their initiative, lost the will to perform independently.

But perhaps the dosage was too strong. Maybe they fell into a stupor, a kind of somnambulism, and had to be disposed of. Remember, he didn't want to call attention to them.

'So there was problem number one: could the dosage be regulated? Could he vary the effect from, say, a mild condition of irresponsibility, perhaps rather euphoric, to a total, helpless dependency, a trancelike state?

'Problem number two would quickly have become more urgent. A simple problem, but critical: he just didn't have enough of the water to experiment much further. The original bottle held half a litre, five hundred c.c.s—about a pint. Could he make more? Or get more? The answer to the second question was no. With war breaking out, the Germans weren't sending any more medical expeditions to Peru. Even if they wanted to, the Peruvians wouldn't let them in.

'The solution was to find out what was in the water, and see if he could produce more of it. I expect that was Schutz's big research project over the next several months—maybe years. And that part of the story we just have to skip. We don't know how he set about it, what equipment he used, how long it took. He must have kept notes, but we don't have them. My guess is they were destroyed, probably by Schutz himself.

'But I know how *I* would have gone about it, and so does the Colonel. I'd have used ultra-centrifuge, electron microscope, X-ray spectroscopy, bacterial cultures, electrophoresis. And we must assume that one way or another he solved the problem. He found out what was in the water, and how to make more of it.

'When we pick Schutz up again he's in Novokuznetsk, and he's made a lot of progress. He's in the late stages of a very precise study: how to control the effects of his Steinkopf treatment by varying the dosage. If you take his "Group 17" reports and leave out the germ warfare stuff—the "meat" of the reports . . .

'Well, to simplify the job I ended up doing it the other way around. I took scissors and cut out all the digressions. I pasted them up in a notebook of my own, following Schutz's own chronological order. When I had it halfway done the whole thing became brilliantly clear, and the rest was apple pie. He has eighteen case histories going—eighteen laboratory subjects, six men, six women, six children—over a period of eleven years. He must have had many more, but we don't have notes on them.

'On these people, he's doing most careful and elaborate testing. He's giving them their treatments by mouth in an aqueous solution he calls (a little private joke, I expect) Dioxymin. He tells the Russians that it's a nutrient solution, duly described in a footnote, designed to keep up their health in the unhealthy prison environment—but the liquid also contains a dosage of Steinkopf material. That dosage he indicates simply by a number, completely unobtrusive but always there in parenthesis. The numbers range from five to twenty, indicating some unit of quantity that Schutz has worked out—it could be a gram, a milligram, a microgram, or something smaller.

'It's interesting—and horrifying—to note that the children get no dosage at all. In their daily Dioxymin there is always a zero in the parenthesis. They don't need any treatment. All six are offspring of the twelve adults. They've inherited the Steinkopf Syndrome from their parents.'

Fergus got up from his chair by the fire, walked to the trestle table, and picked up a black-covered loose-leaf notebook. He handed it to Colonel Attenborough.

'Here are the eighteen case histories, put together as well as I can do it from the material at hand. I've added explanatory notes—some of them just guesswork of my own—to fill in the gaps. Take them with you and study them. You might want to show them to some of your experts at Detrick.

'On these eighteen he has worked out the final details of the most insidious weapon ever devised. But he needed two more things. A real water system of his own, where he could try it out with no one watching over his shoulder. So far, you see, he's mixed it in beakers and bottles and hand-fed it to individuals. Now he needs to prove he can feed it to a city—or a country.

'Having this, he needs a nineteenth victim to test it on. Preferably one he can take with him, wherever he's going.'

CHAPTER TWENTY-ONE

ALLIE THOUGHT something was wrong with the young animal keeper. For one thing, he was covered with sweat, so much it dripped from his chin. For another, he was breathing too hard. Yet he smiled at her, a strange smile that showed his lower teeth as well as his upper teeth.

With the copper-tipped prod in his right hand he walked towards her, his left hand stretched out at his side as if he expected her to run, and was ready to catch her. He had left the door of her cage open. She sat quietly in the corner and looked up at him.

Suddenly, quickly, he jabbed the prod against her wrist.

She did not cry out, since the Doctor had told her she could not; nor did she hurt, since the Doctor had told her she would not. But her arm felt funny. It tingled and jerked back. She did not move it; it moved itself. Then the tingling stopped, and she sat still as before. In the quick motion her sleeve had brushed the cage wall and lost its remaining button, and her shirt cuff hung loosely from her forearm.

The young keeper stared, the sweat dripping down his face faster than before. In his own cage, in the farthest corner, Victor whimpered. The prod came at her again, this time harder than before, so that its metal end left a red mark on her arm. Once more the tingling came, and her hand flew back of its own accord. She sat quietly.

The young keeper's smile disappeared. He said something in the language she could not understand; still it sounded ugly, and though he spoke in a low voice it was angry, like an animal growling. In his cage Victor stopped whimpering and also made a noise like a growl. She had never heard Victor make that sound before.

Unexpectedly, the keeper's left hand lashed out and caught one leg of her slacks near the ankle. He pulled hard and the cloth ripped, exposing the bare skin of her calf and shin. He gripped her ankle tightly and then rammed the end of the prod hard into the calf. As her arm had done, the leg jerked, its muscles cramped and straining against his grip. It had nothing to do with her. The leg pulled itself back, then kicked, then pulled again, taking him off balance. He fell forward, crashing his face against the cage wall, dropping the prod with a noisy clatter. He remained motionless for a minute, lying partly on top of Allie. Then he sat up and shook his head. She saw that he had turned shiny red; he looked at her and raised his hand. He *was* angry; he was going to hit her in the face.

Suddenly he turned and looked at the door of the laboratory. He had heard something, or thought he had. Very quickly he picked up the prod, left the cage, put the prod in its customary place against the wall in the corner. His hands were shaking so that he had trouble locking her cage door. He disappeared into the inner room of the laboratory.

When he came out a few moments later he had stopped shaking, and went out by the door that led up the stairs. Victor left his corner and came to the cage wall on her side, staring at her sadly.

Allie fell asleep almost immediately, without getting up, and in her sleep she moaned and wept.

After his telephone call had been completed Kublitz summoned Dr Schutz for a conference. Actually it had turned into a series of telephone calls; he had been shunted from one sceptical official to another, each one guarded by a cautious (male) secretary, each one available only after a protracted wait. So, frustratingly, was the afternoon passed. Still something had been achieved, and Schutz must be notified.

When the Doctor arrived Kublitz gestured him to the chair and began abruptly.

'The possibility exists that there has been a security failure. It is only a possibility. I do not myself believe it. But precautions will be taken even so. Also I think it is now essential that we conclude the research quickly.'

'I am already at work on the final report,' said Dr Schutz. 'As I have informed you, I will need the earlier reports for reference in preparing it.'

'They are in the safe,' Kublitz said. 'I remind you again of their classification. They must be kept locked in the laboratory until they can be returned to me.'

'Naturally,' Dr Schutz said rather wearily. 'As has been done each time in the past. You will have them back in three days— four at the most. The work will then be finished.'

'All has gone satisfactorily until the present,' Kublitz said. He emphasized his next words: 'But the battle is not won until it is ended. There must be no slip.'

'You refer to the tree? But it has been removed.'

'Not the tree.' He recounted briefly what Nikolai had reported.

'Nikolai is an old lady peering through the window curtains,' said Dr. Schutz. 'Every man who passes is a robber.'

'Possibly.' Kublitz, privately, was inclined to agree. 'Yet the wall is not so easily scaled, and the dock does conceal instruments we do not wish examined.'

'Did the intruders also carry microscopes and Petri dishes? They could scarcely learn much otherwise.'

Kublitz ignored the sarcasm.

'This afternoon Nikolai is, on my instructions, installing a simple electrical-alarm system inside the fence that surrounds the laboratory. It is merely a fine-wire antenna connected to a small transmitter, battery-powered, that we will place in the laboratory. Should an intruder trip the wire it will sound an alarm, a very quiet one, in this receiver.' Kublitz took from his desk drawer a cylinder resembling a thick fountain pen. 'For the next thirty hours I will keep the receiver with me.' He paused, and replaced the box in the desk.

'After that,' he added, 'we will have two additional security guards assigned to the zoo area. Because they must fly from Moscow, they cannot arrive sooner.

'Since it is only for a few days, the Ambassador has agreed to the increased staff. After that, we have assured him, we will dismantle our equipment and move out. Meanwhile, he has insisted that their presence here be as unobtrusive as possible. They will come directly from the airport in the back of a panelled truck. They will set up quarters in the zoo-equipment building. For lavatory facilities they will use the bathroom in your laboratory. They will, of course, be given keys to the laboratory.'

Kublitz noticed that Dr Schutz was sitting very still, his face rigidly composed, as if he were holding his breath.

'I trust these arrangements will not interfere with the completion of your work. There will, of course, be a concealed switch at the gate so that you and Georg Wolter may turn off the transmitter when you enter the laboratory. I will come myself later today to inspect Nikolai's installation. I will at that time bring with me the file containing your reports. Until the alarm is installed, I would prefer that they remain here.'

As Georg Wolter left the laboratory and locked the door behind him the red haze that had clouded his mind and eyes was dispersing, and he was able to think. It was raining, and the water cooled his face. There was, after all, no one near the door. The noise had been imaginary, or perhaps the gusty wind; he could have continued.

Yet the girl's response had not been satisfactory. He knew that the electric shock emitted by the cattle prod was extremely painful, but her reaction had been merely reflexive. It was obvious that she was not feeling anything at all; she had made no outcry—not even a whimper—and there were none of the facial contortions that it was his particular pleasure to watch. What had they called it at the hospital in Frankfort? 'Visual masochistic transference.' Psychiatrists were clever at using long words to describe simple joys, but not clever enough to keep him locked up after he had been caught.

Why? What kind of hypnosis had Schutz used? It was unfortunate that he knew no English and could not talk to the girl;

thus there was no question of counterhypnosis. Schutz had said he had given her the di-phenylitol injection series, but he, Georg, himself a biologist, did not believe it; they were simply not that effective. No, Schutz had found something better. In fact, he had had the feeling for some time that Schutz was up to something— something that had nothing to do with their work on *anthracis*.

As Georg walked back towards the Villa he thought about the girl. When he had first entered her cage she had been asleep, and he recalled now that she had been making a noise, a painful distressed sound halfway between a sigh and a moan. Also, when she awoke as he opened the cage—in that first instant there had been fear in her eyes, he was sure of it. Then, as she came fully awake, it vanished, and from then on her calm expression never wavered.

He had an idea. Suppose the hypnosis, whatever it was, was effective only while she was awake? He had read of such cases: psychiatric patients who could be kept calm while awake, but whose terror and agony returned so violently during sleep that they had to be kept bound. It should be easy to test. The girl slept much of the time. He had only to approach quietly and apply the prod before she woke up. If it produced the desired effect—well, there were injections in the laboratory he could use to keep her asleep. Or perhaps half-asleep would be sufficient. It was, in fact, a brilliant idea. His disappointment diminished. A sense of anticipation returned.

As he approached the Villa he met Schutz walking fast in the opposite direction.

The Doctor was greatly agitated.

'A dangerous situation has come up,' he said. 'We must return to the laboratory immediately.'

Georg was alarmed. Could Schutz know something? Did he suspect?

'But I have just left the laboratory.' He kept his voice even. 'Everything is in order.'

'The idiot, Nikolai, has caused trouble. He has reported intruders spying on the laboratory. I have just seen Kublitz.'

'Intruders? When? How could it be?'

'Twice, at dawn.'

'But the laboratory is locked. And it is underground. What could they see?'

'Also, a fisherman has approached the dock. What does that mean? Nothing. It is idiocy. I told Kublitz, but it is no use. He and Nikolai are coming to install an alarm system.'

'So?' Georg was relieved. It was, after all, not what he had feared. He shrugged. 'Let them. It can do no harm.'

'They are coming *into* the laboratory. The girl is there. We must get her out.'

He had not thought of that. Of course the girl's presence was unknown to Kublitz and Nikolai, and must remain unknown.

'What will we do? Surely you will not dispose of her? We have yet had no time to make tests on her.'

'I think it will not be necessary. I will hide her temporarily. Then we will see.'

'Hide her where? There is no place.'

'I will take her to a place in the woods. When Nikolai and Kublitz have left, I will bring her back. With luck it will be only a brief inconvenience.'

They walked briskly through the rain back towards the laboratory. 'Fortunately the weather is bad,' observed the Doctor. 'There will be no visitors at the zoo.'

In the laboratory all was quiet. The large chimpanzee was in his cage, the girl in hers, and there was no sign of Nikolai. Dr Schutz's near-panic subsided. When Kublitz had told him of the new precautions, the transmitter, the wire, the security guards, he had felt the pulse begin to hammer in his head; he had felt dizzy, for a moment, as if he might fall from the chair. He had seen his plan collapsing before him, a bridge of glass shattered by a hammer blow. The first alarm, and the worst, had been over the reports. He had thought Kublitz was refusing to release them. He *must* have the reports; they contained all of his data, so toilsomely accumulated, so carefully concealed. But at the end Kublitz had agreed to bring them to the laboratory.

The second consternation had been over the girl. He walked now to her cage and opened it. She sat up, awakening slowly. She looked pale. One of her trouser legs had somehow got torn; one of her shirt sleeves hung loose, its cuff unbuttoned. No matter at the moment. He would get pins to fix them later. He remembered the rain, and, entering the inner laboratory, brought out the blue coat. Georg was, on his instructions, counting culture densities under the microscope and noting them in a ledger. The objective was to appear busy and normal.

'If the others come tell them I will return in a few minutes,' he told Georg. 'You need not be specific.'

The girl put the coat on and buttoned it. Taking her by the hand, he led her quickly through the door and away from the

laboratory, into the woods towards the big iron gate, in the opposite direction from the Villa. He looked for a suitable spot. A
hundred yards into the woods, a hundred feet back from the
wall, he found it: a large oak grew close to an even larger beech
tree, their branches intertwining in an arch overhead, their
heavy boles only a few feet apart. Near them a young pine spread
its limbs close to the ground. The centre of the triangle thus
formed was well hidden and the overhead branches would even
provide some shelter from the slow rain.

He seated the girl so that she could rest against the smooth
bark of the beech tree. He talked to her briefly in a low voice.
Then he walked back to the laboratory. The girl would remain,
seated, motionless and silent, until he returned. She would enjoy
sitting in the nice fresh air in the pretty woods.

As he walked he reviewed his personal timetable. At first he
had thought: *disaster*. Kublitz had wrecked it completely. Now
he saw that it made no real difference. He had planned to leave
before dawn on Friday, three days from today. But in thirty
hours, Kublitz said, two security guards would arrive. Taking
turns with Nikolai they would keep the laboratory under twenty-
four-hour surveillance until the work was complete, the final
report turned in. They would be armed. Obviously one could not
leave at dawn, accompanied by a non-existent girl, carrying a
bulky top-secret portfolio, under the eyes of an armed KGB guard.

But as soon as the dizzying effect of this pronouncement had
worn off, the solution had become clear. It required only a slight
change, a small bit of haste: he would leave, instead, at dawn
tomorrow. Perhaps it was even for the better. The girl looked—
not really ill, but pale. It would be well to get her away, out of
the cage, into more civilized quarters, provided with a better
diet. Already she had lost seven pounds: not dangerous, but not
good. Also, leaving Wednesday instead of Friday would avoid
possible complications of a weekend, when people could be
difficult to locate and air traffic crowded.

At dawn tomorrow, then. *No.* The memory came with the
shock of a blow. It had been at dawn—Kublitz had said clearly
—*twice* at dawn, that Nikolai claimed a prowler had been seen
near the zoo. From where would Nikolai watch? Probably from
his room in the Villa, which was high in the attic; very likely he
had a glass, a telescope or binocular. No matter. Having achieved
his small sensation, one would wager Nikolai would be watching.

Not at dawn, then. At midnight, in the dark. It would mean a
few hours of waiting outside after they left the laboratory, but

the rain seemed to be subsiding, and in any case they would survive. The road leading to the highway seemed to be well wooded on both sides. They would walk out the gate, up the hill, up the road until they were near the bus rendezvous, find a secluded spot, and wait for daylight. He wondered how early the buses began. Surely by seven. . . .

As he approached the wire fence surrounding the laboratory he saw Nikolai at work, rounding the far side of the building, stringing the antenna wire, which was so fine as to be invisible from where he stood. He waited a moment until the walls were between them, then let himself through the gate that led to the laboratory door. It was well that no one noticed the direction from which he approached. He observed that Nikolai was doing his job with speed and efficiency, concealing the strand at knee height, here between bushes, there among small trees. At night it would be quite undetectable.

Dr Schutz unlocked the laboratory door and let himself in. Just inside, on the floor, he saw that Nikolai had already placed the transmitter, an oblong object the size of a shoe box. A small wire led from it up the side of the door jamb and out the top. From there it would run first to the fence somewhere near the entrance. He must be sure Kublitz showed him the off-on switch; there must be no alarm when he entered at midnight.

He glanced at the girl's empty cage and at the chimpanzee crouched in the cage next to it. Then he entered the inner laboratory. Georg Wolter was still at work with the microscope, copying figures in orderly tables.

Dr Schutz said quietly, 'The girl is hidden. When Kublitz and Nikolai have left I will bring her back. Tomorrow we will begin tests with the *anthracis*—oral intake first, as planned, through the water system.'

Georg said, 'The cultures are ready.'

'The pump?'

'In order.'

Dr Schutz went to a desk on the other side of the room and, opening a filing cabinet beside it, methodically began removing the sheets of notes he would need for his final report—the report which would never be seen by either Kublitz or his leader, General Vasilovsky.

Thus, when Kublitz arrived half an hour later, he found a scene of routine activity. With relief, Dr Schutz saw him deposit on the desk the bulky loose-leaf binder containing the earlier reports—all of the Group 17 reports, all of his own private data.

'Remember their classification,' Kublitz said again. As on the few previous occasions when he had visited the inner laboratory, he held a handkerchief to his nose, and looked with nervous distaste at the glass cabinets along the walls where the cultures were kept.

'I am not likely to forget it,' said Dr. Schutz. 'You will recall that I wrote them myself.' Still, rather ostentatiously, he picked up the file, placed it in a drawer in the steel cabinet, and locked the drawer.

At that moment Nikolai entered. He spoke to Kublitz in Russian. There followed a brief dialogue which Dr Schutz could not understand. Kublitz explained in English.

'The antenna is completed and the transmitter turned on. It will emit a signal only if someone disturbs the wire. If you and Wolter will follow, Nikolai will show you the disconnect switch so that you may enter and leave the laboratory without sounding the alarm.'

Ten minutes later Kublitz and Nikolai, having sprayed themselves generously with disinfectant, walked off through the drizzle in the direction of the Villa. Georg and Dr Schutz returned to their work in the laboratory.

When they were inside, Dr Schutz said to Georg: 'As you see, it has all worked out quite simply. I will now get the girl and return her to the cage.'

As he went through the gate in the wire fence he was careful to turn the transmitter switch to 'Off.' It was turning dusk as he walked into the woods.

CHAPTER TWENTY-TWO

IMAGINE A WEAPON,' Fergus continued, 'so gentle, so painless, so quiet, that no enemy would ever suspect it was being used against him. A weapon which kills no one, makes no one sick, and produces no detectable physical symptoms, no discernible mental disorders in its victims.' He stared at the fire and puffed his pipe, sitting with legs outstretched, speaking softly as if to himself.

'Well,' Mr Bayles said, 'it doesn't sound very dangerous.'

'On the contrary, it would be the most dangerous form of attack ever conceived. There would be no defence against it, because no one would know there was anything to defend against.

'I read a science-fiction story once,' Fergus continued addressing the fire. 'An extra-terrestrial enemy was attacking the earth, the human race. Attacking? They didn't use any weapons at all, not in the proper sense. Instead, they put up harmless little buildings near all the population centres. When they pushed the button, all the buildings gave off a humming noise, not unpleasant but pervasive, all the same pitch, and everybody in the world could hear it. The idea was to get everybody's nervous system vibrating on the same wavelength and then transmit orders, thoughts, ideas on that frequency. Ingenious. No bloodshed, no pain, no tears.'

Colonel Attenborough said, 'And no resistance. As you said, not really a weapon at all.'

'Strictly,' Fergus said, 'maybe you can't call what Schutz has a weapon, either.'

'Then what *do* you call it?' Mr Bayles sounded mildly irritated. 'What exactly *does* he have? If it doesn't hurt anyone, what harm does it do? What are the symptoms?'

'Take the last point first.' Fergus walked the length of the room and came back carrying the English translation of Diaz-Rodriguez's journal. 'Do you remember this part? It's the old man, as he died, describing what had happened to the people in the Steinkopf valley:

' "They were not ill," the old man insisted. "No one was stricken with fever, or pain, or cough, or sores on the skin. At first it was noticed only that they talked less and laughed less; they had been used to singing in the evenings, sometimes dancing, but now they neither sang nor danced at all. They slept long, and sat, and looked at nothing. When their roofs leaked and needed thatch, they did not mend them. When the weeds choked their gardens, they did not pull them up.

' "All of this did not happen at once, but over the years, perhaps even two generations. Then the men of my house, my great-grand-father and his brothers and sons, feared that these people, who were most of those in our valley, would suffer and starve. So they ordered them: mend your roofs, and they did as they were told; cultivate your gardens, and they did so. But they did only as they were told, and little else; and each successive generation grew worse." '

'So,' said Colonel Attenborough, 'the symptoms——'

Fergus closed the book and looked at the fire again. 'What we have is a total lack of physiological symptoms. The disease—the syndrome, as Dr Schutz calls it—manifests itself socially. In a primitive mountain village, unthatched roofs and untended gardens were the first noticeable signs. But what would you look for in a modern, complex, mechanized society?

'Let's suppose, as all his reports indicate, that the Doctor has the dosage worked out very precisely. And let's say that whoever uses the weapon has the intelligence to grasp its greatest value, its total lack of detectability. Thus we assume it is applied in its mildest, subtlest form.

'What would we, as victims, notice? Or, more likely, not notice? Perhaps, at first, minor malfunction in the most complex workings of our society. Our two biggest single machines are the telephone system and our electric-power network; both are highly automated, yet both demand constant human attendance. Maybe one day, one month, one year, they begin not to work as well as they used to.

'Our biggest factories mass-produce automobiles. Maybe the intricate machinery of mass production begins to go wrong—the automobiles emerge defective; bolts left loose, wiring wrong, parts installed incorrectly. Somehow the factory workers and inspectors can't seem to keep up with their jobs any more. Or they just don't care.

'Whatever the disease hits, I think the deterioration would show up most acutely and quickly in the most intricately complex areas—the big cities.

'Those are possibilities; in any case they'd be the start of a slow, creeping degeneration. I think we'd see a general slackness—in dress, perhaps, in promptness, in neatness. Relief rolls would rise; so would absenteeism. There'd be a decline in productivity per man-hour, which would be duly noted by the Bureau of Labour Statistics. But—and here's the frightening part of it—probably not noted otherwise, not internally, not by the people to whom it's happening.

'Oh, there'd be some outcries at first, probably, but they wouldn't amount to much. Because, of course, the people who should be making the outcries would be suffering from the same malaise themselves. No. Not suffering. But afflicted nonetheless. They wouldn't really *see* what was going on, because they'd be part of it.

'But the decline would be highly visible—and fascinating to watch—from across the sea: from whatever alien group is applying the treatment. The leader-nation. *Its* telephone system would remain efficient. Its machines would run smoothly. How greatly in demand its exported cars would become—and, in the end, its exported engineers, plant managers, technical advisers—leaders.

There would be no struggle in this conquest, just as there was no struggle in the Steinkopf valley.

'It would all be very quiet, very gentle and gradual. Maybe that's the most beautiful thing about it, from his point of view. A bit in the water supply here and there—he doesn't have to infect everybody. One or two per cent will do. It will spread from there.'

Fergus paused in his quiet soliloquy and Mr Bayles stirred. 'Eloquent. Reasonable. Horrifying. But all, as yet, hypothesis. You still haven't told us what Dr Schutz's weapon *is*. To be credible, to be real, to be applied, it's got to have a physical form.'

Fergus laughed, but did not sound amused. 'I have not, and for the soundest of reasons. I don't know. All I have is a wild guess, and I'm not sure I believe it myself.'

Colonel Attenborough looked incredulous. 'But surely in all his written research Schutz must indicate what it is he's working with? A virus? A bacterium? A protozoan?'

Fergus added, 'Or a protein molecule, or an amino acid, or an enzyme. There's quite a list of possibilities. Some we can eliminate, of course—for example, a protozoan is unlikely. It's just too big an animal, too detectable, too vulnerable. Remember, it's got to get through a water-purification system, and it can't show up in a normal analysis.

'But the fact is, all the research Schutz did in those first months, or years, when he was studying the water to find out what he had, what was in it—we haven't a shred of material on that. By the time the Russians got him that work was done, complete. In his Group 17 reports, when he refers to the substance at all (which he does as seldom as possible) he uses only the symbol "s-k", an abbreviation, I assume, of Steinkopf.

'So we don't know what he discovered. Or even, in fact, if he himself ever learned what it was. It's perfectly possible to work with something, to learn what it will *do*, without ever knowing what it *is*. Magnetism, for example, or gravity——'

Colonel Attenborough said, 'Or a filterable virus.'

'Filterable, undoubtedly. But not necessarily a virus. In fact, I'm betting that it's not.'

'The name of the game,' Fergus added, 'is cytogenetics. The pieces you play it with are mutagens. Definitions: the science of manipulating cell growth right at the core—the nucleus, the chromosomes, the genes, the DNA, and the so-called messenger RNA. A mutagen can be animal, vegetable, mineral, a particle of energy, a photon of light.

'But there's one big difference in classification of mutagens.

Some are classed as "somatic". They affect cell structure and growth of an organism for one generation only, and then die out. Cancer is one of these—one of many; mostly they're believed to be caused by viruses or subviruses, and they're not inheritable. But other mutagens affect the germ cells, and if they're not fatal at an early age, they're passed on from one generation to the next.

'Dr Schutz has a mutagen that does both. That is, it's somatic—it affects the organism immediately, but it's also inheritable. The immediate effect seems to be on the brain cells, and through them on the psyche, the personality. Hence the lassitude, the decline of initiative, both in the Steinkopf valley people and in his laboratory subjects.

'This effect is the one he can regulate. But the genetic effect, the children, the second generation, he can't. All his notes indicate that the syndrome shows up more strongly in the offspring than in the parents. As the old man said to Diaz-Rodriguez, "and each successive generation grew worse".

'Judging by all this, and by other hints in his notes, I think Dr Schutz didn't find a virus or a bacterium in that bottle from the Steinkopf valley.'

'What kind of hints?'

'One kind in particular. A lot of his measurements seem to deal with specific gravity. He's concerned with weight and density. You don't ordinarily measure viruses that way, nor the bacteria count in water.

'What do you measure that way? Something where specific gravity makes a crucial difference. A substance where the chemical structure is familiar, but the density is different. Where the elements are all there in the right proportions, but the behaviour has changed.' Fergus looked at Colonel Attenborough. 'You work with biochemists—doesn't that sound familiar?'

'A polymer,' said the Colonel.

'Dr Schutz's bottle contained no new germs. But it did contain a new kind of water.'

'Polywater!' exclaimed the Colonel. 'Of course! Water 2.'

'Or maybe Water 3. Or better still, call it Water X.

'Somewhere in his early testing, Dr Schutz made a startling discovery. Although the Steinkopf water seemed quite pure, it weighed about twice as much as it ought to.'

Fergus tapped the dottle out of his pipe on a log in the fireplace. 'Every chemistry student knows what water is. The molecule is one oxygen atom, two hydrogen atoms—H_2O. That is, they knew it until 1962, when a group of Russians at the U.S.S.R.

Academy of Sciences discovered it wasn't necessarily so. Until then, water was a constant. It was the basis for the metric system of weights and measures: one cubic centimetre of water weighed exactly one gram—that's what a gram *meant*.

'I believe the story is that a Russian physicist, working in one of their research centres in northern Siberia, looked out the window at some winter wheat waving in the wind. It occurred to him that it shouldn't be waving, it should be snapping off—the temperature was twenty below zero, hadn't been above zero for months, and the green wheat stalks, like all grasses, contained more than fifty per cent water. Why didn't it freeze? Why weren't the stalks brittle?

'He gathered some of the wheat, extracted the water, and discovered the reason: it wasn't ordinary water at all. It had changed. Its density was fifty per cent greater than normal water, and its molecules had polymerized—that is, they were multiple molecules. Instead of one oxygen and two hydrogen atoms, they had formed long chains—written not H_2O, but H_8O_4, or $H_{32}O_{16}$, or even higher. Hence the name polywater. It doesn't freeze until it gets down to $-40°$, doesn't boil until $1,000°F$.

'The upshot, after quite a lot of lab work in Moscow, was a scientific paper announcing the discovery of Water 2. American physicists disputed it, and the argument is still going on. One result is that water, as a substance, is getting more study than ever before, and all kinds of new things are cropping up. For instance, some biologists think it also changes its structure when it's enclosed in certain animal cells—red blood cells, for instance.

'What nobody realized—until here and now—is that Helmuth Schutz started this same research in 1937. He's thirty-five years ahead of everybody else.'

'Interesting conicidence,' Colonel Attenborough said. 'The Russian saw the grass waving in the Siberian breeze—and didn't Diaz-Rodriguez mention the lichen waving in the wind up in the Altiplano?'

'Where it also stays frozen six or seven months a year. That occurred to me, too. What I've been thinking is that an earthquake, back in the time of the old man's great-great-grandfather, diverted a mountain stream into an ancient bed of those lichens. They were dead and compacted like peat, but they were still loaded with molecules of the altered water. The stream emerged from the mountainside as a waterfall——'

'—and a village in a valley went to sleep,' Mr Bayles concluded. 'All right. I'm with you so far. But there's still a puzzle. Schutz has his bottle of "Water X". He's got his own laboratory. Over the next five or six years he finds out what it will do.

'But then the Russians come in. They blow up his lab. They capture him. Then what? Can you imagine the Russian army intelligence, and then the secret police, searching him, interrogating him, moving him from a prisoner-of-war camp to a Siberian research centre—all the while letting him carry his little bottle of polywater? How did he keep it, and how did he keep it secret?'

'There's only one way he could have done it,' Fergus said. 'His notes show that in small enough quantities—below the concentration he indicates as "5"—Water X has no discernible effect on the subject's behaviour. When the Russians were closing in, he took the gamble. He had to. Not such a desperate gamble, perhaps, because he already had the ratios pretty well worked out. He injected a few micrograms of Water X, in a weak solution, into his own arm. He became, in effect, what doctors call a "carrier". When he needed it, all he had to do was to draw a sample of his own blood, and in it would be enough Water X, or s-k as he calls it, to serve as the nucleus of a new supply. A few molecules would do.

'How does he make more? Simple enough. Since what he's got is a molecule, not a crystal, not a living organism, it doesn't reproduce itself except in a roundabout way. Nonetheless easily done. When Water X is metabolized into a living cell—when it locks into the molecular structure of the chromosomes—and the cell divides, the characteristics of the water are present in both the new cells. In other words, he feeds it to a culture. As the culture grows, so does his supply of polywater.

'He doesn't specify just what the culture is. He may have found half a dozen or more that will work. But that's why he always needs—and lists—so many Petri dishes, many more than he'd normally need in his b-w research. But who counts Petri dishes? They're a dime a dozen.'

'So,' said the Colonel, 'he not only has the weapon, he *is* the weapon. The only available source.'

'Almost,' Fergus said, 'but not quite. I've never hoped so hard that I'm wrong, but I think there's now another source.'

'The girl,' said Mr Bayles.

'We can't just knock on the door and tell them, "We know you've got her in there—let her out." Because, for one, we don't know they've got her in there. We only think they have.'

'Worse than that,' said the Colonel, 'if Fergus is right, *they* don't know they've got her in there.'

'We can make a formal protestation,' Mr Bayles said. 'It will have to go through the State Department. But if we do, they'll make a formal denial. And their indignation will be genuine.'

Fergus asked, 'Can't we tell them that we know Schutz is working there? I mean maybe not official proof, but good enough to convince them we do know.'

'Probably,' said Mr Bayles, 'but it's the last thing we want to do. You know what the result would be? At worst, nothing at all, only more denial. At best, they'd spirit Dr Schutz out of there, out of the country and back to Siberia, in a matter of hours. And if they found there was a girl there, they'd spirit her right along with him. Or get rid of her in some less pleasant way. This is the KGB. They're not nice guys. In either case, we'd gain nothing. And I hate to think of what we'd lose.'

'We'd blow the cover off every agent we have between here and Novokuznetsk. Our biological-warfare intelligence network would be wiped out. Twenty-five years of work.'

'I'd do it in a minute,' Fergus said cheerfully, 'if it would get the girl out. Your agents know the risk they take. But the girl didn't. She was kidnapped. And she's only twelve years old.'

Mr Bayles sighed. 'You're right. I would, too. But the point is, it wouldn't get her out. It would almost certainly get her killed.'

'The real point is,' said the Colonel, 'what *do* we do?'

Fergus stood up and looked at his watch. It was three minutes past five. 'Officially there's nothing we can do. But as of now, I resign my job as a paid consultant. I have, therefore, no further connection with the U.S. government. As a private citizen, I'm going to do some trespassing on Russian soil. I'm going to try to get Allison Adam out.'

Colonel Attenborough said, 'Alone?'

'No. I have a friend. If you listen, I think you'll hear his car coming up the drive. When he gets here, I will ask you to excuse us. You have no official knowledge of our plans.'

CHAPTER TWENTY-THREE

'WHAT'S YOUR FIRST NAME?' Fergus had liked Officer Simon on sight. He had expected to see a camouflage suit; it had been replaced by khaki drill slacks, tan hunting jacket, and brown canvas shoes. Yet the dark-tanned face and startlingly light grey eyes were unmistakable now as in the early morning mist.

'Sebastian.'

'Fergus.' They shook hands.

'I know.' He smiled. 'I checked you out, remember? Fergus O'Neil, Ph.D., research biochemist with the Institute for Advanced Biological Studies, Cambridge.'

'You have a good memory.'

'I rechecked the file. I also have information, pretty vague, that you're on assignment to either the State Department or the Army. A consulting job. Something to do with biology. I'm not asking questions about it.'

'The plan,' said Fergus, 'is to climb the wall, find out if the girl is in there, and if she is, how to get her out. We can talk on the way. If we start now, we'll still have some daylight.'

'And then some dark,' said Officer Simon, 'which may be more to the point. She's in there, all right. Or was.'

'We'll need rope.'

'I brought some.'

'The same one you used this morning?'

'You know about that?'

'I was looking around, outside the wall. You wore a camouflage suit.'

'Yeah. I decided that was a bad idea. It's government issue—Marine Corps. On this trip I'm a private citizen. I also don't have my badge.'

They set out from Fergus's cabin at a brisk walk. The rain continued, lightly but steadily.

Fergus said, 'What makes you so sure she's in there?'

'What makes *you* so sure?'

'Quite a few things. Mainly, her little brother Willis told me. It was supposed to be a secret between them. I talked it out of him.'

Officer Simon said, 'At first, I just had a hunch. I guess the other brother, John, started it. But the more I thought about it, the more I didn't believe that bicycle bit. He was right: it did seem impossible for her to ride through all that mud, just by mistake.'

'I met John,' said Fergus, 'and heard his argument. It's pretty convincing.'

'Then I scouted along the wall,' Simon continued, 'and there was a pretty big aspen tree growing near it. Generally, they keep the wall clear of trees, but they missed that one. Aspens grow fast. I figured she could have climbed the tree—that's why she sent her little brother home first—and dropped down the other side. I was still just guessing. But then, the next day, I saw the tree had been cut down. That was one too many. I climbed over the wall for a look.

'I grew up in this neighbourhood. When I was a kid we used to fish the river down there. Two or three of us climbed the wall now and then, just to see what was in there, the way kids do. So I knew my way around pretty well. But they've added some stuff, a zoo, for one thing. And behind the zoo, with a fence around it, a new building and some pretty funny-looking apparatus. If I ever saw a place that looked like "secret—keep out", that's it.

'They're up to something in there, I don't know what. But what I thought was this: the girl, Allison, climbed over the wall right near that building—because that's where the tree was. She walked over to it, saw something she shouldn't have seen, and they grabbed her.

'Then I looked around a little more, and I learned a little more. Maybe they didn't just grab her. Maybe they spotted her and chased her. Down the wall a couple of hundred yards there's a gate.'

'I know the gate.'

'She must have run for that, hoped she could get out that way. And that's where they caught her. There's a driveway, not much used, that leads to it. About ten feet off that, I found signs—not what you'd call a big fight, more of a scuffle, broken brush. Somebody thrashed around a bit there. And on the ground in the brush I found these.'

He stopped, reached into one cavernous pocket in his hunting jacket, and pulled out a small box, held shut with a rubber band. He opened it and shook the contents into his palm: two small, bright blue buttons, pathetically feminine, obviously from a shirt, a dress, a sweater.

'You didn't show those to Mrs Adam—the mother.'

'No. I thought about it. To tell you the truth, I was afraid she'd break up, and I didn't want to see that. There's something about her that gets you——'

'I know,' Fergus said.

'But I asked her, and found out the girl was wearing a blue shirt, and it had buttons on the cuff. It adds up.'

'It does.'

He put the buttons back into the box and the box into his pocket. They walked on, approaching the wall through the brush beside the road, near where Fergus had found the chipmunks.

'At first,' Officer Simon said, 'I thought: maybe they knocked her out and threw her in the river—then moved the bicycle to make it look like an accident. But I couldn't really believe it. During the war I was in Marine Intelligence—I still am, in the Reserves—and I worked with the Russians quite a lot, up in the Aleutians, joint operations against the Nips. I got to know them pretty well. They like kids. I don't think they'd do that. The bicycle—yes, to fool us. But I think they didn't know *what* to do with the girl. That's why I'm betting they've still got her in there, waiting for instructions from Moscow. That's what they do.'

Fergus was thinking: Officer Simon had, with nothing at all to go on, come astonishingly close to the truth. The truth? In actual fact, those two small blue buttons he had found were the only real evidence that it was the truth. He also thought: This was not the time for details about Dr Schutz and his work; yet Officer Simon ought to know a bit more—eventually probably the whole story. So he said: 'I know a little about that building. It's a laboratory.'

'You know, I thought you might.'

'Why?'

'Well, you're a scientist. You suddenly show up in Wilcox's cabin—he's a wheel, or used to be. You're working for State, or Army Intelligence, or both. It figures. Again—I'm not asking questions.'

'You'll get the answers anyway, but they're long ones.' The wall loomed before them, and Fergus, thinking again of the buttons, felt an excitement and sureness he had not felt before. 'Right now, let's leave it at this: the building's a laboratory, and I have good reason to think the girl is in it. Let's go and look.'

Officer Simon pulled a coil of rope from the game pocket of his hunting coat and knotted a loop in the end.

'What's short for Sebastian?'

'There isn't any. My friends call me Sim.' He firmed up the knot with browned hands. 'In school, when I was a kid, they used to call me Simple Simon. I developed a pretty good left hook, and they shortened it.'

'Just as well,' said Fergus. 'The name didn't fit.'

'Thanks.' The rope flew deftly up, and the loop settled over one of the iron spikes.

'After you, Sim,' said Fergus. 'Here's luck.'

They did not drop from the wall, but lowered themselves silently on the rope, leaving it in place, ready for exit. Inside, under the big trees, the light was dim, and Fergus calculated that up behind the grey rain clouds the sun was not far from setting. Sebastian

Simon gestured, and they moved towards a grove of still larger trees; then they turned left, heading away from the gate towards the laboratory Fergus had never seen.

Almost immediately Simon stopped, caught Fergus's arm, motioned him down. Barely fifteen yards ahead of them was a man, walking quickly through the woods. He wore a nondescript dark suit; he had thin grey hair and heavy, thick-lensed spectacles. As they crouched, scarcely breathing, he walked another ten strides, then turned and stared back—at first, it seemed, directly at them. No. Beyond them, a little to their right. It seemed impossible that he would not see them, but he was intent on the grove just behind them. Had he heard them? Possibly. He peered past them for another moment, turned around, and walked on. He did not pause again.

When he was fifty yards away, disappearing among the trees, Simon whispered: 'He's heading towards the laboratory. Let's watch him.'

They followed, Simon in the lead, Fergus grateful now for the rain which made the dead leaves soggy and noiseless underfoot. They lost sight of him, caught him again, lost him again. Then the woods thinned abruptly and ended, and the man came into full view, striding towards a squat, square white building with a chest-high chain fence around it. They stopped, staying in the shadows and out of sight.

'There's your laboratory.' Simon spoke softly. Off to the right, farther away, stood a long, low, barn-like structure, a C-shaped series of sheds, a small pavilion, a few benches. 'The zoo,' said Simon.

He stared ahead again. 'Hold on—look at that.'

The bespectacled man, having reached the fence, started along it towards the gate that led through it. Abruptly he stopped and stepped back. Beyond him, on the far side of the laboratory building, there was another man working at something they could not quite see. But it was as clear as hide-and-seek: man Number One did not want to be seen by man Number Two; he was keeping the building between them. Something else was clear to Fergus: the second man was his monosyllabic friend from the dock.

They watched Number Two, who was moving forwards, backwards, crouching, standing, purposefully, handling something they could not see. Simon reached into another pocket and came out with a small grey-green monocular. 'Marine Corps property,' he said, then focused it on the man working—who would, in another minute, be out of range behind the building. In half that time Simon handed the glass to Fergus. 'What did you say about luck? You're looking at it.'

Through the glass, which was sharp and astonishingly strong, Fergus saw that the man was holding a strand of shiny copper wire that looked as fine as thread, uncoiling it from a spool in his left hand.

Fergus handed the glass back. 'I'm not sure what kind of luck.'

'Bad and good, mostly good. They've turned scary—that's an antenna for an alarm system. That's bad, but the good is that we got here just in time. Now we know it's there. Let's watch where he puts the rest of that wire.'

Sitting on their heels in the drizzle at the edge of the shadow of the woods, they watched during the next half-hour a series of small manœuvres, not all comprehensible. When the wire-man disappeared behind the laboratory, the man with the spectacles rather furtively let himself into the building. Fergus noticed that he took a key from his pocket: the door was locked. Five, perhaps ten minutes later, the wire-man reappeared, having rounded the rear wall.

'Now,' murmured Simon, 'let's see how he closes the circuit. That's what we want to know.'

Still unreeling wire from his spool, the man threaded it through a low bush, wound it once around a sapling, walked it to the gate, and headed for the laboratory door.

'Pretty makeshift,' Simon said. 'Temporary. But it will work. I've strung them that way myself now and then. Mainly, I'd say we've lucked out.'

Fergus said, 'Knowing where it is, we won't stumble into it.'

'Knowing where it is, I can deactivate it with a scissors. But more important—we know the transmitter's got to be in that building. That means, a hundred to one, they don't have anybody guarding it. The receiver will be in somebody's room in the main building. If we're careful . . .'' He stopped. 'Wait. Here comes a guest.'

A small, sallow man carrying an umbrella picked his way gingerly along the wet walkway leading from the Villa to the laboratory.

'The boss,' said Simon. 'You can tell. He's not used to getting his feet wet.'

The third man paused to inspect and touch with one finger the newly placed antenna, then, with his own key, let himself into the laboratory. A few minutes later all three men re-emerged, accompanied by still a fourth, younger than the others, wearing a white laboratory smock. Together they walked to the gate in the wire fence, where they gathered around something Fergus could not see. Simon had his glass to his eye.

'A switch,' he said, 'fastened behind the gate post. Of course. To turn the alarm off while they're in there. He's showing them how it works.'

But Fergus was interested in something else. When the four came out of the laboratory, he noticed that the man with the thick glasses had also donned a laboratory coat. It came to him with a jolt that that man must be Dr Schutz. The other was too young; he would be the assistant, the other German—what was his name?—Wolter. The group separated. The two in the white coats re-entered the laboratory. The other two turned back towards the zoo and the Villa.

Fergus was disappointed. This particular scenario was ended. It had provided, as Simon thought, possibly useful information, but it was not what he had wanted. He had hoped for something—what?—some indication that the girl was there. True, there were the buttons. Yet a nagging worry stirred in his mind, difficult to grasp clearly.

'We may as well go,' said Simon. 'We've seen the show for today.'

'You mean we give up?' Fergus was incredulous.

'Not at all. If you think the girl is in that building, then we've got to get in there. But not now. That alarm system tells us what we need to know: the place is unmanned at night. We could sit here in the rain for six or seven hours—but why should we? I say, let's go home for supper, meet again, and come back tonight. Also, I got a pretty good look at the lock on that door through the glass. I'll need a couple of tools to get it open.'

'Can you do it?'

'I can.'

'All right,' said Fergus. 'Midnight?'

'Let's give them a chance to get to sleep. One o'clock.'

They crept back from the edge of the woods, and as they stood up to walk, the creeping worry in Fergus's mind also stood up and identified itself. It was this: All his thinking, his study of Dr Schutz's papers, his painstaking piecing together of the Steinkopf research, had produced a clear—to him—picture of what Dr Schutz was up to. Fergus's primary conclusion, as it pertained to the girl, was that her presence was unknown to the Russians. She and the Steinkopf Syndrome were the private possessions of Dr Schutz. Yet in the last hour he had seen four men enter the laboratory where he thought she must be.

That was too many. The young German assistant—yes, it was conceivable, even likely, that he knew about Schutz's plan, or at least about the girl; perhaps he had to. But the other two could hardly enter the building without noticing the presence of a young female prisoner.

Which meant either of two things: Fergus's theory was wrong, or Schutz had the girl hidden away somewhere else. But if not in the laboratory, then where? The worry added to, rather than decreased, his urgent desire to get a look at the inside of the building.

Still puzzling, he followed Simon in the gathering dusk through the wet woods towards the grove of big trees, to the right of which stood the wall from which their rope would be hanging.

When Jennifer Adam came home from work Willis was in his room, playing quietly at something or other. Worried, she called up to him:

'Willis?'

'Yes.'

'How was school?'

'It was okay.' He sounded quite matter-of-fact. So he had got through his first day back. She was relieved; that would be the hardest day.

'What did you do?'

'Reading and numbers. It was rainy, so we couldn't go out, so we played inside and watched the gerbils.' He came to the door of his room but did not come down the stairs. She waited to see if he would say anything about the morning visit from Fergus O'Neil, or what he had told about Allie, the tree, and the gate. Then she realized that he was waiting to see if *she* was going to mention it; she felt his apprehension and at once decided that she would not. John was in his room studying, his door shut. Better to let the subject remain dormant if it would.

She said, 'I'll call you when supper is ready.'

Through the day, her own first day back, as it had been Willis's, her mind had been busy with the simple work of catching up with her job after her absence, a soothingly superficial kind of preoccupation. Now she thought again of her morning's conversation with Dr O'Neil—Fergus—and it came to her suddenly, as it had not this morning, what a painfully difficult thing he had undertaken to tell her, and how gently, how kindly, he had done it. He had said, in effect, be patient, neither hope nor give up hope, and somehow he had made that seem possible. He had injected a feeling of rationality and strength into her confusion and despair. After he left her she had felt, for the first time, calm enough to face the thought of going back to work, and had gathered her strength and gone.

She wondered again who and what he was. Fergus sounded like a Scottish name, but O'Neil must be Irish. From what he had said, a teacher of some kind, a professor or a scientist, but young— surely not much over thirty-five, her own age. From Cambridge— that would be Harvard, or maybe M.I.T. Though not necessarily; there were a dozen research institutions in the area. On a fishing vacation, yet he seemed too serious to be on vacation. Staying in the Wilcox cabin on the big estate. Nunneley Wilcox had been Undersecretary of State, and was still, so she had heard, in and out of the White House and the State Department. If Fergus O'Neil was not really on vacation, then what? Was it possible that there was something—that they had some idea that the Russians, for some strange reason. . . . She put the idea out of her head. It was unbelievable, and it was too painful.

She kept busy with the dinner and set the table, thinking. Willis had stayed in his room since school, a thing he would not have done when Allie was there, and should not do. His routine was broken. All their routines were broken, and they would have to start anew, a second time, building new ones.

CHAPTER TWENTY-FOUR

ALLIE ENJOYED SITTING in the nice fresh air in the pretty woods. She sat absolutely still, as the Doctor had said she would, so she did not see him while he walked away, because he was behind her, behind the big grey tree she sat against. But she did see the two other men.

They came walking up in front of her, one in a grey jacket, one all in brown. Even his face looked brown, except his eyes. At first she thought they must be friends of the Doctor's, and they were coming to meet him and to see her. Then one of them, the brown one, caught the other by the arm, and they both crouched down quickly, as if they were hiding. They were not looking at her after all, but staring after the Doctor, keeping quiet. They stayed there quite a long time, saying nothing, just looking. At last the brown one whispered something to the other one. They stood up again, and stepping very carefully—*sneaking*—they walked off in the same direction the Doctor had gone, and she could not see them.

Then it was quiet, except for the soft sound of the rain. She looked at the pine tree in front of her. It was small and wide, the ends of its branches almost touching the ground. Under them she saw some brown pine cones. She used to pick up pine cones at Christmastime, so long ago she could hardly remember, to put them on the Christmas tree, or sometimes to watch them burn in the fireplace. They burned with a fine blaze, but they always made your hands sticky.

She looked at her legs, sticking straight out in front of her. One of her slacks was torn, ripped all the way up to her knee, and where it fell open she saw there were blue-and-red marks on her skin. From the prod. A black fly, sluggish in the chill, had landed on her shin and crawled to one of the spots, where it walked around in small circles as if searching for something. It did not bite, but it tickled. Then a big drop of rain, having collected itself on a leaf somewhere above her, fell with a *splat* next to the fly, frightening it away. The raindrop felt cool and the tickling stopped.

After quite a long time she heard a scratching sound. To her left, quite close, grew a very large oak tree, its trunk a yard wide, its grey-brown bark rough and scaly. She saw a feather-duster flick, and then the rest of the squirrel came around the trunk, stopped, spread flat, its bright eyes watching her. Since she did not move, had not moved, it decided she was not there and came the rest of the way down the trunk. Staying close to its tree at first, it scratched among the roots and leaves, finding bits of green and sitting up on its hind legs to eat them, nibbling delicately and throwing away the parts it did not like. As it ate it grew bolder, until finally it was feeding only inches from her sneaker.

Then it pricked up its ears, gave a quiver of alarm, and was gone, around and up the far side of the oak. A moment later she heard what it had heard: footsteps. The Doctor? No, the two men, walking more quickly and somewhat less cautiously than before, coming up behind her, talking in quiet voices. Once again they came almost to her tree, then turned off to the right, towards the wall, towards where they had come from. Now she could see their backs, just a few feet away, and hear what they were saying, though she did not understand it.

'. . . using the place as a laboratory to run biological warfare tests.'

'B-w tests? Here?'

'You can see the advantage of the location.'

'My God. Yes—just a mile upstream from the water plant. . . .'

They walked out of earshot, their backs disappearing among the trees. But the squirrel did not return. It was almost dark now and suddenly, although she did not want to, although she felt nice, she began to shiver. She was still shivering when the Doctor came.

He noticed it immediately, and looked closely through his thick glasses at her face, placing his hand on her forehead. He looked, too, at the blue and red spots on her leg, which had grown bluer and redder than before.

'Pins,' he said to himself. 'I must remember pins.' To Allie he said: 'Come. We will go back inside where it is warm, and you will sleep and rest.' He took her elbow, not unkindly, and helped her to her feet. She stumbled at first; she had not realized how stiff her leg had grown

At the edge of the woods the Doctor stopped and looked carefully, and she suddenly realized that the scene was familiar, she was seeing the animal place, almost from where she used to watch it long ago with Willis. Right over there was the wall where she climbed the tree, only now she was inside and the tree was outside; she could not see even its top branches. The Doctor, having peered long and seen no one, led her to the wire fence, through the gate and back into the low white building.

When they reached the cage he took her coat, looked again at her torn slacks and her shirt cuff dangling open, and once more muttered, 'Pins.' He touched her forehead again, and then her wrist, feeling her pulse.

'You must rest,' he said. 'Tonight we will take a nice long walk up the road. But now you are tired. You will sleep. When I go, you will sleep, sleep until I wake you. Do you understand?'

Allie whispered, 'I will sleep until you wake me.' She lay on the floor of the cage, in the corner near Victor, closed her eyes, and was immediately in a deep sleep. She did not hear the Doctor close the door behind him as he left the building.

After a time the dream began. It was one of the best she had had. It started with a long walk up the road. Up the hill with no bicycle to push, and there, on the top of the hill, her own house. It was night, dark outside but in the windows of the house the lights glowed so she knew they were home. She ran up the driveway. To be home again! Her excitement was so great she decided to make it last a little longer. She would look in the windows first, see what they were doing, and then surprise them. How glad they would be!

She looked first into the kitchen. There was her mother at the stove, wearing an apron, cooking chicken, brown and plump. How hungry she was, how good it would taste, how long since she had eaten chicken! Her mother looked as pretty as ever, but sad. Had she missed her?

She ran to the living-room window. There were John and Willis, they had made a fire in the fireplace, and John was just tossing in a pine cone. It glowed and flamed up, a beautiful orange light. Last, she looked through the glass window of the door leading to her own bedroom. Her light had been turned on; her bed was made up and turned back (as if she were sick!), and on the pillow someone had placed a book. The book was *Heidi*—she could see the cover picture—so she knew Willis had put it there.

She had an idea. She would open the door to her bedroom very quietly and slip inside. Then she would walk out among them as if she had never been away at all. She would say something ordinary: 'Isn't dinner ready yet?'

She had her hand on the doorknob and then she fell down. She must have fallen down, because she was lying on the ground. Her leg began to hurt, just a little at first, and then much worse, horribly, a vibrating, cramping, tearing pain as if her muscles were pulling themselves loose from her bones. She screamed and screamed again. Couldn't they hear her? Why didn't her mother come, or John? There was a crashing noise—a door opening? But no one came, the house was gone: she was lying alone in the dark. The pain came again, and then stopped. She vomited without waking, and slept on.

Since she could not awaken, could not open her eyes, she did not see Georg Wolter, who had entered very quietly from the inner laboratory, not letting the door click; did not hear him approach the cage, the electric prod in one hand, a hypodermic syringe in the other. He set the hypodermic down carefully on the table. He would test his theory before using it. Since she was sleeping near the corner of the cage, he pushed the copper end of the prod through the wire wall rather than risk awakening her by opening the cage door. He tried to stay calm, but already his breath was coming too fast.

Her reaction was better than he had hoped. At the first slight touch of her leg she groaned; when he pressed more firmly, she screamed, a muted scream, true, almost whispered, but a sound of pure agony, a lovely, high, thrilling cry of pain. And her face: her jaw clenched and knotted, then snapped open; gasping, her mouth twisted into a grimace that rent her cheeks; one hand clawed the floor wildly. Tears gouted from under her closed eyelids. And she had not awakened! He would try again—the needle could wait. But he wanted to watch her from closer up.

He pulled the prod back through the wall and walked around to the cage door. He was panting now, his hand shook as he undid the catch; the mist was beginning to suffuse his eyes. He heard only vaguely, over the pounding in his ears, the commotion in the next cage as the big chimpanzee hurled himself from side to side against the walls.

The doors to both cages opened simultaneously, the one unlatched, the other burst from its hinges. As the prod touched the girl for the last time, Georg Wolter felt himself seized from behind in a grip that forced the breath from his lungs. He staggered backwards out of the cage. The incredible scissor grip on his waist tightened and now two enormously powerful hairy arms encircled him, one chokingly around his neck, the other around his head and face, its long fingers gouging deep into his right ear and his right eye. The arms pulled in opposite directions, and his head turned farther around on his shoulders than it had ever turned before. His knees buckled and he crashed forward, knocking the syringe from the table: it rolled across the floor, leaking its contents in a small puddle. In Georg's neck a vertebra snapped loudly, then another. Blood trickled from his nose and mouth. Still the ape held on. Georg had been dead a good five minutes before it released its grip and crept back into its cage, where it huddled in the corner next to Allie, staring at her sadly as she slept.

Fergus's luminous wrist dial showed one-fifteen when he and Simon reached the wall for their second invasion. The rain had stopped but the chill remained and the clouds hung thick overhead, hiding any glimmer of star or moon. They fixed their rope, this time, farther down the wall, nearer the zoo. 'Hard to move through those woods in this dark,' Simon explained.

As soon as they had scaled the top they saw that there were lights turned on in the laboratory, shining faintly through the two small barred windows. 'Means nothing,' Simon whispered. 'They leave them on at night.'

'Still—' said Fergus.

'Might be somebody working late?' Simon crept forward. 'It's possible. We've got to chance it. At least with the lights we know where it is.'

They reached the chain fence. Simon led the way along the outside to a point just opposite one corner of the building. 'Here,' he said, 'if I remember there should be a shrub on our left and a small tree on our right. The antenna runs from one to the other about eight feet inside the fence, about two feet above ground. I'll try to cut that section out without grounding it.' He put a hand on top of the fence and vaulted over it, lighting soundlessly on his crepe-soled canvas shoes. Fergus followed less gracefully, stumbling as he landed. 'Steady.'

From one of the pockets of his hunting jacket Simon produced equipment. He handed Fergus a pair of soft cotton gloves. 'Better wear these from here on.' He pulled a pair over his own hands. He gripped a small rubber-handled shears; in the other hand he held a slim, hooded flashlight. Turned on, it emitted a beam as thin as a pencil. The beam scanned the blackness ahead briefly, caught the gleam of copper, traced it to the bush, and flicked out. 'Got it.' The shears snipped. 'Hold this—keep it off the ground.' Fergus held an end of wire in his glove. The light traced the strand to the tree; the shears snipped again. 'Done.' Simon rolled up the ten-foot section of antenna and tossed it back over the fence.

'Come on through.'

'Why the gloves?'

'Because from here on we'll be touching things that might pick up fingerprints. Our Russian friends will know how to trace them. I'd just as soon they didn't know who broke into their germ lab.'

At the door they met the first hint that all was not as it should be.

'I'll be damned,' whispered Simon. It was an inquiry rather than a statement, and Fergus stared with him at the narrow rim of light around the door frame. The door was open, only a fraction of an inch, but open, and obviously not locked.

They stood back from the faint glow, in the deeper shadow, puzzling. 'There *must* be someone in there,' Fergus said.

'Why? They lock it when they're in as well as when they're out.'

'A trap?'

'For whom? They don't know we're coming.'

'What do we do?'

'I'm for taking a look. You wait here. If anybody starts shooting, sprint for the exit—just the way we came in. I'll be right behind you.'

Simon crept forward, approached the door from the side and pushed it hard. As it swung open he leaped back out of sight. Nothing. Forward again, crouching, he peered in, straightened, and entered. The door closed behind him.

Fergus waited for perhaps a minute, then started towards the door. As he did it opened again, just enough for Simon to slip through.

'Come on in,' he said, 'but brace yourself. It isn't pretty.'

'What do you mean?'

'One of our friends is dead, very messy. As far as I can tell, he's the only one here except for a chimpanzee.'

Fergus, veteran of innumerable cadavers and dissections, felt nonetheless instantly sick when he saw the body. He looked away; calming himself, thinking, it's only dead tissue, he forced himself to look again.

'I've seen stranglings,' Simon said, awed, 'but none like that.' The neck had been literally wrung, twisted like a braid of rope; the head, still tenuously connected with the shoulders, lay at an impossible angle in a pool of blood. Fergus recognized him by his distorted face and stained laboratory coat as the one he had seen in the afternoon, the one he had assumed to be Georg Wolter.

'What could have happened?' Fergus, feeling now confused and bewildered, looked around him, saw two heavy-gauge wire cages, a cracked hypodermic syringe lying on the floor in a puddle of clear liquid, a long wood-and-metal rod he recognized as a cattle goad. One of the cages was empty; in the other a large chimpanzee sat quietly and stared at them with a mournful expression. The hair on its arms was black, matted with dried blood; the door on its cage, broken, had been crudely—hastily— wired in place to keep the animal in.

'First,' Simon said, 'let's make sure there's no one else here. That door must lead to another room.'

It did not, but only to another door three feet distant. The two doors enclosed a closetlike hallway, its ceiling and one wall covered with metal reflectors and glass bulbs; a shelf on the other wall held aerosol canisters.

'Disinfectant spray,' said Fergus. 'A decontamination lock. Those light bulbs will be ultraviolet.' He said to Simon: 'Take a quick look inside, but don't inhale. That's where they keep the bugs. No telling what's loose in there.'

Fergus opened the inner door. They looked into total darkness. Inside he felt for the light switch, flicked it, and the ceiling glowed into fluorescence. The laboratory stretched before them, all white enamel and stainless steel, workbenches, sink, burners, refrigerator, sealed glass cabinets, microscope, an array of equipment instantly familiar to Fergus. Familiar and, at a glance, totally in order and unoccupied. He pulled the door shut.

'Looks all right,' he said. 'Apparently all the trouble was out here.' He looked at his watch: two o'clock. 'Let's split up. I'll take a look in the lab, see what they're doing, see if I can find any clue about the girl. You check out here and try to figure out what happened.'

Inside the laboratory Fergus made a quick survey. The glass cabinets were filled with jars and Petri dishes. He wondered which was the *anthracis*, what the others might be. Probably mutant varieties of the first. The refrigerator held more jars and bottles: nutrient solutions. On shelves along the walls stood a miscellany of standard equipment of steel, glass, porcelain, and rubber. The microscope was a Zeiss binocular, Model 120-C, triple objectives, 1,400-power maximum. He had used a dozen like it.

A six-foot square in one corner held the water-purification system: pump, pipes, filters, a pressure-tank of chlorine, another of fluorine. Beside it stood a tall glass object, a complex of plates and tubes, electrically heated at the base. Fergus recognized it: a multiplate distillation column, a sophisticated version of a still. Why? Of course. The polywater—Water X—would have a higher boiling point than the rest. Schutz would want to be able to distil it out, recheck his concentration.

There was a desk and beside it a filing cabinet. The desk was neat, and its drawers yielded nothing useful—blank worksheets, sharpened pencils, a solitary forceps. The filing cabinet—smallish, two metal drawers of Pendaflex folders—might be more profitable if there was time to study it, but there was not. Its folders were filled with painstakingly recorded data, the statistics of bacterial culture, daily growth rates matched against temperatures, analyses of water content, frequency of cell division and mutation—Fergus recognized them all, but they were meaningless because the bacteria were identified only by letters and numbers. Thus the first half of the first file drawer was filled with statistics on Set A, Groups 1-20. But what kind of a germ composed Set A? And sets B, C, D, and on down the alphabet? He realized that there would be a code book containing the necessary identifications, but it was nowhere in sight. With his gloved hands, he riffled through the folders, each neatly labelled in the upper-right-hand corner, each holding from two to a dozen sheets.

Only one of the folders was different. It had been pushed slightly apart from the rest, at the back of the bottom file drawer. It was labelled 'S-K.' It was empty.

Someone was knocking gently on the closed laboratory door. It opened a crack and Simon's voice came through:

'Fergus?'

'Just finishing up.'

'Come on out. I've got something.'

In the outer room, Simon entered the unoccupied cage. 'They had the girl in here,' he said. 'Look at that.' He held in his hand the box and the two blue buttons he had shown Fergus. In a corner of the cage, almost invisible in the shadow, lay the matching button.

'She was here,' Simon went on, 'and not very long ago. And before she left'—he pointed to another corner of the cage—'she threw up.'

'If she saw that,' said Fergus, with a glance at the twisted thing that lay outside the cage, 'I don't wonder. Especially if she saw it happen.'

'You're a biologist. Ever work with chimps?'

'Yes. Quite a lot.'

'Could—or *would*—a chimpanzee do that to a man?'

'It certainly wouldn't be typical. But sufficiently provoked—yes, I suppose it could happen. They're strong enough. And that's a big one—I'd guess a hundred and fifty pounds, maybe more.'

'Well, I can't say what did happen, but I can guess what may have happened. That man on the floor——'

'That was Georg Wolter.'

'So I figured. Didn't somebody say he was a nasty character? All right, here's a theory: he was teasing that ape with the cattle goad. Being that type, maybe he liked it even better because the girl was there to watch. Anyway, the ape got into a frenzy, broke out of the cage—you can see the door's been broken—and attacked him. You noticed the blood on its fur.'

'Yes.'

'Besides, I don't think a human could do that. But an ape, with those long arms——'

'All right,' Fergus said. 'That's an explanation of the killing—maybe. But where's the girl?' He sat on the bench, facing away from Wolter's body, staring at the empty cage, thinking.

Simon said, 'Of course that's problem number one. This killing has nothing to do with us. Strictly speaking, it didn't even happen in the United States. But does it have anything to do with the girl? Maybe yes, maybe no. You said you thought Schutz was planning to defect—probably try to get back to Germany with his secret weapon and his ex-Nazi friends. Possibly take the girl with him.'

'Possibly.'

'Now put yourself in his place. Obviously he's got things planned out—he's been planning for years. Suddenly there's this mess. Was he here when it happened? I doubt it. But somehow he found out. Maybe he mistrusted Georg and followed him back to the lab, and found him with his neck broken. That part doesn't matter. What matters is this: Schutz sees his plans going all to hell. Because the Russians aren't going to like this. They'll hush it up, but they'll get excited. They'll keep a sharp eye on Schutz, maybe pop him right back to Siberia.

'So Schutz is standing here, feeling panicky, and then the simple solution comes to him: take the girl and leave now.'

'Tonight?'

'If I'm anywhere near right, some time within the past couple of hours. That body on the floor is still warm.'

Fergus said: 'You've got to be at least partly right. Somebody had to be here after Wolter was killed. Somebody got the chimp back into its cage and wired the door shut.'

'And why didn't he use the other cage? Because the girl was in it.'

Fergus was thinking: that would explain why the S-K file, alone of all the files, was empty. If Schutz had fled, he would have taken those papers with him. It also explained the unlocked door— Schutz had been upset, had been rushing, had been careless.

'All right,' he said. 'They've gone. But where? How?'

'If I were Schutz, and had planned it all out, I know what I'd have done. I'd have stolen a car. Somehow or other, eventually, he's got to get to an airport. He's not going to walk it.'

'Could he have done that?'

'They have a couple of cars full-time at the Villa. One's a sedan —an Olds, I think—with DPL plates. The other is a panel truck, regular plates. They use that for shopping, groceries and stuff, over in the village. On weekends, of course, there may be a dozen more, including the Ambassador's limousine. But what I'm thinking—those two regular cars. It wouldn't have been hard for Schutz to filch a key to either of those, keep it in his pocket until he's ready to run. The Russians would have missed it, but everybody loses a key now and then. They'd have a spare, or have one made.'

Fergus looked at his watch. Two-twenty. A sudden, jarring thought came to him.

'How long do you suppose they'd have been gone when we got here?'

'Who knows? Might have been two hours. Might have been two minutes.'

'Where do they keep those cars?'

'There's a parking area near the Villa—to the left as you come in.'

Fergus stood up abruptly.

Simon said, 'Are you thinking what I'm thinking?'

Fergus said, 'While we're sitting here talking . . .'

'I'm with you.'

In the dark, the mass of the Villa loomed like a mountain visible only as a deeper blackness. A solitary light glowed palely somewhere just inside the front door, emerging from a groundfloor window too dim to cast a shadow. They walked wide around it, keeping off the gravel and on the grass. Fergus, staring up, wondered which room was Dr. Schutz's and if he was even now, fooling them all, in it and asleep, dreaming of *anthracis* and *coryna*. They had come most of the way at a run, exchanging faint hopes in faint whispers. Caught by surprise, Schutz might not have had the key with him, if there was a key; might have had to go back to his room for papers, notes, money, a clean shirt; might have put the girl in the car, if there was a car, and told her to wait.

'There it is,' said Simon. A hundred feet past the Villa the driveway, having curved under the *porte cochère,* emptied itself between two hedgerows into a simple asphalt-surfaced square. There were cars parked, dark oblongs on the black surface. How many? Four? Three. Two big, one small. 'Damn this dark,' Simon whispered. He had his light out of his pocket. They crept closer. 'There's the Olds.' 'Look inside.' The light probed quickly and went out. The front seat was empty. Again, the back seat. 'Nobody.'

'Now the truck,' Simon said. 'I think it has no windows in the back.' But there was no truck. When they walked across the lot to the other two cars, the big one was a sedan, the small one a sports Mercedes. Both were empty.

'Damn,' Simon groaned, 'he's done it. He's got away.'

CHAPTER TWENTY-FIVE

THE ROAD WAS DARK, narrow, and deserted. It had been one o'clock when they left the laboratory, Dr Schutz carrying his papers under his arm, the girl wearing her blue coat. Together they had walked along the wall to the gate, opened it, and stepped out of Villa Petrograd for ever. They had five hours until dawn, five hours for a walk of three miles, and Dr Schutz was glad for the time. The girl now seemed definitely ill, though not seriously, and limped as if one of her legs hurt; they would have to stop and rest frequently. 'We will go for our walk now,' he had said at the outset, 'but since it is night we will go quietly. We must not wake anyone.' So when they came to the top of the hill and passed the first house, a white house on the left, although she stared at it she said nothing.

The delay in leaving had been caused primarily by shock. When he had entered the laboratory to get the girl he had found Georg Wolter dead, newly and grotesquely dead, on the floor. His first reaction had been panic: the spies—Nikolai's spies—had been real, had broken in and killed Georg. He would run, forget the girl. Then he realized he could not run without the papers from the inner laboratory. He forced himself to stand absolutely still for a minute. The silence reassured him. He looked again, and slowly it became clear what had happened. He saw the bloodied chimpanzee cowering in the corner of its cage, saw the electric prod, saw the broken cage door. He had known for some time that Georg was a sadist; all of the animals had shown fear of him. And this time he had gone too far.

But the girl was still sleeping quietly, unharmed, in her cage. He did not think the ape was likely to attack him or her, but to be sure he took some wire from the tool cabinet and refastened the door, crudely but well enough. Next he entered the inner laboratory and flicked on the light. It was quiet, undisturbed, and contained no spies. He sat at his desk and tried to calm and collect his thoughts. He had not been fond of Georg, and now that the shock had passed had no particular feeling about his death; their association would have ended tonight in any case. But he needed to think: what effect would the death have on his own plans?

After some consideration he decided, perhaps none, but possibly two effects, both good. The first was that it might confuse the Russians; it would take them longer to determine where and why he had gone. The second was that it might delay their finding out he had gone at all, for Georg would certainly have been the first to notice his absence, and report it to Kublitz.

Now, on the dark road, he wondered how long it would be before they found Georg. When that happened his own departure would be immediately discovered, and a pursuit be started. How intensive a pursuit he did not know. They would be more concerned about the papers than about him—their reports from Group 17, their secret research on biological warfare. They could not know that he planned to make no use at all of that research. His own, which they had never grasped, made it obsolete.

He thought it might be as much as twelve hours before they found Georg—perhaps not until the new security guards went to use the laboratory bathroom.

The girl stumbled and almost fell. He caught her arm and held her up. They must rest again. 'We will sit down,' he said. Where? There, ahead, pasture on one side of the road, woods on the other, no fence. They could walk a few feet into the woods and sit. It would be wet—no help for that. But by good luck he found a large and reasonably dry log; they sat on it. The rain had stopped, the wind had changed and the sharp chill was gone from the air.

He looked at the small, silent figure sitting beside him and had a feeling almost of pity for her. He could not see her face in the dark, but back in the laboratory he had noticed that she looked pale, thin, and tired. He had at least found pins and fastened her torn trousers and her loose sleeve. The blue coat hid most of it in any case. He had washed her face and even tried to comb some of the tangles from her hair with his pocket comb, but it was hopeless and he had finally given up.

He thought: once in Washington, once he had contacted the organization whose number he had memorized—then there would be money. They could buy her new clothes, a pretty dress to wear on the air flight; there would be better food and someone who knew how to fix her hair.

He said, 'Now we will walk some more.'

She stood up obediently, but just as they reached the edge of the road he said, 'Wait.' He led her a few steps back into the woods. A car was coming, moving fast, in the direction they had been walking, coming from the direction of the Villa. Now he saw its headlights and realized it was not one car but two. For a moment his heart sank. Could they have found out already? But as the cars sped past he remembered that they had walked, a mile or so back, past a driveway leading into a very large estate. His fear was foolish. They must have come from there—two American speedsters on business of their own.

The Virginia Transit Company's 7 a.m. express commuters' bus carried mostly regulars. Fred, the driver, knew them all by face and half by name. 'Good morning, Fred.' 'Good morning, Mr Booth.' Mr Booth was a lawyer in the Commerce Department. Fred got them all to the terminal in downtown Washington, Eleventh and H, by eight-twenty.

But this morning there were two strangers, and strange was the right word. They got on at River Crossing Road, the next-to-last stop he made before the locals took over. A ratty-looking kid in a coat three sizes too big, a girl with hair that looked as if she had washed it in mud. She looked half-dead for sleep. She looked sick. With her a man with grey hair and thick glasses, needing a shave.

'What is the fare, please?' A foreign accent. A Dutchman.

'To Washington?'

'Please.'

'A buck apiece.'

'I beg your pardon?'

'Two dollars, mister, two dollars.'

The man looked pleased. He stuck his hand in his pocket and came up with two wrinkled singles. When they went to their seat the man whispered something to the girl. She closed her eyes and went to sleep, her head leaning against the window. Had they been waiting all night at that bus stop?

Fred reached Number 123, the Bridge Highway, and from there on turned all his attention to getting his blue-and-silver monster through the rush-hour traffic.

Mr Bayles, aroused from sleep by telephone at 4 a.m., had made some calls of his own from home to set certain large machinery in motion. One of his calls would trickle down eventually to Officer Simon's lieutenant, so Mr Bayles had, by request, left his name out of it.

He reached his office in the big white building at seven. It was a large office, secure behind two secretaries, furnished in walnut and a dark green leather sofa. Through a double window one could look out between the trees and glimpse a flash of the same river where, fifteen miles upstream, Fergus had gone fishing. Fergus and Simon sat on the sofa; Colonel Attenborough arrived at seven-

fifteen. At 8 a.m. the phone on Mr Bayles's desk began to ring
The first call was a long one. Mr Bayles took notes, said little,
and at the end thanked the caller and asked him for a written
report. When he hung up he said to Fergus: 'We checked your
hunch. A good one. If Schutz is defecting, he's got a lovely friend
at the top. Ever hear of Friedrich Kassel?'

'The name is familiar—I've read it.'

'My God,' said Colonel Attenborough. 'He's Secretary of War.'

'Minister of Defence,' Mr Bayles corrected, 'of the German
Republic. But in the old days, in Silesia, he was Hauptmann Kassel, a captain in the Army of the Third Reich. He had military
command of the district where Schutz had his laboratory—the one
that produced the zombies. They became close friends, and co-
operated beautifully. Kassel had an amateur's interest in Schutz's
experiments. Schutz had a scientist's admiration of Kassel's military efficiency—his ability to produce human laboratory subjects
of a specific size, sex, age, weight. Real teamwork. Young Kassel
got away when the Russians came. Young Schutz got caught.'

'With that on his record, how did Kassel ever get elected Defence
Minister?'

'That was twenty-seven years ago. He was a young army officer
doing his duty. Most of the records were destroyed. Most, but not
all. We have a pretty good dossier on Kassel.'

'And he's still interested in—new weapons?'

'Of course. That's why he's Minister of Defence.'

The phone continued to ring. By eight-thirty Mr Bayles had
private confirmation from inside Villa Petrograd that Dr Schutz
had, in fact, flown the coop.

'They don't know anything about the girl,' he said. 'We can't
confirm her presence at all. But they've found Wolter, and they
found a big hole cut in their antenna. They think Schutz did it.'

'Who else?' said Simon.

'What are they going to do?'

'So far, nothing—waiting for instructions. But they'll have to
try to catch him. He took some secret documents. Probably his
own reports.'

'The Group 17 reports,' Fergus said. 'Of course. They won't
care too much about him. They can disown him. But they've got
to get their papers back.'

By nine o'clock, Mr Bayles had another report.

'No Russian car has been stolen. Your panel truck, with its

regular driver, spent the night at the Embassy. It's there now. It's supposed to go to the airport to pick up some packages for Villa Petrograd. Sort of hush-hush. Probably a load of vodka.'

Simon said, 'Damn. Then how *did* they go?'

By ten, Mr Bayles had received another call and could tell him.

'The simplest possible way. They took the bus. The driver noticed them because they looked strange. The man wore thick glasses and spoke with an accent, didn't seem to understand American money. The girl looked dirty and sick. When they got to the Washington terminal the man went to a phone booth. The driver went into the coffee shop. When he came out they were gone. He's been shown a picture of Allison Adam, and he's positive it's the same girl. We have no picture of Dr Schutz.'

Simon said: 'But how could he know about the bus?'

'Apparently he knows more than we suspected. As you yourself said, he's got to have a plan worked out. He didn't just run off into the woods. And he isn't just going to wander around Washington.'

'So the important question,' Fergus said, 'is whom did he call from that phone booth?' But even as he said it, he felt like cheering, felt like running to tell Mrs Adam that her daughter was truly and demonstrably alive, if not yet safe.

'There is an organization,' Mr Bayles said, 'or there used to be, of ex-Nazis—or, say, extreme right-wing Germans. It had a branch in Washington. I'm not up on it, because, being here, it's FBI business, not ours. It may have dissolved, but I doubt it. The Israelis would know, and maybe the FBI—we're checking with them. But I remember how it started. In a way I was in on it.

'I was working in the State Department, Intelligence Section—there wasn't any CIA then, you remember. In December of 1941, the German Embassy in Washington closed down and its personnel were ordered home. They were allowed to leave, of course, since they had diplomatic immunity. But eight of them refused. They claimed to be anti-Hitler and asked for asylum. I was one of those at State who were assigned to evaluate these sudden changes of loyalty.

'Some were real, but a couple at least had got their instruction from the Führer. They were agents; of course we couldn't prove it, and in the end they were all allowed to stay. I even remember one of their names: Peter Zimmer. He'd been the press attaché, and he was a real Nazi-boy if ever I saw one.

'They weren't worth a dime as spies, because we watched them too closely. But after the war, as "good" Germans they were in a pretty spot to help their ex-Nazi friends. They worked as business-men, lobbyists, propagandists, and when the U.S. started pouring in money to rebuild Germany, they made sure some of it got to their buddies. They also helped some of them escape to South America.

'As I said, I lost track of them when I came over here. But if they're still around, and Schutz can find them, they'll help him.'

'Help him how?' Fergus asked.

Peter Zimmer's hair was still blond, with only touches of grey, and was parted in the middle. He wore a grey suit, white shirt and dark tie. Though he was in his fifties, he had the trim look of an athlete, which he retained by vigorous hiking and by playing football, German style, with his three sons. He had learned the vigorous life style long ago with the Hitlerjugend. His eyes were clear, blue, and chilly.

He had an office downtown in the Ring Building, a home in an elegant northwestern suburb, but was at the moment in a sub-stantial red-brick house in Georgetown, a home-away-from-home for visiting German businessmen and officials on unofficial busi-ness. It bore no identification but a street number. Its staff were competent, trusted, and all bilingual. It was not an office building, but its large and rather sombre library did contain a business-like desk of dark oak inlaid with leather.

From behind this desk Herr Zimmer spoke to Dr Schutz, who sat before it.

'We have arranged a room for you on the third floor. I believe you will be comfortable there. It has its own bath and quite a pretty view of the Dumbarton Oaks park. I suggest that you stay in the room as much as possible until it is time for you to leave. Meals will be brought to you, and you may order what you need —clothes, toilet articles, luggage—through the man who brings them. His name is Hans. The girl has been placed in the charge of his wife, Hilda, who will get her cleaned up and buy her some presentable dresses.

'I have talked to our friend in Bonn, and read him very precisely the message you gave me. He was, to understate things, quite astonished to hear that you are still alive. However, he remembers you well, sent you his greeting, and agrees that you will be a valuable asset to the new Germany. He seemed especially inter-ested in the part of the message about—what was it?—the Stein-kopf effect. He will make the arrangements necessary for your—

reception, shall we say?—in Hamburg. Meanwhile our own arrangements are progressing.

'The passports will take a day to prepare. The airline reservations—those we must study a little. It is not yet clear how hard our friends at Villa Petrograd are going to try to stop you. It is possible that a devious route will be safer than a direct one. It is also possible to trick them—a very simple trick, but it has worked before. Washington has two airports. We send them to one, and you to the other. You say you are sure they know nothing of the girl?'

'Only Georg Wolter knew,' said Dr Shutz, 'and he is now, as I told you, quite unable to tell.'

'That will help. Even so, I think it wise to return to the Villa the secret papers you took.'

'Return them!'

'As you yourself have realized, the KGB will be more concerned about those papers than about you. If they find the papers, most of the pressure will be off.'

'But they contain all my data.'

'While you rested, I took the liberty of having them photocopied. The originals may now be found by the Russians. I will have them placed—perhaps a bit scattered—in the woods near the gate, where you dropped them in your haste to escape.'

Dr Schutz looked dubious. 'I think they will not believe it.'

'Possibly not. And yet I think your friend Kublitz *will* believe it. It will save his skin.'

'May I see the copies.'

Herr Zimmer unlocked a drawer in the desk and handed a sheaf of papers to Dr Schutz. 'You will find them quite complete, and somewhat clearer than the originals. We have a very fine copying machine, a German make, much superior to the American and Japanese models. I am, among other things, the American representative of the firm that manufactures it.'

Having examined the papers, Dr Schutz said, 'It is a pleasure to deal once again with efficiency. I express my gratitude for all you are doing.'

Peter Zimmer opened another drawer of the desk and took from it a grey stone bottle and two small glasses. He poured, and handed one glass to Dr Schutz.

'When one has an efficient apparatus,' he said, 'it is a pleasure to use it. In recent years we do not often have the opportunity.' He held up his glass.

'To the new Germany.'

'Prosit!'

CHAPTER TWENTY-SIX

THE NEWS, while not entirely satisfactory, was better than any that had gone before it, and too complicated to transmit by telephone. So he had called from Mr Bayles's office only to say that he would like to talk to her again. At a little before noon Fergus knocked on the door of Mrs Adam's house.

She opened it, looking frightened.

He smiled. 'Ease off,' he said. 'Allison is alive.'

'Oh God,' she said. 'Thank you. Thank you.' She was not looking at Fergus, but over his shoulder, out the door, at the sky. Then she looked at him and startlingly, as he watched, the colour faded from her lips. Her face turned dead white and she swayed forward. He caught her and her head fell against his shoulder, muffling a single violent sob. After that the tears flowed gently, the first female tears ever to stain his clothing. He thought to himself, the life of one daughter is more important than all the countries in the world, and all the wars.

At length she said, 'I've been praying since you called. Trying to pray without hoping. It's a hard combination. Where is she?'

He led her back into the room. 'Sit down. It isn't quite time to stop praying. But from now on I think it's safe to hope, too.'

When Fergus had told her the story, omitting as much painful detail as he truthfully could, he looked at him, now with trust, and said simply, 'What am I to do?'

He had asked Mr Bayles the same question earlier that morning, and Mr Bayles had said, 'What we've got now is a kidnapping. For the time being the other aspects don't matter. The FBI will look for them in Washington, though they think the organization I spoke of doesn't exist any more—there just isn't any action for it, hasn't been for years. And of course it was pretty shadowy even when it did exist. Still, it's obvious that he has contacted somebody, and it's a good bet he's going to try to get to Germany. So our best hope is to watch the airports, especially German flights. Every airport employee will have, or will have seen, a photograph of Allison Adam. Our biggest advantage is that Schutz doesn't know we know about the girl—or, for that matter, about him.'

Sitting in her bright living room, Jennifer Adam said to Fergus, 'And if they find them?'

'When they find them—when they think they've got any trace at all—they'll call me, because Simon and I are the only ones who can identify Dr Schutz. They'll call you, because none of us has ever seen Allison. They'll want us to meet them, wherever it is. Meanwhile, we wait.'

'And we don't know how long it may be.'

'Mr Bayles thinks a day or two at least before they try the airport. Somehow they have to get papers. Schutz may have a Russian passport, but he won't dare to use it. Allison has none at all.'

'Poor little Allison.' Her hand went to her face as if she might cry again, but she did not. 'Locked in a cage. And now——' She stopped. 'I keep thinking how frightened she must be.'

'Mrs Adam——'

'My name is Jennifer.'

'Jennifer, you have to get used to the idea that she probably isn't frightened at all.' He had told her about the Steinkopf Syndrome. 'For the moment, at least, that's a benefit.'

'When we find her—what will she be like?'

'You understand I've never seen it. But I think she will seem as if she's under hypnosis, or heavy sedation.'

She thought for a minute. 'You know, I keep thinking: I won't even care. Just as long as she's alive. Just so I get her back.' She fell silent again. 'What I dread——'

'Yes?'

'You've done so much, I have no right to ask you to do any more. I dread the waiting—for the phone to ring. And I'll have to tell the children when they come home. I don't know how to do that. Could you stay? Please.'

Fergus felt a surge of pleasure, and felt guilty, because he had had the same feeling when she had rested her head on his shoulder. For the second time he told himself: it is not wrong to like someone you have to help.

'I'll stay as long as you like.'

'Then stay until they call—until they find her.'

The call came from Mr Bayles on the following day, just before supper. The time was five-forty-five.

'We've got a pretty good possibility. A flight from Dulles to Frankfort, non-stop, eight-thirty tonight. A Mr David Schmidt and Miss Schmidt, his daughter, have reservations.'

'What makes you think——'

'When the tickets were picked up, Pan American, as routine, asked for the passenger's phone number to call in case there's a problem. They were given a number. We checked it. It's a phoney.

And the man who picked them up—it wasn't Schutz—had a German accent.'

'Sounds good.'

'Maybe a bit too good. But it's the only lead we've got, so we have to check it out.'

'All right,' Fergus said. 'When do we go?'

'Come to my office at six-thirty. We can drive over together. Bring Mrs Adam.'

In the late afternoon Allie went out from the big red house to the big black car. She and the Doctor got in the back seat, the other two men in the front. She leaned back to rest as the Doctor said, so she could not see out the window, but she knew where they were going: the airport, where they might, he said, go for a ride on an aeroplane. She had a new dress, and a new coat, new shoes—new everything. And her hair was clean. The big blonde lady named Hilda had tried to brush the tangles out, but finally she took a scissors and cut most of it off. Then she washed it.

The men talked on the way to the airport. The one in front, the nice-looking one, not the driver, was telling the Doctor something long and complicated, but it was all in the language she could not understand. She was pretty sure it must be German. As he talked he gave the Doctor a set of tickets in an envelope, and then another set. She knew about aeroplane tickets, though she had never been on a plane, because a long time ago someone—her father!—used to go away on trips. The Doctor put the tickets in his inside coat pocket.

When they reached the airport—it was the old airport, not the new one with the curvy roof—the two men in the front seat stayed in the car. She and the Doctor got out, he shook hands with the two men, and they went in. Her leg still felt stiff when she walked, and made her limp.

Inside, in the big long room with the high glass wall, the lights were bright and it was full of people walking fast, walking slow, and sitting in seats waiting with little cloth bags at their feet. Through the glass you could see the planes moving, and most of the time a voice kept calling numbers in the air. In the middle of the big room a stone stairway led up to a balcony sort of place, where there were not so many people.

All around the edges were counters. People stood in front of them, and young men and ladies in uniforms stood behind them writing tickets and talking on telephones. The Doctor looked at these counters and read the signs over them. He walked, carrying his small suitcase, to one near the middle, not far from the stone stairs. There were three men at the counter buying tickets, and three men in blue uniforms behind it. It was there that the strange thing happened, and everything changed.

She was standing next to the Doctor, and another man, wearing a tan raincoat, stood next to her. Two of the men behind the counter were talking on telephones, but the other one, when she looked up—stared hard at her. Then he stared even harder, and reached under the counter and took something out. He looked at it, then back at her, then at it again. He turned to the other two, but they were both still busy on the telephones. He put down the thing he was holding, whatever it was, and then, suddenly, he ran —out from behind the counter and down the long room as fast as he could go, his footsteps thumping on the stone floor, ducking around people who stared after him. He was gone.

The man in the tan raincoat said, 'Hey, what got into him?'

The Doctor moved a step forward and looked over the counter to see what lay on the shelf behind it.

Without seeming to be in a hurry, he turned away from the counter and gazed thoughtfully around. He took Allie by the hand and they walked to the stone staircase. At the bottom he bent over and told her some things to do; he took from his coat pocket a small white paper bag and pressed it into her hand. It looked like a candy bag, but there was nothing in it but a little bottle. Slowly, because her leg was stiff, she went up the stairs to the balcony place. The Doctor went in another direction, walking quite fast, and disappeared through a door that had a sign over it: 'Gates 8-14.'

Up on the balcony she walked as far as she could, to the back corner, and sat down. It was darker there, and no one was near except a young man, dozing over a book. She looked at the clock in the middle of the main room. She could see it clearly from here; it had four faces and said six-fifteen. She looked below, and saw a commotion at the counter where she had just been.

A crowd of policemen had come running up, followed by the young ticket seller who had run away. He pointed at the man in the tan raincoat, and the policeman grabbed him. They also surrounded the other two men. The man in the tan raincoat was angry. He shook off the policemen, shouted, and punched one of them. Three more policemen held him, and he fell to the floor. Now they had handcuffs on his wrists, and they pulled him away, still shouting. She wondered what he had done. More policemen came, and ran through the doors with the signs over them listing gate numbers. The Doctor was nowhere to be seen, but the young man with the book, having watched the excitement, stood up and walked away.

She looked at the clock again. Six-thirty. At ten o'clock, if he did not return by then, she would take the medicine in the little bottle.

When Jennifer Adam met Mr Bayles she thought he looked like a doctor, not a CIA man. She worked with doctors, and recognized the combination of professional and yet quite genuine concern with which he looked at her. In the car, on the way to the airport, he explained, 'I know this has all been extremely painful for you, Mrs Adam, and Fergus has told me how well you've faced it.'

'Not so very well, I'm afraid.'

'I would have expected you to be close to hysteria at this stage.' He even sounded like a doctor. 'You obviously are not. Still, I thought I should warn you that the part we're coming to may be the hardest of all. Try to remember, you're here to identify your daughter, not to rescue her. We'll have professionals on hand for that, and they know their jobs. When you see her, and you're sure, tell us, and then stay put. Remember that Schutz is desperate. He's been a prisoner for almost thirty years. This is his only chance to escape. He's not going to give up meekly.'

'You sound,' said Fergus dryly, 'as if you're trying to induce hysteria right now.'

'Better now than then,' Mr Bayles said. Jennifer saw him inspect her carefully through his rimless glasses. He added, 'But I think I don't need to worry.'

At the great glass aerodrome with its soaring Saarinen roof, their car turned off the passenger road to a service entrance. An airport policeman in a brown uniform was waiting and led them to an elevator. When they emerged they were in a room Jennifer Adam, who had been to this airport many times before, had never known to exist. It was a control centre, a large busy room full of desks, telephones, and people. Its tinted glass walls looked down on the whole vast interior of the building. She was led to a place near the wall where some chairs faced the glass. She sat down, Mr Bayles on one side, Fergus on the other.

In the area below them a thousand people bought tickets, checked luggage, bought insurance and postcards, waited for flights to be called.

'Right there'—Mr Bayles pointed at a long blue counter below them—'is the Pan American section. Mr Schmidt and daughter are booked for Flight 341. If Allison comes to that counter, will you know her from here?'

'I will.'

'We have binoculars if you need them. Six of our men, all FBI, all good, are watching the counter. You can't see them, but they're there. We have another one behind the counter.

'The plan is as simple as possible. If you see Allison, or if Fergus sees Schutz—let me know, I'll let them know. There will be a coded announcement over the public-address system.

'If, on the other hand, Mr Schmidt and Miss Schmidt check in, our man behind the counter will signal the others and call me on this phone. You will both take a hard look. If they aren't Schutz and Allison, and if they actually board the flight—no last-minute substitutions—we all go home.

'Right now, we watch. Check-in time for Flight 341 is seven-thirty, and it's coming up.'

They watched. Each time a girl of Allison's size and age came in sight Jennifer Adam forced herself to stay in her seat and look carefully, and each time it was not Allison.

Mr Bayles exclaimed, a wordless noise, and picked up the binoculars. He was looking at two men in grey suits, chatting near the Pan American counter. Simultaneously the telephone at his elbow rang. He picked it up.

'Yes,' he said, 'I just spotted them myself. Be sure the others know.' He hung up.

'Those two are Russians,' he said. 'One of them is a KGB man named Dranovitch, very nasty. We thought he was in Moscow. How they got him here so fast I don't know.'

'What will they do?'

'Shoot Schutz, grab his bag, and sprint. They'll have a car running outside with a driver in it. We sort of expected them.'

'What will you do?'

'Get the girl out of the way. Let them run. If they kill Schutz, it's no loss to us. Not worth a lot of gunfire in the airport. We'll chase their car, but I don't think we'll catch it.'

Seven-thirty. A queue formed in front of the Pan American counter, grew longer, grew shorter; bags, boxes, and golf clubs rode the conveyor belt out of sight.

At eight-ten the check-in, theoretically, was over. Mr Bayles's phone rang, and he answered with a single word: 'Wait.'

But at eight-thirty the doors to the mobile lounge closed; Flight 341 to Frankfort was under way, and Mr Schmidt had become, in the parlance of the airlines, a 'no show', as had his daughter.

'A decoy,' Mr Bayles said. 'I was afraid of that. It was all too simple.'

Jennifer Adam felt her tension sliding away like undertow, and braced against the bitter wave of disappointment that surged in behind it. They sat a moment in silence, and still she watched: two figures might yet appear, hurrying, late, having missed the plane.

The phone beside Mr Bayles rang again. He answered, listened, spoke again more urgently, listened further, and hung up. Jennifer saw his doctor's face turn towards her, saw him composing his words cautiously.

'That was from the other airport—National. They say they've found her. Alive, unharmed, and alone. It could be a mistake, a false alarm. But they sound quite positive.'

In the car, riding behind a siren in the car ahead, they made the one-hour drive from Dulles to National in half an hour. Fergus sat beside Jennifer in the back seat and saw the pallor and exhaustion in her face. He felt her shoulder tremble against his, and placed his palm lightly over hers where it lay on the seat between them.

'Hang on,' he said. 'It's almost over.'

'Thank you. I'm trying.'

As they approached the airport—this one older, a rambling group of low white buildings around a central glass tower—the siren was turned off. Again they turned to a service entrance, and again a uniformed officer met them.

'Captain McTigue,' he introduced himself. 'The girl is still sitting upstairs. She hasn't moved in an hour—just keeps watching the clock, holding a bag of candy. We think he brought her and then got scared off. But he might come back for her, so we've left her alone. How bad do you want him? What's the charge?'

Mr Bayles said, 'At the moment, just kidnapping. But there's worse on his record, including murder. We want him pretty bad.'

'All right,' said Captain McTigue. 'It's up to you. Is this the mother?'

Fergus saw him look at Jennifer Adam, saw his face soften as he spoke. 'Ma'am—Mrs . . .'

'Mrs Adam.'

'You look pretty beat. Do you think you can go with us, look at her, and still hold back for a while?'

Jennifer said, 'I can. If it's really Allison.'

Fergus said, 'I'd better go with her.'

'All right. But just the two. We don't want a crowd, it wouldn't look natural.'

He led them inside, down a corridor marked 'Staff Only', and into the big glass-walled room. He nodded towards the stone stairs leading to the mezzanine lounge.

'Up there,' he said.

Mr Bayles said: 'I'll wait here. As soon as you're certain, come on back. I want to know how it happened.'

They ascended the stairway slowly, McTigue leading. At the top he turned right, led them a few paces farther, and then said quietly: 'All right, now, make it casual. Turn around and look behind you, all the way back in the corner.'

She sat alone, a white-faced girl in a new grey dress, looking at the clock, motionless, a white paper bag in her lap.

Fergus heard the sharp intake of breath. 'It's Allie,' she said, 'it's Allie.' And then again, looking over his head, looking past them both, she said, 'Oh God, thank you.'

She looked back at the girl. 'But so thin, so pale, and they've cut her hair. Poor Allie, she's sick,' and she would have started forward; but for Fergus's firm hand on her arm, would have run to her.

'Wait,' he said. 'Remember.'

She shook her head to clear her mind. 'I'm sorry. I forgot. Can I sit somewhere—can I watch her?'

Captain McTigue smiled. 'All the way to the other end,' he said. 'Both of you—sit and watch the planes take off. You can see her from there.'

Mr Bayles controlled himself with difficulty, remembering that he was dealing with, despite their uniforms, civilian amateurs.

'You saw the girl,' he said to the Berkshire Airlines ticket agent, who was very young and now on the defensive, 'and then what?'

'She looked like the picture we got this morning, but not exactly. So I pulled out the picture and looked again. Then I saw it *was* the girl, but her hair was cut. She was with a man in a raincoat— that is, she seemed to be. So I ran——'

'You *ran*?'

'To get the police. What else? Both the phones were busy—Ed was on one and Jerry was on the other——'

'What did you do with the photograph?'

'I—I guess I just dropped it on the desk.'

'And when you came back the girl was gone but the man was still there.'

'The man in the raincoat—yes. And two others.'

Captain McTigue said morosely: 'We arrested the man in the raincoat. He was Congressman Frederick Boynton of Vermont. He was very angry. He missed his flight.'

'What flight was it?'

'The seven-thirty to Boston, non-stop.'

'The other two men?'

'Both absolutely okay,' said McTigue. 'Neither one could be our man. I've got the dope in my office.'

Mr Bayles glared at the clerk: 'When you—*ran*—was there a fourth man?'

The young man said dejectedly: 'I told the Captain—I think there was. But I'm not sure.'

'What did he look like?'

'I don't know—I was so sure she was with the other one. I have an idea he wore glasses, if he was there at all.'

'Did *he* get the seven-thirty to Boston?'

'No.' Both the clerk and McTigue were sure. 'We've checked that.'

'Is there any other flight to Boston he could have taken?'

The young ticket agent could now be helpful. 'None. Except——'

'Except what?'

'Well, he *could* have got the Eastern shuttle to New York. It leaves at seven. And then, if he was lucky, he *could* have got the shuttle from New York to Boston. But you can't check those—there's no reservation. You just pay when you get on.'

'Can you check this: is there a flight tonight from Boston to Germany?'

'Where in Germany?'

'Anywhere.'

'I'll have to get my book.'

The big, black international airline timetable, showing departure times from anywhere to anywhere all over the world, was brought out and the young clerk, now on his own home ground, riffled expertly through the pages, ran his fingers down a column, and said: 'Yes. A Lufthansa out of Chicago. Flight 233. Stops in Philadelphia. Stops in Boston. Then non-stop to Hamburg.'

'What time?' roared Mr Bayles.

'Leaves Boston at nine-thirty.'

Mr Bayles looked at his watch. It said that the time was now ten minutes to ten. He sighed. 'Can you get the Lufthansa office in Boston?'

'Sure. On the telex.'

Four minutes later they had the simple answer, teletyped in block capitals. Mr David Schmidt and daughter, Miss Schmidt, had booked yesterday for tonight's Flight 233 to Hamburg. Mr Schmidt had boarded but had, at the last minute, cancelled Miss Schmidt's reservation. Mr Schmidt was now twenty minutes out to sea, heading for Hamburg at five hundred miles an hour.

Now Captain McTigue was helpful. First he notified his airport police that the heat was off. Then he said, 'We'll pick him up at the other end. He's got to go through immigration, so they're bound to spot him. And those German airport police are good—we've worked with them before. They're not the regular police, they're military—Ministry of Defence—really efficient.'

'I know,' said Mr Bayles.

'I'll get on the pipe,' said the Captain, picking up his telephone, 'and let them know he's coming—just the bare outlines.'

'Good idea,' said Mr Bayles. But he could not dispel a conviction that they already knew.

At the top of the stone stairway he found Fergus and Jennifer sitting at one end of the lounge, saw the girl in the corner at the other end. She stared at the clock, which was closing on the hour of ten.

Mr Bayles said to Jennifer Adam, 'You can go to her now. Schutz has got away.'

She ran the length of the mezzanine to her daughter, a daughter as unresponsive as a stranger.

'Allie, don't you know me?' Touching her cheek, so hollow, so thin; seeing for the first time the bruised and angry welts on her leg.

'You're my mother.' The girl spoke in a whisper, glanced at her briefly, and then looked back to the clock, whose little hand was now squarely on the ten, whose big hand had reached the twelve. She opened the paper bag that lay in her lap, took from it the small bottle, and turned the cap.

Before she could get it open, Fergus had seen, comprehended, and reached over Jennifer's shoulder. He held the bottle in his hand.

'Allison,' he said, 'what's in the bottle?'

'It isn't candy,' she said, so softly they must strain to hear, 'it's my medicine. The Doctor said take it at ten o'clock if he didn't come back. Or if anybody tried to make me go away.'

Fergus sat down beside her. 'Allison, the Doctor has gone. He isn't coming back. I'm the new doctor. When I tell you something, it will be true. Do you understand that?'

She said, 'You're the new doctor. What you say will be true.'

'Allie,' Jennifer said, putting her arm around the thin shoulders, 'we're going to take you home. You've been sick, but we're going to make you well again.'

With her mother holding one hand and the new doctor holding the other, she walked, limping, out of the airport, into the car, and they drove home. She held her mother's hand all the way home. She had not taken her medicine, but even so she felt nice.

EPILOGUE

PART 1. Colonel Attenborough, with some pride, showed Fergus through the gleaming new laboratory, built to Fergus's own specifications and filled with exactly the equipment he had ordered. It had taken only a few meetings, attended by the Colonel, Mr Bayles, a number of generals, and two distinguished elder biologists, to secure allocation of funds to build it. It had been necessary for Allison Adam to attend just one of the meetings. The project had been given the highest priority. It bore the cryptic title: 'Analysis and Reduction of Water X as to Mutagenic Effects on Human Tissue.'

Fergus was particularly pleased that he had already received a reply to one of two letters he had written to the other members of the b-virus team; Jerome would be joining the project in a week; he expected John would also accept.

The PTS was over. He had found a new problem.

PART 2. A dispatch carried by the United Press International ran as follows: 'Lima, June 27. A team of four German geologists, prospecting for oil in the Andes Mountains, were expelled from Peru today for setting off an explosive charge that destroyed a valuable archaeological site. The explosive, designed for seismic testing of the mountainous substrata, caused a landslide which completely demolished and buried a recently discovered stone ruin believed to have been built by the Incas, near the present village of Ayucalpa. The landslide also diverted a picturesque waterfall that formerly flowed through the ruin. The Peruvian government, in addition to expelling the geologists, filed a formal complaint with the West German government, which had sponsored the expedition . . .'

PART 3. Professor-Doctor Hans von Bruckner, a well-to-do biologist, lived in Edelburg, a town in the Lüneburger Heide not very far from Hamburg. He lived in a comfortable house, large but not ostentatious, with a touch of Gothic in its architecture; his own well-equipped laboratory stood a suitable distance away in a separate building on the same spacious grounds. He lectured once a week to a respectful group of graduate students at the University of Hamburg, and after the lecture, in an hour of relaxation, shared a glass of wine in the *Stube* with some of the graduate students. They discussed genetics.

Once a month Professor Von Bruckner paid a visit to his old and close friend Friedrich Kassel, Minister of Defence of the German Republic. There, in the Minister's own living room, they talked about the state of science in Germany, and particularly about progress in some biochemical research related to the national defence.

It was, of course, progressing well.